Neither of them moved for what seemed an eternity; she because she was transfixed, and he because above all he wished only to crush her so thoroughly that no thought nor sight of her would ever disturb him again. He seized her by the shoulders, pressing her against him so hard she cried out, a helpless, nearly silent cry, for his mouth covered hers, expressing for him all the ruthless passions she had set loose in him. His arms were around her, holding her until she couldn't breathe. She struggled against him. As quickly as he had kissed her he released her; and as quickly as she found herself free, she wished herself imprisoned by his arms once more.

"Adam..."

He bent his head toward her waiting mouth with a shy boyish tenderness. There was no force to his kiss now. Silently, by his actions, he was telling her, talking to her, saying all the things she had longed to hear all her life. . . .

Books by Day Taylor

THE BLACK SWAN
MOSSROSE

The
Black
Swan

Day Taylor

A DELL BOOK

Published by
Dell Publishing Co., Inc.
1 Dag Hammarskjold Plaza
New York, New York 10017

An excerpt from this work first appeared as an insert in
Flames of Desire by Vanessa Royall,
Dell Publishing Co., Inc., 1978

Dell ® TM 681510, Dell Publishing Co., Inc.

ISBN: 0-440-10611-7

Printed in the United States of America

First printing—July 1978
Second printing—August 1978
Third printing—August 1978
Fourth printing—September 1978
Fifth printing—July 1980
Sixth printing—September 1980
Seventh printing—October 1980
Eighth printing—May 1981

BOOK I

Adam
1852-1859

Chapter One

A land of bakingly hot summers, white with cotton, green with tobacco and sugarcane, scented by magnolia and gardenia, drenched in sudden rainstorms from cloud-piled blue skies, gave birth to a special breed of man. It was a land whose climate and weather determined its soil, its crops, its way of life. Growing seasons were long, the pace of living leisurely, its men soft-spoken, and its charming women protected.

The land was the Deep South before the War of Secession. The year, 1852.

Tom Pierson, Edmund Revanche, and Ross Bennett relaxed in the Orleans Club, playing brag. Together, in the usual way of Southern gentlemen, they had hunted bobwhite and wild turkey, easily gambled a hundred dollars on a single roll of the dice, and easily smiled at loss.

This day the trio was alert and watchful as Edmund Revanche closed upon the ownership of Josiah Whinburn's plantation, Marsh House. Inexorably, Edmund had been maneuvering Whinburn to place his plantation in the pot. The other two played with cool precision, neither approving nor disapproving Edmund's implacability.

They presented a solid front of friendship. They had squired chaperoned belles, savored the delights of bordellos. Ross had killed a Northerner over a business matter. Edmund had married at twenty-three. Two years later he was widowed without issue. Tom and Ross had not yet married.

Each was well dressed, athletically graceful, restless, and gallant. Swift to both murderous rage and gracious forgiveness, they were more inclined to physical action than intellectual achievement. They were the self-confident products of a doomed civilization.

Edmund barely stifled his grin as Josiah Whinburn stared bleakly at his losing hand.

"This isn't your day, Josiah," Tom said. "Want us to deal you out?"

"What do I owe you now?"

"You can make it up in the next hand," Edmund said. "Put up Marsh House."

Josiah looked uncertain. "My daddy'd roll in his grave."

"Put up the cane crop," Ross suggested. "Do somethin'. We're not gonna sit here all night. You in or out?"

Goaded, Whinburn said hastily, "I'm in. I'll put up the cane crop."

Edmund smiled. Ross began to deal.

Tom watched the sweat-beaded young man. "Josiah, you sure about this?"

"Hell's bells," said Ross. "Tom boy, you're always wet-nursin' somebody. Gonna land you in a pile o' trouble someday."

Tom grinned, deaf to jibes about his easy sympathies. He had mild blue eyes set in a pleasant, clean-shaven face. His thick sandy hair, wild with waves and opposing cowlicks, fell in an unruly mass onto his collar. A stocky man with big hands, he was heavy in the shoulders and without the fashionable tapering at waist and hips. He could never achieve the smoothly tailored elegance that sat so cozily on the long-limbed bodies of the other two. Tom Pierson all his life would look like a dressed-up bull.

Tom played his cards without any sign of his distaste for the proceedings. Repeatedly, Josiah's eyes sought his. Finally Tom complained, "I've had a bellyful of brag."

"Last hand." Ross dealt, waiting for Josiah to ante his cane crop. He patted Josiah on the back. "That's the spirit, boy! We've all lost an' won back all we own."

Ross Bennett's straight brown hair was matched by a drooping moustache and sideburns that stopped cleanly at the level of his full, sensuous lips. He was saved from overwhelming beauty by a high-bridged nose that gave him the aristocrat's permanent sneer.

Of the trio, Edmund Revanche was the most calculating and ambitious. He was graced with a cynicism that allowed his morality to shift with the needs of expediency. His face was inherited from his French Creole father. From his high narrow forehead sprang fine black hair mingled sparsely with gray. Under hooded lids, his brown eyes moved suspiciously. His nose was long and straight, with deep grooves on each side running down toward thin lips.

He was a man of exquisite tastes with ample means to indulge them, a discreet, almost secretive man who lived excessively and had a constitution that shrugged off as nothing the most flamboyant of his excesses.

Revanche, like the others, had come into his patrimony at twenty-one. Unlike Ross, who in a few years would exhaust his, and Tom, who allowed other men to manage it for him, Edmund handled his own affairs. His large sugar plantation twenty-five miles east of New Orleans was prospering. Recently he'd paid gold for the extensive adjoining property and fifteen slaves willed by Old Man Pickett to his charmingly helpless young widow.

It was not incidental to Edmund's plan that Josiah Whinburn's property connected to Pickett's. Windfalls were the stuff of which Edmund Revanche would build an empire. Soon, Edmund would possess a considerable amount of Whinburn money and the cane crop. Without capital for the coming year, Josiah would gamble Marsh House. Or be forced to sell.

"You still playin', Edmund?" Ross asked peevishly. "Josiah's sho' got us whupped."

Edmund looked into Josiah's face, bright with anticipation and relief. One at a time he laid down his cards. With each card the young man's face fell, until it looked as if he might weep.

Josiah rose, bowed to Edmund, and gestured toward the note on the table. "Excuse me for a moment, gentlemen. I feel the call of nature."

Tom had a flash of insight: *Good God! The boy's goin' to blow his brains out!* "Mind if I trail along, Josiah?"

Out of Edmund's hearing, he said, "Know anythin' about keepin' accounts?"

"Is that meant for an insult?"

"Great Jehoshaphat! You're mighty touchy. I'm askin' if you can do figures and keep track of crates and hogs-heads and suchlike."

"I beg your pardon, Tom, I sho'ly do. Losin's got me crazy as a bessie bug. I used to do accounts for my daddy."

"Come to my house on Clio Street, Thursday evenin'. I want your word you're gonna be there, hear?"

"Well, I . . . You've got my word."

"Jes' fine! Now, come on, boy, let's us go get drunk as ten ol' boar hogs!"

Inside the club, Tom pounded on the bar with his huge

fist. "Gentlemen! Gentlemen! I'm proposin' a drinkin' match. Edmund won himself a right smart pile o' money. We're gonna celebrate this grand occasion with wine, women, and song! 'Course the women'll have to wait!" He paused for the coarse laughter to die down. "Anybody willin'?"

From all over the room there came shouts of "I'm on!" and "I'll take a shot at it!" and more laughter.

"I'm gonna put a thousand dollars in the purse. All you boys with real sportin' blood ante up!" Tom shouted.

More shouts, laughter, and jibes came for those who backed down. Twenty-five men had agreed. The purse was locked in the club's safe. Then the requirements for the match were set.

"Eight bottles of wine apiece!" cried Josiah.

"Nine bottles!" said Ross, who knew Josiah's capacity.

"Make it ten," growled a beefy planter.

Edmund's voice rang out. "Twelve bottles each man, an' a quart of anisette."

Josiah, visibly pale, echoed, "Twelve bottles an' one of anisette!"

"Done!" Tom pounded on the bar again. "On a purse of one thousand apiece, awarded the first man finished."

The first bottles of wine were set out. Some men dropped out relatively sober, mounted their horses, and headed dreamily toward less incapacitating pleasures. Josiah drank too quickly. In a remarkably short time he reached oblivion and was carried to the *garçonnière* to sleep it off.

The evening gun had long ago sounded. In the dimly lighted room a dozen young gentlemen in their cups raised an unseemly din. Black waiters ran to constant calls of, "Boy! 'Nother bottle heah!"

Edmund, sipping on his seventh bottle, felt heavy-eyed. He lifted his brows. Ross and Tom were still joking and slapping each other's shoulders.

An argument would clear his head. Edmund put one hand on Tom's arm, making Tom splash wine onto his coat sleeve. Unmindful of Tom's irritated outcry, Edmund said, "Where do you think the South would be if ol' Hen-Hennery Clay hant puh-puhposed his Com-puh-mise? Jus' tell me that."

It angered Edmund that the Compromise of 1850, with its stringent law requiring all persons to assist in the return of fugitive slaves to their masters, could not be enforced. Once a fugitive reached a free state, the nigger-lovers were willing to flout Federal law. Aided by darkness, they guided the fugitives toward Canada.

"Well, Edmund, no law could keep us from bein' right heah. We'd be sittin' in the Orleans Club gettin' drunk."

Ross Bennett laughed, then hiccuped. "Yeah, Edmund, we'd be heah with the nigras still scamperin' to follow our orders. No pukin' law is gonna change us."

Revanche signaled for his eighth bottle. "Like hell!" He glared savagely. "Last month ol' Daddy Bill an' his woman got clean away. Never even rousted the hounds. Black bastards! Two best house niggers I'll ever see. I don't take kindly to any law tamperin' with my business, 'specially nigger property valuable as mine. I only keep the finest."

"What'd you do 'bout it?" Ross licked his lips in sly amusement.

"Flogged 'em. Every damned nigger in their cabin." Revanche said, enjoying Tom's sudden pallor. "Happened your precious Ullah was servicin' my guest, so she didn't get it—then. Wish like hell I could lay hands on the damned doughface that gave them the idea. Jesus, but I hate an insurrectionist!"

"Maybe if you'd go a mite easier, your people wouldn't run."

Ross snorted. "Catch old Tom! Ten house niggers he can't get to do a lick, an' now he's tellin' you how to run a fifteen-hundred-acre plantation!"

Tom thought of his elegant Greek Revival mansion on Clio Street, clean and polished, lavish menus prepared daily, spotless brick walks, and formal gardens, all pridefully tended by loving black hands. He thought of the whip he'd nailed over the kitchen door on the day his father died. "My people do their work to suit me. Matter, Ross, quit drinkin' already?"

Ross drained his glass. "I aim to win that purse, Tom boy."

Revanche reached unsteadily for his wine and knocked it over. Tom jumped up, his coat and trousers stained red. "Great J'hoshaphat, Edmund! You tryin' to fumigate me?"

" 'Pologies." Edmund clutched at the table for balance. "I don't appear to have the proper function of my hands f'some reason. Y'all comin' to the house later on?"

Tom said, "Sure."

"Ol' Tom don't want to risk his life spendin' the night in the bachelor house. He wants cool quadroon han's on his fevered—" Ross laughed.

Tom grinned with the sudden knowledge that he was going to win the purse. Casually confident, he sipped on his ninth bottle. He hardly felt giddy yet.

Sometime later Ross got up, reeling unsteadily toward the outhouse, and relieved himself instead into a brass spittoon. A waiter hurried to carry it out. Ross swung his fist at the man, missed, and turned in a dizzying circle. With peaceful suddenness, his knees buckled.

Tom grinned vacuously as the first of his two most serious competitors went down. Edmund's head lolled. Tom had never seen Revanche so sloppy drunk, yet he was midway into his tenth bottle. At this rate, Edmund would be awake to the very last. He looked around. Three men sat at a table near the back door. One sat rigid as death, his eyes shut, his jaw slack. He looked at his own bottle. Number eleven and nothing left but the dregs.

Tom stood up. His head was buzzing like a beehive, and he was walkin' whopperjawed. How'd he get himself into this *bambache?* Sho', get Josiah drunk so's he wouldn't kill himself.

Edmund swung his head around. "Tom! Where a hell you goin'?"

"Don't stay awake on my account, Edmund ol' frien'. Drink up!"

"Sinsh when you tell me . . . wha' to do?"

"I don't tell you. I jus' sit here an' guzzle it down. Ever notice how the taste goes flat?"

Edmund took a long swallow. "No, I don't believe I do. No diff'nce a-tall." As he looked at Tom, his eyes slowly crossed.

"Ballsafire, Emmun', I never seen you so drunk! You better quit while I can still git you home!"

Edmund drank again deeply. "You never outdrunk me yet."

"Le's talk. Keep awake. Nobody lef' 'cept us." He swept his hand over the room; the revelers had all been helped into their carriages or to the *garçonnière.*

"*Talk!* Whadda we talk about?"

"Money. You like money, don't you, Emmun'?"

Revanche sat there smiling for some time. "Got Josiah's, dint I?"

"I'm talkin' 'bout my money. I'll give you some of my money."

Edmund blinked rapidly several times. "Wha' for?"

"I wanta buy Ullah."

"You're gettin' all the cream off that cow anyway. Wha —wha—"

"I need me a house servant. Bessie's gettin' too ol'."

"Whash"—Edmund blinked and glared horribly trying to keep his eyes open—"your . . . offer? Whash your offer?"

If he offered too little, Edmund would refuse. "Thirty-five hunnert."

Edmund leaned toward him. "Make you a bargain. Four thousand."

"Shit, four thousand ain't no bargain. Get me a edu-edu . . . get me one can read for tha' much."

"Lemme finish. Four thousand, gold, and you gotta out-drink me."

"Emmun', you b—bas—you bass-turd, your price is too high."

Edmund's eyes closed. He popped them open. "Fair's fair. Bargain's a bar . . ." For a moment Tom thought he'd passed out.

Tom nudged him. "Shake hands, an' drink up, ol' frien'! We got a deal. Four thousand an' I drink you unner th' table, an' Ullah belongs to me." He had to look away then. As drunk as he was, he still couldn't let Edmund see how much it meant to him.

Tom grasped Edmund's limp hand. "You're fallin' be-hind, Emmun'!" he said heartily. "A toast! To my new house nigger!"

"Damn if you'll get 'er," Edmund crashed his glass against Tom's. His eyes fell shut. Soon he was snoring, his cheek pillowed in spilled wine.

Tom motioned to the bartender. "You countin' the bot-tles, Jarvis?"

"Yassuh, Mastah Tom. Mastah Edmun' done quit on bottle numbah eleven."

"Anybody else outdrink him?"

Jarvis's black face split in a grin. "Ah b'lieve you finish yo' bottle numbah twelve, suh. All de odder gent'mens gone to sleep out back."

"Fetch me the anisette, Jarvis. An' fetch over that big spittoon, 'cause I declare I'm gonna need it."

"Don't drink dat stuff, Mastah Tom. It look like watah, but dat bottleful gwine kill you."

"Won' hurt me." Tom took a few sips. His stomach rolled in rebellion.

Jarvis's face puckered. "Mastah Tom, you ain't lookin' so fine. You already won de *bambache*, but you cain't collec' if you dies."

"Fair's fair." Suddenly Tom's words slurred, his head reeled. "Got to drink the res'. Made a deal."

Tom rocked himself desperately back and forth to stay awake. He sipped the anisette. Behind the bar, Jarvis and the other waiters whispered. Jarvis came toward him smiling. To Tom the black man's face looked like a big dark moon glaring hideously. He shut his eyes to blot out the distortion.

Jarvis touched him, making him jump. Had he almost been asleep?

"We made a 'rangement, suh. We gwine keep de bottle an' bring it you w'en you ready. Yassuh, we gwine he'p you win dat nigger."

As time slid by, the liquor seemed to lose its usual tang and odor. It looked like water. It tasted like water. The whole world was going crazy. The waiters seemed a-bustin' to take turns serving him, but then they giggled and spilled things. Not a one of them was walking straight. He'd almost think they were getting drunk too.

Tom's real prize was Ullah. Ullah, his caramel-and-cream quadroon love. At first he'd just used her as Edmund's guests were invited to do. But he had been her first man. He remembered Ullah's sweetness, her innocent love when she told him she would bear his child. "Only gwine be one man Ah 'llows give me children, Tom." Her shy humor, her patience, and her unending affection overwhelmed him. Long before Angela was born, Tom was slaphappy in love with Ullah.

Yet he did nothing. He knew Edmund. If Tom asked to buy Ullah, right quick Ullah would become too valuable for Edmund to part with. Worse, Edmund might sell her.

But tonight! Edmund would never remember, but he'd take Tom's word. And bet your boots, Edmund would ask Jarvis, just to make sure.

"Jarvis!"

"Yassuh!" Jarvis beamed fit to blind Tom. "You ready fo' de las' glass?"

Tom's stomach jumped uneasily. "Hol' off on that. Lis'n, Jarvis, 'member how much I 'greed to pay Emmun' for my house nigger?"

The black face took on a crafty look. "Ah wa'n't lis'nin', Mastah Tom."

"Grea' day, Jarvis! It's yo' duty to lis'n! Emmun' gon' ast you!"

"'Spect Ah do 'member," Jarvis smiled happily. Tom shut his eyes against the flash of teeth. "Fo' thousan' dollahs, gold. She mus' be some fancy house nigger!"

Two of the waiters were circling slowly in a dance, while a third beat rhythm. As Tom watched, one of the dancers fell over. The others burst into hilarious laughter, picked him up, and staggered out with him.

Tom pointed. "Wha—?"

Jarvis laughed richly. "He plumb tuckered out, suh. This yo' las' glass."

"Po' it on out, then, an' hol' that gobboon up heah, 'cause it's comin' right back up. Then you get us in the carriage, so's we can go to Emmun's."

"Mastah Ross an' Mastah Edmun', dey's asleep, Mastah Tom."

"They won't gi' you any trouble." Tom shut his eyes tight and downed the anisette, as choky-strong as ever. He felt as if he'd been hit with a mallet. But he had won.

Chapter Two

The soiree at Pickett's plantation was in full swing. Miss Carrie's beautiful old rosewood piano tinkled accompaniment to her silvery soprano voice, raised in a haunting new tune, "My Old Kentucky Home." She'd be going back to Kentucky soon.

She hadn't been able to make her late husband's plantation pay. She didn't lack the spirit. Though she had tried hard for three years, a succession of overseers and factors had taken advantage of her ignorance and good nature, robbing her shamefully. But for Edmund—who must have been a little sweet on her—she'd be sitting on the doorstep of the poorhouse.

Tom handed Sable's reins to a black boy and flipped him a large penny. The boy stuck the penny into his mouth for safekeeping. Tom mounted the steps to the broad, shady veranda.

"Tom! I was beginnin' to think you were goin' to insult me, not comin' to my pahty!" The Widow Pickett wore a low-cut dress of magenta silk that complimented her black curls and creamy skin. She put a dainty hand on Tom's arm.

Tom bowed low, kissing her hand longer than politeness demanded. His practiced gaze skimmed her small waist and bosoms, laced into complaisant prominence.

He looked deep into her eyes. "Miss Carrie, if I insulted you, may I pick the weapons?"

She laughed, a happy gushing sound. "What might youah weapons be, Tom?"

"Would you accept sweet nothin's at two paces?"

She blushed clear down to the top of her gown. "Tom, youah *awful!* Merton better fetch you a drink, so's you'll have somethin' to hol' besides mah hand!"

Tom squeezed her hand gently. "Miss Carrie, you're pretty as a hibiscus blossom today. I plumb lost mastery over myself."

"I've taken off my mournin' for the pahty." She cast down her eyes. "I'll always miss deah Calvin, but life goes on, doesn't it?"

"Wouldn't surprise me if you'll get a whole raft of proposals this evenin', Miss Carrie. You're enough to make a sane man wonder why he's single."

She giggled. "If I don't sound too bold, Tom, I been meanin' to ask you that myself." In her long-lashed dark eyes there was invitation.

"I don't believe I rightly know, Miss Carrie. Maybe I've had my eyes shut."

Ross's grating voice cut in. "Wish you had, Tom boy. I was jus' beginnin' to think I was the one makin' time with the lady. Miss Carrie honey, the gentlemen have been askin' if you'd favor us with another song."

"I certainly will if *you* ask me, Ross." Carrie gave him a melting look and drifted inside. Presently she was heard singing, "Drink to me only with thine eyes, and I will pledge . . ."

"Who won the purse, Tom?"

"Thought you said you were goin' to win it."

"Only thing I won was a bustin' head. You don't know, then?"

"Sure I know. I won it."

Ross's jaw dropped. "Well, I'll be damned!" He gave Tom a hard, appraising stare. "Edmund's not in the habit of losin'. He's gonna have a real blood rush."

Tom said uncomfortably, "What happened to you last night? You must have had a lot while we were at brag."

Ross shrugged. "Three, four drinks. Did you slip me a Mickey?"

"I never did before, did I?"

"You never won before."

"Jee-hoshaphat, Ross! Once in my life I do everythin' right—"

"Cheer up, ol' frien'. Here comes Edmund."

Edmund, Tom observed, looked peaked. "I see you survived," he said heartily.

Edmund's smile was bleak. "The carrion crows are welcome to my mouth. Pfaugh!" Tom and Ross laughed. "You're lookin' suspiciously well, Tom."

Tom braced himself. "That anisette must have cleared my head."

Edmund's nostrils flared. "Congratulations, Tom!"

Tom's heart raced as he accepted Edmund's handshake. "Thanks, Edmund. I'll give you a bank draft for that four thousand."

"Four thousand?" Edmund's eyebrows raised in puzzlement.

Ross said, "I don't recall you losin' money to Edmund."

Edmund had never taken his eyes off Tom. "What four thousand?!"

"You sold me a house nigger. Sho'ly you recollect that. Ask Jarvis."

Edmund's face grew pinched and pale.

Ross laughed softly. "Son of a bitch! You're talkin' about Ullah, aren't you?"

"Yes," said Tom, smiling. He told Edmund how it had happened. "I kept my end of the bargain."

"And so shall I." Revanche's eyes glittered.

Ross said, "We got to toast ol' Tom for outfoxin' everybody."

They touched glasses just as the laughing crowd came from the parlor.

Tom took little part in the soiree. His mind was already

in the future, when the dancing would have grown weari-some. He endured the gala midnight supper and the final gallantries in honor of Carrie Pickett's departure.

It was one o'clock by the time the three men were seated in Revanche's study. Though Tom was anxious to be with Ullah, he talked and joked with Ross and Edmund. "I b'lieve we all had a narrow escape. Miss Carrie looked ready to take up the first proposal."

Ross laughed. "I nearly made her one myself. And hey, Tom, did you?"

Edmund Revanche was not listening. Drink in hand, he lounged in a high-backed chair, booted legs crossed. His full-lidded brown eyes roved over the numerous rows of books, bound in finest Moroccan leather. Mentally he approved the meticulously waxed sheen of the Chippendale chairs and the parquetry floor.

He had made himself a rich man, and he would soon be richer still, with holdings far beyond the South. Already he had begun carving out a foothold in the lucrative North. Not even Tom or Ross knew the extent of his ambition. Edmund believed he saw the weaknesses of the South in a way neither of his friends would. The slave system would not go on forever. One day, Northern fanatics—helped by Southern traitors—would see to it that labor had to be hired.

He couldn't stop that, but by the time it happened, he'd be well entrenched in Northern manufacturing. It would be Abolitionist money he'd use to pay his Southern hired help. His lands would most likely be worked out anyway. He'd still have the best of it. Then he'd take up something else. Politics? *Governor Edmund Revanche.* That had an impressive ring to it . . .

Ross Bennett's raucous laughter shattered Edmund's pleasant reverie, jerking him abruptly back to his guests.

"Hey, Edmund, you heah that? Tom says he is *tarred,* and wants to go to bed!"

Revanche, his earlier fury well hidden, joined in the laughter. He said too solicitously, "Hope nothin's wrong, Tom. Not feelin' poorly or anythin', are you?"

Tom laughed ruefully. "I don't know how you do it, Edmund. It's been a long night—"

"Now Tom's fixin' to make it a longer night! Pour yourself another drink, Tom boy."

Grinning broadly, Tom said, "Ross, why don't you go to hell?"

Edmund's and Ross's eyes met in amusement. Edmund said, "I'll see you to the staircase."

"Sleep good!" Ross called, still smiling.

At the foot of the stairs, Tom turned. "You'll send her up, Edmund?"

The taller man clasped Tom's shoulder. "I've never left you wantin', Tom."

Half an hour later Edmund summoned Ullah. He motioned her toward the stairs and watched as she climbed slowly, gracefully, her head with its pale brown curling hair held proudly, her breasts and full buttocks moving provocatively under the cotton shift. A handsome wench, he thought. Why had he never thought so before now?

Ross was sprawled comfortably across the leather sofa. "I made myself at home in your liquor cabinet." Airily, he waved a glass of absinthe at his host. "My God, Edmund, I've heard of men being faithful to their wives—but to a quadroon slave? How long has it been this same nigra?"

Edmund shrugged. "Three years . . . maybe four."

"Why don't you give him a different one? You gettin' miserly, Edmund?" Ross grinned, holding out his empty glass to be refilled.

"Tom can have any wench he wishes. He doesn't want anyone else. What about you? Is there one you haven't tried, Ross?"

Ross's face grew still. "Just one."

Edmund sat back in his chair.

Ross prompted him. "Aren't you goin' to ask who?"

"I already know."

Ross jerked his thumb toward the ceiling. "Tom won't share her. But damn my eyes if I wouldn't like to try that little nigra."

"You'll have to ask Tom, since he's buyin' her."

Ross sighed. "Well, I guess I'll never know what Ullah's got."

Revanche smiled slowly. "Tonight she still belongs to me."

Ross sat up, excited. "What a joke on old Tom!"

His host shifted irritably in his chair, his good humor suddenly soured. His anger was back, anger at Tom for making a complete fool of him. "If you want her, take her. I haven't seen Tom's money yet."

"You're gettin' het up at the wrong person, Edmund. It wasn't me that fast-talked you into sellin' her. Besides, this is a joke . . . somethin' to laugh about in the mornin' . . . among three old friends—"

"She's a slave! *Property!*" Revanche snapped. "If you want her, take her! Good night, Ross."

"Ahh, Edmund, don't be like that. I didn't mean to insult you. Have a nightcap with me. Like you said, she's of no account. Sit down, now."

In his room Tom Pierson was trembling with anticipation. He sat on the edge of the bed, his hands clasped tight, his heart pounding in joy and relief. Edmund had given his word to sell Ullah. Tom hadn't mentioned the child. Surely Edmund would realize that if he wanted Ullah, he would want Angela, the child that was his out of her.

Abruptly his mind veered to Ullah. What words does a man use to tell his woman that she was free now—and his?

Tom shivered, glancing anxiously at the door waiting for the moment Ullah would appear there, knowing that with her securely in his arms the right words would come. Somehow then, close to her, one with her, he'd know how to tell her. To him she was a woman, neither black nor white, slave nor free, but a woman he loved with all his heart.

Lost in his dreams of her, he didn't hear her light steps across the room, didn't know she was there until she knelt before him, her eyes wide and love filled.

"Sleepy, Tom?" she teased. Her voice, like all the rest of her was soft, gentle, inviting.

Tom stood, catching her up into his arms and whirling around the room holding her, laughing until she laughed with him. "I'll never be sleepy again!" he declared, and laughed again. His breath grew short as her scent flowed into his nostrils. He buried his lips in her neck, her hair, and felt her warmth against him.

Quickly he untied the cord that bound her shift, and slipped the rough garment over her head. She stood proudly before him, knowing how he loved to gaze at her naked body. Almost reverently his hands lifted her small breasts. Hungrily he kissed each one until the dark nipples became erect.

"Shall Ah draw yo' boots off, Tom?" she asked. It was the start of their familiar love ritual.

"Please," he said, more aroused than ever before. He seated himself, and she straddled his legs, her round buttocks toward him. Eagerly he watched her in the lamplight as she bent gracefully, tugging each boot off. His hands sought and caressed her as she moved.

"Yo' coat, Tom?" Her practiced fingers undid the buttons and slid his frock coat off. Each time asking permission, she removed his waistcoat, his cravat, shirt, and breeches, lingering over each movement as he had taught her, arousing him with slow, sensuous touch, until, naked and erect, he took her in his arms. At last his lips met hers, his tongue seeking, hers replying.

Abruptly he let her go and lay down. This again was a signal. Obediently she knelt and began to stroke his temples, moving her strong fingers down to the cords at the sides of his neck. She bent her head and kissed him lightly, her tongue teasing his lips. He pulled her to him so that she was straddling his body, leaning so that he could kiss her nipples.

Expertly the slave girl kneaded his body, finally stroking upward, inside his thighs, until he thought he would explode with desire for her. His fingers cupped her breasts. He held himself still, feeling her fragrant warmth slowly envelop him.

They lay together, shuddering in mutual delight. Now he could tell her that he had bought her freedom. He could offer her a new and more precious kind of bondage, one they could share all their lives.

But only minutes from now, he would become Ullah's slave. It would be he who awaited her signals. It would be his hands that massaged her, feeling on her lovely breasts and belly the delicate striations that told of her having carried his child. And it would be Ullah who would lie quietly or move under him as she wished when they joined again. Ullah, his sweet love, his wife.

Late, when Tom had fallen heavily asleep, Ullah rose and put on her shift. It would be the last time she'd ever have to leave him, God be praised. It was too much that He should have given her Tom, her freedom, and her child as well—it was more than anyone could hope to have. Never before had she known the airy lightness in her heart that she felt now as she crept warm and content from Tom's bed.

She padded softly down the unlighted servant's staircase. Lights still shone on the main floor, though the house was silent.

"Somebody's gonna git it." She began to extinguish the lamps to save someone from a good thrashing. She opened the study door. Ross Bennett lay on the sofa, nodding groggily, the glass held loosely in his hand tilted, spilling liqueur on the shining floor each time he exhaled.

Ullah had always been a little scared of Mastah Ross. He wanted her, wanted her bad. In his eyes the glintings of desire mixed with covetous hate. A cruel gent'man, the other women told her after he had used them. She shivered, gooseflesh rising on her arms.

Stealthily she took the glass from his limp fingers. With the hem of her shift she wiped the floor. Ross's hand reached out, hunting his glass, and found Ullah.

The slave girl stiffened, then she rolled out of his grasp.

"Nigger!" His voice was harsh, drunken, but commanding.

Ullah knew better than to try to run, even to Tom. She took a deep breath and looked straight into his eyes. "Yessuh, Mastah Ross." God knew what he'd do to her, but he would not break her spirit. Tomorrow she would be a free woman. She'd keep thinking on that.

Ross grinned sloppily, saliva glistening on his lower lip. "Hot damn!" he grabbed for her breasts.

Ullah sidestepped his groping hands. They faced each other, Ross weaving slightly. "Nigger, you better not move away from me again, or I'll thrash your yeller ass myself."

She said with dignity, "My name is Ullah, Mastah Ross." Hatred gleamed from her large, dark eyes.

Ross's hand darted out and caught her on the cheekbone, nearly knocking her down. "Don't you put no evil eye on me, nigger, you heah?"

Ullah lowered her eyes. "Yassuh, Mastah Ross."

He was enjoying himself hugely. "Ease my britches off, wench. An' mind you don't make any mistakes, for I got a mighty big yearnin', an' I aim to have you tend to it for me."

Silently, skillfully, she removed his breeches. Then Bennett's large hairy hands were at her neckline, ripping the flimsy shift open.

"Hot damn! So Edmund sent you! Well, come here, yeller gal, and le's see what you got."

Ullah hesitated. Ross grasped her hair, jerking her head to one side. She winced. "Tom never been rough? You're gonna like it." He laughed. "They all like it that way."

He threw her to the floor, falling heavily on her, biting her fair skin, sucking greedily and painfully at her nipples, twisting handfuls of her flesh in his uncontrolled rutting.

Ullah held herself rigid, waiting in fear for his next move. She was always afraid of what Revanche's guests would do to her. When folks thought you hadn't the same feelings and spirit they had, there was no telling what they might do. But Ross was worse than the rest; this night was worse. Tom was upstairs sleeping, never dreaming of the dreadful thing that was happening to her. He had promised her that for the first time in her life she could count on the pleasures of love and not the devices of lust. Tom would never lie to her. It was a nameless cruelty that in this moment, only hours from freedom, with the warmth of Tom's loving still heating her own blood, this insane, drunken animal should take her.

"On your hands and knees, bitch!"

She braced herself against the sharp pain and indignity, trying not to hear his grunts as he lunged into her. When he rolled away from her, panting heavily, he said, "Don't you move, heah? There's somethin' more you're goin' to do for me! Only got one time with you . . . make the best of it." He lay back, skinning her with his eyes, laughing cruelly.

Trying not to sob, not to feel the fire that gnawed inside her, Ullah waited, trembling with fear. Ross Bennett got up and sat, his legs sprawled. "Crawl over heah an' put your head on my lap."

Ullah made her mind a blank. She did what he made her do, then stayed on her knees in front of him, uncertainly. He raised one foot, planted it in her face, and sent her tumbling backward.

As she scrambled for the remnants of her shift, fighting against the urge to vomit, Ross Bennett turned on his side and went smiling to sleep.

Ullah crept to her cabin, tiptoeing in so as not to wake the other occupants. She lay on her cot, her head turned away from Angela, curled up peacefully in one small corner. Ullah muffled her sobs in the shuck-filled tick. She had never cried like this before. But never before had she thought of herself as a person like anyone else. Never before had she been Tom Pierson's promised wife.

There were two sides to this world, the clean beauty-filled place she had glimpsed with Tom and the side populated by men like Mastah Revanche and Mastah Ross. That side was dirty, the abode of devils and demons and hell's fire nipping up from the dark regions to sear those who tried to walk this earth decently.

Tom awakened feeling happier than any other day in his life. The sun shone brighter. In the air was a perfume of blossoms. He would start for home right away. Edmund expected him to stay several days, but he had much to do before he dared make Ullah his own.

Edmund would understand Tom's unquenchable appetite for Ullah. He would never understand marriage between them. Edmund would rigidly support the vicious Black Code that forbade miscegenation. And for his resentment and humiliation that Tom had taken his slave to wife, Edmund would make Tom pay dearly.

He glanced outside. Ullah should have been here by now. This morning of all mornings he had expected her to be early. He finished dressing. Perhaps, like him, she wanted no more of their master-slave relationship.

Then too, it would be like Edmund to keep her busy until the moment Tom had her papers in his hand. Edmund could be petty like that.

"Good mornin', Edmund." With a grandiose bow, Tom placed the four-thousand-dollar bank draft on the desk.

Subtly Edmund's expression changed. He did not move to pick it up.

Tom's heart plummeted. Wasn't the man going to keep his word? Then Edmund opened a drawer, withdrew a paper, and signed it. "I wish you the joy of your purchase, Tom. I hope you are as wise as you are enthusiastic."

Tom felt as though Edmund were staring at his innermost thoughts. "Thanks, Edmund, I'm very—happy 'bout it." Suddenly he wanted to be away from the house, away from this room and Edmund that very minute. "I hate to leave so soon, but I've got an afternoon appointment. I hope you'll understand."

He left the study red to the ears, feeling like a youngster caught in wrongdoing. He went down the rows of whitewashed cabins to Ullah's. Two women stood talking by the cabin door. Their talk stopped abruptly. With wary, anticipatory looks they eyed him and moved off. Tom did not notice their unusual behavior; he was too anxious to be on his way.

Smiling again, he entered the cabin. Ullah sat dispiritedly on her cot, her hands folded limply on her lap. A golden-haired three-year-old child shrieking, "Mas' Tom! Mas' Tom!" grabbed him around the shins and hung on, giggling in delight. He swooped down, taking Angela in his arms, raising her squealing and laughing until her small hands could touch the ceiling. Ullah sat unmoving, her head turned away.

Tom put the child down. "Honey, you go play. Pretty soon we're goin' for a ride in the carriage." Tom watched her fondly as she scampered into the bright patch of sunlight just outside the door.

He looked uncertainly at Ullah, huddled in the dimness. "You're not sorry to be leavin' here, are you?"

"Ah could never be sorry 'bout you, Tom," she whispered.

"Then what?" Gently he turned her face toward him. She jerked away, but he had seen. He said harshly, "What happened?"

Her eyes were fearful. "Ah . . . Ah fell."

His arms went about her. His tenderness should have thawed the awful feeling of cold shame. But Ullah had never felt soiled as she did now. She had been resentful, hurt, and humiliated other times when she had been used by Edmund's guests, but Mastah Ross had dirtied her in a way none of the others had—all because Tom had showed her what it was to be clean and purely loved.

Always before she had been able to ignore these dark thoughts or hide them away in some deep recesss of her being. But before, she had never believed there could be a better life.

"Ullah, tell me what's wrong," Tom pleaded. "We can't start this mornin' with secrets and private hurts. What happened to you?"

Ullah said nothing, unable to tell him how his friend had abused her, afraid of what Tom might do.

But he had her by the hand, leading her over to the light. He slipped off her shift. As his shocked eyes darted over her body, she saw the veins in his temples swell.

"Keep Angela with you. I'll be back soon," he said hoarsely. He saw his daughter standing in the doorway, looking curiously at her beloved Mas' Tom. "Go stay with your mama now."

He knew it hadn't been Edmund. Edmund was simply too arrogant and fastidious for this particular method. It had to be Ross. It was like Ross to do this, to think it a great joke, never seeing the hideous cruelty of it.

As Tom strode up the rise that separated the slave quarters from the house, Ross was on his way to the stables. Tom shouted, "Hey, wait a minute! I'll ride with you."

Ross stood waiting. "Edmund tells me you're leavin' already."

Tom managed a smile. "I've got time enough for a ride."

"Sure you won't stay? The Quadroon Ball's tonight."

"I've already got my quadroon."

The grooms led out the horses, and the men mounted. "It isn't the same," Ross said. "Now those quadroons . . . they're taught to please a man. They *know!*"

"Ullah is pleasin'."

Ross grinned at him, his look slyly knowing. "Yeah," he drawled, "but a good mount isn't all there is to a woman."

Tom urged his horse to a full canter. As Ross caught up with him again, Tom turned shortly. "You liked Ullah?"

"Slow down a little. Sure I liked her. You angry?"

"Why should I be angry?" Tom asked indifferently.

"Well, you could be a little riled. Where's the fun if you don't care who has her?" He laughed. "We had you wrong. Edmund and I thought you wanted her all to yourself. Looks like the joke's on us."

Tom dismounted at a grove of live oaks, festooned with lacy gray Spanish moss. "Let them cool down a bit." The horses headed for the stream that divided the grove from Edmund's fields. Several blacks stopped their plowing to stand silently watching. "Got a bottle with you, Ross?"

"Sho'ly." Ross sprawled comfortably against the tree. He drank, then handed the bottle to Tom.

Tom swallowed deeply and set the bottle between them. "Don't ever come near Ullah again, Ross."

Ross stared at him. "You back on that? I thought you didn't care."

"Did I say that?" His eyes met Ross's coldly.

Ross, reaching for the bottle, stopped. "Wait a minute,

Tom," he said, edging away. "It was just a lark . . . you know me . . . it didn't mean a thing."

Tom stood up, towering menacingly over Ross. The Negroes in the field crowded closer to the edge of the stream. "Stand up, Ross old *friend*. I don't like kickin' the shit out of you while you're still on the ground."

"Look . . . Tom!"

"You heard me."

"I'm not goin' to do any such damned thing," Ross whined. "My God, Tom, Ullah's been with damn near every man we know. Why me? What'd I do? You goin' after all of 'em?"

"No. Just you." Tom grabbed Ross by his lapels, jerking him to his feet, his face only inches away. Ross stood like a stunned rabbit as Tom's fist crashed into his mouth. Ross's punches were wild. Tom, cold with rage, found every target: Ross's chin, his eyes, the pit of his stomach. As Ross doubled over, Tom's knee lifted viciously into his groin.

Ross groaned and fell to the ground, his stomach and vitals paining sickeningly. Tom leaped on him, reaching in blind fury for the bottle they had shared. He hit it against the tree, showering liquor and glass. In his hand was the neck, jagged and sharp.

Ross looked up, terrified. "Tom, no! Please! For God's sake, I didn't mean anythin'—she didn't mean a thing to me! Please! Oh, God, please—Tom!"

Tom, straddling him, let the bottle come down almost to Ross's horrified eyes. After a long moment he shuddered and tossed it away. He hardly recognized his own voice when he spoke. "Don't ever come near her again, Ross. I'll kill you."

He left Ross lying on the ground, moaning. The black faces stared across the stream at him, approving yet sullen. He mounted his horse, riding toward Ullah's cabin.

Her eyes widened with fear when she saw him spattered with blood, one eye reddened and already turning dark. "Tom!" She reached out for him, but he brushed her away.

"I don't need any help. Gather up your belongin's!" He stalked out of the cabin to get the carriage.

Ullah hurriedly bundled up her ruined shift, the rough blanket that had been folded neatly on her tick, and a small battered wooden box.

Tom returned holding Angela frightened and clinging to

his neck. "Is that all? Leave it. You won't need any of it."

Slyly Ullah kept the battered box under her arm.

"Leave it!"

Tears came to her eyes. "It's mah *things.*"

Tom shut his eyes for a moment. He said gently, "Let's go, Ullah."

In minutes he was driving through the outer gates of Gray Oaks. He would never again return to the welcome he had so long enjoyed or to the life he had led so casually until this morning.

Ullah sat quietly beside him, while the blond child on her lap bounced and giggled with the novelty of a carriage ride. Held tightly between Ullah's bare feet, was the scarred box that held her things.

Tom Pierson touched Ullah's arm, and they smiled at each other, more in hope than in certainty that everything would be all right.

Chapter Three

In New Orleans, Tom stopped on Rue Royale and, blushing, bought shoes, stockings, gloves, and petticoats. He selected for Ullah a shaded-silk dress of blue and green, with a matching bonnet. For Angela he found a flounced dress of gold muslin. Last he bought Ullah a veil and a fine cassimere shawl.

He drove to an abandoned shed, standing guard while Ullah and Angela made their transformation. Tears came into his eyes at the sight of his handsome woman and child.

Ullah, knowing they were unobserved, kissed him on the mouth. She said softly, "Tom, you the onliest person ever make me feel so feelsy. Ah gwine do for you the bes' Ah ever did."

Tom took Ullah, primly veiled, along the streets of the city he had always loved. They passed through the Vieux Carré, resplendent with lushly flowering plants, dignified in its fine brick homes with glimpses of intimate courtyards and lacelike ironwork balconies, safe and settled in the rich, joy-filled life of the Creole.

He wanted Ullah to see it as he did, to feel the soft,

tender air, to sense the blue sky and its thick creamy clouds that moved swiftly ahead of the Gulf breezes. He wanted her to know the odors of the waterfront, its faint fishiness, its heady smells of molasses and coffee beans. He stopped the carriage by a huge Negress in a white apron and tignon, calling, *"Belles calas, Madame! Tout chauds, Madame!"* and bought them all the thin, hot Creole fritters.

He was looking for a particular man, one he had frequently seen on the busy fringes of Circus Square. At last he saw him, a wizened, smiling black man in a tattered cast-off green coat. He stood on Rampart Street, clapping two grimy blocks of wood to punctuate his joyous singsong invitation.

"An' breth'en an' sistahs *(tap, tap)*, if yo wants to git to heb'n *(tap, tap)*, yo got to heed de Gospel *(taptaptap)* an' yo gotta do good *(tap, taptap, tap, taptap, tapppp!)!"*

Tom made his arrangements. In a few minutes they were in the formal garden behind a church, facing a fragrant riot of blooms. On the old man's face was a look of intense pride as he married the lovely dark-eyed quadroon girl and the obviously enamored ruddy-faced man. Tom had never given thought to weddings, but he knew his own was beautiful.

He had no ring to place on Ullah's finger. No one bore witness to their marriage. It was an event important only to those two and having no legality.

Their marriage was a vow taken against the Black Code, a law already one and a quarter centuries old. Tom Pierson became a felon liable to be hanged by the righteous for marrying the only woman he ever loved.

After they left the church, Tom turned into the American section where he lived. Here, street sounds and familiar faces seemed more sharply drawn on this momentous day. To those who called greetings from the banquettes, Tom nodded, acutely aware that he had made himself an alien to all he had ever known and loved. While he spoke to these welcoming faces with a smile stretched on his own, beside him, shawled and veiled, he hid his wife to protect her from them.

It was impossible for him to live in New Orleans now. He would have to leave without saying any farewells to these people he had called friend. With the awful clarity of a thought vaguely considered but largely ignored, Tom now foresaw he could not, even for a night, bring Ullah into his house as his wife. His own servants would mutter in the corridors where he could hear them; they would spread word of his deed; they would take their subtle revenge on Ullah for thinking herself above her natural station.

He made another stop, another purchase. In the barn behind his house, Ullah changed once more. When she emerged, she wore the servant's full-skirted calico dress. Her only visible nod to vanity was a striking seven-pointed tignon that covered her head. Until he could get them safely away, Ullah would be his new servant, barred from him in every way he wanted her to be near.

Their most serious threat, while they remained in New Orleans, came from Angela. At three, she was too young to be drawn into the deception.

As they approached the front porch, Ullah hesitated, then dropped behind them and walked around to the servant's entrance. Tom went on, Angela hanging onto his finger, pointing and, in her peculiar darky patois, commenting on everything she saw.

Tom's butler, William, grinned when he saw the blond, pale-skinned child, whom Tom introduced as his sister's daughter. William's expression flickered. Mercifully, Angela did not call for mamá or try to find Ullah when he lifted her into Bessie's arms to be entertained, coddled, and cosseted as she had never been in her life. She would be safe, kept busy and away from Ullah.

Tom told his housekeeper, Jewel, of Ullah's arrival and outlined her duties. He had never felt so dishonorable or so much a sneak as he did in that moment.

He went to bed that night, minutely aware that Ullah slept in his slave quarters, separated from him, and too near the male servants, who did not know she was married at all, much less to their master.

By dawn he hadn't slept at all. Miserably he stared at the ornate ceiling. His eyes felt like sand grating along the shore. But slowly the cherubs embossed on the ceiling had their hypnotic effect. Tom's eyes closed.

He was sound asleep by the time Angela awakened to a strange room, hearing strange sounds. The smells and feel of the place were different, and Ullah was not there, warm and close beside her. Frightened, Angela began to whimper, then to cry in earnest for her mother.

Downstairs, Ullah could hear her daughter. Preparing

Tom's breakfast, she listened anxiously for the sounds that would tell her Tom had gone to Angela. Nothing broke the quiet of the house but Angela's small, frightened cries. Nervously Ullah started toward the staircase, only to turn back, knowing if she walked up those stairs to her daughter now, it would end their secret.

It was too late. Angela was peering down the staircase. At the bottom she saw Ullah. "Mama! Mama!"

Ullah looked around anxiously. From the dining room came the round, jowled, curious face of Jewel, the house-keeper. Ullah stammered, "Po' li'l thing . . . she misses her mama." She scooped Angela up into her arms and held her fast as she cooed and comforted, trying to make it sound as though the child cried for a mother who wasn't there at all. Ullah had only to glance back at Jewel's face to know it was a matter of minutes before every slave on Tom's property would be speculating about Masta Tom's new servant and the child.

She took Angela upstairs and knelt by her, drying her tear-stained face. "You be a good li'l gal now. You let Bessie dress you, then mebbe they'll be somethin' special happen to you today. Mebbe they's a pony cart for you to ride in . . . that right, Bessie?"

New tears formed in Angela's eyes. Her hand clutched at Ullah's bodice.

Tom, immobilized, viewed the scene. "Bessie! What's goin' on here?"

Bessie's eyes widened as she mouthed words. "Ah doan know, Mastah Tom."

"Does it take both of you to manage one small child?"

"No suh, but—"

"But nothin'. Come here, Angela." He lifted her into his arms. "Go back downstairs, Ullah. Bessie can manage now. You *can,* can't you, Bessie!"

"Oh, yassuh, Ah sho' kin. Yassuh!" She nodded vigor-ously.

Tom took Angela with him, making her laugh as he showed her her own image in the mirror, then lathered her small face as he shaved his own. Once he had Angela content, he gave her back to Bessie.

"We'll have to leave here immediately," he muttered to Ullah in the dining room. She bustled around serving him breakfast.

"You shou'n'ta brung us heah. They knows, an' what

they knows eve'y darky in Nawlens is gwine know afore the evenin' pinks up tonight. Won't be long till yo' white frien's knows too."

"No one knows!" Tom looked at her in alarm, then frowned. "Not for sure . . . everythin' will be all right."

Ullah smiled at him, removing his coffee cup from his hand to refill it before he absentmindedly drank the dregs. "It gwine be all right, 'cause you say so." She looked mischievously at him from the corner of her eye. "But they knows. Ain't no darky gwine be bamboozled by a ragtail story like our'n."

He'd hardly finished breakfast when William came to announce Josiah Whinburn. "My God, I'd forgotten!"

"My apologies for bein' so early, Tom," said Josiah.

"It's fine, Josiah, fine. I'm glad you came early."

"I . . . got an offer to sell Marsh House." Josiah looked miserable.

"Who made the offer?" Mentally, Tom put his money on Edmund.

"Mr. George Andreas, the lawyer. He wants to move to the country."

"Are you goin' to accept?"

"I've got one hundred dollars cash. Edmund won the money I was countin' on to see me through the rollin' season. I can't let my people starve."

"You were a God-damned fool, not thinkin' of this until now."

Josiah nodded, his head down. "I'm gonna lose mah daddy's plantation."

"Guess you don't know George Andreas is my attorney."

Josiah's head jerked up. "What does that mean, suh?"

"He's Edmund Revanche's attorney too. That's what it means."

"Why, the low-down . . . you think he's actin' for Edmund?"

Tom put his hand up. "I can't answer for Edmund. But I know you need money, and I'm offerin' to lend it to you. Twenty-five thousand ought to carry you through the year."

Josiah's face seemed to dissolve. "My—God, Tom! I knew you for a kind man . . . but"—he buried his face in his hands and sobbed.

Tom squirmed uneasily. "Think you might get it paid back in ten years?"

"Yes . . . yes, I can." He wiped his eyes. "You're a blessin' straight from the Lord, Tom, an' Him willin', I'll pay you back."

"There's one condition on this money, Josiah." Josiah's eyes never wavered from Tom's face. "There'll be no more gamblin'."

Josiah's voice caught on the laughter of relief. "You got my word, suh." He thrust out his hand to Tom.

"Good! Let's go down to the bank and get this drawn up."

Later that day, about fifteen miles northwest of New Orleans, Tom found the Welkins holding nestled in tree-shrouded isolation, its back against the bayou. The land around it was owned by poor whites, Arcadians of a forgotten past eking out a living by their own independent code in the lengthy shadows of the great plantations.

Mr. Welkins's bayou farm was sixteen acres, and perhaps not that.

"Watah changes the face of the land sometimes," Welkins drawled. He spat at a huge cypress, hitting its trunk dead center with a wash of tobacco juice. "Bes' I recall, that tree marked the east boundary." He grinned at Tom. "Never know for sho'. Trees grow. Change."

Tom said nothing. He entered the yard through a disrepaired opening in the split-rail fencing and walked toward the house.

"Bad storm hit the house 'while back. Never did get 'round to fixin' it."

The mud chimney needed repairing. On the ground lay sodden cypress shakes. Behind the house was a large barn. Welkins took care of his outbuildings: The barn, chicken house, and smokehouse were in good repair.

Tom saw a flat-bottomed boat. "That goes with the house."

"Hadn't figgered on that. Hadn't figgered on sellin' a-tall."

Only days ago, Tom wouldn't have spoken to this man, wouldn't have looked at land whose boundaries changed with the growth of trees or the coming of rain. Today was a different time, a different life.

"You've sold your farm." Tom tried to smile.

Like an animal smelling fear, Welkins's watery eyes

narrowed as he sensed Tom's need. "Never said I was
sellin'. What's a fine fella like you want with my ol' place?".
He fingered the cloth of Tom's coat.

"I've stated my price, Mr. Welkins." He waited, hiding
his anxiety as the old man considered his chances of dick-
ering. Welkins took the money, his bundle of possessions,
his mule, and left that same afternoon.

The next day Tom took Ullah to see the house. She stood
amidst the rubble cluttering the house Welkins had
abandoned for the shelter of the barn and looked at the
tattered mess of quilts and upholstery that mice had
chewed up for nests. The leavings of a family of raccoons
were on the floor. Bright sunlight came vivid and sparkling through the holes in the roof. Tom winced, seeing
with Ullah's eyes the home to which he had brought her.

"We got some fixin' to be done, Mastah Tom." She
laughed as Tom marveled that she could still tease.

"I didn't think to look at the inside," Tom apologized.
"I guess I was too anxious to find a place—any place. I'll
keep lookin'."

"What fo'? This'll be a fine place, soon's it's fixed up."

"It's all that was available in such short time, but I'll—"

Ullah shoved at him playfully, her hands against his
chest, before she pulled him toward her. She kissed him,
smoothing away the frown from his face and the worry
from his eyes. "Quit yo' fussin'. Get up on that roof, man.
Ah ain't gwine stay heah with the rain po'in' down on me."
She took the sage broom from the corner. He watched her
for a minute; then she turned to look at him, her eyebrows
raised.

Tom patched the roof with whatever he could find. He
would have to make more cypress shakes . . . learn how
to make them. He looked down at his red, raw hands. He
had always considered his hands manfully hardened; now
they looked like uncooked meat, scraped and bristling with
splinters. He was far less prepared than Ullah to live this
primitive life. Servants had always done his manual labor.
It would be weeks before his hands would toughen enough
to give him a day's work he could take pride in.

"Stop awhile," he said as he came back into the house.
"You're puttin' me to shame."

"Looks mo' like a house again, don't it?" she asked
proudly.

"Yes, it does. I don't know how you did it. But it'll be

sunset soon." He grinned at her. "Spare a bit o' time for me."

Ullah set the bucket of scrubwater on the sideboard of the cookroom, placed her hand in Tom's, and let him draw her near.

"I want to show you the rest of the property. It's not as bad as the house." He kissed her, his hands skimming her torso.

Ullah, her head thrown back, laughed, the sound deep in her throat, soft and enticing. "What prop'ty you talkin' 'bout showin' me, Tom?"

His voice quavered as he laughed and moved away from her. Together they walked out into the dusky light. The trees and grass glowed deeply verdant in the rosy hues of the evening. All around them the bayou shimmered, reflecting earth and sky until they were engulfed in its eerie charms, no longer able to tell the bayou mirage from the solid ground.

"We gwine be happy heah." Ullah shivered in pleasure against him, then they walked on, moving away from the house down a winding path.

He led her to a small grove of trees near the woods and knelt, dipping his fingers into the bayou. "It's warm." He looked hopefully at her, his eyes glowing dark as she hesitated, then moved toward him. "Come on, Ullah. Don't be afraid."

Reluctantly, she slipped off her dress and followed him. He swam effortlessly; she floundered dangerously. He put his arm under her, and they floated dreamily watching the evening sky.

Then Ullah laughed, a rich, carefree sound. He drew her closer, her arms twined around his neck, and carried her from the water. Ullah sat down in her graceful way on the long grass that edged the bayou. She looked sidelong at him. "This mighty near sof' as a bed."

"I been wonderin' 'bout that," he said softly and reached out to cup her breasts.

Her fingers ran swiftly, adoringly, down his body. "You a mighty fine gent'man, Tom. Doan reckon any nigger ever been lucky like me."

His hands stopped their teasing movements. "Don't say 'nigger', Ullah. Don't ever say it again. Promise me."

She smiled. "Ah try, but Ah doan promise. Now, kin you tell me again how much you love me? Ah like hearin' that."

Like most men confronted with such a request, Tom fell mute. He kissed her eyes, her ears, her mouth, her breasts. His desire rose with the stroking of her fingers; his heart beat faster. In the warm evening glow he gazed upon her lovely face and saw in her drowsy eyes ardent invitation. He lay on top of her, in her, with her legs wrapped over his back. They moved together and then were still.

Tom lay back, content, the grass cool and lush beneath his bare skin. He plucked a long shaft of grass. He ran it over Ullah's skin, making her laugh.

Suddenly he sat bolt upright. "What was that? Did you hear it?"

"Heah what?"

"Someone . . . somethin'—by God! I did! Cover yourself!" He ran toward the woods, following darting flashes of color.

Three adolescent boys ran like startled deer, cannily keeping to the protective covering of trees and bushes. They spread out, running in different directions. In deference to his bare feet, Tom ran as hard as he could after the smallest of the three. He was no more than two paces from seizing the boy when he was hit from behind.

"Run, Beau! Run! I've got him!" the young rapscallion yelled. Then, as Tom regained his feet, the boy began to run again. Tom bellowed at him, angry at having been felled, furious at the look of taunting triumph on the boy's face as he stared back at Tom, daring him to continue the chase.

Stark-naked, Tom leaped bushes and hurled himself forward, chasing around trees, bellowing at the boy like an enraged bull. In a stretch of clearing Tom knew he had his prey. He grabbed thin air as his quarry made a diving leap for an overhanging bough, swinging himself upward.

"You damned monkey, get down here!" Tom glared into the foliage, meeting bright, devilish blue eyes. "Son of a bitch! Get down!"

The boy didn't move, nor did he lose the bold, defiant smile that played around his lips.

"By God, you'll come down if I have to bring you down myself." Tom shook the tree. He began to climb the curving, gnarled trunk. "God be with you, boy, if I do myself harm climbing this damned tree!"

The boy laughed and leaped to the ground. Helpless, halfway up the trunk, Tom stared back at him. The boy didn't run, nor had he any decent appearance of fright.

Tom pushed off from the tree with all his might, hurling himself at the boy, knocking them both to the ground. Holding his captive securely by the ear and pinning an arm behind his back, he marched him back to the edge of the bayou where Ullah waited.

"You all right, Tom?" At his jerky nod she relaxed, her lips twitching at the sight of her naked husband and the very indignant youth being pulled along by his ear.

"Who the hell are you?" Tom released his hold, having no idea why he trusted the boy to remain still.

But his instinct had been correct. The boy stood his ground, his blue eyes blazing and arrogant. He was a handsome youth of about fifteen, tall, broad-shouldered, and well made. His hands and forearms, emerging from the rolled-up sleeves of his rough work shirt, were tanned, as tough and muscular as any man's. His hair was midnight black and curled, unruly and soft, to frame a face that promised strength in every feature.

It didn't improve Tom's disposition to have to look up several inches into the dancing blue eyes of the young hellion. "By God, answer me or I'll lick the livin' lard right outa you, boy."

"You'll not lick anything out of me."

Tom, bristling, moved forward. Ullah put her hand out, her palm warm on Tom's bare chest. Still smiling, she said, "What's yo' name, boy?"

Tensed again, poised to run, the boy looked at her. He relaxed visibly. "Adam Tremain," he said with defiant hauteur.

"Well, Adam Tremain, you been lookin' at somethin' no nice boy dint ought t'be lookin' at. You got anythin' to say fo' yo'seff?"

He seemed about to make another rebellious reply, then his gaze dropped to the ground. "No, ma'am."

"You will when I'm done with you!" Tom snapped. "It's high time somebody taught you manners."

Adam looked straight at Tom's penis, put his fists on his hips, and said, *"You're* going to teach me manners? What kind of manners?"

The blood rushed to Tom's face. Ullah stepped smoothly between them, stern and reproving. "You a mighty sassy youngun, Adam. If you was mine, Ah'd have a mighty lot o' shame over you. You better get yo'seff on outa heah."

Adam's haughty expression drained away. He started to speak when Tom said, glowering, "Go on! Don't show your face here again!"

Ullah and Tom watched until Adam disappeared into the thickening dark of the woods. Ullah sighed, her heart aching. She felt flat and sorry. The way he had left, it seemed as though she and Tom had been wrong.

"Ullah! Where in the hell are my britches?"

"You were too harsh with him, Tom." She handed his clothes to him.

"Harsh, hell. I shoulda whaled the tar outa him."

"If you'da thought that, you'da done it. Ah know you, Tom."

"Impudunt young pup! Prob'ly some damn redneck's kid."

"He's no white trash. Not that'n."

"Says who?" he asked sourly.

"Sez somebody that knows," Ullah replied sassily. "That's the trouble with you white folks. Doan know yo' own kind even eyeball to eyeball."

"Will you stop that talk! It's all behind us now!"

"Not fo' me, Tom. Ah's a nigger. It never gwine be behind me."

"Damn it, Ullah, what's got into you tonight? You're as good as anyone. Better than most. You're no nigger." He put his arm alongside of hers. In the faint light of the moon his showed darker. "See there, by God, you're whiter than I am."

Ullah laughed brittlely, but her voice remained serious. "Ah never say Ah ain't as good as the res' o' them, Tom. But Ah's still a nigger, an' Ah doan wan' us to forget it. Ah's a nigger 'cause somebody come over to Affica one time an' took my gran'daddy an' make him a nigger. That's the way Ah gets to be one, and it hain't got nothin' to do with the color o' my skin. It's got to do with people. People who plays the Lawd and make us somethin' we was never meant to be."

Tom put his arms around her. "What is it, Ullah? What are you tellin' me?"

She shrugged. "White folks never sees 'ceptin' they wants to see."

"Why are you makin' me one of those white folks an' you a nigger?"

"Ah doan know. Ah jes' doan know, Tom. Mebbe

Ah's jes' feelin' a little low. Mebbe a little shame fo' lettin' mahseff believe you could take me away from all Ah is by makin' me yo' wife."

"But I have!"

"Oh, Tom, mah people doan make things real by wishin' 'em into bein' real. We lives by the way things is, an' the way you white folks make 'em. Those things is bad, Tom, an' we done make 'em worse. We broke that preten' worl' yo' folks fixed up nice fo' theyseffs. They ain't gwine let us do that. They let us, purty soon somebody else try it, an' afore you knows, that purty worl' they has is all gone."

"You're talkin' gibberish."

"Ah'm seein', an' yo' dreamin'!"

"Then for the love of heaven dream with me, Ullah. I'd rather not live than to lose you now."

Her hand caressed his face. "Ah's not gwine away from you. Not never," she promised softly. "But it doan change nothin', Tom."

He sighed deeply and began to walk back with her toward the carriage. "All this on account of some pukin' little shirttail boy."

"That's a good boy," Ullah said positively. Then she opened her arms, gesturing and talking as though she saw a scene before her. "It's jes' like watchin' a big ol' flock o' swans come down on the lake. In they midst is one big one, a fine big black swan. He different than the res', an' you know that one, he gwine be special. Adam be special."

Chapter Four

Ullah stood to the side of the dray, waiting patiently for Tom to admit it was already loaded to overflowing with supplies for the house on the bayou.

He looked over the wagon again. "I'll get everythin' on. How many trips do you think we can make before someone notices where we're goin'? Damn house niggers are talkin' their fool heads off now."

There was no room, and Tom knew it as well as she; but he was letting go of the life to which he was accustomed, one small piece at a time.

Changing wouldn't be easy for Tom. He had never been poor. He wasn't poor now, but he was learning to live as though he were, and he was learning to live with the continuous threat of reprisal.

There was nothing she could do to help him. Even in the simple things there was a barrier that Tom could cross only by coming to know life as Ullah had always known it. The house on the bayou would never be like the one in New Orleans. It would never hum with the activity of slaves or sing with the gaiety of visitors' revelry. It would never be adorned with the elegance of respectability. The wind would always come through the chinking in the walls and make him cold at night. In the morning there would be no one but him and the dictates of the swamp.

Tom was going to be a mighty lonely man. He would be tending to things he didn't understand when he'd rather be out riding one of the fine horses he'd no longer own or in New Orleans gambling and chatting with friends he'd no longer have. Ullah sometimes wondered why he had done it. He could have had her in any way he wanted. There were laws about concubinage, she knew, but no one paid much attention to those.

But to marriage there was a lot of attention paid. Two equal people married. Anything different gave people, black and white, ideas. He didn't have to marry her, but he had done it. She wondered if it might not have been better for them both if he hadn't. Not understanding him, she left him alone when he struck up against something from his past that would no longer fit into his future and let him find the answers for himself.

In silence Tom drove to the house on the bayou, struggling to understand how a leisurely carefree life had overnight turned into days filled with problems. Only Ullah and Angela made it worthwhile.

He glanced over at Ullah, her face, as always, a picture of sweet patience, and knew his irritation was wrong. He was balancing the value of things against the worth of this woman. Slowly, Ullah was changing his entire outlook on the things he had regarded as true, changing his thoughts and his desires.

As soon as he had finished unloading the wagon, he began to cheer up. The furniture filled the small rooms, making them seem complete and homey. "It looks nice, Ullah."

"When you gwine start lis'nin' to me, Tom, when Ah

tells you we doan need mos' o' this stuff?" She smiled and kissed him before she moved away to fix his lunch.

He watched her thoughtfully. "When you think about it, most people don't know what it is to live like I have. An' they get along just fine."

Ullah laughed, placing his food before him. "Got yo'seff convinced?"

"Just about." He grinned.

"Mebbe some li'l ol' mosquito hawk, he fin' his way into this house and bring us good luck." She looked wistfully through the open windows at the dragonflies skimming low over the water.

Tom laughed, amused and tolerant of the numerous superstitions she lived by. He stretched lazily, not wanting to leave her. "I expect I'd better git. Those old cypresses just keep on a-waitin'."

Ullah kissed him and watched as he went to the wagon. It wouldn't do her a bit of good to imagine what-all he might do to himself before he learned to use his new tools.

Slowly she began to think of other things, and the boy they had met the night before came into her mind. It surprised her a little. But there was a steady memory of those bright, defiant blue eyes that bespoke more hurt and loneliness than rebellion.

She arranged the parlor and stood back to admire it. Smiling, she glanced toward the open door.

Her hand fluttered to her breast as she gave a little cry of fright. It was almost as if she were a conjur-woman fetching him up by the power of her thoughts. "What you doin' here, Adam? You done give me a start."

He was tense and ill at ease. "I'm sorry," he said.

"No time for sorry now. You gwine stan' there, or you comin' in?"

Adam glanced about, then entered. Ullah was shaking her head.

"Tom gone to the bayou. Good thing fo' you he is. What you want?"

Adam's eyes ran approvingly over the tidy room, look-ing at everything in minute detail, everything except Ullah herself. "What happened to Old Man Welkins? He never said anything about leaving."

" 'Pears as how he did, doan it?" she said saucily.

"He always said he'd stay here as long as it took for the Yankees to come South and—" Adam shrugged.

"Do tell. That what you come fo'? Tell me 'bout Mistah Welkins?"

He met her dark, expectant eyes. "I came to apologize for last evening. I shouldn't have talked to you as I did. I'm sorry for that."

Ullah relaxed and smiled in satisfaction. "Ah knowed that already."

He looked up at her, surprised.

"Sho' Ah did, an' Ah tol' Tom. But he wasn't much fo' lis'nin'."

Adam shifted his weight, began to speak, then bit his lower lip.

"Mebbe you wasn't 'tendin' to 'pologize to Tom."

"I've got to be going. Beau—my friends are waiting for me. I just wanted to tell you that you were right last evening. My mother would have been ashamed, and so was I." Hurriedly he made for the door.

"Adam!"

He turned on the path from the house, looking back at her.

"You come back heah, Adam. It ain't me you owe a 'pology. It's Tom."

His expression was closed and stubborn. "I've got to be going."

"You a gent'man, Adam?"

"Yes, ma'am. Well, most of the time."

"If you wanta be a gent'man you proud o' bein', you starts today. Go make yo' manners to Tom. Then you come back heah, an' I'll mebbe have some lemonade an' mulatto bellies all hot an' ready fo' you." She smiled.

He stood where he was, stubborn, desiring to obey, yet uncertain.

"Prideful!" she scolded him gently. "Go on, now!"

Ullah went into the house. She began to make the batter for the ginger cookies. *No use lookin' on the dark side o' things when there's a hope the bright will come out.* She began to sing. She wouldn't even go to the window to see if he was going toward the swamp. He was her black swan. That Adam boy would be the first friend Tom would have in these bayous. He was a sign.

Adam took his time. It was one thing to apologize to Ullah. He had wanted to, had instinctively liked her from the outset. But Tom was another matter. Adam had never felt trusting toward any man. His memories of Paul Tremain were filled with hostility bred out of fear. He had grown up seeking his satisfactions out of range of his father's eye, encouraged to by his mother, driven to do so when Tremain's baleful glare was directed at him.

He knew the bayous intimately, having spent days there sometimes alone, more generally with his friends Ben West and Beau LeClerc, exploring the many channels, visiting with the families that lived nestled within its confines.

Even before his father's death, Adam was determined to become a better man than Paul Tremain. But widowed Zoe Tremain had no men friends. There was no individual her son wished to emulate. So he read much and observed and analyzed his friends and the men he knew. He created for himself a lofty pattern of perfection.

Only sometimes, Adam admitted ruefully, the pattern slid out of reach. Right now all the old hostilities were with him as he moved with the quiet, easy grace of one familiar with the marshy terrain.

He winced as he saw Tom, his knee pressed tight against a fallen tree, wielding the broadax with an ungainliness that defied the continuance of life. Fascinated, he forgot his reluctance to apologize. "Mr. Pierson."

The ax hit crookedly on the trunk, jolted, and flew from Tom's grasp. Tom clutched his throbbing hand, holding it tightly between his legs.

Adam stared. "Did you cut yourself?"

"No! Damn! I told you never to show your face heah again." Tom began to walk with menacing determination toward Adam. The boy didn't look as cocky today as he had yesterday; still, there was that air of self-sure calm about him. Tom would make him show some respectful fear if it was the last thing he ever did.

Adam moved a few steps, angling away from Tom's path.

"That isn't gonna help you. I'll get you if I want you."

Adam bent over and picked up the ax. Tom looked warily at the boy standing with the broadax held loosely in his right hand. Adam turned the ax, to give to Tom handle first. "I was in the wrong last evening," he said begrudgingly. "I already apologized to Ullah, and she said it was you I owed the apology."

"What makes you think an apology is going to make any difference? If you're thinkin' it excuses you, it doesn't."

"I didn't say that it did," Adam said flatly.

Tom's face tightened. "You don't look all that sorry to me anyhow."

"I am for last evening." The sincerity in Adam's voice was not reflected in the hard blue eyes. "I'll be on my way. My friends are waiting."

"Why didn't they come with you?"

"They didn't do anything wrong. I was the one who sassed you."

"Think you're quite the man, don't you, boy?" Tom said sarcastically.

"I am the man in my family. I disremembered that last evening. I won't again. Good day, sir." He walked off, leaving Tom to stare after him bereft of words.

Ullah was waiting by the worm fence when he returned. "Did you see Tom?"

"Yes, but you're right. He's not satisfied with just an I'm sorry."

"It's what he feels that matters. Tom's fair an' honest. He come 'round when he's done some thinkin' on it. Heah Ah thought you didn't want them cookies."

Adam looked at her questioningly, then grinned.

Ullah listened as Adam talked and ate in turns. He lived alone with his widowed mother beyond the woods, two miles away. He was nearly finished with his academy and would be going to the university next year. To him it all seemed a bother, for his interests lay in ships and the sea and not the classical subjects he was to study, except for mathematics.

"You sho' doan wanta grow up like some iggerant no 'count, does you?"

"Of course not, but I want to be about making my way. I would read and study twice as hard if I didn't have to go to college."

"Sez you. Shows how much you knows. You better go to college like yo' mama say. She knows what's good fo' you."

He enjoyed Ullah's gentle scolding. He liked this sort of argument.

"What you think you gwine do that cain't wait fo' yo' schoolin'? Why, you ain't much mo'n a shirttail boy."

"I'll be sixteen, and I've got my own business," he said indignantly.

Ullah made a face at him, her eyebrows raised. "Well

now, ain't that somethin'. What kin' o' bizness you got fo' yo'seff, Adam?"

"I haul railroad ties, settle the accounts, and pay the bayou men. I get a percentage of their pay and a fee for the use of my boat."

She smiled. "So you cap'n of a bugboat."

He ignored the amusement in her voice, looking down in serious concentration at the cookie in his hand. His voice was low and quietly moving. "I will be the captain of a ship. As soon as I'm out of school, Beau LeClerc, Ben West, and I—we're all going to sign on as apprentices."

"What's yo' mama say to that?"

"Oh, she likes the idea fine. If I go to the university first."

He was deeply engrossed in telling Ullah how he would one day own a ship and sail the seas of the world when Tom came into the house, a handkerchief tied around his hand.

Ullah hurried to him. "What you gone an' done to yo'-seff, Tom?"

Adam jumped to his feet. "I didn't intend to come here—"

"Ne'mind the sorryin' now!" Ullah snapped. "You done say enuf!" Tom had gouged out a piece of flesh. "Well, thank the Lawd, it's not bad." She made a poultice of roots and herbs to draw out the poisons in Tom's hand. "Stay where you is, Adam! Be jes' a minit afore Ah get Tom all set, then he kin have some lemonade an' a mulatto belly with you, if you lef' him any."

"Ullah . . ." Tom began, scowling as he looked from her to Adam. He couldn't refuse anyone the courtesy of his home, but Ullah damned well didn't have to extend it further.

She spoke quickly. "He the cap'n o' his own boat, Adam is. Even got a bizness goin' fo' hisseff. Wouldn't think that o' him, would you?"

"Ullah!" Tom said, louder and more insistent.

"I'd better be going."

"Set down, Adam. Cain't you see Ah got enuf without you hoppin' up like a frog on the run eve'y time he speak up? Set down, both o' you. Time you did some talkin'."

Both Adam and Tom obeyed. Tom looked up at Ullah, his eyes twinkling. "We're being bullied."

Ullah turned to Adam. "How much you know 'bout bayou work?"

"You mean the crabbing and logging? I know some."

"Well, Tom heah, he a good man fo' some things, but his foot's in mortal danger soon's his han' touches the ax."

"Looked to me it was a lot more than just his foot when I saw him." Adam, suddenly amused, was having difficulty suppressing a smile.

Tom glared at him. "Ullah, damn it, I'm not gonna listen to some smart-mouthed boy belittle me in my own house in front of my own wife!"

Adam looked curiously from Ullah to Tom. He had realized that their relationship was more than just that of servant and master, but marriage between them was something he had never thought of.

"Yes, she's my wife." Tom glanced crossly at Ullah. "Thanks to your damned meddlin' we'll have to leave heah right away. Next time I tell you I don't want someone nosin' around, listen to me. You don't feed your enemies lemonade and cookies."

"You our enemy, Adam?"

Tom pounded the table. "Damn woman! Do you never listen?"

Like hurricane shutters to protect the house from pounding rain, Adam's eyes closed, shutting him off from what he knew was coming between Ullah and Tom. He didn't know what to say or how to get out, short of turning tail and running. But he did want out. He didn't want to see them fight or see Ullah lose, as she would. As he had looked at his mother many times when his father was alive, he now looked at Ullah, wishing he could help and knowing he couldn't. Then he cleared his throat, daring to try—once. "I could show you how to handle that ax, Mr. Pierson."

Tom glared angrily at Adam. Ullah's voice was subdued when she spoke. "He's tellin' us he's yo' friend, Tom. Cain't you hear nothin' but the words? You run us away from heah 'cause of a boy who wants to he'p us, what you think will happen anyplace else we kin go?"

Tom sat down heavily in helpless surrender, letting his hands fall to the table.

Adam watched him with new interest. He hadn't hit Ullah, nor had he abused her verbally as Adam had expected, had learned to expect from a man. Intense discomfort gave way to a wary curiosity about Tom.

"Ben and Beau could help. Ben is good with tools."

"I might as well take out an ad in the *Picayune* and give our location to the whole world," Tom said dispiritedly.

"Why, lis'n there, Adam. You heah that? Sound like a ol' she-cow mooin' outa sorrow fo' herseff. You feelin' that sorry fo' yo'seff, Tom?"

"Sure as hell am! No one else does," Tom grumbled, more good-naturedly. His eyes met Adam's. "You say Ben is a good hand with an ax?"

"Yes, sir."

"He ever hire out?"

"No, sir. I didn't mean we'd hire out. We'd help. That's all."

Tom watched Adam quietly for a moment. "Tom. Call me Tom. Anybody catches me without my britches has a right to use my first name." He grinned. "I'd be proud to accept your help, Adam." He extended his hand.

It was the first time Adam ever had, or considered having, the friendship of a grown man. Even now, faced with this stocky, plain-faced man with his eyes once more twinkling with good humor, it was not a totally comfortable feeling. "I'll get Ben. And Beau too?"

"Why not?" Tom said, his capitulation complete and his humor restored. Gently, Ullah's arms wrapped around his neck.

Adam hadn't exaggerated. Ben West was as handy with the ax as Adam had claimed. The first afternoon Tom looked on with amazement as shakes for the house mounted in neat piles. The next day, with a humility he didn't know he possessed, he became the willing pupil of a fourteen-year-old taskmaster. Alternately gritting his teeth in annoyance and roaring with laughter at the boys' antics, Tom learned the rudiments of woodworking. As the days went by, Ben criticized his every mistake, making his pupil repeat the same process until Tom threatened to beat the lard outa him if he told him to plane the piece of wood one more time. "My God, it's smoother'n my ass now!" Tom howled.

As the month passed, Ullah longed to have Angela brought from the house on Clio Street. In September they added a room for the child. To Tom, who had done a good portion of the work, it seemed the most marvelous piece of craftsmanship he had ever seen. The task of finishing the roof fell to Beau LeClerc, for he was small, delicately built, and wiry, the lightest and fastest of them all. He skimmed across the roof, tapping shakes into place with the grace and agility of a heron scooping up fish.

In the pink of the evening, when the roof was complete and the bayou came alive with color, shimmering and casting its eerie images, they gathered around Ullah's charcoal fire, smelling the delicious odor of her hot hoecakes. It was an easy, pleasant time at the end of each day before the three boys climbed into Adam's boat and went back down the channels toward their homes.

Tom lay back listening to the soft sounds of the gourd guitar Ullah had made and was teaching Beau to play. Tom still went nightly to New Orleans, but Ullah stayed in the bayou house. He had come to love being in the bayou. There was a sense of contentment and rightness over him these days, one he had never known before.

As he listened to the music, which was tentative at first, then became surer as Beau got the feeling, Tom dreamed of other nights far in the future. Though the only people he knew here were three adolescent boys, it seemed to Tom that one day this house would be alive with the sounds of laughter and music as the New Orleans house had never been.

Ullah, flushed with success in teaching Beau how to make music on the crude guitar, now turned to Ben and Adam. She gave Adam a drum and Ben the bleached ribs of a cow. The music, as it swelled, thrummed with a primitive cadence that beat deep into the marrow. Even Tom felt himself wanting to move and keep time to the beat. It throbbed through him, making his blood race. The three boys played as though their lives depended on it, their eyes shut, their bodies swaying.

Alone in the light of the fire Ullah danced to the ancient ancestral rhythms, small bells in her hands tinkling, her steps at first slow and sensual. She put out her hands for Tom to dance with her. She placed the bells around his ankles. His movement and the sound of the beat brought the bells into eerie harmony with the bones, the drum, and the guitar. They danced until their bodies were wet and glistening in the firelight.

Ullah sank down laughing. "Oh, Lawd! Ah ain't never danced like that!"

"I can't stop," Tom gasped, falling to the ground beside her.

"Ah gwine haf to take you boys to Juneau Nuit."

Tom pulled her back to him. "You're not goin' to any voodoo queen."

"Ah sho' is. Juneau Nuit's mah frien'. No harm gwine come to me. Anyways, Adam an' the boys 'tect me. They's gotta go, Tom. Ah never knowed white boys make music like them."

"I said no. I'm not goin' to any voodoo ritual, and that's final."

"Ummm, Ah s'pose not. Somebody got to watch over Angela."

"God's eyes! You're wantin' me to watch after the baby? Ullah!"

"If you doan wanta look after her, Ah'll jes' take her with me."

"Like hell you will."

"Den what we gwine do?" she asked wide-eyed.

"I don't know what you're goin' to do." He smiled, pleased with himself. He got up and dusted himself off. "I'm havin' some lemonade. You goin' to get it for me, or do you want me to do that for you too?"

"You mos' likely drop it afore, you got it to us. Ah 'spects Ah bes' get it," Ullah said sweetly.

After she left, Tom said, "Don't s'pose your mama would ever think of comin' out here, would she, Adam?" He tossed blades of grass one by one into the embers. "No . . . she wouldn't like Ullah and me. . . . I mean, ladies wouldn't approve of us. Forget I said it."

"She'd most likely come if she was asked," Adam said softly.

"Ahh, it wouldn't be right. I get crazy notions. I was jes' thinkin', I have to go into town next week to close the house. When I get back, those hogs will be set right for killin'. Be awful nice to make a day of it—games and a barbecue, maybe some music in the evening."

"Lemonade. Fresh, sweet lemonade," Ullah sang as she walked down the path, the full tray balanced perfectly on her head. Beau kept his tongue, his look informing Adam they would be talking of this later.

Soon after, Ullah and Tom stood arm in arm as the

boys pushed off in the flatboat. As always, Ullah spent some time teasing with Adam, poking gentle fun at him. Tom looked on with some small envy at the easy camaraderie that had grown between them. With Ullah the boy was relaxed and happy. Frequently Adam considered Ullah's safety far more quickly than Tom himself did. It gave Tom a feeling of warmth and security, but a pang dug at him. Without realizing it, Tom had begun to look on the boy with a fondness that surprised him. There was something in Adam too elusive to name, some quality rare and good.

Yet between himself and Adam there remained an unrelenting wariness that Tom neither liked nor understood, as though Adam were always waiting for Tom to show himself in the wrong.

"Why does he take to you so, and not to me? What did I do?" Tom complained when the little boat was out of sight.

"He doan trus' you."

"Why the hell not!? Ben and Beau trust me. My God, Ullah, I've never had trouble gettin' along with anyone. Everyone always likes me!"

"Well, now, ain't that nice," she teased.

"I'm serious. What's he got against me?"

She shrugged.

By the end of that week Ullah wanted Angela with her. Tom brought the child from New Orleans the following day. It seemed to Ullah it had been a lifetime since she had last held Angela in her arms. "Why, jes' look at her, Tom. Ain't she big an' fat an' purty?" She hugged the little girl to her again. They took Angela into the new house, letting her explore. By this time Angela had grown accustomed to her big soft bed in Tom's house, and she spent the morning wandering from one room to the next, hunting for it.

Tom didn't return to New Orleans that day as he had planned. One day at a time he put off going. He found he didn't want to leave the bayou or see ever again the now alien world he had left. He was far too content tending to his small house and family, watching Ullah and Angela blossom in the amiable surroundings he had provided for them.

Angela took to Adam as quickly as her mother had. Ben

made her a small paddle, and she spent part of each day in Adam's boat. Adam treated Angela with a consideration few girls ever receive from a brother, taking her for rides atop his broad shoulders, teaching her to swim in the shallow waters, holding her on the back of Tom's horse as he walked it around the yard. Angela pestered him, clung to him, begged constantly for more—and usually got her way.

By Friday, Tom decided he would return to New Orleans the following Monday. On Saturday he told Adam to ask his mother to the barbecue. On Sunday night, with Ullah's head resting pleasantly on his shoulder, he said, "We're goin' to have a party when I get back from N'Orleans."

Ullah raised her head in alarm. "A party! We cain't have no party!"

Tom laughed, and pulled her close to him. "Sure we can, Ullah honey. I got it all figured out. We'll ask the boys and Adam's mama."

"The boys is fine, but not Adam's mama. Ah doan wan' no uppity white woman nosin' 'round heah, givin' me orders in mah own house."

To ease his own misgivings, Tom said heartily, "Adam's mama's likely to have better manners than that."

Ullah sighed. "Mebbe." She lifted troubled eyes to his. "How long you gwine stay in Nawlens, Tom?"

"A week or two. I want to sell the furniture and close down the house. I don't know what to do about the house servants."

"Ain't none of 'em comin' heah," Ullah said flatly.

Tom laughed. "I promise." He turned on his side, facing Ullah. "Haven't we talked enough for a bit?"

Ullah chuckled softly. "You sho' a busy man 'long certain lines, Tom. Nex' thing, there be a arm baby heah, cryin' in the night."

"A lap child and an arm baby. That sounds pretty good to me." His hands, work roughened, gently stroked her. He kissed her shoulders, her full lips, her fingers. In all the tender hollows of her, he tasted the cleanness of her well-shaped body.

Ullah responded with an intensity of passion rare in her, clawing lightly down his arms, nipping his shoulders with her teeth. It was she who pulled him onto her eagerly, breathlessly, open-mouthed with desire. Tom, caught by her fire, joined his body with hers as their excitement mounted, hung suspended, and spiraled downward, leaving them both elated and pleasured.

After a long time Ullah said, "Gwine be another girl, Tom."

Tom felt himself quicken at the thought. Against her lips he said, "I'd rather have girls anyway. Jes' like you, Ullah."

She chuckled. "Hush yo' mouth, you sweet talker."

But that night, instead of dreaming about all the things that crowded her mind in a kaleidoscope of happiness, Ullah dreamed of a mud-clogged pool of water that whirled and spun, pulling her into it. Frightened and shaking, she begged, "Ah doan want you to go to Nawlens."

"Don't be silly," Tom said easily. "Adam'll be lookin' out for you."

"It ain't me an' Angela Ah'm afeerd for. It you, Tom. Ah had a dream 'bout muddy water. Dat means troubles. It's a warnin'. Ah knows."

"That's only superstition, Ullah honey. Dreams can't hurt you."

Tom left in the morning as he had planned. Ullah, still fretting, said, "Stay heah a few mo' days, Tom. Mebbe the trouble go 'way."

"Ullah, I can't put it off any longer. But while I'm gone, promise me somethin'. Promise you'll be thinkin' about the barbecue, not worryin' about some old-time sayin' of your grandmammy's."

Ullah gazed at him, her eyes bleak. "Mah granny knew. But Ah promise, Tom. You watch an' take care o' yo'seff, heah?"

"Don't you worry on my account, Ullah," he said, hugging and kissing her. "Nothin's goin' to happen." He added, grinning, "Didn't you tell me I'm gonna be a new daddy come next summer?"

Her eyes gleamed. "I was mebbe braggin' a li'l, but we gwine try."

She smiled and waved until he rode out of sight. But as she went back to the house, her heart was cold and heavy with foreboding.

Chapter Five

Tom looked with new eyes at New Orleans, on the crescent bend of the Mississippi. It waited for him, an oasis enclosed by dikes, encompassed by the turbid yellow river, the low delta lands, and the lakes. New Orleans: a gem in a mounting of black, oily soil, soaked for eons in the water.

It was a unique city, steeped in sophistication and sin, with untutored violence coexisting beside a hospitable gentility. My city, Tom thought, and felt himself, like it, unique. To be a New Orleanian was to be of a special breed.

Tom entered the Vieux Carré, with its shade-dappled narrow streets that became a bed of dust in summer, a sea of black, slippery mud in rainy season. Now it was dry. And this morning the city, glowing with life and color in the midday sun, reeked of the strangely mingling odors of rot and the perfume of flowers.

In the wooden gutters lay garbage and refuse decaying in the heat. The rough-plumaged black carrion crows with their obscene bald faces pecked about in the filth, not even troubling to fly up or squawk when the carriage passed. The offal would be cleaned up when someone got around to it. Negroes waiting in the calaboose because of some crime or to be collected by their masters after having run away would be brought forth in neck irons, chained together in gangs to sort out the refuse of a metropolis, freeing the gutters of the carrion just as the vultures did. Black carrion crows, both human and animal, ridding the city of the dregs of itself.

From the loud, raucous laughter and yells that emanated from the bordellos on Perdido Street, Tom could turn and look down the serene, palm-shrouded coolness of the most sedate and aristocratic streets in the entire country. Streets lined with houses blending the gracious French and Spanish architecture of ancestral lands, styles brought over the ocean along with the customs and habits of generations past.

Tom had taken the long way to his destination, but he had the time and the desire to look again at this city he had always loved, the most sensually pleasurable in the world. There was no more lovely music to his ears than the chanting of the street hawkers melodically touting their blackberries, strawberries, and bananas in their soft, sweet-sounding voices. The cries of the green sass men with their baskets of okra, snap beans, and garden greens, mingled with the hot-blooded racket emanating from the cock pits, and the bells of the grinder man, the tapping on window and door by the lightwood man. New Orleans lived and breathed to its own peculiar tempo.

He rode past Joseph Bruin's busy slave mart at the corner of Esplanade and Chartres Streets and found he couldn't peer into its courtyard with the same amiable curiosity he'd once felt. The male slaves would be lined up on one side, the females on the other. All standing according to height, waiting for a prospective buyer to take them from the ignominy of being unowned, unknown, and unwanted merchandise. It was out of such a line Edmund Revanche had taken Ullah when she was no more than eleven years old, close as she could reckon.

Tom didn't know what to do with his own slaves. He couldn't free them without drawing vastly unpleasant attention to himself. A man who suddenly freed his slaves without acceptable reason was a fool, or one with abolitionist sympathies.

But Tom couldn't see himself putting Bessie, William, Jewel, and the others at the mercies of the nigger traders. A month ago he would have given it scarcely a thought. Like most Southerners, he had looked on his slaves as property, things to be bought and sold, or at best as childlike creatures given to imitation of their masters and not knowing or feeling as white men did.

Ullah had smashed that delusion by saying that somebody made her granddaddy a nigger. Without meaning to, she had made Tom see himself as a nigger maker too.

It was the worst thing Ullah had ever done to him. She made him doubt the attitudes he'd grown up with, without giving him the insight to answer those doubts. She had made him question the worth of his world without giving him a new one in which he could be at ease. God above, he was no Yankee lover! But what was he? He despised the abolitionists and the Northern bigots more than the way of life that enslaved Ullah's people. Wrong as he considered that system, its proponents cared about the blacks, and they knew them far better than the fire-breathing Yankees. Yet, he could no longer live under that system either.

He turned down the street where George Andreas, his attorney, had his office. Carl Dorn, Andreas's secretary, looked up from the papers neatly stacked on his desk, his expression guarded and cool.

"What do you say, Carl." Tom handed him his card. "Tell George I want to see him, will you?"

In silence Carl took the card and scurried toward Andreas's office.

"Don't let him tell you he can't see me today," Tom called, smiling.

Carl gestured for Tom to enter George's office.

"What the hell's got him, George? You'd think I had the plague."

George Andreas sat in easy dignity behind his inlaid mahogany desk. His hands met precisely in front of him. "Perhaps he thinks you do," he said with a touch of winter in his voice.

"What does that mean?" Tom sat down, alert and anxious.

"There have been a number of ugly rumors about you. Where have you been, Tom? Your darkies are acting guilty as hell about somethin'. You ought to know if you want a secret kept, it can't be kept by a darky."

Tom rubbed his temple unconsciously; his head had begun to hurt. "There's no secret, George. I've just moved out of town . . . got a small piece of land." It was difficult going for him. He didn't know how much he dared let George know. "Thought I might consider plantin'."

"What would you want with the headaches of a plantation? Aren't your real estate holdin's enough for you, Tom?"

"I'm satisfied. The saloons alone bring in enough and—"

"Lately, they've all fallen off in business."

"All right, George, what you got stuck in your craw?"

"You always were too soft with your darkies, Tom. Folks think maybe you're more than just soft. There's also the matter of a slave you bought from Edmund Revanche. Seems a little peculiar that the quadroon should disappear about the same time you left New Orleans."

"That it?"

"There is the question of the slave child you took from Gray Oaks."

"Edmund knows he can't legally separate a mother from a child under ten years of age."

"He expects to be paid for the child. I have managed to convince Edmund not to do anythin' about the pickaninny, but it hasn't sat well with him. What's come over you, Tom? It's a damned good thing your daddy isn't here. He'd take the buggy whip to you."

Tom felt as though the room were closing in on him. "I paid Edmund four thousand dollars—even with his inflated ideas, that should have been enough." He said spiritlessly, "Aside from rumors and Edmund's pique, is that all?"

George's eyebrows rose. "Is that all!? Dear Lord, man, what names you haven't been called in recent weeks aren't worth mentionin'. Your business is off, you're suspected of consortin' with rebellious niggers, some say you incited them, and you ask if that is all?"

"They are sayin' that, are they?" Tom wiped his hand across his forehead. "I'm closin' the Clio Street house, George. Get the best price you can. Auction the furnishin's. The field hands go with the house. I'll arrange for Bessie, William, and Jewel."

"This is going to add fuel to the talk."

"I can't help that."

"What about the other house slaves? You've educated them, haven't you?"

"Yes, they should be all right."

"Be all right! You aren't actually thinkin' of freeing them?"

"George, I don't know. Would it be so wrong to give them their papers? They've served the family for years."

George Andreas's face hardened. "If that is what you wish to do, Tom, I'm sure nothin' I might say would dissuade you. However, if you've got any sense, you'll return to New Orelans. Reestablish yourself. Give folks a chance to see there is no truth in what they hear."

"I'm not comin' back, George."

"Where shall I mail your correspondence?"

Tom looked baffled. "I'll be in now and then."

George's mouth was drawn in a thin line of disapproval.

"You're a damned fool," he snarled. "Get yourself another attorney."

Tom hesitated, then gave him the Tremains' address.

George's face brightened. "You courtin' Paul Tremain's widow? That's the first sensible thing you've said today. Zoe Tremain is a fine lady."

"Yes, she is." Already Tom felt guilty that he had involved her. "Just send my mail to her. She'll know how to reach me."

When Tom left George's office, he felt more tired than he did after a full day's work. His head buzzed with old worries and new ones. Without thinking, he headed toward the coffee shop where he and Ross and Edmund had spent so many pleasant afternoons.

He ordered his favorite, café brûlot. The place hummed with the deep, harmonious sounds of men's voices. Through foreign eyes Tom looked at the too familiar sight of men at a leisure that neither time nor circumstances changed. With some discomfiture he saw Edmund Revanche sitting with Ross Bennett, Mark Wilford, and Etienne Bordulâc.

Ross ostentatiously moved his chair so that his back was to Tom, but Edmund's cold, snapping eyes waited with knowing patience for Tom to greet him.

"What'cha say, Edmund?" Tom asked softly as he approached their table. "Goin' to have a big cane crop?"

"Looks good, Tom. Pull up a chair. You've kept yourself scarce these days. Old friends forgotten, Tom?"

"You know better than that. Hello, Ross, Etienne, Mark."

Ross made a sound somewhere between a clearing of the throat and a laugh. He downed the remainder of the warmed sling in his glass and hailed one of the scurrying bilingual waiters to refill it for him.

Tom spoke briefly to the other two men and fell silent trying to concentrate on the conversation his arrival had interrupted.

Mark was saying, "The Underground stations are only a day's ride apart. My God, they'll have 'em in a line door to door if it isn't stopped. I tell you, Etienne, these damned nigger stealers won't give up until they've forced us into war!"

"If anybody's gonna start a war, it should be us," Ross

agreed. "The Abolitionists are challengin' us, an' there ain't a Southerner worth his salt that don't show a challenger who's boss. Ain't that right, Mark?"

"The boys are a bit riled." Edmund balanced his chair on the two back legs enjoying the spectacle. "There's been the usual talk of uprisings and conspiracies. Now there's been a passel of rumors that some of the nigger-lovin' bastards are of our own kind. That won't go down in these parts. But, of course, our friends miss the main point."

Tom kept his eyes in earnest study on one of the many paintings of voluptuous and licentious women that adorned the walls. He said, "No one is goin' to start a war over the niggers."

"That is precisely what they will do. Of course the war, when it comes, won't really have anything to do with the niggers, but the loyal patriots who promote war will use the inalienable rights of mankind guaranteed by our estimable Constitution to serve their own ends. What a noble war it will be for future historians!"

"Damn, you're the most cynical, cold bastard I've ever met," Tom said, awed, as though seeing Edmund clearly for the first time.

Edmund laughed comfortably. "Because I say people are asinine enough to blunder into war? You've mistaken cynicism for clear-sightedness, Tom. We Southerners are a political minority. Political minorities get defeated and overlooked *for their own good*, particularly when their economic mainstay is a target of active fanaticism of the Northern majority.

"Abolitionists attack us on moral grounds. *Save the soul of mankind!* Yet their true attack comes at our economy. Whether they believe in their bigoted preachments is beside the point. What matters is that profit-seekin' Northerners will parrot the words of their abolitionist preachers. The South will become the symbol of evil."

"Who the hell cares what they think!" Mark shouted. "We don't mix in with their way of slavery. They kill 'em in their sweatshops! Damn, they don't give a good spit about any o' their people."

"We oughta hang the damned abolitionist bastards," Ross said sullenly.

Etienne said, "Do go on, Edmund. What of cotton? Would they risk closin' their own mills and factories to rid us of slavery? Our cotton and raw exports represent sixty per cent of the export value of the entire nation. New Orleans is a more active port, by value as well as volume, than even New York. Can they do without us?"

A knowing smile played on Edmund's mouth. "Can *they* do without *us?*"

Ross laughed in satisfaction. "Hell no, they can't!"

"Can't they?" Edmund laughed bitterly. "Cotton, gentlemen, mountains of cotton. That's our Achilles heel. We need the North. We can hurt them economically, but, by God, they can bring us to our knees. We've already given away our rights to an equal voice in the government a word at a time."

"Then, the great Compromise was just another loss for us."

Edmund shrugged. "It drew the battle lines for the admission of each new state and territory, did it not? Did not the people of California lose all voice in the matter of slavery? Where are their inalienable rights? The Northern industrialists are imposin' their way on us and the new state, because their needs are not the same as ours.

"The North," he continued, "isn't agricultural in the same way we are. Theirs is subsistence farmin'. In fact, gentleman, no section of this vast country is agricultural in the same fashion we are. It makes our politics and our lives different. Our government is becomin' a toady of Northern interests to the detriment of other sections.

"You talk of war, gentlemen? I talk of survival. We need manufacturing, railroads, shipping. Of course there will be a war. The question is when, and will we be prepared."

"Calhoun was the only damned man who knew what he was talkin' about. Our daddies shoulda been uniting the South back in the thirties," Mark said. "Damned Yankee insurrectionists."

With a thickening tongue, Ross boasted, "No Southerner is gonna let no-count Yankees make no never mind. There's ways of takin' care o' insurrectionists and niggerlovers. There's ways, an' I'm one Southerner who believes in doin' what has to be done." For the first time he looked directly at Tom, his handsome face contorted by hostility and drink. "Ain't those your sentiments, Tom, or have you had a recent change of heart?"

"You know how I feel, Ross, how I've always felt."

Ross laughed harshly.

"That's no way to treat a new bridegroom, Ross. Last thing on Tom's mind is politics," Edmund said smoothly.

Tom's head snapped up. Mark and Etienne looked at him curiously. "You have been married, Tom?" Etienne asked.

Tom's heart was hammering so hard he began to shake. He placed the cup of café brûlot on the table to avoid spilling it. Edmund Revanche followed the movement with amusement.

"Yes, I am, but—"

"That calls for a toast and an apology!" Mark said. "Not a one of us invited to the festivities, Tom! What have we done to offend you?"

Tom squirmed, his mind working sluggishly. Edmund, as intended, had caught him off guard. "She . . . uh, my wife is an . . . uh, she's an orphan. We married quietly, at her home."

"We don't know her?" Etienne stared. "She's not a New Orleanian?"

"No. You wouldn't know her," Tom said hastily. His head and heart still hammered as he tried to sort out what mistake he'd made that told Edmund of his marriage to Ullah. Likely, the Negroes had talked along their infamous grapevine. At least Edmund had not told the others. It was as obvious that Mark and Etienne did not know the full import of his marriage as it was that Edmund did. Now Tom wished Edmund had been cold or disapproving when he'd first come in. Edmund's easy assumption of friendship was a bad sign.

Uneasily Tom glanced at the four men, their faces high-lighted and shadowed by the numerous lamps that bright-ened the coffee house. "Well, gentlemen, it's been nice seein' y'all, but I must be on my way."

"Not without a toast," said Mark. "We'd be mighty insulted, not bein' invited to the weddin', if you reject our toast to your happiness." He signaled the waiter.

"Whatever happened to that slave gal, Ullah, Tom?" Ross asked, as though the thought had just come to him.

"I sent her to my sister . . . in Kentucky."

"Sister!? Lawd, you are *full* of surprises today. Damned if I didn't recollect your whole family was wiped out by yellow fever."

Tom was sweating like a hog in August. "See y'all."

"One moment, Tom." Edmund's hand was on Tom's arm. His dark eyes glowed, betraying the fury that burned inside him. "We can't have your wedding go unheralded. Your bride will want to meet her neighbors and friends. It isn't fittin' to neglect the amenities. Sunday next, at Gray Oaks y'all, we'll have a barbecue and ball in honor of Mrs. Tom Pierson. We've got to get a look at Tom's lady, haven't we?"

"I thank you, Edmund, but—"

"You're not goin' to refuse me, are you, Tom? There isn't somethin' about this weddin' you don't want us to know, is there?"

"No! Edmund—"

"Then it's agreed. I'll provide the party. You provide the entertainment, Tom. We'll put on a soiree no one will ever forget. It's settled, Tom?"

Edmund had left Tom no way to refuse, knowing full well he dared not show up. "It's settled, Edmund. Excuse me if you will, gentlemen."

"Hey, Tom!" Ross called after him. "I'm gonna nut me a dirty nigger lover pretty soon now. Want to be in on the fun?"

Tom hurried from the coffee house, Ross's crude laughter in his ears. He strode quickly toward his attorney's office. Damn Edmund Revanche! He'd seen him play such cruel tricks on others. He'd watched innumerable times as Edmund took one then another oblique step, leading his victim into position. Just so, Edmund had won today. He'd set his trap, springing it as soon as Tom allowed himself to be lulled by the war talk. And what would come next?

He burst into Andreas's office unannounced. "George! I want you to sell everythin' . . . stocks, warehouses, saloons . . . everythin'!"

Andreas half rose, his cheeks quivering in indignation. "What is the meaning of this, Mr. Pierson? This office is private!"

Tom glanced shame-faced at an elderly man whose eyes were wide in startlement. "I'm sorry, George." He bowed in deferential embarrassment toward George's client. "I beg your pardon, sir, I'll—I'll wait outside. I must see you, George, it's urgent."

Tom stood up immediately when the elderly gentleman made his way out of George's office, his cane tapping in unrhythmic cadence to his faltering steps. More in control, but no calmer, Tom entered the office. "George, my apologies. I was in a lather, and—"

"No gentleman conducts his business in a lather, Pierson. What is so urgent?" He folded his hands on the desk top, elaborately patient.

In Andreas's eyes it would be Edmund who was behaving in a civilized manner, not Tom. It would be foolhardy to explain that he simply loved Ullah and wished to conduct his life as he saw fit. George would fix him with a baffled blank stare as if faced with the logic of a maniac.

More clearly than Edmund would ever have guessed, Tom understood Edmund's wrath against the North. While Edmund cried out that the Southern planter had the slave's well-being at heart in a way no Northerner could understand, Tom cried out silently within himself that he was no insurrectionist. He was only one man who had taken one slave to heart and to wife.

Bleakly he watched George making notes.

"Assuming I can find buyers for your holdings, what do you want me to do with the proceeds?"

"I'll still do my bankin' on Carondelet Street," Tom said, saddened at the hard-drawn disapproval of his father's best friend. "George . . . I can't explain, but I know what I'm doin'."

"So do I," George said implacably. "You're destroying your life. You are making the good name of Pierson anathema in New Orleans."

"George—"

"There's no more to be said between us, Tom. I'll have your affairs in order as quickly as possible. Good-bye." George's face, along with his friendship, was closed against Tom.

Saddened and subdued, Tom rode through the Streets of Nine Muses to his house. The elegant Greek Revival mansions stood as symbols of wealth and position. As George had pointed out, Tom was on the verge of throwing it all away. In the bayou house, warm and tended by Ullah, it seemed easy. Here in New Orleans, faced with what he had been and all his father had labored to make for his family, Tom was finding it a task most painful. He was not merely leaving a house, he was turning his back on his own father, his city, his people.

His tread on the piazza was slow and heavy. The front door flew open, and William's purple-black face smiled down at him.

"Welcome home, Mastah Tom. We sho' does be missin' you."

Behind William came Bessie, puffing from the exertion her speed had cost her. "Where y'all been? Folks sayin' bad things. An' two o' dem wuthless niggers done run off. Wa'n't a body to gits 'em back."

"Two ran off, did they, Bessie?" Tom repeated wearily, and thought about how there were two he wouldn't have to worry about.

Bessie followed him into the study. "Sho' dey did. Things is bad 'round a house when de mastah doan watch out fo' his niggers. You come home jes' in time."

"Bess, have you ever thought of bein' free?"

"Nossuh, Ah ain't. What you gwine do 'bout dem wuthless niggers?"

"I'm goin' to send you all North."

"Nawth?! What yo' gwine do a thing like dat fo'? Who gwine look aftuh you? What we all gwine do effen you do a thing like dat?" Her black face glistened and quivered in disapproval.

"Sit down, Bessie."

"Siddown! Wid you? Ah ain't doin' no sech a thing, Mastah Tom."

Tom put his head in his hands, leaning heavily on the desk top. He couldn't make anyone understand, not even the people he wanted to free.

After supper he wrote the letters of manumission, sending them North in groups of four. He gave each of them ten dollars and directions to the first of many Underground Railroad stops. "These people will give you food and shelter, and guide you onward. Whatever you do, be sure you keep your freedom papers. Once you are out of Louisiana, you may stop wherever you wish and live as free persons of color. Just be certain you leave Louisiana. As most of you know, feelin's are runnin' high regardin' me. You won't be safe heah any longer."

Some left eagerly, giving Tom thanks and assurances they would remember him. Some left with trepidation, facing an uncertain world. Others, like William and Bessie, left like the exiles they were, their eyes filled with hurt and rejection, their lips pursed in silent accusation: He had turned them out of their home and away from him, away from all that was left of their family.

When the last of them had gone, Tom remained alone in the splendid, hauntingly empty Clio Street house. A few more days and the house would be closed. The only trace of Tom Pierson left in New Orleans would be the bulging bank account on Carondelet Street.

Chapter Six

Ullah put Angela to bed, then went, as she had every night since Tom left, to sit on the front stoop. Wistfully, her eyes fastened on the path on which he would appear. She had wished him near so many hours of so many days that when his horse, Sable, lathered and tired, trotted into view, Ullah sat momentarily stunned, the breath gone out of her. Then she ran to the barn, crying his name.

"Yo' safe," she breathed, her hands running over his body, finding each curve where muscle met bone. She laughed and cried as he held her, turning her face to his. In her naked emotion, she was startlingly beautiful. She didn't know how to play at love. Hers had the power to strike like lightning right to the heart of him.

Her hands fluttered back to his face, her fingers tracing vibrant paths around his eyes, down his cheeks until they rested against his lips. "Nothin' bad happen to you, did it, Tom?"

He looked into the deep darkness of her moist eyes. To be once more in Ullah's arms was as soothing to Tom as the cool waters of the bayou after a day in the merciless sun. He smiled. "Nothin' bad. I'm home, an' neither one of us has to look back. It's all finished."

She sighed in relief, wiping her eyes with the back of her hand. "What you do 'bout Bessie an' Will'm?"

"Sent them North with their papers. I sent all of them North, except two that ran off while I was heah."

"Dey run off! What you gwine do 'bout that?"

Tom laughed, walking her toward the edge of the sun-struck bayou. Overhead wild pigeons flew, blackening the purpling sky with their bodies. In the distance they heard guns begin to sound.

"Hurry on, li'l bird, big man-hawk after you," Ullah said softly.

Tom put his hands on each side of her face. "Let's let the blacks go like the birds."

"But . . ." she began, confused with her own feelings and the beliefs she'd been taught at Gray Oaks, "niggers cain't run . . . lessen you wants a passel o' troubles with the res'."

"Ullah, love, I have no others. They're all gone. There's only you and Angela and me now."

"Doan seem like that's possible."

He smiled. "Maybe not, but it is. Now, tell me what y'all have been up to since I left."

"Hog's ready to kill t'morra. Adam gwine do it iffen you din't get back. An' his mama doan jes' say she proud to come to the barbecue, she sen' me a letter. Adam read it to me."

"What did she say?"

"Miz Zoe a fine lady, jes' like Ah 'spects. What she write come from the heart," Ullah said earnestly, her hand against her breast. She hurried to fetch her battered little box of treasured belongings accumulated over her lifetime. "Ah's gwine keep this fo' Angela. Mebbe when she ol' enuf to be knowin' 'bout her mama, this letter he'p. Nobody ain't never spoke to me like this 'ceptin' you an' Adam, Tom."

Tom read the letter, finding nothing exceptional in it. He handed it back and watched her carefully enclose it in its envelope to be returned to its place of honor in the chest of treasures.

The next morning dawned crisp and clear. Tom felt vividly alive, stretching and giving out a yelp that caused Ullah to leap upon him, wrestling playfully until the bed sheets tangled around them.

"My God, it's good to be home." Tom dangled his arms over the edge of the bed as he looked up into the azure patch of sky that showed through the window. The soft, fragrant breeze crossed over his body, as caressing and sensual as Ullah's hands. They would be leaving all this behind them, going off yet again—to what or where Tom didn't know. For a moment the knowledge hardly bothered him. He would say nothing to Ullah until after the barbecue on

Saturday night. Whatever Edmund might do, it would not be hasty or haphazard. It would be precise, and exquisitely cruel.

He sprang up from the bed, giving Ullah a smart slap on her rump. "Bring on the hog! I'm ready for anythin'!"

"You sho' is!" she laughed. "It's a wonder Ah didn't jes' waste away, not havin' you 'round to pester me all the time."

"If it's pesterin' you want, it's pesterin' you'll get," Tom roared, charging at her like a happy calf. Ullah squealed, running from him in a welter of delight and anticipation.

Adam and Tom spent what remained of the day preparing the hogs. Tom knocked the largest in the skull, laying it flat. Ruefully he looked at the other two, thinking it a pity that he and Ullah would not be here to use the meat. Ullah would not stand for any waste. From hoof to hide, Tom would present every scrap of usable material to Ullah for processing. He slit the animals' throats and hung them to drain over the big-pans Ullah had scrubbed clean.

Adam stood looking at the fattened razorbacks. "You'll have meat for five barbecues, Tom."

Tom grinned and shrugged. "I don't guess Ben's and Beau's mamas'll mind the boys comin' home with a good slab of meat. Yours either."

"No, but Ullah might," Adam said. "She's already fretting about you not having enough grain and feed to last through next harvest."

"We have enough." Tom dumped the bark he had been collecting for the tanning into the primitive bark mill he had found in the back of the barn. As Adam brought more bark for the mill, Tom said, "No more."

Adam looked at him quizzically but put the bark back into its pile. They hitched up the horse and watched its dizzying path around the mill as the bark was ground. The leach pit filled, and Tom and Adam added the water that would sit for the next few days until it reached the proper strength for Tom's hides.

"That should take care of it," Tom said in satisfaction. "I've only got a piddlin' amount of skins anyway."

Adam tried to decide if Tom were simply lazy or if the signs were true. "You planning on leaving soon, Tom?"

Tom straightened up. His eyes met Adam's, startled, then slid away to rove over the landscape. His mouth was set hard. He didn't want to leave. It was the first place that had ever truly been his; the bayou house bore the marks of his own labor and sweat. He was happy here in a way he had never considered. There were no soirees with their obligatory flirtations, no drinking bouts or wild hilarity that had marked his friendship with Ross and Edmund; but here were satisfaction and purpose. And here was the quiet sweetness of having Ullah and Angela as his own.

Adam watched him, then looked down at the ground. He said softly, "I guess things didn't go as well in New Orleans as you let on."

"No. They didn't."

"Someone knows about you and Ullah?"

"I think so."

Adam stared at him for a moment. "You're not bothering anyone. Why should anybody make trouble? Maybe nothing will happen."

"Nothin' is goin' to happen. I'm goin' to see to that, boy."

"By leaving."

"By leavin'."

Adam was silent. He had let this unassuming man become his hero; now anger and disappointment clouded his eyes. "I don't see why you let anybody chase you out! Who are these people? What business is it of theirs what you do? And what do they know anyhow?"

Tom saw the look of pugnacious indignation on Adam's face. He realized two things. He wouldn't run if it were anyone but Edmund Revanche. Tom would have faced his attackers and he would have defeated them.

Edmund Revanche was different. He wouldn't come at Tom as Ross might. Edmund held his hatreds long, nurturing them as he would a fine wine, waiting for the moment when they would blossom into ripened action. Edmund was a shadow, a threat without tangible substance, coming up behind silently by sun or by moon to seek his revenge. Tom had never completely trusted Edmund, his friend. Today he knew he was afraid of Edmund, his enemy.

He clapped Adam on the back and managed to smile. "I don't want Ullah to know yet—not 'til after the barbecue. Come on, boy, you promised Angela some fishin'."

Adam hung back. "You know we'd help, Ben and Beau and I. You can count on us. We wouldn't let anyone hurt Ullah or Angela . . . or you."

"I know. God, boy, I know. But you can't help this time. I'm not a fearful man, Adam, but I'm not a stupid

one either. Sometimes the only way to tell the difference
is in judgin' whether to fight a thing or walk away from it.
If I were alone, I'd fight any way I had to. But I'm not
alone. This man won't take his hates out only on me. I
can't risk Angela or Ullah on my pride. Can you understand that, Adam, or are you too young? Blood runs high
in the young."

Adam nodded, because Tom wanted him to understand,
but he didn't. He wanted Tom to stand his ground. He
wanted victory over Tom's enemy.

The days until the barbecue saw Ullah scurrying around
her cookroom in a spate of anxious activity. Adam, his
mouth full of Ullah's delicious concoctions, yielded to
Tom's restless desire to see and travel all the bayou paths,
discovering the secrets of its intimate world before he left
it for good. They spent long afternoons on Adam's boat,
with Adam poling as effortlessly over the shallowest strips
of watery land as he maneuvered with deft speed through
the deeper channels.

Angela sat on her father's lap, delighting in the fish
Adam caught each day for Ullah and his mother. She
screamed in indignation whenever he and Ben went eeling.
She wasn't allowed to play with the wriggling creatures
they brought in buckets to her mother's door. But her
frustrated anger was always soothed as soon as Tom picked
her up and headed toward Adam's flatboat.

Though Tom could not have said it, Adam, more than
even the bayou house itself, held him here. There was a
strength about Adam that was more than muscle and
sinew, a visionary quality that outdistanced his youth to
look squarely and sensibly into tomorrow. Tom questioned
that Adam had ever been a boy at all in the usual sense.

Just of late he'd begun to wonder what it would be like
to have a son of his own. But when his mind conjured up
pictures of what that son might be, it wasn't the little arm
baby he and Ullah talked about. It was a six-foot young
stripling with black hair and the brightest, most piercing
blue eyes heaven had been able to fashion.

Tom's feelings about Adam were easy to define. About
Zoe, they were mixed. Adam had dropped into his life that
evening in the woods. He had appeared before Tom and
Ullah without attachments or family, like a comely young
satyr. Tom had grown used to thinking of Adam as Ullah's

black swan, belonging only to the water and the woods of
the bayou . . . and to Tom himself. It would be a heart-
wrenching day when they left and Adam remained behind.
The day of Zoe's visit was to be the beginning of losing
Adam.

On Saturday, Zoe Tremain dressed simply in a full-
sleeved pink lawn gown with a rose-colored sash and presented herself to her son for approval. Not that Adam
would be much help. He approved of everything she did.
Too much so. No mortal woman could live up to what
Adam thought he saw in his mother. The man who sought
such unrealistic perfection in a life mate could only be disappointed. As he grew older, and looked far more like a
man than a boy, his idealism worried her.

This day, however, wasn't the occasion for such worries.
She placed a dainty hand on his arm, a picture of impec-
cable simplicity. Zoe, only five feet tall, looked up at
Adam in wonder; how had she ever produced a son of
Adam's proportions? Then she smiled in secret happiness,
remembering his father, the source of both her greatest
joy and her greatest sorrow.

In her youth she had carried Adam within her, thinking
herself blessed beyond measure to have that child. After
his birth came the long trial-blighted years—hardship and
abuse at Paul Tremain's hands. None of it had been able
to mar the intrinsic beauty that shone through Zoe's soft
hazel eyes.

Like Adam's, her hair glowed with the bright sheen of
health, covering her well-shaped head in a mass of unruly
black curls. In it were the first traces of gray, making her
seem more like a child with whitening in her hair than a
middle-aged woman past thirty-two.

"You'll like Ullah, Ma," Adam said, helping her into the
flatboat.

"I'm certain I will. And Tom as well."

"Angela too. She's like a little fairy princess."

Zoe listened as Adam talked about the bayou house.
She'd heard most of it before. He spoke of little else these
days. In the beginning he'd rarely mentioned Tom, but of
late Tom was as much a part of Adam's conversation as
Ullah and Angela.

Tears formed in Zoe's eyes whenever she heard Adam
speak of Tom. After Paul Tremain's death she never

wanted to be near another man. So Adam grew up first
with a man who loathed and resented the sight of him and
later with no man at all to guide him. Then Tom had come,
freely giving Adam what Zoe hadn't been able to provide
and what Paul Tremain had sullenly withheld.

Zoe could never explain to Tom all he had done for her
son and herself, but she could express her gratitude. She
could be Ullah's friend without reservation, and without
revealing her secret reluctance. She'd never been the equal
friend of a Negro. She knew no one who had or who would
approve. Zoe had practiced for days thinking of Ullah as a
woman, not a black woman. Her hands clenched slightly
as Adam sniffed, smelling the succulent odors of the barbecue.

"We're almost there, Ma."

She'd rather die than embarass Ullah and thus her son
and herself. Once again it would make Zoe responsible for
hurting Adam, and Adam's sense of honor would bar him
from the people who represented the best thing that had
ever happened to him. She said a quick prayer that she'd
know what to say and how to act.

A squarely built sandy-haired man turned from the roast-
ing pit to wave a greeting. In the middle of the yard stood
a small golden-haired child, dressed in a white ruffled
dress embroidered painstakingly with tiny rosebuds. She
was the picture of her name—an angel. Behind them was
a weathered-gray patched house. On its stoop stood the
woman Zoe knew to be Ullah, uncertain and nervous.

Zoe's heart went to her. She remembered afternoons
when she felt as Ullah now looked. Afternoons when Zoe
had prayed that just once Paul Tremain would leave the
cork in his whiskey bottle, that just once he would lack the
drink-induced courage to reduce her to shame, making her
plead that he let her son alone. Ullah stood with her hands
wrapped in her apron, prepared for her humiliation.

Zoe, placed on dry land by Adam's sure strong arms,
headed straight for Ullah, her hands extended in greeting
as though they had been friends for a lifetime. "Mrs.
Pierson, what a pleasure to meet you! Now I can thank
you in person for your many kindnesses to my son."

Ullah, coached by Tom, said softly, "Welcome to our
home, Miz Tremain." Then the mask of tension broke as
she smiled happily, looking first to Adam, then to Tom.

Angela ran up to hug her mother just as Ben and Beau came hooting their way from the woods.

The barbecue had begun. Zoe laughed freely at the boys' antics, eating, at Tom's and Ullah's persuasion, more than a lady should or her stays would allow.

The afternoon sped by, with easy talk and laughter. The sky changed from blue to the multihued ribbons of sunset. She watched as the birds passed over the bayou. In the woods crickets and katydids made their music.

"We'd best be getting home, Adam. Much as I hate to leave such pleasant company, it is going to be dark soon."

"Oh, no! We can't leave yet!" he cried. "Not until Ullah dances."

Ullah protested, frowning fiercely at Adam before her eyes darted to Zoe.

Adam grinned at her. "Where'd you hide my drums? Come on, Tom. You've gotta dance too."

"Can't," Tom groaned, his hand resting on a jug of wine. "I'm a set-down hog."

"Would you dance for me, Ullah?" Zoe asked softly.

"You're going to dance too, Ma," Adam declared, his eyes merry.

Zoe's mouth opened in surprise. "Adam . . . I . . ."

"With me, Ma. Ullah, where are the instruments?"

As they had so many other nights, they sat around the low-burning fire. The evening breeze made the glowing warmth welcome. The scent of roasted pig was still thick in the air. Angela sleepily rested her head on Ben's knee as he began tapping a slow rhythm on the bones. Beau played the gourd fiddle.

Zoe's eyes lighted softly as she watched, hardly able to recognize her son and his two best friends. Then she looked at Tom, who had managed to get to his feet in spite of his protests, performing some sort of nearly indecent dance with his wife. Zoe found she liked watching the strangely entrancing movements. She even liked the idea that Tom was so unabashedly in love with Ullah that feelings more properly kept private were not being hidden this night. But she would never, never allow Adam to lure her or bully her into moving her body about in so sensual a fashion.

Adam, reading his mother's thoughts, put down his drum and whispered into Beau's ear. Before Zoe knew what had happened, she was in her son's arms, being whirled swiftly over grass tufts and patches of bare earth with joyous abandon. The pace was the fastest, and Adam by far her wildest partner. Her skirts flew out behind her as she clung to him.

"Adam! Please! 'Greensleeves' is not a polka!" she begged breathlessly. "Do slow down, dear, please!"

"I can't. Beau is playing it like a polka." He laughed and kept her dancing. Her black curls came loose from their pins, caressing her face as her cheeks flushed and her eyes brightened with excitement.

She went from Adam's gracefully reckless stride to Tom's shorter-stepped solid version of Beau's waltz. Ben and Beau also took turns, until, exhausted, Zoe sat down on the log next to Ben, no longer caring if she remembered to lower herself gracefully to her seat as a lady should. Ullah came and sat near her. "Ah jes' wanta thank you, Miz Zoe. Ah ain't never had a day like this in all mah life."

Zoe placed her hand on Ullah's. "Neither have I. I'll be eternally in your debt, Ullah. May I say we've both gained from this day?"

Under the light paths of the Hunter's moon Adam took his mother home. They were singing, Zoe's soprano blending with her son's baritone and the tenor voices of Ben and Beau.

> Oh, potatoes they grow small over there!
> . . . 'Cause they plant 'em in the fall—

and then they laughed to hear Tom's voice calling over the water—

> And then eats 'em tops an' all over there!

Chapter Seven

"We have to leave, Ullah," Tom said. The barbecue was over. The time had come.

She was quiet for a time, pondering. "Where? What place gwine want us any better than they do heah?"

Tom had no answer. In the South he knew they wouldn't be welcome. In the North he would never feel welcome. "Maybe Southwest . . . into the new territories. I'm not sure, honey. We'll look until we find a place where people haven't already got their minds set. Most likely that will be West, where folks are just beginnin'."

She said no more about it, that day or any other. It was not in Ullah to defy her master or husband directly, but she had her ways of procrastinating so that Tom might have the time to reconsider.

Tom didn't hurry her, for he too believed he had time. The longer he stayed, the easier it was to think that he had allowed himself to panic when he saw Edmund in New Orleans. The peaceful tempo of life in the bayou house lulled him falsely. The days slipped into weeks.

December fifth was warm and pleasant, with the breeze from the Gulf pushing heavy white clouds in long, smooth streamers over the patches of woodland and water. The air was fresh, the bayou inviting. Early that afternoon the three boys came to the landing near the woods. Adam gave the sharp whistle that Tom could hear anywhere on his property.

Tom strolled through the woods to meet them. "What are you monkeys up to today?"

"Filling Ma's larder." Adam gestured toward the rifles and some large kettles. "We spotted a bee tree yesterday. Couldn't you use some honey?"

"I'd better not come," Tom said regretfully. "If I don't get Ullah to packin', we're never goin' to get out of heah."

"What's one more day?" Ben teased.

Tom shook his head. "You three are worse than Ullah. Next year I've got to plant somethin' or starve. The way we're goin', we won't be anywhere when plantin' season comes."

"You're not going to leave tomorrow, are you?" asked Adam.

Tom scratched his head, his eyes already shining in agreement. All reason cried out against it, but they were tipping the boat crazily now, laughing and shouting, tempting him with their antics. And as always, he wanted to go. Just one more time before he left the bayou behind forever.

* * *

Ullah had sent Angela out to play after breakfast. Angela wandered everywhere, causing her mother to spend most of her day worrying over what had taken her daughter out of sight so quickly. Now she peered anxiously out of the cookroom window.

Running as fast as she could on her short, sturdy legs, Angela was making her way toward the woods. Ullah shouted her daughter's name, then gave up, knowing she would have to go after the child.

She removed her apron, deftly folding it and placing it on the table, and hurried to the main room. Her smile faded. She stopped suddenly, her heart thumping wildly.

In the outer doorway stood a tall, slender man, impeccably attired down to the brilliantly shining black leather boots. In his left hand he loosely held a whip, its tails dangling. On his head was the outsized grotesque Mardi Gras mask of a boar with sharp, curling tusks. Behind him, crowded into the opening, were five others. A Goat, a Snake, an Alligator, a Raccoon, and a Bear all thrust their huge, leering heads into the room, tipsily jostling each other for the clearest view of her. The laughter from the menagerie was drunken, distorted, hollow.

Ullah backed away. Their laughter and their unintelligible talk ran together deafeningly. She grabbed the folded apron, pressing it against her as though by some magical power it would shield her from the boisterous animals advancing with terrible purpose into her house.

"What you want?" she stammered. "Who are you? What you want?"

The tusked Boar laughed. "Why, Ullah, don't tell me you've forgotten so soon. You know all of us . . . intimately, I would say."

Ullah's sight darkened. More terrified of what he would do if she fainted than she was of facing him, she grabbed hold of the back of a chair and forced herself to keep looking at the tusked mask.

"What you want, Mistah Revanche?" she asked, her throat dry. "Tom ain't heah. Ah jes' cleanin' up this house fo' him."

The whip spanned the distance between them before Ullah even realized he had moved his hand. She felt the cutting sting, then looked down to see the neat slashes across the front of her dress.

"I don't tolerate niggers lying to me, Ullah. Seems like

you've forgotten most of the training you got at Gray
Oaks. You're not cleaning for Tom, you're his wife. Now
isn't that so, Ullah?"

"Nossuh. No! Ah ain't nobody's wife. Nossuh, Ah ain't.
You wrong. Ah ain't nobody's wife."

Edmund flicked his whip, slashing her arms, her face,
until she was screaming and crying for him to stop.

"You're his wife." The words were no less menacing for
their calm tone.

"Yassuh! Yassuh, Ah is," she babbled, clutching at herself.

"You're a damned uppity nigger, Ullah. You've gotten
above yourself."

"Yassuh. Ah do dat. Ah do dat, suh!"

"What happens to a nigger who forgets her place, Ullah?"

"Ah . . . Ah doan know . . . Ah—"

"What happens, Ullah?" Edmund's cold, controlled
voice sent her into spasms of fear. He fingered the length
of the three-tailed whip.

She felt the hair on her neck rise. Gooseflesh covered
her lacerated arms as she hugged herself in terror.
"P-please, Mastah, Ah didn't mean nothin'—"

"What happens, Ullah!"

"They gets punished . . . . they gets punished!" she
screamed, all but incoherent. Wildly she glanced from one
of the looming masks to another. Inescapable, they moved
toward her. Ullah backed away sobbing and trying to stifle
the screams that wanted to loose themselves.

"You've played enough, Edmund. Let us have some fun
with her now."

Ullah sank to the floor, curling up, trying to protect herself from the sight of the animals and the dread of what
was to come. She moaned, crying and pleading to deaf ears,
"Oh, please, suh! Mastah Edmund, hol' 'em back! Oh,
Lawd! Oh, Lawd!"

"When do we get her, Edmund? This is a citizens' committee, not your private party," the Goat's head said, with
more authority now.

"All right. She's yours, but take her outside," Edmund
commanded. "When we get Tom, I want him to see everything."

The whip cut across Ullah's buttocks. She made a sound,
half scream, half whimper.

"Get up off that floor!" Revanche commanded.

She scrambled up. The Snake and the Alligator grabbed her roughly and forced her through the front door into the yard. Suddenly the Snake jerked her off her feet and leaped on her as she fell backward to the ground.

"There won't be any fun and games this time, nigger," said a voice that sickened her with remembered fear. As he had done that terrible night, he grabbed her dress by the neckline and pulled. He jerked her again and again until the fabric gave way and she was exposed.

There was laughter from the masks that crowded closely around her.

"Chrissakes, Ross, can't you get it in?" growled the Alligator. "We can't spend all day!"

Ullah, her heart pounding, watched the fangs of the Snake come nearer. It was useless to fight this man; he would tear her apart. She lay waiting, limp, feeling her legs jerked apart and his harsh invasion of her body. She braced herself, held herself stiff until he was done and the Snake's head rattled with his hoarse breathing. In a daze, she heard the drunken cheers and shouts from the other animals as Ross withdrew from her and the Goat moved to take his place.

The leering face and the long curved-back horns terrified her even more than the Snake had; but worst of all, she recognized the rank odor of Sleath, Revanche's overseer. She knew he would kill her if the others didn't. Sometimes late at night he would come to her cabin, pulling her out of bed and sleep, and force her ahead of him down the long row of whitewashed buildings, his whip biting through her thin shift every step of the way. When at last they would reach his cabin, he'd throw her onto his putrid bunk and . . .

"Oh, Lawd! Lawd!" He wouldn't do it to her this time without a fight. As he came near, her knee came up forcefully into his crotch. He gasped and fell heavily onto her. She thrust her hands through the openings of the mask and drove her thumbs as hard as she could into his eyes. Sleath screamed, drew back his fist, and broke her jawbone.

Tom, laughing as he watched the shouting boys in their crazily rocking boat, heard Sleath's cry, "J'hoshaphat, what was that?" He heard nothing further, except Adam, Ben, and Beau. "Sounded like a painter!" he said jovially.

Then Ullah's animal screeches were the only sound he could hear. They went on and on, mindless, hair-raising, sending a taut tingle through all his veins. Ashen, he began to run. Never had his legs seemed shorter then when he went crashing up the woods path, splashed through the clinging muck of a small pond, climbed its bank, and emerged, still running, from the edge of the woods.

What he saw was something out of hell. In a rough circle were three gaudily painted animals, yelling, leaping, and prancing insanely around a fourth who was attacking a flattened object on the ground. A Goat sat nearby, holding himself and drinking clumsily out of a flask. The animal heads bobbed in outsized grotesquery, urging the attacker to greater speed, to greater heights of lust and brutality. Slightly out of the radius of the circle stood a curved-tusked Boar, his arms folded and his booted legs apart, holding a three-tongued whip. Somehow, on the evil painted face, Tom sensed a smile of satisfaction.

Tom caught a glimpse of blue calico with white flowers on it. *Ullah!* Mounted on her, rocking obscenely to and fro, was a soft-eyed Raccoon with his fawn-colored breeches pulled down.

Screaming Ullah's name, he raced for the circle of attackers. Only the Boar noticed his approach. Tom plunged into the group, knocking aside two of the animals as he dived for the Raccoon, hitting him with the full impact of his hurtling body, rolling into the dust at the feet of the Boar. He grunted in pain, feeling a sharp crack as the Boar's shining boot kicked him in the side.

"Ullah! Run! Run!" he screamed, struggling to regain his feet. He swung his fists wildly, his wrists absorbing the shock each time he connected with a solid body. He heard her voice strange sounding, piteously cry his name once, then a hard slapping noise and a hollow laugh of unholy glee as the next man took his turn.

After that Tom hardly knew what he was feeling. The Snake and the Alligator caught his arms, wrenching them from their sockets as they pulled them up and behind him. As they stood still for a moment panting, the Boar walked near, raised his right boot, and planted the point of it into Tom's stomach just below his ribs. Tom's breath left him in a hard grunt. The earth grew gray and spun nauseatingly. The Snake let go with one hand and chopped Tom in the windpipe.

The Boar spoke sharply. "Hold him, Ross! I want him to see."

The dread fears of the past weeks hit him. It was Edmund Revanche who was the Boar, Edmund who stood to one side smiling evilly, whip in hand so Ullah couldn't possibly escape, taking his vicious, perverted pleasure in watching while his friends wrought his vengeance on Tom's wife.

The Goat was not content with rape alone; he hauled Ullah to her feet, ripping the shreds of her dress away so that she was naked and trembling, barely able to stand, the blood dribbling out of her mouth onto her breasts.

With the Goat's first blow Tom lunged mightily against the two men who held him. He got one arm loose, but then the Bear grabbed and twisted, and he felt the bones break.

"Please . . . let her go!" Tom cried, sobbing. He strained forward, dragging the Snake and the Bear with him. The Boar stepped in front of Tom, the butt of his hand forcing Tom's head back as he drove his knee into Tom's groin. Everything became a haze of blows and pain and Ullah's pitiful broken cries echoing in his ears. Blindly, futilely, he struggled against the hands that held him prisoner, until there was nothing but searing agony in his shoulders and down his arms. He felt and heard his ribs crack as the Snake kicked him.

Then Edmund Revanche threw aside the Boar's mask. He stood before Tom, a cool, cynical smile on his cruel features. "As you see, Tom, I am keeping my end of the bargain. What a pity you are not in better condition to enjoy the spectacle."

Tom, pinioned by pain and the grip of others, whispered hoarsely, "Let her go . . . you've done enough." Ullah had fallen to the ground. The Goat squealed like a hog as he satisfied his lust.

For answer, Edmund slashed at Tom with calculated expertise, first with fists, then with boots, reducing his face and genitals to pulp and gore.

Tom's world turned to a blood-red haze. Yet his hearing remained acute. Ullah was still alive, could still moan from the torture they were inflicting on her. Through tears and broken lips he begged, "My God . . . Edmund . . . please—"

"You God damned nigger-loving traitor." Edmund delivered a final kick that doubled Tom over in agony.

THE BLACK SWAN 79

The Alligator released Tom. "I ain't had my turn at the nigger yet. Leave some for me." He shoved the panting Goat out of his way. The awful green head with its pop eyes and the garish white rows of teeth bobbed and strove over Ullah. Her screams grew more horrifying, even after the Alligator had rolled off her.

Then the Snake, holding his hunting knife by the tip, expertly snapped it, to plunge nearly to the hilt in Ullah's belly. She gasped and went limp. She did not move as four other hunting knives struck her.

But the screams continued, bloodcurdling to Tom because they were his own.

"Oh . . . my . . . *God!*" Adam breathed, and swallowed. The three boys crouched, gasping in horror at the brutal beating taking place halfway between the house and the barn. Ullah swayed on her feet, a mass of bleeding wounds and bruises, while a Goat-headed man knocked her around, then leaped on her as she fell. Tom, trying to go to her defense, was being held by a Snake, an Alligator, and a Bear, while a Boar attacked him mercilessly.

Adam started forward.

Ben grabbed his shoulder, hard. "We'll all get killed if you go out there!"

Adam turned around and glared at him. His head jerked back toward the clearing. "Where's Angela?"

Three pairs of eyes strained for the sight of a small body. "Find Angela, Beau. Don't go near the house . . . . If she's there, it's already too late. Look around that thicket."

Beau had already taken several steps. "What'll I do with her, Adam? What if they come after her?"

"Take her through the woods to my Ma. Run, Beau!"

Adam and Ben ran back down the path toward the boat. Adam grabbed up the guns, handing Ben his, then loading his own and Beau's.

"You're not going to try to shoot them all?" Fear was making Ben's hands shake, but he worked with desperate skill as they moved toward another path. "We can't, Adam!"

"No—they'd kill Tom and Ullah right off. But maybe we can scare them. Run through the woods. Keep down.

Shoot as often as you can. Maybe it'll sound like we're a lot of men. Don't stop shooting!"

"Adam, it'll never work! They'll never believe we're a whole party of hunters. We'd better shoot a couple of them."

Adam's voice was commanding. "Damn it, Ben, do as I tell you!"

The two boys weaved back and forth among the covering brush and shrubs, keeping out of sight as well as they could. In fast succession their guns went off, Adam with the two rifles able to cover Ben's reloading time.

Edmund Revanche looked in the direction from which the shots came, and, listening, narrowed the repeating sounds to a twenty-yard area.

"Finish," he said flatly. "There's a hunting party nearby." He replaced the Boar's head, hiding his face. "Get Tom's horse, Sleath. We don't want any damned fuss over this."

The Bear pulled out his pistol and shot two or three times into the woods before the Boar shouted angrily, "You fool! They'll be shootin' at us if you don't stop!"

The Alligator and the Raccoon bent to lift Tom's barely conscious body upright. The Boar tossed a long rope over the limb of a large cypress. He placed the noose around Tom's neck and jerked it tight. "Put him on the horse," he commanded. He held the loose end of the rope securely to a cross member of the fence, taking up the slack as Tom was lifted onto the horse's back.

"Stretch him a little or he's gonna fall right off," shouted the Goat. The Boar pulled the rope tighter. Only its tension kept Tom erect in the saddle.

"Let's go," the Boar said.

"Want us to tie his hands?" asked the Snake.

Shadows passed overhead. The Boar looked up into the sky. It was growing black with the slow passage of the vultures, flying to the nearest roosts in trees, strutting alertly at the perimeter of the carnage. He looked at Tom's arms, dangling useless at his sides. "No need. Look at her, Tom! See her there on the ground? That's what you're dying for! That's what all insurrectionists come to in the end."

The others were waiting. The Boar mounted his own horse, then gave Sable a smart blow with his riding crop.

Sable, already rolling her eyes in fear, jerked and leaped forward. Tom's limp body was pulled backward, coming to life as it swung through the air in spasmodic jerks and twitchings.

Adam ran out of the woods as the Boar struck Sable. He lowered his rifle, aiming for the Boar's head. The bullet whizzed past the cheek of the mask, gouging it. Without looking back, the garish menagerie whipped their horses into a canter and rode out of sight.

Adam raced wildly across the open yard. He dropped the rifles and grasped Tom around the waist, holding him up. He buckled and strained under Tom's dead weight as Ben ran from the woods. Tom's body sagged again, taking up all the slack Adam could give him. Tom would hang right then, with Adam holding him.

"Hurry, Ben! He's slipping! I can't hold him! Cut the rope!"

Ben sawed frantically.

Under Tom's suddenly released weight, Adam staggered, trying to regain balance, then fell with Tom on top of him.

Ben ran to him, rolling Tom away. Then suddenly he paled as his eyes focused on Tom and couldn't let go of the sight. He turned away, retching. When he looked back, his eyes streamed tears.

"Adam, he's dead. What are we gonna do?"

"I don't know." Adam fought his own fear and nausea. He crawled over to Ullah, stirring up a buzzing cloud of insects that had gathered on her. The warm, pleasant sun struck brightness off the hilts of the hunting knives. "They've killed her, Ben." It was all he could do not to break down and cry.

Ben's voice was quavery. "Adam! Tom's still breathing! God, what if they come back?"

A vulture flew over Adam's shoulder, no longer intimidated, and landed on Ullah, ripping viciously at her.

Adam leaped to his feet, screaming and flinging his arms wildly. Ben, nearer to a rifle, shot one bird. The others fluttered up but continued to fly or to strut like gross chickens nearer and nearer to Tom. Soundlessly, more and more of them gathered in the trees. The stink of them pervaded the warm air.

"Adam, what can we do?"

Adam looked around frantically. "I don't know. . . .

Tom's dying. . . . We—" With sudden decision he said, "Get him down to the boat. We'll carry him between us."

He and Ben gingerly found places where they could lift Tom. A dozen carrion crows left their perches and swooped across the yard onto Ullah.

"Put him down. Keep the crows off him!" Adam ran into the silent house, tearing the bedding off Tom's and Ullah's bed. A quick glance told him Angela wasn't there. He could only pray that Beau had found her safe. He ran back to the yard. So frantic was he, and so menaced by the vultures, that he scarcely noticed the way Ullah's flesh clung to the knives as he jerked them out. He wrapped her in a sheet, struggling with her arms and legs, which flopped about, strangely unwilling to be captured.

Ben spread the blanket, and they lifted Tom onto it. Hastily Adam threw the coverlet over Tom, for the birds were gathering again. They carried him down to the boat. Ben looked anxiously about. "Hurry and get in, Adam. Those men'll come back. They must have seen you. They'll know we can't stop them."

Adam looked from Tom's silent, limp form back toward the yard. "She's . . . the carencrows . . . they'll—" Suddenly he burst into a sob. "I can't leave her, Ben!"

More frightened now than he had been before, Adam ran back to the house. Warily he looked down the path the men had taken. He rummaged in the barn for Tom's shovel, thinking to bury her. Then his heart stood still as he heard the pounding hoofs of a horse.

It was only Sable, seeking her stall, but he had had enough of terror. He ran back toward Ullah. The carrion crows had lighted on her again, pecking and ripping at the sheet that covered her. He chased them off, slung Ullah's body over his shoulder, and moved as quickly as he could toward the boat. Ben's eyes grew wide, but Adam said decisively, "We have to take her with us."

Seated on the wide plank, Ben edged away as far as he could. He wasn't sure what he thought about ghosts and spirits, but he knew he didn't want to sit close to Ullah.

The vultures circled purposefully overhead as Adam poled the boat into the main channel. He had loved these two people next only to his own mother, and one was dead and the other nearly so. Unashamed of his emotion now, he let the tears stream down his face.

"Damn them! May God damn them all," he said over

and over. "I'll repay them, Ben. I'll find out who they
were, and I'll repay them."

Chapter Eight

The night outside was black and starless when the muffled
thudding came at the back door. Zoe snatched up a lamp
and ran through the house. She opened the door just as
Adam's booted toe kicked it again. She gasped, and nearly
dropped the lamp.

There stood her son, his face smeared with blood, his
eyes swollen, haunted, and sad. His mouth was grim and
determined as he stepped up to the house with his hideous
burden. Behind him stood Ben, pale enough to be dead
himself. In his arms he carried Ullah's broken body,
swathed in the tattered, stained bed sheet.

Uncertain, Adam remained in the doorway, his eyes
fixed on his mother's face. Having finally reached the
safety of home, he no longer knew what to do.

"Bring him into the house, Adam," she said in a voice
so calm that it frightened her nearly as much as the sight
of Tom and the rigid, bewildered look of shocked pain on
Adam's face.

More than anything she wanted to close the door, re-
open it, and know that neither Adam nor Ben would be
standing there holding the two corpselike bodies. Ever
since Beau had come running to her with Angela and
garbled tales of animal heads, the day had turned to nightmare.

As one should in a nightmare, Adam walked with the
slow buoyancy of a man moving through water into the
front parlor. There he stood stupefied, his face a dry-eyed,
staring mask.

"Ben . . . is that Ullah?" Zoe hardly believed what she
saw.

Ben nodded, not able to look directly at her.

"Put her on the sofa," Zoe said more firmly. Her concern was for Adam, but it was Ben to whom her words
gave release. He laid Ullah down, rubbing at his arms
where she had touched him, and he cried. In his eyes was

the desire to share the hurt and shock of the day, a longing to be touched, to be comforted and healed by the
warmth and imperfect understanding of the living.

Zoe looked at her son, but could not speak to him.
"Help Adam take him upstairs, Ben. I'll wake Mammy.
She'll know what to do."

"They killed her, and we couldn't stop them," Ben
sobbed.

Zoe pressed her hands against her mouth. She wanted to
run from the room to seek the security of Mammy's all-
knowing affection. Taking a deep breath, she tried to
sound calm. "I know, dear. You did all you could, and
that is all that can be asked of any of us. But now we
must see to Tom. Do as I ask you, Ben. Help Adam take
him upstairs." How unfeeling her words sounded to her
own ears! She walked over to Adam, placing her hand on
his back.

Adam flinched away as though she had hurt him, and
grasped his unwieldy burden tighter. "Let him alone. I'll
take him upstairs," he said with a cold, hard possessiveness.

"Let him do as he wants," Zoe said hastily, and hurried
to the back of the house, where Mammy slept.

Mammy was old. She had been old for as long as Zoe
could remember. She had reared Zoe's mother, Zoe, her
sisters, and Adam. In Zoe's eyes there was nothing on this
earth that Mammy hadn't seen or known about.

The old woman was a mountainous bulge beneath the
cream-colored blanket, her face a huge black oval against
the white sheets. Zoe shook her gently. "Mammy! Mammy,
wake up." The old servant's mouth moved, mumbling. She
rolled over, snoring again. "Mammy, I need you. Please,
Mammy!" Zoe said urgently.

Mammy's eyes fluttered open. "Miz Zoe," she muttered.
"Miz Zoe!" She turned her great white woolly head to see
Zoe's pale face in the darkness. "What you doin' heah,
baby? What's wrong?"

"Oh, Mammy, there's terrible trouble!" Zoe cried, no
longer having to be calm and strong. As she had told
Mammy of her fears and sorrows during her life with
Paul Tremain, she now told her what little she knew about
the afternoon. "Adam, Mammy . . . he's so strange. He
won't even let me touch him. I don't know what to do."

"Fetch me mah wrappah," Mammy ordered. Zoe hurried to do as she was told. "Miz Zoe, doan you be lettin'

de young masta sees you all upsot. You does yo' cryin' on Mammy's shouldah, you heah?"

"I hear."

"Den dry yo' eyes. You be strong, Miz Zoe. Ah takes care o' Masta Tom. Doan you worry no mo'." Mammy gave her favorite child a pat, then rumbled down the hall to the main part of the house, the stairs and rail creaking under her ponderous assault.

Shivering, cold as ice, Adam knelt by the bed where he had placed Tom. His eyes were still dry and staring, his face set in the same horrified grimace, as though he would never again see anything but the loathsome spectacle of that afternoon.

"What you done brought home dis time, Mas' Adam?" Mammy asked. Then she saw Tom lying on the bed, and her face creased in a deep frown. "Git outa mah way. Ah gots plenty to do." She ordered him about as she always did. Now, though, no twinkling blue eyes deviled her, no fond teasing remark replied to her high-handedness. He didn't seem to have heard her at all.

"You in mah way. Now, git up. You heah me?" she said sharply.

"Mammy . . ." Zoe said hesitantly from the doorway, "maybe you shouldn't be so brusque."

Mammy turned on her. "Doan you go tellin' me mah bizness, Miz Zoe. Ah knows what Ah's about. You go down stairs an' see to Mas' Ben. Ah takes care o' Mas' Adam an' Mastah Tom."

Zoe touched Adam's head, feeling beneath her fingers the soft, springing curls, but she did as Mammy asked.

Mammy pulled Adam to his feet. "You does what Ah sez. You ain't no li'l boy, not affer. dis. You gits up an' be's a man."

Adam stared blankly at her.

"You gwine he'p me or stan' 'round all grieved up fo' yo'seff? Dat's bettah. We got to gits his clo's offen him. Take dem boots."

Adam moved stiffly, with fumbling fingers. Mammy worked with youthful efficiency, praying for Tom, praying for strength, and roundly cursing the Devil, whose work this was.

"Mas' Adam, fetch me a bucket o' col' watah, a bar o' dat white lye soap, an' lotsa clean rags. Heah me?"

He nodded jerkily, moved a few steps, and stopped. His

face, greenish white, covered with a sheen of perspiration, twisted as he looked back at Tom.

"You done brung him dis far, boy. You wanta lose him now?" Mammy roared, and shoved him through the door. She went back to Tom, her deft old fingers moving over his body, seeking broken bones and internal injuries through the swollen puffiness of his flesh. She shook her head, muttering angrily.

By unspoken agreement Zoe and Ben had moved into the kitchen, avoiding the mutilated thing that lay on the parlor sofa. As Adam came near, Ben was telling Zoe, "My daddy's gonna raise Cain. He'll see those men strung up."

Adam rushed into the room, grabbed Ben's shoulders, and shook him. "Don't you say a word! Do you hear me, Ben? Not a word to anyone!"

"Adam!" Zoe gasped at his look of venomous hatred. "Please . . . your behavior!"

"I'm warning you, Ben. Don't you let anyone know where Tom is!"

"What about those men? They should be punished— they—"

"What men?!" Adam screamed at his friend. "Who are they? What men?"

"The ones with the masks—"

"We don't know them. But they know Tom. And Angela."

"But what will I tell my parents?"

The veins of his neck stood out, but Adam's face remained ghastly pale. "Nothing!" he shouted. "We went hunting! That's all!"

Zoe got up from her chair, no longer able to bear watching him. She tried to put her arm around his waist.

He jerked away from her. "Let me alone!" He ran out into the washhouse. He came back carrying the water, rags, and soap.

Zoe heard him climb the stairs. Ben sat at the table, staring at his hands. "I just don't know if I can hide this. I never had to . . . had to keep something like this a secret before."

"One seldom does." Zoe was barely listening. Her mind had followed Adam. Her ears were more acutely tuned to the creakings Mammy's feet made on the floor above.

"The man with the Boar's head said Tom was an insurrectionist. He wasn't—was he?"

"I don't know. It would be hard to believe that of Tom. I think he just loved Ullah. It's too bad she wasn't . . ."

Ben nodded in agreement with Zoe's self-consciously unfinished sentence. "Adam and I talked about that some. But Ullah seemed special. I mean, she wasn't like the darkies we have. Ullah was so . . ."

Zoe patted at his hand. "I know. Drink your hot chocolate. It's time you were getting home. Do you think you're up to it now?"

Ben emptied his cup. "I'm all right, Mrs. Tremain. I—I won't say anything. Not to anyone. Ma'am?"

"Yes, Ben?"

He hesitated, then burst out, "Is a citizens' committee the law? Did we do wrong in bringing Tom here? Will you get in trouble for it?"

"I don't know, Ben, but you didn't do wrong in bringing Tom here. What you boys did was right." Zoe patted his shoulder gently.

She felt ashamed as she closed the door. Ben made her feel guilty as he spoke aloud the things she was afraid to put into words. He took her inadequate explanations and was comforted by them. Ben had seen something terrible, but it would not affect him overlong.

Adam was different. He would argue with her explanations. He would find scant comfort in anything she said. Zoe, seeing with unusual clarity how she had repeatedly failed him, wondered if she'd ever learn to guide her son properly. Her love for him was deep and abiding—but love was not enough. Today in the bayou some demented men had destroyed Tom and had taken Ullah's life. In what ways had they maimed and twisted her son?

She hurried up to the bedroom. Mammy had cleansed Tom's wounds and layered his broken body with cold, wet rags. His ribs were bound in a tight casing of white muslin.

Adam stood at the foot of the bed, his hand grasping the post so hard it looked bloodless.

Mammy said matter-of-factly, "Boff dese arms is outa dey joint. Bes' we fix 'em while he still not knowin'." She raised one foot, intending to place it against Tom's side, up near his armpit and away from the broken ribs. Her knee caught in her nightgown; her balance was in peril. "Too ol' an' too fat," she muttered irritably. "Mas' Adam, you gwine hafta do what Ah tells you."

"Can't I do it?" Zoe asked.

"You ain't strong enuf to do nothin' 'cep' hurt him."

Adam walked to the side of the bed. He took off his heavy boot and placed his foot as Mammy showed him. She glowered at him. "You hol's him heah, an' heah. You gots to do jes' like Ah tells you. Cain't be gentle, gots to be a quick, hard jerk, you min' me?"

Adam nodded dumbly. He grasped Tom's hand in his, his other hand fast on Tom's wrist.

"When I tells you, you pulls back hard. De Lawd will do de res'."

Beads of cold perspiration shone on him. He bit hard on his upper lip, his eyes squeezed shut as he waited for the sound of Mammy's voice. As he pulled, Tom screamed.

"Doan you pay no never min' to dat. Only hurts goin' in," Mammy said sharply as Adam released Tom's arm, covering his own face with his hands. Mammy felt Tom's shoulder and grunted in satisfaction. "Now do de odder arm."

Adam was shaking. "I can't . . . I can't."

"You sho' nuff kin. Dis gent'man yo' frien', an' he gwine need dem arms. You git ovah heah wid me an' do what's gotta be did."

"Mammy . . ." Zoe began.

"Hush, now, Miz Zoe, ain't no time fo' you to take on. Mas' Adam, he a man, an' he gwine do man's work."

"Oh, but Mammy, I can't stand to see what it's doing to him!"

Mammy said implacably, "It be makin' dat young man strong, dat what it doin' to 'im."

Adam wrenched Tom's right arm into its socket and stood sobbing.

But Mammy was not finished with him. "Breave thoo yo' nose, boy, den you doan boff up," she said, watching him until the nausea passed. "Now go down an' git de woman laid out on de kitchen table. We gots to make her propuh fo' her burial. Miz Zoe can watch out fo' dis one. You keep dem rags cold, Miz Zoe. Mas' Adam, keep on movin'. You an' me got a heap o' hard labor 'heada us 'fo' de rooster crow."

* * *

Mammy would not allow him to stop, gave him no time to think or argue, as he toted buckets of water up and down from Tom's room so the cold paddings could be changed to try to keep down the swelling. As the night wore on, Tom began to slip into and out of consciousness, moaning in pain, bringing the sharp edge of memory closer to Adam. Mammy sent him into the pecan grove at the far end of their property to dig Ullah's grave.

"Mammy! You can't make him do that! Not after all he's been through. I won't have it! It's nearly four in the morning. Oh, Mammy, you've never been heartless before —why are you doing this to him?"

"Miz Zoe, mebbe you de sof'est li'l lady in de whole worl', but ain't sof'ness dat's gwine git him thoo dis night. Dat boy eatin' he heart out. Dat's what he's doin'. When Mammy done wid him, he gwine sleep, 'cause dat's all dat's gwine be lef' in him to do. Ah watch dat li'l boy fend fo' hisself all alone when Mas' Paul still alive. All dem yeahs Ah say to mahseff, Mammy, dat ain't right, but Ah doan do nothin'. Dis time Mammy gwine he'p him. Ah knows what's bes' fo' him. He gotta think he done it all hisseff. An' we gotta he'p him so's he res' when he finish up."

"He's too young for this!"

"Mebbe so—but it done happen, an' we cain't do nothin' 'bout dat."

They buried Ullah in the grove just before the sky began to lighten, Zoe reading from the Psalms as Mammy held the candle high so she could see the print. Mammy stood proud and erect, her hand touching her breast as she sang softly in her low, sorrowful voice, resonant with the echo of the centuries, a lament for all the losses of all men of all times. Adam lowered Ullah into her grave. The sound of his shovel, replacing the moist earth in the gaping hole, made an eerie accompaniment to the gentle voices of the two women repeating the words of their Maker.

Adam looked like a sleepless specter when they returned to the house. His face was drawn and gaunt, marked with guilt and remorse as only the faces of the very innocent can be. From time to time he would glance up at the staircase, afraid to go back to Tom lest he find him dead, and afraid not to, for if he didn't give his own strength to Tom, what hope was there?

Mammy was halfway up the stairs. "Ain't you comin', Mas' Adam?"

He followed her.

Zoe remained in the parlor. She had never felt so useless as she had this night. She'd wanted Mammy to take over, but . . . but . . .

When she finally went upstairs, she heard the sound of Mammy's voice filling the hallway. Standing outside the door where Tom lay, she listened, remembering the countless times when those same dulcet tones had lulled her into believing the morning would be sweet with the promises the night denied.

Adam's head was in Mammy's lap, his arms loosely around her waist.

"Iffen you git him a piller an' a blanket, Miz Zoe, we bed him down right heah."

"He's asleep?"

"Yes'm, he 'sleep, an' he all cried out. It gwine take a whiles, but dis boy be all right. Dey boff gwine be all right. De Lawd see to dat." Then she added, as though the fiery determination of her will would make it so, "De Lawd an' Mammy."

Zoe felt a small creeping sense of shame as Mammy's hand lightly caressed the hair on Adam's neck, and her eyes rested on Tom. Zoe had thought little about Tom tonight. There had even been moments when, unwanted and unable to make herself needed, she had resented him and what he had brought down on her. Now, as though Mammy's strength were the magic key to her feelings, she looked at Tom and felt the pity, revulsion, and hope that she should have felt from the beginning and could not.

Zoe wondered if she'd ever be able to take what the world thrust at her without freezing inside. She had her own moral principles, but never the courage to impose them on others. Instead, she had always let someone or something stronger pull her along; time and again she was defeated and rendered ineffective to those she loved the most. How many times could she fail before there were no chances left?

During the following days Tom clung to the threads of life, his survival more a tribute to Mammy's tireless ministrations and kind-hearted bullying than to Tom's will to live. She cleaned his wounds until he screamed in agony, but no trace of putrefaction or infection developed. She force-fed him. During his conscious moments she forced words from him, giving him a target for his hatred and an outlet for emotions, still cutting-sharp in a weak body. Mercilessly she dragged his beaten body and his unwilling mind away from death.

Adam was another matter. With him Mammy's ruthless hectoring didn't work. In body he was as sound and healthy as a young colt, but Adam already had a target for his hatred, and he wouldn't let go of it. He clung to the memory of that December day; it fired his rage and pushed back the monstrous guilt he felt for having failed to save Ullah or to help Tom soon enough. He learned to hide his guilt and fears behind the spearpoint of a single-minded desire: to find the man who had worn the Boar's-head mask.

As Tom slowly recovered, Adam hovered constantly in the sick room, silent, somber, brooding, and unnatural. During these days it was hard for Zoe to feel sympathy for him. He frightened and angered her. He hardly ate at all. He wouldn't go out with his friends. There was no laughter in him—nothing but the nightly dreams that awakened him in a cold, shaking sweat.

Zoe wanted to scream at him, shake him until he would do the things she thought he should. The sameness of the days became intolerable—the endless climbing of stairs, the changing of awful bandages, the reluctance of both Tom and Adam to face living again. Zoe hated every minute of every day.

For two weeks she kept her silence and did Mammy's bidding. Then, against Mammy's warnings, Zoe took Angela to see her father.

"Dat gent'man ain't gwine wanta see dat li'l baby yet, Miz Zoe. He ain't ready fo' dat," Mammy said, her mouth drawn down in disapproval.

"Don't be silly. It will cheer him up. Goodness, Mammy, it's about time someone around here smiled!"

"Ain't no smile gwine come o' dis," Mammy growled.

Tom's eyes opened in horror when he heard Angela say, "Papa?" Groaning, he put his hand over his face, shielding himself from the sight of the child who reminded him of Ullah. "Take her out!"

"Tom, Angela has missed you," Zoe said softly. "Don't

you want to see her? It will make you feel so much better."

"Get her out of here! Get her out!" He turned his head away.

Adam got up from the chair in the shadowed side of the room. Glaring at his mother, he picked Angela up, holding her whimpering against him. Her arms found their way around his neck, clinging to him. He took her downstairs to Mammy, then returned to Tom.

Zoe, waiting in the hallway, said apologetically, "I thought he would want to see her."

Adam took the seat Zoe normally occupied near Tom's bed. He seldom sat there, for Tom didn't seem to want to see him any more than he had Angela. Now Tom closed his eyes, his face expressionless.

Awkwardly Adam shifted in his chair, fiddling with his hands. He didn't understand why Tom turned from him, nor did he know what to say when Tom maintained this aloof, hostile silence.

"Angela is all right now. Mammy has her downstairs." When the silence became more than he could bear, he asked, "Can I get something for you, Tom? Are you thirsty?"

There was no reply. Unlike other days when he had made attempts to talk to Tom and given up, Adam persisted until Tom opened his eyes. In them was none of the friendly affection of the past.

"Get out of here, Adam. There is nothin' you can do."

Adam smiled tentatively. "How do you feel, Tom?"

"How do the livin' dead ever feel?"

The smile faded from Adam's face. "But . . . you are much better, Tom. Mammy says you can sit up by the window soon, and then—"

Tom laughed harshly, a sound that could hardly be heard. Neither his voice nor the sounds of his laughter would ever ring clear again. The rope had damaged his vocal cords, leaving him with only a hoarse whisper. "Then I will be able to walk around, a freak, neither livin' nor dead, not a man, not . . . Christ, Adam! Leave me alone! Stop meddlin' in what doesn't concern you!"

"You concern me, Tom." Adam looked away, embarrassed by his need to reveal his own feeling for this man. "I'm just sorry I couldn't get there sooner. If I'd been quicker you wouldn't—"

"Relieve your mind," Tom hissed. "I wish you hadn't

gotten there at all. I'd have died then, an' it would be all over. Is that clear enough? I didn't want your heroic rescue, an' I don't want to see you now. Go away, boy."

Tom closed his eyes again, his mouth drawn down and set. For several minutes Adam sat, unable to move or speak. Then, lifelessly, he went downstairs.

Angela ran to him as soon as he entered the kitchen and held fast to his hand. Next to Tom and Ullah, Adam had her heart. Now it was Adam who banished the inexplicable exile she had been living since Beau had taken her from the bayou house. She turned her huge questioning brown eyes to him.

Adam gathered her into his arms. Her father had turned from her; Adam would give to Angela what Tom could not. That night it was Adam who heard her prayers and kissed her before she went to sleep.

Like all the other things in which Zoe saw the beginnings of hope, she saw it in this and was disappointed. Adam stayed by Angela, delighting her and keeping her occupied, but he did it with the same grim joylessness that he did everything these days.

Soon Zoe was willing to accept anything that might break the morbid spell that cloaked them all. The sound was like music to her ears when on a Sunday afternoon, after an absence of four days, Ben hammered on the front door.

His face was alive with excitement. He grabbed off his hat, saying, "Evenin', Mrs. Tremain. Where's Adam? Boy, have I got news!"

"Good news, I hope. You'll find him in the kitchen."

"Thank you, ma'am. Excuse me, I gotta see Adam right away." He skipped past her, tossing his hat on a chair as he went.

Adam looked up with indifference as Ben barged into the room.

"Wait'll I tell you! You're never gonna believe it!"

"Then why bother telling me?"

"Damn! What's the matter with you, Adam? Don't you care about anything?"

"You know what I care about."

"It happens I've got news about that."

Adam turned his chair to face him. "What did you hear?"

"We're having a barbecue. People everywhere. Daddy

invited half the county. A couple of the men there used to know Tom when he lived in New Orleans. Did you know Tom was rich? He lived in one of those great big mansions on Clio Street and just left it. Can you imagine that?"

"Is that all?"

"One of the men—Etienne Bordulac—said some man really has it in for Tom. Tom stole Angela from his plantation. This fellow thinks Angela is his slave and wants her back. Now he's hunting for them. Mr. Bordulac said that when Tom took Ullah, he stirred up the other slaves. He wants my daddy to tell him anything he hears. It's a good thing you told me not to say anything. Jeez!"

"Sounds like Bordulac was there in the bayou that day."

"No, no, Mr. Bordulac heard it from the other man, the one who owns the plantation. Adam—you're harboring a runaway slave as well as an insurrectionist. They're fighting mad about what Tom did. You know how people feel about giving darkies ideas."

"What was the man's name, the one who owned the plantation?"

"I don't know. I wasn't listening until he mentioned Angela."

"You have to know, Ben. How could you be so stupid?"

"How was I supposed to know it would be important? You know how they all talk. Slaves and war and crops. I think he has a sugar plantation."

"It's a place to start. I can find out about sugar plantations."

"Yeah, yeah, but what about Tom and Angela? You can't keep them here now. They're ready to string Tom up again when they get him. He's going to find out about you. Then what can you do?"

"I'm going to kill him," Adam said quietly.

Ben made a face of impatient disgust. "Aw, come on, Adam, I'm serious. If he comes here and asks about Tom, what're you gonna say?"

"Why should he come here?"

"Bordulac mentioned your ma's name. He's gotten it somewhere."

"He knows my mother?"

"I guess so. But my daddy said Mr. Bordulac must be crazy. Your ma wouldn't have any truck with runaways and insurrectionists. But hush my mouth, Adam, I almost swallowed my punch glass and all. Both of them are right here."

"How could he know about my mother? Find out more, Ben. See if you can get the man's name."

"Can't. Bordulac left. He was going to some ball they're having tonight."

After Ben left, Adam questioned Zoe endlessly.

"Adam, I am not acquainted with Etienne Bordulac nor with any sugar plantation owner."

"You must be! How else would he know your name?"

"I'm sure I don't know, dear. You really must stop this haranguing, Adam. I don't like it, and I can't tell you anything. Why is it so important?" She looked at him wide-eyed. "Unless . . . Adam, he isn't one of the men who was at Tom's house?"

"He may be. Ben said he's looking for Tom and Angela."

"How could anyone know they're here?"

Adam rose to leave the room. "I hope he does come here," he said grimly. "I hope he says right out that he wants Tom and Angela. I'm going to kill him right then, where he stands."

Horrified, Zoe faced her son. "God forgive you!"

"God can forgive me when it's over," Adam said coldly. Zoe slapped him hard across the face. She had never struck him before, but she wasn't sorry. He looked at her in stunned amazement.

"How dare you speak so! Talking of taking a man's life as though it were yours to take! I am ashamed to call you my son, Adam. You have been my heart and my pride since the very moment you were conceived, but today you are my shame and dishonor."

"Ma, listen to me! You don't understand! He—"

"We are not discussing him. I am concerned with you, Adam. You would coldly take a man's life in revenge to ease your own mind?"

"No!" he cried. "It's for Tom!"

"Oh, you are a fool!" Zoe spat the words at him as though he deserved the vilest expressions of her contempt. And she felt good. For the first time since he had come home with Tom in his arms, he was listening to her. "It is your pride, Adam. Do you think I am deaf, that I haven't heard you sobbing in the night or talking in your sleep about what might have happened if you had been able to run just a little faster to Tom or if you hadn't missed when you shot at the man? Of course you talk! You talk incessantly when you are asleep. I have listened and prayed, waiting for the day you might turn to me with these thoughts that torture you."

"There's nothing you can do. I could have saved Ullah. I could—"

"You did all you could!" Zoe shouted, bringing Mammy to the parlor door. "Go away, Mammy, I am speaking to Adam!" she said in the same wrathful voice she had used on her son.

"Yes'm." Mammy's mouth puckered into a smile. To see Miz Zoe looking up to her tall son, shouting at him, was like watching a wren attack an eagle.

Fiery-eyed, Zoe turned again on Adam. "You! You! Always what you could do! You're playing the part of the Almighty, Adam Tremain!"

Adam said stonily, "You don't understand." He went as far as the hall before his mother's voice called him back.

"Adam Tremain, where are your manners? When a lady is speaking to you, you do not leave her presence without being excused."

Adam's eyes fell. "I'm sorry, Mother."

In a softer tone she went on, "I understand something you apparently don't, Adam. You're willing to become the same kind of man as the one you want to kill, and you're willing to risk the lives of all the people in this house to accomplish it. It's an arrogant, self-serving man who would do that."

Adam, dismissed, went upstairs to sit by Tom's bed. His mother never would understand, he thought, and he hadn't been able to explain his deep-running feelings to her. This obsession of his wasn't something he could put into words. It was just something that had to be done.

With absolute certainty, Adam knew the day would come when that hated man would appear at the door. It would only be a matter of time before he was face to face with the man who had worn the Boar's-head mask, and then it would be over. On that day, it would end—all the horror and the dreams and the terrible sense of not having done enough.

Chapter Nine

Zoe threw back the draperies, sending shards of brilliance into the room. It was New Year's morning.

"Cheer up, Tom! It's a beautiful day! Not a cloud in the sky. Perhaps that is a sign. Eighteen fifty-three is going to be a trouble-free year. Is that possible?" Folding her hands in childlike anticipation, she sat next to his bed, her eyes eagerly searching his face for agreement.

"Might be a sign that the worst troubles are those never seen," he rasped in his permanently hoarse voice.

"You would say something like that. I declare, Tom Pierson, I'm about ready to give up on you. It's time you thought of the future. Planting season is nigh on us, and seems like you might think about giving Adam a hand with our field."

Planting was such an ordinary thing, so much a part of the permanence of life, that it seemed alien to Tom. He watched her. She was used to talking now without expecting any replies from him. It gave him a grim sense of power to know how easily he'd taught Zoe to expect nothing in return for her efforts. In some small part it made up for the painful lessons he'd had about his powerlessness to control his own life.

She talked with brittle cheerfulness about the time for this and the time for that. But she talked of time to a man for whom time meant nothing, for whom time had lost all meaning.

Throughout January and February Tom healed slowly. He knew that the days passed only because at the beginning of each Zoe came into his room, pulling open the draperies to reveal the light hidden behind them. He counted that action of hers seventy-eight times before Mammy came in Zoe's place one morning. She stood at the foot of his bed like a glowering black cliff.

"Git out o' dat bed, Mistah Tom. You been lyin' 'bout long's Ah kin stan' it."

He stared at her in disbelief, until she placed her gar-

gantuan hands on her broad hips. There was respect in
his voice when he talked to her, and some amusement.

"I'm still weak an' sore as can be. Let me think about it,
work up to it slowlike. I'll get up tomorra." He smiled
tentatively at her.

"You gwine git up, Mistah Tom, or Ah is gwine git you
up mahseff."

Tom got up. Every morning thereafter he got up.

As the days passed, the heat climbed, and the humidity
became more dense until it pressed down with a weight
and urgency of its own. Tom had hours each day to remember. At the end of his rambling thoughts back into
his youth with his two friends was the day at the bayou
house when they had killed Ullah. His smoldering ill
humor fluttered into a flaming consciousness of what Ross
and Edmund had done to him. The more he thought about
it, fueling his resentment and hatred, the more it seemed
impossible for him to remain in the placid security of
Zoe's care. He would have to do something about them.

Tom dressed every day now, testing his strength and
determination with each venture out of the house. He
walked a little farther each day, remained up a little longer,
fought off the quick fatigue that assailed him at every
turn. He grew more careless about allowing himself to be
seen.

Zoe rejoiced in his attempts to recover. He was another
face at the dinner table, a new source of conversation, a
return to ordinary things. But incomprehensible to her
gentle mind was the idea of a hurt anger so deep that its
only cure was to hurt in return.

Mammy simply watched the signs of returning health.
Other than the condition of his body, she knew little about
Tom. To Mammy, a clear day and tolerable health were
sufficient to make life rewarding.

Adam alone guessed that Tom's aimless recuperative
wanderings had a purpose. Seeing such single-minded
hatred work on one he cared for finally gave Adam an
insight into the self-destructive powers of hatred. Tom had
lost the quiet merriment that had always been so much a
part of him. Adam had sat in Tom's room, a patient exile
during the months of illness and sorrow, awaiting the day
when Tom's spirit would overcome the evils men had
wreaked against him. With a sense of dread, Adam now
wondered if that day would ever come.

On a hot, sultry day in late spring, Tom asked Zoe if he could use her lightweight buggy.

"You planning to go visiting, Tom? I'm so glad. It's time you saw some new faces."

"I've got business that should be tended," he said grimly, his eyes fixed on the wall behind Zoe's shoulder.

"Well, you know you're welcome to the buggy, Tom." She tried not to look at him as he painfully shrugged into his frock coat. His arms still troubled him, particularly when the weather was damp and hot as it had been lately. "I'll have Adam hitch up for you."

"I'll do it myself."

Adam was cleaning the barn. Fork in hand, he called to Tom from the loft, and jumped down, landing lightly on the hard-packed floor beside him. "Where you going today? You're taking the buggy?"

Tom cursed his luck. It wouldn't be easy to get away from the boy's watchful eyes. "Tend to your chores, an' I'll tend to mine," he said, and started to harness the horse.

Adam was not ready to give up. Tom grabbed the buggy hitch, angrily pulling it into place. He was sick to death of the hurt expression on Adam's face, but the boy called it on himself. He wouldn't let go of things as they once had been. He glared at the offending presence. "You peeve me, boy. Now get on with yourself an' let me be."

"I can't, Tom. You're gonna do something stupid. I know it."

Tom dismissed Adam with a brusque motion of his hand. Adam's eyes remained fixed on the gun Tom had strapped around his hips. Unlike most men of his day, Tom seldom wore a gun unless he intended to put it to use.

"You're going after those men, aren't you?"

"That's my business," Tom said.

"I won't let you go alone."

"Like hell you won't! When'd you get appointed my guardian? I told you before, boy, I don't want you meddlin' in my life. Get out of my way, Adam, I'm not foolin' you." He climbed into the driver's seat and took the reins. He raised the buggy whip, glaring at Adam warningly.

"You'd hit me with that?" Adam asked quietly.

"Damned right I would. Seems you don't understand talk. You'll understand this, I'll wager."

Adam stepped back. "Then go! Get yourself killed!

This time I won't be there. I don't give a damn. Not any more!"

Stone-faced, Tom brought the whip down on the horse's flank. Harness and hitch groaned and clicked with sudden motion as the buggy sped down the front drive and turned toward New Orleans.

Minutes later Adam was astride his own horse, cutting through woods and across fields to keep pace with Tom unseen.

At the outskirts of New Orleans, Tom slowed his horse. He told himself it was just to take in the view, not because his arms ached and his backbone felt like putty. Over the city hung telltale black clouds of smoke. From it emanated the odors of burning tar and death.

Now he remembered seeing headlines about the epidemic in the *True Delta*. New Orleans would be but a shell, the wealthier people having abandoned their city homes for the protection of their country estates. He wondered how long the fever had been raging and if there were any chance he could find Edmund and Ross still here. It was an impossibly slim hope that Edmund would be in the city. At the first sign of danger Edmund would have made haste to Gray Oaks, a safe twenty-five miles east of New Orleans. But Ross might have stayed.

He brought the buggy down once more, bringing the horse to a smart trot. He passed the cemetery, the gravestones still starkly brilliant from their annual All Saints' Day whitewashing. In blasphemous contrast were the corpses of those who had already succumbed, stacked like so much firewood inside the confines of the otherwise neatly tended cemetery. With unspeakable haste the gravediggers clawed trenches into the earth. Forty thousand would fall prey to the yellow fever this time. Eleven thousand of them would be buried. Staring white stones would glow white in the night, eyeless reminders standing sentinel to the dark scars of the trenches into which all were indiscriminately thrust: black and white, Catholic and Protestant, Jew and Gentile.

Tom shuddered. The city was gone. In its place were the medieval trappings of siege: the sounds of the hawkers silenced, the grogships closed. In their place were the cries of the dying as they stumbled to be nearer the burning barrels of tar set up at every street corner in the slim hope that the smoke would clear the air of disease.

It was a descent into purgatory. The sounds and smell and sight of death were everywhere. People staggered their last steps to fall on the streets. Banquettes held their bodies, the gutters ran with their bloody vomit. Packs of starved dogs roamed, feeding in voracious delight on the dead who lay untended where they fell. Negroes moaned and chanted, their eyes rolling in fear, their hands clasped in awe-filled prayer that they be spared this Day of Judgment.

Adam, following Tom at a distance, had never seen such carnage. He imagined it was what war was like. At least, it seemed much like what Voltaire described in *Candide,* and that was Adam's only basis for comparison. His stomach was queasy, and after the first shocked, revolted stares at the tangle of bodies and rampaging dogs, he couldn't look. Breath held against the stench of rotting flesh, he stared rigidly at the back of Tom's buggy.

This was the worst Tom had ever remembered seeing New Orleans. Yellow fever was common enough. They were plagued with it yearly. There had been epidemics in '48 and '49, but nothing like this. This was the day of the carrion. He was hard pressed to keep his mind on Ross. He turned the horse down the street where Ross kept his sumptuous *bache,* or lodgings.

On him there was a pall of weary disgust. He glanced at Ross's door and saw a black crepe hanging. He pounded frantically for admittance. At once he experienced horror at death and a sense of being cheated of his own revenge.

Gazella, Ross's housekeeper, opened the door a crack. Her face was shiny with oily perspiration. "You doan wanna come in heah, Mastah Tom. We's all sick, an' Mastah Ross—" she stumbled over his name, lowering her voice so it could barely be heard—"he daid, Mastah Tom."

"He can't be dead!" Tom pushed the door open against Gazella. "Let me see!"

"He sho' is, Mastah Tom. He done pass ovah yestiddy. Ah tried, but ain't nobody can save him when de Lawd call."

Tom bounded up the stairs two at a time. At the top he grabbed for the newel-post. His head was swimming, his eyesight darkened as his heart pounded in reluctant fury. He stood for a moment, waiting for his legs to change once more from water to muscle.

Ross Bennett lay on the bed just as he had the moment he died. No one had touched him. His body was twisted grotesquely. His hair was matted on his forehead above his staring eyes. His mouth hung open in a permanent un-answered plea. He had not died easily. Until this moment Tom had thought of the killing but not of the awesome finality of death.

Before he knew what had happened to him, he was on his knees in weak fatigue, crying with the mindless heart-break of a small child.

Adam watched Tom enter the house. What if he barged in, only to find Tom pleasantly sharing a drink with a friend? What if . . . ? At first he heard nothing. A stillness like an abandonment of spirit rested over the house. Then he heard a woman's high-pitched whining and Tom's broken sobs. He walked up the stairs, gagging at the linger-ing odor of illness and death. Tom was huddled on the floor by a man's bed, his fist slowly and monotonously beating against the side rail.

"Tom . . ." Hesitantly he walked over to him.

"He's dead. *Dead!*"

"I'm sorry, Tom. Who was he? Was he a good friend of yours?" Adam asked. He caught his lower lip between his teeth and reached out, putting his hand on Tom's shoulder.

Tom's laughter was choked by tears. "Friend," he re-peated.

Adam stood up. He pressed the man's eyes closed, forced straight the bent limbs that without warning had ceased their writhing. Then he pulled the rumpled, soiled sheet over him.

"You his servant?" Adam asked Gazella, suddenly angry that the man had been left untended.

"Yassuh."

"Then do something for him."

"What Ah gwine be doin'?" Gazella recoiled at the thought of touching her master. In his life Ross had been proud to have been given the designation of slave breaker, saved in most instances for overseers. In death Gazella could only imagine he'd be more demon than he had been in life. He'd get her, his icy fingers rising up from the sheets, taking her and squeezing the life out of her. She glanced at Adam, her head shaking in frantic negation, then turned and ran from the room, her feet beating a wildly clumsy tattoo on the staircase.

"She ran off," Adam said, amazed.

"Let her."

"But . . . what about him?"

"Let him rot." Tom's face was gray with fatigue and the horrible emptiness that flooded through him. He'd had a bellyful of death. It was everywhere. He wanted to run from it, but his legs were going to take him nowhere. He could barely stand.

Adam grabbed his arm to support him. "Tom—"

"I'm just a little light-headed. Be all right in a minute."

Adam steered him toward a chair. Tom sank into it, his head lolling back. His light beard stood out dark against the pallor of his face. "Let him rot." His voice was no stronger than a whisper. "That much satisfaction I'll get for what he did to her."

"This is the man with the Boar's head?"

Tom shook his head slowly.

"Who, then?"

Tom opened his mouth, but made no sound. Weakly he gestured with his hand. Adam looked at the form on the bed. He had been one of the others. A Goat, a Raccoon, a Snake, an Alligator, a Bear. Did it really matter which? *They* had all been things, creatures with animal heads. This had been a man. He could hate and kill the Boar's head. He could not kill the man.

"Let me help you home, Tom."

Adam tied his horse to the back of the buggy. He drove with Tom barely conscious at his side back through the corpse-strewn streets. The lamentations of the grieving and fearful raised inside him a cleansing dread, quenching his own bloodthirsty desires for revenge. Revenge might be sweet, but its sweetness was that of rot, and its aftermath was pure gall.

After they had returned from New Orleans, Adam began to think perhaps everything would be all right again. Sometime. Hope was revived, and with it Adam's spirit. Though he and Tom were not enjoying the once easy affection between them, they had talked, and that helped. The trip to New Orleans had taught them the futility of revenge.

But had the man with the Boar's head learned that? Adam feared not. His conversation weeks ago with Ben still came to mind. That man had tried once to kill Tom. He was still looking for him. If he found.Tom again, he might kill others as well.

It was not a pleasant thing to think about, but the thought wouldn't lie dormant. And with it returned the memory of Tom's intention to take his family away from the bayou house. Tom had told him then that the only difference between a brave man and a fool was that the brave man knew when to fight and when to run. At the time it had seemed so much nonsense to Adam. Now it seemed like the profoundest of truths. Only a fool endangered others for the sake of his own pride. It was time to run now.

But running away would take planning far beyond what Adam had ever done. His mother owned this house. They had lived in it ever since his father died. She wouldn't want to leave. But Tom and Angela couldn't manage on their own. It would be a long time before Tom could work and do the things necessary to care for Angela. He needed Adam. Most of all, Adam realized, he wanted to be with Tom.

Somewhere in the jumble of Adam's half-formed schemes, there was an answer. In the meantime, he began to enjoy afternoons with Angela. He taught her her letters, took her for buggy rides.

As Tom had earlier, Adam now found it easy to push aside a decision about their leaving. He still worried about the Boar's-head man, but the solutions seemed too dramatic for real consideration.

He lay on the grass, staring up at the cloud-filled sky, waiting for Angela to toss her bean bag onto his chest again. As the little polka-dotted bag came at him, he reached up, flipping it higher into the air. Angela squealed with laughter, running to get it, fetching it back like a delighted puppy.

Tom was upstairs in his room. The trip to New Orleans had depleted his strength. He found himself forced to take naps that began earlier and lasted longer than Angela's did. As he fell asleep, he heard her high-pitched child's voice in the backyard. He had just begun to notice once more what a sweet, cheering sound her laughter was.

Mammy was busy in the springhouse, so it was Zoe who answered the door. She looked out to see a stranger, tall, nearly handsome except for his expression, and the not quite healed scar across his right cheekbone.

"Are you Mrs. Tremain? Mrs. Zoe Tremain?" the man asked.

"I am. What can I do for you, Mr. . . . ?"

"Revanche. I am Edmund Revanche, Mrs. Tremain. Please pardon me for presentin' myself unintroduced to your door. We have a friend in common, however, perhaps two."

"Oh? And who might that be, Mr. Revanche?" Zoe asked, unwilling to invite him into the house.

"George Andreas. I believe he was your late husband's attorney and has since handled your affairs. He is my lawyer as well. He was kind enough to give me your address, as he thought perhaps you could help me."

"Do come in, Mr. Revanche," Zoe said then, smiling as she led him into her parlor. She excused herself, going to the back to call Mammy to fix some refreshments for their guest.

"May I compliment you on your home, Mrs. Tremain. It is tastefully done. I can see you have an eye for beauty and fineness of craft."

"Thank you, Mr. Revanche. I believe you mentioned a problem that Mr. Andreas thought I might assist you with —although I can hardly imagine how I could be of help to a man like yourself."

Edmund smiled slowly, his eyes lingering on her approvingly. "You are in a hurry to cut short our conversation, Mrs. Tremain?"

Zoe looked down at her hands, then at him. "Quite frankly, Mr. Revanche, I am not accustomed to entertaining gentlemen alone in my parlor. Please tell me what it is you want."

"As you will," he said nonchalantly. Mammy carried in a tray filled with refreshments. He took lemonade, holding the glass loosely in his hand. Zoe couldn't help noticing his strangely alluring grace, the smooth, almost liquid quality of his movements.

"I have lost touch with a friend of mine, Mrs. Tremain. He left the city unexpectedly, and I'm ashamed to admit

I did not secure his new address. Mr. Andreas said that
he had mentioned your name the last time he was in the
office. You see, Mrs. Tremain, Mr. Andreas was Tom
Pierson's lawyer as well as ours. One never fully realizes
how small New Orleans is until one discusses acquaintances
over a drink with one's attorney. Do you know the whereabouts of Mr. Pierson, Mrs. Tremain?"

Zoe quickly raised her glass to her lips, hoping to cover
her tumult. This man might be a friend of Tom's, as he
claimed. But if Tom had wished to see him, why didn't
Mr. Revanche know of the bayou house? She glanced up
at him. He was nearly smiling as he stared beyond courtesy.

Quite suddenly Zoe was frightened. She looked again
at the smiling face waiting with exaggerated patience for
her reply. She was certain this was the man for whom
Adam waited, the man who had done such unspeakable
things to Tom and Ullah. With effort she kept her voice
steady. "I have tried to think of every acquaintance I have,
Mr. Revanche. But I am afraid you have wasted your
time."

Edmund crossed his legs, leaning back in his chair.
"Don't speak too hastily, Mrs. Tremain. Consider what
your answer might mean to me. Perhaps," he said lazily,
"your memory will improve with effort." The knowing,
patient smile played on his mouth, offensive and threatening.

"Mr. Revanche, if you are implying that I speak falsely,
I find that rude and insulting."

"I should think you would. But, Mrs. Tremain, I know
you are *familiar* with Mr. Pierson. It is even rumored that
your acquaintance is . . . close, shall we say? I want to
know his whereabouts. Now, if you will be wise enough
to—"

"Mr. Revanche! You may leave this house!" Zoe said,
her outrage hiding her fear. "Leave here, sir. You may
tell Mr. Andreas I shall be certain in the future to engage
an attorney who chooses his clients with more discretion."

Edmund put his head back, laughing softly. His hands
clapped in silent, mocking applause. "Magnificent, Zoe.
You're an excellent actress." He leaned forward, peering
at her from under his dark eyebrows. "Now, answer my
question. I have no intention of leavin' here without the
information I seek, or Tom himself. He will tell you I am
a patient man. When I want somethin' I will remain patient

until I get it. Tom would not want you any more involved in his troubles than you already are. Perhaps you don't quite understand the full import of his difficulties."

"Mammy!" She felt a cold fright. He was capable of anything. His was the way of cruelty, a quiet violence that was all the more hideous for the cloying insinuations that preceded it. *"Mammy!"*

It wasn't Mammy who appeared in the room, but Adam. Zoe's mouth flew open, her eyes wide, as she looked frantically from Edmund Revanche to her son. How long had he been standing there?

Between Adam and Edmund there was the air of instant recognition, an instinctive knowledge, a thread from ancient and primitive pasts when man had not yet lost the ability to recognize his natural enemies. Edmund's eyes were bright with the prospect of knowing this man-boy, who was already far more formidable than Tom had ever been. Adam might have been a granite statue blocking the doorway.

From the kitchen Angela's happy chirruping voice interrupted the spell that had fallen over them. Edmund immediately looked in that direction, his eyes glittering.

"I hope you don't mind, Ma. I brought Ben's sister over to play."

Zoe's lips trembled as she tried to smile. Her hand pressed against the throbbing pulse at her neck. "Be sure to tell Mammy to give her some cookies. Sissy loves Mammy's molasses cookies."

Adam hurried to the kitchen. Whispering frantically, he told Mammy to keep Angela out of sight until the man in the parlor left.

When he returned to the parlor, his whole intent was to protect Tom and Angela. "Who are you?" he asked curtly. After all this time he'd learn who the Boar's-head man was.

With raised eyebrows Edmund gave him a dismissing look of disapproval. "Is this rude young man your son, Mrs. Tremain?" he asked. "Then perhaps you will be good enough to instruct the boy in the etiquette of conversations between adults. This one is private."

"Adam . . ."

"What do you want, *Mr. Revanche?*" Adam asked, unable to hide the triumph of knowing the hated name.

"Privacy for the moment," Edmund sat down in the

chair. The now familiar message in his eyes was not lost
on Zoe. "I am a patient man."

Fear seized her. She didn't know what Adam might do,
nor did she believe that in retaliating, Edmund Revanche
would consider Adam's age or inexperience. "Mr. Revanche, I don't know anything about Mr. Pierson. Please,
I can't tell you anything."

"I suppose that wasn't the pickaninny, Angela, I just
heard in your kitchen."

"No, it wasn't. Good day, Mr. Revanche." Zoe's voice
trembled.

"I'll wait until you have a change of heart," Edmund
said calmly.

Adam stepped forward. "No, you won't. Not here anyway. You've been asked to leave politely. Do so, Mr.
Revanche, or I shall help you."

Edmund looked at Adam, estimating his size and weight
and accurately judging the hate that rode so close to the
surface. It was answer enough to his questions. Sooner or
later Zoe or Adam would go to Tom, or Tom would come
here if he weren't here already. He stood up, his attention
on Zoe. "Both your honesty and your hospitality are somewhat lackin', Mrs. Tremain."

"Considering your boldness and abuse, Mr. Revanche,
I think my hospitality has been highly strained. Good day."

Edmund let her walk with him to the door. He stopped
before she could open it. "One last word, Mrs. Tremain.
Just a small warning to guide you in your deliberations.
Mr. Pierson is a wanted man. First, he caused several of
my slaves to break and run. Second, he is a common
thief. The pickaninny you have in your kitchen is my
property. For your own safety, Mrs. Tremain, you should
be aware that Mr. Pierson is a dangerous man. The last
time he was at Gray Oaks, he stirred up my blacks so
badly that three had to be severely lashed and one hanged
as an example of what comes of darkies who run. Think
about that, Mrs. Tremain. Do you really want to harbor
a fugitive slave and an outlaw? A very dangerous outlaw?"

"Good-bye, Mr. Revanche," Zoe said in a weak voice.

Adam stood trembling at her side. If Edmund Revanche
did not stop talking soon and walk through that door out
of their lives, there would be nothing to hold Adam back.
Zoe clasped his hand with all her might. His fingers twined
around hers with a pressure he didn't realize. Tears stood

in Zoe's eyes, but she didn't cry out or remove her hand until the door had closed on Edmund.

Adam flung himself away from her, his fist smashing into the wall at the edge of the staircase.

Zoe shuddered as the pliable flesh gave against the hard plaster time after time, but she thanked the Powers above that had turned Adam's wrath from Edmund Revanche to the wall.

Chapter Ten

Nursing bruised knuckles, Adam watched Edmund Revanche drive away. Edmund's leisurely departure aroused in Adam a sense of urgency that grew with each turn of the carriage wheels. His mind made up, he walked deliberately up the stairs to Tom's room.

Zoe waited a few minutes for Adam's return. Then she went to her bedroom, passing Tom's closed door without hearing anything. The afternoon had left her tired and shaken. She gratefully accepted the quiet of the house.

Half an hour later Adam knocked on her door. "Ma."

She sat up quickly. "Come in, Adam, I'm only resting for a moment."

Hesitantly he opened the door. "I'd like to talk to you, please."

"But of course, dear. Come sit beside me." She smiled as she patted the chair next to her chaise. As Adam remained undecided and standing, foreboding rose in her again. "Nothing else has happened, has it?"

Adam shook his head. He looked at her earnestly. "But I'm afraid it will. Tom's told me a great deal more about Mr. Revanche. Ma . . . I've decided we have to leave New Orleans."

Zoe's breath left her in a sharp gust.

"You've seen that Mr. Revanche is adamant." Adam went on, allowing her no time to protest. "It doesn't matter that you deny knowing Tom and Angela. He's going to come back until he gets what he wants."

"Adam, please! Don't dramatize it just to frighten me. He would never dare do us harm—not in our own home!"

"He will," Adam said softly. "Tom's living proof of it. We're sheltering a runaway slave, Ma, and a man who is accused of inciting insurrection at Gray Oaks. We've broken the law. Revanche will see that law enforced. He might come with officers, or he might choose another citizens' committee. What happened to Tom and Ullah can easily happen to us."

Zoe shuddered, closing her eyes against the thought.

"Ma, Revanche could be back here tonight. Are you listening? He won't wait. It could be this very night. We've got to be gone."

"I am listening, dear, and I understand your urgency—but there's a houseful of furniture and five people to move. One cannot simply uproot oneself. Where would we go? Where would we stay? Adam, this is my home. Perhaps I'm not so anxious to leave it as you are."

"Ma, *please, Ma,* don't be bullheaded now. Please, listen to me. I know I have taken things that concern you into my own hands, but I'm trying to do what is best. I . . . if we can just get out of here with our skins whole, we can argue all the way to Aunt Leona's."

Zoe gasped. "Leona! Adam! She lives in Wilmington!"

"We'd be safe there. Think about it, Ma. Revanche can't be so hell-bent on killing Tom that he'd follow us across country. Can you and Mammy get us ready to leave at dark?"

"No!" Zoe cried sharply.

"We are going. We have to. Even if Tom and Angela left here, we'd have to go too, for Revanche would try to wring information from us. We've made ourselves his enemy as well as Tom. He'll never let us alone."

"I suppose you are sure about this? Don't bother to answer. Adam, I really wish . . ." She got up, smoothing her hair automatically. "We will not leave everything behind. We'll need beds, linens, kitchen utensils, our table and chairs—"

"We'll take the most important things, but if they won't go into the buggy or the big dray, we have to leave them."

Zoe's mouth quivered. "Some of these things belonged to my mother."

Adam put his big hand on her small shoulder. "I know," he said softly. "We'll lock the house and send an agent for them as soon as we're safe in Wilmington. Ma, you will start packing immediately? I'm going to ride down to get Ben and Beau to help."

As he left, Zoe reflected that once again she had made no decision. Circumstances and Adam's young judgment were going to carry her along this time. *Perhaps one day,* she thought, *I may develop some backbone.*

As she went into the hall, Tom emerged from his room, shockingly pale, the scars livid across his face. "How can I help, Mrs. Tremain?"

"There are two trunks in the attic. Are you able to carry them down? Perhaps Mammy could help you," she began, then added, in sudden decision, "keep Angela with you so she won't be underfoot."

Tom drew in a long breath. "Wh—" His voice failed. "Where is she, ma'am?"

"She's with Mammy. I'll send her up."

With ruthless efficiency Zoe listed absolute necessities. Feather ticks. Pillows. Bedding. Suddenly she was immensely pleased with herself. She had told Tom to care for his daughter, and he would have to do it. Even after he'd started to treat Adam more kindly, he had refused to see Angela. Daily he broke Zoe's heart, for when the child asked about Papa, she spoke as of one in a foreign land. And Zoe kept promising that Papa would tell her stories as soon as he got well.

And now stark desperation had brought that day. Zoe completed her brief list. It had been seventeen years since she had left Wilmington to live in New Orleans with Paul Tremain. Now she was going back.

In the short time Adam was gone, his mother and Mammy stripped all the wardrobes of clothing and linens and packed them into trunks. Tom sat watching, a radiantly chattering Angela snuggled against him. "An' then, Papa, what did the baby bear do?"

"He packed all his clothes an' his toys and moved to a brand-new house." Tom said.

"He like the new house?" Angela began to laugh, the question forgotten as she heard voices in the hall. "Adam's home! Papa, Adam's home!"

Tom smiled crookedly at Adam. "Sure can tell who's got her heart."

In another hour the boys had dismantled the beds, carried in barrels from the shed, and carried them out again packed with china and glassware and keepsakes. Somehow by dark, they had made room for everything, leaving a place in the dray large enough for Tom to lie with Angela to nap beside him. Mammy scraped together a competent supper, and they all ate standing up.

"Y'all gonna have enough money?" Beau asked, his mouth full of fried grits and ham. "I can lend you fifty dollars I've got hidden away."

Adam grinned. "Thanks, Beau, we'll be all right. We're so far from the bank that we always keep money handy. And Tom sent me to the bayou for his things, including a tidy little hoard. You and Ben could watch the house for us, though."

"North C'lina is a long way off," said Ben wistfully. "How soon y'all think you might be coming back to visit?"

Tom, as had been his habit in recent months, was saying nothing. But perhaps he'd listened more carefully than he knew. Seeing the boys together, eager as always to help, cheerful as always when they were together, Tom rounded out a thought that had begun yesterday. There had been more than money at the bayou house. There were the last tangible traces that Ullah had ever lived. Doubting his own good sense, Tom had instructed Adam to bring back two items besides the money. He wanted to keep Ullah's box of treasures and the small wrapped package that contained what would have been another addition to her little box.

He still hadn't the courage to unwrap the small black hand-blown glass swan that he'd planned to give Ullah for Christmas. At least he'd had the courage to tell Adam to bring it to him. Perhaps the black swan was only another valueless trinket that Ullah would have kept hidden away in the little box; but to her it would have represented Adam. So it would now to Tom, and someday he would present that swan to Adam himself for Ullah.

Tom looked at Ben, Beau, and Adam, each young face saddened at the prospect of parting. "We can't come back here for a long time, Ben, you know that. But I'm gonna get a place, and you and Beau have an open invitation to come anytime. Angela and I will always be glad to see you." He did not look at Adam, who quickly put his head down to hide a surprised, triumphant grin.

* * *

It was black dark by the time the last items were loaded and tied down, the house left clean and secured. Zoe stood beside the carriage, her eyes going over the familiar lines of the house. She was bracing her emotions against the possibility of never again seeing any of the beloved possessions she had to leave behind. Yet, she knew their next dwelling wouldn't be a home without her grandmother's oval gilt mirror or the pie safe that had been her parents'.

Zoe knelt in the dust. Her sweet voice murmured softly, "Our Almighty Father, we ask Thy blessing on this journey. If it be Thy will, guide us to safety and happiness in our home that is to be. Keep our feet upon Thy paths this night and for the rest of our lives. In Jesus' name we pray. Amen." The others echoed the solemn, final "amen."

Ben and Beau stumbled over each other's words, each trying to tell Adam what his friendship meant to them. Finally Adam said, "Ready, Ma?"

Ben and Beau rode with them to the fork that led to New Orleans. There they parted quickly. Ben and Beau watched until darkness swallowed even the turning of wheels and the jingle of harness.

"D'you s'pose he's forgotten our pact, Beau?"

"Not Adam," Beau answered staunchly. "We've been going to be ship's masters ever since we had our first boat. He'll remember."

The words were comforting, but both feared they were a lie. Adam Tremain had melted into the night. He was gone from them.

Adam led the way, driving the two-horse dray while Zoe handled the carriage. Tom and Angela, almost engulfed in a pile of feather ticks, slept from exhaustion. Mammy was propped securely amid the furniture. "Effen some ghos' tries to git ol' Mammy, he gwine hafta fish me outa dese chairs," she declared, barricading herself. For the first mile or two she watched constantly to right and left, riding backward. Then weariness overcame her fear of the dark, and her white woolly head found a resting place. Soon her snores mingled with Tom's and the occasional snorts of the horses as they strained through muddy places or over broken ground.

The night was alive with noises that frightened Zoe. She was accustomed to the nightly calls of the screech owl

families that lived in the bald cypresses near the house. Out
here, with the woods opening for their passage and seeming to close ominously behind them, their harsh, shuddering cries made her flesh crawl. The underbrush rustled with
cottontails and the tiny furtive scuttlings of shrews and
voles and weasels. For Zoe every noise was a stealthy footstep taken just out of sight behind her open carriage.

Her arms ached. It was one thing to drive the light
buggy on her daily round of visits and errands. It was quite
another to go on hour after hour, scarcely able to breathe
for fear of the unknown predators lurking out there, with
one's arms and shoulders pinched and uncomfortable from
urging on the reluctant horse that didn't like the night any
better than she did.

A heavy, prolonged crashing in the underbrush made
her horse rear and brought a barely stifled scream from
Zoe. "Adam!"

He stopped, but did not leave the dray. "Are you all
right, Ma?"

Zoe got the horse under control. Shaking, she answered.
"No! I'm not all right! I'm frightened to death, and there's
something in the woods over there!"

"Hang on, Ma. I'm coming back, soon's I can wake up
Tom."

"Oh, Adam—hurry!" she called, her voice trembling uncontrollably.

He mounted the seat beside her, letting her hide her face
in his jacket. "Well, hey there, Miz Tremain," he said, and
she could tell he was grinning. Ghosses an' hants aftuh
you?"

"Adam, don't make fun of me! I did hear something!"

He took the reins, and they started up again, Tom driving the dray. "Of course you did, but it was only a black
bear looking for dinner."

"*A bear!?*" she gasped.

Adam chuckled. "He won't hurt you much. But he's got
the horses all excited. You stay awake so you can take the
reins in case I have to shoot him."

The sound Zoe made was between a yelp and a whimper.
But for a while there were no more scary noises. She put
her head on her son's solid-feeling shoulder and dozed.
She awoke again when they stopped. Around them was a
thick wall of mist. The dray, only a few feet ahead of
them, was nearly invisible. "Adam, where are we?"

"Partway up a small neck of land north of New Orleans. We take the ferry there across Lake Ponchartrain. After that, only ten or twelve miles to Mississippi."

Adam handed her the reins and went up to the dray. "How you comin', Tom?"

Tom's hoarse voice sounded eerily through the droplets of mist. "Can't say I'm sorry we stopped," he said. "Think maybe I'll curl up on the tick until this stuff lifts."

Mammy woke up, seeing the swirling fog in the graying light. "Mas' Adam!"

"Everything's all right, Mammy," he assured her. "The horses need a rest. We'll go on as soon as we can see. We're safe now."

"Mas' Adam! Iffen you cain't see us, how kin you tell we's safe?"

Adam laughed. "As long as I can hear your voices, Mammy, I know you're there. Not even a ghost would try to follow us in this gumbo anyway."

Long before darkness waned, they heard the sounds of a bayou morning. Not far in the echoing distance they heard the staccato drumming of the ivory-billed and pileated woodpeckers, louder then growing softer. A blue jay screamed its name. Wings fluttered as a flicker flew across the road, crying *kikikikiki!* The day creatures took the place of the night prowlers with their chorus of whistling, piping, booming, and trilling calls, above the low rasping *kzrrrt!* of the snipes and the nasal *peent!* of woodcocks. The sun, awake at last, burned a hole through the mist to lay a rainbow around the wide-awake, listening group.

"Rainbow's de Lawd's good sign," said Mammy solemnly.

"Mammy, my bellybutton's striking sparks off my backbone," Adam complained. "Any slivers of ham in that lard can you packed?"

"Sho' is, Mas' Adam." So, as the sun burned away the shreds of mist, they shared ham and cold hush puppies and water from the well back of their house. Then they moved on.

By midday they reached the shore of Lake Ponchartrain and boarded the ferry.

After that they traveled by day, away from the coastline with its wet, uneasy ground, into and out of the pungent pine forests of Mississippi, through a rolling land, ne-

glected, its withered dry cotton stalks left to the sun and
wind. Here and there they saw a newly plowed field polka-
dotted with flocking white ibises. They followed wagon-
rutted trails and occasionally cowpaths, having to stop
twice to pry the heavily loaded dray out of the clinging
mud.

With immense relief and excitement they began to smell
the familiar Gulf air. That day they entered Biloxi. The
lighthouse cast its long shadow in the late-day sun as Adam
led them along the wharves. He left Tom with the others
and made inquiries among the steamship offices. Adam con-
tracted for passage on the *Goodenough,* a large vessel carrying passengers and cargo. They would be at Aunt Leona's by the first week in June.

Once aboard ship, they settled down to the long days
on the water. Mammy spent her waking hours preventing
Angela from falling or jumping over the side of the ship.
Tom, surprisingly strengthened and cheered by taking his
turn at the cross-country driving, experienced the first public antipathy to his ruined appearance. As he walked the
decks, the furtive and curious looks followed him. He
heard the hushed comments, blurring into a buzz as he
passed. With steely determination he kept to his daily
walks, and slowly the forced chatting with other men grew
casual as they came to know him. Nightly he engaged in
the games of poker, brag, and ramps. He won his victory.
He was again accepted and liked, because he was likable;
but he'd learned that becoming someone's friend was going
to be immeasurably more difficult than it had once been.

Adam's face was cast in a permanent bronzed smile. He
was in his element. He was on a seagoing vessel moving
through the Gulf of Mexico toward the cold, rolling waters
of the Atlantic Ocean. He was never still. He talked to
every seaman as long as that man's patience and store of
information held out. He watched every activity from the
closest permissible distance.

While Adam was examining the myriad knots that held
the lines, a ship's officer accosted him sharply. Adam's instant respectful answer and his evident passion for ships,
gained him the first mate's permission to stand night watch
and the captain's permission to take a closely escorted tour
belowdecks and into the fo'c'sle. His avid eyes saw and cat-
alogued everything from bulkheads to bilges, stokehold to

galley. He had a thousand questions, but his logical mind stuck to learning as much as possible about one thing at a time.

From the first mate he learned not only about the parts of a ship and their workings but about the men and their duties. Most important of all, he learned that he could sit for his second mate's papers when he was seventeen. By age twenty-one he could be a ship's master.

Halfway through the voyage Adam was standing by the rail, watching to the north an approaching line of small islands. A seaman touched his arm and saluted smartly. A devil's grin was on his face. "The captain's compliments, Mr. Tremain. I'm to escort you to the chart room."

In the cramped area the men worked efficiently as Captain Connacher proudly unrolled his charts. "There aren't many of this quality to be had," he said, smoothing them out for Adam to admire. Turning from the charts, he showed Adam the compass, chronometer, and the binnacle. Suddenly his head went up, a look of satisfaction passing over his face.

"Feel that water under your feet, Mr. Tremain?"

Adam's eyes lighted. "It's different, isn't it, sir?"

The captain nodded approval. "So, you did feel it. We've just come off the Gulf Stream. I'd know that feeling anywhere. It's truer and better knowledge than any chart will give you. Remember it, boy. If you've got the makings of a master, that feel will live with you all your life."

"I'll not forget it."

"Indeed you won't," the captain replied, and laughed. "You'll remember everything the sea has to tell you. She's an awesome mistress, Tremain. She doesn't permit a man many mistakes. And I'll warn you now, while you're still young and full of dreams, once she takes you as hers, she'll never let you go."

"It's too late already, Captain Connacher. I love the sea better than anything else in the world."

Walking again on deck, it was easy to imagine it was his own. He gazed out across the smoothly rolling waves to the darkish line where blue water swallowed blue sky. Around him were netfings, masts, and stacks, and things called bow-chocks, davits, cleats, braces, halyards, sheets, chain plates—all pieces and parts of a steamship rigged for sail, things whose very names spelled mystery and adventure to Adam.

Adam begrudged the years he would have to spend at the university before he could sit for his master's papers and captain such a ship as this. For the moment he gloried in the possessive richness of the borrowed deck, and felt through the soles of his boots the surge and pull of the Atlantic Ocean. Here, he knew with a joyous excitement, lay his destiny.

Long before they came into the Wilmington pier, they sighted the many steeples, the high square tower of Saint James's Church, the fine homes with their shade trees and outbuildings. In the Cape Fear River running west of the city were a number of smaller ships, loaded flatboats, and barges. Over the entire dock area hung the sharp odors of tar, turpentine, and resin being shipped to ports all over the world.

The passengers were being met by a peculiar assortment of Negro men, dressed in oddments of garb they thought attractive. All of them wore the badges that proclaimed them free; all of them clamored for business. "Ca'iage, suh? Ca'iage, ma'am?"

Zoe retreated in indecision, and Adam took charge. "We want to go to the home of Mr. Garrett Pinckney, a lawyer," he said. "He lives—"

The driver's face halved itself in a glad smile. "Yassuh, Ah knows dat house well. On Dock Street near Thud. Yassuh! Mistah Garrett Pinckney is a mighty fine gent'man, mighty fine, suh!"

Mammy eyed the driver distastefully and said irritably, "Den quit chewin' de fat an' take us dere, nigger!"

The driver said respectfully, "You a mighty fine Mammy, an' you thinks you knows ever'thin', but you doan, no'm, you doan. Dis way, ma'am! Dis way, suh! Watch de li'l lady over dem loose planks, Mammy!"

Along the way the driver continued exceptionally loquacious, pointing out the Cassady Brothers Shipyard and the Marine Railway and the home of Mr. James Cassady. On Front Street they passed the imposing Georgian home of Governor Edward Dudley, where plans had been formulated for the Wilmington and Weldon Railroad and Daniel Webster had once been a guest.

"Dar's Saint John's Lodge." The driver pointed to a building with shuttered windows and white-painted steps leading to a second-floor porch. There was a dignified, new double house with stone eyebrows over its five upper windows, near to a handsome brick home whose lines were accented by geometric ironwork. Everywhere were signs of construction.

Leona and Garrett Pinckney lived in a two-story clapboard house, with wisteria climbing the porch and tall black gum and Spanish oak trees shading the yard. A latticed wall led them to the porte cochere, where the driver let them out with more beamings and good wishes.

"Uppity free nigger," muttered Mammy darkly, as the carriage pulled away. "Talkin' up to white folks like he sumbuddy."

Zoe said, "Oh, dear! Suppose Leona isn't at home!"

Adam shrugged. "We'll find a place to stay until Aunt Leona returns."

Zoe looked apprehensively at the door. I can't stand it if we have come all this way and Leona isn't even here.".

Adam laughed and raised the lion-headed knocker on the door, letting it fall with a resounding clank. "One way to find out."

Chapter Eleven

Leona Pinckney opened the door to see her small sister standing on the stoop, tears forming, her face forlorn. "Zoe! Zoe, my dear! My heart can't trust my eyes!" She gathered Zoe into her motherly arms, with Zoe laughing and sniffling in relief as she tried to dab her nose. "Oh, Adam, you're a man!" Leona gave him a hug as strong and possessive as the one she had given Zoe. Then she saw Mammy, waiting with endless patience, approving the reunion of two of the three sisters she had reared. Leona hugged and clung to Mammy's stolid bulk. "I'm so happy y'all are here! I do hope it's to be a long, long visit!"

Zoe's conscience smote her for dropping her problems onto an unknowing Leona. She looked toward Adam. "I'm afraid it's going to be more than a—" A smiling man appeared in the parlor doorway.

Leona rushed to his side, looking up at him adoringly. "Zoe, this is my darling husband, Garrett." They made a striking couple, both gray-haired, tall, and big-boned. They even looked alike, with their aristocratic features and their direct way of looking at others.

Zoe smiled hesitantly at this Yankee, the brother-in-law she had never met.

"Leona, Garrett, there is something I ought to tell you. This isn't exactly a visit—"

"Well, let's sit down and relax a bit, Zoe. Then you can tell us whatever you want." Leona busily ushered them into the parlor.

"Leona, wait, please. We . . . *had* to leave New Orleans—"

Garrett took Zoe's arm. "There's time for that, Zoe. Right now, Leona and I are just happy you made the journey safely. We'll deal with the rest later. You're welcome to stay here as long as you like."

"Thank you, Garrett, but I must tell you right away. Tom and Angela were being hunted—may still be! Some men tried to kill him, and—"

"Dear sister Zoe," said Garrett with maddening casualness, "let us go into the parlor where we can be more comfortable."

"I'll just tell Cooky to put another potato in the pot," said Leona.

Mammy took Angela into the kitchen, while Zoe, Adam, and Tom talked to Garrett. He listened with interest and no visible shock.

Adam said, "We've pretty much put ourselves in your hands. We don't want to stay here under false pretenses. Perhaps you don't want to be involved."

He didn't miss the glance that Leona exchanged with Garrett before she said, smiling, "You're welcome here. My Garrett is just a sweet ol' transplanted Northerner who never acquired all the Southern sympathies."

Garrett smiled with tolerant affection at his wife. "Leona delights in telling people that around these parts I am considered a doughface. Those who know I am Northern think more highly of me than those who assume I am originally Southern. In either case my sympathies, or lack of them, cause some of the local folk to question my sanity. But rest easy, you will be safe enough here."

"Garrett, if people are already worried about your Northern sympathies, we'll only cause you more trouble," Zoe said anxiously.

"Not at all. I am merely the local eccentric, no more."
He looked toward Tom. "My friends will be happy to give
you employment, Mr. Pierson."

"Call me Tom," he said hoarsely. "I thank you for the
offer, Garrett, but employment is about the only thing I
don't need. I have a fair amount of money—if I can figure
a way to get it out of New Orleans. As Adam told you, we
left in a hurry."

"And I had to leave some of Mamma's furniture, Leona.
It nearly broke my heart to go off and leave all that behind." Zoe looked pleadingly at Garrett. "Perhaps you
could help me find an agent—"

Garrett laughed. "I thought Southerners never hurried!
We'll arrange it all tomorrow. Leona, perhaps Zoe would
like to see the house. I'm going to the docks to get their
goods. Adam, will you accompany me?"

When the men left and Tom was resting, Leona proudly
showed Zoe Garrett's law certificate and other treasures he
had brought from the North.

"Oh, Leona, Garrett *is* a fine man!" Zoe exclaimed.

"When I think that I wasn't sure I should marry him, I
actually feel like fainting!" When her first husband, Clay
Thomas, died in the Mexican War, Leona had thought her
life was over. Then she had fallen in love with the attorney who was clearing up Clay's estate. Still starry-eyed
after two years of marriage, she wished the same for her
younger sister. "I don't suppose there's a gentleman in
your life, Zoe?"

Zoe shook her head. "I've only loved one man."

"Romantic tomfoolery! We know plenty of eligible gentlemen, and more than enough young ladies to delight
over Adam. I will never understand how Paul Tremain
sired a boy like him! He is such a handsome thing!" Leona
cooed, mentally planning parties.

"Leona, really!" Zoe laughed. "Please keep in mind he is
only sixteen years old."

"I wasn't judging merely by looks," Leona said, piqued
at the implied criticism. "He is quite mature, and what
else would be expected? After all, with Paul inebriated so
often, *somebody* had to be the man of the house." At Zoe's
pained look she said, "Well, I'm sorry, but it's time you
quit mourning for a marriage that never worked out. If
Papa had realized the kind of man Paul was, he'd never
have allowed y'all to marry."

"Well, it's past and better forgotten," said Zoe pleasantly. "Oh, Leona, it's just like old times with you scolding and bossing!"

Leona laughed heartily. "I never learn, do I? What are your plans?"

"Adam and I will buy a house, I suppose. Tom says he'll do the same. This really is a permanent move. We can't ever return to New Orleans. That Mr. Revanche means harm." Zoe shuddered at the memory, then paused, considering. "But here's the odd thing. He's also very attractive. I've never seen a man move so gracefully. Mind you, I didn't think of this until later. He frightened me badly at first. I was quite ready to faint. What terrified me most is that he is so pleasing to look at, yet he has this deadly air of control and purpose. One simply cannot imagine Mr. Revanche being at a loss. He commands. . . ." She shivered, then laughed uneasily.

"I'm glad you had the good sense to come to me immediately. You're no match for a man like that. And Adam need not be exposed to another worthless man. Paul was quite enough. Garrett will be good for him. Didn't it seem to you he was acting rather fatherly toward Adam?"

Zoe hid her smile. "I do think he was, and I am so glad for it. I worry about Adam, Leona. All he wants is the sea. He dreams of a ship of his own, but I am anxious for him to be properly educated. As soon as it can be arranged, I'd like him to start at the university."

"Garrett will be a strong ally for you," Leona said, and stood up. "I must see to some things in the kitchen. We employ free Negroes, you know, but even the best ones still require some supervision."

"You don't own slaves anymore?"

"Garrett is a Yankee, remember? He doesn't believe in slavery."

"He didn't grow up with it as we did, or he'd see the necessity."

"I grew up with it, Zoe," Leona said softly. "I don't miss it either. Garrett says that historically it has never worked and that he does not wish to claim ownership of other men's lives. Would you disagree with his feelings?"

"Of course not!" After a long pause Zoe added, "But those are just idealistic words, Leona. Garrett may be right in theory, but the South needs her slaves. One man's opinion is not going to change things."

Again Leona smiled but did not reply.

At dinner Garrett proved to be an entertaining host as they all exchanged anecdotes about the past. Then Tom and Adam launched into an exaggerated version of Zoe's fright over the bear. Garrett laughed heartily.

The fish muddle had just been served when the butler came to the table. "An imphotant bizness mattuh has come up, suh."

Apologizing, Garrett left the room.

Tom smiled. "Clients before kinfolk anytime."

Leona excused herself, following Garrett into the hall. When she returned, Zoe looked questioningly at her. "Poor Garrett. I hope his clients don't do this to him often. I can hardly imagine George Andreas interrupting his supper for his clients, can you, Tom?"

Tom replied hoarsely, "Not likely."

Leona, preoccupied, said, "There are only certain clients for whom Garrett will do this. Some matters simply will not wait, you understand."

Zoe smiled. "No, I don't understand at all, but I believe you."

Not another word was said about Garrett's mysterious clients, and within the week he left for New Orleans. Armed with powers of attorney, Garrett would see George Andreas and arrange to sell Zoe's house, ship her household goods to Wilmington, and transfer Tom's and Zoe's accounts to the Bank of Cape Fear. He expected to return within the month.

Tom and Adam explored the streets and wharves of Wilmington, built a flatboat, and poled it in the shallow marshy areas of the Cape Fear River. For Adam it was a schooling of the sort he liked best. He learned the depths and shallows of the Cape Fear and its branches. New Inlet became one of his favorite areas as he went over the shoals and moved along inside the breaker line of the Atlantic. Vaguely he thought of serving as a river pilot for incoming and outgoing ships long before he would be able to sign on as an apprentice.

As Adam concentrated on the land beneath the water, Tom's eyes gazed fondly at the islands and swamplands, lush and inviting to him. "A man could build a house on one of these islands," he mused.

Pulling up his sounding line, Adam glanced at him.

"Aw, c'mon, Tom, you're not gonna take to the swamps again, are you? It was a good idea for New Orleans, but not here. Live near us, among your friends."

Tom looked at him coldly. "Friends," he said contemptuously.

Adam sighed. "You've got to trust somebody."

Apologetically Tom clapped him on the shoulder. "I trust you, and I think mebbe I'm gonna trust Garrett. *If* he comes back with my money."

"He'll be back. Listen, Tom, Ma and I could buy a double house."

"No," said Tom harshly. "Oh, hell, boy, I know you've got my best interests in mind, but I don't want much to do with people jes' yet."

"When we divide the flatboat, which half you gonna take?"

Tom laughed ruefully. "The half that floats, I guess. Give me time, boy. Right now I just want some quiet. You know, I liked the bayou house. It wasn't much, but damn if it wasn't the nicest little place I ever did have. Seems like a spot here in the swamp would suit me fine."

Adam knew what it was Tom was feeling and unable to put into words.

At midnight Adam was sitting in Garrett's study, reading a favorite childhood book, *The Swiss Family Robinson*. He was so absorbed in their building of the pinnace that the soft rapping on the back door startled him. Cautiously he looked out the window. Several Negroes stood in the shadows, looking anxiously at the house.

Adam opened the door and held it with his foot, ready to slam it shut. "What do you want?"

The man on the stoop showed his teeth in a familiar-seeming grin. Adam recognized the carriage driver who had brought them here.

"Evenin', suh," he said politely. "Some people wants to see Mistah Garrett Pinckney."

"Mr. Pinckney is in New Orleans."

"Is Miz Leona heah, suh? She gen'ly takes care of us iffen Mistah Garrett ain't heah."

"It's the middle of the night," Adam protested. "Why don't you come back in the morning?"

"We'ns don't dast, suh. Please, suh, jes' tell her 'Lijah Free be waitin' ovah at Saint James Church."

Adam, persuaded against his will by the sweating earnestness of the man's plea, said, "I'll tell her."

"Right off, suh? We ain't got so much time. You takes mah meanin'?"

Leona responded immediately to Adam's tap on her door. Within minutes she came out, wearing dark clothing.

"Aunt Leona, you can't meet a mob of darkies in a churchyard!"

In the light of Leona's lamp her eyes shone. "You're coming with me. You might as well learn about your aunt and uncle firsthand, Adam."

"It's dangerous being out at night! You're taking a terrible chance. Aunt Leona, I can't let you go!"

She said quietly, "You can, and I will. Here, put on Garrett's gray dustcoat and button it up to cover your shirt."

Adam felt he was being whirled by the force of Leona's personality into some monumental undertaking. Protecting his independent aunt was far more difficult than protecting his mother. "What business of yours are these people, Aunt Leona? What's Uncle Garrett going to think when he comes back and finds out you helped runaway slaves."

Leona, busy stuffing a ham, some cold, boiled eggs, and cornbread into a clean game poke, stopped long enough to reply. "Our house is one of the major stations on the Underground Railroad. You'll find many of our nights are interrupted like this."

"But . . . Uncle Garrett is a lawyer—and this is illegal!"

Leona smiled. "You're absolutely right. And so far we have saved several hundred black human beings from a life of animal degradation. Are you coming with me or not?"

The Negroes were waiting, in a somehow terrible silence, in the shadows behind the church. None moved except Elijah Free, who spoke to Leona in tones so low Adam could hardly hear. "Evenin', Miz Leona. We got to get dem people outa Wi'mton way b'fo' mawnin' gloam. Dey's two catchers follied Ruby an' her fambly all de way from Cha'ston to jes' de fah side o' de ribber. We los' 'em, but not mo'n two hours back."

"Have they got dogs?"

"No'm, not yet."

Leona thought quickly. "The safest way would be all together, by dray, but this time we need speed. How many people, 'Lijah?"

"Ten, Miz Leona."

"We'll use your carriage, plus our two. Adam, help me get hitched up. You'll drive the middle carriage. I'll take Ruby and her family, and 'Lijah will take the others. Adam, be sure to follow me closely. We don't want you getting lost."

A baby woke and began to cry. They all stood rock-still until Ruby managed to start it nursing.

Leona hissed, "Why is that baby awake?"

Elijah said, "It done got de sleep drops, but dey all wo' off, an' Ruby ain't got no mo'."

"Get her in here. As soon as the poor little thing finishes nursing, I'll give it some paregoric from my bottle."

Adam was reminded of Mammy, issuing orders the night Tom got hurt. He wanted to protest, to say that he didn't believe in slave hauling, but Aunt Leona was keeping him too busy. Besides, what protection could a stringy old carriage driver be if there was real trouble? It was just like Aunt Leona to barge confidently ahead, without knowing what she was getting into.

"Aunt Leona, have you got a pistol?"

"Yes, two. Can you shoot?"

"I surely can."

"Here, then. It's loaded. Just be certain whom you are shooting."

In taut silence they sped through dark streets, spooky with half-erected houses of the current building boom. On the outskirts they passed the dilapidated rows of tin and tarpaper shacks where poor whites and freed Negroes lived. Dogs pursued them, barking and growling, for a hundred yards before tiring of the chase. Leona's pace was hard to follow in the pale light of the new moon. But she knew the road, and Adam kept in her tracks.

They crossed Smith Creek, stopped to listen with held breath, but heard no unusual noises. They continued north through the swamp forest, where the cypresses lifted knobby knees daintily out of the water and the gray Spanish moss dripped like dank hair from the treetops.

Crowded against him, but trying respectfully not to touch him, a teen-aged black girl said in a whisper, "Ah's awful skeert."

Her companion leaned forward to peer into Adam's face. "What we gwine do iffen dey catches us? Me an' Pearl is mighty 'pohtant niggers. Ol' Marse give thutteen hunnud dollahs fo' us, an' iffen he catch up wid dis wagon, he's like to pin our ears agin de stocks."

"Is that why you ran away?" Adam asked.

"Yassuh," whispered Pearl next to him. "Ol Marse say Ah was lyin' to him 'bout a piece o' sowbelly Ah got, so he stick mah han's an' feets thoo dem holes in de stocks, an' he take a poundin' iron an' poun' nails thoo mah ears right into de stocks."

Adam had heard of ear pinning, but Pearl's recital gave him goosebumps. More than anything he wanted to reach up and touch his own ear. "How long did he make you stay there?"

"Mos' all day, Mastah. Ah coon't move mah haid fo' a week aftuh Ol' Miss make de overseer pull 'em out."

"Ol' Marse purty mean," the other girl volunteered. "He kin pop dat whup to make it sting like a yellerjacket. Ol' Joe, he a two-head nigger, he carry fish scales an' a li'l ol' dry-up mud turkle in he pocket. Ol' Joe put de evil finger on Marse, on'y Joe doan git de conjur all work out 'fo' Marse catch him, an' he whup Ol' Joe so he can't walk no mo'."

Pearl's courage seemed to be rising. In a nearly normal voice she said, "Ol' Marse go roun' de cabins astin' us does we pray at nights. We sez we doan, but Mastah, we does. We prays wid our haids down low, an' we sings low. We prays fo' de end o' trib'lation an' de end o' beatin's, an' fo' real shoes dat fits our feets, 'stead o' dese red russets dat gets stiff like a anvil when dey wet."

"How did you manage to get away?"

"One day dey ain't nobody 'roun', an' Airy say to me, 'Pearl, le's us run off.' So we run off an' hid in de woods." The three carriages had now come out of the dark and scary woods into even scarier open fields. "Where we-all gwine, Mastah?"

"About twenty miles to a Quaker man. You will rest there, and get food, then this man will take you on to the next station."

" 'Nen we gwine be free?" asked Airy.

"You'll have to travel for a long time, maybe till the next new moon. You'll go across North C'Lina and Virginia into Philadelphia."

"What's dem?"

"They're—places. When you get there, you can find work."

"Oh, Mastah, we ain't gwine work," Pearl giggled. "We's *free* niggers!"

"You'll have to work. But you'll get paid for it. And you'll still be free. Nobody in Philadelphia or New York will beat you. You'll have enough to eat."

"Dat soun' mighty fine," said Airy. "What's it mean, git paid?"

"You do work and you get money for it. You use money to buy your food and clothes and a place to live."

"Ol' Marse take care o' dat," said Pearl, her voice quivering. "We'ns doan know how!"

"People will help you," Adam said, though he was only guessing. Up to now, he hadn't thought about the pitfalls that yawned before newly freed slaves. Pearl, crying softly beside him, was beginning too late to realize that being free wasn't everything she had hoped.

Airy said, "Mah mamma make free one time, but dem slave catchers pick her up an' walk her ahint a hawse all de way back to Ol' Marse. He whup her an' whup her. Mama tell me a nigger doan know no misery till he make free an' gits fotched back."

Adam, thoroughly confused, was not sure he believed the words that fell so true-sounding from the lips of Pearl and Airy. He remembered his father striking and verbally abusing the blacks they'd owned then. But Ben's and Beau's fathers treated their darkies well. Their servants had ticks to sleep on and extra clothing so they could keep themselves clean and garden patches of their own. And Mr. West had it worked out so he didn't need an overseer. He gave his people tasks every morning, and when they had finished, they could stop for the day. Adam wondered if that was why the West's blacks were more efficient than those of Mr. LeClerc, who nervously oversaw everything his darkies did.

But that was one way of slavery. There was a dark and fearsome other side, the side where Edmund Revanche stood. Men who thought like Revanche saw their servants as things, property to be used, bought, sold, punished for small infractions, and brutally murdered for larger ones. Between the two extremes Adam knew about, there had to be a great middle ground of slave owners who were usually kind enough, who kept their slaves fed and doctored, punished them like children if they did wrong, and sometimes rewarded them if they did well.

But they are like children, Adam thought. *Pearl is as old as I am, and she thinks being free is being taken care of somewhere. But how could she know different?* Slaves were better off kept in ignorance, he had heard. They wouldn't crave things if they didn't know they existed. An educated slave was nothing but a danger, liable to start insurrections and all sorts of unhandy activities.

But they did learn things when they wanted to. The darkies stuck together, lying for each other, teaching each other the old traditions and crafts of an ancient people. Those who made free seemed able in some mysterious way to leave behind them some part of their spirit to inform those left behind of new ideas. The slave grapevine seemed more legend than fact, yet it was true the slaves always knew of things that had happened or were about to happen, before their white masters did. Slaves often talked and sang of the spirit; perhaps that was all the grapevine was, the imparting of information by the powerful collective spirit of a people in a common struggle.

Adam had never given slavery this much thought before. He could hardly remember what it was like to have blacks do all the work. When his father died, Zoe had sold all their slaves except Mammy, the only one who had not belonged to Paul Tremain.

People like Mammy, hardworking and competent, would be as well off free as in bondage. But Pearl and Airy, who he suspected were lazy scamps and not too bright, would find that their freedom made them a mighty thin meal. Maybe they would learn to take care of themselves, and maybe they wouldn't.

Leona turned abruptly into a wagon track across a fallow field. Adam followed until they stopped inside a huge barn. Leona climbed down, helped by a stalwart man. "Thee has brought us a goodly number this morning, Leona!"

"Hello, Ebenezer," Leona said. "There's one more load. Has Elijah arrived yet?"

"Not yet. Are thy people hungry?"

"Of course they're hungry. I brought food, but it was too risky to stop."

"Thee was pursued?"

"So 'Lijah says. The catchers want Ruby's man for killing an overseer. Oh, Ebenezer, this is my nephew, Adam Tremain. Adam, Mr. Cline."

The Quaker's work-roughened hand clasped Adam's. "It's good to have thee here, friend Adam. Would thee fetch thy people, please?"

He led them into a large, windowless room. Ebenezer and Leona began to prepare the meal. The blacks squatted on their haunches, watching with apprehension and hope. Adam helped portion out the food, saving some for Elijah's passengers. Ebenezer gave instructions to the fugitives and left them alone.

"Will thee both share breakfast with me and my wife?" Ebenezer asked. "Elijah will eat with the others. They are not yet accustomed to taking meals with white people, Adam, so we do not force them."

"How did you know we were coming?" Adam asked.

Ebenezer laughed. "Pipes buried under the wagon trail carry the sounds of wheels into our house. It is a very effective alarm."

They entered the whitewashed kitchen, with its unadorned walls and sturdy, practical furnishings. Ebenezer's wife, taking muffins out of the oven, smiled at them. "I heard another carriage, husband."

"Thank thee. I will attend to it," Ebenezer replied.

Adam and Leona took a different route home, one more heavily traveled. The sun was struggling to free itself of the clinging morning mist when they entered the Pinckneys' carriage house. Leona said, "Now, doesn't that make you feel that something important has been accomplished, Adam?" She was wearing a wide grin.

Adam grinned back. "I think so, but I've got a lot of questions."

"Better save them. Your mother will have some too, likely."

Zoe opened the porte cochere door. "Adam! Leona! Where have you *been?* I was worried half to death!"

Still smiling, Adam said, "Aunt Leona's been leading me astray." He did feel good, though he didn't know why. Helping a handful of fugitives make free from cruel masters seemed a lot different from emancipating every darky in the South. It was a long step from there to ideas of abolition. And this trip in the black of night had been merely an adventure thrust on him and safely completed.

Adam was pleased with himself, and his attitude did

nothing to calm his mother. Leona attempted to settle Zoe's fears and managed to rouse new, deeper ones.

"How *could* Garrett involve you in this! Leona, I—"

"He didn't persuade me, Zoe. I wanted to. Garrett worries for me. It's dangerous to haul slaves, but I believe it's the right thing to do. Mostly I work through the Wilmington Female Benevolent Society, the one that Mama helped to found in 1817."

"Surely that has not become an abolitionist society!" Zoe said, aghast.

"Certainly not, but some of the women sew clothing and provide food for the fugitives. I'm the only woman who hauls them, though."

"But if you were revealed . . . wouldn't you go to prison?"

"Quite possibly, or perhaps hang if the wrong people caught us," Leona said briskly. "But you're thinking like a Deep Southerner, Zoe. Not all of the South is so bound to the slave system as are the big cotton states. There are a lot of abolitionists right here in Wilmington. Many of us think slavery will die out as the ground becomes too poor for profitable cotton and cane crops.

"Times are changing, Zoe. Garrett and I believe the fugitives should be helped now. We are in the right place to do something. From here we send them to Philadelphia or New Jersey overland, or to New York and Canada by water."

"Slaves are taken by ship?" Adam asked.

"Yes. It is the best and safest way, but as you can imagine, it's not easy to arrange for a ship to carry such a cargo."

Zoe's eyes fastened anxiously on Adam. She shifted the subject away from ships. "Oh, Leona, it is all so dangerous, and it is wrong. You have no right to take these blacks. They belong to someone—"

"Fiddlesticks! They're people. They shouldn't be owned by anyone."

"Aunt Leona, when did you start doing this?"

"On our wedding trip we stopped in Cincinnati. Garrett knows Mr. Levi Coffin, and I met him there. They call him the president of the Underground Railroad, you know. He just laughs about that. He is so kind, Adam, such a warm, gentle person. While we were taking supper with him and his wife, several fugitives came to his door. Garrett and I talked with them. I knew then that I wanted to help these people so they can have a better life. Do you realize what being in bondage does to an intelligent human being? Cruelties to the mind go far deeper than whip cuts and starvation."

"You must have freed our family slaves and never told me," said Zoe.

"Yes, I did. You remember about twenty years ago, when Nat Turner murdered all those people up in Southampton County? In North C'Lina that rebellion caused a big change back toward slavery again, but now I believe not more than one family in four owns slaves here. When Clay was alive, we talked about letting ours go, but he was from Mississippi and just couldn't bring himself to do it."

"So you and Garrett are abolitionists," Adam said. "Wait'll I tell Tom."

Leona's eyes twinkled. "Tom already knows. He's going to work with us."

Zoe sat straighter, her nostrils flaring. "Adam, I don't want you involved in this! Leona paints a very glamorous and noble picture. But Leona is always persuasive when she wants things her way."

Without a smile Adam said, "You've always told me to think for myself, Ma. This is something I'll have to consider."

Zoe sighed. Her worried eyes remained on Adam's face.

Adam said, "I want to talk with Tom about this."

With an attempt at lightness, Leona said, "We might even get you interested in this, Zoe."

"I never would be. Never."

"We have two contacts in New York, Mr. Isaac Hopper, and a gentleman you most likely recall, Mr. Roderick Courtland. Do you remember meeting him the summer before you married Paul?"

She shook her head violently. "No—I don't remember him at all."

"How could you forget him? Then, you don't know he never married?"

"Stop your matchmaking, Leona!"

Leona looked truly surprised. "Matchmaking?!"

"Yes! I don't want to hear any more about Mr. Courtland!" Zoe began pacing back and forth.

Adam stirred uncomfortably. "Excuse me, Aunt Leona. I'm going to find Tom. Thanks for taking me along."

As she followed Adam out into the hall, Zoe glared at her sister. In a low voice she said, "Adam, this has gone far enough."

He looked at her with calm stubbornness.

"We simply cannot stay here. You must find us a house, Adam. Any kind of house, but outside Wilmington."

Adam burst into a relieved laugh. "Big sister's bossing you around?"

"Don't tease me," Zoe said edgily. "You don't know how Leona can be. Garrett will be back with our things any day now. Adam, I just want to be settled. We're getting involved in too many frightening things lately. Please. Just find us a house."

The following day Adam and Tom began a flatboat trip of several days down the Cape Fear River to its opening into the Atlantic. They passed Orton Plantation, with its bountiful gardens in lush bloom. At the remains of Brunswick Town they stopped to explore the ruins of dwellings and shops untenanted since the Revolution.

"Don't b'lieve your ma would like livin' here, Adam," said Tom.

They left Brunswick's alluring deepwater harbor, going on a few more miles. Then, spread out before them on a beautiful estuary was a homey little town. Lining the waterfront were trimly built houses with two-story galleries and widow's walks. Around them bloomed yellow and red gaillardias and sea evening primroses. Groves of live oaks gently nodded their glossy leaves.

Adam, sweating in the late-summer sun, felt and smelled the ocean breezes cooling the air. "I think we've found the place, Tom."

They spent the day in Smithville, talking to townspeople, fishermen, laundresses hanging clothes, sun-browned children running barefoot in the sandy dust. Adam fell in love with a stately shingled house, two and a half stories high, with a widow's walk that looked out far beyond Bald Head over the billows to the curving horizon.

Their nearest neighbor served them supper and bid them stay the night.

Next morning Tom said, "Seems like we got you settled. Now I want to go look at this Crusoe Island I heard about yesterday. That sounds a lot like what I got in mind for my new place."

"Where's that?"

"Oh, a few miles up Green Swamp. Fisherman said he'd take us there. Said to bring our guns against bear."

They crossed meandering streams of dark water and tangled swamplands thick with otter, muskrat, beaver, and herds of deer. Crusoe Island was an elevated knoll, not properly an island at all. As they approached the tiny community, more than a hundred hounds set up a baying and barking.

"Bear hounds," said Caleb, their guide. "Lots o' bears in here. They break into the smokehouses and the stock pens and raise a merry hell. Have to clean 'em out ever' so often."

"What do people live 'way back in here for?" asked Adam.

"They's three stories told. Seth, he sez his kin were pirates that tried to raid the river settlements an' come back in here to hide. Winnabow's people lived along the coast, and when the white men come, they made the Indians go into the swamp. Ol' Jean, he claims he was a Frenchy doctor under Napoleum, an' he he'ped a bunch o' prisoners get away. Napoleum wanted him fer that, so he run for Haiti an' then come here. He's an awful old man, must be past eighty. But you take notice, all them folk look alike, sturdy-set an' towhaired, with pink cheeks like a English woman. I took ship to England as a lad, so I recollect them Englishers well."

With Caleb as their entrée Adam and Tom were welcomed with a reserve that soon bloomed into cordiality. The very nature of the settlement at Crusoe Island, spanning entire lives kept secret from the world, fitted Tom's desire for a place offering undemanding companionship with others who had their own reasons for living in isolation.

Before bedtime Tom had promises of help in raising his cabin. The men of the community, shy of strangers but overcome by curiosity about the man with the scarred face and bent body who wanted to join them, gathered in Seth's cabin to talk in their odd-sounding north-of-England accents and to pass the stone crock of white lightning from mouth to mouth.

As the night dropped abruptly and the candles were lit, Adam's head began to reel. He had had wine before, and liquor as well, but this stuff laid a fiery path all the way from the back of his tongue down his gullet. But he sat on the floor, leaning against the chinked wall, and sipped at the crock each time it passed him.

The candles stuck in their saucers were guttering, and he could hear the voices around him singing, in meltingly sweet harmony,

Enraptured I gaze, when my Delia is by,
And drink the sweet poison of love from her eye.

After a time somebody laughed. "Lookit the boy thayer. Bin struck by lightnin'. Johnnie Mae! Hi! Want you to pack 'im up t' loft."

Adam raised his head from his chest far enough to see dusty bare feet topped by what seemed to be excellent legs and a calico skirt that didn't even cover her knees! He shut his eyes in embarrassment.

The girl laughed, a low throaty sound. "Gimme yere hand, boy. Oi got to carry ye up ladder."

Adam, scarcely able to understand her dialect, raised one hand and let it fall. Then he felt himself pulled to his feet and slung over a strong shoulder. He opened his eyes. The floor was retreating from him in foot-long jumps. The candle disappeared from view, and he was dumped, not ungently, onto a hammock slung from a low ceiling.

Hands touched him, rubbed him in places where hands shouldn't be even when it felt good. Adam moaned faintly and again heard that soft, throaty laugh.

The hands went away. "Ye be'n't a boy," said the voice, with satisfaction. "Ye be a man, a bi-i-ig man."

Her words echoed in his ears as the lightning took him off to sleep.

Chapter Twelve

Tom began to live in Green Swamp, a guest in Seth's cabin while trees were felled and readied to build his own. Adam went back to spend a day now and then helping with the logging. He got to know some of the men. Most of them weren't talkers, but those who were spoke in such an incomprehensible dialect that he missed half of what they said. There seemed to be no women around. If Johnnie Mae existed, it was in a drunken dream long past.

"Of course there's women, Adam," said Tom. "But they're backward females. They're just now beginnin' to come out when I'm around."

"Who was it carried me up into the loft that first night?"

"That was one of 'em. Strong as an ox. I've seen her pack loads that would stagger a man, an' she's not even breathin' hard."

Adam asked casually, "Is she pretty?"

Tom laughed. "She's not up to your caliber by a long shot."

At last the house in Smithville suited Zoe. She wanted to move immediately. Six Negroes were hired to man the boat with its load of furniture to the Tremains' new house.

That night Zoe and Adam had their last festive dinner in Leona's dining room. They sat up late, unable to talk enough to get it all said before the sisters would live twenty miles apart.

Zoe, exhausted, was both saddened and exhilarated at the prospect of her own home. Leona followed a deeply entrenched habit of giving advice. Adam wanted desperately to talk to Garrett alone, to get his carefully formed opinions on slavery, abolition, and emancipation, and what might happen if all the slaves were freed at once.

But Garrett was tired. Only courtesy kept his eyes open and his attentions fixed on his guests. When the tall-case clock in the entry hall struck midnight, he gave Leona a significant look.

Good-nights were said, lamps left on the hall table were lighted and taken upstairs and one by one blown out. For four hours the house slept.

The knocking was so urgent it woke everyone. Adam heard Garrett's heavy tread on the stairs. Soon Leona followed. Adam lay drowsily listening, cozy under the sheet in the black stillness before dawn.

He had drifted back to sleep, when the door to his room was flung open and Leona was shaking him. "Adam! Adam, wake up!"

He came bolt awake. "More fugitives?"

"Yes! The worst mess I ever saw! Get your clothes on

as fast as you can, bring your rifle, and hurry out to the carriage house!"

There were five of them, blacks with eyes rolling and nostrils distended with fear. Two were women. One man was lashed to a horse, barely alive. All were covered with swamp muck. All had wounds bleeding in red runnels down their arms and legs onto the dirt floor. They babbled incoherently to Garrett.

Adam stood rooted with revulsion.

"Hitch the horses, Adam," Garrett said. He and Leona were working over one man with a terrible gash on his arm. "Four horses. Use the dray and put the grays in the lead. Lay out the tarpaulin in the dray bed. Get blankets. You're riding with me."

Adam hitched the horses with difficulty. The smell of blood made them uneasy and fractious. Hysterical keening from one of the women, on her knees praying, made Adam's skin creep. He tried to calm the biggest gray. All they needed in this ruckus was for the excited horses to shove everything through the closed doors of the carriage house.

One of the men, his arm heavily bandaged, came up to him. "Ah hol' de hosses. Ah's a groom." He pointed toward the keening woman. "Kin you he'p Jane, Mastah? Big Mose was her man."

"Adam, help me get this man into the dray," said Garrett. Adam helped lift the slave free of the gore-covered horse. Jane suddenly issued a bloodcurdling scream, pointing to the door.

"Oh, mah Lawd, it's Mose's ghos' come to git me! Oh, Lawdy Lawdy Lawdy—"

"Great Scott!" said Garrett. "Leona, shut her up!"

Adam, who had nearly dropped his share of the burden at Jane's outcry, looked over his shoulder. His mother's hair was sleep-fluffed around her pale face, her long white wrapper flowing around her. "What in heaven's name—" she blanched at the weirdly lit sight.

"You like slavery, Zoe?" Leona asked grimly. "Here it is!"

Zoe shrank toward the door, her hand trembling against her mouth.

Jane kept screaming, "It de Debbil! De Debbil!" until Leona slapped each side of her face. Then she held Jane close until the senseless noise became words and the sobbing ebbed.

"Mose, he daid, Missy!" Jane cried. "We runnin' thoo Green Swamp, an' de dog make to tree Mose. Mose he kick dat dog, an' dat ol' dog he catch Mose laig an' tear he laig!"

In a confused babble the story tumbled out from the others—a tale of horror and death as the terrified slaves had fled the catchers and their dogs, with Mose sacrificing his own life so that the others could make free. In the melee the slaves had killed two of the catchers.

"Big Mose"—Jane's voice broke and another took up the story—"Big Mose yell at us to run, an' he grab fo' de catcher's gun an' pull 'im offen de hoss an' he st'angles 'im wid he han's!"

"De catcher's tongue hang way out. Mastah, dat catcher die."

"Mose, he still screamin', 'Run, Run,' an' us runs thoo de rattlesnake den, an' dat's de time Jason git bit by de snakes!"

"Ain't no mo' racket back dere where de catchers is, so Marcus sneak back. Big Mose lyin' daid wid a big hole in he ches', de fust catcher he still daid, an' de nex' catcher on'y breavin' a li'l bit."

"So Ah takes mah good ahm, an' I chunks dat catcher a goodern on de haid! 'Nen I catches dem hosses so's we kin ride."

."We ties Jason onter de hoss, an' we keeps on tredgin'. We comes to a ol' nigger daddy out lantern-fishin'. He he'ps us cross de ribber—"

"An' de nex' nigger we sees tell us'n to come heah."

Zoe cowered against the doorframe, as if ready to faint.

Leona worked through the hubub. "Zoe, come and tear bandages. We've got to get these people out of here!"

Garrett and Adam were trying to get Jason into the wagon. His leg ballooned as the venom took hold.

"I don't see how he can make it," Garrett murmured.

They were distracted by a thump. The biggest gray horse, whinnying, tried to move toward his neighbor. Marcus, the groom with the broken arm, had fainted under the horses' hoofs. Adam and Garrett dragged him out and laid him by Jason. "Leona, have you got the worst wounds bound up?"

"Yes, dear. Hurry, you people, get up into the dray."

Adam climbed onto the seat, his rifle across his knees, Garrett's extra revolver nearby in a pocket built for it.

Zoe saw the first thing that made clear sense to her. "No! You can't take Adam! I won't allow it! He's too young—"

Garrett took the reins. "Open the door, Leona. Stand aside, Zoe."

"Garrett, I beg you! Please! I don't want him killed!"

"Neither do I. Good-bye, Leona my dear. We'll return as soon as we can."

Leona put her hand on her husband's arm. "God go with you, my love." They smiled into each other's eyes. Garrett shook the reins.

Adam turned to face his mother. "I'll be all right," he said in soft-toned confidence.

Zoe's face puckered as the dray began to move. In the back Jane, rocking to and fro, started her keening again. "Oh, Lawdy Lawdy Lawdy . . ."

Garrett whipped up the horses as Adam looked back. "Zoe'll be all right. Throw a blanket over that girl, Adam. Cover her clear up and have her people tend to her. Then get back up here and keep watch."

Adam scrambled into the dray, glancing back long enough to see Leona catch up with Zoe and pull her back abruptly.

"Zoe, are you out of your senses?" Leona hissed. "You're screaming fit to wake the dead!"

"I don't care! I don't want Adam hurt!"

Leona gripped Zoe's arm firmly. "You keep on hollering like that, and they'll all get killed."

"I don't care about a bunch of darkies! Adam is all that matters!"

"Zoe, *shut up! Shut your silly mouth!* Do you understand me?"

"Turn me loose! I can take care of myself!"

Leona smiled grimly. "Good. Help me clean up this mess."

"I—I can't."

"Then get Mammy to help me if you're too much of a lady. We'll have to hurry. We've got to scrape the floor of the carriage house clean and rake the driveway and scrub everything that's got blood on it."

Zoe stared at her, but Leona was already moving in swift strides toward the carriage house. She turned to say, "Before dawn!"

Zoe looked up at the trees; the dark night was already paling. *Oh; God, why didn't we leave sooner? One day earlier and we'd be safe in Smithville. Please, God, keep him safe.*

Leona shoved a rake into her hand. "Rake the drive," she commanded. "Start around the back, for that's the way they came in. Rake it hard so there aren't any foot tracks or spots. And sprinkle plenty of capsicum. It ruins the dogs' sense of smell."

As Zoe hesitated, Leona said, "It's your neck as well as Adam's and Garrett's. If the catchers come here, we'll be caught too."

"Thanks to you and Garrett!"

"—who took you and your family in when *you* were fugitives!"

Zoe raked with frightened determination.

Garrett got the dray away from the streets of Wilmington before it began to grow light. But there was still the poor section of town to go through. Adam made everyone lie down, and he spread the blankets over them. The high sides of the dray would keep their cargo hidden.

The neighborhood dogs were a lot more noisy and persistent this trip, Adam noticed. Several of them followed the dray, barking constantly until Garrett flicked at them with the long whip and they fell back, still yapping.

Adam took another careful look behind them. They had passed the bend in the road. This side he could see nothing. Their horses were galloping smoothly, with greater speed still in them. Off to Adam's right the rim of the sun edged a field with a rosy flush. Crows flew out of the woods, cawing raucously. Overhead the buzzards were circling, hoping to catch an early cottontail for breakfast. Adam's head pounded with questions he longed to ask Garrett. Finally, he asked, "Do you think slavery is all bad? These people weren't harmed until they tried to fight off those dogs."

Garrett glanced at him, and without thinking looked behind. "No, not all of it is bad," he said. "Some people are better off in a situation where they're taken care of and they're told what to do.

"There has to be something to what these people tell us about the cruelties. The Underground system wouldn't exist if the darkies didn't take such awful chances to break away.

"History shows us that slavery has been a monumental failure, Adam. Man is not willing to be a chattel."

As they rounded another bend, Adam looked behind again. All clear. "But, sir, if it doesn't work, why haven't the slaves been freed through legislation? The planters could hire workers."

"It isn't just a matter of freeing slaves. Those people represent the largest single item of Southern capitalization. There are fortunes tied up in them, actual money. If they're freed, what happens to the money they represent? Where would be the Southern ability to give and get credit? To free slaves, we must also free planters of their financial need for them."

"Then there's no way . . ."

The dogs were on them before they knew it. Running silently behind the dray were two large hounds, powerfully built with deep chests and heavy, dark muzzles. Adam, sweeping the dawnlit countryside with his eyes, glimpsed the fawn brindle animal near the rear wheel. The dog changed its stride, ready to jump into the dray. Adam leaned out, hanging onto the seat with a foot hooked beneath it, and shot the beast in the chest as it rose.

"Good God!" cried Garrett, straining to hold the horses from bolting at the sound of the shot. Before Adam could reload, the blankets popped up, and four frightened dark faces looked out. Jane and the other woman began to scream. The second dog, silvery tan with one white eye, was up in the dray. Adam grabbed the revolver and pointed it but did not dare shoot. Well trained, the dog stood attentive, baying that he had them treed. The terrified women tried to fend him off, frantically waving their arms. The dog snarled, and tore at the women.

Marcus and the man called Boy pounded the dog with their fists. The dog turned on them. Adam scrambled into the bed of the dray, unavoidably treading on Jason, who lay so still. At point-blank range Adam shot the dog in the head. He leaped back, revulsed. Blood and brains flew onto his shirt and trousers. The unearthly howls and screams went on and on.

"Garrett, there's two men!" he said frantically. Hastily he reloaded his rifle. Garrett grabbed his revolver just as

a lanky, sharp-faced man on a swiftly galloping horse
lifted his rifle and fired at the smaller gray. Garrett shot at
the man and missed. Another shot rang out, hitting Garrett
in the arm. He raised his pistol and fired. The sharp-faced
man screamed and fell dead beside the road.

After that everything happened at once. The gray horse
ran several steps after being hit, then, collapsed. The other
horses, pushed onward by the dray, dragged her a short
distance before they piled up on each other, with the dray
crashing into them just before it overturned.

Adam, coming to with a knot on his head, thought the
whole world was screaming. Women, horses, men shrieked
in a cacophony as hideous as doomed souls pleading for
mercy in hell. Only Garrett made no sound. He lay still.
Adam's revolver lay inches away from his hand.

"Ah wou'n't grab out fer thet if Ah was you."

Adam looked up and up. A burly man, seated easily on
his horse, blotted out the sunlight. From the silhouette a
pistol aimed at Adam's heart.

"You jes' rise up slow an' easy, boy. You gonna he'p
me right this-here wagon an' git them niggers in it afore
Ah kills you. We los' three men an' five dogs a'ready,
chasin' this-here bunch. Now git up."

Adam couldn't reach the revolver. But he wouldn't die
without a fight. He rose very slowly. He'd wait his chance.

The fugitives quieted as the slave catcher yelled commands. "Arright now, shut up an' git up! Offa yo' asses
an' on yo' feet!" He punctuated his commands with well-
aimed cracks of the long whip in his right hand. Still he
kept a competent hold on the pistol. Left-handed? Maybe
not. Adam shifted slightly in the direction of the revolver.

He was startled at the whip crack inches from his ear.
Marcus, groggily holding his bandaged arm, flinched as
the lash bit into his shoulder.

"Move yo' ass, nigger!" cried the burly man. "Git that
bigun up offa the groun' so's he kin heft that-there wagon."

Marcus's eyes rolled toward Jason. "He daid, Mastah."

The whip sliced Jason's flesh. He was beyond feeling it.

Boy was helping an injured woman. "Fo' Chrissakes,
you black varmints gonna stan' there all day? Git a move
on!"

Adam, watching the pistol, saw the man's hold on it
slacken. *No, not enough time.*

He looked toward the horses. Tangled in their harness,

held down by the dead gray, they were struggling to rise, whinnying and snorting with fear and frustration, kicking and biting each other.

"You won't have any horses to pull this dray if you don't do something about them," Adam said.

Before the catcher could reply, there came a hollow, eerie sound of absolute terror. It came from nowhere, it came from the air and up out of the ground. The hair on Adam's neck prickled. The Negroes froze, as unmoving as statues.

The catcher looked around, his head moving quick as a snake's. Adam picked up the revolver and aimed it. As he fired, a bullet whined past him, splintering a hole in the dray. The trapped-animal screams stopped.

The silhouette on the horse began to crumple. His whip slid to the ground, but the man raised his pistol, cocked it, and fired at Adam. There was a futile click. Blood spurted out of the man's jugular vein, each spurt marking his weakening heartbeats. With a sickening splat he toppled to bleed his life out onto the sandy roadway.

Adam watched every movement, unable to look away. The ruddy pool spread. The catcher's gurgling breaths grew more shallow, then stopped. The silence became unbearable.

Marcus laughed nervously. "He daid. He ain't gwine chase us no mo'." He stepped back from the still body, robbed of its formidable vitality.

God forgive me. . . . I've killed a man. Adam turned abruptly away from the others and retched into the underbrush.

His head pounding, his mouth sour, he straightened up. He wiped his streaming eyes. He drew in air. It seemed a long time before he could face them again.

The scene was no better. Jason and the catcher lay sprawled. The silver-fawn dog had been flung into a pool of stagnant water. All were black with flies. Involuntarily Adam looked overhead. Yes, the carrion crows were gathering, making smaller and smaller circles, ready to swoop down, and . . . this was the murder of Ullah all over again.

Out of his revulsion, Adam yelled, "What are you standing there like a bunch of sheep for! Get those horses loose! Hang onto them, we're going to need them. Girl, what's your name?"

"Mandy, Mastah."

"Where are you hurt, Mandy?"

"In mah stummick, Mastah. Knock de breaf outa me when dat wagon pick up an' fly like a pigeon."

"Can you help me with Mr. Garrett?"

"Yassuh, Ah he'p, yassuh!"

Adam knelt beside Garrett, putting his face close to see if he was breathing. Blood oozed from Garrett's wounded arm and from a bump behind his ear. Adam touched him. "Garrett! Can you hear me?"

"Ah rub he han's." Mandy chafed Garrett's wrists. He was slow, so slow in responding. At length he opened his eyes a slit, then tried to focus. "Buzzards," he said indistinctly, trying to rise.

Adam breathed in relief. "We're all right, hear? Both catchers are dead. Lie still 'til we get the dray fixed."

"I'll help," Garrett said, but passed out again.

There was nothing to do for him now, Adam thought. He could put a wet rag on his forehead, but the only water was alive with wiggleworms. "Mandy, put a blanket over Mr. Garrett."

Adam and the blacks righted the wrecked dray. Jane was lying flat, her head on the sand. As the dray lifted, she began to scream again.

Completely out of patience, Adam grabbed her and shook her until her teeth clicked. "Shut up! Shut up! One more scream and I swear by Almighty God I'll take you back and sell you down South!"

Mortified with shame, he let go of her shoulders. "Are you hurt?"

Jane shook her head. "Mah laig pinned undah de wagon, but Ah not hut."

He whispered, "I'm sorry, I'm sorry." Her ankle was twisted at a queer angle, purple and puffy. "Just lie still."

Jane's eyes rolled after him. "Yassuh."

The dray's sides were smashed, but it was usable. Marcus had untangled the horses and tied them to trees. They whickered, ready to shy. "Better use de catcher's hosses. Dis'n stringhaltered."

Adam nodded, trying to decide what to do. The buzzards had lit. They clustered down the road, feasting on the brindle dog. Adam's stomach lurched uneasily. They'd be here next. He broke off a small tree limb. "Mandy, stand by Mr. Garrett. If the buzzards come near, shoo them off."

"Bad luck to kill a buzzard, Mastah."

"Bad luck for the buzzard," he growled. "Protect Mr. Garrett, you hear?"

The men dragged the two catchers under the low-hanging branches of a pine. Next they padded the dray with blankets and lifted Jane and Garrett into it. Somehow they persuaded Jane they would have to take dead Jason, so his soul could be released by proper Christian burial. Marcus and Mandy could sit beside Adam, while Boy rode on the back.

Marcus was needed to control the horses, for the catchers' saddle horses were sulkily unwilling to be hitched. He soft-talked them, ignoring the roan's bared teeth. An hour later the four horses were awkwardly moving forward.

They rumbled through the fallow field and up into Ebenezer's barn. His wife came out to meet them, her face pink and wholesome under her dove-gray sunbonnet. "Friend Adam, thee's had trouble?"

"Yes, ma'am. We'll need help."

"Thee heard the horn sound? Eben will be in from the field directly. We didn't expect thee in daylight." She gasped as she saw Garrett.

"He's had a bullet wound and a blow on the head. He keeps fainting. We've got two people with broken limbs, a man dead, and two stolen horses."

"And thee, friend Adam?"

Vignettes from the awful journey flashed through his mind, but he could not speak of them. He said, "It was a hard trip, ma'am."

She smiled. "Thee acquitted thyself well, else thee'd not be here."

They had reached safety, but Adam could not relax yet. He was still responsible for Garrett's welfare.

The fugitives who could walk were helping the others into the windowless room. They laid Garrett on a high bench. Adam helped the little Quaker woman remove his shirt. His bullet wound was minor. She cleaned it with soap and water and bound it with muslin strips.

Garrett's eyes opened. He smiled faintly at her. "Well, well, Prudence, I seem to be . . . on the receiving end of . . . your mercies."

"Thee lie still, friend Garrett," she said good-naturedly. "Thee's a knot large as a goose egg on thy skull. It wants cold compresses."

"Adam. Where's Adam?" He tried to sit up and fell back dizzily.

"I'm here." With Garrett in expert hands, Adam was comforting Jane. She was in severe pain. He felt he could not bear it if she started screaming again. "I'm fine, Garrett."

"Turn thy head a bit," Prudence instructed him. Garrett sucked in his breath as she began to clean dirt from his wound.

Eben came in with two husky field workers. He greeted everyone, then assessed the situation with few questions. He gave instructions to his men as Prudence worked. Adam went out before this was begun. He had no stomach for tasks that Ebenezer and his men could do better.

He looked with dull eyes at Jason in the wrecked dray. He would be prepared and decently interred. The blacks believed the spirit of one who lay dead unburied and unblessed was doomed to wander the earth for eternity. Was it true, he wondered, of the men who pursued slaves for the bounty?

Adam walked slowly out into the bright, hot day and leaned against Eben's barn, holding his face up to the sunshine. Was Garrett in shape to travel? It might be best to leave him here.

Into his thoughts unbidden came the glimpse of a man silhouetted against the morning sun, falling.

Adam shuddered. Then he heard Prudence call him, and he stepped swiftly back into the dark barn.

"Friend Adam, Garrett is asking for thee."

Garrett was still lying on the bench, covered by a blanket. Adam put a hand on his shoulder. "How do you feel?"

Garrett licked his lips. With difficulty he focused his eyes. "I'm fine, Adam. Eben will let us use his . . . spring wagon."

"It's foolhardy for you to travel now. You'd be risking your life."

"I'm going home." He shut his eyes. "You're not to leave without me."

"Rest thee awhile now. Adam will speak with thee again."

The men were still setting Jane's ankle, but Prudence took Adam to the house. Two shy young girls had a hot meal ready.

"I can't eat," Adam blurted out.

"No? Then thee'll have a cup of beef broth." The broth was thick with herbs, and vegetables. As Adam was finishing, she said, "Thy uncle wishes to leave. Eben has the spring wagon ready, with a fresh horse."

Adam said apprehensively, "What'll I do if he—d-dies?"

Prudence's hand was warm on his arm. "Don't fash thyself, Adam. He has promised to lie quietly. The good Lord will watch over thee."

Garrett, deathly pale, stubbornly walked to the wagon. "See? I'm perfectly fine. Prudence has fixed me a kingly bed. Touch up that horse!"

In spite of Adam's anxiety, the trip was uneventful. But as they splashed through the ford at Smith Creek, Garrett said, "Adam, stop."

"What's the matter? Are you getting sick? We'll soon be home."

"I'm going to drive."

"Like hell! Think I want you falling and busting your skull open?"

"Look at yourself. You can't drive through Wilmington like that."

Adam looked down. His shirt and trousers were spattered with large dried blood spots. "Give me your coat, Garrett. I'll cover it up."

"I left it at Eben's. I'm going to drive, Adam. You keep hidden."

They got back late in the afternoon. Zoe, looking anxiously out the windows, saw a white-faced Garrett swaying on the seat of a strange wagon behind an unfamiliar horse. And Adam was not with him.

Chapter Thirteen

Leona was in the carriage house, seated on a hay bale. Her fingers flew as she knitted a blanket to be used on some future trip. Her nervousness was betrayed only in the taut way she held her head, her ear straining toward the doors. Already it seemed that several lifetimes had passed since Adam and Garrett had driven away. She'd gone into the house once to reassure Zoe that everything was all right, but she knew it was not. The men were long past due.

Her knitting fell unheeded to the floor at the sound of wheels biting and spattering the gravel and shells of the driveway. She flung wide the great doors of the carriage house.

Garrett drove the wagon, pale and weak, alone. Leona didn't notice Adam's absence. Her eyes were for her husband, who released the reins and slumped down on the seat. Leona's ears blotted out the sound of Zoe's frightened, mournful shriek.

"He's dead! Ohhh, my God! He's gone! Adam!" Zoe tore wildly at herself and pulled away from Mammy's restraining hands.

"Miz Zoe, you gwine hurt yo'seff. Doan carry on so," Mammy pleaded.

In the back of the wagon the blankets jounced as Adam tried to free himself of them. "Ma!" His voice was drowned out by his mother's hysteria and Leona's shouted orders to the servants.

Adam leaped from the wagon. He pressed Zoe against him, muffling her sobs against his shirt. Her screams abated. Her sobs were deep and heart-rending. "I'm all right, Ma. Nothing happened to me." He put his face in the soft pillow of her hair. "I'm all right."

"Adam, help me with Garrett," Leona's voice was on the edge of hysteria.

He smoothed his mother's hair back. "Go with Mammy. I'll come as soon as we get Uncle Garrett into his bed."

Still trembling and clinging to him, she nodded, then stood back looking at him as if to assure herself he was truly there. Her face distorted in renewed horror as she saw the bloodstains. She rubbed frantically at her cheek where she'd pressed it against his chest. Her screams were long, howling cries that reason could not temper.

"Get her out of here, Mammy!" Leona's fists beat at her skirts. "Adam, help me! Garrett is dying! Help me!"

Adam and the servant called Luster carried Garrett to his room. Leona dogged their steps. Her untidy hair flew about her face in gray wisps. Adam placed Garrett on the bed and hurried out.

For an instant he hesitated at the top of the stairs, wanting to run down their length into the outdoors, away from the noise and the chaos, away from his mother.

Mammy had taken Zoe to her sitting room and there

tried to quiet her. By the time Adam had gained sufficient resolve to face his mother, she was crying in soft, self-pitying hiccupping sobs. Her normally pretty face was swollen and blotched with red.

He said awkwardly, "It isn't so bad, Ma. Mr. Cline says Uncle Garrett will mend. The dray turned over, and he hit his head."

"I wish he had died! I do! I do!"

"Miz Zoe!" Mammy breathed, clasping her hands and rolling her eyes sincerely heavenward. "Doan you talk like dat. De Lawd done heah you!"

"He deserves it, after what he did," Zoe sobbed.

"Ma, quiet down, you don't mean what you say. It's over. Look, nothing happened to me. Everyone is safe."

"Till next time and next time and next time, till he finally gets you killed!" She clawed at his shirt, pulling him toward her. "Adam," she whispered urgently, "promise me, promise me you'll never do this again. We'll leave here today, and then you must promise you'll never see Leona or Garrett ever again. Promise me, Adam!"

"Ma—I can't do that."

"You will! You must! I can't stand any more of this!"

"You'll feel different in the morning, Ma. Wait—"

"I won't wait! I can't! You've dragged me from my home, gotten us into one trouble after another! I *demand* that you do as I say in this!"

Carefully he opened her grasping hand, freeing himself. Zoe, wrapped in her own hysteria, did not see her son's hurt and anger. Adam looked at his mother, who, pathetic but determined, was waiting for him to accede. He said, "Ma . . . I can't do it."

"They mean more to you than I! You'd sacrifice your own mother's well-being for your quixotic notions?" Her voice rose. "You ungrateful ignorant! You know nothing, nothing of what you are involved in. Can't you see Garrett and Leona are taking advantage of you? You're a child! They are using you for their own purposes!"

"No, they're not, Ma. They're good people."

"And what am I? Doesn't it matter to you that my life is being ruined? I love you, Adam. Is it so much for a mother to ask that her son not bring her sorrow every waking moment of her life? Do this for me, promise me."

He took another step away from her. "I can't," he said more quietly than ever, choking on the words.

"Adam!" she cried, coming toward him. "Go to your room! Go immediately, and stay there until it is time to leave for the new house. Do as I say!" she shouted, stamping her foot when he didn't move. "Adam, I am your mother! You will obey me, you will!"

"Ma, don't . . ." he said, his hands out to her. The hurt on her face was mirrored in his own. She screamed at him again. He walked to the door, stopped there, looking back over his shoulder, then ran down the hall. He took the steps two at a time, stumbling as he hurled himself through the front door and out into the soft evening light.

His mind raced, but nothing formed into a coherent thought. Impressions and scenes and feelings sped in and out of his consciousness. Like a wounded animal, he wanted a safe place to lick his wounds and try to mend the awful tearing that had occurred last night and today. Vaguely he thought of Tom. Tom, better than anyone, would understand what he felt over having killed the catcher. Tom could feel what he felt and help him to find sense somewhere.

He ran for the flatboat, jumping into it with such recklessness he nearly capsized the craft. He rowed down the Cape Fear River, then poled his way back into the depths of Green Swamp with hardly a thought to which channels and meandering creeks he was taking.

It was cooler in the swamp. By night it would be cold. The dark creek water that wound its way through the spongy, vine-clogged growth was quiet but swift running, a powerfully tranquilizing, immutable force that always calmed Adam, gave him pause and insight. This time nothing calmed his turbulent feelings. He poled, his eyes fastened unseeing on the blackish water. All was turmoil, disorganizing him, forcing him on deeper and deeper into the swamp, his mind always returning to the moment when the dray had suddenly overturned. After that there had been no thought, only impressions, horrible, sickening vignettes that tormented him.

He wasn't in the right branch of the creek for Tom's cabin, and he no longer cared. He didn't want to see Tom either. He didn't want to see anyone. He didn't want to talk or think or feel. All he wanted was sleep.

He moored in a deep channel, throwing a rope across a bough that hung far out over the water. He lay down in the bottom of the peacefully rocking boat and closed his eyes.

He awakened to the shrill morning songs of the swamp birds. Bright spots of sunlight through thick overhead foliage danced against silhouettes of isolated leaves. Lazily he lay there, cradled by the boat, lullabyed by the woodland sounds on the undulating water. So long as he didn't move, nothing was real. But he felt dirty. The odors of tension and sweat clung to him, befouling the sweet fresh air he breathed.

He climbed out of the boat to relieve himself and looked down at the hardened splotches of crusted blood with bits of dog hair dried into them. Hastily he pulled off his clothes, throwing them into the water. He knelt on the bank, scrubbing the clothes, rubbing them until his knuckles chafed. The bloodstains weren't coming out. He picked up a rock and jumped into the water. Again he scrubbed, pounding the clothes viciously against the rough surface of the rock. The fabric gave until the pink of his hand showed through the thin remains. He placed the garments on bushes to dry. As he looked at them, rippling slightly in the breeze, he felt one part of yesterday had been left behind.

He dived and came up in waist-deep water. With handfuls of grass he scrubbed the day-old sweat and dirt and memory from his body. When he had finished, he let the grass float away from him like tiny green ships on a vast, dark sea. The waters of the creek carried them slowly past its deep-cut banks, covered with tangled late-summer grasses and blue dayflowers, until the little flotilla had disappeared. He ducked again to rinse himself, stood up, and stretched his body. His clothes might be dry enough to wear in an hour or so.

He gave a startled yelp, thinking of alligators as something slithered past him. As if disembodied, long strands of blond hair fanned out underwater like silken snakes. She surfaced, stretching her smooth, tanned body to come out of the water so close to him that her full breasts rubbed his chest disturbingly.

"Mawnin'," she said cheerfully. "What be yere name?"

"A-Adam," he said, backing away.

The girl giggled and let the water carry her against him again. "Then mayhap moi name be Eve!" Her laughter

rang out, echoed by a chorus of birds on the swamp not far
away. "What be ye a-doin'?"

"I, well, I . . . was taking a bath. I didn't know anyone
was nearby."

"Been watchin' ye since afore ye woke up. Watched ye
make water up agin that tree, watched ye wash yere clo's
an' scrub yere body. Oi got plumb tuckered wie watchin',
so Oi come to be wie ye."

In spite of his confusion, Adam found himself fascinated
by her voice and straining to understand what she said.
The strange cadence and pronunciation of her words,
mixing the hard sounds of the Banker with the soft slur
of the hill people, formed a very ancient, very English
language he'd never before known except here in the
swamp.

He realized he was leaning forward as he listened. He
straightened, embarrassed anew. "I'm sorry, I seem to be
in your swimming hole. I'll—I'll—if you'll just turn your
back, I'll—get right out." He kept moving back, getting
nowhere. She was right there no matter what he did.

She shook her head flirtatiously. Her cat-eyed smile was
devilish. "Oi come to be wie ye, Adam. How come do ye
wanta run away, dereling?" She moved closer to him,
looking up into his face.

He hardly knew what to do. She was as relaxed and
fluid as the water itself, gliding in graceful motions against
him and then away. When her flesh passed and touched
his, there came that peculiarly sensual feeling of water
being warmed by skin and skin cooled by water, sensations
so stirring that they were overwhelming his ability to think.

He hoped fervently that the water was cold enough to
prevent a natural display of his desire, yet the growing
feeling of heat warned him. Without frock coat or trousers
to conceal it in the ordinary way, he had no place to hide,
no secret desires to be left secret.

His eyes riveted on her naked breasts. As far as he could
tell, all she had on was a blade of grass stuck to her shoulder. And that was something he didn't want to think about
because it didn't bear thinking about, but he couldn't seem
to think of anything else.

Eve knew. She giggled delightedly as she put her arms
around his neck and 'pressed full length against him. "Ye
be a slow man, be'n't ye?"

He put his hands up to take her arms away. A gentleman, even when he stood naked as the day he was born, remained a gentleman. "No, ma'am, I'm not slow. I'm just . . . just . . ." Her skin felt different from his. Her wrists were so small and smooth compared to his thickly muscled ones, so vulnerable and appealing somehow. He stood there bemused with his hands on her wrists, drowning in the nearly colorless blue pools of her eyes, feeling the seductive smoothness of her skin with every pore in his body. He put his arms around her and kissed her.

It was a long kiss that went on breath after breath. No matter how tightly he embraced her, it didn't seem tight enough for this girl, who kept teasing against him with her breasts and clasping his shoulders with fingers like claws. And the way she teased him underwater was making his knees turn limp.

Then, slick as an otter, she was out of his grasp, dolphining away toward the deeper part of the creek. A Piscean mirage who swam with the quiet rippleless grace of a fish, she hung there treading water and teasing him with her pale sea-nymph eyes.

"What be yere trouble, Adam? Don't ye like a bit o' playin'?"

He could leave now if he wanted. As she had done, he dived, arching back to the surface, making his way toward her. As he neared her, she sank out of sight. He peered down and saw nothing but the soft moving shadows of the swamp creatures. But she was there. Or else it was a mermaid, running her hands over him to lure him down with her. He reached out, feeling for her, and pulled her up by the hair. She came out of the water giggling.

Again she pressed her body to his and took his breath away with her mouth. Slowly they sank and hung just under the surface till Adam thought his lungs would burst. They stroked up for air together, and he smiled at her for the first time. "Never thought I could like drowning."

"Never know what ye might be likin' till it gits tried." She looked at him from the corner of her eyes before she swam away. She stood in the water, her breasts floating at the surface. "Not too deep over here."

He swam to stand beside her, wanting to touch her but unable to break through the rules that decreed he could not.

"Ye know nowt of woman, Adam," she said, sounding half-disgusted. "Oi be a-wantin' ye to reach out an' take aholt o' me boozums."

Adam stretched out hesitant fingers and stroked the curving sides of her breasts. She said, "Purty nice, be'n't they?" and smiled up at him. She was tall. He looked into her eyes, not far below his own. He smiled back and, bolder, ran his fingertips over her taut nipples. He felt his breath getting shorter. He had never held anything so alluringly fashioned, of such a desirable roundness and firmness and softness.

Eve, watching his face, said, "Ye be a-wantin' obleegin', Adam, afore ye be a-goin' off an' a-wastin' it in the branch."

Her hands ran down his body, expending no motions on cleverness or finesse. She grasped his penis and testicles with expert gentleness. Then the end of his penis touched soft, yielding flesh, moister somehow than the water around them, warmer and more inviting than the water. He seemed to go down a long cozy tunnel as deep as he wanted, her warmth securely cradling the length of him. He took a deep breath of delight. Without knowing, he put his arms around her, his hands under her rounded buttocks pulling her desperately close against him.

Eve moved away from him ever so slightly, yet her hands held him as close as he held her. He moved into her again and pulled away, yet her warmth grew and caressed him faster and faster, holding him tighter, pulsating all the way along him until the pulsations came one upon the next and he moaned over and over with a rapture as vivid as the open cloud gates of the sky.

His knees turned to water. His entire body was water. But Eve held him strongly and kept him within her. The current flowed around them, lending a buoyancy the land would have denied. Then her breathing began to sound raggedly, shudderingly, as he felt the spasms of her delight caressing him anew.

They stood locked together, panting, her breasts rubbing against his chest. Then he was slipping out of her. He felt the coolness of the water, washing him clean again.

Adam opened his eyes, and the brightness of the sun-struck water dazzled him. How long had he had his eyes squeezed shut?

She laughed huskily. Across her breasts and her freckled

cheeks lay a rosy flush. "Ye air a purty fine man, dereling. Wie time ye be all an' all any woman be a-wantin'."

With passion's retreat, reality returned, and Adam stood staring at her, dumbfounded over what he had done. In his consternation, he'd been going to beg her pardon. Word-bereft, he dropped his embrace.

"Mayhap ye won't be a-wantin' to do it again?" she said, still smiling.

"Not—not right away," he answered, feeling himself blush.

The girl floated away from him, lying half-submerged in the water like a pond lily. Adam floated near her. There must be something he was expected to say. The only trouble was he didn't know the proper words to use when a girl has come up out of the creek and seduced you for the first time in your life.

It was inadequate, it was foolish, but he said it. "That was nice, Eve. Th-thank you."

Her laughter rang out with the crafty wisdom of the natural child. "Preacher man says it be naughty 'stead o' nice, but it be nice, be'n't it?"

"Yeah." They grinned at each other. Adam took her hand, and they lay companionably together, resting in the water. Presently he asked, "Would you really want to do it with me again?"

"Aye, Adam. Aye. Ye got the kinda cock Oi be a-likin'. Long an' thick. There be a few things ye're not knowin' yet, but Oi'll learn ye a' that, next tuthree days."

"You live around here?"

"Aye. Cabin yonder the turnin' there. Ye an' me'll go in after a bit, an' Oi'll gie ye a mess o' grits an' aigs an' side-meat, an' Oi'll show ye tuthree things fer larkin' about."

"You live out here by yourself?"

She looked at him strangely. "Roy lives with me some-time, an' moi kin when they's a mind."

"They're all at the cabin?"

She shook her head. "Roy's went up to Wi'mton wie a chap. Ye don't injoy folks a-pesterin' wie yere fun?"

Privacy meant nothing to her. How could he explain that it was a part of his life? Feeling captured and capti-vated by this tantalizing creature, he said nothing, but smiled as he looked up into the sun-bright clouds and considered what wonder might befall him next.

Adam followed her out of the water, taking his trousers

and shirt off the bushes. He started to put on the trousers,
suddenly shy again, now that they were on land. She
laughed. "Ye'll have no call fer duds, lad." He walked behind her, insisting on carrying his clothes, feeling gratui-
tously exposed, yet avidly watching her bare brown butt
muscles twitch as she strode along the path to her cabin.
Evidently she went naked in the sun a lot, for she had no
paler areas as he did where his trousers covered him. At her
door she suddenly turned, and her eyes went down. She
grinned. "Ye be 'bout ready agin, be'n't ye?" She fondled
him briefly, then stepped inside the cabin. "Come in, if ye
can git in fer the dirt."

Adam followed eagerly. "Latch thet door, Adam. If
Oi don't go to he'p work today, they'll be a-sendin' one o'
the younguns to see 'bout me. Oi don't 'spect ye'll be
wantin' a bairn lookin' on?"

"No, ma'am."

"Ye be of the gentry, Adam? Ye talk so."

"I—I guess I am," he said, uncomfortably aware of the
differences that lay between them.

"Oi'd injoy bein' a loidy. Roy saw some loidies a-waitin'
fer a sailin' ship in Smithville. Roy said they'd faces white
like milk, an' totin' sunshades up on sticks to keep the
sun off'm."

"You've got beautiful skin," he blurted out.

She was poking up the fire in the fireplace, lifting a lid
off a kettle that hung from a hook. She smiled at him, a
picture of feline grace bending toward the fire, its light
painting flickering shadows along the curves of her breasts
and hipbones. "Oi'm gonna show ye ev'thing Oi got," she
said matter-of-factly. "Oncet ye know what it looks like,
then ye'll be a-knowin' what yere a-feelin' fer in the dark.
Time Oi git a' done wie ye, ye'll be a-knowin' how to
pleasure any woman ye'll ever want."

The idea embarrassed Adam; yet, as the girl had observed, he was ready. But such readiness had a way of
disappearing. When she was willing again, would he be
ready then?

He looked around the cabin. Tidy. Clean enough. A few
garments hung on pegs. A homemade table and chairs and
two chests that stood side by side under the windows. In
the corner, a wide rope bed. Everywhere, furs. On the
puncheon floor he recognized raccoon and fox. Over the

chests and on the bed was fine beaver sewn together into a coverlet. He was even sitting on a fur-covered chair.

"Them furs feel good agin yere privates, don't they dereling?" she asked companionably.

Adam blushed. He wanted to draw his trousers on, so his turmoil wouldn't be so quickly apparent to Eve's observant eyes. At the same time he was enjoying the novel sensation of having nothing on while he watched every move of a girl who also enjoyed having nothing on.

She laid the table, served the plates, and poured out cups of bitter coffee. "Better link in, Adam." She pointed with her knife. Expertly she ate with knife and spoon. When in doubt she used her fingers. There were no forks or napkins. Adam realized he'd had only one meal in the last day and a half and followed her example with gusto.

She licked her fingers and her lips and looked across the table at him with pleasant anticipation. "Fust time Oi see ye, Adam, I seed ye be a man. But ye in no-ways 'bout to be doin' nowt wie it. Now ye kin."

The husky voice, the hands on him . . . "You mean it was you who carried me up into Seth's loft that night I got drunk?"

"Aye, Oi did thet, Adam. Ye be a load to tote, but Oi've got strong arms, an' Oi tote ye."

"But that girl's name was Johnnie Mae! I heard them call her!"

She smiled, her tongue licking across her lips. "Oi was jes' a-larkin' wie ye 'bout me name, 'coz yere name be Adam. Adam be the fust man, an' Eve be his woman. Ma read me thet fable when Oi was a wee bairn. She be a-readin' nice."

"Johnnie Mae," he breathed, looking at her with freshly opened eyes. "I've had dreams about you ever since. I thought you weren't real!"

"What be ye a-thinkin' now?" she asked him invitingly.

Thoughts came easily; putting them into words was more difficult.

She smiled at him. "Be ye thinkin' ye oughtna be a-thinkin' what ye air?" she teased.

Tight-throated, he said, "I'm thinkin' maybe we're going over there and lie atop those furs on the bed. I'm thinkin' maybe you've got somethin' you said you'd show me."

Over the next days Johnnie Mae showed him not only

what a woman looked like but what she felt like. She taught him the areas of most pleasurable sensation. He learned how to arouse a woman without being too rough. She showed him how he could increase his own enjoyment, how to prolong his performance so he could satisfy the woman more than one time. She helped him discover the little signs a woman gave out that said, "keep on going" or "that hurts" or "I don't want you to do what you're doing." Women, said Johnnie Mae, were all made pretty much alike. But up in their heads they were different. Some women didn't like to do it. Some thought they didn't, but a skilled man could persuade them they did. It would be up to Adam to figure out which was which.

To his surprise no one came near the cabin, though Johnnie Mae was gone part of the time. During her absences Adam swam in the creek or lay naked in the sun. It was during these peaceful, solitary times that he found he could begin to think of the catcher, the slaves, and his own beliefs without the terrible, hurting demoralization. And those thoughts no longer had the ability to crowd in on him when he didn't want them. There were times when he could bask for hours, deliberately thinking of nothing, or he could sleep as he waited for her to return to him.

Sometimes when she was there with him and they lay side by side, looking at each other's bodies and talking desultorily, he would try to tell her some of the things he had thought about while she was gone.

She was hard to talk to. There were all sorts of things she had no conception of and no desire to learn. She had never learned to read. Knowing how to read hadn't done her mother much good, except to tell the pretty stories; but Johnnie Mae knew them by heart now and didn't need learning from a book. If a person had the swamp and a cabin and somebody to lark about with, what good was reading? The same with writing. Johnnie Mae had grown up in a community where everything was spoken, nothing written down. Perhaps that accounted for the oddness of her dialect. Strangely, she had a rudimentary grasp of counting and measuring and adding up. But in the main, if it wasn't a physical activity or a literal fact, Johnnie Mae didn't want to grapple with it.

It was the same, only worse, when he tried to tell her about hauling slaves. "Oi seed slaves oncet," she said. "A-workin' in a turpentine camp down thetaway. They didn't look so bad off. If they be a-wantin' to leave out o' there, they coulda."

"But these people we helped couldn't run away."

She looked at him stubbornly. "They coulda run if they'd a mind ta."

His explanations were useless. Johnnie Mae had her notions set, and facts weren't going to change them.

The next time he tried the direct approach. "What would you think of a . . . man who had killed another man?"

"Men allus be a-talkin' about their notches." She looked him in the eyes with avid interest, and his gaze fell. "He be yere fust man?"

"I didn't say *I'd* killed someone."

She looked at him a little longer. "Did he need killin'?"

"I . . . I don't know."

"He did or he didna. One or tother."

"It's not all that simple."

She shrugged. "He did or he didna."

Reluctantly, Adam nodded.

"Then ye done right. Don't fash yereself about it."

He wanted to tell her everything that had happened, how scared he'd been yet exhilarated, how sick-making it was to see life's blood he'd spilled flow into a pool too fast to sink into the ground. He needed to hand over the burden of guilt to someone who understood. He looked at her again, opened his mouth to speak, and closed it.

"Be ye too tuckered to lark about wie me?" She put out a long-fingered, tanned hand and slowly rubbed him beside the placket of his trousers.

Familiar with her now, he slipped his hand inside her shirt and made her nipples come erect. "What do you think, Johnnie Mae?"

She favored him with a slow, sweet smile that showed her uneven front tooth, that stretched the freckles on her nose and accentuated her cat's eyes. She was a girl of the sun, smelling of sunshine and of grass and of her tawny hair that gleamed like a shawl thrown over her shoulders. She lay back, her hair spread under her on the rough, thick grass, gazing at him through her eyelashes. She said simply, "Oi think ye be all man."

He kissed her breast and undid her shirt and pulled off her short skirt. He shed his trousers with newly acquired speed and stood over her. He was not pale now. He liked that, being tanned. He liked the feel of the sun on his entire body. His penis made a shadow across her belly, and that pleased him. What he liked best of all was the way Johnnie Mae looked lying there under him, lazily inviting, yet proudly aware of the perfect picture she made no matter what she did. She posed deliberately, he knew; but then she had a lot to pose with.

"Play like Oi be a loidy, an' Oi don't want to do it wie ye, an' ye be makin' me," she pleaded. It was her favorite game. "Play like ye be a big ol' bear, an' ye wud wrostle me down. Play like Oi be the man, an' ye be the woman." Pretense was her excitement.

He dropped to one knee beside her, and her hands promptly enclosed him. Then she laughed, let him go, and lay looking carelessly away from him. So he stroked her as she had taught him, fingertips running lightly down the inside of her arm to tickle her palm, then up the outside of her body to caress the full curve of her breast. She looked at him then, smiling faintly, and he kissed her at the corners of her mouth.

Johnnie Mae seemed to be at peace, enjoying him, waiting with pleasure-filled patience for her man. He thought he had never seen anything quite so beautiful. The words were out before he even thought them. "Johnnie Mae, I love you."

Her eyes caught his, and he saw the tears start. "Nobody ever said thet to me afore. Be thet coz we be a-playin' Oi'm a loidy?"

He began to kiss her face, the end of her nose, the edges of her eyes. Between kisses he let flow all the words he wanted to say to a girl he loved. "You're the sweetest . . . dearest . . . most beautiful . . ."

Johnnie Mae lay with a look of dazed desire, hungry for his words as much as his lovemaking. He went into her slowly, prolonging his pleasure and hers.

It would be the last time. He hadn't told her, but maybe she knew it the way, animal-like, she sensed things.

They swam afterward, touching each other as they lay on their backs in the easy current. They came out and dried in the sun.

She knew. The way she dressed told him. "Be ye a-comin' back, Adam?"

He embraced her. "You know I'm coming back, Johnnie-Mae," he said softly. "As soon as I can." He could make it to Smithville by nightfall. He kissed her again. "I love you. Don't forget that."

"We lay a cairn to mark a memory." She gathered a pile of rocks from the riverbank, placing them with skill to form a pyramid.

Adam watched, curious and a little amused. "What are you doing?"

"It be a tryst stane," she said, preoccupied with her effort.

He knelt beside her. "A tryst stane?"

"It be a marker o' a time when a man an' a woman have a memory ta keep. Ye wud be puttin' a wee small treasure 'neath it, Adam. Have ye a token ta mark the memory?"

He fished through his pockets. He came up with nothing more precious than a small penknife, but it was pretty, with a mother-of-pearl handle iridescent in the sunlight. He placed it under her pyramid of rocks. Across the small mound he clasped her hands, no longer wanting to leave her ever.

Johnnie Mae was wiser and had said her good-byes. Gently she kissed him, loosened her hands from his grasp, and walked slowly away from him. She didn't stop to see him leave. When Adam looked again, she had rounded the bend and was gone.

He went to Smithville. As he knocked on Zoe's door, he wasn't certain how she would greet him or what he would say.

She threw herself at him, her arms tight around his neck. "Adam, forgive me! I'm so glad you're home. You must be hungry! Where have you been? No, I didn't mean that. I won't ask. I'll ask you nothing. I don't deserve to know."

"Ma! Quit chattering—I can't say a word."

"Oh, Adam . . ." she began, then clasped her hands, pressing them against her lips, her eyes begging for forgiveness. "I thought you might go to Garrett and Leona rather than me. I was wrong. Terribly wrong and hurtful to all of you."

He walked with her into the parlor. "You weren't wrong, Ma. I didn't know what I was getting into. But now I understand. I've been through the worst of it."

"You want to join Garrett. And what of college?"

He grinned at her. "I'm going to school this fall."

"Oh, Adam!" She smiled broadly and hopped up from her chair.

He held up his hand. "But only for two years. Then I go
to sea. That's where I belong."

Garrett was still confined to his bed. "Good to see you!"
he said heartily, when Adam came in. "Leona told me what
happened after we got back from Cline's. I'm sorry, Adam.
It was a difficult thing for you to face alone."

"Perhaps it was to the good. Uncle Garrett—"

"Garrett," he said firmly. "I prefer to think of you as my
friend. A man has little choice in nephews but a great deal
of it in friends. I'd like to count you among my best."

Adam felt a pleased blush scorch its way up from his
neck to his forehead. "Thank you, sir," he gulped. "I'm—
I'm truly honored."

"Now, young man, that understood, let me say that I
don't mean ever again to involve you in the Underground
against your will. It takes more than a flair for leadership
and adventure. Leona and I saw your strength, and we
made an important decision for you. We were wrong. A
man should be dedicated to the beliefs and principles behind a cause. Unless you know why you believe a credo
and you know the kind of man you are, it is impossible for
you to be responsible for that cause."

"I may have come further in my thinking than you know,
Garrett," he said diffidently. "The catcher . . . when I shot
the catcher . . . I never saw a man die like that before. I
kept thinking, I did that. I killed him. All the things he
might have done kept coming to me. His family and
friends, hunting, fishing—I took it all away from him."

Garrett looked sharply at him. "But you do understand
it was necessary?"

"It's different for me. I wanted to kill someone once. I
even prayed it would happen. It was Edmund Revanche,
the man who mutilated Tom and killed Ullah. I thought I
had a right to kill him for what he had done."

Adam was absorbed in his talking, thinking it out as he
spoke. Garrett looked on with warm interest as he waited
for Adam to reach the conclusion for which he struggled.
Slowly Adam raised his head, looking directly at Garrett.
"I think that is like slavery, Garrett. There's not so much
difference. It's taking a life and ending all the wishes and
hopes a man has and thinking you have a right to do it.
Well, not quite the same, but—"

"No, don't belabor the question. Go on." Garrett said.

"I couldn't help what happened with the catcher. But I can help what happens to people like Jane and Marcus. Well, maybe if I don't, then that's the same as . . . I mean, if I let them be caught and returned to their masters, then I am helping him keep them captive, and they can never be anyone except who he tells them they are."

In frustration he drew his hand across his face. He was sure of what he believed, but the elements of that belief, the various links and separate thoughts that combined to form the overall feeling of rightness, were still not clearly defined for him. They tied his tongue and came out in fits and starts.

"I have heard those thoughts spoken more eloquently, Adam, but never more sincerely or truthfully. God bless you, boy."

Adam glanced quickly away from Garrett's misting eyes, blinking rapidly as he cleared his own, but he couldn't keep the pleased smile from his face. "You said once that the water route is the best way to haul slaves."

Garrett listened, again curious as to where this young man was about to lead himself.

"I'm going to the university for the next two years, but after that I am going to get my mate's papers and then my master's papers."

"And then all you need is a ship."

"It'll take me a while, but I'll get my ship."

His uncle smiled with satisfaction and decision.

"Well, when I do," Adam said, looking straight at him, "I'd like to haul the slaves by water, Garrett."

Chapter Fourteen

The platform for the Wilmington and Weldon train looked crowded as Zoe, Leona, Garrett, Tom, Angela, and Mammy all stood together wishing Adam good luck at the university. Adam boarded the train and found a seat by the window. The waving of good-byes continued for as long as the train could be seen.

As his family disappeared from sight, others who had not been there to bid him good-bye came to mind. He,

Ben, and Beau had always planned to go to the same university, study the same subjects, and apply for their mate's
papers at the same time. Now everything had changed but
himself. He would have to go on alone.

As the train took him farther north and inland through
a fine October day, Ben and Beau continued to occupy a
great portion of his thoughts, giving ground only when a
longing for Johnnie Mae would overtake all thoughts and
reduce him to feelings.

Adam left the train at Raleigh and took the coach the
remainder of the way to Chapel Hill. From the first moment when Adam entered the building where he would
begin his classes, he was aware that it was a separate world
to which he now belonged. Within the campus at Chapel
Hill there was an entire small society, enticingly different
from the rural backgrounds most of the students had left
behind them. Both days and nights were crammed with the
learning of things wonderful and tawdry, and all valuable
to growing up. Here were men who spent their days foster-
ing the mental processes of reluctant young minds. This
was not the sea, it was the land of education, but it had its
own kind of exhilaration.

By the end of the first week Adam knew he would always
remember and cherish the two years he was to spend there.
With all the enthusiasm and eagerness any professor could
ask for in a student, he plunged into his studies. He occupied his days with modern languages, chemistry, and
studies for public service.

In the evenings, though he didn't know it, Adam began
to spend his leisure hours as Tom had spent his with Edmund and Ross. There were late afternoons of cards, evenings of courting young women in hopes of finding some
who were nice but not too proper, and there were mornings
of half-laughingly nursing thumping headaches as the previous night's adventures were recounted and appraised with
new friends.

But when the laughter wasn't there and the sense of
adventure had vanished, Adam always felt terribly alone.
Apart from a few hastily scrawled letters, Adam had heard
nothing from Ben and Beau. Now it seemed important that
he should have. Theirs was a dream shared, one that should
have had its beginning this autumn. And yet it hadn't.
Though determined as ever to fulfill that dream, Adam felt

torn from those he loved, painfully aware of the hundreds of miles that separated them.

At moments like these, in place of the usual hilarity of college fun, there came a mellow kind of longing for the countryside, the people he had left. And under it all there was a young man's yearning for the shrouded greenery of the swamp and the low, husky laughter of his sunshine girl.

Johnnie Mae's image grew in his mind. With distance her backwoods dialect seemed quaint and endearing to him, her quick wanting of him more a sign that she had loved him deeply than an immediate physical desire to have her passions slaked. The vision of the rope bed in the corner of her cabin haunted him. Without him there to fill it, whose body would rest by her side, being warmed and soothed by her knowing hands?

Adam knew that his having told Johnnie Mae that he loved her had not been enough. A man who loved a woman gave her more than childish promises. By Christmas he was convinced that he truly loved Johnnie Mae and wanted to marry her.

In January of 1854 Adam returned to Crusoe Island. Certain he would find her at the creek, swimming as she had been with him that last day he saw her, he went there. The little cairn she had built and called a tryst stane still stood near the spot where they had lain together, but Johnnie Mae was nowhere in sight. He walked down the spongy path.

The door to the cabin was open, and he could hear her voice. He entered the cabin as though he were its owner, as he intended he should be. Johnnie Mae turned from the hearth fire. Near her sat a thin, rangy man, at ease and proprietary on the fur-covered chair.

"Adam, be it truly ye come back?" she asked, and got to her feet.

Adam's eyes never left the man. "I want to see you, Johnnie Mae."

"Oi be right in front o' ye, dereling."

"No, I mean I want to talk to you . . . alone."

The man stirred and came to stand behind Johnnie Mae. His hands rested lightly on her shoulders. "This be yere highborn man, Johnnie Mae?"

"This yere is Adam, Roy. He be a bootiful man, be'n't he?"

"Aye. He be."

"Johnnie Mae . . ." Adam began. "I want to talk to you. Is this your brother?" Sure of the answer, Adam put out his hand for Roy to shake.

A cracked smile crossed the man's thin face. "She be tellin' ye faws effen she say Oi be brother to 'er. She sez ye has queer notions 'bout allus bein' alone. Guess that be the curse of the highborn. Oi be goin' over to Lolly's. Oi be there when ye be a-wantin' me."

Roy sauntered off, the long piece of grass still dangling from his lips. Adam looked after him. "What did he mean you told me false? Isn't he your brother?"

Already her hands were all over him, probing inside his shirt and down the front of his trousers. "Oi be wie'out ye fer so long a span o' moons done rode the sky and was lost. Be'n't ye a-wantin' me, Adam? Be it ye've forgotten yere Eve?"

He could scarcely breathe, let alone talk, but he wanted her. As he touched her, he remembered how it had felt to touch a girl who wore nothing under her shift. Johnnie Mae's breasts fit perfectly into the cup of his hands as he gently rubbed her nipples erect.

Confident once more and wanting to play, Johnnie Mae crossed the small room, removing her shift as she walked. Her body shone in the glow from the fireplace. She stood there as he remembered her best in his fantasies alone at school, posing for him. He lay down on the rope bed, watching her, waiting for her. Johnnie Mae, hips thrust forward, rotating slightly as she came near him, walked to the bed. Adam sat up, kissing her breasts. Her hands ran through his hair, pressing him against her as she rubbed her soft, warm belly against his chest. In one motion they lay back on the bed together, Johnnie Mae straddling him and coming down on top of him.

In the dusky firelight Adam's eyes grew dark with passion. With long, slow thrusts he moved with her and against her until her body shone with the same thin coating of sweat as his own. He rolled over until she lay beneath him, his to do with as he wished. He listened as she cried his name, murmuring in her strange dialect the words of wanting and endearment she spoke too quickly and breathlessly for him to discern. But he knew their meaning, and as he trembled and held her close, he knew she was completely his.

They slept, content in each other's arms. Late in the evening she got up to fix them something to eat. She brought it back to the bed, where she sat cross-legged, feeding him a bite at a time.

"Will ye be a-stayin' wie me fer a time, Adam?"

"I want to be with you always. Would you like that Johnnie Mae?"

Head to one side, she smiled at him. "Mayhap ye not be a-likin' me iffen Oi be there fer ye anytime. Mayhap it be better a sometime lovin'."

"I'm askin' you to be my wife, Johnnie Mae."

She lay back, her laughter deep and throaty. "Ye be wantin' me to wed ye, Adam? Be'n't ye a-knowin', man, Oi be wed these many years to another?"

"What are you talking about? You're not married!"

"Aye. I be wed."

Bewildered, he glanced around the cabin. "But who ... where's your husband?"

"Me man be Roy. Yere a fine man, Adam, but Oi—"

Adam was off the bed in a moment. "Roy! You said he was your brother! What are you playing at, Johnnie Mae? No man is going to turn you over to another if you are rightly his!"

"Be ye riled wie me, Adam?"

"Hell, yes, I'm riled with you. What are you trying to do?"

"Oi be a-tellin' ye Oi kinna wed ye. But Oi be a-likin' yere lovin'. Yere a good man wie yere cock, Adam. Oi be a-likin' thet."

"Holy God! That's all it meant to you?"

"Aye. What more be there?"

"But I thought . . ." He shook his head in angry disappointment, turning from her and collecting his clothes like a scolded schoolboy.

"Didna Oi pleasure ye, Adam? Why be ye wroth wie me? Why be ye a-leavin'?" She got up from the bed, unbuttoning his shirt as he fastened his trousers, then unfastening his trousers as he tried to rebutton the shirt. "Stop it, Johnnie Mae. I thought you cared. I thought you loved me. Thank Roy for the use of his bed," he said sarcastically.

His sarcasm and anger were lost on Johnnie Mae. She stood before him, not understanding why he should behave in so peculiar a fashion. She decided that this too must be a fancy of the highborn.

Hurt and humiliated, Adam ran from the cabin. He went to the house in Smithville, spending a quiet, sullen evening with his mother. Next morning he returned to school, vowing never to come home or to see Johnnie Mae again. She was a liar and a cheat. And he was a fool.

During his last year at the university he studied hard and played even harder. Venturing far and wide, his reputation increasing as his escapades grew wilder and the trail of doting young women he left behind grew longer.

Somewhere among the long list of women's names and the half-remembered nights and the small gifts of trinkets and rings he had been given rested the memories of Johnnie Mae, long repressed and unconsidered.

Chapter Fifteen

In the spring of 1859, Captain Adam Tremain, temporary master of the *Reliable*, stood on deck as the ship entered the main channel of the Cape Fear River. It was the end of a voyage that would deliver the *Reliable* to her permanent master, Captain Tyrone Armbrister—a voyage during which Adam had begun to think his boyish dreams of saving the blacks were no more than dreams, until he once more saw the coasts of his homeland.

After a short stint as midshipman Adam got his second mate's papers. Not only was second mate a dog's-body job, Adam had the misfortune of serving under Captain Israel Sloan on a ship plying trade between Norfolk and India. He had felt Sloan's brutal bullying and been educated in the back alley, dockside brawling of Bombay. As quickly as possible he got his first mate's papers, and from then on, experienced a far easier life at sea as well as a quick rise to his captaincy. He had warm memories of good companionship and adventurous travel—Tokyo with its quaint gardens and houses; Rio de Janeiro, brilliant in sun; Nova Scotia smoky green in her mists and turbulent seacoast.

All along the Cape Fear were signs of progress and signs that nothing had changed at all. Great tracts of once stately pines stood denuded and scarred by the turpentiner's ax. In their place were loblollies, eking their existence from soil that would support no other tree.

In fields of cotton, rice, and indigo he saw teams of Negroes laboring in great gangs. But now there were more fields whose yield was sparse, more land that was not under cultivation but lay barren and naked in the hot sun. Men had continued to consume the bounty of the Southland too fast for natural recovery.

Adam had traveled to many countries in the past four years, but nowhere had the land been devastated with such speed as in his home country. Still, men looked upon the open, untouched areas of the South as though the treasure would have no end. For the Southerner, the price of land was cheaper than the price of flesh. Both were expendable.

Being home was to Adam both a joy and a sadness. Memories of bygone days along the Cape Fear and in the Green Swamp crowded in on him. It all seemed long ago and gilded with a golden haze of peace and young contentment.

Once the ship had docked and his papers were in order, Adam rented a pirogue. He felt foolish, perched long-legged and wearing the uniform of a ship's master in the small boat. But he was coming home the same way he had left it. He had had no great ship then. None of the exotic sights of the world had clouded his vision then. And they wouldn't now. To go back to the beginning where he had first placed his foot on the road to becoming what he was seemed a valid and urgent thing for him to do.

His powerful shoulders guided the boat into the once familiar channel through the Green Swamp that would take him to the swimming creek of six years ago. He moored the boat near the swimming hole. By the bank there was a small pile of stones, no longer a cairn. The wind or some creature had knocked it over. The stones held together with primitive cement clung tenaciously in dejected clumps, much like his memories of Johnnie Mae. They were no longer a unit in his mind. There were scattered moments of goodness and bitterness, but they had clung together, bringing back to him a time that seemed lost, and in the losing seemed valuable.

In place of himself and Johnnie Mae swimming, there were three children making mud houses along the bank. They were no more than three or four years old. They stopped playing as he came up, staring wide-eyed at the tall man all dressed in dark blue. He smiled, his teeth showing the whiter for the heavy dark moustache that covered his upper lip. Like scurrying pups they dived for the cover of a hideaway in the bushes. Three pale-eyed faces peeped out from the covering of golden hair and green leaf that shadowed their features.

Laughing softly, he walked down the path to Johnnie Mae's cabin. Less well kept than it once was, it stood in its solitary simplicity in the small clearing of jungle tangle. As it used to, the front door stood open, revealing little of the dusky interior. He came to stand at the stoop. His knock was light. Johnnie Mae stood just inside the door, a tarnished dream that hurt Adam far more than finding her married ever had.

With lackluster eyes she looked at the stranger at her door. "Who be ye?" she asked harshly. At her sagging naked breast rested the head of a contented infant, its small hand patting in a possessive search for her nipple.

As Adam stepped inside, Johnnie Mae reached for the musket. With one hand clutching the baby and the musket held firmly in the other, she faced him. "Oi be a-wantin' to know yere bizness, man. Who be ye?" The gun was pointed at his midsection.

"You don't remember me, Johnnie Mae?"

She stopped all motion; not even her chest moved with breathing. Slowly she smiled, blinking rapidly. The crooked tooth that had made her smile so endearing was gone. "Ye kinna be Adam," she said softly. "Ye kinna be. Ye was gone these many years. Ye be a thing o' the past."

He smiled at her, taking the musket from her. Then he laughed. "I guess maybe I am a thing of the past today." He didn't bother to tell her why he said it or why he had come back to her. She wouldn't have understood, or cared. "You didn't think I'd ever forget you, did you?"

Her head cocked on one side, she looked hard at him. "There be nowt o' the lad left in ye. Me Adam be gone fer aye," she said softly. She looked away, more aware than he of the change in her. "An' yere Eve, she be lost as well. We be like the rain seed, Adam, we let out freshet, an' the mawnin' gloam done smoothed us from the heavens."

He couldn't speak. The sunshine of Johnnie Mae was gone. It was hard and painful to look at this woman, used up and spent by Roy's utilitarian attentions, or to remem-

ber her posing for him. She was Johnnie Mae, someone
special; and he had clung to her image as a last vestige of
youth, never expecting her to change.

"Be ye hungry, Adam?" The baby still in her arms, she
shoved aside dishes from the last meal. Memories flooded
in on Johnnie Mae as well as Adam. Flustered, she glanced
about the messy cabin room. She cleaned a chair of its pile
of children's garments. "There be time fer doin' nowt but
see to the bairns," she said defensively.

Adam's hand caressed the side of her cheek. She pulled
away from him. "Oi be'n't the lass Oi was, Adam."

"Nor I the lad. Put the baby down, Johnnie Mae. Come
sit beside me."

Warily she eyed him but moved to do as he asked. She
sat on a ladder-backed chair, facing him. She was nearly
prim, sitting there with her knees tight, her arms crossed
protectively.

Adam lounged in long-legged comfort over the large
fur-covered chair. Where once he had had the rangy, long-
limbed appearance of a boy, he now had the massive com-
pactness of a large man. Every muscle in his hard body
bespoke power. Too many years and too many nights of
drunken abuse at Roy's hands had passed for Johnnie Mae
not to view this tall, heavily muscled creature before her
with fright. That she had ever had the youthful strength to
carry him up a ladder to a hammock in the loft seemed a
fantasy too fantastic even for Johnnie Mae's freedom-seek-
ing mind. Everything about Adam seemed beyond her.

He saw her uncertainty and fear. "Come sit beside me,
Johnnie Mae," he said softly. "Play you're the lady and I'm
the gentleman come to call."

The tears in her eyes were instant. She shook her head
and held herself more tightly. "Oi kinna play at bein' a
loidy no more. Oi kinna do it."

"But you can." With a large white handkerchief he
wiped away her tears, drew her hair back from her face,
and buttoned the front of her dress. "Now, my lady, call in
your eldest to watch your baby. You're going out for the
afternoon with your gentleman caller."

She shook her head.

"Do as I tell you, Johnnie Mae."

Johnnie Mae called her children, telling them exactly
what Adam had told her to say. The oldest girl looked
with fascination from her mother to Adam.

"Where be ye a-goin'. Ma? Who be the big man? Why kinna we go?"

"A gentleman be one a-needin' privacy fer his doin's, Lily. Mind ye keep good watch on the bairn." She turned to Adam. "Oi be ready, but Oi'll not be a-thankin' ye fer this, Adam."

He took her arm. Together they walked down the winding path. On the way he cut boughs from the flowering trees. As he placed the greenery in the boat to form a carpet, she looked confusedly at him.

"What be ye a-doin', Adam?" Again tears sprang to her eyes. "What be ye a-wantin' wie a pore ol' critter like meself, Adam? Ye be a-makin' a foolery o' me."

"Put your arms around me and forget all you're thinking. We're just taking a day and playing that time hasn't passed."

She looked up into his eyes, the one part of him that had not changed. They were still as clear and startlingly blue as they had been when he was a boy. She stared at him, as though by remaining locked in his gaze, she could chase the present away and go with him wherever he wanted to take her.

As Adam rowed the small craft down the creek, it became easier for her. With a very good contralto, she began singing and miming "I Wish My Captain Would Go Blind" and tossing flowers at Adam, slowly becoming in heart the gamin Johnnie Mae, who had taught him loving was not always the same or as joyous as making love.

It was sunset before he brought her back. He stood at the mooring, holding her hand. Her cheeks were flushed, and she looked happy.

"Oi be a-sayin' farewell to ye, Adam. Be ye ever in need, Oi be here fer ye, but Oi be thinkin' this be the last Oi'll see o' ye."

"It is the last time."

"Why did ye come, Adam? There weren't no need."

He touched the broken cairn with the toe of his boot. "A special time between a man and a woman should be marked for the memory."

"Aye. We made such a marker."

"Yes, but in the years I've been gone, I've learned that what has a good beginning needs also a good ending. There can be no true ending that is not in the nature of the beginning."

Johnnie Mae smiled. "Ye be a good man wie yere tongue, Adam Tremain."

"Then we'll rebuild the tryst stane."

"Aye, we will." She knelt on the soft, damp grass, gathering up the scattered remnants of the stones.

It was nearly dark when they finished. Johnnie Mae leaned forward, kissing him on the cheek, then ran off toward the path to the cabin. At the bend she paused, looking back for a moment. "Ye munna fergit to place a token, Adam. God be wie ye, Cap'n Tremain."

Adam was far down the meandering creek when Johnnie Mae came back to the creek bank. In the light of a new-rising moon she took his ring from under the cairn and held it in both of her hands as she stood staring at the swimming hole, hearing laughter and seeing sights that had happened six years before.

For Zoe, Adam's return was something she had dreamed of and then found herself unprepared for. Adam, in her parlor, filled the room with a masculine presence both potent and exciting. He eclipsed everything around him by his size, the blackness of his hair and moustache, and the air of command that had become as much a part of him as his twinkling eyes and ready smile. She found herself tittering nervously and wanting to call her own son "sir."

As soon as Adam went upstairs, Zoe wrote a message to Leona and Garrett. Periodically she would stop and listen, her eyes fastened on the ceiling. His footsteps on the floor above made her shiver in excited memory. She put her cool hands up to her flushed cheeks. It was impossible that Adam as a man could bring back so sharply those warm, love-filled days of the summer before her marriage. She found herself longing for his father as she hadn't done in years.

She gave the note to a young black boy to deliver to Leona, pressing a penny into his hand.

With great relief Zoe received Leona's reply that she and Garrett would be coming to stay for three days. Tom and Angela would come with them. She hurried to tell Mammy of their guests. With people in the house keeping her mind on what was at hand, perhaps the look in Adam's eyes and the deep, rich sound of his laughter would not make her think so often of the man from whom Adam had inherited those eyes and that voice.

But with Adam sitting across from her, talking easily of the great houses he had seen and visited in Brazil and the beauty of the Canary Islands, Zoe became increasingly conscious of the feel of her clothing against her skin, her smile and manners, the way she looked through his eyes. She found herself giggling, then losing track of the conversation. She couldn't believe at her age it was possible for her to act like such a simpleton. It was not reason enough that Adam had the same crackling, electric sexual vitality as the only man she had ever loved. The door to her memory had been thrown wide in the first few minutes, and she found it far more difficult to close than it had been to open.

Leona, Garrett, Angela, and Tom stood on the stoop. As Zoe opened the door, both men complimented her, and Leona stared as though she had seen a ghost.

"Come in," Zoe said, her smile broad. Her voice was tinged with happy laughter that bubbled up unwanted and unexpected. "Would you care for some liquid refreshment, Garrett, Tom?" She was nearly dancing around the room as she flitted from one of them to the other. Her cheeks were flushed and her eyes bright.

Leona continued to study her in silence. Then she said, "Zoe, I declare, you look like a young girl." At that moment Leona's attention was distracted. "Oh, my stars! Zoe! This can't be him!"

"Dat's him all right, Miz Leona!" Mammy beamed. "He be a fine ol' man, jes' like Ah allers knowed he be."

"You're my woman, Mammy," Adam said cheerfully, putting his arm around her shoulders.

"Ah ain't no sech a thing! Ah's yo' Mammy!"

Leona laughed. "Come sit with me, Adam. I want to hear about your travels. And don't you dare leave out one bit of gossip!"

Tom looked on this man he loved, as his daughter, Angela, shy with a newly awakened ten-year-old's femininity, moved closer. Affectionately Adam took her hand, including her in his magical circle of being. As she listened to his stories of far-off places where kings and queens and princes walked on red carpets and knights rode to the tournaments amid the trumpeting and colors of pageantry, her eyes glowed brightly on the warm presence of her own

knight. There was no one on earth she'd rather love than
Adam.

Adam was Angela's escort to dinner, when Mammy,
caught up in his aura as wildly as the others, appeared in
the doorway with a new apron and a crisp, starched white
tignon covering her head.

"Suppah is suhved," she announced in stentorian tones.

It was a gay meal, filled with more talk of the years that
had passed. Garrett and Leona told about the activities of
the Underground Railroad and the warrish temper of the
Southern people.

After coffee, Adam rose. "If you'll excuse us, ladies, the
gentlemen will retire to the study."

"They always run off to hide," Leona complained.

There was a companionable silence in the study as each
man mulled over his own thoughts and sipped his brandy.
Adam smiled at Tom. "So, Garrett has you thoroughly involved in the Underground now, has he?"

"Up to my eyeballs. Why, aside from Seth an' a few of
the swamp people, I hardly see a white face for days at a
time."

"Tom's cabin is a safer place to keep the blacks then our
house is."

Tom glanced at Garrett, then grinned at Adam. "What
we need is some old tar who's not afraid to put his neck
in a noose."

Adam played with his cigar, turning it in his mouth,
his teeth showing brilliant white as his smile grew. "I know
of one, maybe three."

"Three! Who?" Tom sputtered.

"My last port before I came home was New Orleans.
Captain Ben West and Captain Beau LeClerc are taking
you up on that offer of a visit you extended them years
ago, Tom. They'll soon be heading for Smithville."

"By God!" Tom breathed. "Garrett, they're the salt o'
the earth—sea too, I guess. Damn!"

"These are the two boys you grew up with, Adam?"

Tom was hopping excitely in his chair. "Wait'll you
meet them, Garrett. We'll be takin' slaves out by the score.
These three haven't got a fearful bone in their bodies."

Garrett looked concerned. "A man can hang for stealing
a slave or inducing him to run."

"Don't discourage him before he's gotten started, Garrett."

Adam smiled. "Set your mind at ease. You're not leading us astray."

Garrett asked in a musing voice, "You like the sharp knife of fear cutting at you, do you, Adam?"

"Not the fear, but the challenging of it. I'm ready to begin whenever I can get a ship."

Tom looked impishly at Garrett. "Is it time to tell him?"

"Tell me what?"

"We've got a ship for you, Adam, a kind of gift from Tom and me."

"My God, you've left me speechless. A ship!"

"A steamer. Garrett an' I don't know ships. We're not sure of what we've got."

Adam still had his dazed look of incredulity as Garrett explained. "You'll take the darkies to the north shore of Long Island. Rod Courtland will meet you there, and then he will see to them. The first trip will be nothing but a trial run. Tom and I will be your only passengers."

Adam still did not understand. "Rod Courtland?"

"Yes. As I once told you, Rod Courtland and I went to school in Boston together. The years have fled, but the friendship has remained steadfast. You and Rod will set the schedule of trips when you go up there. He will help you set up a legitimate merchant trade between New York and the Southern ports."

As they talked, the business matters were cleared away one at a time. There were four partners in the shipping venture: Garrett, Tom, Roderick Courtland, and Adam. The profits would be divided evenly among them, and Ben and Beau would be paid according to Adam's own means.

"Well, it sounds promising," Adam said. "But I am certainly the weak link in this outfit. It's your ship, your capital, your goods."

Garrett said gravely, "Don't underestimate the seriousness of your part, Adam. In effect this will make you a criminal in the South and a smuggler in the North. You'd be quite a prize for a few interested parties to capture and turn over to the South."

"Each of us has his own reasons for taking risks. Tom knows mine."

Tom cleared his throat. "Shall we take a look at the ship before it's too dark to see?"

Garrett said agreeably, "I'll go see to the carriage, then."

Adam glanced around at the clutter of glasses and cigar ashes and rang for someone to clean up.

"What you want, Mas' Adam?"

"You can clear away now, Mammy. Isn't there anyone else to do this?"

"Yassuh, but dey's a bunch o' wuthless free niggers. Ain't nobody gwine ten' to you 'cep' Mammy long's Ah got breaf in mah body."

"Sure you won't be my woman, Mammy?"

"You get yo' big ol' han's offen me, or mebbe Ah's gwine change mah min'." Her face screwed up into a stifled smile before she burst out in rolling girlish giggles.

Tom watched their teasing with a half-smile. When Mammy left the room, Adam said, "Garrett should be ready. We'd better go."

Tom shook his head. "He knows I wanted to talk to you alone."

Adam sat back down in his chair, leaning forward, his elbows resting on his knees.

"There isn't an easy way for me to say this to you, Adam. After all the years you'd think . . . but I just never got over Ullah's death."

"Tom, you and I have never had to talk out loud about this."

"There's somethin' she'd want you to know . . . an' now she's not here to tell you herself." Slowly Tom got up and went to where he had left his coat. When he returned, he held Ullah's small, battered box of treasures. He placed it between himself and Adam, then lifted the lid so the contents of the box were exposed.

"She kept all the things that meant the most to her in this box." He touched the shells, the clay doll, several pieces of jewelry. "Mostly I gave them to her." He picked up Zoe's letter. "She meant to show that to Angela when she was old enough. Ullah thought maybe a letter from a lady as fine as your mama would help Angela not to be ashamed of her."

"Angela would never have been ashamed of Ullah."

"Maybe not, but Ullah didn't know that. She didn't complain, mind you, but Ullah's life, well, she'd been taught to expect the worst." Tom's eyes were watering so badly he couldn't see. His hand trembled as he replaced the letter in the box.

"Tom, we don't need to talk about this. I remember Ullah. I'll never forget her as long as I live. I loved her."

Tom nodded his head with deep swoops. "I know . . . I know . . . but see, Adam, you were somethin' special to Ullah. God forgive me, there was a time I was jealous. Right from the very first time she saw you, she knew. She said it was like lookin' at a lake full of white swans an' then seein' a black one. You just know that one black swan was somethin' God made special. She knew that." Trying to impress the import of his words on Adam physically, he clasped Adam's forearm. "She never got to tell you." Tom was crying outright now, and Adam found tears welling in his own eyes.

"Thank you for telling me, Tom. I—"

"That ain't all." He dragged the box nearer to him. With reverential care, Tom took out a package wrapped in gaily decorated paper. Tom held it gently in both of his hands, staring at it as he spoke. "See, Adam, seems like all your life, leastways since Ullah and I knew you, you've been called upon to help her kind, even though you never sought it. But it's like she saw it . . . she knew. Ullah, seems like, knew a lot of things with her dreamin' an' her thinkin'. Around me, she called you her black swan."

He put the package in Adam's hands. "I got this special made for her. I was goin' to give it to her that Christmas." He wiped at his eyes. "You've become what Ullah always knew you would. She'd want you to have this, Adam. Go ahead. Open it. It's a Christmas gift long overdue."

Carefully Adam unwrapped the small package. Cushioned among the wrappings, made of hand-blown glass, was a delicate black swan. The light caught in the dark glass, sparkling off the wings and the gracefully curving neck, taking away his breath with his speech as he looked at the miniature piece of art that had represented him in Ullah's eyes. His chest grew tight as he thought of her, remembered the clear oval of her face, the laughing dark eyes that had teased him and cared about him.

He turned the black swan in his hands and tried to see in it and in himself what she had seen. Before him there lay a tapestry of unfinished threads on which was mapped out the many trips he would make from the South with his cargo of dark-faced people seeking the unfettered North.

But that wasn't all. Even though Adam vaguely realized that the slave hauling was but a small part of the meaning of the black swan, he had no way of seeing what lay beyond the next year.

BOOK II

Dulcie

1850-1862

Chapter One

Dulcie had been fighting again. She had scratched and kicked Jothan, a child who under more favorable circumstances would have been her physical equal. But Jothan found himself in direct jeopardy from all sides. Though they played and took their schooling together, and got each other into trouble several times daily, Dulcie was still his Little Miss. No pickaninny was allowed to hit Little Miss. Jothan knew it was so, for his mother, Ester, had thumped his small woolly head with her knuckles countless times for doing just that.

He was about to risk another thumping and give Little Miss a barefooted kick in the shins, when Ester came boiling out of her cabin to see what the commotion was. As if this wasn't discouraging enough, down the dirt path from the house came Dulcie's mammy. There was fire in her eye, as much for the black child as for the white one.

"Miss Dulcie!" she roared. "You, Jothan! What in tarnation y'all scufflin' 'bout dis time?"

"Jothan, you come right back here!" Ester yelled as her son ran to hide in the cavernous reaches of the stables.

"Mammy, make Jothan give me my marble!" yelled Dulcie, jumping up and down, her red pigtails bouncing. "He won't let me have it!"

Dulcie had made a mistake, staying in one place. Mammy grabbed her arm. "You hesh yo' mouf! Mastah Jem give Jothan dat marble!"

Dulcie twisted in Mammy's grasp. "But I won it, an' I want it!"

"Dey's folks in de hot place wantin' ice water, an' dey ain't gittin' what dey wants neither! Ah had mo'n enuf o' you today! You, Ester, it's 'bout time you learned dat uppity li'l pickaninny some manners!"

"Ah doan see you makin' out so good yo'seff, Mammy," Ester retorted. Quickly she turned away, calling in a stern voice for Jothan to come right out of them stables or she'd tan his hide.

Dulcie squirmed and jerked. Mammy held her firmly.

"You is gwine to bed, Miss Dulcie. How you 'spects to grow up 'n' be a lady if you allers fisticuffin' an' screamin' like a peacock? Ladies doan climb trees an' show dey pant'lettes, an' dey doan chunk odder people in dey faces! Ah gits plum petered out wiff makin' you behave yo'seff!"

"It's mine," Dulcie said sullenly. "I betted him I could jump fu'ther'n him. He on'y jumped from Beauty's stall partway over to Buffy's—so I clumb up the ladder an' jumped from the loft, an' I won!"

"Bless de Lawd, chil'," said Mammy, paling visibly. "Doan you do dat agin, you heah me? Yo' daddy fin's out you jump outer de loft an' he skin me alive. De Debbil muster been 'sleep, or you'd broke both yo' legs!"

"But I didn't," said Dulcie with satisfaction. "And it's *my marble!*"

James Moran stuck his head into the small parlor where his wife, Patricia, sat doing needlepoint in an oval frame. "Patsy love, why don't you come for a buggy ride with me?"

Patricia smiled up at him. "Ah *am* gettin' right bored with shovin' that needle in an' out. Jem, we need to have a pahty."

"There's one next week at the Saunderses."

"Ah mean a pahty heah! A big pahty! Ask Mad an' Ca'line to come an' stay ovah, have a ball an' a barbecue! An' a tiltin' tourney foah the young gentlemen! Ah can staht askin' folks next week."

"Not so fast, Patsy, not so fast." Jem laughed. "We can talk about that later." As though he suddenly noticed the quiet, he looked about the room. "Where's Dulcie? She's not in bed already? She's not sick?"

Patricia sighed. "Oh, no, but Ah very nearly wish she was! Mammy told me she was bein' mean to three of the pickaninnies today, an' she struck Jothan! Sometimes, Jem, Ah jes' don't know what's to come o' that child."

"Jothan brought it on himself, I'll wager." Jem grinned. Secretly he was pleased that his daughter could hold her own. "Don't you worry about Jothan, love. He'll get even with her."

"Well, Ah don't know, Jem, she's all worked up 'bout somethin'. Did you give Jothan a present? Somethin' Dulcie might want?"

"A bag of marbles to be divided among all the little boys is all."

"What would a little girl want with marbles?" She took her husband's arm, looking up at him fondly. "Today, deah, Ah believe Dulcie is all youahs and none of mine. Why, when *Ah* was six, mah mama declared Ah was a perfect li'l lady."

"It's her red hair," said Jem complacently. His own was the same color. "Red hair gives people strong passions."

Patricia blushed hotly and patted him on the arm with her fingertips. "Jem Moran, you have got a very naughty mind! And besides, weah talkin' 'bout youah daughtah, not youahself!"

Jem thought fleetingly that he *was* talking about Dulcie.

They drove down the double line of crape myrtles that separated clover-thick lawn from vegetables gardens and the orchard beyond. In the long open spaces dust devils rose and died down in the constant, drying wind.

Jem stopped the carriage. With a broad sweep of his thick square hand he indicated the field that stretched and rolled before him. The late-afternoon sun cast hot-looking shadows at the feet of the wilted plants. "This is what I wanted you to see. It proves everythin' I've been sayin'. The land's gone barren. Our Mossrose is dyin' on us, Patsy love."

The summer had been exceptionally dry. Now, in mid-August, in the cotton fields stood a poor crop thickly covered with red-brown dust. On the lowest branches the bolls had turned brown and split open to show the snowy locks ready for the first picking. Patricia's gaze moved outward, down the long rows to the dark, ragged pine forest crouched waiting to reclaim the brilliant earth that had been cleared with so much difficulty.

She shivered slightly. Turn one's back and the trees would creep up and take over again. "How big a crop do you reckon on this season, Jem?"

"Unless we get a freshet soon, we'll be lucky to get half last year's. And it, you'll recollect, was mighty pindlin'."

"But it will bring enough to keep the plantation through next yeah?"

"That's why I wanted to talk to you, without the servants eavesdroppin' and chatterin' about it all over the county. Patsy darlin', we're runnin' out of money."

Her eyes widened. "But ouah credit is still good! Isn't it?"

"Not as good as it was before. I've bartered and traded to the hilt, and we're still in need of cash!"

"But the cotton—"

"The cotton crop may pay back the last loan. It won't buy you pretty dresses or see you off on visits to your kinfolk. I can't say positively that the vegetable gardens will feed us through the winter. The field hands are totin' water, but nothin' is doing well. Nothin', Patsy."

She turned soft, confident brown eyes on him. "But you'll bring us out of it all right, Jem. Have you worked out a plan?"

He drew a deep breath and seemed to grow taller and sturdier. "That I have, Patsy love. I'm goin' to spread out, do things different, quit totin' all my eggs in one basket."

"Violet says the hens have got the sulks too."

Sometimes Jem was hard-pressed not to lose his temper with literal Patricia. She was very young, untutored in worldly ways. Her saving grace was that she loved him without reserve and she believed in him. The edge of his impatience softened. "Forget the hens for now, Patsy. They're Asa's job, and I'll have Wolf speak to him tomorrow. I'm talkin' about field upon field of puny cotton. We're goin' to have to let the land rest. You know, Patsy, that's one of the troubles of the South today."

"Jem deah, don't let's get stahted on the whole South. You know how it boahs me. Ah thought we were talkin' about ouahselves."

"I am, but let me lead up to it, Madam," he said, irritable again.

"Very well, Jem," she said with cool dignity. "Ah'll just sit heah quiet as a beetle and listen to you."

"The South," he began expansively, "thinks the land will go on forever, all on its own, without any replenishment, just raising the same cash crops in the same fields time without end. Most planters are too fine-frocked to have their darkies spread manure and plow it in."

"But you've been doin' the same as they did!"

"I know, I know, and me who knows better. You're lookin' at the results right out there. Every stalk of cotton dry as popcorn."

"But next yeah—"

"Patsy, when the land wears out, the planter's got few

choices. He can sell, if anybody'll buy. He can abandon everythin', move his family to a new place, and begin again. Or he can build up his fields for a few years and then start rotatin' his crops."

"A few yeahs! Jem, how can we manage to keep all ouah people fed and clothed and tended if we don't have good credit or cash or a crop?"

"If we don't raise crops, we don't need so many field hands."

"You mean, sell off—"

"Sell off every slave we don't need. Use the money for capital while I'm startin' on my grand plan. Now, the North has a lot of advantages the South hasn't got—"

"James Moran, it was bad enough when mah sister Mad married Oliver Raymer and moved to N'Yawk, but Ah set mah foot down. Ah'm stayin' right heah."

"Quiet as a beetle. Your very words." He touched a finger to her lips. "I figure that the things the North has are as much mine by right as the things of the South. I should have thought of this long ago. With the capital I'll have from sellin' a hundred prime field hands, I'm goin' to do three things. I'm goin' to build the land back up. I'm goin' to invest in textile mills in the North—Oliver is willin' to run a mill for me on shares. And"—he braced himself against her shock—"I'm goin' to turn Mossrose into a breedin' farm."

"Foah hawses?"

"I'm goin' to breed slaves." Into her wide-eyed silence he said hastily, "There's a huge market for them all over the Deep South. Maryland, Virginia, North Carolina, and Kentucky have great farms that do little else but breed slaves."

"Jem, that's wicked!"

"Wicked, is it! No more so than havin' those we've got starve along with us! But they'll have plenty to do besides lie about and make babies."

"James Moran, Ah fin' youah conversation *highly* objectionable!"

"Patsy love, I'll speak no more of it. But my mind is made up. I'm never goin' to let myself get caught with my hat in my hand at the doors of a bank again. My Irish forebears survived worse than this on potatoes, rocks, and manure, and we can do the same!"

After a silence she said, "Well, then, that's all settled, Jem."

"We'll start next week, Patsy." He ran his hands through his thick pale red hair and let the breeze cool his head. "I've talked to Spig Hurd, the slave trader. He'll come by on Tuesday to pick out the first lot."

Patricia shuddered. "Ah wish there was some other way. If it's manure yoah needin', Jem, wouldn't breedin' hawses be just as good?"

"It's all decided," Jem said firmly.

"Jem, youah the head o' the household, and it's youah right to do what you think best for us all. But have you thought about what this might do to ouah li'l Dulcie?"

Jem hadn't thought of Dulcie. "Why?" he asked belligerently. "The darkies breed all the time anyway. What's a six-year-old child going to know?"

"She isn't always goin' to be six. She's goin' to turn twelve and fifteen. She's bound to notice, to heah somethin' a young lady shouldn't ought to heah."

"It will be good practice in stoppin' her ears, then," he said shortly. "Besides, she's already watched me and Asa puttin' the bull to the cows."

Patricia put her hand to her forehead as if about to faint. "Mah baby! An' you been smirchin' up her mind, lettin' her see those animals? Oh! Oh!"

"It wasn't so much let her as not knowin' she was there, Patsy. She was lookin' down from the loft while we were busy. How's I to know she'd be up there in the haymow with the new kittens?"

"You got her right out of there, Ah hope?"

"Well, yes, as soon as I knew she—"

"You didn't *tell* her anythin', Jem?"

"Well, I . . . the fact of the matter is, I did. She asked me what we were makin' the bull do that for, so I jes' said he was helpin' the cow, uh, make a little calf." Into his wife's stunned, glacial silence he added, "She might as well know while she's young enough to see it as a natural event." This not helping particularly, he said, "Unless you want her to grow up into such a fine lady that her husband'll have to tell her how it is between man and wife."

Patricia was red from the roots of her hair clear down inside the modest cleavage of her brown tulle afternoon dress. Tears sprang from her eyes. "Jes' like a man! He wants his bride to be innocent and then blames her because she knows nothin' about men!"

Patricia, Jem observed, was winding up for a high old bawling spell. He said gently, "Now Patsy, have I ever once blamed you? No! You were a lady born and bred, and I've always respected that in you. Our Dulcie was born a tomboy, as much lad as lass. A good thing too, since she'll be our only child. By the time you've molded her into a lady, it will be all to your credit and entirely due to your good sense. But don't curb her spirit and her natural curiosity to the place you stifle them!"

"That's far moah desirable than what you—" She broke off, still blushing, hiding her tears in a lacy handkerchief.

He patted her awkwardly. "I'll look around first, next time. This one glimpse isn't goin' to ruin her, Patsy. Not unless you decide to make a point of it."

"Ah do b'lieve the damage has already been done!"

Jem sighed sharply, his short patience exhausted. "For your information, Madam, our daughter is not goin' to grow up so delicate she doesn't even know that hens lay eggs! Since when is it damagin' to a child's brain to get a bit of knowledge into it?"

Patricia wiped her eyes, but a tear leaked out now and then to punctuate her diminishing sobs. "You did give youah word to keep Dulcie away from the animal breedin' areas."

"I said I'd look around, didn't I? Besides, what's she got Mammy for?"

Abruptly changing the subject, Patricia put her husband on the defensive again. "I s'pose bein' short o' cash means we can't have pahties."

Jem recognized the maneuver; Patricia's solution to everything was always the most socially fashionable. A party might make a breeding farm acceptable to her. "Does this party you speak of mean so much to you?"

"Oh, yes, Jem . . . please!" She put her hand on his arm, her tear-stained face lifted to his. "Ah won't have to have a new dress or anythin'! We can have it aftah the weathah cools off, an' Ah'll weah mah lavendah silk you like so well. An' we can ask the Saunderses an' Chilcotes an' Biggses. . . ."

Jem, relieved to have safely surmounted Patricia's resistance, grinned at his wife. "And you can have a new dress too."

She squeezed his hand rapturously. "Jem honey, youah too generous foah youah own good! No, Ah'll be a thrifty li'l wife! You'll see!"

They rode back to the house in the dusty red rays of sunset, Jem more at ease and hopeful than he'd been the past two summers. Patricia was already planning her party, trying hard not to think about the other thing, for she could feel herself blushing every time she considered telling Agatha Saunders about the farm for breeding people.

Patricia's attention was caught by a flash of white out near the quarters. It moved very fast in several directions at once, then suddenly pounced on an unseen object in the grass. The motions were punctuated by childish yells of rage intermingled with those of attempted conciliation.

"Dulcie!" Patricia gasped. "In her nightdress!"

"Where in hell is Mammy? I'll tan her for this! Mammy!" Jem roared.

Mammy materialized from a cabin, hastily straightening her clothing. She reached down into the writhing mass of nightgown and extracted her charge as Jem and Patricia approached.

". . . an' he swallied it so's I can't have it!" Dulcie was wailing.

"Swallowed what?" asked Jem. "Who swallowed somethin'?"

"Jothan—he put my marble in his mouth an' he let it go down! Now it's in his stummick, an' I want it!" She began to cry desolately.

Jem knelt down. "Dulcie, come over to your daddy."

Mammy shoved Dulcie toward Jem; Dulcie jerked loose and went to sit on her father's knee. Once safely there, she made a face at Jothan.

"Dulcie Jeannette, listen to me. That marble you're scrappin' over belongs to Jothan because I gave it to him. Do you understand?"

"But I want—"

"Hush! You're not to take toys away from the darkies. I absolutely forbid you to have that marble."

Dulcie considered crying some more. Instead she looked into her father's eyes stubbornly. "It had a blue lady in it," she whispered. "A pretty blue lady."

"I don't care if it had a double eagle in it, it's not yours."

* * *

Not another word was mentioned about the marble until, two days later, Dulcie sat in her mother's parlor. She had a small object she was rolling around in her hand, holding it up to the light and marveling at it.

"What is that, Dulcie?" Patricia asked.

"A marble."

Patricia got up from her desk, coming close to her daughter to gaze disbelievingly at the marble with the blue lady in it.

"Did youah daddy bring you that?"

"No, Mama."

"Well, wheah did you get it?"

Dulcie rubbed the marble over her jaw and cheek, smiling in delight. "It's mine. Jothan didn't want it anymore."

"Ah thought Jothan swallowed it."

"He did, but I followed him till it comed out."

Patricia blushed, setting her lips tightly. This was all Jem's fault. He was too careless of a little girl's natural sensibilities. And Patricia, considering Dulcie's store of unchildlike knowledge, knew this wouldn't be the last such problem.

The Morans missed no meals while Jem developed Mossrose into a breeding farm. The initial sale of slaves bolstered his credit. Later he sold timbering rights to a section he wanted cleared. Patricia proved to be thriftier than he had ever dreamed, seeming to take pleasure in making over and making do. As a lady should, she ignored the seamier aspects of their new life, complaining only when Dulcie was involved. Otherwise she let Jem do what he wished. If Jem wanted to send his field hands over to neighboring plantations for wagonloads of manure to spread on the fields, he knew what he was doing. If Jem felt he needed to oversee the human breeding as he did the animal breeding, that was Jem's affair. She pretended to know nothing of it.

To Jem's mind, overseeing the breeding of his slaves was important. Fellie, Darcy, and three of the females were pure Gullah. He would keep the strain pure. Jem permitted Fellie and Ester, his two best Gullahs, to live as a family, because they had done so in the past and because he liked Fellie. For the other slaves, there were no families. There were merely studs and females ready for conception. With the blacks whose African lineage was no longer pure, he bred with an eye to docility, intelligence, size, and length and strength of limb. There was no mating at Mossrose that hadn't Jem's approval. There would be no weakening of his stock by indiscriminate coupling. His animals would be of the finest quality.

Patricia was busy every waking minute with the management of the house and her responsibilities for the welfare of the slaves. However, her main concern was keeping Dulcie innocent. When the slave quarters suddenly seemed full to bursting with gravid females, all apparently due to deliver on the same night, Patricia set her small foot down. "Jem, you've got to buy a midwife."

Jem bought Ludy, calm and intelligent, a slave who had been taught to read. Ludy was exactly what Patricia had specified. The only problem was that she and Dulcie's Mammy hated each other on sight.

Mammy had always been the queen bee, lording her position of caring for Little Miss over the others. Now, Ludy, while not a house servant, held a position as important to the plantation as Mammy's. Ludy also had a good singing voice and rivaled Mammy in another of her strongholds, the prayerhouse.

At Patricia's request Jem had built a small chapel that the slaves called their prayerhouse. Inside were the long backless benches the Negroes preferred, so that if the Lawd moved them to sway or writhe or leap up with the coming of the Spirit, their movements would be unhampered. Up in front was the small area where Mammy stood as she led them in song. The first night Ludy was there, she unwittingly took Mammy's place.

It wasn't the end to the insults heaped on Mammy. Weekday mornings Patricia taught the slaves rudimentary reading, writing, and arithmetic. Ludy could both read and figure, something Mammy had never learned, for Mammy was a grown woman long before Patricia ever held school.

Jem was not enthusiastic about educating his darkies, for education meant discontent, and a discontented slave meant constant little irritations. But Patricia having steeled herself for the inevitabilities of slave breeding, argued that when it came time to sell them, the educated ones would bring more.

In 1852 Jem installed a spinning house, in which rough

linens for the plantation could be made, with extra to sell to neighboring planters. He put Fellie, a regal black of nearly perfect proportions, in charge of his cobbler's shop. Fellie was not only Jem's best breeding stud, he was intelligent and hardworking. Without need of guidance or a driver, Fellie taught others how to make and mend shoes.

By 1854 Mossrose had taken on the look of a prosperous small town. Scattered down the hill from the main house were two neat rows of whitewashed buildings, each housing a separate industry where Jem's people took quiet pride in their work.

The largest building, the best built and equipped, was the nursery. Until a child was old enough to walk, he was kept there, closely supervised. At specified times the mothers left their work and went to nurse their babies. At odd hours either Patricia or Mammy would inspect the nursery. The elevation of Mammy to inspector of the babies had quieted the rivalry between herself and Ludy, who was only a midwife after all, but it hadn't erased the undercurrents of hostility. Mammy took her inspection seriously. As she put it, "Dem chilluns better be took good care of, 'cause Mastah Jem gots a lots o' money tied up in 'em. Dey's quality niggers."

Slowly Jem's dying Mossrose came alive again. The plantation was transformed into something more prosperous and different from what it had been. As it changed, so did Dulcie. At ten she was gangly, all hands, feet, and teeth that didn't fit together yet. Her red hair had darkened to a glinting coppery tone. Her pigtails had given way to curls that bounced when she walked or, more usually, ran.

But some things had not changed. Dulcie stayed in trouble with her parents or Mammy most of the time. Her eyes saw too much. Her swift, undisciplined mind concluded too much. For a young lady she knew too much of the wrong sort of thing. As Patricia had feared, Dulcie saw pregnant women daily and took for granted that darkies had babies every year. Only her mother, Mammy, and Ludy seemed exempt. Dulcie concluded they were too old.

Then one summer morning, as Mammy dressed her, things Dulcie had been noticing all came together. Mammy's heavy body had always been soft and pursy, swathed in osnaburg and covered by her white apron. Now Mammy's apron was higher, the strings were shorter, and her belly, pressing against Dulcie's shoulders as she brushed her hair, was hard, no longer soft.

"Mammy, are you in a family way?"

Mammy dropped the hairbrush. In the mirror Dulcie saw her eyes bulge and her mouth pop open. "What make you ast me a thing like dat, Miss Dulcie? Yo' mama scold you good did she fin' out you astin' questions!"

Dulcie had not taken her eyes off Mammy's face. "You are, aren't you?" When Mammy didn't answer, she went on, "Mama doesn't know yet, does she?"

"Bless de Lawd, Miss Dulcie, doan you go tellin' Miss Trishy! Ah got a swellin'. Yes, ma'am. A swellin'. It go down purty soon."

"What kind of swellin'? Where did you get it from?"

"No kin' o' swellin' you needs to know nothin' 'bout, chil'. Mammy got bit by a trowser worm, dat's all."

Dulcie, with a directness that would have delighted her father and made her mother swoon, asked, "When's it supposed to get born, Mammy?"

Mammy threw up her hands in combined fear and resignation. "Miss Dulcie, yo' mama fin' out Mammy in de family way an' she sell me. You doan wan' yo' ol' Mammy selled, does you?"

"I can keep a secret as well as you can." For the first time in her life Dulcie had the upper hand over Mammy. "I can help you keep it from Mama if you want me to. Is Ludy goin' to help with the birthin'?"

"No, ma'am," said Mammy firmly. "Ah he'p mahseff. Dat Ludy done put de bad eye on me, or Ah doan be in dis fix."

"Where are you goin' to go when it's time for it to get born?"

"Asa make me a baid. Doan you worrit, chil'. Mammy kin manage."

When her time came, Mammy could not manage to leave the house. Closely followed by Dulcie, who had hampered her every move for days, Mammy was in the plunder room, a small storage room where "play-pretties" were kept. In the narrow space between the rows of shelves, Mammy hardly had space to turn around.

"Miss Dulcie, you de wustest chil' Ah evah did see fo' gittin' undahfoots," she said in exasperation. "You got to give Mammy room accordin' to her stren'th, an' Ah feelin' strong terday."

"You don't look very strong," Dulcie retorted. "How come you stop every now and then and bend over and go all sweaty?"

"It's mah swellin'. Kickin' up a stawm dis mawnin'."

Then the storm broke. As Dulcie watched, half-fascinated and half-horrified, water ran over the floor and into the low corners of the room.

Mammy's voice was strange. "Chil', git inter de ragbag an' git a couple ol' rag rugs. Mammy got to lay down on de flo' awhiles."

Dulcie, full of questions, moved speedily, reaching into the pile of washed dark-colored rags. "It's time, isn't it, Mammy?"

Mammy was hanging onto a shelf, her eyes bulging. "Git outer heah. Dis minit. Heah me?"

Instead Dulcie shut the door. "You don't want Mama to find you here, do you? I can help you."

Mammy sank to the floor. "Miss Dulcie," she panted, "you kin he'p me mos' of all effen you go 'stract Miss Trishy. Go out an' git inter a scuffle wiff somebody."

"I don't get into scuffles anymore," Dulcie said coolly. "Except sometimes with Glenn Saunders, 'cause' he's a priss."

As Dulcie watched, Mammy strained and grunted, stopped and strained again. But nothing seemed to be happening. Mammy kept her struggle as quiet as possible, but a groan escaped now and then. She rolled from one side to the other in a sort of rhythm.

"Does it hurt, Mammy?"

"Not . . . so bad. Git on out, chil'." Her tone was pleading.

"Mama's gonna switch us both anyway. What can I do?"

For a while Mammy didn't answer, lying there moving her head from side to side. "Chil'? Mammy got to pull her skirts up. You look an' see effen dat baby's head comin' out."

Dulcie looked. Wonder of wonders, there was a tiny head partway out of Mammy. "It's there! I see it!" she said excitedly.

"Ssshh! Miss Trishy heah you! Take holt an' pull a li'l bit, not too strong, jes' keep steady." Dulcie did as she was told, turning the baby's shoulders until suddenly there on the floor lay Mammy's newborn child. Mammy, panting heavily, said, "Git clean rags an' wrop it up warm an' put it on Mammy's boozum."

Mammy held her child close, patting it hard on its tiny back until it began to cry in thin, short little wails.

"Make it quit, Mammy! Mama might hear!"

"Can't he'p it, Miss Dulcie. Dis chil' got to git breaf someways."

Suddenly the plunder room door opened. Patricia, a bunch of summer flowers in her hand, stood with one foot inside the room. Her eyes flitted unbelievingly from Mammy, on the floor with her skirts up to her knees and an infant screaming on her broad breast, to Dulcie, who had shrunk against the shelves all hunched up as if her mother might strike her.

"Dulcie—Moran! What—is—goin'—on—heah?"

Dulcie and Mammy spoke together: "Mammy just birthed a baby, Mama." "Ah tried to git Miss Dulcie outa heah, Miss Trishy—"

Dulcie added, "It's a boy, Mama."

Patricia's voice, when it came out, was hoarse and ragged. "Dulcie Jeannette, go straight to youah room! *This minute!*"

Dulcie stepped carefully over Mammy and scooted past her mother, lingering partway down the hall hoping to hear what was said.

"Get up those stairs!" her mother screamed in a tone she had never heard before. She ran up and turned the corner, still listening.

Snatches of conversation floated up to her. "Ah've nevah been so shamed—never expected mah Mammy to do this . . . mah innocent child!" There was the humble entreating tone of Mammy's voice but no words. Then the pronouncement of doom: "Mr. Jem will sell you tomorrow!"

"Please, Miss Trishy . . . please . . ."

Dulcie ran back down the stairs. She clutched her mother's hand. "No, Mama, please don't! Don't sell Mammy. I'll be good! I promise forever and ever!"

Patricia Moran, with a terrible expression on her gentle face, turned her daughter over her knee and gave her the only spanking of her life. She took her by the arm and marched her to her room and locked her in. Then she went to find Jem. He and his grand scheme had brought this on them, and he could provide the solution.

Mammy had been right about one thing. Neither of the Morans wanted a Mammy with a newborn baby. Her job was to train Dulcie to become a Southern lady having no knowledge of carnality or its consequences. Almost too quickly to comprehend, Mammy found herself locked up. For Jem, Mammy no longer existed. She was too old to breed; she was a disobedient servant. Worst of all, she had bred indiscriminately, lowering the quality of his stock. In two days, the soonest Jem could reach Spig Hurd, she and her child were on their way to the auction block.

Dulcie, confined to her room alone, was desolate. Even when she had been flouting Mammy's rules, she was very fond of her. Getting into trouble from now on wouldn't be so much fun without Mammy on her heels.

Even mealtimes and dressing and bathing weren't any fun. A house servant, a tiny sixteen-year-old named Claudine, brought her meals. Dulcie tried to engage her in conversation, but Claudine would only look scared and say, "Hush, Miss Dulcie. Ah ain't s'posed to talk to you."

"Why doesn't my mama come up and see me?"

"Hush, Miss Dulcie."

"Where's my daddy? I want to see my daddy!"

"Miss Dulcie, finish up that breakfast an' hush your talkin'."

Dulcie, after two days of the silent treatment, was getting more and more frightened and uncertain. Her mama and daddy didn't love her anymore! They had sold Mammy, for Spig Hurd came and got her in his wagon.

"When will I get to go outside again?"

"Hush, Miss Dulcie. I'm not 'lowed to speak to you."

Dulcie sat at a small table, napkin tucked under her chin. She looked at Claudine, standing with her thin arms folded. She looked at the plate of soft fried eggs, biscuits with jam, bacon, and milk and strawberries. Dulcie picked up the plate and hurled it at Claudine, then cast herself onto the bed, crying loudly.

Jem heard her and came in. Ignoring Claudine's bespattered condition, he made straight for the bed. He picked up his outcast child and held her close. "There, there, Dulcie, it's all right."

"Daddy, I'm scared! And I want Mama!" Dulcie wailed.

"Mama's still asleep. Now stop cryin'. I'm takin' you down to breakfast with me. This damned foolery has gone on long enough."

Released from durance, Dulcie tried to be a model child, a real li'l lady Mammy could be proud of. For several days she sat in nerve-wracking peace, playing listlessly with her dolls, reading books, doing her needlework without being told, and sighing fit to drive her mother wild.

"Dulcie, wouldn't you like to go outside and play in youah swing?"

"No, thank you, Mama. I'll just finish hemmin' your kerchief I'm making."

Later: "Ah can have Hersel take you for a carriage ride. You could visit the Saunderses. Wouldn't that be nice?"

"No, thank you, Mama. I'm readin' *Redburn* again. It's a very interestin' book by Mr. Melville about a sailor's first voyage."

By week's end Patricia was heartily irritated by the constant sight of her suspiciously well-behaved daughter. Though there were no past parallels for her angelic behavior, Patricia feared that, as Mammy used to say, "Miss Dulcie jes' gwine bus' out in a new place." Surely, with a houseful of servants, she should not be expected to entertain her daughter along with her other duties. Patricia talked to Jem about it.

Afterward she said to Dulcie, "Your daddy an' Ah have decided youah almost a young lady, old enough not to need a mammy anymore."

Fleetingly the old fire lit in Dulcie's eyes, but she looked down at the shining toes of her slippers. "Yes, Mama. Whatever you say."

"We've decided to give you a servant—a maid. Would you like that?"

Still watching her slippers, Dulcie said tonelessly, "Who?"

"Daddy an' Ah . . . thought you might like to have Claudine."

Privately except for the two days of imprisonment, Dulcie liked Claudine immensely. Claudine had been born in the quarters, Rosaleen's sixth child. She was a frail infant, unwanted by her mother, who shoved her aside and let her milk dry up. But huge Violet, the cook, who had a new baby of her own and milk for half a dozen, took Claudine into the kitchen to raise as her own.

Claudine was clever-minded, as quick-moving as Dulcie, a happy girl eager and open to all the wonders life could hold. When Jem began his breeding farm, it was already apparent that Claudine would never carry a child in her narrow pelvis. Patricia began teaching Claudine to do her hair and hook up her gowns and to recognize what ladies might properly do and what they might not. Claudine seemed suitable in every way.

Dulcie didn't want to acquiesce too readily. Mama might take Claudine away. "No, thank you, Mama. I don't like her."

"But you've always gotten along so well with her!"

"Not anymore. I'd rather have Grace."

"Grace! But Dulcie honey, Grace is so stupid. Claudine is—"

Dulcie's eyes met her mother's defiantly. "I don't want Claudine!"

She cloaked her triumph when her father insisted. "No more o' this hagglin', Dulcie Jeannette. Claudine is going to be your maid!"

With Claudine in attendance Dulcie was once more interested in going outdoors. She reestablished old patterns, her first stop being Fellie's cobbler's shop.

"Wheah you been, Miss Dulcie? Ah got a heap o' sweets pilin' up since you ain't been 'round." Fellie opened a box on his workbench, disclosing small molasses candy treasures Ester made for him to give the children. Fellie was the favorite of every child on the plantation. He loved his own with a possessive pride and enjoyed the company of the others.

From Fellie's shop Dulcie and Claudine went to the orchard. They climbed trees and sat perched on convenient limbs, sucking on Fellie's candies and talking. Dulcie already rode well, preferably astraddle and bareback. In time, Claudine learned to manage a horse well enough to keep up with her mistress.

Claudine did not, however, neglect her duties. Her gentle affection carried far more weight with Dulcie than Mammy's heavy-handed dictums. She managed to keep her hair and clothing in order and to arbitrate dissension among Dulcie and her playmates, children of neighboring planters. Mostly the arbitration was needed between Dulcie and Glenn Saunders, who generally came out on the short end of Dulcie's pranks and needed soothing. It was not without setbacks that Claudine was slowly molding her young mistress into the outward forms of a lady. But her quick mind and strong passions that Jem had spoken of remained private and independent.

Patricia, in her literalness, saw her daughter's struggles to behave properly and was pleased. "Dulcie honey, Ah'm goin' ovah to Saunderses' to take tea this afternoon. Would you like to go along?"

"Do I get to play with Birdie and Blythe and Blossom?"

"Of course," Patricia smiled. "Weah youah white organdy dress with the bluebirds embroidered on it, so you jes' be lookin' youah prettiest."

The Saunders plantation was several miles from Mossrose, facing, as Mossrose did, the Savannah River. Here grew pecan and hickory groves and peach orchards. Set among the trees were bee gums, hives made from a hollow black gum tree, two feet in diameter and height, with a board nailed on for a cap and a hole bored at the bottom for the bees to enter.

Mrs. Saunders's lemonade was cool and refreshing. Her finger-sized cakes with the rosebuds on top were delicious. Dulcie had three before she caught the warning eye of Claudine from the hallway. Giggles were not far below the veneer of her good deportment.

Blossom, who was fifteen and already receiving serious attention from Mr. Chilcote's son, Jan, led the teatime chatter. Birdie and Blythe exchanged glances with Dulcie, and the game was on. For each subject Blossom attempted to discuss, the three younger girls each had an opinion, sedately phrased, deferential to elders, and infuriating to all concerned. Finally, tea was cleared away.

"Mama, can't these *children* go outside and play jackstones or somethin'?" asked Blossom, brown eyes flashing.

All three girls cast down their eyes to hide their elation.

Out in the backyard, safe from the view of Mama, Dulcie said, "Race you, Birdie! First one to the jessamine bushes!" Off they ran, ruffled gingham and organdy flying. Blythe, who was twelve to the other girls' eleven, ran not to race, but just to be running.

"Beat you, Dulcie!" said Birdie happily.

"Race you again to the first pecan tree! One, two, three, go!"

This time Dulcie won, but as she generously pointed out, Birdie was already tired from her first race. They walked in the grove, arms around each other, crinolined full skirts brushing and bouncing airily.

Dulcie stopped suddenly. "Are those things really full of bees?"

Blythe said, "My daddy says there's ten thousand in one bee gum."

Not sure if she believed it, Dulcie said only, "Huh!"

"And there's honey too," said a voice from the tree above them.

As it was expected of them, the girls shrieked in surprise. Dulcie knew, of course, that Glenn would be in the groves, either following them or hiding behind a tree waiting to jump out and yell, "Boo!" She would infinitely have preferred it to be Todd Saunders who followed them, but it was always her old playmate and adversary, Glenn. Glenn was thirteen, blonde and soft, not exactly a girl, but certainly far from being a boy yet. Being Todd's brother didn't improve his image in Dulcie's eyes. Todd was older, slimmer, and more agile than Glenn. The only problem was that Todd paid not the slightest attention to the younger girls.

Glenn landed with a heroic thump on the ground in front of them. "Want to see a whole bunch of bees, Dulcie?"

"What for?" she asked suspiciously.

"See what they look like, goose. Unless you're afraid . . ."

Dulcie picked up the gauntlet. "Afraid of what? An ol' log full of bugs? I'll bet you're too scared to take the top off a bee gum!"

"That's not bein' scared, only sensible," he said loftily. "That's not the way you do it. Depend on a girl to be too dumb to know." He ignored the snickers of his sisters. "I'll *show* you." He took one of his father's cigars from a hiding place, put it in his mouth, and lit it, sending clouds of blue smoke into the trees. Then he bent near the bee gum and blew smoke into the little hole at the bottom. "That's to let the bees know you're there." He blew in several more puffs.

"I don't see a single bee!" said Dulcie indignantly, bending so she could look up the hole. "That's an empty hole, Glenn Saunders, you're just tryin' to hornswoggle me."

Glenn, starting to pale from the cigar smoke, puffed harder.

Impatient, Dulcie picked up a stick. "I'll see if there's any bees," she said, and poked it into the little hole.

Blythe and Birdie had started edging away the moment Glenn lit the cigar. When he began smoking the hive, they ran pell-mell. By the time the swarm began to pour out of the bottom of the hive in an angry brownish stream, Glenn's sisters were safely out of sight.

"Dulcie, run!" Glenn said, grabbing her arm and following his own advice. "The pond!"

Dulcie started to argue, but a sting on her arm, then on her neck, spurred her to a speed she had never before attempted. Glenn was left behind, yelling, "Jump in! Jump in!" She reached the duck pond and kept right on running until the water closed over her head.

Glenn splashed in beside her. They stayed underwater, coming up for quick breaths, until the swarm buzzed angrily back to the grove.

"Glenn Saunders, you made me ruin my dress!"

Glenn's face was covered with reddening lumps, each with a little brown sprout coming out of it. One eye was swelling shut. He looked at Dulcie through the other one. "I don't feel very good," he said.

Dulcie looked up to see Claudine running down the path toward the pond. "Whatever we gwine tell your mama dis time, Miss Dulcie? Ain't no way we can hide dis one!"

Dulcie climbed out of the pond, her dress streaming mud and water. "I think you'd better tell Mama I'm ready to go home now, Claudine."

Chapter Two

By 1860 Mossrose had the look and the reputation of a successful plantation. And Jem's daughter was the most sought-after belle in the county. Jem's pride knew no bounds when it came to his wife, his daughter, and his land. For them there was no second best, and Dulcie's coming of age was a time in their lives to be marked grandly.

Dulcie's sixteenth birthday party began at nine o'clock on a warm October morning. She had been dressed and nervously waiting for nearly two hours. She had tried to see her father, but he had been closeted in his study all morning, talking a cotton deal with a shipper. Now, hearing the smooth roll of wheels on the sandy drive, she said, "Quick, Claudine, touch up my hair in the back. Oh, dear, I just know I'm going to sweat today. Do I look all right?"

"Yes, ma'am, you sho'ly do. Mastah Glenn jes' 'bout eat you up. Have you got it in yo' mind what you gonna say when he p'poses?"

Dulcie whirled toward the door, her hoops making the full skirt of her amethyst silk dress sway like a bell. "Dear Mr. Saunders, while I do not disregard your expressions of esteem and affection and find your attentions not unwelcome, still I must ask you to wait your turn in line, as I am most desirous of catching myself a more suitable husb—"

"Miss Dulcie!" cried Claudine, scandalized. "You cain't say that!"

Dulcie, giggling softly, swept out of the door into the hall.

She paused on the top step, one hand prettily on the rail. In the wide lower hall with its rose-patterned hooked rug were Birdie and Blythe Saunders, as grown up as herself, and their cousins, Katherine and Roberta Baxter. Strutting around the outskirts were Glenn Saunders and his attractive brother, Todd; Lowell Hume; and Conroy and Leroy Biggs.

Glenn saw Dulcie first. He stood staring, his mouth hanging ajar at the unaccustomed vision of Dulcie in a silken gown.

She was small and delicately formed, with a tiny waist and ample breasts that showed a hint of curve at her modest square neckline. Her deep auburn hair was parted in the center and combed down to form a shining wave toward her high cheekbones. Below the wave, curls hung gleaming to her shoulders. Her eyes were glowing amber, fringed with long thick lashes. Her straight narrow nose turned up a bit on the end; her full lips parted now to show even white teeth.

She descended the stairs in smooth gliding motions as Claudine had so patiently taught her. It was like walking into a maelstrom of hugs and kisses and squeals of delight from the girls.

As always, Glenn stood and listened as the others spoke so glibly, wishing that the fury of feeling that always captured his tongue and his sense in Dulcie's presence would release him just this once. He stood at Dulcie's side, feeling for her hand hidden in the folds of her skirt. With a sense of warm possessiveness he grasped it, pressing it against his thigh; but all he could say was, "Birthday girl, youah pretty as a picture."

Dulcie smiled on them all. "Oh, I'm just so glad y'all could come today! It would hardly be a party if y'all weren't here with me." Then she turned her golden eyes to dazzle Leroy. "Leroy, you're so quiet. Won't anybody let you speak up?"

The grin that spread across Leroy's face was slow and suggestive. "When it comes time for me to speak, Miss Dulcie, no one will keep me from it."

The others laughed, and Dulcie joined them. She wasn't sure it had been a remark meant to be humorous, but it certainly whetted her curiosity and her sense of daring. Before Dulcie had a chance to answer him, another carriage pulled up. Jan Chilcote and his wife, Blossom, whose fourth pregnancy was hardly showing yet, came to greet Dulcie. For two hours the procession of carriages and horsemen streamed through the front gates of Mossrose.

Once all had been greeted and the older people were seated or milling around talking with Jem and Patricia, Dulcie herded the chattering, giggling young people out to the seating places in the folly and under the grape arbor.

As Dulcie took her own seat, arranged to make her the center of attention, she noticed a soft cushion placed there for her. "Who was the sweet ol' thing who put this cushion here fo' me?" she asked, her eyes already dancing for the unknown admirer. None of them said anything. She had only to look at Glenn's pleased, blushing face to know.

"Miss Dulcie, may I have the pleasure of the first Virginia reel?" It was Todd, with his lofty manner and faintly mocking smile.

Dulcie suddenly found good reason to cool herself with her carved ivory fan. "This evenin's a long way off, Todd,"

she said affectedly. "You might fo'get you'd asked me, an'
Ah'd be a lonely li'l wallflowah."

"On youah buthday, Miss Dulcie?" He pretended surprise, imitating her accent perfectly. "Why, Ah'd fo'get
mah own name fust!"

Dulcie laughed.

Glenn, who was not especially enjoying the sight of
Dulcie looking so raptly into another male's face, particularly that of his older brother, took courage in his
hands. "She'll be dancin' the second reel with me."

Todd's eyes grew warmer on Dulcie. "We'll have to let
Miss Dulcie decide for herself, won't we?"

She held his gaze for another second before turning
lightly to put her hand on Glenn's arm. "I really haven't
promised anyone yet." Her eyes sparkled. "I'll dance
with . . . with the winner of the tournament!"

Glenn grabbed Dulcie's hands, and they performed a
few lively steps of the reel while the others laughed and
clapped.

"I sho'ly hope you enjoyed that, Glenn," said Lowell
Hume, "since I'm goin' to win the tourney *and* Miss
Dulcie."

A chorus of young, bantering male voices drowned him
out.

"Miss Dulcie, will we be havin' a gander pull?" asked
Conroy Biggs.

"Ooh, I hope not!" Blythe shuddered with delighted
anticipation.

"Well, I think so. Daddy had the gander penned up last
night."

Everybody laughed. Half the fun of a gander pull was
catching the gander again after he'd escaped from his pen.
"We'll go see," said Leroy.

"D'you need some help lookin'?" Roberta asked coquettishly. She was half in love with Leroy already. She knew
from her last visit here that Leroy was likely to leave her
with memories of stolen moments of delight that few
young men of his age had the skill or audacity to dare.

Dulcie rose, despite the hampering influence of Glenn,
who leaped to his feet in such an excess of politeness that
he nearly knocked her over. She put her hand on his arm.
"You'll excuse me for a few moments, Glenn?"

Glenn bowed to Dulcie while looking daggers at his nearest kin.

Todd, not in the least affected by Glenn's annoyance, walked leisurely away. The gander was in his nailed-up box, running his long neck and vicious beak out of all the slits, seeking escape. Roberta was feeding him blades of grass. "When does the tiltin' tourney start, Dulcie?"

"Whenever the Whitaker boys get here. The course is marked out." She indicated a long bare area between stables and spinning house, decorated with pennons and bunting of various colors. About twenty feet apart were three arches, twined with more bunting and decorated with flowers.

Dulcie took their attention and their illusionary dreams of victory away from the arches and pointed toward the sand-filled square in the far corner of the area that was for Indian wrestling. Again, visions of two stalwart young men, pitting their strength against one another, jumped into the minds of young girls, who wanted their favorites to win, and of young men, who wanted to prove their prowess before an audience.

Jem had insisted that the tournament be a part of Dulcie's party. Tournaments were traditional American entertainment, dating back to Colonial times, and were a less lethal imitation of jousts of the Middle Ages. For Jem they were the perfect combination of European pomp and raw American skill.

Their continuing popularity was aided by the novels of Sir Walter Scott, in particular *Ivanhoe*, written early in the century and still widely read and dreamed over in the romantic South. For young Southern men it was a chance to display horsemanship, athletic skills, and daring, thrilling the ladies. For no young man would enter the lists without flaunting a brightly colored symbol presented to him by a fair maiden. The solemn pageantry, with prancing horses and handsome men in bright costumes, was pleasing to the eye. But the most exciting part, where even the sturdiest young lady was apt to faint, was the flowery speeches of the winner and runners-up in naming the Sovereign of Love and Beauty and her ladies-in-waiting.

Birdie Saunders edged through the group of young people until she came to stand next to Dulcie. Dulcie's eyes sparkled. Turning to Birdie Saunders, she shivered slightly.

"Isn't it romantic, Birdie?" surprised, she saw tears in Birdie's soft brown eyes.

"No," she whispered. "After tonight you'll be all grown up. We won't ever have fun like we used to."

"Oh, Birdie, we will! We'll—"

Stubbornly Birdie shook her head. "It'll never be the same. Remember the naughty, *naughty* things you used to do to Glenn?"

Dulcie's nose crinkled as she smiled mischievously. "Who says that has to end?"

Birdie smiled instantly. "Dulcie! What are you thinkin'? I'd know that look anytime!"

"He's goin' to the stables. Remember when we poured water—"

Birdie giggled, her tears vanishing. "An' got his good clothes all wet?" Her laughing eyes met Dulcie's, and a decision came.

Quietly they left the group, sneaking around behind the bushes and outbuildings. Dulcie said urgently, "Hurry up and distract him, Birdie, while I climb into the hayloft."

Dulcie ran into the stables, glancing hastily toward the loft. The ladder wasn't in place, nor was the hayloft near enough to Comet, Glenn's pampered thoroughbred gray. Chewing on her lip, she stamped her foot, raising little dust puffs. Then she smiled, looking overhead to the storage loft located directly over the stalls of Comet and the black stallion next to him. It would be the perfect vantage point.

She found the ladder, tucked neatly out of sight. She tugged at its weight, pulling it away from the wall. Wobbling, the ladder stood upright. Then it fell to the floor wih a resounding crash that startled the black horse belonging to her father's business guest.

Struggling, she heaved the ladder up. She let it fall into place, slamming against the flooring of the storage loft directly over the black horse. Whinnying and snorting, the black stallion kicked at the sides of his stall, his eyes walling, his neck arching away from the frightening ladder.

Glenn'll be here before I'm ready! she thought. "Hersel! Hersel, where are you?"

"Ah's heah, Miss Dulcie."

"Do something about that horse! He's kicking down his stall."

"Lawsy, lawsy! Whut you done to dat hawse? Dat

animule b'long to Cap'n Tree-main, an' yo' daddy's gwine
holler fit to raise de Debbil." He eased into the stall,
speaking softly. "Easy now. Whoa, hawse!"

A full water bucket in one hand, her skirts looped up
over her arm, Dulcie made her way up the ladder to the
storage loft.

"Miss Dulcie, whut kinda debbiltry you up to?" Hersel
asked sternly.

"You just soothe that horse and don't talk to me."

"Mastah Jem gwine skin both us'ns iffen you doan quit
dat. Dem bo'ds gwine gib way." Then as Dulcie went on
with her struggle, sloshing water below her, Hersel said,
"Ah's gittin' outer heah. Ain't gwine be in no place to git
de blame."

Birdie's eyes danced as she teased her brother. "Guess
I've held you up long enough now, Glenn."

Glenn tweaked her nose. "You're not gonna hold me
up at all. I'm goin' to see to my horse."

Birdie giggled. "Come on, I'll go with you."

"What are you two up to now?" Glenn threw back his
head and laughed. "I figured it out this time. You're not
gonna get me."

Birdie pushed him toward the stables, but Glenn, smiling
maddeningly, did not move.

"Oh, Glenn, please!"

"I'm not fallin' for it this time."

"I'll get Dulcie to dance the reels with you! The whole
set!"

Glenn raised his eyebrows speculatively. "If you don't
come through, I'll . . ."

Dulcie, perched waiting on the floorboards of the storage loft, glanced down anxiously. She could hardly see.
Then a man's shadow crossed the bright patch of sunlight
at the door. Dulcie dived back into hiding. She heard Glenn
below her, moving around. Suddenly the ladder disappeared.

She stood up, alarmed at first, then began to giggle. "Ha,
ha, think you caught me, smarty! Come over here, I have
a surprise for you!"

He hesitated, then overcome with curiosity, he walked
slowly toward the black horse's stall. Dulcie puzzled for

a moment at his silence, then heaved the bucket of water with all her might.

"*Sonofabitch!*" Adam jumped, balancing on the stall gate, reached overhead to the loft flooring, then swung himself up. In the murky shadows Dulcie edged back to hide herself behind a broken sulky.

He stalked her, muttering, "I've tumbled some in my life, but never with preliminaries like this."

The man loomed before her dripping water. He was large, powerfully built, his face shadowed, his eyes dark and inscrutable.

Dulcie quaked, unable to form a coherent sound. Innocent though she was, she felt the male power emanating from him, stirring her blood and leaving her breathless.

Before he even touched her, she could feel the presence of him enclosing her.

He reached out and grabbed her. He was like the force of a hurricane—wild, untamed, unstoppable. He pulled her against him. Dulcie, in a daze, felt the cool wetness of his frock coat, the long animal hardness of his body.

She started, and began pounding on his chest. "No! no! You can't do this to me—I'm Dulcie Moran!"

"Is Dulcie Moran different from other women?" The warmth of his breath stirred her hair.

"My daddy'll have you horsewhipped!"

He laughed and held her more closely. "How will you explain luring me into the loft?"

Dulcie tensed, all the adventure gone. She began to cry. "Oh, please, please—let me go. I didn't mean to soak you! It was a joke on Glenn!"

"Jokes like that are for children—but then, you're not much more than a child, anyway. Have fun, Dulcie!"

He let her go and jumped down to the stable floor.

Dulcie peered down, worried. "Are you going to tell my daddy?"

"Not this time." He mounted his horse, then looked up at her. On her pretty woman's face played the emotions of an inexperienced child. Momentarily he wondered what it would be like to be the man who introduced Dulcie to love, for he was certain someone would, and soon.

He said lightly, "But if you ever play a woman's game with me again, you'll pay a woman's price."

Adam rode out of the stable.

Dulcie sat down and wept.

Birdie and Glenn ran in. Birdie, seeing the splash marks on the stable floor and hearing Dulcie's sobs, said, "Dulcie! What happened?! Was it that man? Did he hurt you?"

Glenn hurried to put up the ladder. Birdie climbed up.

"Oh, Birdie, don't make me talk about it now! I just can't!"

Glenn called, "Dulcie, are you all right?"

"Birdie, sneak me into the house! I can't see anybody lookin' like this!"

As Dulcie rounded the back of the house, the six Whitakers, four sons and two daughters, arrived closely followed by their parents and grandparents. Dulcie and Birdie crept up the servants' stairway. Claudine helped her change her dress while Birdie gently bathed her face, holding cold cloths against her puffy eyelids.

"Dulcie, aren't you ever goin' to tell me what happened?"

Dulcie shook her head wildly. "No—no—it was too horrible!" In her mind's eye Dulcie saw him again. She shivered, confused that the memory of him made her feel both hot and cold at once. It was as though his strong, warm hands still rested in the small of her back. As Claudine stroked her hair, she felt his breath, stirring her hair.

Abruptly she leaned forward and covered her face. "Oh, Birdie, it was awful! Just awful! He was horrible—an' mean! An' he threatened me!"

Birdie, remembering the man she had seen riding from the stables, stared off dreamily. "Oh, Dulcie, I wish it had been me!"

Dulcie, twinged by jealousy, said, "You don't know what you're talking about! You'd have been scared to death!"

Still filled with misgivings, she went back downstairs. She looked around furtively, in case the man had come back. If she saw him again, she'd just faint.

And if she never saw him again . . . it wouldn't matter. He had nothing to do with her. That man had been nothing but a rogue and a ruffian. It was her birthday party, her coming out, and the men of the county were there in her honor. There were all kinds of men, suitable men, gentle men, waiting to court her. She would have her pick of the crop.

The Whitakers greeted her effusively, tangling her in hugs and giggles, the men doffing their hats gallantly. They were blond, all of them. She thought of thick black curls and a teasing flash of white teeth under a black moustache. . . .

Mr. Acton, master of the local hunt, sounded his horn for the tournament.

The pageant began with knights arrayed in brilliant striped satin tunics of two and three colors, mounted on gallant steeds trailing ribbons of the same colors from their bridles. Sedately, in parade formation, they rode past the spectators, sweeping off their ribbon-trimmed hats as they passed the lady of their choice. Behind the knights came their personal servants. After them followed the small children from the quarters, doing handsprings and cartwheels and improvised acrobatics.

Glenn, wearing Dulcie's gold and brown insignia, rode past and bared his long pale locks in the traditional salute.

The first event was Taking the Ring. At full gallop each man sped along the seventy-five-yard course under three arches. With a tapered jousting lance he would attempt to impale a ring suspended from each arch.

Lowell Hume rode first. Cheers went up from the audience as he presented the ring to the judges for inspection. Another ring was hung in its place, and Todd Saunders galloped under the arches. He caught nothing. Then in succession, and with similar results, Conroy Biggs and three of the Whitakers passed through the arches. By now there were catcalls from participants as well as onlookers.

Next Glenn galloped down the decorated arches, looking grimly earnest. He looked surprised at the cheering, but red-faced, he dismounted and swaggered over to the judges. Grandly he bowed to Dulcie. "Miss Dulcie, will you do me the honor of holdin' this ring for me?"

It was almost an anticlimax when Leroy Biggs galloped madly down the lane and speared two rings. Leroy accepted the applause with aplomb, wrapped the rings in his handkerchief, and tucked them safely into his pocket. Lowell Hume won, by taking three rings.

After the applause had died down, Lowell made his speech selecting the tournament queen. "Who here is fair enough to be called Sovereign, the Queen of Love and Beauty? Upon my sacred honor, friends, I cannot cast my eyes in any direction that they do not linger on a maiden bountifully fitted to wear the garland of myrtle."

"Hear, hear!" cried Granddad Whitaker, a dilapidated Englishman whose eye and hand for a pretty girl were legendary in the county.

Lowell went on, "Yet one must be chosen—that one to whom heaven has lent such grace that the veriest dolt will remark favorably on it. That one whose mortal beauty is enhanced by her sweet spirit and her tender kindness. She who will be Sovereign excels the freshest rosebud for purity, the bluebird for happy augury, and the most luminous rainbow in its rareness.

"It would be less than apropos if I did not name the maiden adored by every dauntless gallant of this mighty county, the most captivating damozel of them all—Miss Dulcie Moran, our Queen of Love and Beauty!"

Her speech of acceptance was graciously to the point. This was the world she belonged to—the pageantry, the gentle manners, the honorable men—a world of light and social grace; a world safe from dark corners and the unleashed sensuality of the dark, bold raider of the loft. "I am truly flattered to be chosen your queen for this important day in my life. As for bein' all those delightful things Lowell said I was—I'm goin' to have to work mighty hard to live up to them! But now, let the runners-up select those who shall be ladies-in-waitin'!"

Glenn, looking dour, chose Katherine, his cousin. Leroy said, "Miss Enid Whitaker as the queen's lady!" The ladies-in-waiting were installed with suitable ceremony. The trumpet was sounded for the Indian wrestling.

Leroy came out winner in that event. Todd won the footraces. Only five participants entered the hand races. Cedric and Andrew Whitaker, Lowell, Glenn, and Leroy stood on their hands to follow a course that finished at the feet of the Sovereign. Leroy, so red he was nearly purple, did a somersault to celebrate winning.

The gander pull would be the last event. This was so popular a sport that Jem allowed his servants to watch it. It was as much a treat for the guests as it was for the slaves, for Fellie had his own little band of musicians he had trained from among the adolescent blacks. They led the procession of slaves out to the area, playing and singing as they came. Dulcie glanced over to see Claudine among them. On either side of her were two large young black men. Claudine held the hand of each of them. Dulcie grinned. She knew Claudine had a young man but had no idea who it was; and Claudine wasn't one to talk, fearing Jem would find out and send her away. At least now the field was narrowed to two men. Dulcie would find out soon which it was.

Her attention was wrested from Claudine as the gander was taken out of his pen, his big black feet tied securely. Then, flapping his long wings, nipping desperately at his captors with his heavy black beak, he was dipped into a tub of grease. As a final indignity, he was hung by his feet high over the racecourse, honking and hissing in distress.

The object of the sport was to ride one's horse under the goose at full speed, trying to seize the squirming fowl by its neck. Whoever made off with the goose's head was declared winner.

Dulcie, looking at the big dark body with the black neck undulating like a snake, whispered to her nearest lady-in-waiting. "Oh, Enid, tell me when it's over! I don't think I can watch this."

Enid eyed her curiously. "You always enjoyed it before. What's the matter with you today? Was it your pet?"

"No, no—it's just—I'd forgotten how gruesome the poor bird looks all slimy with grease and—an' waitin' to die."

"Dulcie!" Enid's whisper was shocked. "The boys are only havin' fun!"

Dulcie watched with apparent interest as rider after rider passed under the high-hanging gander. Andrew Whitaker got his hand severely bitten as the gander struck a lucky blow. But the gander was doomed. His strikes became fewer as he tired. Then suddenly it was over. Leroy Biggs let out an ear-splitting yell as the gander's head came off in his hand.

Dulcie's heart was hardly in the presentation of the engraved silver loving cup, though she was glad that Leroy, with his outrageously suggestive eyes, had won.

"Miss Dulcie, as champion, I'm claimin' you now for all the reels."

She gave him her sweetest smile. Leroy excelled at anything physical, including dancing. "Of course, Leroy. I can hardly wait."

"And will you sit by me at dinner?"

Dulcie put her hand on his arm. "I'm so sorry, I've promised Glenn."

"Now that's a shame, Miss Dulcie, a real shame." His gaze slid to Enid.

Glenn appeared quietly beside Dulcie, looking downcast, as she had expected.

"Glenn, I loved your ridin' today!" she gushed. "You went through those arches like a thunderbolt, your lance shinin' like a knight of old! I was so proud of you when you just *snatched* that ring!"

Glenn attempted to look humble. "It was just luck. I'm not really good at things, Dulcie."

"Not good! How can you say such a silly thing! Here you are, part of the Queen's Court! You don't see everybody up here, do you?"

"Well . . ."

"Hasn't all that glorious exercise whetted your appetite? Now you just come along with me, an' I'll see that Violet heaps your plate with the best of everythin'!" Dulcie's voice soothed and encouraged and led. *It is all wrong,* she thought. *Here I am comforting Glenn, and he's supposed to be the strong one. If I marry someone like him, it will always be like this: I'll have to tell him he's wonderful; it will be my duty. No one would ever have to tell that stranger he was wonderful.*

Lowell Hume, seated on Dulcie's left, leaned over boldly and kissed her on the neck. Dulcie squealed girlishly. Glenn got up from his seat, scowling fiercely at the intruder. "Suh, I must ask you to remove yourself to another chair. You are annoyin' Miss Dulcie."

"My apologies, suh," Lowell answered. "I'd-a never suspected Miss Dulcie was promised to you." Still, he made no move to rise.

Glenn was left standing there speechless. He tried once more. "As a gentleman, you must be familiar with the code of duelin'? You have offended me, and I wish to call you out, suh."

It had gone too far. Dulcie stood up, her plate slithering across the grass. "Glenn! Lowell! I beg you to recollect this is my birthday party! I'm askin' you, as gentlemen, not to spoil it. Glenn, do I have your word?" She riveted him with her amber eyes, and his hot gaze fell.

He mumbled, "I only thought to defend your honor."

"Miss Dulcie, I'm not lackin' in personal courage, but I see no purpose to be served by woundin' or—" Lowell added with evident relish—"killing a human bein' of such negligible value as Mr. Saunders."

Glenn would have sprung on him, but Dulcie put her arm between them. "Glenn, you gave your word. Lowell?"

"Miss Dulcie, it's my pleasure to promise anythin' you might ask." He bowed low, flicked a crumb from his handsome waistcoat, and sauntered off toward Camille Whitaker. Glenn glared after him.

Everyone was watching. Dulcie, smiling flirtatiously, tucked her hand under Glenn's arm. "I think a short walk would do us both good."

Once they had strolled out of sight and hearing of the others, she turned on him. "I hope you're satisfied, Glenn Saunders! All by yourself, you've ruined my birthday party for me!"

"But Dulcie, I"—he stopped, his mouth still working.

"You may call me *Miss* Dulcie! You've forgotten I'm not yet promised to any man! Your possessiveness has become extremely tedious. If I want to talk, dance, or walk in the moonlight with other men, I will!"

He nodded miserably. "I'm sorry. I only—"

Her mood changed, lightninglike. "I believe I would like a little more of that punch, wouldn't you, Glenn?"

He looked at her, bewildered. "Well, ah, I guess I—"

"We'd better go back to the party."

"You're not angry with me anymore?"

"*Oh!* You *are* a fool! Yes, I'm angry! But I have guests, and I want them to have a good time even if I don't!"

"Dulcie—Miss Dulcie—I only did it because I lo-lo—" he seemed on the verge of expiring, then gulped and said, "love you."

At any other time Dulcie would have answered in the accepted manner, never revealing her own feelings at all. Instead, irritated beyond measure, she said, "Well, that's your misfortune!" and kept on walking, with Glenn scurrying to keep pace with her.

He evidently thrived on such treatment, for early that evening he was at her elbow, reminding her that he had the first waltz. Dulcie looked up into his honest, loving, and hopelessly commonplace face. "I'm sorry I got so huffy this afternoon. I know you were only doin' what you thought was right. I was so rude to you! Can you forgive me, Glenn?" She drew out his name lingeringly, so that it was almost like a gentle touch of her hand. She knew he would think her words far more meaningful than a simple apology and that later she would once again have to extricate herself from what he read into them.

She danced with him, smiling until her cheeks ached. Then she was whirled away by first one then another to whom she had promised dances. Leroy's turn came during the reels. He led her through them with such tireless vigor that even Dulcie was winded and, as she had feared, sweating.

"It surely has been fun dancin' with you, Leroy," she said, still smiling. "You're very light on my feet."

Leroy laughed and laughed. "Oh, that's funny, Miss Dulcie! Light on your feet!" He seemed to enjoy himself so much that Dulcie laughed too. Eventually Leroy got himself under control. "Care for some of your birthday potion? It's mighty agreeable and refreshin'. I'll get it for you."

"Please. I'll just go sit on the veranda a moment."

"I'll find you, don't you worry. You jes' get comfortable now, an' we can have a nice little chat."

By the time he had made his painstaking way across the ballroom with two cups, Dulcie was surrounded by Todd and Roberta, Enid, Camille, and Lowell. To her relief Glenn was not in sight.

Leroy jostled his way jovially through the laughing group. "Here y'are, Miss Dulcie! A cup o' cool punch, jes' the thing to quench your thirst after dancin' so light-footed—so light—now, what was it you said that made me have that fit?"

"I—I forget," she said, not wishing to start him up again.

"Miss Dulcie has a marvelous wit," Leroy explained to Todd. "After we danced the reels, she said to me, um, well, what she said was—"

Dulcie took pity on him and repeated the thin joke. Then the others laughed, as much at Leroy as at her remark. He might not know it or care, but Dulcie did. When the music began again, Lowell asked her to dance. "Thank you, Lowell, but I'm goin' to rest a little longer."

"Yes, Miss Dulcie and I are goin' to have a quiet talk," said Leroy.

Dulcie eyed him with some misgivings as the others left them alone.

"Let's take a little stroll, shall we, Miss Dulcie? The breeze down by the folly is mighty pleasant."

"Fine, Leroy. But we can't linger. I've promised the very next dance to Andrew Whitaker."

Gallantly he held out his arm. They walked slowly over the grass, blue with moonlight. "Miss Dulcie, there's somethin' I've been thinkin' on."

She said nervously, "Leroy, do you know anythin' about stars? There's one big bright one peepin' over the top of the folly."

"No, ma'am, I don't know very much about stars. But I been thinkin' about this for some long time now, an'—"

"It's real bright, and almost red—"

"An' what I think is, it might be pretty nice."

"Oh, look, the sky is just full of them!"

His voice was reproachful. "Miss Dulcie honey, you aren't payin' no never mind to what I'm sayin'. I'm gonna have to remedy that."

Dulcie gulped, and grasped at one last straw. "I'm sorry, Leroy, it's just that the night is so beautiful—"

"It's like every other autumn night. If you want to talk about somethin' beautiful, we'll talk about you, Miss Dulcie. You're the most beautiful critter that ever walked the earth."

"Why, th-thank you."

"I want you to consent to be my wife."

Her careful training was doing her no good this evening. In fact, it had hardly done her any good all day long. She said breathlessly, "I didn't know you were interested in me!"

"Yes, ma'am, I'm interested. Mighty interested. I like the way you talk an' laugh an' the way you move an' sit a horse an' dance. 'Specially the way you dance, an' fit so fine in my arms—sort of like this."

His arms encircled her, his face came near, shadowed in the deep twilight of the folly. She smelled the spicy tang of his shaving lotion, felt the strength of his arms. She shivered with a sensation so alien, yet so familiar, she didn't dare think of the man who had first stirred it. "Leroy, you're presumin'—"

"You've got fine spirit, admirable spirit I've been admirin' since you were fourteen. I figger I'm jes' about what you need."

"You mustn't hold me so close—"

"Sweetheart, you don't seem to be gettin' it through your lovely head that I'm declarin' my love for you and askin' you to be Mrs. Leroy Biggs."

"Leroy . . . this is so—unexpected."

He was holding her against him now, and somehow it wasn't totally unpleasant. "Don't you think that sounds fine? Dulcie Biggs?"

Leroy lips were on hers in a kiss that was not suitable to give a lady, and his hard-muscled arms embraced her with an insistence completely incompatible with the Southern idea of feminine fragility. She tried to turn away, but his mouth stayed on hers until she realized she was kissing him back. Oh, it was thrilling to feel the hot chills in one's stomach and the shaking of the knees and the breathlessness that went with the first real kiss!

Leroy finally stopped kissing her, but he still held her, his face inches away from hers, his panted breath fanning her. "Miss Dulcie, dearest Dulcie, forgive me. But I love you so much . . . Dulcie!"

Dulcie, dazed with some unmentionable desire, some hot longing so new to her that she didn't even know what she longed for, raised her mouth eagerly for him to kiss.

They stood fused in the moonlight. The music had stopped. Light chatter and laughter floated toward the folly. She pulled away, coming groggily to her senses. "Leroy, I've got to go in! I told Andrew I'd—"

Leroy chuckled. "That was three dances back! Forget about Andrew. You came out here to be with me. You will marry me?"

"I . . . I can't. I just—"

"You jes' need time. I'll give you time, Dulcie. I'll give you a lot of things." Teasingly he pecked at her cheek. His eyes twinkled in the soft light. "Do you like the way I kiss you?"

Dulcie stood dumbstruck.

Leroy grinned. "I got the idea you want me to kiss you some more."

There was nothing Dulcie could say except, "Oh, Leroy!"

"Guess we better do that again," he murmured. His hands slid gently up the sides of her waist under her breasts.

"No! Please. I've absolutely got to go back into the house. Mama will be in a takin'! Could I give you your—" she gulped—"your answer later on? Next week maybe?"

"I can wait. Long's it's not too long."

Dulcie moved with unseemly haste. At the outside entrance to the servants' stairway she excused herself. "I'll just go fix my hair."

"You look beautiful to me." Leroy moved toward her.

Dulcie's teeth were chattering with nervousness. She escaped ignominiously and lifted her skirts to skim up the stairway to her room. "Claudine!" Where was she? She sat down and began gingerly to try to restore order to her hair. She banged the hairbrush down. *"Claudine!"*

Claudine came out of her dressing room, blinking sleep from her eyes. "Miss Dulcie, Ah never heard you call. Why din't you call me?"

"I did! Do something with my hair. Le—I've got it all tangled."

"Mastah Glenn he'p you do this to yo' hair, Miss Dulcie?"

"Glenn! I forgot about Glenn. Oh, Claudine, do hurry!"

"Ah cain't hurry 'lessen you hol' still. You ain't been messin' 'round with dat stranger agin, has you?"

By the time Dulcie came downstairs, the music had begun again, and Glenn was standing alone, looking desolate. She went straight to him. Halfway across the room she saw Leroy, dancing with Roberta. His eye caught hers, holding it until Dulcie, blushing guiltily, was forced to look away.

At the end of the minuet, Andrew and Lowell both came to claim their dances. Then Glenn was back. "Would you like to sit this one out with me?"

Dulcie felt sorry for Glenn. He was fond of her and, given the slightest encouragement, would hang around her forever. But one proposal—so unexpected and still to be answered—was all she could cope with. "That's a very kind offer, but I promised Daddy this dance."

"Dulcie, I want to talk with you!" he pleaded.

Jem came up, beaming and smelling of liquor, and put his arm affectionately around his daughter. "Don't tell your mama I said so, but you're every bit as pretty as she is!" He winked. "Don't you think so?"

Glenn said sadly, "With all due respect, prettier, Mr. Moran."

Jem laughed. "For that, I'll give you my dance with her."

"Daddy! You mean you'd dance with every woman in the county tonight and not even once with your own daughter?"

Jem looked pleased. "Put that way, I've got no choice." He whirled off with Dulcie, his feet a little awkward from the punch bowl.

Then came the last waltz before midnight supper, and Leroy to claim it. He held her lightly, correctly, never touching her body with his. Yet she was acutely aware of his muscular arms and the hard chest under his frock coat, and the warm glow that suffused his face and hers whenever their eyes met.

At the end of the dance he bowed low, took her hand, and kissed it. "You won't forget my answer, Dulcie?"

She smiled at him, reveling in his self-assured virility. "I'll remember."

Hours later, lying in bed still awake and going over every minute of the day and evening, especially the evening, Dulcie felt herself go warm. The man in the loft didn't seem so terrible now. Suddenly she realized he had awakened her to something she really wanted.

"I'm fallin' in love!" she whispered to the gray dawn. "In love with Leroy Biggs!"

Chapter Three

Dulcie slept past noon, woke full of vigor, and sprang out of bed. What she wanted most of all, after a warm bath and breakfast, was a long horseback ride.

"Get out my riding habit, Claudine. I'll be going by myself," she added firmly, knowing full well Claudine's response.

"No'm, you ain't. Last time Mastah Jem 'bout took a chunk o' mah hide."

"Oh, he did not! He's never touched a servant in his life."

"Ah knows dat, but he was thinkin' 'bout it."

"Well, I need to be by myself this morning."

"Miss Dulcie, Ah 'preciates yo' needs, but mo' Ah 'preciates Mastah Jem's head this mawnin'. He had hisseff a pow'ful good time yestiddy."

"You'll have to keep your mouth shut, then."

After a silence while she helped Dulcie into her riding breeches, Claudine asked, "Did Mastah Glenn p'pose to you?"

Dulcie smiled. "No, he didn't."

"He was jes' bustin' to ask you!" Dulcie continued to smile.

"Somebody else proposed."

"Mastah Todd? Mastah Cedric?"

"Give up, Claudine. It was Leroy Biggs."

"Mastah Leroy! Din't never think he gwine settle down to one woman. Bes' you watch yo'seff." She brushed Dulcie's hair with needless vigor.

Dulcie said dreamily. "He asked me beautifully. Very romantic, out in the moonlight by the folly."

"Yes'm, that's where he'd want you to be."

"Everything was proper!"

Claudine wasn't impressed. "You didn't lead him on none, Miss Dulcie?"

"Lead him *on?* Claudine, I tried to lead him *off!* But he had his mind make up."

"What you say to him?"

"I told him I'd think about it. And that's why I want to ride alone."

"Mastah Jem won't let you marry him, so's you doan have to think on it."

"Why not?" Dulcie's eyes met Claudine's, startled. "Leroy's a good person, kind, prosperous—his daddy gave him a quarter of their plantation when he turned twenty-one, you remember."

"Iffen Mastah Leroy had niggers choppin' cotton ovah de entire state of Jawjah, Mastah Jem still say no. He wants you to marry Mastah Glenn."

"Oh, Glenn! Glenn is nothing but a big—white-livered —poop!"

"You din't say dat yestiddy, Miss Dulcie."

"Oh, I know, but he makes me so angry. I wish he'd do—somthin'!"

Claudine giggled. "Mastah Leroy musta done a fine job kissin' you. You sho' look like it when you come tearin' upstairs last evenin'."

"Just fix my hair. I *knew* I didn't want to talk to you about it."

Dulcie had already made up her mind she would take a long ride. She had to figure out a way of wording her reply to Leroy, something nearly as important as deciding what her decision would be. Claudine rode at her side. Not only did she respect Dulcie's need for privacy, but she was far more interested in one of the young men working in the field.

"Miss Dulcie, you still wantin' to be alone?"

"Since you've tagged along, that's hardly worth answering, is it?"

"Could be it is. We's far enuf from de big house now, your daddy won't see. Could be Ah'll go visitin' some o' de fiel' han's . . . iffen you wants to be alone," Claudine said sweetly.

Dulcie's eyes twinkled. "My, but you're considerate of my wishes suddenly, Claudine. There must be a reason."

"Nary a one," Claudine said sincerely.

Dulcie giggled. "Do you mean there are two?"

"Miss Dulcie! Mastah Jem doan 'low me to fool with no nigger bucks. He'd skin me an' use mah hide fo' a umbrella stand."

"An' youah skeered o' Mastah Jem, aren't you?" Dulcie mocked.

By the time Claudine returned from her rendezvous, Dulcie had decided she would tell Leroy she wasn't ready to marry but he was welcome to call on her. It was *almost* an understanding, but she would have time to see if being in love with a man's kisses was as satisfactory as liking the man you might marry. Until she was promised to him, she could still be friends with other men as well. One thing Dulcie knew for certain: She liked the attentions of many men.

When Claudine and Dulcie rode out of the trees, they spotted Hersel heading quickly for the stables. Then Asa furtively disappeared behind Fellie's cobbler's shop.

"They're certainly acting strange."

"Yes'm, Miss Dulcie, dat's a fact."

"Something's wrong . . . and you know about it! What is it?"

Claudine shrugged. "Nothin' you 'n' me kin do 'bout it, so I doan tell you an' 'stress you."

"*Claudine! Tell me!*"

"Mastah Jem gwine sell 'bout twenny niggers t'morra."

Dulcie looked confused. There was nothing unusual about Jem selling Negroes. "That has you and Asa and Hersel stirred up? Why?"

Through tears, Claudine blubbered out, "Ruel . . . an' Jothan, dey's—"

"No!" Dulcie had played with Jothan until she was nine years old, and forbidden near the quarters. He and Ruel were the oldest sons of Fellie and Ester. They were family —certainly not to be thought of as the slaves bred especially for sale.

"Lige, Zekel, Mag 'cause she cain't breed, Eggar. De res' of 'em's fiel' han's."

"But Jothan and Ruel!"

"Miss Dulcie, dey's old enuf to be selled, so Mastah Jem gwine sell 'em."

"He—he can't," Dulcie whispered, stricken.

"Mistah Spig Hurd comin' in de mawnin'."

Into Dulcie's mind flashed a picture of Spig Hurd's wagon coming years ago, that time he had hauled off Mammy and her newborn baby. "I'll . . . talk to Daddy," she said uncertainly.

"Save yo' breaf to cool yo' coffee, Miss Dulcie."

Dulcie found Jem on the veranda with Wolf, the overseer. She disliked Wolf intensely, a surly, obsequious man who sometimes whipped the field hands, though Jem would not let him touch the higher class servants. Now Wolf rose, touching his hat with one black-nailed hand. "G'day, Miss Dulcie. Ah'll do what you tol' me, Mistah Moran. Ah sho'ly will, right off. Yes, indeed!" He hurried away.

Jem smiled affectionately at his daughter. "Did you like your party yesterday?"

"Oh, it was wonderful! You and Mama gave me the nicest birthday celebration any girl ever had. Didn't you see the jealous faces of the Whitaker girls? And I thought Birdie's cousin Roberta was just going to turn green and expire on the spot. It was perfect."

Jem laughed appreciatively. "I'm glad you had a good time."

"Daddy," Dulcie began seriously, "I want to talk to you about something . . . important."

"I thought you might. Young Saunders asked for your hand?"

"No, Daddy, it's not about Glenn, it's—"

"He didn't? The whelp! He asked my consent yesterday. He hasn't been soft-soapin' me so he can trifle with you, has he, Dulcie?"

"Glenn? Oh, never Glenn, Daddy, he's very sincere. I just didn't give him a chance to say anything. He will, though, sometime."

Satisfied, Jem sat back and regained his smile. "Then, it must be Leroy Biggs you're wantin' to talk about."

"Daddy!" Dulcie said in exasperation. "Is Spig Hurd coming tomorrow?"

Jem's face took on a stern look. "Spig Hurd is no concern of yours."

"Is it true, Daddy?"

"Claudine has been talking to you. Well, Miss, it isn't her place to talk, nor yours to listen to darky gossip."

"Are you going to sell some of the children?"

"Children! The only one under fifteen is Eggar, and he's a poor specimen I'm glad to get rid of."

"And Fellie's boys? What of them? Ruel is fourteen, and both he and Jothan are fine servants. Why are you going to sell Fellie's sons?"

Jem, flushed and uncomfortable, tested his reasoning aloud for the first time. "Dulcie, no planter, especially one with a breeding farm, can become attached to his slaves. That's something you'll have to think about. Someday Mossrose will be yours. If you get to feeling they're family, when it comes time to sell them off, you can't do it. You've got big money invested and can't get anything out of it until they're sold."

"*Money!* But these are people!"

"Now, don't you get caught up in that error, Dulcie Jeannette! They speak and work like people, but that's where it ends. They're black animals, daughter. Human-like, but not human. They need guidance and supervision, else nothin' gets done. They have no more responsibilities than—than your saddle horse. Their food is provided, they're housed and clothed. Not a one of them could go out and earn what I give them. Their only purpose in life is to work and breed and live under a white man's guidance. Says so right in the Good Book."

"Oh, Daddy, it never says in the Bible that black people are to be slaves and whites their masters."

"They're not people, daughter! They're the descendents

of Ham, marked always by their skin as somethin' less than the rest of us. They haven't got higher ambitions like you and me, and they haven't the means to satisfy them. Thinkin' different will just get you confused and misled."

Dulcie knew to say another word was to push Jem to anger, but she continued. "Look at Fellie! You've told me yourself how he trained the workers in shoemakin'. No one had to lead him. He's so trustworthy you don't even have a driver over him!"

"Fellie," Jem said angrily, "has gotten above himself, complainin' to you. I'll—"

"I haven't seen Fellie! I'm lookin' at it from his viewpoint!"

"He hasn't got one! Now, you listen to me, Dulcie! Fellie is the same as a stallion or bull. D'you see the bull bawlin' after his calves when they're shipped off? Does the stallion kick down his stall if I trade away his colts? They don't even know which is their get, and neither does Fellie."

"But he does! And Ester knows! Jothan and Ruel have always lived with them!"

"Lettin' them live like a real family is a mistake I quit makin' years ago," Jem said testily. "These blacks have been bred for sale, and sell them is what I'm goin' to do."

"Daddy, couldn't you sell a couple of field hands instead?"

"No, I can't and since you butted in, I'll tell you why. At going prices, I'll get twenty-five hundred to three thousand dollars for two prime field hands. Those two boys of Fellie's will bring five hundred to a thousand dollars more because they're mannersable, and thanks to your mother they can read and do sums. At the slave marts in New Orleans they'll fetch a pretty price from some merchant who'll train them for clerical work."

Dulcie listened to every word and disliked the sound. "It's all so hard and uncaring, Daddy. Can't you understand—"

"I do understand the way you feel, but I'm not such a soft fool that a pair of tear-filled yellow eyes can dictate the way I run my business."

Dulcie blinked hard, looking away. "There's no other way?"

"None." His voice softened. "Now go along, Dulcie.

Have Hersel saddle up Strawberry. Take yourself a nice ride. It'll make you feel better."

Feeling herself dismissed, Dulcie stood up. Her father rose with her. Her eyes met his again, and he held out his arms to comfort her. But he said, "It's right that you should be compassionate, Dulcie. It's a woman's way. But you're never to attempt to interfere again, hear?"

In the cobbler's shop Fellie was bent over a worker, patiently demonstrating how the upper had to be eased onto the sole. Regardless of personal upheaval, he had a job to do, and he was doing it.

"Fellie, come out here."

Fellie looked up. "Yassuh, Mastah Jem." To the other he said, "You go 'head an' patch up dem holes 'till Ah gits back, heah?" He joined Jem outside.

Without knowing he noticed, Jem saw the immense dignity of the man, the self-confident sense of personal worth. His pure-black Gullah face was lined with grief. He waited quietly for Jem to speak.

"What's this I hear about you complainin', Fellie?"

"Mastah Jem, Ah doan complain. You good to me, an' Ah doan say no odder way to nobody."

"What does Ester say?" Jem tapped his riding crop against his breeches.

"De same, Mastah Jem. She doan complain nothin' neither."

"I hear you got the sulks because the boys are leavin' tomorrow."

Fellie lowered his eyes. "Nossuh."

"Well, they're going whether you like it or not! You're gettin' too big for your britches! You could be sold, too, if I'd a mind to do it!"

Fellie raised his eyes to meet Jem's. "Ah ain't nevah complain, Mastah Jem. But dey's somethin' maybe you like to know."

Jem looked sharply at the tall black man. "What would that be?"

Fellie's face took on a kind of hopeful, shining pride. "Those boys o' mine pure Gullah. Dey both ol' enuf to start breedin' babies fo' you. Jothan an' Ruel, both 'em. Yassuh. Dey show me las' night. Dey kin both do it fine, Mastah Jem."

"I've got a dozen men of good breed stock right now,

and that's plenty to service all the women." He turned away.

He was called back by Fellie's soft, desperate tones. "Mastah Jem, please—" Fellie put out both hands in unconscious supplication—"please, suh! Doan sell mah boys! Dey's good boys—strong! Quick in dey haids! Doan give no trouble! You sees dat yo'seff, Mastah Jem!"

"I can see you're forgettin' yourself, Fellie." With sharp motions of his wrist, Jem was softly cracking the crop on his breeches again.

Tears were rolling down Fellie's cheeks. "Ah's afeerd fo' 'em! Mebbe somebody buy 'em what won't treat 'em good!"

"It's all settled!" Jem stalked away, mounted his horse, and cantered off. Fellie's head sank toward his chest. His shoulders heaved.

Hersel watched Jem's diminishing figure, then crossed the path. "Ah's mighty took down fo' you, Fellie. It ain't fittin'. Jes' ain't fittin'.'"

Fellie, unable to speak, wiped his tears with the palms of his hands and went back to work.

That evening the Negroes held prayer meeting in the chapel. The sounds of their songs floated in through the dining room window. "I Am Bound For the Promised Land" was followed by an inexpressibly mournful, "Were You There When They Crucified My Lord?" and "Go Down, Moses, Way Down in Egypt Land." The noise gradually mounted, with shrieks, shouts, and keening that cut the eardrums like a razor.

"Good God! Lucius! *Lucius!*" Jem bellowed.

A wizened black man scuttled in from the pantry. "Yassuh!"

"Shut that window and go tell those darkies to quiet down or I'll lock 'em in the cabins."

Jem got his quiet, but peace of mind did not accompany it.

Spig Hurd and Jem had been business acquaintances for many years. He visited Jem occasionally, looked over the stock, and took everything available for sale in the more than twenty-five markets in New Orleans. Buyers congregated there from all over the Deep South, especially from Texas, annexed only fifteen years before and desperately hungry for workers in their sprawling cotton fields.

On this particular day Hurd and Jem enjoyed sloe gins in the study before going out to load up the slaves Jem had selected.

Spig asked, "You wouldn't have any quadroons for me?"

"Happens I do. I've got three in the kitchen that I bought from Old Man Whitaker because his wife was dinging him about them. I didn't buy them for resale."

"A fancy girl went for over twenty-five hundred dollars a few weeks ago at Joseph Bruin's," Spig said slyly. "Moran, you'd sell your Mammy if she'd bring that kind of money."

"I did sell my Mammy. You ought to remember, you came and got her."

The men laughed together. Chatting easily, they moved toward the compound where Jem had left the blacks under guard overnight. Jem bellowed, "Lucius!" and Lucius came running. "Scoot up to the kitchen and tell Violet I want the three little girls out here."

Lucius was back promptly with three frightened, crying children. "Dese de ones, Mastah Jem?"

"Yes—and get that pout off your lip before I give you somethin' to pout about."

Lucius stood up straight, looking away from the girls. Spig felt them over quickly, lingering over the last one, who, he noticed, was developing early. "How much, Moran?"

"They'll have to go for a thousand apiece."

Spig protested, naming imaginary defects. "I don't know if I can get that much for them—be losin' money."

Jem shrugged. "D'you want them or don't you?"

Spig looked doubtful. "Well, I'll take 'em, I guess." Both he and Jem stood to make a tidy profit, and both knew it.

The girls wailed loudly. They didn't want to leave Violet, they didn't want to leave Miss Trishy, they were afeered to go in the wagon.

Jem said roughly, "Lucius, get these younguns into the wagon." He opened the door of the compound. The reek of fear filled the air. Twenty-two blacks of all ages huddled on the floor and on the ticks. Wolf, glowering, stood beside the door with his large whip in his hand. "Didn't have to use it once, Mistah Moran." He sounded disappointed.

Jem, for all he bred slaves to be sold, always had an uneasiness about this stage of the business. It upset him for his darkies to cry and carry on as if they had human emotions. Wolf, watchful, grinning with amusement, hurried them into Spig's large wagon.

Suddenly a big black shape exploded from the cobbler's shop and flew through the air, knife flashing, to land heavily on Spig Hurd. The knife upraised, Fellie yelled, "You ain't gwine take mah chilluns!" As the knife plunged down toward Spig's throat, Wolf's whip lashed out, caught Fellie's arm, and jerked it backward.

It was all over in seconds. Not a Negro moved. Fellie lay in the dust, and Spig Hurd, cursing and pulling out his gun, scrambled to his feet. Fellie's sons, Ruel and Jothan, sat staring down at the floorboards of the wagon, their eyes dry as stones.

The whip cut open Fellie's shirt. "Get up from there, you black son of a bitch!" said Wolf. Fellie stood, fear in his eyes.

Spig's pistol was pointed at Fellie's head. His face was white with fury. His eyes glittered. "You gonna do somethin' about that, Moran, or do I get to blast his Goddamned head off?"

"Ease that sidearm back into your holster, Hurd," Jem said curtly. "He's my nigger, and he's worth a lot. I'll tend to him my way."

Spig holstered his gun, standing with his thumbs hooked in his belt. "I'll stick around for the show. It better be damned good, Moran."

"Wolf, tie Fellie to that tree. Good and tight, so he won't slide down and ruin himself. Peel his black hide from his neck down to his heels."

Wolf smiled hugely. "Yes, *sir,* Mistah Moran!"

Fellie could beg mercy for his sons, but never for himself. With no outward show of emotion, he walked to the tree and tamely submitted as Wolf tied him by the wrists so that he stood on tiptoe. He held himself as proudly as he could, knowing that before the overseer was done the pain would be past mortal endurance.

Wolf stood back, his whip ready. "You say peel him?"

Spig said, "You niggers there in the wagon! You watch this, just so's you don't get any ideas about yourselves!"

"Fifty lashes, Wolf," Jem said, "No more, no less. I want to hear you countin' 'em. You touch his balls once, and you get the same."

Wolf's unpleasant smile dimmed. "Hell, Mistah Moran! Nuttin' 'em is half the fun!"

Jem said nothing. Wolf laid the whip on leisurely, expertly, chanting, "One. Two. Three. Four. . . ."

Fellie bore the first strokes in breath-held silence. Then the lash struck him as he was drawing breath, and the breath became a sob, until his sobs turned into harsh anguished pleas. "Don't sell—mah boys!" Soon the cries became indistinguishable moans of pain. The Negroes in the wagon cried out with him. Still the whip went on, cuts crisscrossing cuts as Wolf counted slowly, monotonously, "Twenty-five. Twenty-six. . . ."

Dulcie and Claudine, upstairs in the sewing room, heard Fellie's screams and the keening of the others. Dulcie looked out the window, gasped, and drew back hastily, her insides churning at the bloody sight. Wolf—and Daddy standing there with his arms folded, letting him—and Spig Hurd, grinning. . . . *Fellie,* who loved children black or white as if they were all his own. And his sons being taken from him.

She started for the door, then stopped. Her father had said not to interfere, and when he had spoken, he had meant it.

The anguished sounds went on and on. Fighting nausea, her throat tight with pain, she whispered, "Oh, Claudine!"

Claudine moaned with every stroke of the whip. "Miss Dulcie, it ain't fair. Never was a better man made than that Fellie. He's the bes' nigger yo' daddy'll evah have."

Suddenly the counting ceased, and Dulcie went to the window. The bloody whip hung limp from Wolf's hand. Her father and Spig Hurd were talking. Then the loaded wagon rumbled away, and Jem disappeared around the side of the house. "Two of the field hands are taking him away."

Claudine edged nearer.

"He must be still alive. They're taking him to his cabin." She thought for a moment. "I'll go see if I can find Mama."

Her parents' bedroom door was closed. If her father was in there, she didn't want to knock. She went to the kitchen. The servants' backs were turned to her, though no one looked busy. "Violet, where is Mama?"

Huge Violet, tears streaming down her round cheeks, wailed, "She run up an' lock herself in her bedroom, Miss Dulcie."

"Violet, hush. Mr. Jem will hear you! *All* of you stop cryin'. It will only make things worse."

"Miss Dulcie, Fellie gwine die!" said one of the younger girls.

"Oh, he will not!" Dulcie said staunchly, hoping it was the truth. "Stop snifflin'. He'll be all right in a few days." Again she hoped she was right. She had never seen anyone who had been badly whipped. How long did it take to get well?

Jem was sitting in his study, rocking in his chair with considerable agitation. He held a tall glass half full of neat whiskey. But the glow, the mellow, relaxed feeling, wouldn't come to rub out what had happened, what he'd had to watch. Damn Fellie! Damn Spig Hurd! Damn the blacks! If he ever had to whip another slave, he'd sell every last one of them.

Dulcie passed by, saw him glaring belligerently at nothing, and prudently went on upstairs. She tapped lightly at her mother's door.

"Go away," came a muffled voice.

"Mama, it's Dulcie."

"Let me alone!" Her mother was crying.

For half an hour Dulcie paced the sewing room. She couldn't stand waiting a moment longer. Legs trembling, she approached the study. The door was locked, and her father did not answer.

He might be outside. She ran anxiously to the stables. "Daddy?"

"Your tender-hearted daddy's in the big house gettin' drunk," replied a sarcastic voice.

Dulcie jumped. "Wolf! You startled me! What are you doin' here?"

Wolf's obsequiousness extended only to Jem and Patricia. "I'm doin' what your daddy ordered. I'm lockin' up ever' nigger on the place."

"You're what!? Who told you to do that? Daddy never—"

"My advice to you is to stay in the house where you belong."

"Since when do you presume to speak to me like that? My father's goin' to hear about this!"

"Now that there's a real threat, Miss Dulcie. Jes' what you expect he'll do about it?"

Dulcie walked quickly by the rows of cabins. They were all shut. Two of Jem's big drivers patrolled the area, holding whips. "What's happening, Barney?"

Barney rolled his eyes; Wolf was behind her. "We dunno, Miss Dulcie."

Angry and frightened, Dulcie returned to the house. It would be dusk soon. She had no wish to be caught after dark anywhere near Wolf in his present access of power, with her mother locked in one room and her father in another.

Behind her parents' door there were footsteps moving to and fro, and other small familiar but unidentifiable sounds. She knocked firmly. "Mama! Mama! I want to talk to you!"

"Later, Dulcie deah," came her mother's calm voice.

But her mother did not appear for dinner. The study door stayed locked. Dulcie ate alone. The servants came in, put the courses on the table, and left. An air of tenseness was all over the house. And where was Claudine?

"Ah ain't seen her, Miss Dulcie," Violet muttered.

For the first time in her life Dulcie went to bed with her door locked. Sleep would not come. It was not like the night—had it been only two nights before?—when she had hugged her pillow and daydreamed about Leroy until morning light. Everything was dreadfully wrong. A man had been flogged, an unheard-of thing at Mossrose. The blacks were locked in their cabins; the house servants were sullen and edgy. Neither Mama nor Daddy would speak to her. And Wolf was in charge.

Dulcie was still awake when a light tap came and a whispered "Miss Dulcie."

She unlocked the door. "Claudine! Where were you!?"

"That ol' Wolf shet me in a cabin wiff the fiel' womens. Ah tell him Ah'm a house nigger, an' he jes' laugh. He doan let me out 'til dey goes to work."

"Did you find out what happened?"

"Fiel' han's doan know nothin' noways, an' dey doan know nothin' dis time either."

"Is the study door still shut? And Mama's bedroom?"

"Miss Trishy's door shet, but ain't nobody in the steddy."

At breakfast Patricia looked worn, her eyes puffy. "Ah know nothin' o' what happened, Dulcie. Nor would Ah wish to discuss it if Ah did. Ah'm goin' ovah to Mrs. Saunders's today, you'll recall."

Dulcie did remember. Glenn's mother, somewhere in her forties and grandmother of three, was having a late baby. "Do you have to go so soon? Couldn't you wait till she sends for you?"

Patricia's mouth grew firm. "Ah am goin' today, Dulcie."

For several nights more the blacks were locked up. During the day Barney guarded Fellie's cabin. Jem seemed very busy while Patricia was gone. He had selected several new drivers, and they were posted everywhere, in the fields, the cobbler's shop, the spinning house, and the rush-hat manufactory. He came in late for meals, if at all, and was gone in the morning before Dulcie rose. He was avoiding her.

She waited in the study all one evening, sitting quietly without a light, until he came in to sit with his boots off and enjoy a drink before bedtime. "Lucius!" he bellowed. "Why isn't this lamp lit?"

"I blew it out," Dulcie said. "Daddy, I've got to talk to you."

He glanced over at her. "Well, I'm too tired. I don't want to talk. Go to bed, Dulcie, we'll talk in the mornin'."

"You haven't spoken to me in days!" Dulcie burst into tears. "Mama's gone, and you don't want anythin' to do with me!"

Lucius came to the door. "Yassuh, Mastah Jem?"

"Fix me a stiff drink and shut the door when Miss Dulcie goes out." He sank down in his chair, and Lucius pulled off his boots for him. Dulcie remained seated. Jem sighed deeply. "All right, Dulcie, what're you after?"

"I just want to know what's g-goin' on!"

"You'll have to stop that bawlin'. I can't abide it."

"I'm tryin', Daddy!" While her father sipped his drink, Dulcie wiped her eyes and blew her nose and regained some self-control. "Tell me what happened. Please. Why did Wolf whip Fellie?"

"Didn't you find out from the servants? They always know everythin'."

"I'd rather you told me."

"Fellie forgot he's nothin' but a nigger."

"What did he *do?*"

"He tried to kill Spig Hurd."

Dulcie felt as if the wind had been kicked out of her.

"Ohhh." She put her hand to her stomach. She and Jem stared at each other. "I see."

"I doubt it." Jem sipped again. "I very much doubt it." Dulcie, unknowingly, had provided him the opportunity to justify his actions to himself. "If it had been up to you, Miss, you'd have shaken your finger at him and sent him to his tick for a little nap."

Dulcie's temper rose, as Jem had hoped. "I wouldn't have sold his children in the first place! I certainly wouldn't have let Wolf flog him! Of all the cruel, senseless—"

Jem leaned forward angrily. "Cruel, it it? Senseless? Dulcie Jeannette Moran, you've got little in your head if you can't see why Fellie had to be flogged. If Wolf hadn't stopped Fellie's hand, a white man would be dead. Fellie would be hanged. I'd be lucky if I didn't get the same!"

"But he didn't kill Mr. Hurd!"

"No, but he tried to! He tried! Within sight of half the blacks on the plantation, Fellie tried to kill a white man! Just what do you think would have happened if Fellie'd gotten away with that? Tell me!"

Dulcie opened her mouth but was not given time to answer.

"You've lived your entire life on a plantation where the blacks are satisfied. They have their prayerhouse and their frolics. They aren't locked in or punished as long as they behave themselves. I thought I was bein' kind to them— but it was carelessness. They're all feelin' too full of themselves, and Fellie is just one example. He goes back to work tomorrow—under a driver and in chains."

"In chains?" Dulcie whispered.

Jem's voice rose to a shout. "Is your hearin' leavin' you? Yes, *chains!* He's got to be taught a lesson he'll never forget. And the rest of them too. We'll see how fast they try to start an uprisin', with that before them as a constant reminder!"

Dulcie said coldly, "That's spreadin' the punishment a little thick."

"Who are you to judge, Miss! A girl barely turned sixteen! I tell you, the blacks have got to be kept under control! If they're not, they'll take matters into their own hands!"

"Doesn't that prove they're human? Thinkin'—feelin'— hurtin'—"

"We're back to that again are we? No! They don't think,

and they don't feel, any more than other animals do!"

Dulcie's throat constricted as she thought of the Negroes in the kitchen sobbing for Fellie's pain, and those in the wagon, and Claudine, sharing it in spirit. But she could not speak.

"Did you ever see a pack of dogs tear up a bitch in heat because they couldn't get at her fast enough? Does that make the dogs human? Does it?"

"No—but—"

"You're a Southerner, second generation, my own flesh and blood, and damn my eyes if you don't talk like a preacher! You're just like your mother! Too gentle! Too soft-hearted! Wrong-headed and feisty."

Dulcie rose, her skirts rustling. "If I'm feisty, I get it straight from you! You've told me so, often enough. And if I'm wrongheaded, I know where that comes from too!" She turned to go.

"Dulcie Jeannette!" her father roared. "I will not allow you to be impudent to me."

"I'm going to bed!" Dulcie yelled back and ran up the stairs. She locked her door and threw herself on her bed, crying in angry frustration.

Claudine came out of her dressing room, looking fearful. "Miss Dulcie, somethin' else happen." Her voice was pitched low.

"I don't want to hear about it!" Dulcie cried. Then she looked at Claudine. "What did you say?"

"Fellie gwine run off, Miss Dulcie."

Hastily Dulcie wiped her tears and sat up. "How can he? He's not well. He's locked up."

Claudine leaned nearer, whispering. "Dey's not locked up any mo'. Mastah Jem's keepin' the drivers patterollin', but dey's all ca'm down now, so dey ain't lock in."

"How did you find that out?"

"Ah was out foolin' 'round wiff Barney awhiles."

"You mean Barney told you that?"

"No'm, he lets me go in an' see Ester. One de pickaninnies tell me. His mama slap him good. She say he fibbin', but he ain't."

Dulcie stared at Claudine unblinking, her quick, impulsive mind racing. Claudine shrank away. "Ah doan mean to get Fellie in no mo' trouble, Miss Dulcie. He still mighty sickly."

"Hush, I'm thinkin'. Dulcie rubbed her arms where the

delicate gooseflesh of risk had made her chilly. Before judgment could weaken her resolve she asked, "Is Ester goin' along?"

"Ah dunno. Ah wish Ah never tell you."

"Claudine, get out my ridin' outfit. And find that old pair of britches and a heavy shirt for yourself."

"Miss Dulcie!" Claudine gasped. "What you thinkin' on? Oh, no! Oh, no! Lawdy Lawd, what Ah done do?"

"Do you want to go, or stay here and explain to Daddy why you didn't keep me from goin'?"

"Ah doan wanta go neither one! Ah's too afeerd! Miss Dulcie, please! Oh, Lawd, what Ah done!"

"Oh, calm down. We won't do anythin' till Daddy comes to bed. Tell me, who else is patrollin' besides Barney? What's Wolf doin'?"

"Mistah Woof snorin' like a bull in his cabin. Dick an' Barney's all, an' dey's sleepy too. Might be dey take a li'l wink 'fo' long."

"Shove that rug up against the door crack so Daddy won't see my lamp. I've got some work to do."

By the time Jem went woozily to bed, Dulcie had sent Claudine to Fellie's cabin with a message and, in a creditable imitation of Jem's handwriting, had made up six letters freeing Fellie, Ester, and their four remaining children:

On the 10th day of Octo. 1860, I, James Moran, have set free my slave, Fellie, and I hereby make and acknowledge the emancipation paper for his complete freedom.

James Moran

Claudine came back in. "Dick an' Barney ain't gwine bother us. Dick's pleasurin' his woman, an' Ah take care o' Barney. They both sleep like angels."

"Did you look in on Wolf?"

"Yes'm. He a mighty tired man. Bottle on de flo' by his baid."

"Fine." Dulcie blew out the lamp. "I have to get some money out of Daddy's safe and put his seal on these papers. Is Fellie ready?"

"He be hidin' in de stables, time we gets out dere."

Fellie and his family were waiting. With a sinking heart Dulcie realized there were others: Emma and Phyllis, both dangerously pregnant, Myrtle, who oversaw the spinning house, and the handsome Gullah field hand named Darcy. "You people are supposed to be in your cabins!" she hissed.

"Miss Dulcie, dey wants to go 'long," said Fellie.

"The carriage will never hold twelve people!"

"Darcy done figger out 'bout hitchin' up de wagon, Miss Dulcie. We ain't got so fa' to go. Jes' to de piney woods, den we runs."

For a moment Dulcie's courage faltered. Then, thinking quickly, she said, "All right. We'll have to wrap the harness so it won't jingle."

"Me 'n' Darcy fix it a'ready," said Fellie proudly. "We lay quilts all oveh de bottom o' de wagon to keep it quiet, too."

"Darcy, open both doors as silently as you can. Everybody get in the wagon and lie down till I tell you it's safe. Darcy, you shut the doors behind us and catch up as quick as you can."

"Miss Dulcie, you ain't nevah gwine wid us!" said Fellie unbelievingly as she climbed up on the wagon seat.

"Don't worry about it now, Fellie. Get in."

"Den you jes' git us off de plantation an' come on back. It ain't safe fo' you. Ah doan wants you gittin' hurt!"

"Nobody's goin' to get hurt," Dulcie declared. She flapped the reins, and one of the horses whinnied, scaring everybody. She kept the wagon moving slowly on the grass at the edge of the long crepe myrtle lane.

Chapter Four

When they reached the River Road, Dulcie whipped the horses to a fast trot. She wouldn't be safe until she passed Saunders', Acton's, and Whitaker's plantations.

Claudine sat beside her. "Where you takin' us, Miss Dulcie? "

"To Savannah. We should be able to get there and back

before there's an uproar at home. I took enough money
for ship passage for everybody to Philadelphia. They'll be
free once they get beyond North Carolina."

Claudine asked in alarm, "You ain't sendin' me off,
Miss Dulcie?"

"Why, Claudine?" Dulcie teased. "Don't you want to be
free?"

"No, *ma'am!* Anythin' Ah doan wan' is bein' turned
loose! An' somethin' else Ah doan wan' is lookin' Mastah
Jem in his face when we gits back. He gwine take a
piss-ellum club to both us."

Dulcie shivered. "Ugh, Claudine, don't say things like
that! If I'd look back and see Daddy, or Wolf, I know I'd
just swoon!"

As it grew pale daylight, Dulcie and Claudine knew the
plantation bell would be sounding at Mossrose. Soon it
would be alive with activity. Since Dulcie seldom rose
early, no one was likely to notice she was missing. But
Fellie and nine others would be gone.

Dulcie told the blacks to sit up in the wagon and not to
act scared in case they met anybody. Unless they were
asked direct questions, they were not to say a word.

Their first threat to safety was a lone man on horseback.
Patteroller! cried her anxious mind. *If it is, and he finds
out I've got a wagonload of runaway slaves . . .* "Sing!"
she told them. In her clear, sweet voice she began, "Nelly
Bly! Nelly Bly! Bring the broom along."

The harmonious blending of the rich voices made a
lovely sound on the misty morning air. "Keep them singin',
Claudine," she commanded as the approaching rider
reined up. He removed his shabby hat and swept a low
bow. Dulcie flicked the horses again. The man remained
at the side of the road, irresolute.

When Nelly Bly's several verses had been exhausted,
Darcy began, "Oh, brothers, you oughta been dere. Yes,
my Lawd" and on through other songs comforting and
familiar to them from the prayerhouse.

To ease her tension Dulcie said, "Fellie, you and Ester
have to pick yourselves a last name. When you're free,
you can't be just Fellie."

"I's gwine be Fellie Jordan, 'cause we cross ovah Jordan
to make free."

"That sounds fine, Fellie." *And Daddy says they are*

animals who don't think or feel! "What name will you choose, Darcy?"

"Ah doan know no names, Miss Dulcie. What gwine be mah name?"

"Well, let's think. What do you especially like, Darcy?"

"Cain' say Ah knows, Miss. Ah likes de animals. 'Possums make good eatin', an' dey's nice li'l critters."

"Foxes are pretty smart. How about Darcy Fox?"

Darcy beamed. "Yas'm, Ah likes dat. Ah gwine have me dat name."

"Miss Dulcie, me 'n' Ester thanks you fo' takin' us'uns to S'vannah," Fellie said. "We'n have a mighty po' time figgerin' it out fo' ouahseffs. Ah's worrit 'bout you gettin' back safe. What Mastah Jem gwine do?"

Dulcie gave him a smile. In spite of his pain and soreness from unhealed cuts, he had not once asked for comfort or any sort of ease for himself. "You quit worryin' over me, Fellie. I always get out of my scrapes, don't I? Besides I'll have Claudine with me. Daddy'll be pretty mad, but he'll get over it. He always has."

"Dis de wust thing you evah done, Miss Dulcie."

Dulcie said nothing. She wouldn't speak against her father. Her criticism was patent in her presence here. And thinking of him now only made her nervous and timid at the time she needed to be most bold.

They came to the familiar wide sandy streets of Savannah lined with China trees and suddenly thoughts of Jem vanished as the going became harder. Deep sand in the centers of the streets sucked at the wagon wheels and the horses' hooves and slowed them down.

Anxious, Dulcie urged the horses past Factor's Walk and down the steep, curving roadway toward the pier. She could see the islands in the river, the steamships and sailing ships that lay at anchor. Two steamships were anchored close to one another. The first, *Mirabelle,* was grim and rusty, her crew lackadaisically coiling ropes or lounging at the rail staring at Dulcie. "The other one looks neater, don't you think, Claudine?"

Dulcie saw a two-hundred-twenty-five-foot sidewheel paddler moving gently at anchor. Two well-polished black stacks stretched skyward. On the wheel housing, in red and gold, was written *Ullah.* Her upper decks were crisply clean, the gingerbread trim gleaming with fresh white paint.

Dulcie knew little of ships, but she recognized industry and smartness. Several sailors were on their knees holystoning the deck; another polished the brass rail that stood waist-high. Their spirits were good. She could hear them joking with one another. The *Ullah* looked a likely prospect, if only they'd take Negroes onboard. "Darcy, yell at those sailors and tell them I want to see their captain."

Darcy walked near the ship. "Suh! Please, suh!"

Fellie sat in the wagon, staring at the ship. His face quivered. "Miss Dulcie, please, Ah cain't get on dat boat."

"Of course you can, Fellie! There's no reason to be scared. It will only be a short trip, and then you'll be free."

"Yas'm, but Ah cain't go lessen Ah fin's mah boys."

Dulcie stared at him. "What? Fellie! You've come all this way, risked everybody's life—and you won't go North?"

"Ah doan mean Ah ain't gwine Nawth. Ah do dat, yas'm. But fust Ah got to fotch back Jothan an' Ruel."

"Fellie, don't be a fool! They're on their way to New Orleans! You can't find them! Besides, you *can't* stay in the South! You'd be taken right back to Mossrose. And if Spig Hurd sees you he'll shoot you!"

"Yas'm, me 'n' Ester knows dat. Ah knows Ah gots to lay low 'til Ah fin's mah boys agin. But Ah gots to fin' 'em. Ah got a whippin' on account Ah wants mah chilluns, an' Ah still ain' change mah min'."

Dulcie thought. "Would you go North if I try to get the boys back?"

Fellie shook his head sadly. "Miss Dulcie, you jes' 'bout de bestes' lady in de worl', 'cept you cain' get mah boys fo' me. You take too many chances fo' me an' mine a'ready. Ah gots to fin' mah boys mahseff."

"What are you goin' to do? How will you ever—" Dulcie began, when a cheerful voice, only a few feet away, made her jump.

"Miss, is there somethin' I can help you with?"

She looked up at a well-built man in his twenties, with a pleasant smile and blond hair that fell in a wave over his forehead. She had time to notice the blue work clothes, with his sleeves rolled up to show a tattooed anchor within a heart on his right forearm. She took a breath and rallied her thoughts. "Are you from the ship?" She pointed.

"Yes, ma'am, the *Ullah*. Your man said you wanted to see the captain."

"Are you the captain? You don't look like one."

The blond man stood with his thumbs tucked into his belt and his fingers pointing downward, his legs a little apart, his tight-fitting dungarees outlining him boldly. He was still smiling. "Yes, ma'am, I'm a captain. We've got three captains onboard the *Ullah*. We just don't happen to have three ships yet." He seemed to think it a very fine joke.

Dulcie smiled uncertainly. "Then who . . . which?"

"I'm Ben West, Miss, serving temporarily as first mate. Looks as if you've got some trouble."

"No trouble at all—Captain West." She made an ineffectual gesture to smooth her hair. "I just . . . I want passage for these people. They . . . my father freed them, and they're goin' to Philadelphia to . . . to my uncle— Oliver Raymer. He . . . he'll help them get work." She scanned the streets for familiar and therefore threatening faces as she talked.

"Do they have papers, Miss?"

"Oh, yes! Ester, show him yours."

Ben West looked at the emancipation paper and knew immediately it was invalid. But that was the least worrisome aspect. Poorly forged, Jem Moran's signature stood out boldly. Ben's eyes narrowed. The *Ullah*'s hold was filled with Mossrose cotton. What game was this girl playing bringing fugitives supposedly freed by Moran to the ship that carried his cotton as cargo? "Who are you?" he asked brusquely.

Dulcie stepped back, her voice all but inaudible. "Who am I? My name? Why . . . why must you know my—?"

"Look, Miss, you'd better see the captain right now!" He took her arm, pulling her roughly along.

Dulcie staggered, her knees weak with fright. "Oh, please. I'll go somewhere else. Please. Let me go. Don't tell—"

Ben glowered at her, not impressed by the deathly pallor of her face or her wide, frightened eyes. "Who are you, anyway?"

"D-Dulcie Moran. Jem Moran's my daddy. I-I live at Mossrose! Please! I haven't done anythin' wrong!" She choked; frightened, hiccuping tears burst forth.

Ben's jaws dropped. "Oh, God! You're his daughter?" He rapped sharply on the captain's cabin door, then pushed it open, and stepped inside, pulling hard on Dulcie's arm, jerking her beside him. Nonplussed, he said, "We got a bundle o' trouble, Adam. She . . . she claims to be Jem Moran's daughter. Got a wagon full of fugitives and . . . and damn! emancipation papers with Moran's signature forged on 'em. What do you want me to do with her?"

Adam's eyes never left Dulcie. He listened to Ben with only half an ear.

Dulcie was faint with fright. She stared with hypnotized terror at the man she had met at Mossrose the day of her birthday party—her father's business associate. She was too frightened to move or even cry. The tears wouldn't fall. In her ears pounded an unhealthy roar. She couldn't hear what Ben was saying or what the big dark-visaged man replied as his black eyebrows knit together in a forbidding frown.

The next she knew Ben West was gone. She was alone in the small captain's cabin, the door shut, the smell of resin strong, the walls dark with ancient paneling. The captain, judgmental, scowling was waiting for her to drink from the snifter he pressed to her lips.

"Drink it," he commanded.

Obediently Dulcie sipped it, breathed the brandy down her windpipe, and choked.

He swore under his breath, jerked her hands high over her head, and roughly patted her back. Her eyes were watering, and she couldn't speak. She trembled all over.

"Are you all right now?" he asked, his voice still rough and demanding.

"What are you goin' to do to me?"

He sat down at his desk, evaluating her across its expanse. "Why did you choose this ship to bring your fugitives, Miss Moran?"

"Can't you just let me go?"

His eyes narrowed, the blue growing darker and harder. He watched her for what seemed to Dulcie hours. Then he leaned back, his expression bland. "As you wish, Miss Moran. You are free to go."

Dulcie was immobile for a few moments as the import of his words sunk in. Then she stood up shakily, taking an uncertain step toward the door. "I can leave? You won't stop me?"

"Be certain you take your darkies with you."

She felt as if he had hit her. In her own cringing fear, she'd forgotten Fellie and the others. If she ran now to save herself from Jem's anger, Fellie would die as an example to other slaves. "But I . . . I have papers. Couldn't you—"

"You might also inform your father I don't like being tested in so callow a fashion."

Dulcie's head swam. Nothing made sense. "Captain . . . ?"

"Tremain," he said curtly.

"Why should my father test you, Captain Tremain?"

"Why indeed? Suppose you tell me."

Slowly the truth began to form. Dulcie returned to her chair, still frightened, but bolder, determined. "You would have taken Fellie if my name hadn't been Moran, wouldn't you?" she said in amazement. "You *do* take runaways North! It's my father, his cotton. Captain! I can tell on you!"

"What will you tell, Miss Moran? That I refused to take some fugitives North for you?"

As quickly defeated as she had been hopeful, Dulcie slumped forward, her hands covering her face, bitter sobs tearing from her. "I only wanted to help Fellie. Why did I have to choose this ship?"

Adam watched her, outwardly dispassionate. He knew her only to be an imp and a hellion, quite capable of acting as her father's agent to trap him into an admission of hauling slaves. But he didn't know if she were actress enough to put on the heartbroken display that followed as she bawled out the story of how she came to be at his ship with ten of her father's best Negroes.

To trust her he'd have to risk everything—his career, his ship, his freedom. Yet, if she told the truth, she had also risked everything to bring these slaves to him. According to Dulcie, Fellie would hang for threatening the life of a white man.

Reason told him to get her off his ship as fast as he could, protect his contract with Jem Moran, and thus assure that the planters would never suspect he hauled runaways North. Other men had been tricked into an admission of guilt by ruses such as this.

And yet—he believed her. Instinctively he was drawn to her, trusted her, believed her fantastic, unbelievable story. His eyes moved slowly over her. He saw a grubby-

looking girl with wild roan-red curls and an aristocratic
beauty in spite of her unfashionable tan. Her riding jacket
had fallen open, and he glimpsed the full breasts under
her white shirt, her tiny waist. He looked away, angry
that this girl, nowhere near being a woman, could make
him consider throwing caution and reason away. And for
what? Some mad, naive scheme to free an incorrigible
darky who didn't even want to go North. Yet he was! He
was considering it. No, more—he *wanted* to take her
Negroes North. "Wait here, Miss Moran."

He locked her in the cabin, then went to the rail. *"Mistah LeClerc!* Bring the man Fellie up here!"

As Fellie approached him, Adam could see the man
struggling to walk proud despite his pain. "Yassuh."

"Miss Moran tells me you've made free and now have
changed your mind."

"Ah ain't changed mah min', but Ah gotta fin' mah boys
fust, or Ah gwine die tryin'."

Adam played with the tip of his moustache. In his gut
he knew Fellie meant every word he spoke. The man's
pain, his love for his children were strong, filling the air
around them. "Well, Fellie," he said, considering, "what
will happen to the rest of your family if you go hunting
for your boys and get killed?"

Fellie lowered his head. "Ah doan know, suh. But Ah
gotta do it."

Dulcie sat quietly waiting. She was beyond crying, beyond fear. She knew he'd locked her in. She'd tried the
door. She supposed he'd sent for the authorities—or perhaps Jem. She closed her eyes. Did they imprison women
for stealing slaves? Hang them? Tar and feather them?
She'd heard of such things.

Finally the key turned in the lock. Adam came in looking as forbidding as when he left. His face was stern.
How could she have imagined wanting to be kissed by
him? He was a terrifying monster of a man. Just being
in the same room with him made her shiver, unable to
think or breathe.

He paced the narrow cabin, his trouser leg brushing the
hem of her riding habit with each passage. She tucked her
feet closer to the chair. Her knees trembled as cloth
brushed against cloth with his next passage.

Hands clasped behind his back, he spun to face her. "Miss Moran, shall we suppose that I agree to take your people North, what exactly do you intend to tell your father?"

Dulcie looked up hopefully, but the light in her eyes died quickly. She gestured helplessly. "I . . . I have the money for passage. I . . . I thought all I'd have to do was pay you and—but now I know you won't take them. I didn't know—" She swallowed hard, her throat was dry and hot.

Adam raised an eyebrow, his smile mocking. "You didn't know it is illegal to steal slaves? Come, now, Miss Moran, there isn't a Southerner over the age of five who doesn't know that."

Mutely, she nodded. "But I had the papers. I thought they'd be enough."

"An act of the legislature is required to free slaves in Georgia."

Dulcie gaped at him, then hid her face.

He kept questioning her, pressing harder and harder. He no longer knew why he put her through this. The slaves were already aboard. He was already incriminated. He'd already promised Fellie he'd find Ruel and Jothan and bring them to New York. But still he quizzed and tormented this girl, half wondering if his resentment didn't stem from her innocent power to make him feel reckless and wild, capable of performing any feat of heroism. It was the most stupid, irresponsible thing he'd ever thought! she saw on his face. Then she began to realize what he woodenly at his desk, waiting for him to turn her over to the authorities.

"We cast off in fifteen minutes, Miss Moran."

She nodded dumbly. What did that mean?

"Your people are secreted aboard." He tossed the statement at her, his blue entrancing eyes studying her for the smallest reaction.

But she was beyond reaction, resigned to Jem's wrath, the penalty of the law.

He gestured, his long tanned fingers spread wide, a scornful smile on his lips. "It is your move, Miss Moran. The fugitives are aboard the *Ullah*. What will you do now?"

Dulcie stared at him, bewildered at the uncertainty she saw on his face. Then she began to realize what he was saying. Her golden eyes came alive, sparkling, joyful. She smiled tentatively, then broadly, her hands prayerlike at her lips. "You'll take them? You'll take them!"

It was like seeing the sun come out after the rain, Adam thought, as he watched the transformation in Dulcie. She was radiant. She glowed. Affected, he stood up, smiling now too. He put his hand out, and she grasped it with her tiny warm hand. Both of them started at the touch of the other's flesh. Blushing, she primly retracted her hand.

Adam cleared his throat. "I'll have Mr. LeClerc see you ashore. We, uh, we sail in minutes."

Dulcie could hardly breathe. It was relief and gratitude, she knew, but she was terribly conscious of this formidible, handsome man. She forced herself to meet his eyes without blushing again and suppressed the tremulous, nervous giggle that wanted to force its way through her lips. "Thank you—oh, it's not enough! How can I ever thank you for what you're doin' for Fellie?"

He looked almost embarrassed. "You'll be safe going home? You have an escort?"

"Oh, yes! I got here, didn't I?"

Adam nodded curtly and led her to Beau. "See her ashore, Mr. LeClerc." Quickly he turned, disappearing down a companionway.

Gentle and comforting, Beau talked easily with Dulcie, walking her to her wagon leisurely, as though he had all the time in the world.

The deep-throated bellow of the *Ullah*'s whistle sounded. Beau grinned, giving her a quick salute. He ran for the ship. Precariously balanced on the rising gangplank, he waved to her over his shoulder.

As Dulcie climbed lithely onto the wagon beside Claudine, Adam watched from the bridge. The *Ullah* steamed slowly away from the pier. He squinted, then grabbed his telescope. "Beau!"

Beau walked jauntily to his side. "That's some girl, isn't she!"

"Is that little black boy all the protection she has going back?"

Beau laughed. "Better check your spyglass, captain, sir. That little black boy is the cutest little tiny black girl I ever saw wearing britches."

"Reverse the engines!"

"What? Beg pardon?"

"Reverse the God-damned engines! Now, Mistah Le-Clerc!" Adam bolted down the companionway. The crewmen gaped in alarm as the captain raced down the deck, waiting in wrathful impatience for the *Ullah* to back into her slip. He jumped to the wharf before the gangplank was half down.

Adam ran along the waterfront, racing up the steep, curving road to Bay Street. Carriages and wagons moved in steady confusion. But Dulcie was gone. God, he hoped she was safe. Dulcie Moran might have reached the *Ullah* all right, but he doubted her audacity would withstand Moran's fury.

His steps were heavy as he returned to the *Ullah*. He berated himself for not having realized from the start he should have taken her home himself. Even with a horse, which he didn't have, he'd be hard-pressed to catch her now. Nevertheless, he considered going to the livery stables. But the *Ullah* stood at anchor. The slaves—Fellie and the others—waited. Still reluctant, he boarded the ship. "Cast off, Mr. West," he said lifelessly. What would Jem Moran do to her?

Chapter Five

As Dulcie made her way toward Savannah with her wagonload of slaves, the first light of dawn crept across the sky over Mossrose. Neither the owner nor the overseer of the plantation was prepared to face the day. Wolf woke with the ringing of the plantation bell. He swung his legs over the side of the bed, unerringly placing his foot on the empty whiskey bottle. The cold contact of the glass against his warm bare foot brought back both the memory of the needed sleep it hadn't given him enough of and the thundering headache it had given him in abundance.

Groggily, his head throbbing and his stomach rebelling, he peered down the narrow alley of the slave quarters. The blacks were already heading for the fields. He didn't see his drivers, but they were nearby. They knew him well enough not to dare anything else. Strict discipline was critical; he'd spent years trying to convince Jem. It

allowed a man freedom to take a day in his bed. With the
punishment of Fellie, Wolf was confident that finally his
boss realized what came of coddling slaves.

His stomach heaved with the need to relieve itself of its
sour burden. Wolf groaned and lay back, waiting for the
nausea to pass. He was asleep before the last of the slaves
were in the fields.

Jem was in no better shape than his overseer, but in far
worse frame of mind. He wasn't pleased with anything.
Patricia had been angry with him before but never the way
she was this time. Her trip to the Saunderses had been
planned in advance of the incident with Fellie, but he also
knew that Patricia had wanted to go. She was glad to be
away from Mossrose and from him.

While Jem was a strong-minded man, he was not at all
strong when it came to the disapproval of his wife or
daughter, and at the moment he had the disapproval of
both. Often Jem was pleased to note that Dulcie had a
great deal of his blood running in her veins, but when he
was in the wrong, as he felt he was now, it was like having
two consciences. Hadn't he castigated himself enough for
what had happened to Fellie? It could not have been
helped. Fellie had to be punished, or Spig Hurd would
certainly have killed him. Not only was Fellie a valuable
slave that he didn't want to see strung from a tree or
shot, but, Jem admitted, if only to himself, he had allowed himself to become too fond of Fellie, too lenient—
and that small sin had been returned to Jem tenfold.

And Fellie had not really been provoked. It was one
thing for a white man to mourn the loss of his sons, but
Fellie's boys were not exactly his sons, they were his get,
bred for purpose. Jem consoled himself with the thought
that Fellie, being but half human, would soon forget. It
was just Jem's bad luck that these particular boys had to
be sired by the humanest slave he happened to own. Why
couldn't Patricia and Dulcie see he'd done only what had
to be done? He hadn't wanted to whip his best nigger, and
he hadn't liked it.

Feeling sorry for himself, Jem rolled over in bed, convinced he'd never felt so poorly in all his life. He envi-
sioned Patricia's return later in the morning. Perhaps if
she saw the miseries he'd put himself through, she'd understand.

* * *

It was nine o'clock when Wolf finally roused. He dressed quickly, his head still hurting, his stomach in too much of a turmoil to consider food. He felt mean. It would pleasure him to lash those black bastards into line. Ten years he'd waited for Moran to give him free use of his whip arm. Now he meant to demonstrate its value.

It was an overcast day, one of those when a man can feel the pressure building up, tightening all around him. No wonder his head throbbed. The stable boy saw Wolf coming and had his horse ready. Wolf smiled. Already the flogging of Fellie was showing results. Never had this particular boy shown such alacrity.

Wolf rode toward the farthest field. He'd work himself back in toward the quarters and catch another nap. All was quiet. The sun peeped through the clouds, wiping away the threat of rain, and yet the feeling of something impending remained. When he reached the last field, he realized what was wrong.

A hush had fallen over Mossrose like a smothering blanket. He scanned the field and saw the slaves, all with bent backs, diligently at work. It should have made his heart glad, but it was as unnatural as anything he'd ever seen. There was no noise, none of the buzzing undercurrent of talk and laughter. All was still, as it was when a storm was brewing.

He rode down the rows, flicking his whip indiscriminately. None of them flinched, begged, or showed the customary fear of him. It was as if he weren't there at all. Uneasy, Wolf went to the end of the field. Neither Barney nor Dick was anywhere to be seen. "Where's your drivah?"

'Simmon, a wizened old black man nearly at the end of his picking days, didn't stop his rhythmic bending motion. "Cain't say Ah knows who you talkin' 'bout."

Angry at the insolence, Wolf brought his whip down across the old man's shoulders. A groan was forced from 'Simmon's lips and a line of blood showed through his shirt. As if on cue, one by one every slave in the field stopped work. Backs straightened. Faces turned toward Wolf. An ebony chain stretched out across the seven-acre field, their triumphant faces daring him to use his whip on 'Simmon again.

In spite of the lightning-fast anger that struck him, Wolf shuddered. Visions of the Nat Turner rebellion flashed into his mind. A kind master, an intelligent slave with dreams of freedom and retribution festering in his animal mind, gone beserk, slaying women and children, men and boys indiscriminately, without cause or mercy. He remembered stories his daddy had told of people, white people begging for their lives.

Wolf backed his horse a step, then two. He yelled at them, brandishing the whip, but far enough away that it touched no black back. It was show, now, a means of saying he wasn't afraid while his insides turned to water.

In front of him a black twig of a woman, a dark stick covered with osnaburg that hung on her like a shroud, began to sing. The old woman, mate of 'Simmon, her voice quavering and tremulous, gazed up at him through old and rheumy eyes, and defied him to strike her down. One by one the blacks took up her song. The words rolled out across the open fields, filling up the waiting air:

> De good time comin' is almost heah,
> It was long, long, long on de way.

Their voices came at him like a physical presence. The sounds surrounded him as the Negroes in the other fields took up the singing. The plantation reverberated with the rumble of the black voices.

Wolf no longer tried to hide his terror. He rode the perimeter of the field, lashing with the whip, screaming for them to go back to work. Slowly the black human chain began to move, walking with an untouchable courage away from him, away from their work, away from the fields. He couldn't stop them. He couldn't rekindle the fear he'd always been able to light in their eyes.

By ten o'clock Jem couldn't bear remaining in bed any longer. He was unaccustomed to the inactivity and bored with the idea of making Patricia feel sorry for him. He was the master of Mossrose, and there'd be no more sniveling over his decisions by his wife, his daughter, or his darkies.

"Lucius! Lucius!" His voice echoed in the empty house. "Lucius! You black bastard get your hind end up here!"

By the time he'd yelled for Lucius several more times, the unnatural quiet of the house pressed in on him. "What in the devil?" he muttered, and began walking from one room to another. When he entered the kitchen and found no Violet standing at her cookstove, he knew something was afoot.

He was headed for his study for his rifle and his whip, when Wolf burst in through the front door.

"Since when do you bust into this house when you damn please?"

Wolf's face was a pale, shining globe. He fought for words and breath to tell James Moran that there was an insurrection on Mossrose. "Oh, Gawd, suh. It's the niggers, suh. They's in a takin', and' ain't nothin' I do that can get 'em back to the fiel's."

"What in thunderation are you talkin' about?" Jem had no sooner spoken than the sounds of their singing could be heard through the open door and windows. The sound was loud, jubilant. Jem looked warily from the window back to Wolf. "They in the chapel?"

"Yes, suh. I lef' 'em to come an' warn you."

"Nothin's goin' to happen as long as they stay put." Jem leaned far out the window, still not willing to believe his ears or his overseer. "What they worked up for?" He knew the answer before Wolf swallowed hard, taking all his pride into his gullet with the word "Fellie."

"Sweet Jesus."

"They're headin' for a real bust-out. What're we gonna do 'bout it, suh?"

Jem wiped his forehead nervously. There wasn't a Southerner alive who didn't live in dread of something like this. "No way we can hold back four hundred niggers if they've a mind to come at us. Only thing we can do is fortify the house, protect the women, and warn the other planters. Ride to Saunders, warn him, and tell him to pass the word. Bring Miz Moran back here with you. Hurry, Wolf. Tell Saunders and the others to gather their dogs an' all the men they can. Meet here."

"Yes, suh! You shore you want Miss Patricia back here?"

"Yes, yes, I'm sure. No tellin' how far this will spread. I want her home where I can look after her. She and Dulcie can go to the root cellar. Nobody's gonna break in there—got a special door on it. Where the hell is Dulcie? She couldn't have slept through all this racket."

"Can't say as I know, suh. Haven't seen her this mornin'."

Jem ran to the staircase, returning no more than a minute later.

Wolf reached for him. "You all right, suh?"

"Ohhh, my God. She's gone," Jem moaned. "Goddamned nigger bastards have got her. Took her."

Wolf's skin tightened and prickled in fear. He knew better than to wait. He hurried from the house, riding fast on the River Road toward the Saunders plantation, shouting to all he passed, "Insurrection! Took Miz Moran captive! Meet at Mossrose! Bring hounds! Insurrection!"

By the time he reined in at the Saunderses', panic had spread across the county. Houses were barricaded against their own slaves. Overseers worked furiously, lashing at any suspected sign of insolence or rebellion.

Cal Saunders tried to persuade Patricia to remain. Her face frightened and pinched, she refused.

"Mah Dulcie may be lyin' dead this very moment, Cal. If Jem can fin' her, Ah'm goin' to be right theah in mah home when she needs me."

Patricia mounted the narrow buggy, sitting beside Wolf and his loaded rifle. On the way she had him repeat every detail of the slaves' activity that morning and of Dulcie's disappearance. Finally, she asked, "But have they actually done anythin' threatenin'? Dulcie has always been a favorite of the blacks. She—"

"I think they took Miz Dulcie off somewheres. Keepin' her there. One of the wagon's missin' an' four o' the horses. That good-fo'-nuthin' Fellie an' his woman is gone too. I'm thinkin' they took her off, so's we couldn't do nuthin' to stop 'em."

Patricia's hands clasped at her breast and throat, but she said nothing. The distance to the house seemed interminable. Patricia jumped from the carriage as soon as Wolf reined the horses to a stop.

"Jem, the men are comin'. Cal Saunders and Glenn are just behind me. She threw herself into his arms. "Oh, Jem, if weah goin' to be slaughtered. . . . Jem, Ah love you."

"Aw, Patsy love, it'll be all right. No one's goin' to be slaughtered." Carefully he kept his betraying eyes from her sight.

Patricia kissed him, then buried her face in his shoulder again. "We gonna get ouah Dulcie home again, Jem? Will that happen too?"

"We'll get her back," he said grimly.

"Free 'em all if you must. Promise me you will, Jem. Give 'em Mossrose itself if that's what they want to bring her back safe to us."

"We'll get Dulcie back, Patsy, and there'll be no concedin' to the niggers." Jem felt far stronger and more manly now that Patricia was once more depending on him.

She moved away from him. "No, Jem, you can't do anythin' against them—not until Dulcie is safe. They . . . they could kill her. Nothin' is worth that. She's ouah daughtah, ouah only chil'."

"Hush, Patsy. I said I'd take care of it." He took another rifle from the gun rack, methodically loading it as she watched.

"You aren't gonna do this, Jem Moran."

"Hide in the root celler, Patsy. Lock the door and stay there 'til I tell you it's safe to come out." He handed her a gun. "If things go wrong, don't hesitate, Patsy. Pull the trigger."

The fear that had been held in abeyance now overwhelmed her. She pushed the gun away. "No! You talk to them, Jem. You go out theah to the chapel, an' you talk to them! Ask them what they want. Doesn't matter what it is. You give it to them if they bring ouah Dulcie home! You heah me, Jem!? You promise 'em the moon if they give you Dulcie alive and well!"

"Calm yourself, Patsy. There's no reasonin' with a nigger. They don't understand reasonin'. I hear the Saunderses comin'. Be my good love and go to the root cellar. You'll be safe there."

Cal and Glenn Saunders's voices could be heard in the front hall as Patricia screamed, near hysteria, at Jem. "It's youah fault! You brought this on us with youah whippin' an' youah brutalizin' of Fellie! He took her 'cause o' what you did to him. Now youah gonna listen to me! *We will promise them anythin'!*"

"Patricia!"

"She's mah daughtah, an' Ah intend to fight fo' her, even if it's you Ah have to fight, James Moran!"

Glenn and his father stood in the study doorway, astonished. Glenn nudged his father.

The older man nodded, then turned, looking toward the front door. "Those are the Biggs's hounds. I'd know that lead hound's bugle anyplace."

The Chilcotes, Biggses, and Actons arrived in a group. The Matthewses, Carsons, and Redgraves rode in from the south across Jem's fields. The yard filled with pawing, nervous horses and the sounds of eagerly whimpering hounds. In the background was the melodious singing of the slaves.

Glenn Saunders jumped onto the rail of the veranda, shouting above the noise for attention. He told the men of the situation at Mossrose, of Dulcie's capture, and of the threat to their own plantations.

Inside the house Patricia had worked herself into a frenzy. Everything she had worried about over the years came tumbling out. "You nevah treated youah slaves bad 'til you began this breedin' business. Now look what it's done to us! Ouah Dulcie gone—maybe lyin' dead, 'cause o' you, Jem. Ah won't stan' quiet this time. Ah won't let you do anythin' to prevent her from bein' returned to us. You heah me, Jem!"

"I can't help but hear you, Patricia, but I wish to God I couldn't. How can you blame me? I love you and Dulcie better than my own life."

"Then you'll free the slaves? Let 'em go if that's what they want?"

"No." He turned from her, ready to leave the room.

"Fellie's got her," Patricia said flatly. "He'll kill her 'cause you took his sons. An eye for an eye."

Jem shook his head, cold fear taking over. "He wouldn't . . . gentlest nigger on the place—"

"That gentle nigger nearly killed a man fo' those boys o' his. Ouah Dulcie's blood is on youah hands, Jem. Ah won't foahgive you fo' that. Set 'em free and get Fellie's sons back. Spig Hurd was gonna stop at other places before he went on South. You can still get 'em. Do it, Jem. I'm beggin' you!"

But Jem had already walked out into the crowd of men and boys and hounds that cluttered his lawn. They had divided into two groups. Glenn was organizing one group. The tick from Fellie's cabin lay on the ground. Each man took a strip of it, giving their hounds the scent.

Glenn divided the party. He gave them the signal for calling the others for help as well as the signal to indicate that the fugitives had been treed. One group would take the River Road to Savannah, another would ride toward the piney woods, the third to the coast, and the fourth heading south and inland. "No shootin' unless necessary. We don't want Miss Dulcie harmed by us."

On the other side of the yard Dulcie's other suitor was talking with as much earnest vigor as Glenn. But Leroy Biggs had devised a much more direct and brutal scheme. The men with him marched in a mass, guns loaded, toward the small chapel with the blue door that had been meant to bring good fortune to the plantation. As they neared, the singing stilled, then rose again more thinly, marring the easy harmony.

Leroy kicked at the blue door, sending it back on its hinges. Black faces, now silent, looked at him. He appeared a dark phantom, outlined as he was by the brilliant light. From Jem's ledger Jan Chilcote read the name of the lead man of each cabin.

"Stand by the door when your name is called," Leroy ordered. The chosen formed a line. Leroy selected six of the best, the most popular or the biggest men. "That's how many hours you got, one hour for each man's life. Six hours to spread the word an' bring Fellie an' Miss Dulcie back here. Each hour that passes an' you don't bring 'em back one man dies. He won't die kindly. I'll gut-shoot him."

Keening and chanting rose and swelled, filling the chapel with lamentations and pleading. "We doan know where's Miz Dulcie! Please, mastah, we'ns doan know! Doan hurt Hosea! 'Pollo a good man, doan hurt nobody."

Leroy's face showed no softening. "Six hours. One dies at the end of each until Miss Dulcie is back here safe and sound."

The six men were herded into the yard, in plain view of the chapel. Each was tied to one of the trees lining the driveway. Leroy stood in front of them, his feet planted firmly, his legs spread. His rifle rested on his crossed arms. From his belt hung a pocket watch, which caught the sun and sent signals of the passing minutes to those in the chapel.

As soon as Dulcie reached the outer boundaries of Mossrose, she left the River Road and jolted across the fields in the heavy wagon. "It's just eleven o'clock. I've often slept later than that. With a little luck, Claudine, we can come in the back way, and no one will ever know I was gone."

But Claudine wasn't listening. She was looking all around as Dulcie tried to think her way into the house unseen. "Miss Dulcie," she whispered breathlessly.

"Oh, what is it now!?"

"Look 'roun' an' what you see? Where the fiel' niggers? Dey's not a one o' 'em in de fiel's. Oh, Miss Dulcie, Ah'm jes' 'bout as skeered as Ah kin be."

Claudine's small hand on her arm transmitted the fear to Dulcie as she saw the eerie emptiness of the fields. She slowed the horses to a walk. As they neared the back of the quarters, they heard the baying of hounds, the lamenting in the chapel, the sounds of angry, excited male voices. "They know we're gone, Claudine," Dulcie whispered.

"Yes'm. What we gwine do now?"

At the rear of Wolf's cabin Dulcie stopped the horses. "We're goin' to run for the house, go up the back stairs, and come out just like we don't know what's happenin'."

"Miss Dulcie! Ain't nobody gwine b'lieve dat!"

"Nobody has to. They won't say a word—'til later, and that's all we need. Not a word about what we did—no matter what!"

Dulcie sped through the servants' entrance. Outside she heard Leroy's voice. "Ten more minutes, you darkies, an' 'Pollo gets killed first. Any o' you got somethin' to tell me, or y'all jes' goin' to let these niggers die?"

With trembling hands Dulcie changed into a fresh and pretty morning dress. "Look out the window. See what's goin' on."

Claudine moaned. "Oh, Lawd, Miss Dulcie, we done it dis time."

"Don't stand there groanin'. Tell me!"

"Dat's a huntin' pahty. Mastah Glenn jes' rode off with the houn's, an' Mastah Leroy, he a-shoutin' at the niggers in de chapel. Lawd, Miss Dulcie, he say 'Pollo gwine die!" Claudine began to cry. Dulcie remembered vividly the sleek brown body of the young man in the fields the day after her birthday party. "Mastah Leroy say he gwine shoot 'Pollo in five minutes. He cain't do dat! Mastah Jem—"

Dulcie spun Claudine from the window. "They'll hear you! Fix my hair. Hurry! You don't want anything to happen to him, do you?"

"No! No, coon't stan' dat, Ah coon't."

Dulcie ran down the stairs, remembering to slow her steps as she reached the door. Her father stood on the porch looking bewildered and unhappy. 'Pollo had been unbound from the tree, his arms tied behind his back. Jan Chilcote and Conroy Biggs dragged him in front of Leroy. They forced him to the ground, where 'Pollo remained kneeling at Leroy's feet, in plain view of those in the chapel.

Taking all her courage, Dulcie stepped onto the veranda. "Mornin', Daddy! Why, I declare! What's goin' on?" She smiled broadly, her eyes glowing in innocent wonderment as she scanned the clusters of men, all armed, all attentive to Leroy until Dulcie appeared in their midst. Jem stood rooted, looking as though he'd been struck unconscious. As the others cried or murmured her name, Dulcie greeted each as though it were a Sunday outing, but she made her way without faltering toward Leroy. She stood beside 'Pollo and looked up into Leroy's face.

"Where have you been?" His voice was low with fury.

"Why, I've been in my bed sleepin', Leroy, 'til y'all woke me up with your racket. What's goin' on? We havin' a party?"

Leroy alone of the men in the yard was having no part of Dulcie's performance. "You can call it a party if you like. But it isn't one for a lady. Get back inside the house where you belong."

Dulcie's eyes sparkled with all the angry things she'd like to say. Instead, she smiled sweetly. "Thought you'd come to see me, Leroy, wantin' my answer to your proposal. Here all you came for was to shoot poor 'Pollo, who hasn't done anythin'."

"I don't take to women interferin' with a man's business, Dulcie."

"An' I don't take to bein' ordered. Your answer is *no*, Leroy!"

He laughed at her. "Dulcie honey, I don't need an answer from you now. I already got one." He glanced up and saw Jem headed toward them. "What you need is a man strong enough to break you to harness, an' I'm that man." He grasped her by her arm and took her to her red-faced father. Dulcie struggled. Leroy only laughed. "Here's one worry off your hands, Mr. Moran. She's safe enough, an' never was in any danger. Now all we got to do is stop these blacks from goin' on a bloody rampage. Soon's I shoot a couple o' these bucks—"

"Daddy! You aren't goin' to let him shoot 'Pollo! You can't!"

Jem seemed incapable of speech. From the slave chapel 'Simmon and his old black stick of a woman approached Jem. They came slowly, clinging to each other. Behind them the others filed out of the chapel walking in quiet order back to the fields.

"We's ain't rampagin', Mastah Jem," 'Simmon said in his crackling voice. "We's jes' singin' fo' Fellie an' his woman. Dey done made free, an' we's a-singin' dem on dey way. We ain't causin' you no mo' troubles, Mastah Jem."

Jem remained silent. His hand shook as he clutched at Dulcie's arm. His face was red except for the deathly white patches that stood out like half-moons under his eyes.

"Get back to the fields," Leroy ordered. "Mistah Moran will see to you soon enough. You can tell the others your singin' cost you dear. Six men. Tell 'em that."

"Please, mastah. Cain't punish niggers dat ain't been bad," 'Simmon said humbly. " 'Pollo, he ain't wan' come wiff us. 'Pollo doan like singin' noway, 'lessen his mama say he got to, an' she say he got to."

"Daddy . . ." Dulcie said in a tear-choked voice.

"Put 'Pollo and the others in the stables. Tie them up. I'll see to them later," Jem managed to say. The decision seemed to snap him out of his stupor. "Leroy, seems like this uprisin' is of my daughter's makin'. I've got to ask your help. Send these men on their way."

"You don't want me to call the others back, the hounds?"

"No, I want Fellie brought back. Can't have them runnin' and gettin' away with it. We'll have to make an example of Fellie. Got to hang him, I suppose." Jem wiped his brow. "The hounds'll get him. They've got his scent." Without looking at Dulcie, hanging his head to avoid his neighbors' eyes, he walked to the house. He would have to think up some reasonable lie to explain his daughter's disappearance and reappearance and the insurrection at Mossrose, but for now, he hadn't the heart or the arrogance to try.

Lucius had returned to his usual post, waiting to be given Jem's hat. Violet was making a racket to announce she was back in the kitchen. Young house girls scurried around the lower floor polishing and dusting with a fury no driver could ever induce.

Jem steered Dulcie into his study. He shoved her against the chair so hard she sat down with a thump. "Daddy!"

Jem waggled his riding crop under her nose. "Don't open your mouth without my permission!" he said with menacing calm. He ordered Lucius to tell Miss Trishy she could safely come out of the root cellar.

Patricia entered the study well after Jem had worked himself out of his quiet, humiliated anger into a screaming rage. Patricia had never seen Dulcie cower from anything, but she cowered from her father now. She huddled in the big leather chair, sobbing out the tale of her taking Fellie to Savannah, while Jem loomed menacingly over her.

"Jem Moran! What is the meanin' of this?" Patricia pushed him aside as she went to Dulcie, holding her, and giving thanks that her daughter had been returned safely to her.

"Your daughter, Madam, was never in the least danger."

"We were all in mortal danger, Jem. You said so yourself."

"From your daughter! This young woman has nearly caused an insurrection right here in our home! She has succeeded in makin' me a criminal and has aided ten of my prime slaves to run off. Ten of them!"

"I only wanted to help Fellie. I didn't know . . . I didn't mean to make you a criminal! Oh, Daddy, please listen to me—"

"In the state of Georgia, Miss, it requires a legislative act to manumit a slave. Your daddy is now a criminal."

"But I didn't mean it! I'm sorry!"

"Jem, no one is goin' to know . . ." Patricia was not actually listening, but only trying to pacify her husband. "A criminal! What did you do, Dulcie?"

"She forged my name to documents of manumission."

"Oh, Jem," Patricia breathed.

"You've gone too far, Dulcie. I won't stand for this in my home. You've made a laughin' stock of me in front of the whole county. When a man can't handle his own daughter, he's no man at all."

"Jem, you've always been so good with Dulcie. Everyone knows that."

"I've been soft with her, Madam. Everyone knows that, and everyone knows she's completely out of hand. Well, no more!"

"What are you goin' to do to me?" Dulcie asked in a small voice.

"What I should have done the minute Leroy Biggs asked for your hand. Patricia, I want you to arrange that weddin'."

"I won't marry Leroy. I don't love him, Daddy. You saw what kind of man Leroy is. I couldn't—"

"You have no say in the matter. Perhaps Leroy can control you. It's apparently what a woman like you needs."

"Daddy, no! Please, I don't love him. I . . . I couldn't stand to be married to Leroy! Anyone else . . . Glenn! Daddy, please let me marry Glenn. He loves me. I know he does, Daddy. Please let me marry Glenn!"

Jem ignored her. "Patricia, I want them married. This month."

"Jem, you're angry now. Can't we decide this later?"

"It is decided, Patricia. I'll hear no more about it."

"Jem, marriage is something sacred to a woman. It's her whole life," Patricia said earnestly. "Let Dulcie marry the man of her choice. You've always wanted Glenn and Dulcie to marry. . . . Jem?"

Jem glanced at Dulcie. There was no soft, admiring love in his eyes as there normally was. Dulcie truly believed he loathed her. "She'd run him ragged. She needs a man like Leroy who'll keep her in line."

Dulcie stood up, her eyes red and tear-filled. She began to speak but couldn't bring anything out but a strangled sob.

The hunting party returned at sundown. They reported failure as Jem now knew they must. He thanked them and said, "I think it's best to leave Fellie to the catchers. I'll take an ad out in the papers tomorrow." He explained Dulcie's return using the same lame excuse she had. "Seems like she was too warm last night and went to sleep in the guest wing. Not a soul knew she was there."

Sick at heart, Jem returned to the study. Patricia was waiting. She would fight for Dulcie, even if it meant fighting Jem himself.

Dulcie was still crying when Patricia came to her room

hours later. She smoothed Dulcie's damp hair. "Hush, now, it's goin' to be all right."

"It'll never be all right," Dulcie moaned, her tears coming anew. "I can't marry Leroy. I can't! He was goin' to kill 'Pollo—just shoot him right where he knelt. I didn't know Leroy! Oh, Mama, I'll die before—"

"Dulcie Jeannette, hush youahself, an' listen to me. You won't be marryin' Leroy, nor anyone else you don't choose fo' youahself."

Dulcie's sobs waned. She raised her head.

"Get Miss Dulcie a towel with violet watah, Claudine," Patricia said gently, still smoothing Dulcie's damp, curling hair from her face. "Why youah pretty li'l face jes' gonna look like a puff addah's tomorrah, Dulcie."

"Mama, is it true? I don't have to marry Leroy?"

Patricia smiled as she dabbed at Dulcie's red and swollen face. "Not as long as youah mama lives, you won't. Did you think Ah'd evah let somethin' like that happen to mah li'l girl?"

Dulcie flung her arms around her mother's neck. "Oh, Mama! Oh, Mama, thank you. Oh, I love you, Mama!"

Patricia disentangled herself from Dulcie's embrace. "Don't you want to know what is goin' to happen?"

"Glenn?" Dulcie asked weakly, knowing if that was the victory her mother had won for her, she couldn't say a word.

Patricia shook her head. "Youah goin' to N'Yawk—to Mad. She an' Oliver'll be goin' to Europe, an' you'll go with 'em. Would that be moah to youah likin'?"

Dulcie blinked at her. "Europe?" It would be exile.

"Mad wrote to me some time ago. She asked me if Ah would considah lettin' you go."

"Mama, will Daddy let me go?"

"You did youah daddy a terrible wrong, Dulcie. Ah'm not absolvin' you of that, you understan'. But I don't want you married off to a man you can't abide."

Dulcie hung her head. She was truly ashamed she had hurt Jem. But as he himself had said of Fellie's whipping, some things just had to be done. She had done it.

"Be nice to youah daddy, Dulcie. He loves you mightily, an' you lowered him in the eyes of his frien's and neighbors. A man's got to have his pride."

"Do you think Daddy will forgive me?"

"I 'spect so, in time. Just don't ask too much of him, Dulcie, not right now." Patricia wondered if there were any truth in the hope she offered Dulcie. She'd never known Jem to be more unhappy, or so adamantly angry. But he had given into her wishes. He must want what was best for Dulcie in spite of his anger.

Patricia forced a smile, her hand cupping Dulcie's chin, making the girl look at her. "Now, tell me, aren't you even a li'l bit happy about goin' to Europe with youah Aunt Mad an' Uncle Oliver?"

"I don't want to leave you and daddy, Mama," she said truthfully. She was always most pliant and loving when she was in trouble, realizing only when it was withdrawn how much she counted on and needed the love and approval of her parents.

Patricia Moran knew her daughter well. She shook her head at Dulcie. "It's time you were growin' up, Dulcie Jeannette," she said softly.

Chapter Six

Adam avidly read through the *Mercury* and the *Courier*. Most of the news he had heard as gossip in port, but reading it lent the gossip credibility. He sighed, leaning far back in the chair, his long body stretched out.

"No good news," Garrett commented.

Adam tapped the newspaper. "Have you read this? A confederation of Southern states. Think of it, Garrett. A new government, a new country. If Lincoln is elected, he'll never allow that."

"We'd be fools to allow Lincoln or anyone else to push us into war." Garrett looked at him, deliberately silent. The South would eventually collapse under the pressure as states' right, property rights, social rights were all forced against it; or it would be consumed in the flames of insurrection. Some Southern states were already moving away from slavery. Virginia had comparatively few slaves. In North Carolina, seventy-two percent of the population owned no slaves at all. In those states development had advanced sufficiently to warrant use of other forms of labor.

The North had had its turn at embracing slavery, found it unworkable, and discarded it. But many Northern states had existed for one hundred or more years longer than Southern states. Texas, which had not entered the Union until 1845, was still raw frontier needing immense numbers of laborers. Ten decades, three generations of men, had passed as the North developed its resources and industries. Southern development was far behind; yet the North judged both sections as though they were equal in terms of existence and advancement.

Adam, thinking of this, said, "I don't believe slavery is right, Garrett, but neither do I believe destroying a country is moral simply because that country does not conform to certain beliefs."

They closed the subject, but each knew he had seen the anxious stirrings of mob hysteria behind the coldly impersonal *Mercury* and *Courier* reports.

Daily the hysteria mounted. In Black Oak a vigilance committee was formed to seek out and identify Northern Abolitionists disguised as teachers, hawkers, and ministers. Committees of five patrolled their designated areas, swearing to uphold law and, when necessary, to draft new law by majority vote. Their vigilant actions were to be only group actions to prevent an excess of zeal. However, all was accomplished in communities that were anxious, angry, suspicious, and fearful.

Adam and Garrett spoke about personal safety only once during this time. "Neither Leona nor Zoe can be involved in the Underground, Adam. In fact, it would seem best to allow them to think you and I have curtailed our activities as well. Before you protest, hear me out first. It's far more dangerous for you to haul slaves now than it was before. These vigilantes may be hysterics, but they are hotheaded and unpredictable. The Orangeburg vigilantes are expelling visitors simply because they are strangers. It is not uncommon for them to arrest a man for talking to a Negro in his home. They are afraid. Fear is the worst adversary of all. No one can prophesy when panic will drive one of these vigilante groups to irremediable action. I don't want to see you caught up in it."

Adam laughed uncomfortably. "Nor do I."

Garrett went to Adam, placing his hand affectionately on the younger man's shoulder. "If I can't persuade you to give up slave hauling, promise me you'll be cautious. The

Ullah is becoming well known. You may be subjected to harassment or even search at any time."

Adam did not reply. He knew the dangers all too well.

On October 8, 1860, South Carolina elected a prosecession legislature.

On November 7, Lincoln's election was confirmed.

The spirit of the Confederate South began to take form.

One did not have to agree with the trend of events. It was impossible for a man not to be affected by the enthusiasm that raced like an electrical current from person to person.

Adam was no exception. On November 9 he brought the *Ullah* into Charleston and attended a large public meeting there. A number of Georgia politicians and railroad men pledged their state would follow South Carolina out of the Union. Adam listened to the speeches fanning the flames of Southern pride, spoken in firebrand terms of a Union already dissolved by the horrendous North. Around each speaker rose the sounds of a populace gone mad with their cause. Their voices more thunderous than a storm at sea; thousands rose from their seats to shout approval. They waved their hats overhead, flapping and fanning the air like thousands of cormorant wings.

Adam, Ben, and Beau left the meeting together, walking slowly back toward the Ashley River. Beau was disturbed and quiet. Adam was thoughtful. Inside him stirred hungry, burning feelings of dedication to the South—a need to protect his home, an emotion he could not quench with reason.

Adam elbowed Ben, who was still craning, taking in all the sights, still luxuriating in the excitement that permeated the city. "I think we could use a few more good solid orders," Adam said conversationally.

Beau looked solemnly at him. "We've got as much as we need."

They walked down a narrow passageway, stacked with cotton bales, barrels, and boxes. From a side alley four men fell into step behind them.

"This is a good time to approach some of the larger planters," Adam persisted. "They are all in an expansive frame of mind. What do you say, Ben?"

About a block ahead a lone man detached himself from the shadows, moving toward them.

Ben laughed. "I say that if you want to stay here and nose aroun' Charleston, y'all ought to come right out and say so."

Adam grinned. "I do. But I also want those orders. We can get several to ship with us if we approach them now. They all have cotton on hand. With all the war talk, and some raising their own regiments, they're eager for cash."

Beau, not sharing his friends' enthusiasm, was watching the approaching man, whose face was hidden by a slouch hat. Reluctantly he agreed that Adam should remain in Charleston. Ben, in command of the *Ullah*, would take her cargo to New York and then return to Charleston to pick up Adam.

Behind them a man hawked and spat. Beau looked over his shoulder, then he turned, his eyes riveted on the man now only yards in front of them. His voice low, he said, "Hey, fellas, we got some nasty company."

"Hot damn!" Ben said. "I could use a good fight!"

The lone man shot a wad of tobacco at Adam's feet. "You men from aroun' heah?"

"What business is it of yours?" Adam snapped.

The man opened his hand. In his palm lay a battered homemade badge: Chastn Vijlanty Comity.

Adam said sarcastically, "I do believe we've met up with self-appointed law."

"Don't smart-mouth me, jack tar. We got a duty to perform." He touched his pistol. The other four men moved in closer.

On either side of Adam, Ben and Beau took a quick step, forming a triangle. Adam barked, "You want trouble, Mister, you'll get it!"

"Don't take any more crap off'n him, Bob. We know damn well he floats a nigger ship. Make him show us!"

The four vigilantes charged. Ben let out a bloodcurdling battle cry. Using his clasped hands as a hammer, he smashed one man behind the ear. The toe of Beau's foot caught the next vigilante in the groin. As he doubled over, Beau's knee came up, crushing the man's nose. Adam seized two men by their necks and cracked their skulls together. They slithered to the ground. Adam stepped forward, going for the leader.

The man backed away, his hands up. "Di'n't mean no harm. We was only protectin' our own."

Adam grabbed his badge, crushing the hated symbol of

mob authority in his hand. Ben whipped the man's gun from his belt and pointed it at his gut.

The man paled. "Hey, wait a minute. All Ah wanted was to ast you some questions."

Adam said, "You got all the answers you're gonna get. Beat it!"

The man took several steps, watching his companions scuttle into the shadows. "Hey, ain'cha gonna gimme mah gun back? Ah di'n't do nuthin' to you. It was them."

Ben shot into the street at the man's feet. "Christ!" The man screamed, jumping back. Ben shot again and again, emptying the revolver as the man danced and squalled in fear. Laughing, Ben tossed him the empty gun.

Brave again, the vigilante shook his fist. "Ah won't forgit you bloody bastards! Not never! Ah'll gitcher." He ran.

Ben and Adam laughed, sparring playfully. Beau did not join in. The other two turned on him, punching lightly. "Come on, Beau. Did ya ever see such a bunch of left-footed clods? We clobbered 'em. Did ya see that guy run?"

Beau pushed them away. "I know we agreed, but I don't think you ought to stay here, Adam. They're suspicious of the *Ullah* now. One shred of real evidence and they've got you."

"Oh, shit, Beau, that guy wouldn't have the balls to look me in the eye again."

When they returned to the *Ullah,* Adam wrote a letter to Garrett:

> Charleston is set for rebellion. With Georgia promising to follow the lead of South Carolina, the Union will most probably be broken before the new year.
>
> The 1860 Association has become a network spreading secessionist news throughout the South. It is no longer the voices of radical politicians carrying us toward the precipice of war. The people are one in their hearts. The South is going to secede, and the North cannot permit it.

The streets of Charleston were crowded with militiamen drilling, their flamboyant blue cockaded hats bobbing in time to their marching feet. Vigilance patrols alternately spread or quelled wild rumors of incendiarism and restlessness among the blacks—elsewhere. "Ouah darkies," they said fondly, "is jes' natch'ly tranquil."

Adam bid Ben and Beau and the *Ullah* good-bye amid the noise of a busy pier. "Give this to Garrett personally, Ben. I don't want to chance the mails."

Beau pleaded, "Please, Adam, come with us. You're not safe here."

Ben's hazel eyes danced. He, no more than Adam, could damp the urge to be a part of this thing he feared but desired. But behind the youthful appreciation of danger lurked a mature worry. "Y'all watch yourself, Adam. Beau's right. The *Ullah*'s gatherin' herself a reputation, an' so's her number one master. Those vigilantes know our business as well as we do, an' they're just itchin' to catch us at it. Steer clear of 'em, will you?"

Adam saluted briskly, grinning.

Secession fever showed no signs of abating. Everywhere Adam went during the next month he saw the blue cockades, the marching and drilling troops. Rumor had it that arms were being brought in from the North and being stored. Lincoln's name, when it was spoken at all, was vilified. He was a minority President who had snuck into Washington like a thief in the night. The wave of Southern pride would not crest but kept on gathering voice and force.

By December Adam had secured five shipping contracts and the promise of three others. Of more immediate importance, he had gained entrée to several prominent homes, where information about the Southern temper was as accurate as any to be had: There would be war.

All Charleston felt it as the city decked itself for the momentous convention of secessionist delegates. State flags were displayed everywhere. Streets were decorated in bunting. On storefronts were artists' paintings symbolic of the bounty and prosperity expected after secession. In Saint Andrew's Hall, convention president D. F. Jamison Barnwell called the convention to order with a gavel on which *secession* was branded in bold black letters.

Adam, along with throngs of people in and about Saint Andrew's Hall, reached eagerly for the Charleston *Mercury*. In bold print he read, "Extra! Passed unanimously at 1:15 o'clock P.M., December 20th, 1860: An Ordinance to dissolve the Union between the State of South Carolina and other States united with her under the compact entitled 'The Constitution of the United States of America.' " His

eyes dropped to the bold print at the bottom of the page.
"The Union Is Dissolved!"

That evening the delegates marched in procession
through the streets. A mob of three thousand thronged the
entrance to Saint Andrew's Hall. On either side of President Barnwell's chair stood large palmetto palms. On his
desk lay the document. Shouts of "Hurrah" and "Huzzah"
burst forth as the delegates placed their names on the
paper. At last Barnwell announced, "The Ordinance for
Secession has been signed and ratified, and I proclaim the
State of South Carolina an independent commonwealth."

The city went wild. The decorations on Saint Andrew's
Hall were torn down and then into small bits so everyone
might have a souvenir. The night air was clamorous with
the melodious pealing of church bells. Cannons fired sa-
lutes. Throngs surging through the streets raised their
voices deafeningly. Inspired by their common bond,
stranger turned to stranger, avid to share his elation.

It was a glorious night for prostitutes. Men drunk with
power of a war they already imagined having won sought
any ear receptive to their braggadocio, any body eager for
unquenchable virility. The women made it a night of feminine patriotism. On this happy and historic occasion fees
might be lowered or even forgotten.

After being approached by an odd assortment of women
and having his back pounded by hearty men, Adam no
longer wished to be a part of the raucous celebration, yet
he wanted something, something to break the uncertainty
secession had brought. It had fired his blood but given him
no outlet. He was restless and discontented.

He pushed his way through the crowd, ducking the fre-
netically waved palmetto fronds, avoiding the arms that
beckoned him to join the street dancers. Finally he broke
free of the milling hordes, hurrying down a darkened resi-
dential street. Behind him were jubilant shouts, drunken
laughter, and the sounds of thousands of feet.

He returned to his room in the Mansion House. But
once inside, he was skittish. He paced the room, then lay
down on his bed, only to rise and begin pacing again. Perhaps he'd go back to the streets after all.

He left the Mansion House by the front door and walked
east on Broad Street toward the Cooper River. He came to
the corner of East Bay and stood looking at the Old Exchange. Stede Bonnet had been captured and imprisoned

there in 1718. Adam smiled ruefully. He wasn't far from being a pirate himself. It was a strange night, he mused, strange thoughts, strange feelings. Suddenly, his legs crumpled. He was on his hands and knees staring at the boots of the "Chastn Vijlanty Comity."

"Tol' ya Ah wou'n't fergit. Git 'im, boys! Show 'im how we feel 'bout nigger lovers in Charleston. Give 'im a taste o' our hospitality afore we hang 'im!"

Adam tried to get up. The man's boot cracked against his ribs. He gasped, the wind forced painfully from him. A boot crunched down on his hand. Adam screamed. Pain jabbed as he was kicked from behind. "Nigger-lovin' bastard!" A frenzy of blows rained down on his back, neck, and head. He couldn't move, couldn't breathe. No time— fists, boots, distorted faces. He curled into fetal position, his hands and arms drawn up to protect his face and head. One man viciously pummeled his kidney. Another kicked at his knees, wildly seeking his groin.

Over the grunting noise of the cursing men and their blows, came a high, piercing wail. Electrified, the men halted.

In the soft winter darkness stood a dusky, beautiful woman. She seemed to float in her ethereal pink satin gown. In her steady hand was a pearl-handed derringer. Her unearthly high-pitched laughter rang out. "Pahty's ovah, boys. Li'l ol' Melody wants the leavin's."

Silence. Then: "Hell, that's only the nigger-bitch from the hat shop!" The man turned and hit Adam sharply in the back. Then as Adam kicked out, the vigilante screamed, falling to the ground, moaning, crying, grasping his shattered kneecap.

"Good-bye now, boys—lessen y'all wants to die. Ah only got one mo' shot, an' it's gonna be fo' keeps."

"Jeezuz Chris', Melody. You know us. This bastard's a—"

"Sho' Ah know you, Jeb. You too, Bill . . . Bob. 'Cou'se Ah ain't met yo' wives. Think mebbe Ah should."

Muttering and threatening, the men shuffled, then slowly left, two of them carrying their wounded companion.

"Kin you git up, Cap'n?"

Adam struggled painfully to his knees, taking Melody's offered hand.

"Y'all right?"

He groaned, then smiled crookedly. "I hurt like hell."

"Not too much, Ah hope, Cap'n." She smiled cryptically. "Ah got a surprise fo' you. Ah sho' would be disappointed if that bag o' white trash spoiled it fo' me. Hol' onto me. We kin make it back to yo' hotel."

She walked him to his door but refused to go in. "No, Cap'n. You go on, clean yo'seff up. Ah'll be back, jes' like nothin' ever happened." Again she flashed her dark eyes at him, her smile seductively mysterious.

He had just splashed cold water on his face when she knocked at the door. Hastily he mopped himself with the towel. He opened the door and stared in amazement.

In the dim hallway, carrying an oversized hatbox, stood Melody Cox, as though nothing had happened. Her dark, suggestive eyes glowed like coals in her tawny-complexioned face. She said, smiling, "Jes' bringin' you a li'l somethin' you din't ordah, Cap'n Tremain."

Occasionally on his trips to Charleston he'd gone to Melody's shop to purchase a bonnet for his mother or Leona. Melody's talents were legendary among the ladies. She ran her exclusive shop because she liked to, and she ran it as she wished, catering to no one's tastes but her own. Melody didn't have to, nor did she answer to anyone but herself.

She was equally well known and sought after by men. A well-trained New Orleans quadroon, she had been the pampered mistress of a prominent young Creole gentleman until he married. Then Melody had removed herself and her financial settlement to Charleston, to become one of its most discussed courtesans. Her actual talents in this respect, however, were known privily to only a small, select clientele. Melody Cox dispensed her personal favors with the same lofty arrogance she ran her hat shop—with authoritarian selectivity and at an unconscionable cost to the client.

The scent of her perfume pervaded the air. Once in the room, Melody posed, teasing with her eyes and body. "Here's a li'l somethin' y'all might be needin' in the future to recall who y'all are," she said lightly, presenting him with the box.

He opened it and brought forth a hat topped by a ridiculously large rosette of blue ribbons. His own blue cockade. With a laugh he placed it on his head, tapping and poking until it had a jaunty tilt. "You think I need this to know who I am, Melody?"

She shugged and her shawl fell free revealing one naked shoulder. "Everybody else goin' mad, you might's well do the same. Do you like it? Ah made it mahseff, jes' fo' you." She stood close against him as she meticulously adjusted the hat, then swept it off, throwing it to the floor.

His arms slipped around her waist, pulling her closer yet. Melody offered no resistance. Her slow smile disclosed beautifully white teeth as she raised her head exposing the long golden curve of her throat.

"How did you know I'd need you?" he asked between kisses he rained on her neck and shoulders. Her perfume and the uniquely feminine scent of her skin was intoxicating.

"Ah watched you. Saw all those girls comin' up to you an' you sendin' them away jes' as fast. Ah say to mahseff, 'Melody, there's a man who ain't gwine know what he wants 'til he's all alone in his room an' he ain't got it. Then them men—"

Adam laughed softly. "Are you here to give me what I want, Melody?"

"No, sir, Cap'n, Ah'm here to get somethin' Ah been wantin' mahseff," she murmured. With silken expertise she began to loosen his clothing. "Now, y'all jes' turn youah back an' be patient fo' a minute, Cap'n. Ah got somethin' Ah wanta show y'all." Her dress fell to the floor in a pool of pink satin. Immediately his hand caressed the soft roundness of her buttocks. "Youah not s'posed to be lookin', Cap'n. Youah gwine spoil mah show," she said petulantly. "Now, get back ovah theah on the bed an' let me come to you the way Ah likes."

He kissed the nape of her neck, then went to the bed to await Melody's sensuous, well-choreographed progress toward him.

This was what Melody enjoyed most. She blossomed under the deep, slow gaze of a man's eyes as he devoured the contours of her undulating body. Melody smiled. The sight of her naked body never failed to excite a man or herself. Since she'd lost her Creole lover to his wife, about the only pleasure she got from these passing gentlemen was what she gave herself. She hoped, but didn't expect Adam to be different. Few men were good in bed. They were too eager, too rough, too cock-minded to know how to pleasure a woman. She had learned to pleasure herself.

She arched her back, thrusting out her bosom, the flat of

her hands moving down the curving length of her torso. "Ain't Ah jes' about the prettiest thing you evah did see, Cap'n?" Sidestepping his slight movement, she said, "Ah, no! Not yet. Melody ain't ready fo' you yet, Cap'n." Her voice grew huskier as she moved about the room, unwilling to be hurried or cheated of her pleasure. She danced and postured, glorying in her own sensuality. She played with her shawl, using it as a veil, drawing it across Adam's naked body as she danced toward him, then away. Mesmerized, he watched, the heat mounting in his loins, as she neared him again.

Then he was springing from the bed, pulling her toward him, forcing her to move to his rhythm. His mouth crushed against hers, hard and demanding. Melody laughed, deep and throaty, girlishly giggling at having a man take command of her. "Not yet, Cap'n. Not quite yet. Ah ain't ready yet."

He pulled her to the bed, caressing her, his hands moving over her lush body, his lips and tongue touching her and titillating her until she cried out for him. "Now, Cap'n. Now!"

Chapter Seven

When Adam awakened the next morning, Melody was gone. All that was left to give evidence that the strange girl had been there at all was the blue cockade hat she had placed on the post of the bed. Slowly the memories of Melody's indefatigable body washed away, and he began to think of other things. He sat on the edge of the bed in numbed silence, to give the moment the respectful awe it deserved. It had happened. The secession of the South had begun.

The rest of the week Adam spent talking to every planter he knew, reaffirming their shipping contracts and gleaning whatever other information he could regarding the intentions of the other states either to follow South Carolina's lead or to remain in the Union.

He sought out Melody only once, just before he was due to leave Charleston. As he walked into her shop, she looked up, saw him, and smiled broadly. With a wave of her well-manicured hand she turned her customer over to her shop-girl and led Adam to a small refined sitting room at the rear. She refused his invitation to dinner that evening in his hotel.

As sure of her charms as ever, she walked around the room as she talked, giving him full view of herself. "Ah cain't afford to come with you, Cap'n."

He laughed. "From what I've been told, it is I who am likely not to be able to afford your company." He took her hand, drawing her onto his lap.

"What you cain't afford is money. What Ah cain't afford is bein' spoiled by you." Her hands were busy as she talked, moving across the broad muscles of his chest. Then her hand slipped inside the soft material of his shirt front, her fingers twining in the hair of his chest and belly as her searching fingers moved downward. "Mebbe jes' once more," she murmured, leaning back and allowing him to carry her to the sofa.

It was a memory-filled farewell Adam bid to Charleston when the *Ullah* came into port. He returned to Wilmington on January 9, 1861, the day Mississippi seceded. Florida and Alabama followed suit. Then all eyes turned to Georgia: Her central location made her a vital link between the Atlantic Seaboard states and those of the Gulf. Of all the Southern states, Georgia possessed the greatest industrial strength, desperately needed for the economic and military well-being of a Southern nation.

Garrett, sharing news over cigars and whiskey with Adam, sighed heavily. "The whole bloody conflict may still be avoided, Adam, if Georgia refuses to secede."

"And if South Carolina, Florida, and Alabama refuse to reenter the Union, they'd bear the brunt of any reprisal alone," Adam retorted.

"What reprisal? Put yourself in Lincoln's place. Would you not be more than happy to see the Union intact once again?"

"What, then, about the questions of slavery and states' rights?"

Garrett shrugged unhappily. "Another postponement. Perhaps another compromise. Perhaps the Crittenden Compromise could be made into something, given the chance. My God, Adam, anything is better than secession!"

"I don't know what's good and what's better. On the one

hand, we are destroying the Union of a nation born of a dedication to freedom. How can this be good? And yet, so long as that Union exists, the North will judge us morally and dictate to us legislatively. That cannot be better."

"That is why time is so valuable," Garrett said tensely. "If we regain our objectivity, surely Congress will recognize the desperation of our situation. We must pray that the people of Georgia listen to men like Alexander Stephens who speak for unity."

But there were other voices in Georgia. Senator Robert Toombs said, "Throw the bloody spear into the den of incendiaries!" Then, "Make another war of independence. Fight its battles over again; reconquer liberty and independence." These voices the people followed.

Governor Joseph Brown ordered Fort Pulaski on the Savannah to be occupied on January 3, 1861. By January 19 the Georgia State Convention had voted 208–89 in favor of secession. Georgia left the Union. Governor Brown secured the surrender of the Federal arsenal at Augusta on the twenty-fourth.

A chain reaction began. By the first of February, Louisiana and Texas had seceded. Three days later representatives from all seceded states except Texas met at Montgomery, Alabama, to form a provisional government for the Confederate States of America. In the eyes of the secessionists a new nation had been born.

With the news of the appointment of Jefferson Davis and Alexander Stephens as President and Vice-President, Garrett stood in the entry of Zoe's house looking dumbfounded. To Zoe's eyes Garrett had seemed to age hourly since word of secession reached them two months before.

"Adam is in the study, Garrett," she said, then indicated the door as he gave no sign of having heard her.

Adam looked up from his ledger. He immediately rose, coming over to the older man. "Sit down, Garrett, I'll get you a drink."

Garrett fumbled his way to a chair. Adam, making him a stiff whiskey and soda, was seriously worried. His friend's face was pale and strained. He had seen men look so just before they collapsed. He handed him the glass, making sure Garrett had ahold of it. "Drink this, sir."

Garrett drank slowly. "I'm all right, Adam, as all right as a man can be amid so much wrong." He stared at the wall and sipped his whiskey. At last his eyes rested on Adam's face. "What will you do now?"

"I don't know. We'll keep the *Ullah* running, but I don't know where that leaves us with Mr. Courtland. I doubt he's going to want much to do with a Southern vessel."

"I'd hardly given Rod's position in this a thought. His desire to free the blacks most likely will override his repugnancy to Southern trade."

"Perhaps, but I'd like to be prepared to buy him out should he decide to make things difficult for us."

"You don't like Rod?" Garrett suddenly realized the latent hostility in Adam's voice.

Adam shook his head, smiling. "I like him immensely. He's a fine man, and I admire him. I'm merely beginning to realize how much of a Southerner I am. This hatred of the damned avaricious Yankees is contagious. I find myself envious of the damned fools who parade in full dress uniform. I'm tempted to join the glorious fight for liberty and right!"

In spite of his talk, Adam did nothing. He and Ben and Beau tried to keep the *Ullah* to a regular schedule. The number of runaways Tom held for them in the Green Swamp declined, mostly due to the zealous activities of vigilante groups and patrollers.

Daily some new step toward war was taken until all eyes focused on Fort Sumter. To the North it was a symbol of the Union. To the South, Sumter was on their soil, a fort manned by soldiers of a foreign nation.

On April 11 General Pierre G. T. de Beauregard, commander of the Southern troops and a man with an eye to the way his name would look in future history books, demanded surrender. At 3:30 A.M. on April 12, Beauregard sent a message to Major Robert Anderson, commander of Union forces in Fort Sumter. He would fire on the fort in one hour if it was not surrendered.

A Confederate howitzer fired on the fort at 4:30 A.M., beginning a thirty-three-hour bombardment. Major Anderson lowered the American flag on April 14, 1861.

On April 15, Lincoln called for seventy-five thousand militia to be drawn voluntarily from loyal states. North Carolina seceded rather than fight against her sister Southern states. On the seventeenth President Davis issued letters of marque authorizing privateers to plunder under the guardianship of the Confederacy. It was a remarkably bold move, for the United States was involved in international talks to outlaw the use of privateering on the high seas.

Lincoln's response was no less bold or remarkable. On April 19 he issued a blockade of all Southern ports. Not only would that create the largest blockade ever attempted, over three thousand miles of coast, but it meant Lincoln was violating international law by preventing international trade in ports of his own nation. Since Lincoln did not have a navy anywhere near capable of blockading the territory, his blockade existed more on paper than on ocean waters. Ships continued to go in and out of Southern ports in these early days, somewhat chary, but mostly derisive of the pompous little navy that sought to guard so immense a coast.

With the blockade, however, Adam gained a special worry. The security of the *Ullah* became precarious. She was liable to capture by the North and confiscation by the South. Since President Davis had been issuing letters of marque for privateers, Adam had twice been encouraged by prominent planters to register his ship as a privateer. Each time he had evaded their questions. He did not want to spend his days seeking and capturing Northern ships for booty and bounty.

But there was no place for a neutral in the South. The pressure grew. He would have to come to a decision soon, or no planter would ship cotton or any other cargo on the *Ullah*. Their business was for the loyal. Adam had to start showing his colors prominently.

He called a meeting of the interested parties in the *Ullah*. Ben, Beau, Adam, Tom, and Garrett met in Garrett's parlor. "Ben and I have discussed our situation, Garrett. It seems our best move is to keep the *Ullah* running. There is pressure to register her as a privateer, but I hope that will die down. I think it is just another manifestation of war fever. Waiting seems worth the gamble."

Ben added enthusiastically, "One thing is certain: the South is dependent on the North and Europe for manufactured goods, and Europe needs our cotton. Why, we could make a bloody fortune if the war lasts long enough for England to use up her warehouse of stored cotton."

"More likely y'all land us in some pesky jail," Beau grumbled.

Adam's attention focused on Garrett. "The one question

we have is where does Rod Courtland fit into our scheme. I still cannot feel comfortable about him. The South is determined to win its independence; in that respect we're at war with a foreign nation. Mr. Courtland has an excellent business mind, but he's definitely a patriot—a Union patriot. Now he has a quarter interest in the *Ullah*."

Garrett glanced at Tom. "What do you think, Tom?"

Tom slumped down in his chair, vaguely uncomfortable in the confines of a proper house; he had grown accustomed to his rough life in the swamp. "Courtland knew conflict was comin'. He's gotten what he wanted from the *Ullah*'s trade. I don't think he's goin' to start squawkin' now."

Garrett agreed. Ben stood up immediately, unable to keep still. "We had another thought," he began, then turned to Adam. "You tell them about it. It's really your idea. You deserve the credit. Or the blame."

Tom laughed. "Here it comes, Garrett. Hold fast to your pocketbook."

Adam laughed with Tom. "It would be only a temporary cost if I'm right."

"What'd I tell you, Garrett. It's gonna cost us. Do I know these boys or don't I?"

"Lincoln can foul normal shipping with this blockade of his, but if there were ships specially designed to outrun his cruisers and slip into river channels, the blockade would pose no threat. The longer the war lasts and the longer the blockade exists, the greater the market will be both for manufactured goods in the South and raw materials in Britain and France. There is already talk that shallow draft steamers are being built for the purpose in Liverpool and Glasgow. They sail under British registry and use Bermuda or Nassau as home port. We've got three captains and a golden opportunity. If we can finance three fast ships, we can aid the Southern cause, continue the slave hauling, and make our fortunes."

"Three," Garrett repeated. "Then this is not a new idea, Adam."

"Beau and I figure we can manage a quarter interest in one ship," Ben said earnestly.

"Among the five of us, we can raise nearly enough for two ships if we all stretch to the limit," Adam said. "Now, what about Courtland, Garrett . . . Tom? If he were Southern, I wouldn't hesitate."

Tom scratched his head. "You say we can swing one of those special-built steamers on our own? Doesn't seem to me it'd take much time to raise money for the second, seein' as how you claim we're all gonna make a fast fortune. What do you need the third ship for anyway? You've got the *Ullah*."

"We were hoping to keep the *Ullah* out of any blockade running, Tom. She's a good ship, but her best speed is just over thirteen knots. Mr. Lincoln's a determined man. He's rigging everything from whalers to river steamers to man that blockade. He's also building new ships—fast ones. I don't want the *Ullah* to become a prize of war." Adam paced back and forth.

"You don't want to use her at all?" Tom asked.

"I don't want to lose that ship, Tom. Ben and I agree that for now she can safely make the New Orleans–Nassau run. But the new ships are being rigged for sail and steam. We'll be able to make sixteen knots or better with a favorable wind. There won't be much the Union can float that could outrun us in one of them."

"Then, it would seem that your solution is to deal directly with Rod, Adam," Garrett said. "I suggest you stop in New York, talk to Rod, then proceed to England. You will be ordering at least one ship, and with a little luck you'll be able to place the full order for three."

Adam had visited Rod Courtland's fashionable brownstone house before, but he was no less impressed by the extravagant bachelor quarters this time than he had been previously. He liked Rod Courtland, though he found him a strangely aloof man who defied understanding.

Rod stood slightly over six feet, an inch or two shorter than Adam. His hair was iron gray, stark in contrast to his deeply tanned face. He had the most vivid blue eyes Adam had ever seen. But for all his charm, good looks, and business acumen, Rod Courtland remained a stranger to most people. By his choice, he seemed to attract acquaintances rather than friends. And he was unmarried. In itself that was not remarkable, but from previous visits, Adam knew the man's appetites. Rod liked and was liked by all manner of women, but he remained the charmed admirer or the occasional lover. "Each man is permitted one serious error in love, then he is expected to become wise enough to avoid the next." Rod had left the remark unexplained.

Adam was shown into Rod's thoroughly masculine, booklined study by a pretty, plump-bottomed Irish servant girl who looked him over with minute attention. He returned her admiring stare.

"That will be all, Hannah," Rod said wryly as he entered the room. He turned a warm smile on Adam as he extended his hand in greeting. He glanced toward the slowly retreating girl. "That one," he laughed. "She's just come over, and damn, with her bold eyes, if some yokel isn't going to knock her up before I get her properly trained. It's good to see you again, Captain Tremain. Our meetings are far too few. How long will you be here this time?"

"I'm sailing for England as soon as we've completed our business."

"One of these times I'm going to convince you to see New York."

"I'd like that, sir, thank you."

"Then I'll extract a promise from you right now. The next time you come into the city, I have your company for at least three days."

"Agreed."

"Good. Now, then, what urgent business carries you here and on to England with such haste?"

Among the characteristics that Adam liked best in Rod Courtland was his unwillingness to waste valuable time on meaningless talk. Neither man pretended there was anything between them but a ship and a business and a wary respect for one another. Adam settled into his chair and told Rod concisely and without embellishment the details of his proposition. Uninterrupting, Rod listened, then sat back deep in concentration.

Finally he shifted his weight, studying Adam. "I suppose you already realize that I have no sympathy with this insurrection."

"I'm a Southerner, Mr. Courtland. Had I been asked, I would have advised against war, but I was not asked. We are at war."

"So we are. Undeclared perhaps, but war nonetheless. It is a quirk of fate, Captain Tremain, but that same hapless toss of historical dice that placed you on the side of the Confederacy has placed me on that of the Union. We've become enemies."

Adam bristled slightly but showed no outward sign except a tightening of his mouth. "I've become no one's enemy. If I must defend my homeland, I'll certainly aid her in whatever way I can, but the South hasn't made any offensive move against the North. She will not unless forced to do so."

A look of baffled amusement passed over Rod's face. "You don't consider firing on Fort Sumter an aggressive act?"

"No, sir. Fort Sumter is on Confederate soil. Major Anderson was asked to vacate the fort several times before action was taken. It was Mr. Lincoln's decision to maintain Federal troops in the fort. I would call our action a defensive one. But we're straying from our purpose. What I propose is a business venture likely to make a fortune for both of us."

Rod laughed. "Do you realize, young man, the Southern commercial debt to the North is approximately two hundred million dollars, and most of that is owed to New York City merchants, of whom I am one? Now, you propose a shipping venture in the midst of a civil uprising in which I must purchase the ship, supply at least part of the cargo, and become a traitor to my own country!"

Adam was on his feet, as angry as Rod. The two men stood glaring at each other. "There is no point in discussing this further. Good day, Mr. Courtland. Doing business with you has been memorable if not pleasant."

"Sit down!" Courtland snapped. "You and I have a few things to clear up, not the least of which is the *Ullah*. Or has it conveniently slipped your mind that I have a quarter interest in that ship?"

"I'll make arrangements through Garrett for you to be bought out."

"Sit down, damn it! You're the most hotheaded man I've ever dealt with. Where's all the slow Southern charm, Captain? Or is there a cold-blooded Yankee hiding beneath all that Rebel skin?" Rod looked up into Adam's angry face. He began to enjoy himself. "Let me hear your proposition again. A man should always be thoroughly informed of golden opportunities he is about to refuse, don't you think?"

"I see no point in wasting my time or yours on explanations if your mind is already made up."

"I see. You have no faith in your powers of persuasion

or the irresistibility of your business venture. In that case—"

"Just a minute, Mr. Courtland, what kind of antagonistic game are you playing?" Adam demanded.

"It's called testing the mettle of a man, and you, Captain Tremain, have more temper than sense."

Adam stood poised to leave in a flurry of righteous anger. Rod Courtland's face was as hard-set and unyielding as his own, but Rod's eyes shone with the bright blue light of victory. More than losing Rod Courtland's investment in the ships, Adam was nettled by this man's infuriating ability to challenge him as no one else could and make him look like an inexperienced, hotheaded cub. Always in Courtland's presence he had the need to prove himself, to be somehow the man's equal. Even more than to Tom, he was instinctively drawn to this man.

He took a step back toward the center of the room, then walked swiftly to the chair he had vacated. He said coolly, "If you're able to keep a reasonably open mind, Mr. Courtland, I'll convince you you'd be a fool to turn my venture down."

A small smile played on Courtland's mouth, a smile that could no longer deceive Adam that Rod Courtland would easily be convinced of anything. He would not be tempted by greed. Nor could he be appealed to on solely idealistic grounds. He would agree only if the facts appealed to him. It was Adam's task to discover what combination of information would please Rod.

"If we can, let's keep our opposing patriotisms out of this," Adam began. "Both of us are aware that neither the North nor the South will give up this war until one or the other is the decisive victor. In spite of Mr. Lincoln's early optimism in calling for three-month volunteers, it is likely to be a long war. I propose we provide each side what they need. No matter what my sympathies, Mr. Courtland, I do not wish to see Northern mills idle or Yankee men without work. I cannot believe you would want to win a war over people unable to supply themselves with food or call yourself a victor because the South cannot clothe or arm itself. If it is true that the South battles for its avowed cause of independence and the North carries the banner of unity and moral right, then the war should be one of equal adversaries, or nearly so. Should it not?"

Courtland's expression did not change.

"And should you still be concerned, I intend to continue hauling out of the South those blacks who want their freedom." Adam pulled from his inner pocket a sheaf of papers Garrett had prepared, delineating the terms of the agreement and the responsibilities of each man.

Rod read through the papers. "You have Garrett Pinckney's approval?" He put the papers down. "I'm surprised."

"Why? Garrett got me started slave hauling, and he, along with yourself and Tom, purchased the *Ullah*. Why would he change his mind?"

"Several reasons. For one, Garrett was a Northerner most of his life. He was a staunch Unionist until now. Most important, this proposition would make me a traitor. I wouldn't expect a lawyer of Garrett's caliber to propose such a thing."

"We were going to keep politics out of this. Your feelings about being labeled a traitor have no place. If it comes to that, sir, you have had no compunction in making me a traitor for the past two years as I hauled slaves out of the South. Nor did you complain when I said I would continue to do so. As to technical disloyalty, Mr. Courtland, each of us is making a traitor of the other," Adam said, angry again.

"What you do, you do by your own choice, Captain, and so do I," Rod said with infuriating calm. "President Lincoln has issued an order stating that no loyal state shall engage in trade with those in the condition of unlawful insurrection. Legally, I cannot trade with the South at all."

"That kind of unreasonable control of states' and citizens' rights is precisely why this war originated. True enough, it has come to rest on the shoulders of slavery, but slavery is an issue only in the context of property rights, Mr. Courtland. No one is fooled that the North wants the problems of the blacks. More than once I've questioned to what freedom I bring the runaways. They live here in squalor and misery. They are beset by disease and racial hatred. They are stacked in tenements so decrepit and decayed that no planter would tolerate them on his plantation. They are despised by those whose jobs they take, and their education is as severely neglected here as in the South. The Northern war is one of interference with the way of the South, Mr. Courtland, not one of ideals or humanitarianism. No one here wants the freed slaves. No one here wants their problems. Those you wish to dump on the South."

"But I suppose you do consider the Southern cause one of ideals?" Rod asked sarcastically.

"To a degree, yes. Butchery of Southern land and resources to feed Northern manufactory has not resulted in economic good for the South. We have been judged and condemned, interfered with, threatened with Abolitionist-incited insurrection, driven to the wall.

"You claim to loathe slavery, Mr. Courtland, yet you see nothing wrong in making the South no more than a raw-material bank for the Northern mill. Is there a difference in the loathsomeness of an individual man being made a slave and a whole section of the country held in bondage to another?"

Rod listened with interest as Adam defended the South and its unique problems, citing incidents that had occurred in the three decades preceding the war that Rod had never considered. One political blunder after another had led to war. If there was ever a war reflecting the wishes of the people, this war reflected those of the Southern people. Rod admitted he couldn't say that of the North. There were those who were deeply concerned for the Union and those who deeply hated slavery, but there were many more who looked upon Lincoln and his war as a damned nuisance. And there were those who wanted peace at any cost.

Where Rod himself fit into the broad spectrum he didn't know. But it was obvious that Adam knew exactly where he belonged. Rod admired more than anything else the young man's passionate love for his land. Adam wanted peace and he wanted union, but only with the South holding its head high.

Rod knew Adam believed slavery to be entering its final phase in the South but was not willing to support immediate abolition. Three and a half million idle blacks in a rural population of nine million was sufficiently devastating in thought alone. Rod could imagine the complete chaos it would bring in reality. "Damned kid's going to turn me into a Rebel yet."

It was nearly frightening for Rod to sit there and see Adam's naked faith in honesty and justice, sensing that his own had become so tarnished through the years that he could remember them only by seeing their purity shine forth in the eyes of a young, untested, and unbeaten man. Rod wondered when he'd lost his idealism. Perhaps when he'd lost Zoe McCloud.

"I'll admit I like your proposition from a business viewpoint, Captain Tremain, but I cannot place my name on an agreement that would show me disloyal to my country. I'm sure, feeling as you do about the South, you'll understand that."

"I don't consider the South my country. I'm an American, Mr. Courtland. I simply don't want to see my section of this nation disrespected. If it takes a war to gain respect for the South, then I must support it. In the end I hope both sections will see the need each has for the other."

"I have underestimated you, young man. You have made me out to be the sectionalist. However, I still can't see my way clear to becoming disloyal."

"On principle or in appearance?" Adam asked suddenly.

Rod's instinct was to assert that his principles were being violated, but in truth he knew his beliefs were closer to Adam's than he'd ever admitted.

"Appearance," he said honestly, then began to chuckle at having been bested.

Adam relaxed a little. "Then, I suggest our agreement be private. Your name will never appear on the ownership or registry papers of the ships. All monetary transactions will be done privately between you and me."

"So, for a bank draft you would give me an interest in your ships, a profit for my cowardice, and you reap all the risks of capture and confinement. Isn't that a bit like selling your soul for three ships, Captain Tremain?"

"I hope not, sir, but if you'll agree, I'll make the bargain."

Courtland thrust out his hand. But Adam had gained only part of what he sought. He could purchase two ships, but would still need the *Ullah.*

After some deliberation both Adam and Ben concluded that the only practical thing they could do to protect the *Ullah* was to register her as a privateer. "As soon as I return from England, I'll procure the letter of marque for her," Adam said. "Then you'll have to take the two new ships from Glasgow to Nassau. Beau and I will meet you there with the *Ullah.*"

"We'll have our three ships, Adam. But who gets the new ones and who gets the *Ullah?*"

Adam shrugged. "We haven't got the ships yet. If we can, we'll purchase ones already in the works. We don't want that old war to pass us by sitting in dry dock. Besides, I doubt Mr. Lincoln will leave his blockade so poorly manned for long."

Three days after the meeting with Rod, Adam and Ben left for England, Adam's mind buzzing with the details of what he would have to do in the next few months. Ben would remain in Glasgow while Adam contacted Alexander Collie and Company, a British shipping firm willing to serve as agents for the Confederate States. Then he would sail back to the United States from London, leaving the supervision of the Clyde-built steamers in Ben's hands.

Glasgow was a bustling city, the largest in Scotland, smoky with shipbuilding and industry, fearsomely crowded by its energetic population. Adam's thick wool uniforms felt cozy in the wet chill of a Scottish summer. In the misty mornings he and Ben set out for the Clydeside shipworks. The riverside docks were kept frantically busy building these specially designed ships, constructed purposely to be able to slip past the Federal cruisers or to outrun them on the open sea. The smoky skyline was thick with tall belching smokestacks and the bare masts of ships nearly ocean-ready.

Englishmen flocked to the prospect of enormous profits to be made from the American war. Men were given mysterious and lengthy leaves of absence from the Royal Navy to man the blockade runners under assumed names. Young gallants glowed with the borrowed glories of men of the past such as Sir Francis Drake, freely roaming the oceans, outwitting the enemy in the dark of night, all to win or all to lose on the quirks of fate and the expertise of the Federal guns.

All of them, like Adam, were waiting anxiously for their ships to be completed. Their eagerness for the adventure infected Adam with the same fever. He had to calm himself before he arrived in London. Tending to British registry for the ships and contacting the Confederate agents there, he was hard pressed to keep his mind on business. His heart had long ago left him, to stand on the bridge of a sleek, dark-gray sidewheel steamer that was taking recognizable shape on the River Clyde in Scotland.

In June he boarded the *Tunbridge* for home, a man
divided: his heart still in Glasgow, his mind leaping the
Atlantic to New York.

Chapter Eight

Dulcie found the process of growing up one of mixed
blessings. She loved being with Aunt Mad and Uncle
Oliver, and the European tour was something she had
dreamed about but never dared hope would come true.
But leaving Mossrose as she did, under the heavy cloud
of Jem's disapproval, was a constant sorrow to her, something that lay at the back of her mind, momentarily forgotten when she became enchanted by the wonders of
Europe and the gallantry and effusive admiration of the
young men she met, remembered when the thrill of flattery
had worn thin.

The first six weeks of her Grand Tour were spent in the
British Isles. Aunt Mad and Uncle Oliver delighted in
taking her across green and foggy Ireland in wagonettes,
swathed in great heavy plaids that laughed at rain and
chill. They had several days in sooty, hospitable Dublin.
In the faces, crag-lined with the marks of robust indi-
viduality, tempered by a natural chivalry, Dulcie saw the
origins of the people who had made the South what it was.
Everywhere she looked, seeing the gardens, the fierce love
of the land, she knew more keenly than ever what Jem
felt for his beloved Mossrose.

In England they marveled at Hadrian's Wall, sixteen
hundred years old and crumbling, still standing sentinel
over the harsh Northumberland countryside. From London
they sailed on a French trader to Dunkerque, then traveled
north overland by *diligence* to Belgium and the Nether-
lands. From Marseilles they took another boat to Livorno
and spent a leisurely winter and early springtime touring
Italy.

Then it was March 1861, and they were in Milan.
Though Oliver had checked at all the previously agreed-
upon post offices on their journey, there had been no mail

from Jem or Patricia. Dulcie concealed her disappointment and smiled. "Perhaps when we get to Paris."

Oliver beamed on her gratefully. "Of course there'll be a letter in Paris." Then he gave her a totally unexpected compliment. "You are a very satisfactory traveling companion, Dulcie. You never get tired or seasick, never downhearted."

Dulcie blushed. "I can't thank you enough for bringing me and Claudine with you. I don't think I could ever tire of traveling."

Yet she was tired, of the potholed miles over haphazard roads, of the meals that made her stomach queasy, of inns where the bedding was sour and grimy. And though she tried not to think of it, she was homesick. She wanted to see her mother and father and Mossrose. With her own eyes she wanted to look at her father and know he had forgiven her. There were so many things she understood now that she had not been able to see before. If only she could tell him. She yearned to see corn and cotton waving in the winds that blew over Mossrose. She wanted to hear the plantation bell tolling out the arrival of dawn. She wanted to smell the fragrance of Violet's home-baked bread. She wanted home.

After a few weeks in Milan they moved north with the sun. The variflamed torch of May lent splendor to the chestnut trees along the Seine, the gardens of the Palais Royal, and to the kiosks, cafés, and the flea market. "Paris in springtime," breathed Mad.

Dulcie drew in a quivering breath of delight. "I see why it's your very favorite city. It's beautiful!"

"It's also ugly," Oliver harrumphed. "It stinks of its sewers, but it's famous for its perfumes. All the best and all the worst can be found right here."

They took a furnished apartment at the Chalon in the Faubourg Saint-Germain. For most meals they went to a clean little *ordinaire* a few blocks away. Their *propriétaire*, Monsieur Bas, was knowledgeable and accommodating, helping them to find agreeable guides and carriage drivers who were no more reckless than the average.

Their time in Paris was leisurely. While Oliver spent his days talking business in a passable French and visiting sooty factories, his languid gaze missing no detail of foreign manufacturing procedures, Dulcie, Aunt Mad, and

Claudine enjoyed themselves thoroughly. European charm and exaggerated displays of courtliness did much to enhance their stay in Paris, as well as enliven the hushed girlish conversations at night in their room.

Daily Oliver inquired about the mail. Then finally there was a letter from Jem, dated a month before.

"My dearest daughter," Jem began, and Dulcie could feel the tears spurting from her eyes. Blindly she ran to her bedroom, where she could read and weep as she needed to, and unfolded it before her:

> This letter finds your mother and myself well. We trust you are the same, as we have rec'd. only two letters from you. [*But I've written every Sunday!* thought Dulcie.] I have posted letters to you at every known stop to keep you and Oliver informed of our situation here.
>
> President Davis has called for volunteers. The brave men of the South have responded eagerly to defend their country. I cannot believe that any war between the North and the South will last long.
>
> I am sorry to terminate your journeyings, but I do not want you to come back to New York only to be held prisoner in the North. As always the Abolitionists and the Black Republicans under President Lincoln's guidance continue to harass. There have been changes in passport regulations, and many innocent Southerners on leisurely travel have been accused of being Confederate spies.
>
> Convey my greetings to your aunt and uncle and tell Oliver that I am ordering you home without delay. I will be fearful for your safety until you are at Mossrose again.
>
> Your loving father,
> James Moran

Dulcie read the letter twice. Heedless of tears, she rushed to the sitting room. "Daddy sounds so urgent about us comin' home, Uncle Oliver. Is the South truly at war?"

Carefully he read her letter. "I've been reading news of it in all the European papers. So far it has been all wind and bombast, but the storm is gathering. We shall start for the United States tomorrow."

Oliver looked at his niece. As though a limb had been

severed by so sharp an instrument that no pain was felt, this abominable war had severed Dulcie's nationality from his.

Mad was far less willing to confront such unsettling realities. "Oliver, I declare, you're as bad as Jem, scarin' poor Dulcie half out of her wits. There's nothin' to it, Dulcie, so don't you be frightened."

"Now, Mad," said Oliver softly, "we don't need to treat Dulcie like a little girl."

"Jem is just an alarmist, Ollie dear." Mad dismissed him, seeking comfort in less perplexing things than the division of a nation. "Besides, we have a personal introduction to the Countess Archambeault, whose first name is also Madeline, only she spells it differently than I do."

"If she lives in Calais, you can visit her," Oliver said mildly.

"Well, it's just on the way, Ollie dear."

"Just on the way in which direction? Toward the Mediterranean?"

Mad laughed and patted his shoulder. "No, you goose, only a few miles off the post road toward Calais."

"Then a visit won't be possible, as we'll be traveling by train."

Dulcie recognized the initial skirmishes in a marital battle; the mild hint from Aunt Mad, the quietly decisive reply from Uncle Oliver, the subtle suggestion of opposition from her aunt. Mad's next move, Dulcie knew, would be a sidestep.

"I guess this will be our last night in Paris," Mad said. "But I insist we not make it serious or sad. Let's make it a real celebration!"

"We just had a big night last night. Dear Mad, I believe I am getting too old for late nights."

True to form, Mad gave in gracefully—this time. "Of course, Ollie honey, that was very thoughtless of me. We'll go to Monsieur Honfleur's and have a really splendid repast! Then we'll retire *quite* early."

Oliver appeared to have won the first engagement, because Mad had retreated. "Oh, Oliver! How is it that you can always get around me? You never want to argue with me, and yet you always come out best!"

Oliver nudged Dulcie. "The last time I recall getting the better of her was March of 1841, when I got her to say she'd marry me," he whispered.

But the battle was scarcely joined. Mad began it again after a superb dinner of delicately browned fresh fish, duck stewed with cucumber, a tongue with a mouth-watering tomato sauce, sweetmeats and puddings, finishing with peaches flambée, and wines to enhance each course. Oliver had been particularly appreciative of M. Honfleur's choice of wines and was nodding a bit over his dessert.

Dulcie, delicately spooning the last bites of peaches flambée, caught her aunt's eye and burst out giggling. "Give up, Aunt Mad."

Mad had a face made for smiling. Her high round cheekbones, her wide mouth with straight white teeth, and eyes that crinkled but not too much for beauty's sake, combined to bestow upon her a radiant look of cherubic joy. She smiled now on her beautiful niece, thinking once again that since she had no children from her twenty years of marriage, how nice it was of Patricia to lend her Dulcie. So much more soothing to be with than any of her sister Caroline's flighty daughters.

"I never give up, dear. I have it all worked out!" she cried happily. "We'll hire a carriage large enough to carry all our trunks. We'll take the post road as far as Chantilly and just *endure* the customs men. The castle of the prince of Condé is there, you know."

Dulcie had not known.

Mad went on dreamily, "We might just spend a day in Saint Denis. The Benedictine abbey there holds the French crown jewels and a number of holy relics, including, I believe, a thorn from our Blessed Savior's crown."

Oliver said unexpectedly, "We've already seen enough nails and wood from the True Cross to build a ten-foot fence around the castle of Chenonceaux."

Mad squeezed his arm conspiratorially. "Just the same, Ollie dear, one of them might be real, and think what a thrill that would be!"

"You do realize, dear Mad, that this whole scheme is completely irresponsible?" Oliver said mildly. But Mad had already won. All thoughts of war and safety had been banished. Oliver looked fondly at his women and agreed silently that a few days more could hardly matter.

Mad broke forth in her angelic smile. "Oh, yes, Ollie! I'm sure it is the height of naughtiness, but doesn't that just add flavor to the adventure? It will be such a grand end to Dulcie's Grand Tour. Oh, yes!" Her eyes were sparkling and happy as Oliver looked on with tacit approval. "From Chantilly we work our way north and east to Pierrefonds. The Countess Soulier gave me *explicit* directions."

"In that case we shall surely become lost," Oliver mumbled. "We'll have to have postilions, you know, Mad. We'd never find the way without them."

"Nasty little creatures," said Mad, wrinkling her nose as if she smelled one. "I can never decide which feature about them is most revoltin', their saddle-sore beasts, their noisome garments, or those *very* peculiar jackboots."

"Their manners," rumbled Oliver. "I've known goats more civil. We could take the train to Calais, get there in less than a day," he added in one last weak thrust at good sense. Then he appeared to doze, his round face and bulbous nose shadowed by the candlelight, his superfluous chins tucked comfortably into his cravat.

Mad had gone conveniently deaf. "Will you be terribly disappointed at having to leave Paris so soon, Dulcie?"

Dulcie smiled at her aunt and looked away. "Of course I'll be sorry to leave, Aunt Mad, but I know I'll enjoy seeing the other places on the way to Calais. And the Marquis duBois did invite us to his ball, remember?"

"Ah! Might there be a certain marquis's son you'd like to see once more?" Mad asked brightly, then darted a testy glance at her husband. "We certainly won't miss *that!* The very idea! Just because Jem is crying wolf! By now Alain will be positively spoiling to see you again!"

Dulcie blushed, remembering good-looking Alain duBois of the liquid brown eyes and the ardent kisses. "Oh, he's not serious, Aunt Mad. He's just being extravagant and complimentary."

Mad wagged an admonishing finger. "You're not to discourage him, Dulcie. Not every Southern family has a real French marquis in it!"

Dulcie grinned. "Daddy'd love that! You know how he is about foreigners."

"I sincerely doubt that he ever met one of any importance. We must go. Ollie, we're leavin' dear, hadn't you better open your eyes?"

"They were never closed," Oliver rumbled. He might have spoken truly, for all his vague, sleepy manner. When he seemed to be furthest away, he would suddenly utter some remark, some wise conclusion that astonished them all. Many a shrewd businessman, assessing Oliver and thinking him a bit lacking, had discovered his error expensively.

Back at the *appartement* Mad went into a frenzy of activity. She issued orders to Claudine, to Dulcie, to Oliver, who simply fell asleep in his chair, to M. Bas to bring down their trunks, to arrange for a carriage, to go out and buy them another trunk.

They were ready at dawn. Guilbert, the carriage driver, was surly and apparently weak-muscled, for he dropped anything he tried to load. In the end Oliver and M. Bas put on the luggage. M. Bas sent his son to fetch the postilion. An hour passed before they returned.

Mad's pet peeves were all combined in the postilion. His official duty was to ride ahead on his pony to warn the driver of large potholes, washed-out bridges, bandits, and other dangers. He was, in effect, their protector. It was quickly plain that the meagerly constructed, wizened wisp who drunkenly sat his bony mount would not do. His looks would sooner inspire hilarity than fear, should they be beset on the highway. On his small head sat a large cavalier's hat, complete with plume. He wore a blackened sheepskin coat that came down to his enormous jackboots. His legs would be well protected, for an iron rim ran around the top of each boot, emphasizing their impressive diameter. To complete his costume he wore wickedly long brass spurs encrusted, as it proved, with the blood of his hapless pony.

"Good God!" Oliver exclaimed.

Even M. Bas, accustomed to such creatures, was taken aback. He recovered quickly. "A *tigre*, Monsieur Raymer! François, expose for Monsieur Raymer your *pistolet*."

François's hand darted into his boot and produced a half-empty wine bottle.

M. Bas grew apoplectic. "You fumbling ninny, son of a pox-ridden hag and a three-legged mule! Your *pistol!*" Then he ducked with astonished nimbleness as François hauled out an ancient pistol, pointing it into M. Bas's face. He screamed, "Put it away before you kill us all!"

"I do not keep it loaded, Monsieur," François retorted mildly, and dropped the weapon back into the cavernous boot.

Mad recovered first. "Oliver, I don't believe we'll need a postilion after all."

Oliver's eyes gleamed. "Surely, dear Mad, you haven't been frightened? It was your idea that we should suffer the discomforts of carriage travel."

"We are *not* goin' to take this shriveled caricature of a horseman who reeks of the scrapin's from the stable floor!"

Oliver laughed comfortably. "Very well, my dear. "I'll just settle up with M. Bas, and we'll be off."

The first few miles were quiet, Oliver snoring lightly, Mad exhausted from her efforts of the night before. Dulcie and Claudine were gazing out the windows, afraid to catch each other's eyes and start giggling. The carriage rolled over the hard-packed post road. Mad's eyelids fell.

Dulcie saw him first. Hearing acrimonious discussion, she stuck her head out the window. Then, smothering laughter, she pantomimed to Claudine the pulling on of enormous boots and pinched her nostrils. They started laughing.

"Fermez les bouches," said Oliver in his lowest rumble.

"What is that disgustin' stench!" Mad exclaimed. She poked Oliver with her forefinger. "Ollie, that pipsqueak postilion has followed us!"

"On the contrary, my dear, he is leading us."

Mad digested this briefly. "Ollie dear, stop the carriage and tell that revoltin' little wretch we won't need his services any longer."

"It's the law."

"Ha! The law according to Monsieur Bas!"

Oliver snored.

They stopped for midday meal in a shady spot along the road. From her baskets, Mad extracted bread, baked by Mme. Honflour only yesterday, pungent Camembert cheese, and wine. The festive air was only slightly spoiled by the odor of the driver, who had not bothered to climb from his seat but with a mild, "Pardon, Mesdames, Monsieur," had relieved himself copiously over the far side of the carriage; and of the postilion, who showed his respect by sitting some distance from them, unfortunately upwind.

"I am told," said François, cleaning his black teeth with the point of his knife, "that there has been a *voleur* very near to where we are sitting. Should the rumor prove itself, you shall be happy of my services."

"What's that? A what?" Mad looked around hastily, as if for a mouse.

"Nothing, dear, he's only speaking of bandits. Don't

concern yourself," Oliver said soothingly. Then he began
to talk in French with the postilion.

"What's he sayin'? What are they talkin' about, Dulcie?"

"A bandit, Aunt Mad, but it turns out he's miles from
here, in the district between Morienval and Pierrefonds."

"Oh, bosh, he's only tryin' to frighten . . . Pierrefonds?"
she asked. weakly.

"Aunt Mad, *that's* where the countess has her château,
isn't it?"

"Ummm, yes, dear, but I'm sure—well, of course nothing exciting will happen." Then Mad brightened. In her
best party voice she added, "Except possibly that we shall
all die of inhaling bad air." She rose, dusted her skirts,
and directed Claudine to put away the leftover food.

So they went on. They left the post road to follow cart
tracks alongside vast cornfields and rich pasturelands, then
through a wood that stretched endlessly. Ahead of them
the little postilion, fairly sober and mindful of duty, trotted
on his cadaverous pony. The bedraggled plume on his hat
dipped jauntily. Oliver, who had been sitting up alertly,
yawned and rested his head.

"We should be comin' to an old château soon," said
Mad, consulting directions. Now that they were on the
spot the route did not seem as clear as it had in Paris.

"That might be it," said Dulcie, nodding to Mad's left.

"Of course! Now, at the fork we go east. Dulcie, motion
the driver to turn right."

At the fork there was a third road, and a hot debate
between driver and postilion. Finally François came back
and stuck his head in the window. "Monsieur, I believe it
is the center road you want to Morienval."

Oliver did not open his eyes. "If you do not take the
extreme right-hand fork, I shall rise up from my seat and
kick you in your skinny ass."

François's head disappeared. He said to the driver, "It
is just as I have said, you are to follow the road to *that*
side. Monsieur agrees."

"*Nom de chien!*" exclaimed Guilbert, and turned his
horses east.

Chapter Nine

The road was long and tortuous, charming at a glance but monotonous with the hours. They spent the night at a large farmhouse. The driver and the postilion by preference slept in the stable. Oliver and Mad occupied their host's bed, sleeping on snowy sun-dried sheets. The farmer and his wife in the kitchen, and Dulcie and Claudine in the parlor, slept on pallets.

Dulcie turned over. The shucks rustled under her. "I shouldn't say it, Claudine, but now that we have to go home, I don't think I mind very much."

"Ah been prayin' right along we git to go home soon. Ah been missin' 'Pollo's lovin'."

Into Dulcie's mind flashed a vignette of Claudine, bursting into sobs in the Louvre when she discovered she was in the Gallery of Apollo. They had shared many unexpected confidences during this trip. Sometimes Claudine would slip out for a while to meet the carriage driver or another of the passengers on their coach for what was apparently a fulfilling physical interlude.

Thinking of this, Dulcie said, "What about your Spaniard, Hernando? I keep seein' him pop up at the oddest places."

"He got the notions an' the wherewithal, but he sho' ain't 'Pollo. I been hopin' yo' daddy gwine let us jump ovah de broom."

"You know he doesn't like his darkies to marry."

"Oh, Miss Dulcie, Ah hope he change his min'. Ah love dat 'Pollo a pow'ful lot. Ain't dere somebody you's wantin'? Somebody you jes' keep a-thinkin' 'bout no matter what else is goin' on?"

"Well, Glenn, I guess." Her voice quivered. "I don't love him, like you love 'Pollo, but I miss him." Tears leaked out of her eyes and ran into the edges of her hair. But not for Glenn. She cried because there was no one anywhere she cared for enough to want to marry.

She didn't want to cry. She wanted to grow up and be all the things Patricia expected. When she returned to Jem, it would be as an accomplished woman, able to make correct decisions, able to hold herself with poise and dignity. No longer a foolish girl playing flirtations games in the summer house with Leroy Biggs, but Dulcie Moran, woman of the world.

"Oh, Claudine, will I ever find someone?"

"You gwine meet yo'seff a fine man. You see. It gwine happen."

She couldn't bear to talk about it anymore. She was too weepy tonight. "Oh, there's always tomorrow, then another tomorrow."

The next afternoon they had passed through Morienval and were within sight of the countess's château. Mad sat up excitedly as they entered the woods that hid the château from view. "We're nearly there, Dulcie! Oh, I do hope she is receivin' today! But, then, she'd nearly have to be, wouldn't she, since we have the letter from her sister?" From her reticule she brought forth the stiff, crested stationery with the spidery European handwriting on it. She stared at it hard, as if the French words would magically turn into English so she could read them.

The carriage stopped. Mad gave a little yip of surprise when a long-barreled pistol, followed by a sad pale face, stuck itself in at the window. "Madame, your *bijouterie*," said the hesitant voice.

"Who are you!? What do you want?" Mad asked frantically. "What did he say, Dulcie?" she whispered, as if he might not notice.

"He wants your jewelry, Aunt Mad."

"My jewelry!" Mad's hand went to her throat. "Certainly not!"

The man repeated his request, more firmly this time.

Mad punched Oliver with her forefinger. "Ollie, Ollie dear, it seems we have a bandit at the window and he says he wants my jewelry."

"Has he got a gun?" Oliver rumbled.

"Yes, dear, he has, but—"

"You'd better give him your jewelry, then." He appeared to doze again.

"*Oliver!* Oh, where is that nasty little postilion? *François!*"

François, lying unconscious under the feet of his grazing pony, did not reply.

"Donnez-moi votre bijouterie, Madame, toute de suite!"

"What's he sayin', Dulcie? Ooh! What is that stupid driver doin'? Guilbert! *Guilbert!*" Mad rapped in frenzied movements on the roof of the carriage. The driver, likewise unconscious, did not move.

The bandit's face was taking on a kind of bewilderment. *"Sacre bleu!"* He gripped his pistol more decisively. *"Madame,* your *monnaie."*

This much Mad understood. Again, his demand banished her fright. "Oh, do go away! We're goin' to see the countess today."

The pistol wavered and came to a stop an inch away from Dulcie's cheek. "Aunt Mad!" Dulcie squealed. "Give him your purse. Oh, please!"

Mad dipped into her purse and came with two coins of little value. One by one she gave them to the bandit. He gestured for her to give him her rings, one set with rubies, two others with garnets and diamonds. Reluctantly, with an obedience born of Dulcie's peril, she stripped off the rings. "I certainly hope you are satisfied now!" she spat. He became possessor of Mad's treasured cameo lavaliere, Dulcie's amethyst ring, and all her money. Growing bold, he reached into Mad's lap and snatched the countess's letter.

"Give me that!" Mad made a brash, ineffectual grab for it. He held it upside down and sideways, trying to shake it or make sense of it. She attempted his own tongue. *"Monnaie, non! Un laitue!"*

"That's lettuce, Aunt Mad. *Lettre, Monsieur."*

The bandit's eyebrows rose. Plainly he did not receive much mail.

"It's worthless," Dulcie said. *"Un souvenir sans valeur."*

He handed back Mad's letter. Indicating Claudine he asked in French, "Why is the lady's face so black?"

"Claudine is . . ." Dulcie paused, glanced at Claudine, then went on, "diseased, Monsieur. *Un maladie de peau."* She shrugged sadly.

The bandit shuddered. "And Monsieur? Why does he not awaken?"

Oliver was awake, Dulcie knew. Why he had done nothing she didn't know. "A bad heart . . . a *coeur pauvre —très pauvre, Monsieur."*

The pale face lengthened. "But that is so sad, Mademoiselle. I shall not even disturb him. Give to me his money belt."

Dulcie, understanding only "money," reached into Oliver's waistcoat for the coins he kept for beggars and tips. "That is all, Monsieur."

The bandit repeated his demand, accompanying it with wild gesturings.

Mad tapped Oliver with her forefinger again. "Ollie dear, he wants somethin' else. Did you understand him?"

Oliver rumbled in French, "Tell him I do not possess a money belt. I am without funds until we receive a bank draft at Calais. Tell him that I will die if we do not soon get to Calais."

"But Monsieur, you are not on the road to Calais!"

"More's the pity," Oliver rumbled.

"I have not yet searched your luggage, Monsieur."

Oliver groaned. "I am unable to lift heavy objects, so perhaps you would like to climb up on the carriage and do that for yourself."

The bandit, still on his horse, disappeared. "Uncle Oliver, what can we do?" Dulcie whispered.

"Let him take what he wants. His pistol has a bad barrel and will explode if he fires it. We could all be injured."

Guilbert of the surly disposition and the weak muscles was roused to consciousness by a cold pistol jabbed in his rear. He found an unsuspected strength and began throwing down boxes, baskets, and trunks.

Oliver stuck his head out and roared, "Guilbert! Stop throwing our luggage about! I'll tear off your balls and have them for breakfast!"

"But, Monsieur, the bandit threatens to shoot them off with his pistol!"

"Then throw them *carefully!*"

"You will please get out, Mesdames, Monsieur. I wish to keep you in my sight while I select a few trinkets."

They stood in a row as the man pawed through the numerous containers, strewing the woodland path with dresses and paper wrappings.

Behind him, an expression of revenge on his dirty face, crept François. He held his pistol pointed toward the bandit's head.

Oliver said plaintively, "Monsieur, do you not have

enough trinkets? My illness is worse. We must continue
our journey."

Dulcie held her breath for the explosion of François's
pistol. There was no explosion, only a rusty click. As he
said, he did not keep it loaded.

"Hit him with it!" cried Oliver. François raised his
weapon dramatically just as the bandit turned. Faced with
a pistol even larger than his own, François shrank into his
boots.

"By the Holy Rood!" exclaimed the bandit. "Guilbert!
Fetch nails and a mallet! You are going to nail this mouse
to a tree!"

As best he could in his huge boots, François fell to his
knees, gabbling for mercy. His wife and ten children would
starve. Had not the bandit done enough to him, knocking
him senseless? Not only did he have the pain of the head,
but also his pony had stood on his chest while he ate the
plume from his hat. Besides, he was not fit, he was too
worthless to die the brave death of the Blessed Savior.

"Stand on your feet, impious nincompoop! Would I
shadow the name of the Savior by granting a cockroach
like you His glorious demise? *Jamais!* It is your boots we
will nail to the tree, with you in them!"

With Guilbert holding up the hapless postilion, the
bandit nailed his boots so that he faced the tree. Though
no injury was being done to him, François screeched constantly.

"I believe we've had quite enough of this lunacy," Oliver
rumbled. Mad and Dulcie pulled him back and stood
clinging to his arms.

"'low me to tend to him, Mastah Olivah." Claudine
stepped forward. She pulled up her sleeves and unbuttoned
her dress down to her waist, so that her small brown
breasts bobbed in the V formed there. Switching her hips,
waving her brown arms in snakelike gestures, she approached the bandit.

Claudine did not speak French, but hers was a universal
language. She thought he was mighty appealin', said her
eyes. She was available, said the saucy sway of her hips.
She rubbed first one brown hand, then the other, up her
arms and over her breasts. The bandit stood transfixed,
his mouth gaping, fascinated and horrified by the malady
of the black skin. Almost, he wanted to reach out and
touch it.

Claudine extended her fingers toward him. The bandit moved away uneasily. Then Claudine slowly, tantalizingly, pulled up her skirt. Because of its fullness, the watching group saw little except her bare ankles, and the popping eyes of François and the highwayman.

Up to her knees, ever more slowly up her thighs to her waist, went Claudine's skirt. Her hand rubbed lightly up her bare thigh. The bandit's eyes grew glassy. Saliva showed on his lower lip. Then, with a lightning-quick motion, Claudine thrust toward him both her pink palms.

The bandit screamed, clutching himself, and bolted for his horse.

After a silence assured them the bandit was gone, Dulcie and Claudine hugged each other, dancing around.

"Ollie dear, shouldn't you close your mouth now?" said Aunt Mad, her calm restored. "Claudine, that was very fine and brave of you, but you are exposin' yourself."

"Look, Aunt Mad, he forgot his trinkets!" Dulcie said, still laughing, and pounced on the greasy sack the bandit had carried.

"Fine, dear, take everythin' out, but watch for lice."

"Monsieur, I beg you, get me down from this tree!"

Oliver's reply was unspeakable, even in French. He repacked the carriage, and they headed again toward the countess's château.

The countess was delighted to receive them once she had scanned the letter from her sister. *"Quelle belle demoiselle!"* she exclaimed, looking at Dulcie. She went on for some time about the purity of Dulcie's skin, her hair of the flame, her eyes of the amber. Then she said, in English, "But you must hunger!"

Over thin cups of strong coffee, and assorted delicacies, the countess chatted with them. Hearing that they planned to attend the grand ball of Réné, marquis duBois, she exclaimed, "But he is my cousin! You shall go with me in my barouche! My servants will follow with your luggage. *C'est entendu!*"

Theirs had been a long journey, and all of them, even Mad, were happy to place themselves and their plans for the next few days in the capable hands of the countess. She got them to Calais without further incident.

As they entered Calais, Dulcie became acutely aware that this was the end of her Grand Tour. The ball at the Château duBois tonight would be the last time she would dance with men like Alain duBois, son of a marquis. She wanted it to be a night she would never forget. A perfect night.

She already felt as if she were part of a wonderful dream, and the night was not even near yet. Alain's eyes softened with admiration as soon as he saw her step from his cousin's carriage. From that moment he was her constant companion and servant. Whatever she wished, she had it at her fingertips before she was able to speak the words. Her head was spinning with a myriad of gay, romantic visions, each one fulfilled and made real by Alain.

The château was magnificent. Each room was decorated to represent the countries in which the marquis had traveled. Alain whispered to her as he took her through miniature versions of Italy, Bavaria, India, and China, with authentic furnishings and wall coverings. He spoke softly of the thousand moments he would keep her in his arms or the amorous miles they would travel through these gaily decorated replicas.

Dulcie's heart thudded in girlish anticipation of being won and loved by Alain. That she didn't know if she wanted to be loved or won by Alain made the coming evening all the more exciting. All manner of heavenly things might happen to her, all against her wavering will.

Dulcie looked like a small flower in full bloom when she entered the room in her softly shaded apple-green gown that emphasized her tiny waist and her flamboyant coloring. Alain was at her side immediately. *"Ravissante!"* he declared, with the deepest of bows.

He held her at a decorous distance for the waltz, though his eyes plainly told her he wished it otherwise. Dulcie's cheeks were already flushed, and her eyes answered the desire in Alain's with messages she did not know were there. The sparkling crystal chandeliers, ablaze with color, melted into swiftly running rainbows as Alain whirled her through India and China, then into the dimness of the English ballroom.

Her head filled with the glory of being irresistible; she had no chance to resist before Alain's lips were on hers. "Alain . . ." she said, quivering with the feelings he had suddenly aroused.

"Ahh, Dul-see!" he breathed. "I cannot lose such a jewel as you. Why do you not linger here in pleasant Calais?" He squeezed her to him, heedless of the dancers who might in passing catch a glimpse of apple-green silk and know it was the American girl whom Alain was compromising. "But I must persuade you, *non?*"

"Alain! Please, the others, they will see us! Aunt Mad—"

"You will stay here with me. No more Aunt Mad. *Voilà!*"

Dulcie's eyes shone, contradicting the rising panic that warned her she could no longer handle the situation. Alain moved closer. "Ahh, but you are adorable! So modest! So innocent! Mmh! Mmh!" He kissed her twice. She tried to move away from him. Alain smiled knowingly. Between men and women it was all a game, retreat and advance. For one so young she played it well. American ways and her undoubted innocence added just the spice to whet his somewhat jaded appetite. He held out his arm. "Come, Dul-see." They went down dazzlingly white marble stairs into the cool night.

The moon was nearing full. They strolled with studied aimlessness; when they stopped, they were completely hidden by tall surrounding shrubs. "You are mine now," Alain said lightly, and kissed her again. "You are my prisoner in the maze, Dul-see. You cannot get out until you have promised me that you will never leave me."

Dulcie's heart thudded. Could the impossible be happening? Was Alain thinking of marriage—so soon—and with her, of no aristocratic lineage? She tried to speak casually. "I promise not to leave you for five minutes, Alain, then I must go back to the ballroom, or my aunt and uncle will be lookin' for me. Will that be long enough?"

Even in the shadowy maze she could feel his hot gaze on her. "Five lifetimes would not be enough, Mademoiselle." He kissed each fingertip. "Listen to me, Dul-see, for I wish to speak my heart to you. I cannot bear to lose you to your Southland. I have a proposal, *ma fleur.* I am asking if you will become my mistress."

Dulcie was speechless. She stood staring at Alain while her mind screamed with shock and hurt. *"Mistress!"* she whispered. "Alain—"

"You are afraid! Ah, but *ma petite,* what joy I would have in teaching you! You would also, in your own way, enjoy the learning."

"I don't believe—"

He held her closer, while Dulcie stood stiff within his arms. "Dul-see, *ma belle,* attend to me. My father can

provide us with every material want. He is a man of the
world, understanding of these affairs of love. You would
have a fine apartment here in the château, servants, new
gowns, jewels, travel. And in me you would have the perfect lover—handsome, finely clothed, and attentive. Already I speak your language. You, *cherie,* would speak
mine in every way."

"Alain, I could not begin to consider . . . Americans
cannot do things like this," she said desperately.

"You are in France, *ma douce amour,*" he murmured
softly into her ear. "For us it is entirely proper, and very
sensible." He covered her face with kisses, murmuring,
"Do not refuse me, Dul-see. Tell me that you will belong
to me, and to me only!"

Dulcie felt the warm, confusing surge of passion consuming her, melting away her careful rearing, debasing her
chastity.

Alain's seeking mouth found hers. "Oh, Dul-see," he
murmured, between kisses, "my desire for you burns red
as the harvest moon. Say you will receive me in your
boudoir tonight, moments from this moment! Let me fold
you in my deepest embrace, let me pluck the blossom from
your so dainty flower of love!"

Dulcie gasped. His lips were on her breasts where they
mounded creamy above the lace of her low square neckline. "Alain . . ."

He burst into French. "My Dulcie, sweeter than the
honey from the perfume fields of Grasse! I will make you
sing with joy, my little nightingale—"

"Oh, Alain, is it so wonderful?" she breathed, wanting
to believe Alain was the one she had waited for. Was this
marvelous passion he spoke of the magical thing all women
yearned for? She didn't know—oh, she didn't know.

Alain drew back, his expression sympathetic, understanding. "Ahh, *ma pauvre enfant!* You worry about the
uncle. My father, the marquis, will explain to Monsieur
Raymer. All will be well, *ma petite.*"

Dulcie's heart was pounding sickeningly when he took
her back to the ballroom. Alain relinquished her graciously
to a young man who approached them. As Dulcie was
whirled away, she saw Alain and the marquis walking with
Uncle Oliver toward the library.

They were still talking when the music stopped. Oliver
was laughing and perfectly agreeable. Her heart was in her

mouth as Alain quickly excused himself and led her to a secluded corner.

As the other guests leaped and whirled in the gavotte, Alain told her, "Your uncle has regretfully refused me, *ma cherie*. Your father would be desolated if you were to remain in France."

Dulcie blinked at him for a moment, then made her face sad. "I am . . . disappointed, Alain. I had hoped—"

His gesture was one of negation. "A miniscule obstacle, Dul-see. There are always ways of avoidance, *n'est-ce pas?*"

"Oh, but I couldn't defy my uncle—"

"You have not the hair of flame for nothing, Mademoiselle. I will come to your boudoir to be with you this night, *cherie*. Together we will discover the mysterious delights of *l'amour*."

Dulcie's face grew hot. She whispered, "I cannot, Alain."

He chuckled softly, regretfully. "My little wild flower, you have the sweet shyness, but you have the desire for *l'amour. Mais oui!* In you is the passion only waiting to be set free." He pressed his lips to her hand. "Perhaps you will change your mind, *ma douce*."

A passion only waiting to be set free, he had said. Did it show, then? Had her shameful need to be loved by a man begun to show so that all could see? She blushed as she thought of the reckless desire that rose in her at the touch of a man's lips. Such thoughts she normally kept under tight control. Only to herself, in one small dark corner of her mind, could she admit the constant hunger to be loved, to be taken and used in love. One day it had to be someone, but each time the chance came, it seemed she would reach the point of decision and then run away from it. Again she wondered if she had made a mistake. Was Alain, after all, the man to set her free of all the longing?

Two days later a large party stood on the pier with Dulcie. Behind them were low, bleak houses, huddling along the Calais waterfront. Around them the gulls wheeled endlessly, crying in their strange voices.

It was time to board. Last kisses of the hand, fond gazes from eyes never to be looked into again, courtly bows and adieux from the marquis and the marquise. Alain took ahold of her arms and gave her a ritual kiss on each cheek, lingering—oh, so briefly!—on her lips, desire and regret still on his face. "*Au revoir,* my Dul-see. *Bon voyage.*"

"*Merci,* Alain. I shall think of you fondly."

Then they were on the ferry, waving good-bye across the widening stretch of water, and Dulcie's eyes were wet. Good-bye to Europe, to Alain forever. She was going home.

Chapter Ten

In London the Raymer party boarded the *Tunbridge* for New York. Dulcie found an open spot at the rail where she and Claudine could watch the busy scene on the docks. Carriages and drays arrived, disgorging passengers and baggage, wealthy families with their retinue of servants; the not-so-wealthy, who lugged their own baggage and their infants, with toddlers clinging wide-eyed to their mothers' skirts. A bevy of well-dressed young girls, fussily chaperoned, chatted together as they approached the gangplank, followed by five animated and attractive young men, evidently going home from their Grand Tour. Home to what? Dulcie thought idly, then uncomfortably, *going home to war.*

It did not bear thinking on, and she turned abruptly away to gaze down the long deck. Except for a few like herself, nearly everyone was moving toward the companionway that led to the passenger cabins and staterooms. Two little boys chased each other in and out around obstacles, laughing and screaming, until without warning each found his arm held firmly by a big man in a dark blue uniform. Dulcie watched, fascinated, as he quickly squatted down to the boys' level and appeared to be explaining things to them. He pointed, gestured, smiled, and the boys seemed to listen. One evidently asked about his cap, for the big man laughed and put it on the boy's head. Then he rose and sent them on their way, mildly subdued. He continued to stalk the deck, his hands behind him, his restless eyes seeing everything.

Dulcie nudged Claudine. Claudine smiled dreamily. "A real prime example o' manhood, there, Miss Dulcie. Git yo' eyes full, 'cause a man like dat, he got him a wife in eve'y poat."

Dulcie fastened her eyes on the opposite side of the deck. He would pass in front of them in a few seconds. Then, as if it were his duty to do so, he deliberately turned his head toward her. In the moment before he lifted his hand to his cap in a courteous salutation, Dulcie saw the brilliant blue eyes widen in recognition.

She got a blurred impression of a clear, warmly tanned complexion; of high cheekbones, a finely sculptured jaw, and a thick, coal-black moustache that curved over his upper lip to stop just below the corners of his handsome unsmiling mouth. She went hot from head to foot, drawing in her breath involuntarily; but he walked on, his smooth long-legged pace unbroken.

For a moment Dulcie stood paralyzed, then her eyes darted after him. He showed no signs of looking back. She found the courage to turn her head and stare frankly at his broad shoulders, moving slightly under the well-fitted dark blue frock coat that tapered down to his slim hips. Dulcie liked the purposeful way he put each shining boot down, like a man in command of himself as well as others, a man with neither braggadocio nor false modesty, whose step had an energetic liveliness that bespoke his long acquaintance with decks in every kind of sea.

He was suddenly swallowed into the companionway. Dulcie realized she had been standing with her breath held, every muscle tensed. She managed to close her mouth. She blinked rapidly. She turned to Claudine, to find her maid gawking much as she must have been.

"Ooh my, Miss Dulcie," Claudine breathed.

They strolled the length of the deck once more, then went down to help Aunt Mad unpack.

"We saw the captain, Uncle Oliver," said Dulcie. "Tramping up and down the deck with the weight of the world on him."

"As he should," replied Oliver. "This is his first voyage in command of the *Tunbridge*. He has three hundred sixty passengers to worry about, as well as his crew."

"I certainly hope he has a postilion," said Mad placidly, and they all began to laugh.

Dulcie said, "You know the captain, then, Uncle Oliver?"

"We sailed under him last year on the *Fairwinds*. Surly fellow, bullies his crewmen."

"Oh! He bullies his crewmen? But he's so handsome!"

"Captain Sloan? I shouldn't have described him so. But, then, I don't have your fresh viewpoint."

"But his name isn't—" Dulcie stopped herself. She had given him her word she'd never mention him, his ship, or that he'd helped her.

That night at the second dinner sitting Dulcie saw him again, two tables away. His black curls gleamed in the lamplight as he bent his head to take a forkful of food. He was making perfunctory replies to an attractive girl next to him. "There, Uncle Oliver, how can you not call him good-looking?"

"Oh, that one. That's someone else. Yes, he's got a nice face. A bit too sensitive, but still strong." Oliver smiled. "Shall I find out about him, my dear?"

Dulcie saw him frequently on deck the next few days, staring preoccupied over the ocean for an hour at a time or pacing with that restless impatience of a man with not enough to do. She sometimes glanced at him if they passed each other; but his eyes stayed straight ahead of him across the miles to New York City.

The voyage could be over if she waited for him to approach her. There was not that much time to waste being shy and ladylike. Driven by impulses she only dimly understood, she slipped away from Claudine, slipped away from them all in search of Adam Tremain.

By the time she had climbed the companionway and forced herself to walk sedately the length of the deck, her heart was pounding in something approaching panic. He was there—he usually was—staring out at the water cleaved by the prow, wrestling with private problems she could scarcely have imagined.

She gathered her courage. "Cap-Captain Tremain."

Moving with the alertness of a man who lives always with danger, he had already turned toward her, sweeping his cap off to tuck it under his left arm. "Yes, ma'am?" he said with a half smile, the intense blue eyes lighting.

He was tall, almost threateningly large, a rock of a man one could break oneself on. Suppressing the urge to shiver, she drew in her breath. "I'm sorry to disturb you, Captain."

"It's all right, Miss Moran." His voice was deep, accented by the South. "How can I be of service to you?"

Dulcie took herself in hand. She had business with this man, even if she did find him troublesomely attractive.

Surely she could handle the asking of a few questions!
"I brought you a number of passengers. You took them
North—to freedom." His expression had changed, closed,
become withdrawn if not outright combative. Dulcie
stumbled on, "Surely you remember, Captain Tremain!
There were ten of them, and you promised one man you'd
find his sons for him."

He looked out to sea a moment, and his eyes returned
to strike into hers again. From the time they'd first met,
this girl had meant trouble. "I don't remember, Miss
Moran."

She persisted, filling in details. "Can't you tell me about
Fellie? Did he get away safely? And what about his boys?"

"I can't tell you anything because I haven't got the least
recollection of the man you're asking about."

"But you promised!" Dulcie's eyes filled with tears. "It
meant so much to Fellie . . . and to me."

Relenting a little, he said gently, "Miss Moran, if I gave
my word, I kept it."

The interview was over.

She turned to go. It had been an utter failure. Not only
had she found out nothing about Fellie and his family but
now Captain Tremain would see her as a pushy, forward
female. She had been a fool, a shameless fool.

Adam watched her proud retreat, his eyes troubled.
The man Fellie had been a favorite of hers; she had gone
to great risk to help him make free. Naturally she wanted
to know about him.

Heavy steps on the deck behind him brought his thoughts
to a halt. It could only be one person: Captain Sloan.
Adam studied the water, tense, braced against Sloan's too
boisterous slap on the back. At the last instant he faced
him and saluted smartly.

Israel Sloan's brutish expression had changed only for
the worse since Adam had served under him as second
mate. "Well, *Captain*," he said with a joviality that showed
his tobacco-stained teeth. "You remember one thing I
taught you—respect for your elders and betters. Even if
that was a pretty God-damned sloppy salute."

Adam looked him boldly in the eyes, aware that Sloan
would take fullest enjoyment in embarrassing him, if indeed he could not find sufficient excuse to clap him into
irons or have him flogged before the crew. "Sorry, Captain, guess I've gotten out of practice."

"Too busy tryin' to take over my command, that it?"

"No, sir."

Sloan's voice was menacing. "Come on now, Mister, don't go tellin' me no friggin' lies. I got eyes, and they see real good. I been watchin' you trampin' my decks from stem to stern, nosin' into every little thing, lookin' for somethin' to go crosswise so's you can be Johnny-on-the-spot to set it right. Ain't that so, Mister?"

Adam held Sloan's gaze. "That's not so, Captain. I'm a passenger on your ship, and that's all. I have my master's papers in good order. I suggest you call me Captain Tremain."

Sloan guffawed. "Just happens I like to call you Mister. Helps keep you in your rightful place. I see you got all the pretty little quiffs marchin' right up to you to make your private arrangements, too." He leered, revoltingly suggestive. "Just let one of my men catch you holed up someplace—anyplace—with one o' your whores! I'll make you so sorry you'll wish you'd been born dead, do you understand me, Mister?"

"Perfectly," said Adam. "As a paying passenger, I don't take kindly to being threatened. Do you understand *me*, Captain?"

His thick fingers smacked Adam's lapel heavily. "I don't like your uniform, Mister. On this ship there's only one captain, and I'm it. Hereafter, you find something else to wear."

"Yes, sir." Adam saluted as Sloan left, and turned back to the sea. God forbid that he'd ever become like Sloan! Rank was such a privilege. "Find something else to wear." Adam's eyes suddenly sparkled.

At dinner that night Dulcie sat with her back toward Adam's table, a maneuver that Adam observed wryly, and devoted her attentions to Goodman Hastings, one of the five Grand Tourists. Skits would be presented in the lounge so that the ladies would have an evening of entertainment before their escorts attended Gentlemen's Night as guests of the captain. Goody invited Dulcie to accompany him to the skits, and with Mad's permission she agreed.

After the entertainment they strolled leisurely around the deck. Goody tucked Dulcie's hand under his arm, quoting humorous incidents of the presentation. Dulcie took an unexpectedly fierce delight in being with some other

gentleman when they happened on Captain Tremain standing in his eternal spot along the rail, smoking a fresh cigar
and watching the sea.

Then Goody nearly spoiled it all. "Ah, there's Adam!"
he cried happily. "Come along, Miss Dulcie, I'll introduce
you."

"Good evening, Miss. Evening, Goody," said Adam. In
the pale lights his teeth flashed in—at last—a smile. He
seemed to have a genuine liking for the irrepressible Goody.

"Miss Dulcie, may I present Captain Adam Tremain?
Captain Tremain, Miss Dulcie Moran of Savannah, my
own hometown."

Dulcie was afraid Adam would say they had already
met disastrously. Instead, he said with another smile for
her alone, "It's a real pleasure to meet you, Miss Moran."

He could not see her hot blushes. "Thank you, Captain
Tremain. Would you please tell me somethin'? What do
you see out there in all that water that continues to hold
your interest?"

"Whales. Porpoises. Seaweed. Little pale things that
glow."

Goody had been willing to flaunt Dulcie to Adam; he
was not so willing to share her. "Going to Gentlemen's
Night, Adam?"

A broad grin answered that.

The next morning Oliver, arising late after the Gentlemen's Night, was shaving. Suddenly he burst out laughing.
"Oh Mad, you'll never see the point of this, but it's too
funny to keep." He started laughing again. "You bring to
mind Captain Tremain? Handsome devil, I know you
recognize him. Well, it seems he served as second mate
under Captain Sloan, and now that Tremain's a captain
himself, Sloan is smarting under the competition."

"But not smartenin', I'll wager."

Oliver chuckled. "That's very good, Mad. Deep." He
patted her hand. "So Captain Sloan tells Captain Tremain
not to wear his uniform, to find something else to wear.
Oh, ha! ha! When Captain Tremain comes in, long after
everyone else has arrived, he's wearing—now get this, dear
Mad—he's wearing his trousers and his boots—and a
string tie! Oh! ho! ho! ho! And nothing else—except a
coat of suntan! Isn't that rich?"

Mad mumbled over the items of Adam's attire. "He'd forgotten his shirt, Ollie? Is that it?"

"Yes!" Oliver howled, shaking with his glee. "And his coat! But he did it on purpose!"

Mad looked at him blankly. "Ollie dear, why would he do that?"

"Because Captain Sloan had ordered him to, and he didn't have any other clothes along except his uniforms!"

In her years of marriage with Oliver, Mad had almost forgotten how to make herself blush. Suddenly she remembered. "Ollie, I don't believe I need to hear any more. This is *quite* embarrassin', dear."

"But it's funny! Don't you think so? A room of perfectly attired gentlemen, behaving very properly, then suddenly in comes this magnificent young savage. All aplomb, smiles, and sunshine and shaking hands with everyone. Then gradually a hush fell over the room as it dawned on everyone what he'd done. I glanced at Captain Sloan, and I vow, my dear, I thought I'd see the man have an apoplectic fit. He roared out, 'Captain Tremain! Get your uniform on!'"

Mad tittered in spite of herself. "What then, Ollie? Oh, this is just shockin'!"

Oliver chuckled again. "Captain Tremain saluted grandly and said, 'Yes, *sir!* By your leave, sir!' Then everyone in the room started laughing, Sloan last of all. He knew when he'd been bested. When Tremain returned, everyone was slapping him on the back, and he went over to Sloan and apologized handsomely."

Mad smiled a little. "Men are so terribly vulgar!"

Oliver laughed. "Oh, no, nothing vulgar about it at all. He did the whole thing with such style and grace that it positively made the entire evening. Hardly a man there but envied him his savoir faire, not to mention his display of muscles." He lowered his voice. "Mad, do you know, I would nearly believe he's tanned all over?"

Mad, sitting straight up in bed listening avidly, shut her eyes tightly. "Oliver, I don't think I need to know any more."

"Well, as you wish, but wasn't it a fine joke?"

"Yes, Ollie dear, a very fine joke."

So good, in fact, that Mad and her deck-chair friends analyzed it endlessly, whispering behind their hands.

"Scandalous!" said one. "Incredible!" said the next, who in forty wedded years had never seen her husband in less than his union suit. Somehow everyone heard, even the young ladies, for whom discussion of such behavior was beyond the pale.

And Captain Tremain, restlessly patrolling the deck of a ship not his, was no longer allowed to remain aloof. He was drawn into deck games, debates, and the entertainments he had been ignoring. His smile, which so few had seen previously, appeared frequently enough to dazzle the sourest dowager, who outspokenly called him a shameless rogue.

Dulcie heard the story, whispered between giggles, from her shipboard friend, Mandy Thomas. "I have even heard that his body is tanned from the sun!" said Mandy, her eyes large with speculation. "That must mean he appears in the out-of-doors without his—without his shirt! Isn't that awful, Dulcie?"

Dulcie, who had formed altogether too vivid an image of Captain Tremain wearing only trousers and boots, blushed deeply. "He should be ashamed of himself." She pushed the image away.

Thereafter, although it was impossible to avoid him, she passed the man as though he had become invisible. Such reckless boldness as his frightened her in some way she didn't care to examine. She strolled in the afternoons with Goody Hastings and Toby Dobbs. She played battledore and shuttlecock with Mandy and her sisters. There was music and dancing nightly, and Dulcie was often invited, but Adam was never there, to her great relief.

An Atlantic voyage would hardly be complete if all its days were sunny and its nights starlit. Two days out of New York Dulcie awoke to find rain gusting in. She sat up in her sodden bed and slammed and secured the porthole. "Claudine, would you get me a dry blanket?"

"Ah's seasick, Miss Dulcie. But Ah'll do it d'reckly."

Then Dulcie noticed the lurching motion of the ship, wallowing like a hog in mud. "Never mind, Claudine," she said quickly. "You stay in bed." She wetted a cloth and put it on Claudine's sweating forehead.

"Ah's so col', Miss Dulcie," said Claudine, her teeth chattering. "Ah got to git up an' fin' me a quilt."

Dulcie put more covers on her maid and tucked them

in. Claudine gave her a weak smile of thanks, closed her
eyes, and dozed.

Dulcie dressed in her riding clothes. She had used them
only a few times in Europe. But on a sloppy day like this
they were practical.

There were few at the tables this morning. Oliver was
cheerfully spooning down steaming oatmeal and crunching
his toast and kippers.

"Poor Aunt Mad and poor Claudine," said Dulcie as
she sat down. "I wish there was somethin' I could do for
them."

Oliver's eyes twinkled. "Take them a few kippers?
They're delicious."

Dulcie laughed. "Uncle, you're a terrible, terrible man
—and I love you madly just the same."

Oliver harrumphed, and looked in some other direction.
After a bit he said, "My dear, do you suppose your father
would come North to live? There's good tillable land in
New York and New Jersey."

"What made you think of that, Uncle Oliver?"

"Merely an avuncular desire to see my favorite niece
more often."

"Thank you for the compliment, and what else do you
have worked out?"

"Now, really, Dulcie, am I that transparent?" he asked
indignantly. "As you deduced, I've thought about this quite
a lot. You're mature enough to look at this rationally,
Dulcie, or I'd never dream of discussin' it with you. Once
the North invades Southern lands, you can see where that
will put large landholders like your father. He'd be clever
to sell immediately at the best price he can get and invest
in Northern land or business."

"I understand what you say, Uncle, but there's nothing
I can do. It's Daddy you should talk to."

"I have. And I will again. But I wanted you to hear my
side, from me. I don't want to lose you—in any way." He
looked at her fondly. "I believe I could use a touch more
salt, please, Dulcie."

Dulcie stood on deck, wrapped in her riding habit and
oilskins. There was no one about except some of the
sailors. "Wind's mighty chancy today, Miss," said one.
"Better go back below. Or else keep hold of a line."

"Thank you, I will." She made her way to the rail. It was

terrifying, it was elemental, it was supremely invigorating to be out on the ocean in the midst of such a storm. The clouds were a solid char-gray sheet overhead, the rain a wall around the ship. Smoke and soot from the stacks blew around her as she moved forward, holding the rail tightly. The ship heaved and shuddered, rocking from side to side, but its bow stayed pointed toward New York. Dulcie watched the foaming water, hypnotized by its endless motion.

"Pardon me, Miss, did you lose your horse?"

Dulcie swung around in surprise, and wanted to run. It was Captain Tremain, his white teeth bared in an exuberant smile. "I beg your pardon?"

He gestured toward her riding outfit. His gaiety was irresistible, and she smiled back at him. "It was so stuffy downstairs—I mean, below—and I wanted some air. I'd have been foolish to ruin a gown for that."

"You're getting drenched, you know."

"I like storms, Captain Tremain," she said defiantly.

He ran his eyes over her face for a long moment before he said, "Yes, I believe you do." His lips curved up in a little smile, and he looked away, toward the rolling, breaking waves. The rain curtained them, set them apart from time and place and propriety.

Adam turned to look softly at the girl beside him. "I bought Fellie's boys in New Orleans for a ruinous price and gave them their freedom papers on the spot." He smiled. "They're with their family in New York now. My partner hired both as clerks in one of his businesses. They're proud people, that family. The boys are buying their freedom, paying us back a little at a time."

Dulcie hugged herself, doing a little two-step dance. "Oh, I'm so *happy!*"

Adam's eyes were warm on her. "So am I, Miss Moran."

"How can I ever thank you enough, Captain Tremain? You simply can't *know* how much it means to me, to find out at last!"

"No?" He grinned at her.

"You don't know the entire story, Captain." She told him then what had happened after she left Fellie in his care. "I haven't seen my father for over a year. All his letters went astray until we got to Paris, and I didn't know if he'd forgiven me." With his sympathetic eyes on her, she felt tears coming. She turned her back so he wouldn't see her mouth tremble.

After a moment he said casually, "I've been to Paris." With a little grin meant only for himself, he went on, "I probably saw a different side of the city, but the things I remember best are the chimney pots on the Left Bank and the chestnuts beside the Seine and the itinerant violinists—I've never heard so many bad violins played so badly."

Dulcie, in control of herself now, giggled, partly with embarrassment. "And the windmills, hundreds of them, catching the winds above Montmartre."

"The carriage drivers, every one of them a wild man."

"And Calais, Captain? Were you ever there?"

"Yes, but I was sick with fever. So now you'll go home to Savannah?"

"Actually to Mossrose. And you? Where is your home?"

"My mother lives south of Wilmington, in a little resort town. My home is—several places, usually onboard a ship."

She made the question casual. "Are you married, Captain?"

"No, ma'am," he said, with a finality that made her blink. "Except maybe to the sea."

She caught his eye, and he was teasing her. She retorted, "That must explain why you spend so much time starin' at it." After a short silence, with the rain still slashing at them, she said, "So now we are both goin' home to the war. Which side shall you take?"

"I'm a Southerner, Miss Moran."

"Captain Tremain, is it true that the South is poorly armed? And that the North will invade us soon?"

Adam laughed a little. "For a beautiful girl, you ask some ugly questions. Are you a spy?"

"A spy! Oh, you're makin' fun of me! I'm serious. I want to know!"

"Undoubtedly you do, but you'll have to ask someone else, for I don't wish to discuss it. Tell me, did you tour the British Isles? Was it as wet as we are now?"

Dulcie glared at him belligerently, longing to crush him for his flippancy. Then she caught the sparkle deep in his eyes, and they laughed.

"Miss Moran, there's a nice dry lounge below, and stewards to bring us hot coffee. Don't you think we must be simpleminded to stand here in a raging storm for over an hour?"

She met his half-rueful, half-derisive smile with one of her own. "What other reason could there be, Captain?" Her gaze roved over his finely chiseled features. It was there even though he didn't know it, that first look of tender awareness, that recognition of like spirits. Her eyes clung to his, yearning, passionate, submissive.

By evening the storm had passed. The sea was calm, but an air of excitement pervaded the *Tunbridge*. A traveling troupe would present its specialty in five acts, a full four-hour performance of that stunning hit *Uncle Tom's Cabin*.

"Aunt Mad, Toby Dobbs asked if I'd be able to go with him. May I?"

"Do you want to, dear? I know he's from a wealthy family, but, gracious, he has such hard-looking eyes. Not respectful at all."

"You let me promenade with him."

"But that was in a group, dear, and quite different."

It was no use arguing with Aunt Mad; besides, Dulcie didn't care to spend four hours in Toby's company. It was just that she would look like a wallflower sitting with her aunt and uncle, and Adam hadn't asked to escort her as she had hoped he would.

The 'tween-decks lounge was stuffy with cigar smoke and perfume, blown about languidly by the many fans with which the ladies were prettily cooling themselves. Onstage the mulatto fugitive George Harris was declaiming: "There isn't, on earth, a living soul to care if I die! I shall be kicked out and buried like a dog."

With a melancholy quiver in his voice, Mr. Wilson said, "Take HEART, George! Trust in the LORD!"

George pressed his fingertips to his forehead. "IS THERE A GOD TO TRUST IN? There's a God for you Christians, but is there any for US?"

Dulcie's head was aching with the smoke and scent and shouting. "I've got such a vile headache, Aunt Mad. Would you mind if I just went to bed?" She made her way out, down the aisle, as Aunt Mad watched. The moment Mad turned her back, a man sitting two rows behind her made his exit.

Dulcie started toward her cabin, changed her mind, and went up the after companionway, moving quietly on deck to stand in the darkness by the rail. She saw no one else.

She took a few deep breaths of the cool salt-smelling night air and began to feel better.

Suddenly arms flew out of nowhere to grab her. She screamed in fright.

Adam, needing a distraction from his tedious idleness, had gone early to the lounge, taking a seat in the last row. He had already seen one of the dozens of versions of *Uncle Tom's Cabin*. Tonight, however, he was too warm, restless, impatient with the slowness of the *Tunbridge,* impatient with the turbulence of his own mind to watch the play. For the first time in his adult life he was alone and found himself lonely. Such realizations were treacherous shoals.

He turned his attention to the stage, where Eliza Harris was speaking to her husband. The girl Eliza was a gross version of Ullah, a caricature that Adam didn't care to see more of. He rose and departed, mounting the forward companionway.

Half an hour before, all had been clear. Now banks of clouds were obscuring the stars, and the wind was rising. By tomorrow they'd be into rain again. He moved to the rail where they had stood—was it only this morning? He sighed, reproving himself for dwelling on a slender auburn-haired girl with rain in her hair and on her lashes, a girl with a giving heart and no one yet to give it to. A girl who held convictions so strong that she dared her father's wrath. A girl who met the sea unafraid, who liked the gale, who had a womanly virtuousness that fought in her with a boldness creditable to any man.

A girl any man, if he were not blind or otherwise committed, would . . .

He heard her scream. Instantly he was alert, moving noiselessly toward the sound. Then Toby Dobbs's hearty laugh rang out, and Adam stopped. To him, Dobbs was a boor, given to coarse jests and male crudities that spoke ill of one of New England's oldest families. He'd seen them strolling together, Dulcie talking vivaciously and flirting with him while Dobbs looked at her possessively.

He stood listening. Words were swept away. Only the tones remained. Hers, lashing out at him in a fury. His, conciliatory, then pleading. Hers, forgiving. His, triumphant, frolicsome. In moments now, they'd be kissing and making up. Adam threw his fresh-lit cigar into the water. He'd go below and read. If a girl of Dulcie Moran's distinctive qualities could endure an oaf like Dobbs, she deserved anything that happened.

"Really, Toby, you nearly frightened me to death!"

"I've already said I'm sorry. Why don't we just drop the subject?"

"Certainly," said Dulcie frigidly. "I have a headache, Toby. If you'll excuse me, I'll go lie down."

"Don't go yet," he pleaded. "Please stay awhile. Talk to me, so I'll know I'm forgiven."

"Toby, you're an incurable rogue."

"Will you stay in New York? Perhaps we could do the town."

Dulcie clapped her hands. "Oh, how excitin'! That sounds like such fun! Except I must take the first passage I can book to Savannah."

"We'll go to the theater, dine at Delmonico's, see the lights of Broadway after dark." His arm stole around her waist; Dulcie moved away. "I'd like to keep you in New York as long as I can." He looked earnestly into her eyes.

She looked down, but Toby Dobbs was not to be circumvented. He turned Dulcie to face him, holding her too tightly. "There's no need to be coy. I saw you leave the lounge, saw you look right at me. I knew you'd be up here where it's nice and dark, waitin' for me."

"I couldn't see a thing in the lounge. I left because I have a headache."

He laughed indulgently. "Now you've saved your pride, but you're still here with me, just where you wanted to be." He bent to kiss her, and Dulcie pulled back, turning her head away from him.

"Toby, stop it!" she hissed. He held her tighter, his mouth coming closer to hers. As he kissed her, Dulcie began to struggle.

Toby muttered, "I'll teach you to tease me, you little bitch." He forced her against the rail, holding her with one arm while his free hand groped at her neckline. Then his fingers were hurting her breast, his mouth bruising hers, while Dulcie fought, trying to push him away from her.

As Adam stepped into the companionway, her voice was no longer light-hearted or teasing. At a glance he knew the girl wasn't being coy.

His hands reached out, grabbing Toby Dobbs by his

coat collar and the seat of his trousers, sending him
sprawling down the deck. With a quick glance that told
him Dulcie wasn't going to faint, he strode over to Dobbs,
picked him up, and sent him sprawling again. He stood
over him, feet apart, arms crossed so he wouldn't forget
himself and lay hands on the boy once more. In a deadly
quiet voice he commanded, "Mister Dobbs, go to your
cabin."

He turned to Dulcie. She stood where Dobbs had
pinned her, wide-eyed, her hands protectively over her
breasts, trying not to cry.

Forgetting the slightness of their acquaintance, forgetting the impropriety of addressing her so, he said, "Dulcie,
are you all right?"

"Oh, A-Adam!" She hurled herself against the rock that
was Captain Tremain. He held her warmly, securely,
while she cried in deep, terrible sobs. All the tears she
had held back throughout Europe, the tears of homesickness, of nobody to love, the tears of meeting only to part,
all, all flowed onto Adam's comforting shoulder.

Her voice, punctuated by sobs, came incoherently. "I
didn't lead him on, I didn't! He wanted me to go to the
Tom Show, Aunt Mad said no. I got such an awful headache. He followed me." She raised her head to look at
him. "You think I'm a perfect little fool, don't you!" She
cried some more while he patted her back with his fingertips, thinking how small and fragile she seemed, how
needful of his protection.

He murmured, "No, no, I don't think that at all, Dulcie,
don't cry for that—"

"He's been a gentleman 'til now. I never dreamed he'd
—I didn't even know he was *near* me!"

Courteously Adam tried to loose his hold, but she did
not move away from him. "Did he hurt you?"

"No, no . . . I mean, yes, he hurt my mouth—and my
b—" She had almost said the word, and the shameful
thought brought on a fresh flood. "He had his hands on
me."

"There, there, now, I'm sure you'll feel better soon," he
said in an attempt to be soothing.

"What'll I do"—she gulped—"the next time? When
you're not around?" Her breast heaved against his.
Strangely Adam had no answer for her. He was too busy
fighting down some base impulses of his own to be hyper-

critical of someone else's. "Oh, Adam, why are these things always happenin' to me?"

He thought he'd met every kind of woman created, the bold ones, the shy ones, the saucy, and the sly. He'd never met any that befuddled his mind and sent his senses reeling as this small, trembling red-haired girl did. She had drowned him in the passion of her sorrow and with her trusting touch aroused him, until unguardedly he spoke the thought most vividly on his mind. "You're a virgin on the verge, Dulcie," he said softly, holding her gently to him. "A man—"

She stared up at him, shocked almost out of her tears, then put her face back against him and howled. "I might have known."

Hastily Adam tightened his embrace and tried to mend his remark. "I'm sorry, please believe me, I wasn't thinking—"

"Yes, you were! And I know what you were thinkin'!"

He put his hand up and stroked her hair.

She raised her head, her eyes still streaming. "What did you mean? Tell me! Go ahead and tell me!"

He pressed her head back against his shoulder, still petting and stroking her tenderly. "All I meant was that you have a sweet innocence about you, and a man can see it. For some not very pleasant reasons, sometimes men want to—destroy the very innocence they find so attractive."

Dulcie, her face pillowed on the very nicest chest ever, listened to the pounding of his heart. "Adam, do I invite men like that?"

"You're a very invitin' young woman, but—no, I don't believe you do it on purpose. Men—some of them—read the signs according to their own hopes."

She shuddered against him, though she was no longer sobbing. "I'm so grateful. I don't know what might have happened if you—" With utmost reluctance she pulled away from the safekeeping of his embrace.

Adam reached for his handkerchief, meaning to hand it to her, but instead he wiped at her face gently. He made a rather long job of it. He had never before wanted so much just to go on holding a woman. And from the look in her eyes she wanted to be held.

Suddenly shy, she looked away. "I ought to get back to my stateroom."

"Stateroom air is very bad for headaches. Wouldn't you recover more quickly if we strolled the deck?"

They walked together, talking, watching the clouds and the sea, joining the others who came up on deck at intermissions. They sat for a while in the deck chairs pulled close enough that Adam's sleeve touched Dulcie's shawl; but he did not reach for her hand. He told Dulcie a lot more about himself than he realized, about his parents, about Ben and Beau and their childhood pact to become ship's masters.

"Why does your ship have such an odd name?"

The old, buried ache stabbed at Adam. That made twice tonight. "Ullah was . . . a woman I knew. A very fine woman."

"Were you in love with her?" Dulcie waited, interminably, heart hammering, for his response.

"No, nothing like that. She—was my partner's wife."

Dulcie's throat tightened. His pain was almost a visible thing, shimmering there in the darkness. "Somethin' tragic happened, didn't it?"

"Yes." Their hands found each other's, and they were silent.

It was long after midnight when he took Dulcie to her cabin door. They stood in the wavering light, a little apart. Dulcie looked up into his handsome face with the intensely blue eyes and the tender mouth. Around Adam's lips hovered a half-smile, just a curve at the corners. He didn't know that Dulcie read into his expression all the pulsing emotions he was carefully keeping out of it.

"Oh, Adam," she whispered. "Is this love?"

He looked away, withdrawn again. Yet his voice trembled as he sad, "Dulcie, Dulcie . . . how can I tell you?" If he didn't leave her now, if he stayed another second . . . "Good-bye, Dulcie."

It rained hard the following day, a hard rain that fell straight down from morning until night. Adam stayed in his cabin trying to read. Frustrated, he flung himself onto his bunk and lay with one arm over his eyes, thinking.

Dulcie might be out on deck, hoping to see him, or possibly, just as she said, enjoying the rain.

He packed his uniforms. He took his meals in his cabin. He sent his regrets to Captain Sloan that he would not be able to dine at the captain's table this evening. By morning they would be in port. He'd have other things on his mind then.

It was a festive evening for Captain Sloan. He had invited his most influential, his most attractive passengers to share his table. Dulcie was there, her cheeks flushed, her gold gown gleaming in the lamplight. Goody Hastings, Oliver, and Mad, and some other couples made up the table.

The champagne flowed freely. The captain was expansive, baring his brown teeth endlessly in the smile of a good host. He said, indicating Adam's empty chair, "Too bad about Captain Tremain. Very odd, for a ship's master. He's in his bunk seasick!" A laugh went around the table, but Dulcie felt herself go white. He was not there because she had embarrassed him last night.

They tied up at New York the next morning. Dulcie threw her pride to the winds and stood at Adam's favorite spot by the rail, hoping—yearning—to see him once again. Oliver, supremely unaware of his niece's pale listlessness, stood nearby among the other passengers.

Finally the gangplank lowered. Adam lifted his sea chest to his shoulder and was one of the first to disembark. Dulcie's heart thudded hurtfully. A tall gray-haired man she assumed to be his father stepped forward to shake his hand. He was nearly as handsome as Adam, with blue eyes almost as dazzling. They climbed into a gleaming rockaway and melted into traffic.

"By George, that was Roderick Courtland that met young Tremain."

Hope crept back into Dulcie's sad eyes. "You know him, Uncle?"

"I certainly do. The most tight-lipped poker player I ever dropped a thousand to. A shrewd businessman. Got a finger in every pie. But a fine man, Rod, a true gentleman. We'll have him to dinner while you're still in the city."

Chapter Eleven

The first day of enforced relaxation in Courtland's elegant brownstone was sufficient to bring Adam to a fine edge of irritability.

Courtland, lounging in a chair while Adam prowled the sumptuous parlor, chuckled. "I can see the quiet life doesn't appeal to you. I didn't think it would. I've planned a theater party for tomorrow night. Perhaps an evening out and the company of a charming young lady will set you to rights."

"I'm enjoying it here. There's no need to put yourself out on my account." A memory of Dulcie flashed into his mind. He pushed it away.

Rod laughed. "You'd make a disastrous diplomat. Remind me of your woeful talents should I ever need to use you as emissary in a delicate situation."

Adam laughed ruefully and came to sit near his host. "Inactivity does not agree with me," he admitted, and found it a far easier truth than the other that crowded into his mind unbidden. Dulcie Moran was not a woman he could trifle with. She was of a breed to set fire to a man's blood, but of a class one must marry.

He made himself pay attention to Rod Courtland. "Who'll be in the theater party? Anyone I know?"

"I doubt it. Theodore Sizemore is an old friend. He married a pretty New York girl I might have married myself."

"Why didn't you?"

Rod sighed good-naturedly. "Oh . . . I loved someone else and lost, then Nan met Ted. These things work out for the best in spite of ourselves. I seem to be the perfect bachelor, and Nan is very happy with Ted. They have two lovely children. Ruth Ann is eighteen, and Miranda is ten. Though Ruth Ann is of age, it is Miranda you must guard against. She's likely to have your heart dislodged from your breast before you know it."

Adam smiled. "She sounds like Tom's daughter, Angela. I envy the man that girl marries." He paused again in thought. It wasn't Angela's kind of sweetness he wanted at all. It was spirit and fire that drew him. He wanted a woman who would never be demoralized by disappointment as Zoe had been or in need of the gentle handling that Angela would require. Bringing himself back to the conversation, he said, "She sounds fascinating."

Unknowing, the Courtland party entered the Astor Opera House soon after the Raymers. Dulcie sensed Adam's presence behind her in nearly the same instant she heard his deep baritone replying courteously to Ruth Ann's fluting description of her shopping expedition on Fifth Avenue.

Before she could think what to do, his voice was lost among the buzzing hum as Rod led his party out of the main stream of people. Dulcie kept her eyes riveted straight ahead. Having made an utter fool of herself with him once was enough. He had never been so courteously solicitous of what she had to say as he was of the female he was with tonight. She could well imagine his cutting remarks had she told him of one of her shopping trips.

She started, losing her composure as well as her vindictive thoughts, when Oliver suddenly steered them through the richly attired throng.

"Rod! Rod Courtland!" Oliver shouted with hearty good cheer.

Rod turned from Ted Sizemore. Oliver Raymer emerged from the crowd, Mad on one arm and on the other a strikingly beautiful young woman whose eyes smoked with a golden haze of fire.

Dulcie greeted Rod and the Sizemores with her best smile. From time to time her luminous eyes darted from Ruth Ann to Adam, fixing there long enough to sear him with her thoughts. "It is . . . *pleasant* to see you again, Captain Tremain. Some things have been made far clearer by tonight's meeting. I can now understand your impatience to reach these shores with so charming a young lady waitin' for you here."

Ruth Ann giggled, flicking her fan up deftly to hide the faint blush that came to her rice-powdered cheeks. Confidently, she glanced up at Adam, her short dark lashes ringing her hazel eyes.

Adam flashed a quick obliging smile to Ruth Ann, then glared at Dulcie. "You are too perceptive, Miss Moran."

His voice was clipped and hard, with none of the melodic resonance she remembered. Dulcie wondered what she had done this time to displease him.

Ruth Ann's hand tightened slightly on his arm, a small motion of shy possessiveness not lost on Dulcie.

Flustered at having annoyed him again as soon as she opened her mouth and more than a little jealous, Dulcie spoke with irritated haste. "Well, it's been nice seein' you. Perhaps we'll have the fortune of meetin' again, Captain Tremain—under more pleasant circumstances. Although I can't imagine when. I'm leavin' New York very shortly."

"Surely, seeing me can't be that upsetting, Miss Moran. Have you no mercy for a poor man's feelings?" He grinned wickedly.

She knew instantly that once more he had made her sound like a besotted shrew. With a grandiose tug at her full skirts she swept away, only to hear Ruth Ann whisper, "She might be quite beautiful if only she knew how to present herself . . . terribly *earthly* look . . . a pity."

Dulcie didn't want to hear his reply; it could only be humiliating. She sought security between Mad and Oliver, gripping her uncle's arm while Mad dramatized their welcome by the Countess Madeline Archambeault.

Dulcie thought the house lights would never dim and Mad would never cease chattering. She was overwarm. She knew she wouldn't like the melodrama, *Nellie, the Beautiful Cloak Model.* Fragments of conversation drifted all around her, detached, mixed together, loud. *Too earthly!* she seethed. *I've seen better complexions than Ruth Ann Sizemore's on dead fish.* For pride's sake, she longed to return to verbal combat with that ninny. She had already lost her opportunity to improve the impression Adam had gotten of her aboard ship, but she could certainly give Ruth Ann something to think about.

Then Oliver's conversation caught her ear and Dulcie's face paled to rival Ruth Ann's. She grasped his sleeve, wanting above all to have him keep quiet!

"Mighty nice of you, Courtland," he was saying. "Dulcie and Mad were certainly taken with the young captain on the voyage over. There's nothing we'd like better than to join your party. Isn't that so, Mad dear?"

"Of course, Ollie dear. And Nan, the marquis's ballroom was . . ."

Dulcie smiled her agreement to Oliver, then glared up at

Adam just to be certain he knew she was going against her
will. It didn't improve her disposition even slightly to see a
twinkle in his blue eyes.

Once the melodrama had begun, she was so distracted
she could scarcely distinguish heroine from soubrette.
Along with Miranda, she had been relegated to the two
front children's seats, to be escorted by "Uncle" Rod. She
had never felt so humiliated in all her life.

Dramatically she considered throwing herself from the
box to die onstage, with her life's blood dribbling majesti-
cally from her in front of Adam's very eyes. Severe prac-
ticality forced her to dismiss the idea. She could never
jump far enough to reach the stage. All her efforts would
be for naught if she splattered all over the spectators below. She shrank into her seat, the surrounding darkness of
the theater box her only comfort. She could not recall a
worse night.

Ruth Ann's and Adam's voices drifted to her from time
to time as they hissed or cheered the performers, laughing and enjoying themselves. Mad was still chattering to
Nan, and in the background the placid, soft sounds of
Uncle Oliver's snoring reached her ears.

Intermission was dreadful, except that it meant the night
was half over. The houselights went up, exposing her sitting there with Miranda. She contemplated desperate
means of escape as Oliver roused himself sufficiently to invite the entire group for a late supper at Delmonico's. The
evening was *not* half over; intermission lost its meager appeal.

The invitation accepted, the group rose, leaving the box
for a change of air and some refreshments. Dulcie pretended to follow, then dropped back. She was staring
woodenly into the parquet section when Miranda came to
her side. The little girl's eyes sparkled conspiratorially.
"A very handsome gentleman asked me to give this to you,
Dulcie."

Dulcie took the folded note. She read the firm, bold
writing. "Dear lady of uncommon beauty, will you grant
this admirer one moment?"

"Who gave this to you?" Dulcie spoke severely, but her
eyes danced, betraying her excitement. Oh! What a coup if
there really were a handsome man she could be seen with
—by Adam and Ruth Ann.

"A man." Innocently Miranda shrugged her shoulders. "What shall I tell him? Are you going to meet him?"

"Certainly not! One must be properly intro—" But Miranda had already scampered out of the box. Dulcie leaped from her seat and pulled the curtain back, looking down the corridor both ways. There was no sign of Miranda or a handsome stranger. She returned to her seat feeling terribly sorry for herself, but the excitement lingered.

Miranda reappeared five minutes later. Dulcie snatched the note before Miranda could say a word. "Don't you leave here until I tell you you may." She scowled, then read the note. "Is one moment so much to ask of you, most beautiful lady, when you will be safeguarded by the innocent chaperonage of Miranda?"

"Where is he?" Dulcie asked. She patted her hair and smoothed the front of her gown. Perhaps if the man turned out to be presentable, she could tell Uncle Oliver that he was an old friend she had asked to join them. At least then she would not be sitting unescorted, and she would only have to suffer his company for one night.

"I'll show you, Dulcie." Miranda took her hand, pulling Dulcie into the box next to theirs.

He said, "I knew you'd never be able to resist an admirer."

"Oh! You conceited beast!" she exclaimed as Adam, grinning, swept into a low bow, then put out his hands for her to take. He laughed aloud as she, unladylike, placed both fisted hands on her hips and tried to think of something sufficiently cutting to say to him. "Is it your habit to collect unsuspectin' young women as trophies, Captain Tremain? Isn't one per evenin' sufficient for you?"

She was magnificent, he thought. Dulcie, all fire and beauty. Heedless of her anger, he came toward her. "I see only one trophy worthy of collection here tonight."

"Murderous flattery!"

"Truth." His voice was soft, almost a whisper.

"Truth?" she cried shrilly. "Have you kissed the Blarney Stone, Captain Tremain, or did you manage to swallow it whole?"

Her anger was disproportionate and incongruous matched against his amused, soft-spoken pleasure in her. He took her hand, his eyes barely concealing laughter. She tried to free herself, winding up to give him another tongue lashing.

"Ssshhh." He placed his fingers on her lips. "The house-lights have dimmed. They'll be coming back. You don't want them to think—"

"Think what!? If you say one more—"

"Shh. Remember you granted me one moment. I've still not had it."

"You misled me. I would never have come if I'd known it was you!"

"Exactly why I did not sign my name. But you did come. And you promised by your coming that I could have a moment with you. I should have stated that it was to be a quiet moment."

"Are you finished now?"

"No. I want to apologize for our last meeting."

Dulcie's eyes widened. "*This* is an apology? Well, I *am* honored! Please spare me the next one! Now, may I please return to my seat?"

"Then, you won't listen to me?"

"There is nothin' you could possibly say that I might be interested in, Captain Tremain." She instantly regretted that, for his eyes darkened. He glared at her, making no move to escort her back to her box.

At dinner Oliver jovially arranged everyone's seating, talking as he went. Adam was placed between Dulcie and Ruth Ann Sizemore.

"Why, Captain Tremain," Dulcie said with eyes too bright. "This must be our lucky day. We seem destined to enjoy one another's company again."

Without smiling, Adam looked directly at her, his eyes challenging her, staring so hard she became uncomfortable. "Destiny seems to have taken us farther than you realize," he said. "Your Uncle and Mr. Courtland have seen fit to arrange your passage home on my ship, Miss Moran."

Dulcie looked toward Oliver. "Uncle, you arranged for me to travel on Captain Tremain's ship? But you said nothin' to me!" She added desperately, "We shouldn't impose on him like that. I can't possibly be ready to leave . . . I appreciate it, but I really think—"

"Nonsense, dear Dulcie. You have three days. Adam has assured me it is his pleasure to see you home."

She swiveled to look at Adam's noncommittal face. "Uncle Oliver, I'd—"

Oliver, already full of good cheer, raised his glass high.

"To your homeward voyage. May it be both pleasant and safe."

Dulcie let out a deep breath. Would this evening never end? She sat quietly as Oliver expounded on Adam's sterling qualities as a gentleman and a captain. "Dulcie, my dear niece, you'll be as safe as a caterpillar in a cocoon. Count your blessings."

"And," Mad added dramatically, "Captain Tremain has vowed on his honor to deliver you personally into the arms of your father."

"Thank you, Captain. You are too kind."

"Not at all," he replied silkily. "I failed to convey my good intentions to you earlier this evening. Perhaps my actions will speak more clearly than my words."

"Your actions have always been perfectly clear, Captain Tremain," she said in a low voice. "It has been mine that have caused the misunderstandin's. I assure you I shall stay out of your way on the voyage home. You'll have no cause from me to regret your generosity."

There was no fight in her words now. He liked that less than he could fathom. He was tempted to say or do something outrageous just to rekindle the fire in her eyes.

It was a strange leavetaking compared to her arrival in bustling New York harbor. Beau had sent a telegram informing Adam that he should meet the *Ullah* on the north shore of Long Island, for he could not risk taking the *Ullah* into the port of New York without being arrested as a Southern agent. The development lent an aura of intrigue.

Oliver voiced his misgivings as Rod's coach jolted over the rutted country roads. "By Jove, Courtland, you never said Tremain ran a hidey-hole operation. Why can't he leave New York like any decent law-abiding person?"

Rod rested his head comfortably against the seat, knowing Oliver was mostly bluster. "What do you expect, Oliver? We're at war. Your niece and Adam are Southerners. He can't come in and out of the North at will. If they knew who he was, they'd clap him into prison for a spy."

Oliver grunted. "Mucky thing, this war. Think Dulcie's safe with him?"

"She's safer with him than anyone else. I told you he's a business partner. Have you ever known me to consort with any but the best?"

When Oliver finally spoke, his voice was no longer worried. "Can't say I have. You're always first-rate, Court-land."

Dulcie looked out of the window into the night. She could see nothing. The coach plunged blindly into the thick wetness of a murky-dark rain. The trip was endless. She had talked with no one, not even Claudine, who huddled, shaking in one corner.

When they finally arrived at a desolate sandy beach, both she and Claudine were tense and tired. Oliver climbed into the jolly boat with them. A seaman rowed with long strokes over the chopping sea. Adam stood on the *Ullah*'s deck, covered by a heavy dark slicker. He had never looked more forbidding to her.

Oliver bade her good-bye. Dulcie clung to him. After the long, slow hours in the coach their parting seemed so sudden and final. The trip seemed so dangerous, the meeting with her father so imminent.

Dulcie, Adam, and Claudine stood watching as Oliver was rowed ashore. "Oh, Lawd, am Ah glad yo' heah, Cap'n!" Claudine shivered as Oliver's form disappeared into the murk. "Dis boat ain't gwine warsh away in all dis rain, is it?"

Adam's arm slipped around her comfortably. "Not the *Ullah*. She'll bobble right along, a cork in a gale." He laughed, a reassuring sound.

Claudine's eyes rolled upward to meet his and then to look into the sky. "We ain't gwine thoo no gale, is we?"

Adam took her by the shoulders, forcing her to look fully at him. "There's nothing to fear, Claudine. Just do as I say and trust me."

She nodded, quaking and shivering under his fingers. He handed her over to Beau. "Fill her full of hot coffee and get her warmed up."

"Adam, I got a ship to get under way," Beau reminded him plaintively.

Claudine, clutching Beau's sleeve as the ship rolled, said, "Ah'm gwine be pow'ful sick."

Beau glanced at her in alarm, then shouted for the second mate. "Get her below! See she's comfortable and has everythin' she needs."

Dulcie hadn't moved. She stood soaking wet, clutching her shawl around her shoulders. There was no trace of her customary independence as Adam led her to her quarters and unlocked her door.

"Thank you, Captain," she said meekly.

"Dulcie . . ." he began, but said no more. He didn't know to what place his fierce little adversary had fled, but the Dulcie he faced this night was not she. He had never felt so closed off from anyone as he did from her now. She was behaving like a perfectly brought-up lady, soft spoken and correct. He hated it. Disturbed deep inside without understanding it, he murmured she was welcome and left her.

Dulcie sat down in her wet clothing, not caring that she felt clammy or that Claudine would be too seasick to help her change until the storm had passed. She had managed what she wanted to do. She had not made a fool of herself with him again. She had not lost her temper nor had she allowed herself to become lost in his blue eyes. She had been victorious. Why then, did she feel so miserably unhappy?

She greeted him the next morning. Her comments were light, polite, dealing only with the beauty of a sunny day after so much rain. She walked on airily as if she had planned to take a solitary stroll on deck. She met Beau, approaching her in search of Adam.

"Good mornin', Miss Moran," he said, smiling, sweeping his cap from his head to reveal a mass of brown hair. "I hope you found the *Ullah*'s accommodations to your likin'. I made certain you had the finest cabin."

Dulcie smiled and assured him she had never slept better. She liked Beau and deliberately prolonged the conversation. His was a gentle, soothing manner that Dulcie found far more appealing in her present state of mind than she ordinarily would. He was so unlike Adam. He was slightly built, without trace of Adam's sheer physical power. His features were delicate. And what Beau thought and felt were plainly revealed in every line of his expressive face. He was certainly a man more suited to a civilized conversation and harmless flirtation than that great brute of a Captain Tremain, whose whole manner kept her wary and unsure of her control.

She answered his last question sweetly. "Why, thank you, Captain LeClerc. I'd love to take a tour of the ship." She allowed her eyelashes to cover her eyes, suggesting demure invitation. "I'll be waitin' in my cabin. Don't you take too long to attend to your duties, now."

Beau was whistling when he finally came up to Adam's

side. "Mornin' there, Captain, sir," he said cheerfully, his face split wide in a grin. Adam glowered at him. " 'Scuse me, sir, but the storm's passed. What's eatin' you? Can't you see it's a damned beautiful day?"

Adam, unmoved by Beau's mood, said sternly, "You shouldn't take her on a tour of the ship."

"Why not? Nothin' I'd enjoy more—well, almost nothin'. Think I'd pass up an opportunity like that with a girl who looks like Dulcie Moran?"

"You can't pick and choose certain passengers for special treatment. A captain has to be impartial. She's no different from Mrs. Bush or Mrs. Pease. Or are you planning to start a guided tour as part of the *Ullah*'s service?"

Beau shook his head. "I thought Miss Moran *was* a special passenger. You sure as hell gave me that idea sometime."

"She's the same as any other and to be treated accordingly." Adam gazed at Beau, still feeling mean and out of sorts.

"I've never seen you act like this before," Beau said. "You gonna tell me what's behind it?"

"Since you insist—I like a tight ship, *Captain*. We don't chase skirts while on duty. Keep your mind where it belongs, Mister. We're at war. We're about to run a blockade. You've no time to think of anything else."

The expression on Beau's face was hurt, then angry. "As you wish, sir. As you are a passenger on this run, I suggest you remain in your cabin for your own protection in these dangerous waters."

Adam stared at Beau's set and belligerent face. It would have been funny another time, but this morning nothing seemed funny. "Damn it, Beau," he said plaintively, but Beau tossed him a sloppy salute and marched off. Adam slammed the butt of his hand down on the rail.

They were in the fo'c'sle checking the coverings on the lights and the hatches that might alert a Federal cruiser when Adam finally apologized.

Beau said agreeably, "Forget it. It doesn't matter, long's you're feelin' better. You gonna tell me what it was all about?"

Adam looked uncomfortably blank. "I don't know."

"Aw, c'mon, Adam. You know as well as I do. All you have to do is say you want her for yourself. That's gotta be it. Why else would my walkin' Miss Dulcie over the ship cause—"

"You took her on a tour of the ship after I expressly ordered you not to?"

"Now, you get somethin' straight, Adam. I'm master on this run. You don't give me orders for anythin'! If you're wantin' Miss Dulcie for yourself, just say so. For the rest, just shut up and let me tend to my job."

"Miss Moran has nothing to do with this."

"Then I suggest you stop gettin' hot under the collar every time I go near her. Do I make myself clear, sir?"

Adam was silent for a while. "What are we arguing about, Beau?"

"Damned if I know, but I'm sure as hell mad about somethin'."

"I'm sorry, Beau. It's my fault—"

"Damned right it is!"

"Son of a bitch! You don't back off a minute, do you! I'm tryin' to apologize to you!"

"Keep it!" Beau shouted. "And get the hell off my bridge!"

The next several days did not improve the relationship between Beau and Adam nor Adam's temperamental state of mind. With equal fierceness he glared at both Dulcie and Beau. While Dulcie was coolly polite to him, she seemed to become radiantly alive under Beau's gentle companionship. And Beau hardly seemed to know he had a ship to run.

Alone, Adam stalked the decks searching for some flaw in the fittings or preparedness of the *Ullah*, shouting irritable orders to the crew, making them check and recheck perfectly sound equipment. Their grumbled comments, spoken to be overheard, only added to his intense ill humor and wounded pride. He had always prided himself that his crews were justly and fairly treated. But despite his constant resolve to improve his temper, the nagging irascibility continued to plague him.

This night, as he had for the past three nights, he churned along the deck, hearing the sounds of Beau's guitar accompanying Dulcie's and Claudine's harmonious singing. The clear feminine voices lent an eerie sadness to the constant smack and wash of the sea against the *Ullah*'s hull. He gazed down into the dark water, feeling deep inside a cold, heavy loneliness, not unlike hunger, but not to be eased so readily.

He turned his back to the brass ship rail, staring toward the warm sounds of laughter that followed the song. He heard Beau run his fingers across the guitar strings, then begin to form the chords of "Greensleeves." The ache inside grew deeper, and like a man driven, Adam stalked the length of the deck, running from the haunting melody that reminded him of a firelit night when Tom and Ullah danced as Ben and Beau accompanied them on the gourd fiddle and drums. He had danced with Zoe, laughing and teasing as her hair flew wildly. It had been a night bright with happiness—so long ago. All the loving memories were long ago, and somehow lost from him.

He shook himself, annoyed at his self-pitying weakness. Scowling until his dark brows knit themselves into a straight line, he walked purposefully toward the captain's dining room and the music.

Dulcie was perched on a stool near Beau, her brown skirt draped gracefully, her cheeks flushed rosy from her efforts and enjoyment. Her amber-gold eyes met his as he entered. Without thinking, she smiled happily.

They waited expectantly for him to join them. He couldn't. In spite of his determination, he felt no more a part of the festivities now than he had been when standing outside on the deck. Beau looked up at him, his hand faltering on the guitar strings. He began to strum with defiant strokes. "What shall we sing now, Miss Dulcie? Make it somethin' lively and gay." The harshness in Beau's voice heightened the tension that had entered the room with Adam.

Dulcie paused, smiling at Beau, then feigned a delicate yawn. "I'm about sung out, Beau. Maybe tomorrow night, if you'd like."

Adam leaped from his seat, striding the short distance to the door. "Don't stop on my account," he said angrily, slamming the door. He returned to his station on deck, gazing once more into the heaving waters, filled with anger and some unbearable frustration he couldn't name.

He didn't know how long he had stood at the rail, glaring out into the night, before he heard the rustle of skirts behind him. "Well, Captain Tremain, you certainly know how to enliven a party, don't you?"

He pretended he hadn't heard her, didn't know she was

standing so close that the delicate scent of her perfume surrounded him. Driven by her own failure to make anything ever come out right with him, she went on tormenting herself and him. "In less than five minutes you managed to—"

Her words died away as he turned to face her. The light of the waning quarter moon couldn't banish the shadows that hid his fierce, stormy face from her, but it played its ghostly light along his cheek, illuminating the spot where—if only he would smile—a long, deep dimple would appear.

Neither of them moved for what seemed an eternity; she because she was transfixed, and he because above all he thought he wished only to crush her so thoroughly that no thought or sight of her would ever disturb him again.

He seized her by the shoulders, pressing her against him so hard she cried out, a helpless, nearly silent cry, for his mouth covered hers, expressing for him all the ruthless passions she had set loose in him. His arms were around her, holding her viselike until she couldn't breathe. She struggled against him. As quickly as he had kissed her, he released her; and as quickly as she found herself free, she wished herself imprisoned by his arms once more.

"Adam . . ."

He bent his head toward her waiting mouth with a shy, boyish tenderness. There was no force to his kiss now. Silently, by his actions, he was telling her, talking to her, saying all the things she had longed to hear all her life. Dulcie trembled in his caress, then responded with a woman's instinctive recognition of her mate. Her arms encircled his neck as his closed around her, drawing her against him, molding her soft, curving body to his hard, masculine one.

Adam was as shaken as Dulcie. He was reeling with an elated passion he'd never known. It seemed to consume him. She was desirable. He sensed her surrender. He wanted her, and yet there was something deeper that kept him from her. In a welter of confused need and desire for a woman—for the qualities of this woman that made her different from any other he had known—he turned away, closing off all emotion rather than drown in this new feeling.

Dulcie was too happy to see the turmoil on his face or to sense the rigid withdrawal he forced on himself. She

stood beside him, placing her small white hand on the rail
next to his muscular tanned one.

Adam stared down at them as though they belonged
to two people he had never known. Recoiling, he moved
his away from hers.

Dulcie looked up at him and saw there none of the love
or tenderness she had been certain of moments before.
She stared at him, blinking in hurt amazement. "You . . .
did that on purpose!"

He said nothing.

Nearly in tears, Dulcie cried at him, "You kissed me
just to mock me! It meant nothin' to you!"

Adam took a step toward her, reaching out for her
hands. "Dulcie—"

"Oh, I *do* hope you had your fun, Captain Tremain!"

"Dulcie, don't. Listen to me, please."

Tears streamed down her face, but she didn't care.
"Never!" she sobbed, and ran pell-mell toward her cabin.

She remained in her cabin for the rest of the trip,
venturing out only for meals or in the company of Beau
or Claudine. Though he tried at first, Adam couldn't get
a moment alone with her. After two days of trying, he
decided things were best left as they were. He had recovered from his ill humor; he would forget Dulcie soon
enough. Hadn't he always known that virginal girls were
the most romantic and least satisfying of all women?

Once Dulcie was delivered safely to her father, he would
be free of her, free to seek his pleasure with more accommodating partners.

The last day of the voyage seemed endless. Beau couldn't
head the *Ullah* toward port until dark. A lookout was constantly posted, searching the horizon for ships. Adam
didn't worry overmuch about Mr. Lincoln's blockade. At
last report the Atlantic Squadron could boast only twenty-
two ships to guard the entire coast from Fort Monroe to
Key West.

What did worry him was overconfidence. Only carelessness would cause the *Ullah* to be fired upon. It was difficult
to keep oneself aware that their worst danger lay in the
apparent lack of danger. Neither he nor Beau had any
experience in running at night without lights, piloting the
river channels with nothing to guide them but the water
soundings taken in the dark.

The *Ullah*'s engines kept a steady thrum, the noise

absorbed by the lapping roar of the waves beating against the shore. He had been told that one ship could pass within fifty feet of another in the dead of a moonless night without being seen or heard. He believed it, but he didn't want its truth tested this trip.

Adam acted as pilot. None knew the peculiarities of Southern waters better. With countless adjustments, the *Ullah* churned toward the black shore, slipping without a scrape into the channel of the Savannah River.

Late as it was, eager faces on the pier gazed up at the ship in hopeful anticipation of a cargo of munitions from England. Told the *Ullah* carried only passengers, the welcoming committee vanished back to their cots to await the next arrival.

At first light Dulcie and Claudine stood on deck ready to meet Jem. Adam sauntered up to Dulcie's side, offering her his arm. She hesitated, her face stubborn and defiant, then she smiled the closed, polite smile reserved for stuffy dinner partners. She placed her gloved hand on his arm, allowing him to escort her down the gangplank.

"Do you see your father?" he asked as they stepped onto the pier. The wharf area was crowded with drays, carriages, and dock workers. "If we haven't located him within a few minutes, I'll hire a carriage. He may not know when we were due to arrive."

"Don't you bother to keep schedules on the *Ullah?*" she asked bitingly.

He grinned, appreciating the spirit she showed. He had half-expected her to act the helpless, well-bred young lady. But she had her own sense of pride and honor. "We keep schedules, Miss Moran," he said with measured formality. "But ships like the *Ullah* run to a schedule of the moon and tides, not the appointment calendar of gentlemen farmers."

"Come, now, Captain Tremain. Are you tryin' to impress me with the danger of our voyage? If so, you needn't bother. We were in no danger whatever. Not once did I see another ship anywhere near to us."

"That, Miss Moran, is the desired object of running at night. Had we seen another ship, most likely it would have been a Federal cruiser eager to blow a sizable hole in the *Ullah*'s hull."

"Twaddle."

He laughed. She glanced up at him, then scowled, looking with renewed purpose for her father.

* * *

Jem Moran was not certain how to greet his errant daughter, particularly now as he realized she was not only beautiful as ever but she was grown. She was every inch a woman. Seeing her beside the tall, dark-haired captain shook Jem more than he liked.

Dulcie released her hold on Adam's arm and ran to him. "Daddy! Oh, *Daddy*, I'm so glad to be home!"

Jem held her close, cherishing one of the last moments that she'd ever recognize her father as *the* man in her life.

After he had kissed her cheeks and wiped away her happy homecoming tears, he greeted a teary Claudine. He thrust out his hand for Adam to shake. "You must come to Mossrose, Captain. We haven't seen you for a long time. Let Mrs. Moran and me thank you properly. Was it an easy voyage?"

"Oh, Daddy, we had to . . . run at night without lights. There were Federal cruisers that might have shot holes through us if they'd seen us. Captain Tremain guided us through all the dangers."

Adam looked at her, one eyebrow raised, a smile playing at the corners of his attractive mouth. "It was an uneventful trip, sir."

"You're just being modest, Captain! You told me be———"

"As you suggested, Miss Moran, I was merely trying to impress you." He grinned lazily.

"Well, you're safe now, and home. That's all that matters," Jem said, interrupting the silent communication that flashed between Adam's and Dulcie's eyes. "How long will you be in port, Captain Tremain?"

"A day perhaps two. We'll take on whatever cargo we can and go out as quickly as possible. The dictates of the moon, sir."

"Then you must be our guest while you're here."

"I'd enjoy that," said Adam regretfully, "but I'm anxious to be on my way. The *Ullah* is too slow to make an effective blockade runner. My ships are being delivered to Nassau any day. Soon as I leave Savannah, I have a stopover at New Orleans, then I go to Nassau. My return trip will be my first true run with war supplies. Perhaps then?"

His eyes never left Jem as he spoke. Then, too soon, they had made their good-byes and Jem's hand was at her elbow, guiding her to the carriage. Dulcie looked back.

"May the road rise with ya, Adam," Jem shouted.

Dulcie waved at him. She wanted to see him again with all her heart, but he'd never have consented to visit Mossrose had she been the one to invite him. The knowledge left her bewildered and unsure. She had always been victorious in her romantic conquests. Now, when it mattered more than it ever had, cotton and a war had defeated her.

Chapter Twelve

As Adam boarded the *Ullah*, he was acutely aware of the subtle difference in this trip. When it was over, not only would the *Ullah* be signed on as a Confederate privateer, but Adam would have officially begun a career as a wartime blockade runner.

It was a dangerous occupation, for the blockade runners used unarmed ships. A hardy, adventurous breed, their most effective and immediate bond was the network of information they shared. In any Southern port, as well as Nassau, Bermuda, Mexico, or Cuba the scuttlebutt was gathered and remembered, the information used to evade prowling Federal gunboats.

Only ten Federal ships patrolled the Gulf of Mexico, guarding Pensacola, Mobile, New Orleans, and Galveston. But they were more dangerous than the larger Atlantic fleet, for there were not the one hundred eighty-nine openings for commerce in the Gulf that there were on the Atlantic Coast.

Adam's greatest security rested in the fact that the Federals were as inexperienced at blockading as he was at running through. They worked in the same pitch-blackness, and on a moonless horizon one ship looked much the same as another. Already tales were told with great hilarity of cruisers who had been tricked into firing upon each other.

In the last moments before they weighed anchor, Adam stood on the bridge with Beau, every muscle tensed, as he waited for time and tide to be right. Except for the comforting thrum of the engines, there was no sound aboard.

There were only the thoughts of what might happen. The *Ullah* was loaded to her upper decks with Jem Moran's cotton. Everything Adam and Beau owned would be won or lost on this trip.

Adam gave the last order he could shout aloud. "Weigh anchor!"

They slipped through the first tier of the blockade without unusual incident. Federal lookouts in small rowing barges, moving unseen on the waters, waited to alert the cruisers by rocket flare of the appearance of a blockade-running ship. Adam had vowed he'd make no effort to avoid hitting the small craft should one enter his path; but when the time came, he touched the helm, moving it the two strokes required to avoid the boat. A flare shot up immediately, bursting nearer to one of the cruisers than to the *Ullah*. Guns peppered the night with grape and canister. A Parrott gun boomed so near, it seemed to be aboard the *Ullah* with them. Adam held the ship near the coast, then arced her course straight out to sea.

They had successfully passed the first barrier, but dawn brought renewed danger. There was no release from constant vigil. The *Ullah* steamed steadily at ten knots, sitting low in the water because of her heavy load of cotton. It was a crowded sea and dangerous waters. Several times the lookout spotted a ship. Each time tensed muscles relaxed when it turned out to be a merchant vessel and not a cruiser.

By noon the sky was overcast, a bluish gray haze lowering to the water's surface every hour. Throughout the early part of the day Adam and Beau were alert, expecting to be attacked momentarily. By late afternoon, when they had not sighted the cruising blockaders and the weather grew steadily worse, their nerves were raw with tension.

"I can smell the son of a bitch, Beau. Where the hell is he?" Adam squinted at the vast expanse of moving gray haze. He strode to starboard, peering at what seemed to be a deserted ocean.

"See anythin'?" Beau asked, searching too.

"Nothin' . . ." Then: "Sweet Jesus! There she is," as the cruiser emerged from the fog, five miles astern of the *Ullah*. "Full steam ahead!"

Beau raced below, bellowing orders to his firemen to build a full head of steam in both *Ullah*'s boilers. His crew was about to be tested for the first time. He checked the bunkers, trying to guess how much scarce and precious anthracite coal it would take to outrun and outmaneuver the cruiser.

As Beau's crew built pressure in the boilers, the heat grew intense under Adam's feet on deck. The vibration made everything creep that wasn't secured. His men made bales of cotton fast, shifted others aft. With the ship vibrating so hard that Adam expected it to lift from the water, they were making no better than thirteen knots. The cruiser gained steadily on them, rapidly drawing near enough to fire upon the *Ullah*. The cruiser, having no bow gun, began to yaw, sending hundred-pound shot from the long-range Parrott gun over the *Ullah*. Then their aim improved. Part of the passenger deck shattered, spraying decorative gingerbread and splintered lumber onto the cotton bales. Losing speed because of the yawing, the cruiser dropped back, the shots falling short.

Adam knew as well as the Federal captain that the *Ullah* couldn't outrun the cruiser. His only remaining course was to pit his knowledge of the waters against the superior speed of his pursuer. As soon as he saw the cruiser enter the Gulf Stream, he angled toward its outer reaches, slipping out of its two- to three-mile current. If the cruiser remained in the stream going against the powerful current, Adam could make up some of the speed the *Ullah* didn't possess of herself.

Beau, satisfied with the efforts belowdecks, ordered the cotton bales on the foredeck shoved into the sea, lightening the load. The white bundles bobbled along in the *Ullah*'s wake. Lightened and giving everything she had, the *Ullah* was barely reaching fourteen knots. Her decks shuddered. The flooring was almost too hot to bear standing on. From her stacks billowed smoke and cinders blown from the overheated furnace. But was giving Adam what he needed.

The cruiser, beating against the Gulf Stream and the time she lost by yawing, had dropped about seven miles astern. With dark approaching and the Florida Straits near, Adam began to believe they'd make it. He glanced at the sky.

There was a loud but strangely muffled *crumpp!* A ragged red hole bloomed in the deck sheathing. Flames burst around them in one great fiery gasp. Pieces of splintered planks, cinders, and large murderous metal

shards flew up to land on the deck. As though by a giant
hand, Adam was slammed against the helm, his breath
knocked out sickeningly. Beau and the crewmen were
flung across the deck amid the debris.

Belowdecks, men screamed.

Adam stumbled to his feet, grasping the helm, testing
it gently to see if the *Ullah* still responded. Satisfied, he
ordered the mate to take the helm. He catapulted down the
ladder to assess the damage to ship and crewmen.

He ordered injured men hauled to the captain's dining
hall while those still whole were to keep the remaining
boiler full of steam. Beau and the crew worked feverishly
to put out the fire that would act like a beacon, spotlighting
them as darkness fell. Men worked with scalded skin, un-
complaining and determined as Adam again asked for all
the power *Ullah* had left.

With the number two boiler blown, the *Ullah*'s speed
was reduced to a maximum of eight knots. He set a course
straight for New Orleans, then veered sharply, reversing
the engines, coming to a stop in the dubious protection of
a fogbank just beyond the western Florida coast. The
Ullah blew steam beneath the surface, causing no dark
billowing clouds to give them away.

Adam, Beau, and the crew stood in rigid silence on the
ruined deck and bridges, each man praying that the cruiser
would pass them by. Adam held his breath as it neared.
Its guns roared and spit fire, certain that somewhere before
them lay the crippled, easy prey of the *Ullah*. The Federal
ship passed, a ghost more felt than seen, shooting its Parrott guns wildly at the night air.

At New Orleans the Federal ship *Brooklyn* guarded the
Pass à l'Outre. Thirty-five miles away the *Powhatan*
guarded the Southern Pass. In between were the unguarded South and Northeast passes, both open to small
vessels, both possible for ships of shallow draft, but not
the *Ullah*. Adam thought longingly of the sleek blockade
runners waiting for him in Nassau.

He headed for the Pass à l'Outre, both he and Beau
braced for the guns to begin roaring once more. Rain came
down in a steady drizzle, threatening a coming storm.
Thunder rumbled, nearer with each drumming roll. Only
the thick cloud covering near the shore saved the *Ullah*
from being dangerously illuminated by the distant flashes
of lightning out at sea. Unable to risk the storm coming

nearer, Adam again called for all the speed the ship could muster. Low on coal, Beau dismantled the wood fittings from passenger cabins to burn. He broke into one of Jem's cotton bales, saturating it in kerosene and adding that to the firebox.

As they neared the Pass à l'Outre the *Brooklyn*'s rockets shot up into the air, warning the *Powhatan* a blockade runner had been spotted. Adam tensed at the helm. There was little evasive running the *Ullah* could do now. He watched awestruck as the *Brooklyn* sailed with a full head of steam away from her post, leaving the Pass à l'Outre clear.

"God bless the poor bastard she's chasing." Adam laughed in relief. He steamed through the pass into a two-mile square of water called the Head of Passes. From this point they were safe. Exhausted, he turned the helm over to a crewman, clasped Beau's arm, and steered him to the captain's cabin, where they broke open a bottle of French brandy Adam had brought back from Europe and drank until both were too sleepy to lift the glasses to their lips.

By morning the *Ullah* had limped the remaining ninety-five miles to New Orleans proper. They docked at Poydras Street. The injured were transported to the hospital. Repairs on the ship were begun.

The New Orleans docks rang with the melodious yell songs of the dock workers as they loaded and unloaded cargo:

> Bend yo' back, tote it to de lift,
> White boss hollers if you ain't swift.

Beau and Adam hired a carriage, a room at the hotel, and a hot bath. After that their first stop was Brennan's Restaurant on Royal Street. For the first time in more than a year they ate a New Orleans meal: pompano toulouse, roasted quail in a potato nest, grillades in creole sauce.

Sighing contentedly, they left Brennan's, their minds back to business. The courthouse was open daily until 6:00 P.M. to accommodate any man wishing to sign on as a privateer with the Confederacy. Adam signed the open book of subscription, designating the *Ullah* as a privateering ship manned by fewer than one hundred fifty men. He placed before the registrar the papers proving her a cleared vessel, then paid the five-thousand-dollar bond.

Others waited their turn, talking of ships already commissioned and plying their trade: the *Triton*, a schooner; the *Phenix*, a steamship of 1,644 tons and 243 men to man her; and a privateering submarine, the *Pioneer*. There was no limit to the imagination, daring, or hopes of the men who signed the subscription books.

Adam placed the commission papers in his pocket. Beside him Beau's eyes sparkled, filled with an eager love of this city. For Beau New Orleans was home. In no place on earth did he feel so alive or so much himself as he did here.

With some dismay he discovered that many gaming houses were closing because of the war. The gamblers had formed their own regiment, pledged to protect the city. "We're goin' on the town tonight, Adam. Look there—they've scribbled *'Aux Armes, Citoyens!'* on the wall. Before we know it, New Orleans'll be as closed down and stodgy as—"

Adam laughed deeply. "New Orleans could never be stodgy. Close down the city, and the bordellos'll open business in the bayous."

"We're still goin' on the town. We've done our business, and I'm not takin' no for an answer. I haven't seen a good comique at the opera house for over a year."

"Wrong night for that." Adam chewed absently on the tip of an unlit cheroot. "Just vaudeville for the hoi polloi."

"I feel like the hoi polloi," Beau said, undaunted. "We'll see my mother, meet my future brother-in-law—jeez, Adam, can you fathom that? Barbara's gonna be married, my little sister. That damn Morgan Longworth better be the best damn husband a man ever was."

"With that clan of yours looking out for Barbara, the poor bastard's probably afraid to piss for fear he does it wrong."

Beau laughed gaily, feeling considerably kinder toward Morgan.

The front door spewed an assortment of demonstrative LeClercs, kissing, hugging and crying over Beau and Adam. Mrs. LeClerc insisted they stay for supper.

Morgan Longworth III was a handsome man of nineteen. He stood straight and proud beside Barbara in a spanking new gray captain's uniform. But his best credential was that he loved Barbara with a winsome, tender adoration.

Barbara, basking in Morgan's love, turned shy, enraptured brown eyes to her brother. "You won't miss our weddin', will you, Beau?"

Beau leaped from his seat, bounding over to his sister to embrace her. "Sweetheart, I'll be here if I have to swim the blockade. You can count on it. Come spring, Beau LeClerc is gonna dance at his sister's weddin'. Morgan," he said, taking the younger man's hand, "I'm truly honored to be your best man."

They left LeClerc's house with Beau still eager to taste the fruits of New Orleans' peculiar pleasures. Like a bee in a blooming clover field, he leaped from suggestion to suggestion, talking of his sister between times. "Did you see her face, Adam? She loves him! They'll be happy—don't you agree? He's a good man. What did you think?"

Adam said thoughtfully, "They seem to love each other very much."

"Yeah." Beau sighed. "Makes me wonder what you and I are missin' out on. No one ever looked at me the way Barbara looks at him."

Adam mumbled his agreement, his mind in a fluttery turmoil as he remembered the soft vulnerability in Dulcie's eyes after he had kissed her.

"And seein' them . . . I don't know. Sure gave me a powerful yearnin' for someone nice and soft—"

"We sure as hell aren't goin' to find anyone like that, walkin' the streets with you chatterin' like a magpie. Where do you want to go?"

"Orleans Ballroom." Beau turned on Chartres Street. "Let's take a look."

"What do you want to go to a Quadroon Ball for? Those girls won't come with us. Their mamas are makin' permanent arrangements for them."

"We can look."

"Looking isn't exactly what I had in mind."

They paid the two-dollar admission and entered what was considered the finest ballroom in America. Here, under lofty ceilings lit by brilliant crystal chandeliers, on romantic balconies overlooking the gardens of Saint Louis Cathedral, were the famous beauties of New Orleans, flamboyantly gowned in silks and satins, arrayed in plumes and flashing jewels. Schooled in the subtle arts of pleasing men, they were women whose sole aim was to become the

faithful mistress of a wealthy white patron in return for
financial security and one of the small white houses that
sat in a neat row on Rampart Street.

Here, too, were the elegant men who had come to select
a quadroon woman and, having made the choice, enter
into artful negotiations with her mother so that he might
pay court to his chosen beauty. It was an elaborate and
dangerous ritual: Frequently more than one man desired
the same girl, and the Quadroon Balls were renowned for
duels precipitated by a fit of jealousy or a fancied insult.

Adam grumbled at Beau as they walked with slow non-
chalance to the wine table in the flagstoned courtyard.
"You realize all we can accomplish is to have some dandy
hot to put a bullet in us if we touch the wrong girl." He
surveyed the room as he spoke, eyes lingering on the lush
feminine forms all around him. It was enough to make
a man wonder if fighting a duel wasn't small price to pay
for an evening in such a paradise. He hesitated, watching
Beau, with his ready smile and gregarious nature, thrust
himself into the midst of conversations private or otherwise. Somehow he managed it without calling disaster upon
himself, Adam noticed with a twinge of envy.

Adam stood near the balcony, enjoying the playful
breeze that gusted erratically through the open doors. He
had been standing there for about fifteen minutes when
a statuesque woman in her forties approached him. "Well,
Captain," she said, fingering his lapel, "you already spoken
for, or are you more selective than most?"

"A little of each, Madame." He introduced himself and
offered to fetch her some wine.

They walked together to the seat she had vacated.
"You'd make the perfect man fo' mah baby, Captain Tremain."

"If she's your daughter, Madame, I'd find her irresistible. But I'm not in the market. I sail day after repairs are
made on my ship."

"What? So sure, Captain? Cannot a man be made to
change his mind once, as a woman wisely does a dozen
times in an hour?"

"Perhaps . . . on rare occasions."

"This will be such an occasion. No man can look upon
Solange Plafond and resist her, Captain. Not even a man
with so determined a jaw as yours." In one graceful movement Madame Plafond rose from her seat and crossed the

room, disappearing onto the balcony. Moments later she returned, leading to Adam a young woman of breathtaking beauty. He noted her lushly sensuous mouth, her charmingly direct gaze. Her flame-red silk gown, artfully draped to reveal her full breasts and long slim waist, was adorned with a large diamond clip. An expensive woman—and worth every penny.

"My daughter, Solange, Captain Tremain." Madame Plafond stepped back, assessing the look on Adam's face as she translated bewitchment into dollars. She gave Solange just enough time to entice, then spoke precisely. "Solange has already received a preliminary offer from another gentleman, a very rich gentleman of old New Orleans lineage. But my daughter's wishes are as important to me as financial considerations, Captain. Within reason, of course. I can see she is taken with you."

Behind them the lilting sound of the orchestra beckoned. Solange lifted her slender, perfectly shaped arms to Adam. Madame Plafond's gloved hand came down on her daughter's arm. "We will negotiate first."

"Oh, Mama!" Solange frowned with an ineffectual severity that merely accentuated her well-bred beauty. "If my Adam is the man I wish him to be, he will return to your negotiations. What would a man be worth who had no honor? That would not be *my* Adam, Mama." She gazed at him, her exotic beauty radiating the exhilaration that coursed through her.

Adam took her in his arms, guiding her onto the dance floor without thought of the implications of his action. Aside from a small, fiery auburn-haired girl, no woman had fitted into his arms with the ease and comfort of Solange Plafond. But tonight there was no room for thoughts of Dulcie Moran. Solange's soft pliability had relieved him of such unexpected and unwanted visions. And should he ever need it again, he'd know that the cure for one woman was another, a woman like Solange.

Madame Plafond gazed after them, satisfied, and went in search of her daughter's other gentleman. She had observed Solange's moment of choice when she had defended Adam, as well as the captain's surrender to her dark, liquid gaze. Now she had only to curtail previous arrangements before there was trouble.

Having a duel fought over one was high flattery yet it had distinct disadvantages. There was always the possibility that the wrong man would win. Even in victory, a paramour with a pistol wound or rapier puncture was incapacitated, sometimes for weeks.

Her daughter's patron fancied himself a master with the sword. Somehow, Madame Plafond did not envision the dashing young captain a virtuoso of the rapier.

Edmund Revanche was enjoying himself immensely. He had selected a woman who appealed to him with a thoroughness he had believed impossible. Solange, however, had the power to obliterate comparisons. She was unique and total. A woman who filled a man's eyes and blood. Had she been white, he was not certain that he could not learn to love her. As it was, he was proud he owned her.

With preliminary arrangements already made to the satisfaction of Madame Plafond and himself, he had turned Solange over to her mother without suspicion or misgiving when she had said she wanted Solange to meet someone, while he remained with the friendly, high-spirited people Solange had introduced him to. With perfect grace the women flirted mildly, flattering and complimenting Edmund's urbane charm. He was in his glory with an appreciative audience, who hung on every *bon mot* he chose to utter.

He drew deeply on his thin cigarillo, glancing over the dance floor. Abruptly he excused himself, hastily threading his way through the dancers.

Adam and Solange, lost in the music and one another's eyes, started as Edmund clasped Adam's shoulder roughly, bringing them to a halt. Adam turned to look into the cold fury of Edmund Revanche's aristocratic face.

"Edmund . . ." Solange breathed, placing her hand over her heart. "You have given me such a fright! I shall expect an apology at once. This is truly inhospitable behavior, unworthy of you."

Edmund's eyes remained on Adam. "Perhaps you are ignorant of our customs, sir, so I shall enlighten you. In New Orleans a man does not prostitute another man's woman by makin' love to her, in public or in private."

Adam's eyes turned the cold blue of ice. Edmund had changed little in the past eight years. The gray at his temples had grown whiter, giving his handsome face an added dignity. But the hardness in his eyes was unaltered.

His lips remained unchanged, so ready to curl into the grim smile that betrayed the cruelty of which he was capable.

"I know the customs of New Orleans, Mr. Revanche."

Edmund's eyes narrowed. "You know me?"

Adam's smile was tight. "I know you quite well. Better than most."

"Pray enlighten me, sir. You have the advantage in that respect."

"Shall we leave it that I was and still am a close friend of Tom Pierson," Adam said coldly, taking perverse pleasure in the smoldering hostility that flared in Edmund's eyes.

Edmund couldn't recall Adam's name, but he remembered the unsheathed hatred of the boy in Zoe's house. Shaking in fury, he slowly and dramatically drew off his white kid glove, prelude to the ancient act of tossing it in challenge at Adam's feet.

Around them the ballroom grew quiet. The laughter and talk died away, to be replaced by murmuring and whispers. The space around them emptied. People formed a circle for the challenge.

Solange called frantically for her mother, truly alarmed as she recognized the hatred that existed between the two men.

Madame Plafond hurried forward. Beau, startled by the sudden contretemps, peered over the obstructing shoulder of the man in front of him. "Mother of God!" he breathed. Heedless of the outraged cries, he pushed his way to Adam through the wall of people.

He arrived at nearly the same instant as Madame Plafond. "Adam, there you are!" he cried with false heartiness. "I've been lookin' for you. We've got to leave right away. We'll be late—Barbara's soiree—"

"Shut up, Beau," Adam said through his teeth.

"Mr. Revanche," Madame Plafond gasped, "please, dear sir, this is a terrible mistake. Solange and Captain Tremain—"

Edmund grinned. "Ah, yes, Tremain. Now I recall . . . Adam, isn't it? Well, Tremain, I shall never forget again."

"No, you won't," Adam said. "I'll see that you don't."

Edmund laughed, relaxing. His outward manner became as smooth as it would have been had Adam been a welcome acquaintance. Cunning to the last, he would assess Adam's strengths and weaknesses before he decided how to handle him and with what weapon.

"Mr. Revanche," Madame Plafond said with greater authority, "I insist you end this ridiculous posturin'. Captain Tremain is a . . . dear friend of my former mistress. It is expected he meet my Solange."

"I shall handle this situation, Madame Plafond, without instruction from you," Edmund said coldly.

"No, sir, you will not. At least not in this fashion. I am not without powers of my own."

"Adam, come on—let's get out of here. Back down," Beau whispered.

"If you persist, Mr. Revanche, our arrangement shall be at an end. My daughter would never consent to being courted by a barbarian!"

"It's true, Edmund, I could never forgive you or forget this night," Solange said softly. "Do you think so little of me that you would threaten the dear friend of my mother?"

"Have you made up your mind, Revanche? Will you meet me one to one?" Adam asked, smirking.

Madame Plafond stirred restlessly, then fixed Edmund with a surprisingly ferine stare. "Mr. Revanche, should you persevere . . . ah, but it would be such a pity, were you to be the subject of idle gossip—"

"Dare you threaten me?" Edmund gasped.

Madame Plafond smiled. "There are no threats here tonight, Mr. Revanche. There are only threats of threats. Shall we keep it that way? Solange, I believe your gentleman would like some refreshment."

Edmund stood indecisive, weighing his desire to lay waste to Adam against the risk to his own reputation. As an adversary Adam would be direct, relying on his enormous strength. Edmund could overcome that. But Madame Plafond—there was an adversary more to his own mold, a torturer, an exquisite tormentor who would take delight in ruining his good name.

Jauntily, as though he had never had other intentions, Edmund smiled, placing Solange's hand on his arm. "I am yours, dear one." He thrust his hand into his glove. "This has been an interesting renewal of our acquaintance, Captain Tremain. Be assured we shall meet again."

"You can count on that, Revanche. Perhaps then you won't have the skirts of two women to protect you."

Edmund laughed easily. "How strange, Captain, that you should utter the thought I was thinking about you. The skirts seem to be fluttering in your direction, do they not?"

Adam watched as Edmund with unflawed poise strolled with Solange to the balcony.

"Adam, for the love of God, let's get out of here before he changes his mind and comes back."

"Such malignance between you! He is a very bad man in your opinion?" Madame Plafond asked.

Adam said fervently, "He shouldn't be permitted to touch the hem of Solange's gown. You did her no favor in preventing this duel."

Madame Plafond was silent for a time. Then she said, "The arrangement will be voided. I saw the look in my Solange's eyes as she danced with you, Captain. For all her femininity, my daughter is no fool. She is a good judge of men. She trusted you. I do too. I will see Mr. Revanche never comes near her again; but alas . . . the same must be true of you. With such enmity between you, agreement over my daughter with either of you is impossible."

"My loss and regret, Madame," Adam said with sincerity. He took her hand and kissed it, then kissed her on either cheek. "For Solange," he whispered, then tapped a goggle-eyed Beau. "Shall we leave? It would be a pity to be late for your sister's soirée," he said sarcastically.

On the street once more, Beau followed Adam's long strides without thought to where he was leading. "My God, Adam! Of all the women in the room, you have to end up with *his* quadroon!"

Adam turned down Ursuline Street then onto Gallatin Street, an avenue reknowned and reviled for the underworld of harlots, garroters, footpads and thieves that existed there, alive by night, hidden by day. Adam grabbed Beau's sleeve, pulling him abruptly through the open door of the Green Tree dance hall. He was spoiling for a fight, and the Green Tree was one of the most likely places to find one.

"Jesus Christ, Adam, you're goin' to get us killed yet tonight!"

"You wanted to see the town. Beer!" he shouted to the bartender. He leaned against the fender, waiting with easy anticipation for the slatternly woman across from him to leave her companion in answer to the invitation in his eyes. She smiled at him. He beckoned to her. She got up from her perch on her man's knee and walked unsteadily to Adam, then lay back in his arms, wanting his probing hands to stroke and caress her.

The man hit him before he could release the woman. She sprawled to the floor as the brawl sprang full force into being. Chairs overturned, glasses shattered. Adam swung indiscriminately at all comers. The mirror behind the bar splintered as a chair flew over his head. Pickpockets rummaged through the clothing of the fallen, making off with money, rings, and watches as the dance hall became a tumult of flailing arms, enraged cries, strangulations and pain, and sour breath.

Having had his fill and still on his feet, Adam disentangled Beau from his three adversaries and plunged into the street laughing as he wiped the trickle of blood from his mouth. His hands were scraped and bruised. There was a long, thin line along his jaw where someone's ring had caught him in a glancing blow. It would be purple by morning.

"Now where?" Beau asked glumly, his hands against his midriff. "How about Archie Murphy's place? He's good for at least one murder a night."

"Not me," Adam said, stretching luxuriously. Suddenly he spun around, letting out a tremendous bellow, frightening a skinny juvenile footpad out of a dedicated life of crime. Adam halfheartedly chased the boy for a block, then returned to Beau.

"Remind me never to go out with you again," Beau moaned.

"What's the matter with you? You're game for a fight now and then."

"Yeah . . . now and then. Just not *now*."

Adam laughed, his eyes teasing as they walked past the ten-dollar bordellos and the fifteen-cent Negro cribs that lined Gallatin Street. "How about some gentler sport?"

"Damn, Adam, don't you ever get tired? Some bastard back in the Green Tree kicked me in the gut, I'm not gonna straighten up for a week."

"Awww . . . want me to go back and hit him for you?"

Beau glared at him. Ignoring him, Adam stopped in front of a house where two young girls stood leaning suggestively against the doorjambs. "How many . . . customers in a night?"

She shrugged, "Two, mebbe three. 'Pends effen Ah likes 'em or not."

Before their avaricious eyes, he lined three silver dollars on his palm. "Him and me." He indicated Beau.

The girl smiled. "C'mon in!"

"No. My place."

"You ain't gwine do nothin' funny, is you?"

"Dåmn right I am. You're gonna get a bath like you never had before."

"You crazy man! It ain't Satiddy."

He began to walk away. The two girls followed. "Ain't you gwine take us wiff you? Doan you wan' us?"

"Not much. You're too damned young." He handed the larger girl the three dollars. "Go home to your mamas where you belong."

The girl bit the dollar, then giggled. "Yo' crazy, man."

Beau smirked. "Adam, you're all bluster."

"Aaah, they were still children. And dirty at that."

Running the blockade out of New Orleans was easier than entering. One had only to anchor at the Head of Passes. From there one could watch all four passes. As soon as the *Brooklyn* left her post, Adam shouted orders, and the *Ullah* steamed out into the Gulf.

The short voyage across the stretch of Atlantic was uneventful. Two days after they left New Orleans the *Ullah* approached the limestone and sand islands of the Bahamas. The waters around the islands were unfamiliar to Adam. He studied the strong tidal currents, making notes to himself on the complicated navigational problems of the area: partially submerged cays, crosscurrents, and eddies. Though these waters were British domain forbidden to Federal ships, the cruisers often chased a blockade runner right into port. With the many reefs and peculiarities of the area, he needed to know these waters as well as he did the Southern coast. His life might well depend on it.

The harbor at Nassau was excellent, a natural deep harbor guarded by Paradise Island. Old ship's charts named them the Fragrant Islands, and as he neared,

Adam thought it apt. He and Beau looked across low-lying green islands lush with poinsettia, bougainvillea, flaming red poinciana, hibiscus, the spiking orange heliconia. Parrots of vibrant hues flitted between trees of a purplish shade that reached with fingerlike roots to the water.

The wharf was as busy as any he had ever seen, but with a difference, a strange sound, a rhythmic cadence as native conches lustily sang and made music as they worked. Ships made fast three abreast. Drays clattered between warehouses and wharves, stirring clouds of pulverized limestone dust. Drivers bawled at Negro roustabouts, who shouted commands to workers amid the screech of axles and cargo blocks and steam donkey engines, in a curious blend of British colonial flavor and the easy enchantment of African rhythm.

Adam scanned the ships anchored in harbor for the two that were his.

"There's Ben!" Beau shouted, punching Adam, waving to Ben.

They slapped at each other's shoulders, laughing, all talking at once, until Ben said in mock dismay, "Hey, aren't either of you interested in seeing the new ships? They're beauties!"

The three of them, each prouder than the next, gazed lovingly at the two sleek, low-riding sidewheel paddlers. Gray ghost ships, 350 feet long, double stacked and built for speed. A tremor ran through Adam: In his imagination it was already a dark moonless night and he was at sea approaching the Carolina coast.

"What'll we name 'em?" Ben asked.

"The *Sea Gull* and the *Heron*," Beau suggested.

"The *Liberty* and the *Independence*," Adam said with quiet authority. Neither Ben nor Beau said anything. The names fit as if the ships were very old and had always been so named.

A toss of the coin decided which of them would captain the new ships. Adam and Ben looked at the gold pieces lying on their palms heads up.

"I get the *Ullah*," Beau said happily. "Truth to tell, I'd have hated to give the old girl up. She and I have come a long way together."

"I'll take the *Independence*, Ben."

"Fool, you've given me the best ship." Ben tucked his thumbs inside his fancy waistcoat and grinned proudly at the *Liberty*.

Ben guided them around the island. Adam drank in the strangeness and beauty: brown fruits called sapodillas, green ones called sugar apples, scarlet plums, tamarinds, papaws, and jujubes. With the relish of a small boy set free in a candy shop, he sampled them all.

At dusk the cicadas began to chorus. From the street they could see the anchor lights swinging lazily from the halyards of ships in the harbor.

They stayed at the Royal Victoria, a four-story hotel completed just that year. It boasted bathrooms with water on tap, porticos, a glassed-in courtyard, winding paths, shrubs, trees, and exotic flowers—the pride of the island and strong temptation for men to linger there forever.

The clientele in 1861 was composed of Confederate officers and agents stationed in Nassau to handle the flow of war material and the cotton that would pay for it. There were blockade-running captains with connections in Boston, Philadelphia, and New York who dealt in almost any cargo available. Adventurers drawn by the lure of war to its perimeter rubbed shoulders and exchanged stories with others of their kind. Gossips in the lobby of the Royal Victoria spent leisurely afternoons speculating on who among the guests was a Northern spy. High-class prostitutes, dancers, and entertainers had their own suites or shared them with their benefactors, giving Nassau society morsels for spicy conversations.

The morning of their second day, Adam, Ben, and Beau sought out the various agents on Bay Street. They spoke first to "The King's Conch," Mr. J. B. Lafitte, head agent for Fraser, Trenholm and Company, which handled all cotton and shipping transactions for the Confederate government. Adam would work closely with them throughout the war.

Next they saw Mr. L. G. Watson, who represented the Glasgow firm of Alexander Collie, from whom Adam had purchased the *Liberty* and the *Independence*. Expecting to order another ship after his return voyage, Adam wanted to know the man with whom he would be dealing.

Alexander Collie and Company, ship builders, also acted as agents for the Confederate Trading Company and pri-

vate Confederate brokerage consignment and shipping
concerns. While the South needed ordnance, there were
other items the populace desired: fine cloth, toothbrushes,
foodstuffs, whiskey, brandies. An enterprising man could
net two to three hundred thousand dollars on one trip.
Adam intended to be such a man. Capture seemed a re-
mote possibility in the safety of a British port where the
blue jacaranda blooms and makes a man think of im-
mortality.

Adam returned to the Royal Victoria that evening feeling expansive and optimistic. Not only did blockade running seem a profession that had sprung into being with
him in mind, he had learned there was no British duty on
cotton and the tonnage fee was only a shilling a ton.

And growing in the back of his mind was a plan to get
even with Revanche. Not for a quarrel over a woman, but
for Tom—and Ullah.

On the veranda of the hotel several blockade-running
captains were engaging in their favorite pastime, pitching
pennies with ten-dollar gold eagles. Confidently Adam
drew out his own coin, tossed it, and, laughing, stooped to
pick up his winnings.

The dining room held one hundred fifty people. It was
always crowded. Seamen exchanged the latest news of
Federal cruisers, their positions, and the safest running
routes. It was also a showcase for the prostitutes, who displayed their wares in the latest Paris fashions gleaned from
Godey's Lady's Book and reproduced by frenzied seam-
stresses.

Adam, Ben, and Beau finished their meal and sat drinking a brandy with their fruit. They all stared as a lushly
built red-haired woman wandered into the room and
paused, as if searching for someone.

Ben whistled silently. "Suppose that's all her under that
dress?"

"She looks lost to me," said Beau.

Ben laughed, and Adam asked, "Why don't you ask her
if she wants to be found? You're always helpful, Beau."

Beau glared at both of them. "I will." He got up and
brought her back to their table. Flashing angry warning
signals at Adam and Ben, Beau still blushed. "This is . . .
this is Miss . . . Miss Glory Hallalooya. Adam, Ben."

"I'm so pleased to meet you!" Glory's voice was bubbly,
her smile wide. "You-all are new, aren't you?"

"Your name can't really be Glory Hallalooya," Adam said, grinning.

"I don't see why not! What's wrong with it? Say, you men don't mind if a lady has a drink, do you?"

Adam motioned to the waiter. He poured her a brandy.

"Oh, thank you!" she said, and the bubbling giggle rose in her. Except for a particularly well-endowed body, Glory looked like a little girl, with her sparkling eyes, upturned nose sprinkled liberally with freckles, and wide mouth that wasn't comfortable unless it was smiling.

Though she was nearly ridiculous with her outlandish name, her little-girl face, and her harlot's dress, Adam found Glory Hallalooya engaging. As often as she emptied her glass, he refilled it. Ben and Beau tactfully left as Adam leaned back in his chair smiling, and Glory leaned forward in hers, earnestly telling him how she came to be in Nassau.

"They just left me. And with not a word or a penny," she hiccuped. "When I woke up in the morning, Mr. and Mrs. Packer—" she giggled—"had packed. And left me. With a hotel bill. Now, do you think that's any way to treat the governess of your children? I didn't either."

"You were a governess?" Adam asked, astonished.

She waggled her finger at him, then wrinkled her nose, smiling happily. "I was Eleanor Brooker then."

"Aha! So your name isn't Glory Hallalooya."

Her enormously expressive face took on all the lines and planes of worry. "Don't you like my new name, Adam? I thought it had a certain—flair, considering the war and all. But it you don't like it, maybe . . . Adam," she said, lowering her voice and leaning across the table to whisper in his ear. "I want to tell you a secret. I'm going onstage, be a dancer, *you* know. Want to know the truth?"

"Yes," he whispered back.

"You won't think I'm awful?"

"How could I possibly?"

"Well, some people think it's awful—immoral, but I want to be one of *those* dancers!"

"A stripper?!"

"Ssshhh!"

"But sweetheart, if you're going to take all your clothes off onstage, it can't be a secret, at least not for long." He glanced down into the cleavage she'd managed to display nearly under his nose.

"It's different onstage. Do you think I'm awful now?" Her eyes were wide and incongruously innocent.

He smiled at her. She was like an irresistibly frisky puppy, affectionate and funny. "I think you're wonderful."

Her gray eyes danced. "Oh, I'm so glad, because I love to take my clothes off, and right now I love you too! Wouldn't it be awful if you didn't love me back?"

He laughed aloud.

Glory wriggled out of her gown before he could close the door to his room. He stepped over a pile of discarded green silk. By the chair he sidestepped her petticoats. Near the bed he stumbled over her discarded shoes, camouflaged by her pantalettes. Glory giggled. She sat among the pillows wearing only her profusely plumed green velvet hat.

"Do you love me, Adam? I mean only for tonight. I love being loved."

He took off his jacket, then began methodically to unbutton his shirt. Glory leaped up, prancing across the bed. "Wait! Don't be so businesslike. Follow me!" She began leading him around the room. Somehow she managed to unbutton a cuff, then a shirt front. "Drop a shirt here and a collar there," she said gaily, and deposited his clothes on the floor as she had her own. "Isn't this fun? I used to do this for Johnny Packer when he was just a little tad."

"Johnny must have gotten one hell of an education."

"Oh, he did! The Packers shouldn't have gone off and left me like that, do you think? I was a good governess, and Johnny learned a lot."

He dropped his breeches in a comfortable heap beside her pantalettes. "No one should ever leave someone like you unattended. Come here, it's time the governess learned to play follow the leader."

Glory flew into his arms, laughing and kissing his face and neck. "How could I have just met you? Haven't we been lovers all our lives?"

He laid her down against the pillows, her child's face beginning to change subtly as he kissed the hollow of her neck, touched her breasts until they rose and swelled into hard buds beneath his fingertips. Glory nibbled at his ear, then gasped with a sharp intake of breath as he stroked the inside of her legs, spreading them to accommodate him.

Her blue eyes glowed as she looked up into his darkly

tanned face and they filled with passion. She put her arms around his neck, drawing herself up to kiss his lips. "Oh, Adam," she breathed, "I want you so, but I don't want this ever to end."

She wrapped her legs around him as he slid his hands under her buttocks, raising her as he entered her with a slow rhythm that built and beat like the rapid waves of an incoming tide.

Glory lay with her eyes closed, a contented smile on her face, as Adam rolled off her. She took his hand and placed it low on her belly. She said lazily, "I want to feel the warmth of your hand on me."

His hand slipped down to the moist patch of softly curling hair. She smiled. Adam rose up on one elbow to look at her broad, open features with the strangely innocent look. He couldn't imagine her on a stage in front of a howling audience of rowdy seamen. But he didn't doubt that if it was what she wanted, she would do it.

"I think I like you better than any other man I've ever met," she said with disarming directness. He kissed her, but her brow had wrinkled into its worried look. "You won't spoil it, will you, Adam?"

He looked questioningly at her. Her face crumpled. She buried her face in the mat of black hair on his chest. "Oh, I'm truly a sinful, sinful woman, Adam. I have hardly any shame at all."

He touched her hair, lifting it and kissing her neck. He tried to make her face him, but she clung to him, her face pressed against him, her voice muffled. "I could never be faithful—not even to you, Adam. Will you get terribly jealous and hate me?" She began to cry.

He caressed her until the small sobs subsided and the rhythm of her breathing changed, and his own desire rose. "I want you just as you are, Glory, dancing, laughing, flirting and . . ."

Teary-eyed but smiling again, Glory bounded up from her refuge on his chest, throwing her arms around him in fresh delight.

Adam remained in Nassau until the moon darkened. Every day and some nights he saw Glory. He never knew when she would appear in his bedroom, but her unpredictability made her all the more fascinating. He never wondered whom she was with those other nights, and he

didn't care. From Ben's guilty responses, Adam guessed
he was one of Glory's men. But he never asked, and Ben
never volunteered the information.

Each time she came to him, she wore one of her outlandish, brilliantly colored costumes, which she left in gay
little heaps across the floor in a path to his bed. They had
made love in every way they could devise.

She came to the pier the day he boarded the cargo-
laden *Independence* for his return to Savannah. "Keep
the bed warm for me, Glory, I'll be back," he whispered
into her ear.

She squealed in joy, kissing him long and passionately,
cheered on by the delighted hoots of the watching roustabouts.

Chapter Thirteen

As the carriage entered the long sandy lane to Mossrose,
Adam smiled wryly at his strange misgivings. There was
only one suitable name for a man doing what he was doing
now: fool. It was playing with fire, gambling on vagary.
Nothing would come of it between him and Dulcie.

Her caprices intrigued him; her fiery temper and her
contrite apologies, her capacities for joy and sorrow and
concern. But Dulcie's singularity went deeper than that,
and because of it he should stay away from her for both
their sakes. She was not a surface person. She looked beyond what she saw and heard, and she understood things.

But would she understand his passion? Dulcie would
never freely give herself to him out of wedlock. Yet he
would not marry now. He didn't even want to think of it.
So why had he been fool enough to accept Jem Moran's
invitation to Mossrose?

Abruptly his thoughts shifted to a humbler vein. Perhaps he had figured it all wrong. Dulcie had certainly been
romantically inclined toward other men. Toby Dobbs
could not have been the first to take advantage of what
was basically a harlot's nature in a well-bred woman.

He got an uncomfortable picture in his mind: Dulcie,
freezingly polite for her parents' benefit while he tried to

pretend everything was quite as usual. He crossed his arms
on his chest, scowling at the imagined coldness of this
woman for whom he had returned to Savannah.

The house loomed in front of him. Facing east, sited
on a natural knoll, was Dulcie's home. Mossrose was three
and a half stories, a pleasant house of soft pinkish-brown
brick, its tall windows framed in white, shuttered in green.
Fragrant pink moss roses softened the lines of the house.
To the south and west immensely tall, spreading live oaks,
dripping Spanish moss, shaded the house from the hot
afternoon sun.

Down the hill Adam could see the folly, its pillars
twined with white wisteria and honeysuckle. Wrens sang,
and blue jays scolded; a catbird cried. He heard horses'
hooves pounding down a dirt lane and male voices raised
in jeering tones. Out of sight, young children played noisily.

He paid the driver, and a wizened black man materialized from the house to take his sea chest. Then everyone
had come at once to meet him: Patricia in yellow voile
with ribbons at her waist; Jem, sweating, smiling. Half a
dozen youngsters boiled around the corner of the house,
closely followed by two attractive youths and Dulcie on
horseback.

"See? Strawberry beat you!" Laughing, Dulcie jumped
from her horse and walked toward Adam. Her hair had
tumbled from its snood and curled riotously around her
face. She was covered with dust, and her face was
scratched. Beads of perspiration dotted her upper lip and
forehead. He'd never wanted anything so much as he
wanted to grab her and hug her tight.

She was in far greater command of self than he was.
Standing just the proper distance away, she held out her
hand. "Welcome, Captain Tremain." Her golden eyes
danced, taunting him.

Adam's mouth curved into an appreciative, rakish smile.
Fully recovered, he kissed her hand. He had the satisfaction
of watching her blush as the other riders laughed and
teased her.

Captain Tremain," Jem said, "my nephews, Waite Price
and Philip Tilden."

Inside the cool entrance hall there were more introduc-
tions: Aunt Caroline and Uncle Webster Tilden from
N'Orleans; their children, Jenny, Jeannie, Gay, and Robert;
Dulcie's aunt Mildred Price from Jonesboro; and Mildred's

daughter, Millie, who was just fourteen and looked up at Adam through worldly wise lashes. Other cousins had resumed their joyous chase through the back gardens toward the orchards.

Adam searched the room, but Dulcie had vanished.

Patricia said, "Would you like to freshen up aftah youah journey?"

Adam followed her into a small, cheerful room. His chest stood open in a corner, and Lucius was hanging and smoothing his new dandy-ashore wardrobe, an extravagance he could hardly explain even to himself. Adam looked out the window onto a long balcony, down past the cedar grove to the quarters.

Refreshed, he stepped into the hall as Dulcie emerged from her bedroom. Poised and cool, she waited for him. Her hair had been redone, the dust and evidence of scratches erased. The touchable, errant little girl had been covered over by a virginal white eyelet piqué frock.

Adam stopped, looking her over carefully and leisurely.

"Well, do I pass inspection?"

He moved close to her. He touched her cheek where a scratch had been, tracing the outlines of dust streaks he could no longer see. His gaze was sensual, his expression mocking. "I liked you better messed up."

Dulcie slapped his hand. "Ohh! Still your same charmin' self, aren't you, Captain!" Her eyes flashed, raking him the length of his uniform. "Haven't you anythin' to wear besides that blue suit?"

He grinned. "Your temper didn't wash away with the dust, did it. My arm, Miss?"

"Do I dare risk havin' you push me down the stairs?" But she took his arm, with Lucius trailing behind.

They talked politely in the cool, dim parlor until the sun went down and the shutters were opened. Then Jem said, "Captain, you've never had time to look over Mossrose before. Would you like to see my setup?"

Adam rose immediately. "It would be a pleasure, Mr. Moran."

Chattering, Dulcie and her girl cousins moved from the parlor to the cooler veranda.

"Where did you *find* him?" Gay sighed ecstatically. "He's *beautiful!*"

"Well, but he's more than that," Dulcie said.

"What, then?"

Words like *compassionate* and *brave* raced through Dulcie's mind. None seemed adequate. "Noble," she said, then blushed hotly. "Oh, do let's talk about somethin' else! He certainly didn't come here on *my* account. He ships cotton for Daddy, and that's *all*."

Millie said, "Dulcie, when you blush like that, the back of your neck goes all red like a turkey's."

"Well, Millie, then just look down at your fingernails. To me they look all black, like a Minorca hen's."

Millie stuck her tongue out at Dulcie.

"Oh, Millie, stop!" said Jenny. "What if you freeze that way?"

Jeannie said diplomatically, "Dulcie, tell us again about tomorrow."

Millie, forgetting her pique, asked, "Who-all's comin'?"

Dulcie smiled at her. "Just nearly everybody in the county, Millie. Plenty of boys just the age you like."

"Oh, it's goin' to be so excitin'! How many proposals do you think will happen? Tournaments always inspire the men!"

The morning threatened rain, but by ten o'clock the sun was shining on the elaborately decorated tournament ground. Jem had spared nothing to welcome his daughter home and to put on a rousing display for Captain Adam Tremain, whom he already acknowledged as a possible suitor.

A month of slave labor had gone into building the stage for the small acts and band concert, and the stairstepped stands for viewing the different events of the tournament itself. Over the viewing stands and the three pavilions, one of each regimental unit represented, stretched a sunshade of broad stripes of Confederate gray and gold. As they had at that other tournament, now nearly a year ago, pennons and ribbons of every color fluttered in the warm July wind.

But everything was different now, Dulcie mused. Old swains had married; younger girls than she were wearing shiny new wedding rings and shyly hiding their prompt pregnancies. Now there was the war.

She missed familiar faces: the Acton boys, Cedric Whitaker, Todd Saunders, all serving under General Beauregard up in Virginia. Soon Glenn's company, the Savannah True Grays, would join General Johnston. Leroy's Rough and

Readies, and his brother, Conroy's, company, the Invincibles, were spoiling to get into the war before it was over.

The ages-old tournament was infected with a martial spirit. As the preliminary parade passed the stands, there was Glenn in his very proper gray uniform with the gold braid down the trouser legs; Leroy Biggs, Andrew Whitaker, and Lyman Matthews in their fringed buckskins, slouch hats pinned up rakishly on one side; and Conroy Biggs and Arthur Redgrave in gray with scarlet sashes dripping like blood from their waists. Each represented his regiment and would compete against the other regiments.

Addie Jo Acton squirmed in her seat as Glenn doffed his hat to her. "Oh, Dulcie, isn't he fine? I'm so proud of him!"

Dulcie smiled at her. "You're goin' to be a very happy bride next weekend, Addie Jo."

"I hope we'll be invited to *your* weddin' soon, Dulcie," she said kindly. "Has he proposed yet?" Though she was too polite to point to Adam where he sat beside Patricia, Dulcie knew whom she meant.

"He's here on business with Daddy," Dulcie said, wondering if the back of her neck had turned red.

"Oh! Is *that* why he isn't competin?"

Dulcie was annoyed. Addie Jo almost seemed to be purposely stupid. "I don't know. Oh, look, the magician pulled a rooster out of his hat."

"He's just one of the servants. He had it there the whole time."

Strong with trumpets and heavy with drums, Jem's hired brass band offered a stirring rendition of "Bonnie Blue Flag." Then the trumpeter, with a special long silver trumpet, blew fanfare for the first event.

The units raced through the decorated arches, spearing the bright brass rings with their lances. Leroy won the honor of choosing the queen.

"Seein' how I'm elected cap'n of my regiment, it seems to me I deserve the greatest pleasure of pickin' out our Sovereign o' Love an' Beauty," Leroy began. "As y'all know, my lovely wife, who used to be Camille Whitaker before she improved her station"—he shot an impish grin at Granddad Whitaker, who rose and good-naturedly shook his stick at him—"my wife is easy the prettiest girl in seven counties, maybe even eight, if I could name eight of 'em." His audience laughed with him. "But so happens Camille tol' me this mawin', now, Leroy, don't you go choosin' me up for queen, 'cause I don't wanta git up outa my rockin' chair today." A slight, uneasy titter stirred Jem's guests. Camille was a bride of three months, but her pregnancy was obviously older.

"An' I ain't pickin' Miss Dulcie, though she mighta been my second choice. She's already got a feller. One who ain't got the guts to compete against real men." He smiled contemptuously at Adam. 'So, friends and neighbors, I'm namin' purty li'l Addie Jo Acton to be Rulin' Sovereign o' the 1861 Confederate Tournament!"

Cheers greeted his speech. Addie Jo was a favorite; and wasn't she soon to be a bride, and this her last chance? Then there were more cheers, mostly from the men, as Leroy daringly kissed the queen.

Glenn chose Gay as the queen's lady. She went radiantly down to stand by the throne. Arthur Redgrave chose Millie, and suddenly Dulcie was left sitting alone.

It seemed no one noticed but herself. She picked up her skirts, ready to go elsewhere; but Adam was there beside her, large, male, and protective. "Pardon me, Miss, do you allow yourself to be seen with outcasts?"

Dulcie laughed, mostly in relief that he had rescued her from the same fate. "Adam, why aren't you out there competin'?"

"Is that where you want me to be?"

"They'd let you join one of the teams."

"Look at them. Except for a few, they're young boys. Do you want me taking advantage of weedy youngsters like Waite Price?"

Dulcie giggled. "Knowin' Waite, he'd probably trick you and throw you over the roof."

Adam laughed. "Is that what it takes to please you? Perhaps it's worth risking a broken neck."

"Adam . . . don't." Dulcie shuddered.

"At last, an honest expression of feeling! The lady does not want the brave seaman to injure himself."

"Don't flatter yourself, Captain. I could hardly care less."

"Should I believe that, Dulcie?" He stared at her until she was forced to pull her eyes away from the crowning of the queen and look at him. She had so little will of her own when he was near. She felt herself swaying toward the sparkling blue of his eyes and the tender set of his mouth. "If I should be wounded honorably upon the field, would you tend me? Stay me with flagons? Comfort me with apples?"

Dulcie, recognizing the words from the Song of Solomon and remembering what came after, dropped her gaze. It was unfair of him to make love to her in public, and in such a way. "Adam, please don't tease me."

"Is that what you think I'm doing?"

Looking out over the sunny field where the pennons flew, she said quietly, "I think you ought to be out there."

"To save my Southern honor? Or yours?"

"To save my father's pride. You're his guest, not mine. And not a planter in the county will want to do business with a man who won't risk his hide in harmless tournament games."

"I didn't realize there were so many blockade runners to choose among."

"There are enough. Oh, Adam!" she said in exasperation. "You know what I mean!"

"I'm beginning to get the idea."

When the guests left the viewing stand and began drifting toward the house and the barbecue pits, Adam walked with Dulcie toward the little knot of people clustered laughing around Jem and Patricia.

Dulcie's cheeks were burning with indignation. Couldn't Adam see how people felt about a—a coward?

Leroy's raucous voice cut into her thoughts. "Beggin' yo' pahdon, Cap'n—I did hear you're cap'n of a ship, didn't I?"

"You heard right."

Leroy punched him on the arm. "Sorry to be laughin', Cap'n. Just seems there's an awful lot o' funny people made into cap'ns these days. Anybody'd think we was desp'rate or somethin'."

Adam, still smiling, looked Leroy's fringed buckskin uniform up and down. "They might at that."

Leroy's face grew red. "I take that as an insult, Tremain."

Adam looked grieved. "I thought I was being agreeable. My apologies, Mr.—?"

"*Cap'n* Leroy Biggs, o' the Rough and Readies. Seems to me, you bein' a officer, you'd join in the fun. Less'n youah scared o' competition. That bein' the case, I can

see you don't wanta look like a damn fool in front o'
Dulcie. Hit home with that'n, didn't I, *Cap'n?*"

"Oh, Leroy, don't be such a boor!" said Dulcie.

"You let her do all youah fightin' fo' you, Cap'n?
Wouldn't s'prise me if you spread that story about bein'
a blockade runner yo'seff."

The muscle worked at the side of Adam's jaw; his eyes
narrowed. Deliberately turning his back on Leroy, he
offered Dulcie his arm. "Shall we have a cool glass of
shrub, Dulcie?"

Behind them Leroy said, "One kind o' skunk I purely
hate is a coward, ain't that right, Lyman!"

Dulcie stiffened. "Are you goin' to let them say—"

Adam imprisoned her hand under his arm. "Keep walking, Dulcie."

"But they're insultin' you! You just can't let them—"

"They're playing a game, and I don't care to play, that's
all."

"But a challenge—"

"A challenge has to be worth takin'."

Dulcie was bewildered. Brave men fought when challenged. No one ever questioned the worth of a challenge.
Honor was to be defended at all costs.

Her cousin Robert Tilden was at the refreshment table.
Robert was twenty-two, swarthy and dark-haired, with a
waxed moustache that curled up to points. He was a member of a Zouave army company in New Orleans. Today
he wore the high-necked red Garibaldi smock, belted with
a sky-blue sash over full-cut blue breeches that tucked
into shiny black boots.

On a visit to New Orleans at the age of fourteen Dulcie
had briefly fallen in love with her good-looking cousin.
She was quite certain Robert would not have walked away
from Leroy's taunts. She smiled at him fondly, glad of a
respite from her disturbing doubts about Adam. "I declare,
Robert, no one but you could make those baggy britches
look stylish!"

Robert's white teeth flashed. "You'll turn my poor head
with your flattery. Cap'n Tremain, we missed you out on
the field. I'm afraid the Savannah True Grays are over-
supplied with boys and short on men. I hear you're orginal-
ly from New Orleans. I figure two New Orleanians should
even the odds for them. Would you care to join us tomorrow?"

Dulcie felt herself cringe. But Robert's smile was genuine; so was Adam's.

"Thank you. Perhaps I will. Captain Biggs also extended an invitation."

To Dulcie's amazement the men laughed easily together. Robert, whom she'd known all her life, was no stranger to a fight. And she had seen Adam's temper flare over less. Aboard the *Tunbridge* he'd disposed of Toby Dobbs without hesitation. But both of them seemed to take Leroy's slur on Adam's courage as a joke. What did they see that she was unable to?

Dulcie could not help remembering the lavish ballrooms in the Castle duBois. Her own home was as beautiful in its way tonight, softly lit by lamps and candles reflected in gilt-framed mirrors. Yet she realized she was looking at it with detachment. Perhaps her year in Europe had removed her from the self she had been before.

More likely, Adam Tremain had made her look at herself and question the desirability of a prearranged life. Only now did she realize she wanted none of it. He had made it impossible for her to live the contented social life of her mother or dream the limited domestic dreams of Camille Whitaker Biggs.

By first intermission Dulcie felt old and very mature. The young belle was gone, as were the courtiers. Aside from Adam and Glenn she had hardly danced tonight with a male over the age of sixteen. Glenn's seriousness became him now, in spite of his constant talk of Addie Jo. Dulcie was half-amused, half nettled: after all, Glenn had grown up in love with *her*.

She walked in the garden with Andrew Whitaker, who claimed her for the next dance. "Miss Dulcie, I want to apologize for my brother-in-law. He ain't scarcely mo'n half-tamed anyway, an' there's not a gentleman here who's not ashamed o' the way he's baitin' yo' daddy's houseguest."

"Captain Tremain can take care of himself, Andrew, but thank you."

"Me'n Leroy's friends, but many's the times I've hauled off and fisted him good. He just loves a fight, an' he's gonna make a fine soldier—if one o' his friends don't kill him first on account o' his mean mouth."

"What about you, Andrew? Are you anxious to get into the war?"

"Yes an' no, Miss Dulcie. I never backed off from a fight yet, but somethin' about this one makes my stomach clench up. I ain't jes' positive I'm gonna get back from it."

Dulcie felt her blood go suddenly cold. War and death went together, but not for men like Andrew or Glenn or Adam. "Of course you will, Andrew! What silly talk!"

He produced a grin. "Jes' in case I don't, could I kiss you now?"

She hesitated. It wasn't proper, but Andrew was nice. "All right, but on my cheek. And no hands!"

Andrew laughed. "You sho' know how to plumb ruin a good thing, Dulcie!" He leaned forward, his hands behind him, and kissed her softly on the mouth.

As Andrew drew away, Adam said pleasantly, "Excuse us, please." Gay, clinging to his arm, said nothing. Wide-eyed, Dulcie watched them pass.

"Miss Dulcie, I'm truly sorry," Andrew whispered. "I wouldn'ta done anything to make him think ill of you."

"He seemed happy with Gay," she said flippantly.

Andrew grinned. "You promised me the next dance. That way some big tall ship's cap'n can't take exception when I got both arms around his girl."

"But I'm *not* his—"

"No, but you're a-gonna be." He swept her onto the floor, giving her no chance to reply.

She danced with Andrew and giggled at his jokes. Robert came up, tremendously attractive in a muted plaid coat and trousers, and swung her off her feet in a reel. Leroy, quite drunk, appropriated her for a waltz. He could hardly walk, yet he danced as lightly as ever. But whoever held her, her eyes constantly sought and found Adam.

Adam, she observed resentfully, was the belle of this ball. Not enough that his wine frock coat, pale gray trousers, and ruffled shirt fit him as though they were molded to his body. Not enough that one glimpse of him made every woman aware of her sex and his. Not enough that his ways were endearing him to every female from fluttery-lashed Millie to old Grandmother Whitaker. Not enough that he had made her long to be with him. *It wouldn't kill him to ask me for one dance,* she thought almost tearfully.

The long intermission was nearly over before he came up to her. "May I get you a cup of punch, Dulcie?" His expression was unreadable, almost dangerously neutral. Was he angry still? Or did he not care?

"Yes, please, Adam."

They strolled onto the front veranda. "Are you enjoyin' the dance?"

"Of course." He smiled down at her. "Aren't you?"

Something in his voice made her look at him, then quickly away. "Yes!"

In his silence her fib stood out boldly. Adam took her hand in his.

There were others nearby, couples strolling toward the gardens and the folly. He had nothing to say to her, for the intermission ended and they were alone, and he had not uttered a word. Yet, there was a union in their silence. Her jealousy eased. Perhaps now she could stand seeing him dance with other girls and not feel diminished by it.

"Dance with me, Dulcie."

Her heart leaped with gladness. "I'd—I'd like that."

They whirled over the smooth lawn to the strains of "Wait for the Wagon." His eyes never left hers. They were laughing, then came the applause. Waite and Phil leaped into view, clapping. "Bravo! Bravo!"

Dulcie was annoyed. Waite said, "Robert says you'll be on our team tomorrow, Captain."

"We need somebody that can get outa his own way better'n Glenn!"

"You think I can, that it, boys?" Adam asked lightly.

"Sure," Phil piped. "Anything'd be an improvement over what we got."

Adam laughed heartily. "One thing all your family seems to believe is that no man should be allowed to think too highly of himself."

The tournament resumed in the morning mist. When the long silver trumpet blew, Jem announced the javelin throw.

The contestants had shed yesterday's finery. Most wore riding breeches and soft shirts. Dulcie quickly decided that Robert was nearly as handsome as Adam, that Leroy was nearly as well built. Adam was wearing breeches of a warm earthy brown, that fit snugly over his flat belly and narrow hips, stretching across his powerful legs and buttocks. His shirt, damp in the mist, clung to his chest, sleeves rolled up to reveal thickly muscled forearms. His hair curled riotously, making him look younger and more rakishly masculine than ever. Dulcie couldn't tear her eyes from him, nor could she ignore the intriguing pictures of him that flashed through her mind.

Gay poked her. "Why are you blushin'? What happened? I didn't see anythin'."

"There was nothin' to see!" Dulcie tried to watch calmly as Adam took his position on the field. He picked up the javelin, testing its balance, flexing his arm, getting the feel of the instrument in his hand. Then he ran, his powerful legs setting a rhythm, torso turning, arm out, his chest thrust forward as he hurled the spear out toward the markers. Dulcie could barely sit still as Glenn's team became victors on the strength of Adam's and Robert's throws.

She was nearly breathless when the steeplechase began. Down the course were bales of hay, sections of snake fence, and a barrier of large flat rocks. At the starting gun the contestants were to clear all barriers, turn around at the end, and run against the tide of laggers back to the starting point.

Phil and Waite took off at the "get ready" count, and were ten feet down the lane before the shot sounded. "False start! Go on back!" Phil turned in one direction, Waite in the other. The mass of contestants pounded down the track toward them. The cousins ran heavily into each other and went sprawling. Those in the rear had to leap over several fallen bodies before the casualties picked themselves up and continued running.

The steeplechase was grueling, requiring tremendous strength and stamina as well as speed. Contestants fell, agonizing over cramps in legs and sides. By accident or in malice some stepped on the heels of men in front of them, battling to be first over the barriers.

Adam, running in front with Andrew, Robert, and several teen-age boys, had cleared the hay barriers and fences. Just ahead was the rock pile, too high to leap over, too wide to clear, and treacherous to climb. There was a mad scramble as others leaped for the same spot. The hurtling bodies, Adam among them, crashed down on the far side of the pile. With a triumphant "Yaa-hoo!" Leroy Biggs hurdled the rock pile and landed with both hands in the small of Adam's back.

"You son of a bitch," Adam gasped.

"Somethin' botherin' you, Cap'n?" Leroy smiled, then fell back as Lyman slid face first down the pile onto him.

Adam, limping for the next few strides, went on. He leaped the last barrier—hay bales with slithery hay scattered on the far side—and sprawled again. He felt as bruised and mauled as he had when, as an apprentice aboard his first ship, he had learned to climb the rigging.

On the way back he concentrated not on his competitors, but on the course. The rock barrier looked less formidable now. The runners had knocked it down to more manageable height, merely an ankle-spraining obstacle. At the hurdles Adam made up distance, his long stride and powerful legs taking him over the snake fences with ease. He was ahead, sprinting strongly down the quarter mile to the finish line.

Leroy's heavy footsteps behind him spurred him on, knees high, kick strong as he gauged his steps to the last hurdle. Leroy pulled up beside him. Again their eyes met, grim determination on both faces, mingled with the contorted grimaces of agonized lungs.

"I'm a-gonna whup you, you smart-assed boat driver," Leroy gasped.

"Like hell."

They ran down the long lane, faces red, hearts slamming, pushed on by cheers and the sight of the finish line. At the last barrier something—someone?—hit against Adam's foot. His rhythm was gone. He couldn't clear the barrier. He could go through it or . . . He dived in a forward roll, regained his balance, and kept running. At the finish line he was two paces behind Leroy and five ahead of Lyman Matthews and Robert Tilden.

When the last contestant had straggled in, pandemonium reigned. Men bent over trying to regain their breath. Several vomited into the bushes. One teen-ager turned brilliant red, then ghost white as he passed out. Men were draped over the hay bales, chests heaving, sweat pouring.

"Keep moving, boy, keep moving," Adam panted, forcing Phil Tilden to keep jogging with him, slowing the pace until they could stand it.

There was a break while thirsty competitors crowded the refreshment table, laughing again and jostling each other. Leroy was lording his triumph. "Yes, sir, it just don't take much a-tall to beat out-a-town boys. Seems like if they ain't got a boat under their feet, they better get wheels!" The laughter was general and good-natured, and Adam joined in.

"Hey, Cap'n," Leroy beamed, "how 'bout a good ol' boxin' match? Jes' you an' me, jes' us two big boys? Whaddaya say to that?"

"Sorry," said Adam, and finished his drink. "Too dangerous."

Leroy's laughter boomed out. Dulcie, approaching with Gay and Jeannie, said, "What's he up to now?"

"Haw! Haw! Haw! Too dangerous, the cap'n says. Well, by damn, Cap'n, even if I wasn't holdin' my cotton for better prices, I sho' wouldn't want to ship it with you!"

Adam said, with a little smile, "I didn't say who it was dangerous for."

Leroy's eyes narrowed. "I say you're afraid to face me fair and square."

Adam's mind flashed back to dock brawls in London, Tokyo, Bombay. Then it had been learn quick or lose his life. "I'm not going to fight you, Biggs. Save it for the Yankees."

Andrew said plaintively, "Leroy, ain't you never a-gonna grow up?"

Camille tucked her hand under Leroy's arm and gave him a strained smile. "Honey, that was a mighty fine race y'all ran. I'm right proud of you!"

Leroy glowered at her and shoved her away. The others, embarrassed, covered up the awkward moment. Dulcie and Gay, chattering lightly, took Adam's arms, and they headed back toward the tournament grounds.

The horn sounded for the rope climb. Jem said, "Now, friends and neighbors, we've got an easy-lookin' little competition here, just a short trip up to that first limb"—heads went up, up to the sailor's knots in the rope, sixty feet above the ground—"and down. Everybody gets two tries."

The younger boys went first. As one then another tried and failed to go up the rope, the audience and other contestants became eager to see somebody, anybody climb it. Glenn went higher than anyone before him; then he made the mistake of looking down. Leroy, who had sneered at the failures, was next. Like the others, he had watched the techniques of the better climbers. He pulled himself up until his feet could grip the rope. He went up hand over hand, more and more slowly, then he lost the hold with his feet, panicked, and started the rope to twisting. He slid back down.

He blew elaborately on his burning hands, spat on them

while glaring at the circle of watchers, and attacked the rope again. But it buckled and spun out of his grasp. His feet kicking furiously, he whirled until he was dizzy, then fell heavily to the ground. He lay there, then shook his head to clear it. "Whooo-eee!" he crowed. The audience laughed. "Well, I got higher than anybody, so I win."

"Mind if I take a shot at it?" Adam said, walking past Leroy.

"You already had your turn!" Leroy yelled.

Waite cried, "He did not! You're cheatin', Leroy!"

Leroy smirked. "Let's see what ya got, Cap'n. Mind you don't fall and hurt yo'self."

There were shouts and some jeers from the audience.

Adam grasped the rope, failed to catch it with his feet, and dropped back to the ground. The audience moaned its disappointment.

"You're wastin' yo' time, Cap'n. Let's go to the next event," Leroy said.

Adam looked at the spectators who crowded around them. "Everybody back now. I'll give it my second try."

There were hoots and catcalls, and grins on every face.

He strode up to the rope, examined it carefully, hoisted himself a few feet off the ground, bounced a few times, then hoisted himself up another ten feet. The shirt stretched taut across his powerful back, shoulder muscles working smoothly under the thin fabric. Silence grew as each man stepped back to watch. Adam unhaltingly raised himself thirty feet in the air. The rope stayed meekly still. Forty feet, and not a slip or faltering motion, no sign of fatigue in the muscular arms, no hesitation as he smoothly lifted his weight to fifty feet.

Dulcie had never seen a man so high off the ground. He pulled himself to the limb, swinging his body over it with ease. With a wave to the astonished spectators gathered like curious ants below him, he came back down the same effortless way.

Dulcie's heart leaped from her breast as the men, laughing, pounded him on his back, wrung his hand, and congratulated him.

The Indian wrestling was the last event. Waite was the champion of the youths' division of wrestlers but promptly lost to his cousin Robert. Robert defended the title against several and lost to Lyman. Finally it was Adam defending, Leroy attacking.

"Two falls out of three," Jem called. The audience, well aware of the animosity Leroy had for Adam, stirred and strained for a better view.

"Two out of three it is," said Leroy cheerfully, and before Adam knew it, he was off balance. "One outa three," Leroy crowed.

Adam was ready for him, and Leroy shifted his foot first.

"One even, one to go," said Robert, watching closely.

Adam assumed the position. Leroy said, so low that only Adam could hear, "You an' me's goin' to fight, Cap'n. If you don't, that yella liver o' yours is gonna be hangin' right out fo' Dulcie to take a good look at."

"Leave her out of this, you stupid animal."

"Oh, no, Cap'n. You been gittin' it in the only girl I ever loved, an' I'm takin' exception to that."

Adam felt his heart speed up. There were murmurings and restless stirrings in the viewing stand. He said, "You're wrong, Biggs."

"She let me, Cap'n, so I 'reckon she's a-lettin' you. How d'you like yo' second-hand goods?"

Adam's fury nearly blinded him. "Tell Moran to announce the match. I'll fight you. No holds barred."

Leroy grinned. "My kind o' fight, Cap'n."

Jem, looking from Adam's white fury to Leroy's mean smile, said, "I don't like this a bit."

"Your guests should enjoy it, Mr. Moran," Adam said tightly.

Jem looked at Leroy, then at Adam, taut with suppressed anger. "I guess you've got to get it out of your systems. But I reserve the right to stop this any time I see fit. Agreed?" When they nodded, he warned them, "Then, this will settle it, or I'll throw you both off my plantation."

Jem's announcement electrified the guests to screaming applause. Some of the servants inched nearer to watch. Claudine clung to 'Pollo's arm. Dulcie shrank in her seat. Adam hadn't wanted to compete, hadn't wanted any part of this, and she'd told him he ought to. Whatever hatred drove Leroy, it had to be powerful. He'd try to hurt Adam and wouldn't care how he did it.

Leroy and Adam stood face to face. "Go," said Robert, acting as referee. The two big men circled, taking measure of each other. They looked like jungle cats, graceful and ferocious.

Leroy punched at Adam's mouth. Adam, knees bent slightly, pulled his head back a few inches. Leroy's body tilted forward. With one foot Adam tapped a muscle in Leroy's ankle, and Leroy's feet went out from under him.

Dulcie sat still, her hand up to her mouth.

"One fall—Tremain," Robert intoned loudly.

"You ain't makin' no fool outa me," Leroy declared. He crouched, then leaped, his right foot shooting out, aiming for Adam's crotch. Adam's back flexed as he caught Leroy's foot and flipped him over. Leroy fell heavily face forward onto the ground. The watchers shouted joyfully.

"Two falls—Tremain! He wins!"

Leroy rose, his nose bleeding, sand ground into his skin. Roaring, he charged at Adam, both fists swinging. Blood spurting from his nose and mouth, he came on like a demented bull. Adam dealt him a staggering blow to the belly, then came back with a left that laid Leroy out cold.

The guests went wild, screaming for Leroy to get up. They surged out of the stand toward the impromptu arena. Adam made his way through the throng unsmiling. He was followed by several contestants. He was deaf to their cheers.

Dulcie stood to one side. She knew that look and was afraid to meet his eyes. In some way not clear to her, she was the cause of his anger.

Adam's entourage, mostly youths except for Robert, gradually fell away, realizing their hero had nothing to say to them. As they neared the house, Adam said to Phil, "I'll be back in a few minutes. D'you mind?"

The boys left, but Robert stayed. "I'm comin' with you, Adam, so if you need to be alone, you're goin' to have to say so."

Upstairs, Adam quickly stripped and washed in the cool water that was kept on the washstand, while Robert stalked around the room. Finally he turned to Adam, who stood, his muscles tensed, leaning over the basin, clutching the sides of the stand. "What'd Leroy say to you?"

In one swift motion Adam picked up the washbowl and hurled it, spewing water, across the room until it crashed against the far wall.

"About Dulcie?" Adam did not answer. After a while Robert said, "She likes to flirt, but that's all."

Adam struggled into clean trousers. The room was hot, and his skin was still moist. "I wouldn't know."

By the time they rejoined the other guests, Adam was polite and outwardly sociable. Only his eyes and the firm set of his jaw betrayed his cold, jealous anger. Whenever Dulcie came near, her golden eyes unwittingly provocative, the hot, searing anger stirred in the frozen pit deep within.

He left the parlor, where clusters of young people played a variety of games, half-expecting Dulcie to follow him. He paced the grand entrance hall alone, tormenting himself with thoughts of Leroy Biggs and Toby Dobbs and Andrew Whitaker and he didn't know how many other men.

When she finally came out of the parlor, he was at her side in two long strides. He took her wrist, dragging her into Jem's empty study. He shut the door, leaning against it. Dulcie backed away from him.

His eyes glittered dangerously. Tightly reined emotion worked on his face, threatening to break loose into violence as he stared at her. He stalked her, his voice low and intent. "Have you ever been with a man—any man?"

She opened her mouth, horrified and frightened to the core of her being. Her face crumpled. She drew back, slapping him. He grabbed her shoulders. "Answer me, Dulcie!" he rasped. *"Answer me!"* He began to shake her.

"No!" she cried. "No! No! No!" Her voice rose on the edge of hysteria. The door opened. Adam stared into Robert's stern face.

"Go to your room, Dulcie." His eyes were steady on Adam. "I'll see to your guest."

Dulcie ran to Robert. He gently pushed her toward the door. When she was gone, Robert said, "You should have taken my word. She flirts, that's all. She doesn't even understand why you are so angry."

Adam stared bleakly at him, the anger draining away, leaving only remorse and jealousy to haunt him.

It was unusually sultry even for Savannah in July. The young ladies were resting, refreshing themselves for the festivities that evening. Quiet fell over Mossrose.

Dulcie hadn't invited anyone to share her cool room. She was tired of whispers and trivial girlish secrets. She wanted to lie alone on the crisp sheets, her hair unbound. She wanted to languish in the hopeless luxury of dreaming about Adam.

She stirred restlessly, her voice dull. "Oh, Claudine, Adam will never propose to me. It'll all come to nothin'."

Claudine smoothly changed hands on the heavy fan cord. "He'll come 'round, Miss Dulcie. Ah jes' doan know when."

"Oh, if it could be true." She grew pensive and flopped back onto the bed, then leaped up to pace the room. "I can't stand bein' closed in here another minute."

"Wheah you think yo' gwine? You ain't traipsin' aroun' by yo'seff."

"Please don't fuss at me, Claudine. Come with me."

Hersel complained, "Miss Dulcie, it's too hot to be takin' hosses out."

In an excellent imitation of Jem's roar, Dulcie said, "Hersel! Shut your mouth and get me that horse!"

"She ain't saddled yit."

"Who cares!" She vaulted onto the horse's back. She laid the whip on Strawberry. They seemed to float ahead of the dust that rose from the red earth. Once she had crossed the pasture, scattering the milk cows, and put the hilly cornfields between herself and the house, she slowed the mare to a walk. She shook her russet hair free and let it ripple down around her shoulders like live flame competing with the sun.

"You ain't gwine fin' nothin' but trouble feelin' like you is, Miss Dulcie."

"Don't nag me, Claudine! Shut up and ride!" They trotted through the piney woods, then out into the sunshine, heading for a cool green grove of willow oaks. Dulcie's mood cleared, and she turned to Claudine with a grin. "Why don't we swim? It's a perfect day for it."

"How you gwine 'splain yo' wet clo's?"

"I'll swim in my shimmy. Come on, Claudine, nobody'll see us."

"Wheah de young mastahs be at? Sho' doan wan' 'em catchin' us."

"Why, they . . ." Dulcie reined in, putting her fingers to her lips. "Are they down at the dam? I thought I heard somethin'."

Stealthily the two girls crept along the woodland path until they could see the large pool in the small swift-moving creek.

"Oh, Lawd. You din't oughta look. Dey's mother nekkid."

Claudine was looking, avidly. Dulcie usurped the small hole in the bushes. She had never seen a man without any clothing on.

Nearly all the young men were there. They were playing in the water, splashing and yelling. One or two at a time they scrambled up the sloping bank facing the watching girls, stood poised for a moment, then dived back into the clear depths. Dulcie stood statuelike.

"Miss Dulcie."

"Shh!"

"Ah found a bigger peekyhole iffen you squat down heah."

Everything that had been obscured by leaves and twigs sprang into view. Once more the war inside her began. Patricia's lifelong teaching waged furious battle with the hot-blooded feelings coursing through her. She fought hard to press the sinful thoughts away. She gasped, "Men without their clothes on look terrible!"

Claudine giggled softly. "No'm, dey doan. Mastah Andrew dere, he got a middlin' nice body. Lots o' real strong muscle. Mastah Leroy lookin' purty good. Mastah Glenn's real slendah, ain't he?" She stifled a giggle. "Ooh, my, jes' catch a peek at his li'l twiggy thing! 'Taint hardly bigger'n mah thumb! But them's the kin' you wanta watch out fo', Miss Dulcie, sometimes they puff up nice an' give you a real happy s'prise."

Dulcie glared at her. "Hush! What do you know about men's things?"

"Ah seen a plenty things on black mens an' white mens. Lots o' dem big bulls got li'l horns."

Dulcie sucked in her breath. Adam Tremain stood on the bank. The midafternoon sun highlighted his heavy muscles and his smoothly tanned skin, casting soft shadows along the firm planes of his face.

Water ran in gleaming rivulets from his glossy curling hair to make bright streamers that lay across his collarbone and sparkled among the black hairs that covered his broad chest. Dulcie's gaze followed the hairs as they dwindled to a narrow path down his belly, then formed a wide triangle at his loins. She stared, then jerked her eyes away, on down his tapered thighs to the green grass at his feet. Unwillingly, her gaze rose again and lingered.

He was proud of his body.

Dulcie felt her heart hammering. Surely Adam would hear. Her voice trembled, and she shivered in the heat. "Let's go, Claudine. They'll see us."

"Yes'm. Mastah Adam got a body dat know what to do wiff itseff."

Dulcie, red to the roots of her hair, said, "You see too much!" She didn't want to talk of Adam as they had the others, not even with Claudine.

"Yes'm, but he got it all right out dere for lookin' at."

"We shouldn't have been lookin'!"

"Take mah word, white folks has got the wrong ideas 'bout dey bodies. Lawd done made 'em somethin' to enjoy, not somethin' to be 'shamed 'bout."

"All *right!*" She mounted Strawberry and swatted her irritably. If only she were a lady, like Mama wanted her to be, she wouldn't have all these confusing fancies that made her blood stir and her body long for . . . something. She lashed her horse again, trying to escape the image of Adam Tremain, posed in naked beauty on the bank of a cool stream.

Claudine, riding some distance behind, had much the same thoughts as her mistress. But Claudine was enjoying hers.

Late that night Adam was still lying awake. He punched his pillow for the hundredth time and sought a cooler place in the hot feather ticking. Finally he sat on the edge of the bed, running his fingers through his hair and yawning. He missed having a deck to walk on, a breeze to cool him.

He pulled on trousers and shirt, tucking in the shirt tails with unnecessary vigor. Barefoot, he walked down the hall, his eyes flicking to Dulcie's closed door and went downstairs into the blessed coolness of the yard.

The grass was soothing under his feet. He walked aimlessly, his mind seething. He'd never seen Dulcie act toward anyone the way she had toward him that evening—almost desperately flirtatious, roguish, then as if she realized she was taunting and unmaidenly, coolly ignoring him. He deserved whatever she chose to deal him, he knew, for his atrocious behavior toward her; but a nagging doubt wouldn't be dislodged.

Perhaps Dulcie had really wanted Leroy to win, to put

him in his place, to humiliate him. He'd ignored her barbed remarks. Did she think Leroy could accomplish what she could not? In spite of Robert's reassurances and Dulcie's denials, was there something between her and Leroy? Leroy had married during her absence. Suppose she had been in love with him and was merely using Adam in some girlish intrigue?

The idea made him walk faster, his hands behind him. After a number of paces he automatically turned about as he would on deck. Then he stopped short, laughing wryly at himself. He made himself continue down the hill to the folly.

He sat on a bench, listening to the crickets and the liquid notes of a mockingbird. Above the night sounds came another, a shuffling across the grass. Adam stood up when Claudine came hesitantly into the folly.

"Mastah Adam, you be all right?" Her voice was soft, concerned.

"I just needed a walk." He smiled. She continued to look at him, her face unreadable in shadow. "What are you doing out here, Claudine?"

"Ah got me a lover-man Ah gwine visit wiff. Ah done pick up yo' shirt an' britches an' warsh an' mend 'em fo' you, Mastah Adam."

"I saw they were gone. Thank you." He tried to see her expression. Surely there was something she wanted, something to tell him. "What is it, Claudine? Miss Dulcie?"

"Yassuh," said Claudine, sounding relieved. "Ah see you a man what got a pow'ful need. An' Miss Dulcie a mighty con-foozed lady. She gittin' notions 'bout gent'mens she ain't nevah had befo'. You know dat's a itch ladies cain't git scratched. Ain't nothin' dey kin do 'bout deyseffs, not iffen dey stays ladies. An' de way she actin' this evenin', it try de patience o' a mahble saint. She cain't he'p dat either. Cain't you jes' kinda ovahlook Miss Dulcie's manners 'til she gits herseff set right?"

Adam laughed. "I can try, Claudine."

"Thanky, suh." She turned away.

"Claudine . . ."

She tensed, though she did not turn toward him. "Yassuh?"

"Oh, never mind. Nothing."

She looked over her shoulder. "Miss Dulcie never send me out heah. Servants gotta see an' doan see, heah an' doan heah. Ah do dat, Mastah Adam, an' sometimes Ah does somethin' 'bout it, an' sometimes Ah doan do nothin'."

Chapter Fourteen

During the days following the tournament Adam visited neighboring planters. By the end of the week he had shipping commitments from Whitakers and Actons. Country people enjoyed visitors. A ship's captain was a curiosity, and it was an honor to have such a well-spoken, attractive man call on a county family, even on business.

It was much the same wherever he went: the leisurely talk with the family, a hearty noon meal, the numerous personal questions asked in a tone of consuming interest. Business was tended to last, for once it was concluded, Adam would leave, taking the one bright patch of the day with him.

He usually tried to get back to Mossrose by three o'clock. He wanted to spend the time with Dulcie, who had recovered from that one evening's foolish mood. On their walks and rides with the cousins she was gay and spirited. Yet they were seldom alone. She had other guests; and Adam was struggling against a growing desire for her that he did not want too severely tested.

By Friday morning he could no longer resist. He took her, chaperoned by Claudine, to the Chilcotes'. They had a pleasant day, Dulcie talking to Blossom with a newly dawning interest in household and marriage, while Adam and Jan conducted their business. They rode home in the hot, golden afternoon.

Suddenly Adam stopped. "Claudine, will you hold the horses for a few minutes? I saw something in here the other day that I think Dulcie will enjoy."

He led Dulcie down a narrow woodland path high with weeds to a turning where they were completely hidden from the road. "Adam, where are you takin' me?" Dulcie laughed. Her hair blazed, her creamy skin with the blush of rose glowed in the afternoon sun. "What is it you want me to see?"

He walked a few paces farther. "Come here, Dulcie." He took her in his arms, her mouth open against his. It was not enough. There could never be enough of Dulcie. He was working himself up fruitlessly—but how good it felt to have her body against him. He pulled his mouth away from hers and pressed her cheek against his wildly hammering heart. "Listen to it, Dulcie, it's telling you all the things I can't."

Her hand moved across the broad curve of his chest. "Oh, Adam. I've wanted to be with you. Why is it so difficult?" She raised her head. His lips, touching hers in exquisite tenderness, turned harsh, almost brutal. He held her away from him.

"We're going back to the road," he said grimly.

"Why?" All her heart was in her gaze.

Desire stood naked and exposed in Adam's eyes. "We'll go back now, Dulcie, or you'll walk with me deeper into the woods."

She threw her arms around him, holding herself against him, for his own arms were limp at his sides. "Don't make me decide. Just . . ."

Slowly his hand caressed her back. He looked down at the mass of red hair that covered his shirt front. He wanted her, how much he wanted her. But not to be taken like a field hand in the woods. Not with Claudine waiting and knowing. Not with Dulcie a sacrifice to his lusts.

He kissed the top of her head, raising her face so she looked into his eyes. He kissed her forehead, then placed her hand in his, looking at the slender white hand resting in the cradle of his large tanned one. Tears formed in Dulcie's eyes but did not spill. "I'll come with you, Adam."

He smiled at her, shaking his head. "Now I know what I wanted to show you—a man who's a fool." They walked down the narrow trail together.

Claudine's surprise was only too evident when they returned so soon. Quickly she dropped the reins and moved into the back seat, puzzling over what had happened. She knew about men, and she knew about women. But when a lady met a gentleman, there were such heavy consequences to pay for being pleasured. She wasn't sure what took place before nature defeated convention.

That night Dulcie could not sleep. She pretended to, waiting for Claudine to slip out to the quarters, not to return until the rising bell sounded. At long, long last Dulcie's door was closed stealthily. She was alone.

She stood at the window. The moon was bright, throwing the front lawn into deeply sculptured light and shadow. The folly and the white iron benches, ghostlike, wavered in front of her eyes.

Slowly, as one in a dream, Dulcie untied the blue ribbon of her thin silk nightgown and let it drift into a pool at her feet. She stood naked, bathing in moonglow, smiling to herself at this secret ritual.

She stood on tiptoe, running her palms sensuously over her hips and along her breasts as a lover might, until she held her hands lifted to the brilliant moon. Adam. Oh, Adam. Hold me, love me, make me yours.

Though it violated every precept of her time, though it flaunted the stringent rules of moral purity that had guided her from birth, Dulcie had come to recognize and accept her own driving need. She would offer herself to the man she loved. A man who, perhaps not knowing it yet, loved her in return.

Dulcie drew on her gown and a lacy silk robe. She tiptoed down the hall, past Adam's room and out onto the balcony. Her heart beating quickly with excitement, she stood against the wall, a wraith in the moonlight gloom.

She would go in Adam's window, motionless as a shadow. She would stand beside his bed, reach out her fingers, and touch him in his sleep. He would wake, and . . . Adam would know why she had come.

Or she would tap lightly on his window. He would not be sleeping. He would hear her and come to her.

In the end Dulcie did none of these things. She could not. The step was too big, too final.

She stood with her palms pressed flat against the wall that separated them and could not bring herself to go to him.

Adam, restless in his bed with pent-up passion, was savagely considering going to Savannah to find relief that any woman could provide, but only Dulcie could fulfill. Only Dulcie. He groaned and turned over, his penis hot and engorged between his belly and the smooth sheets. In his fantasy Dulcie lay with him, held him, cradled him. Dulcie, my sweet, my darling.

He let out a long breath and fell asleep.

* * *

He went on Tuesday to see Cal Saunders. Their business was finished within an hour, and Adam was on his way back to Mossrose in an afternoon so stifling it was like being smothered in moist blankets. It would rain soon. He'd welcome a hard rain.

He galloped up the lane and dismounted outside the stables. He could hear Hersel arguing. "Miss Dulcie, it be swelterin' terday. You gwine give dis hoss de sunstruck. Mastah Jem woan like dat."

"Hersel, this makes twice in a week you've refused to do your job. Do you want me to report you to Mastah Jem?"

Adam looked into the stables. Hersel, his lips in a pout, was tightening the saddle on Dulcie's mare. "You gwine git caught in de stawm."

"I'll go with her, Hersel. Miss Dulcie'll be all right."

Dulcie saw him, and her eyes lighted. She smiled. "Thank you, Hersel," she said sweetly. They moved sedately down the lane to the fields.

"Where am I to escort you, Dulcie?"

"Anywhere," she said, still smiling. "As far as we can go."

"Don't tempt me. I might take you to New Orleans with me."

She flicked Strawberry lightly, and the mare broke into a canter. Adam's blue roan stayed at her side. "Don't tempt *me*. I might accept."

They rode across the cotton fields into the willow oak woods along the creek, following paths Dulcie knew well and Adam had come to know.

They crossed a dry, fallow field, then entered the piney woods.

Dulcie reined in. She tore off her snood, shaking her hair until it spilled in a russet cascade over her shoulders. Feeling wild and free, she gazed at the towering pines, conical, spearing the heavens. She searched through the heavy boughs for sight of the wonder the forest promised, then her eyes lowered and met Adam's. They laughed in delight. "Doesn't it smell good, Adam?"

Around them the calm settled. Birds stopped singing and returned to nest, foxes sought their lairs, deer with folded legs snuggled into the brush. All the woodland creatures sought mate and home before the coming storm.

Adam dismounted. "All I can smell is your perfume. Just flowers." His eyes held hers, and his smile dimmed. He held up his arms, then she was off her horse and standing in front of him. He said her name only once. The dark green trees soughed. His mouth came down on hers hard, his moustache coarse against her lips. With one viselike arm he cradled her against him as though he would never let her go.

He drew his head away, his breath coming hard. "Dulcie." His lips met hers again, and she was open to him, letting him in, letting his tongue taste hers. His hand moved under her jacket to the edge of her breast, unfettered except for the thin shirt.

She turned a little toward his hand, wanting him to touch her, explore her, know her fully.

He rained kisses on her face, her throat, on her breast through its fragile covering, murmuring without knowing it the words he had spoken only in a waking dream. "My darling. You're all I can think about. Dulcie, let me make love to you. I want you so."

The summer storm heat closed around them, was within them, throbbing, pressing, urgent, struggling to be free. Slowly, then faster, creeping in sighing gusts, the wind blew through the pines.

In the distance a sharp crack of thunder rolled across the greeny-gray heavens.

Dulcie said breathlessly, "There's an old log house . . ."

The horses stamped uneasily. The first rain fell softly on the boughs above them. Adam glanced at the restive animals, then looked back into Dulcie's languorous eyes.

The wind rose swiftly then, the tops of the pines bent and rubbed against each other in a melancholy music. Suddenly mobilized, he lifted her to her horse. They rode quickly down the seldom used forest path.

They tied the horses in front of a low door that sagged on its hinges. He held out his hand, and Dulcie followed him trustingly. He pushed the door to, its primitive hinges protesting as he closed the world out.

Dulcie moved away from him, looking into the murky corners of the room where Adam would take her. There was a gaping hole in the roof. There were no windows, no opening for light to enter. She looked at Adam uncertainly. "Well . . . we certainly are here."

A loud booming of thunder, followed by brilliant flashing lightning, made her flinch. Rain poured through the hole in the shingles.

"You weren't afraid of a storm at sea." He stood tensely, feet a little apart, hands loosely at his sides.

She was nervous, shivering despite the heat. Her eyes clung to him. Doubts assailed him. Flexible as his tastes were in women, his honor bound him to the customs of the society he lived in. Some women existed for his pleasure alone, and he used them for that. Could he vent mere lust on Dulcie?

He loved her. The thought rocked him, robbing him of the remorseless desire to take her as he had the others. "You're getting wet, Dulcie," he said, softly teasing. He put his hands out, motioning her to him.

She lurched into his arms. He held her gently, stroking her. His mouth on hers was tender. More than to possess her, he wanted to protect her. "Nothing has happened. It's not too late to turn back, my love."

"Oh, Adam . . . Adam . . . Adam, hold me! Don't let me go—ever."

He buried his hands and face in her hair. She pressed her breasts, her loins against him, wrenching inarticulate sounds of love from the depths of him. With his tongue he forced her mouth open, seeking, and the flame swept Dulcie as it was sweeping him, making his arms tremble as he held her.

Presently she felt her jacket being unbuttoned, and obeying his murmured commands, she began to undress him. His coat fell to the floor, covering hers. His fingers were at the green silk tie around her neck. It floated away in the gloom. Then her shirt slipped from her shoulders.

She stood quivering, resisting the impulse to hide her bared breasts from this large man to whom she thought to give herself. "Take off my shirt," he whispered. With shaking fingers she obeyed. The curling black hair that matted his chest sprang into view. He took her hand in his, placing it against his breast as he touched hers. His fingers burned against her flesh, sending an unbearable thrill through her.

"Touch me as I touch you. Let me feel you caress me, Dulcie." Hesitantly at first, her hands moved over the heavy muscles that mounded smoothly across his chest, feeling their taut contours with growing excitement.

His arms were around her, bending her backward in the crook of his arm so that his mouth moved down, down to kiss each breast longingly, lovingly. Her long riding skirt fell around her ankles.

Her voice shook as she said, "I . . . I came to you in the night, Adam."

"What?" He was barely listening.

"Friday night, very late. I . . . was awake. I stood . . . unclothed. I wanted—I wanted to come to you."

A bitter vision of himself sprang into Adam's mind.

"I . . . stood outside your window. Oh, Adam, why didn't you know? I wanted to go on, but I was so afraid."

He kissed her and held her tenderly. "Are you afraid now, Dulcie?"

"A little, but I need you. Adam, hold me."

"Dulcie." He drew her hand down to his throbbing penis. His tongue went into her mouth, moving back and forth, probing, tantalizing. She responded, trembling, eager, caressing him through his trousers.

He jerked the tape that held up her pantalettes. Dulcie gasped, her breath searing her lungs. She stood naked. The lightning played on her breasts, the gentle swell of her hipbones, on the dark triangle below her belly.

He ran trembling fingers over her breasts, holding them almost reverently, bending to kiss each taut upturned nipple. The scent of her perfume, sweet as flowers, cool with her innocence yet spiced and warmed by her rapid heartbeats, mingled with that aphrodisiac other fragrance, the strong, sharp scent of her readiness for him.

His head grew light. His blood raced.

His hands moved down flat against her belly, his thumbs caressing her thighs where they parted.

Dulcie looked into his darkened eyes, her own half-closed, her nostrils flaring with passion. It was this she wanted, the touch of her lover's hands upon her secret flesh, the union of his body with hers, holding him within her as she had held no man.

His hands moved on her gently, making them both shudder.

He placed her fingers on the top button of his trousers. His lips were on hers, his tongue sliding against hers, as she fumbled shakily with the tight fastening.

Adam moaned softly as he murmured her name. She

jumped away from him, drawing in her breath in a screaming gasp. Rain and the wind whirled through the small room as the door let go of its hinges and crashed to the floor behind Adam. Then her heart exploded in her breast, leaving her without the means to breathe.

Wolf.

The torrential rain poured down on the overseer, funneling off his sodden hat down his neck, streaming down his filthy shirt and trousers. He smiled hungrily at Dulcie, a grimace of broken, tobacco-stained teeth, his face flushed with lust. With one hand he held his erect penis, moving the hand away from himself and back with rapid purpose. Then his body curved forward, his face growing red and tight, his body twitching in pleasured spasms.

Adam instinctively moved toward Wolf. "Oh, God! You stinkin' *bastard!*"

Dulcie's breath came in sobs. He took her in his arms, pressing her face against his chest, shielding her from Wolf's obscenity.

It was over in seconds. "I been a-watchin' y'all," Wolf grinned.

Adam, unable to move without exposing Dulcie, was white with impotent rage. His voice shook. "Get out of here!"

"Naow don't y'all worry none. I wouldn't tell Mr. Moran." Wolf grinned again. "But I ain't a-gonna fergit what-all I seen, neither."

"You son of a bitch. I'm going to kill you." Adam's voice was deep and grating.

"Cap'n," said Wolf in the burlesque of respect he loved to show his betters, "you ain't a-gonna kill me. Dulcie's treated me like shit ever since she was a snot-nosed brat. Naow things is changed, ain't they. I seen her fer what she is. I ain't a-gonna fergit that. No sirree!"

Adam's hands tightened painfully. He pressed against the back of Dulcie's head as though he would drive her inside the protective shell of his own body.

Wolf moved out of sight. Quickly Adam picked up his frock coat. He wrapped it around her. She turned her face from him, shamed and horrified. She stood paralyzed with humiliation, clutching his coat against her.

They heard the sharp crack of a whip and Wolf's shouted "Giddap!" As the horses whinnied, Adam sprang through the door. Strawberry and the blue roan cantered riderless into the pines.

Wolf was mounting his own horse. Adam, running, was almost on him when, laughing, Wolf whipped his horse. The animal leaped forward, taking him out of Adam's reach. He reined in and turned around. "Cap'n, y'all ain't a-gonna do *nuthin'*." He disappeared into the storm.

The rain pelted down coldly on Adam. His breathing hurt his chest. In frustrated fury he returned to the cabin. Dulcie cowered in the darkest corner. She looked up in fear as he stood in the doorway, water running from his body to make darker pools on the dirt floor.

Adam shuddered. "Oh, God, Dulcie." He wanted to erase the terrible moments by his presence, to hold her against him to stop her shaking and make her feel loved and safe once more.

She cringed at his touch. Her voice was high. "D-don't touch me!"

He put out his hands to her. She pressed herself against the filthy damp wall. He touched her hair, his face sad and tender. "Don't do this, Dulcie, don't."

"Don't look at me!" she shrieked, her eyes wide, filled with shame.

He laid her clothes in a pile near her. "Get dressed, Dulcie," he said gently and reached for his coat. She grasped at it, clawing at the material as she held it tightly against her. "No! Go away. Let me be!"

"Don't be ashamed, Dulcie. You . . . you could never be anything but beautiful to me. I'm sorry it happened."

A strangled sound tore from her throat. Once more he tried to touch her, and she shrank from him. "I won't look at you, darling."

"Don't call me darling! Don't call me anythin'! Don't speak to me—ever!"

"I was just going to hold the coat for you, like a screen."

With a quick bend of her knees she grabbed for her pantalettes. "Turn around!" She struggled one-handed to put the pantalettes on, still holding his coat against her, not trusting him to keep his back turned. He heard the rustling of cloth as his coat fell to the floor, her hysterical commands. "Stay as you are! Don't look!"

"Dulcie, please—listen to me."

She swept past him, running for the door. He grabbed her arm, spinning her around so that she stood pinned against him. "What do you think you're doing? You can't go out there alone."

She struggled, then gave up, staring past him, her mouth set, her eyes fixed on nothing.

He released her, gently caressing her arms. "I'm sorry, Dulcie. Things seem to turn out wrong for us."

"So you said." Her voice was toneless.

"It would have been an act of joy, not a thing to remember in shame—"

"Oh?" Her eyes flickered over his bare chest, then rose to his mouth and to his eyes. Her gaze was filled with bitter self-pity. "Shall I undress for you again?"

Blood swept his face like a dark flame.

Tears formed in her golden eyes, but she held herself straighter and disciplined her trembling mouth. "Adam, if you had said once, just one time, that you loved me, even if it was a lie . . . But you didn't say it, did you?"

Adam hesitated too long, her hypocrisy choking him.

Her tears spilled over. "You needn't bother, Captain Tremain," she said woodenly. "Your opportunity has passed. I no longer wish to hear—anything."

"And you won't, Miss Moran."

She turned away from him, her back stiff. But she waited until he was dressed, and they walked together out of the cabin into the heavy rain.

As they neared the edge of the woods in sight of the plantation buildings, Adam said, "I'm going to carry you."

"You are *not!*"

He scooped her up, holding her so tightly she could not kick him. "Put your arm around my neck. Your horse fell. You hurt your back."

"I'm not goin' to lie."

"You are, and I am. And if you must stay in bed for a day or two to preserve your reputation, consider it worthwhile."

It was a long distance across the fields to the house, and all the way Dulcie was forced to listen to the regular beating of Adam's heart.

Patricia, standing anxiously at the window, saw them coming. She flew to the back door. "Dulcie, honey, what's happened to you, baby?"

"I'm all right, Mama," Dulcie said hastily. "Strawberry caught her foot and threw me. And when Adam picked

me up, a terrible crack of thunder made the horses bolt.
He's had to carry me the whole way home. I've strained
my back, I think."

With Patricia and Claudine hovering anxiously, Adam
laid Dulcie very gently on her bed and departed immediately, closing the door.

"Is the pain very bad, honey?" asked Patricia as Claudine began stripping off her sodden garments.

Now Dulcie let the scalding tears flow. "Oh, Mama, it
hurts. It hurts!"

The flurry of activity and attention ended. Patricia went
downstairs. Dulcie lay in bed, a book open by her, but she
was looking out the window at the rain.

"Miss Dulcie, you dint hut yo' back. Somethin' else happen."

Dulcie looked at Claudine without answering. She began
to read. Soon Patricia would gently lecture her about the
inadvisability of being alone with a gentleman. Dulcie
would say that it was happenstance, how lucky he had
come along then, and explain that Adam had been very
kind.

"You ain't cryin' 'cause o' yo' back."

"I'm not cryin' at all!"

"No'm, but the tears leakin' anyway. Did you an' Mastah
Adam fin'lly have each other?"

Dulcie's look was at first shocked, then defiant, then the
bitter despair overlaid her features. "Oh, Claudine, he
could never love me now!"

She knew that nothing she would say could astound
Claudine. In words poured out against the pillow while
Claudine rubbed her back soothingly, she relived the moments of being lovingly held and—almost—taken. The
revulsion of seeing Wolf, the glimpse of his hand before
Adam had shielded her. Now, the awful, abysmal sense
of dishonor, degradation, of utter loss.

"Miss Dulcie, you got to put a good face on it. Iffen
you does any mo' cryin', yo' mama gwine know somethin'
ain't what you says."

"Claudine, I'm ruined anyway, I might as well—"

"De only way you ruin' is in yo' own min'. An' dat's
de worst way. But you ain't gwine do it wiff him, not any
mo'."

"What would be the difference? If my mind is soiled,

then my body might as well enjoy it. That's all that's left
to me now."

"No, ma'am!" Claudine said emphatically. "You tries it
now, you jes' gettin' even wiff yo'seff, an' it won't be no
fun no way! You is gwine stay in baid 'til Mastah Adam
leave. Dey ain't gwine be no slippin' out an' makin' ev'thin'
wuss!"

"Since when are you my mammy?"

"Jes' hesh yo' mouf. We gwine git you thoo dis 'thout a
scratch."

The house stayed quiet, too quiet, until dinnertime. Even
the youngest cousins tiptoed in deference to Dulcie's injury. After dinner Jeannie, Jenny, Gay, and Millie came
hesitantly to her door. Soon they were twittering like
gaily dressed birds. At dark Claudine left, making Gay
promise that she would sleep overnight in the trundle bed
by Dulcie. "Ah got a lots o' warshin' to do," she explained.
"Might take me a long time."

So Dulcie was imprisoned, though with her favorite
cousin.

Adam endured the evening with forced smiles, pretended
hilarity, and good nature as the men played poker. After
a run of poor luck he put down his cards and concealed a
yawn. Without hurry, he excused himself.

As he lit the lamp in his room, a movement caught his
eye. "Claudine! Is Dulcie—?"

"She fine, Mastah Adam. Ah come to tell you dat," she
said with a strange calm.

He looked at her thoughtfully.

Claudine moved deeper into the room, nearer to him.
"You a fine gent'man." Her eyes admired him, too lingeringly.

"Did Mr. Moran send you here?" he asked harshly.

"Nossuh!" she said indignantly. "Mastah Jem doan do
dat wiff his niggers. We's too val'able. Ain't nobody send
me."

Adam crossed his arms in wary silence.

"Ah come to you 'cause you needin' a woman bad."

"Well, that's nothing to do with you." He indicated the
door.

"Ah knows how to pleasure a man right smart. Ah'd
in-joy pleasurin' you." Her smile was gentle and dreamy.

His voice was hard as steel. "When I'm a man's guest,

I don't use his servants for my private gratification. Get the hell out of my room!" He held the door open, then closed it firmly after her.

He changed into dark gray trousers and sweater. Every muscle tense, he sat on the balcony, listening for the noises of the poker party to cease. His eyes, accustomed to night watching, saw the lights go out in the quarters and an occasional subtle change in the dark as someone moved across it.

He waited another hour, then swung over the balcony railing, and made his way down the ornamental iron pillar. His clothing blended in with the murky darkness. He ran through the yard, keeping to the trees, stealthily slipping past the slave quarters.

Wolf's cabin stood out from the others. It was larger, and a lamp lit its windows. He kicked the door open. The overseer lay with a slatternly looking Negress, wearing only his filthy union suit, a pointed lump in its front.

Both Wolf's and the woman's eyes bulged. Adam filled the low doorway. He motioned to the woman. As she sidled past him, Adam moved pantherlike, his hand chopping sharply at Wolf's erection. Wolf shrieked and clutched himself with a grimace of surprised pain.

Adam stood over him. "Wolf, I hear you've been telling lies about me. I don't like that."

"Jesus Christ, Cap'n," Wolf groaned hoarsely. "What you talkin' 'bout? I ain't said nothin' 'bout nobody!"

Adam's hand shot out, palm up, fingers stiff, and caught Wolf in the pit of his stomach. Wolf groaned. His hand moved to protect himself. "I never told nothin'—I swear! I ain't a-gonna say nothin'!"

Outside the Negroes began to gather. Black voices started singing. "Ah's dreamin' now of Hallie, sweet Hallie, sweet Hallie."

Then, as the noises in the cabin grew louder, so did the chorus: "Lissen to de mockin' bud, lissen to de mockin' bud!"

Panicked, cornered, Wolf grabbed his whiskey bottle, hitting it on the table. Glass and liquor splattered. On his toes, prepared to spring, Adam circled. Wolf's breath came in sharp, painful gasps. Adam lunged with a knife-edged chop that broke Wolf's left arm. Enraged with pain and crazy with fright, Wolf struck down with the broken bottle neck, grinding it into Adam's shoulder.

Adam broke two of Wolf's ribs with a sickening snap. Oblivious to the pain in his shoulder or to the overseer's agonized howls, Adam worked Wolf over with painful jabs that made the man's muscles writhe.

Wolf lay crumpled in the corner. Adam stood over him panting, fury still distorting his features. "Go near her, breathe a word to her or about her—I'll find out. I'll come after you. I'll kill you."

"I . . . won't . . . talk," Wolf moaned.

Adam strode out of the cabin. As he passed the blacks, a hundred hands reached out to touch him. Old 'Simmon whispered, "Thanky, Mistah. Thanky."

Behind him Barney closed Wolf's door. The others melted into their cabins. Deaf to his pathetic whimpering, they would let Wolf lie till morning.

Adam went up noiselessly the way he'd come down. He stripped off his clothes. Naked, he went to the washbowl, soaped and rinsed himself. Toweling his body, he realized blood was still dripping down his arm.

He lit the lamp and leaned toward the mirror, struggling to reach the wound.

"Ah fix it fo' you," said a soft voice.

He jumped nearly out of his skin. *"What—?"* He suddenly remembered to lower his voice. He hissed, "I told you to get out."

"Ah seen what you doin' an' Ah come back 'case you need help."

Adam, aware of his nakedness, looped the towel around his loins and tucked it in. "All right," he said angrily. "Get that damned cut stopped!"

"You got to set down. You's so high up, Ah cain't see nothin'."

Claudine's fingers moved skillfully along his shoulder, cleansing the gouge, soaking it with bay rum, finally stopping the bleeding. She poured the bloodied water into the slop jar, dropping the used towel into it. "Ah take that out after a bit," she said, gazing at him steadily.

Adam remained seated, not wanting to risk standing up and losing his towel. She blew out the lamp. Then she was kneeling in front of him. She undid his covering, and her quick fingers circled his penis. "Ah's gwine pleasure you real fine." She bent her head down toward him.

* * *

Adam roused to a tapping at his door. He looked around hastily. The sun was high. Claudine was gone. "Just a minute!" He dressed and opened the door.

Jem was standing there, a shotgun in his hand. "There's trouble at the quarters. Some' o' the darkies gave Wolf a hell of a beatin'."

Adam, Robert, and Jem, all armed, walked to Wolf's cabin. "He in heah, Mastah Jem," said 'Simmon. "He say he bad hurt."

Wolf lay on his stinking bunk, groaning. His eyes flew open when he saw Adam. He tried to rise and fell back. "Don't hurt me anymore!"

Jem looked sharply at Adam. "Is he talkin' to you?"

"Are you talkin' to me, Wolf?" Adam asked, incredulously.

"Nossir, nossir. Thought you was somebody else." Wolf was holding his left arm, breathing with evident pain.

Jem demanded, "Who did this to you, Wolf?"

"Nobody, Mr. Moran," Wolf asserted stoutly.

"Don't talk crap! Was it the darkies?"

"If anybody's missin' that's who it was, Mr. Moran."

"Out with it, Wolf! Were you foolin' around with somebody's woman?"

"Yeah, that's it, Mr. Moran. I got me into a whorehouse brawl in S'vannah." His eyes darted to Adam. "Jes' barely made it home."

"That was damn stupid. One more time, Wolf, and your ass is off my plantation. Barney!! Get Ludy and have her put Wolf back together."

"Yassuh." Barney moved with leisurely relish toward the nursery.

As they walked back to the house, Adam began, "I'm sorry to tell you this—now that you're having trouble with your overseer—".

Jem eyed him apprehensively. "You know somethin' about this?"

"No, sir. I'm leaving earlier than I had planned. I've got to be in Savannah to see to my cargo."

Jem's face was a mixture of relief and disappointment. "You know I'm mighty sorry that you can't stay. We've got a fine big soiree planned for you on Saturday evenin'. Maybe you could make it back for that?"

Adam shook his head regretfully. "We'll still be loading

then, sir. Mr. Moran, your hospitality has been first-rate. It's been so pleasant here, I wish I could stay."

Jem beamed. "I'm sure Dulcie will be sorry to see you go, Adam."

The unspoken question hung between them.

"Perhaps so, sir. Dulcie is a charming lady. It'll be a lucky man who marries her some day." His tone was properly respectful, properly detached.

Jem, understanding his message, sighed and went into the house.

Adam and Robert strolled around the yard, smelling the aroma of breakfast bacon and biscuits. Robert mused, "Last time I saw a man take a beating like Wolf did, it was Leroy Biggs. Funny . . ."

Adam scowled at his companion. Robert's lips twitched. Their eyes met in understanding, and both looked away.

Dulcie had her own ideas about playing invalid. She did not intend to be stuck in her boresome bedroom, with Adam unable to come in or even pause in the doorway to inquire after her well-being. It was unbearable not knowing if she'd see scorn or caring on his face. Did he loathe her now? Think her cheap? Or had he spoken truly saying she was always beautiful to him?

When Patricia appeared, she smiled wanly. "I'm feeling better, Mama. I could lie on the parlor sofa today, if Daddy would help me downstairs."

"Now, honey, it'd be foolish to rush. Youah guests will undahstan'."

"But I'll be so lonely! Mama, would it be all right if Adam . . . and Robert . . . came in to visit? Claudine would be here."

Patricia looked her shock. "Dulcie Jeannette! Suhtainly *not!* Wheah is youah modesty?"

Dulcie sighed. "I didn't think you'd let me."

"Very well." Patricia tried to sound severe. "You may come downstairs."

Dulcie, propped up with pillows, wore her prettiest *canezou* and skirt of orchid Swiss muslin, and held court. But she was a wan queen, her face showing the strain and doubts of the night. The girls drifted in and out. The boys waved at her from the doorway.

Adam came in after breakfast, with Robert and Gay.

Dulcie teased Adam, laughing at his sallies. But she was thankful they were not alone, for her careful pose would crumble. They would be back at that terrible scene, wanting to speak of the thing that had nearly happened between them, needing to talk it away, but having to pretend instead that their mutual passion had never existed. Face to face, she doubted she'd have words strong or sharp enough to cut Adam to ribbons as her outraged chastity demanded.

"Oh, Dulcie, you'll enjoy this," said Gay, giggling. "That reekin', awful man Wolf got himself beaten up last night!"

Dulcie did not dare look at Adam. "He did?"

"Yes. Uncle Jem thought the darkies had done it. But Wolf admitted he'd sneaked into Savannah and gotten into a fight! Your daddy's goin' to cut off his pay until Wolf can work again!"

Dulcie said briskly, "I'm sure he deserves it."

"Adam's got news, too—but maybe you already know," Gay added coyly.

Adam said, "It can wait."

"Come on, Gay," said Robert. "Let's leave them by themselves."

Adam's eyes met Claudine's. Behind her mistress's back she smiled at him lovingly. Adam, though unsmiling, spoke gently. "You too, Claudine."

"You don't have to leave," Dulcie said quickly.

But Claudine obeyed Adam.

He got down on Dulcie's level, squatting on his heels. Dulcie glared at him, her despair of the night before replaced by an indignation that would let her cope. "Well, what is it that's so important, Captain Tremain?"

On a drawn-in breath he said, "I'm leaving today. I thought you'd want to know."

Dulcie's mask, all the sham, fell away. "Leavin'!" The thought was even more monstrous than . ... that other.

"It's the best thing I can do for you." His eyes betrayed nothing.

After a long time she felt she could speak normally. "Will you return?"

"I don't know."

Her mouth twisted. "How you must despise me now!"

She caught his naked look of despair. "I haven't changed in any way toward you. So I must go. Dulcie . . ." His voice became so soft she could barely hear it. "A man like I am doesn't use the words 'I love you' lightly. If I ever say them to a woman, it will be because I am willing and able to pledge my life to her. That is something I cannot do right now, no matter what I want."

Dulcie's eyes were dry, dark golden, filled with pain. "Adam . . . are you sayin' that you love me?"

"Don't ask me now." He touched his fingers to her lips. As he left the room, he did not say good-bye or look back.

Dulcie stared after him, her heart dead in her breast.

But at lunchtime she walked, supported by Robert, to the dining room. By Patricia's standards her decorum was perfect. Toward Adam she expressed a mild flirtatiousness, a stronger regret that he was leaving, an uninvolved liking for him.

All the relatives joined the Morans as they wished Adam Godspeed. If he was a shade too hearty when he said, "Miss Dulcie, it's been the greatest pleasure!" still, his hand squeezed hers, and his moustached mouth kissed her hand with brief tenderness.

They waved until he had gone partway down the lane, then Dulcie stood alone with Jem and Patricia, watching him retreat out of sight.

"Come along, Miss," said Jem not unkindly. "Cryin' will get you nowhere."

She turned bleak, dry eyes on him. "That's why I'm not cryin', Daddy."

"He'll be back soon, Dulcie honey," said Patricia comfortingly.

Jem cut in briskly, "If he's back, it will be on business and not to court our Dulcie. I as good as asked him his intentions only this mornin'."

"What did he say, Jem?"

Jem repeated the conversation he'd had with Adam. "I don't believe he found Dulcie . . . wantin'. But there's a cold-blooded man, Dulcie Jeannette. His kind seldom settles down. If you were to marry him, he'd snap your heart like a fiddlestring. You're well out of it, Miss. He's gone, and you can forget about him."

"Theah's still the soiree Saturday night, Dulcie. We'll have that anyway," Patricia said brightly. "Ah do b'lieve Andrew Whitaker is quite taken with you. You couldn't do better than a Whitaker. Andrew's family is—"

Dulcie looked down the empty lane. She turned a stubborn face to her parents. "It's Adam I love."

Jem's anger rose. "A one-sided sentiment that does you little credit!"

Dulcie began walking toward the house, remembering to limp slightly. She had said it! Her resolve formed itself, making her feel light and clean again. Wherever Adam Tremain went, she would follow him. She would belong to him—whatever his terms, whatever the cost.

She slowed down so that her parents could catch up with her, and took the first irrevocable step.

"Mama, Daddy, it's goin' to be terribly lonesome around here when Aunt Ca'line and her family leave Monday. Would it be all right if I went with them for a little visit? I haven't seen their new plantation, and I've always loved New Orleans."

"You've hardly been home a month!"

"Just a short visit? Please! Long enough to . . . forget."

"Daddy and Ah will talk about it," said Patricia decisively.

Chapter Fifteen

Nassau lay before Adam like a multihued jewel, while Savannah and New Orleans were an ocean behind him. Yet, all his thoughts were of those distant cities. Visions of the time he had spent at Mossrose blinded him to the hubub of Nassau's colorful Bay Street. Remembrance of moments of exquisite passion intertwined with those of humiliation and impotent fury. Twice this month a man had dirtied and destroyed a time that was good. In Savannah it had been Wolf, a lowly, self-serving man. The tender moments could not be salvaged, but Adam had taken care of Wolf as he would any small-minded blackguard.

But in New Orleans it had been Edmund Revanche, a different matter. Adam's confrontation with him at the Quadroon Ball concerned more than Solange. It had begun with Ullah, and it wouldn't end until there was a reckoning.

He was gruff as he made cargo arrangements with Fraser Trenholm and Company, not taking time to chat as he normally did. From the Confederate agents' office he went to the Royal Victoria Hotel. Neither Ben nor Beau had returned. He lay across the bed and tried to sleep while Revanche and Wolf and the ruined moments with Dulcie paraded across his mind.

Later he went to the dining room, feeling a loneliness he hadn't known since he was a boy. He glanced around the room as he toyed with his food. Men in uniforms, men who ran the blockade as he did, sat laughing and eating, enjoying the easy company of their temporary women.

The brilliant colors, the cacophony of bright, cheerful sound made his own isolation complete. He called for brandy, emptied three snifters as he might have downed rum, then walked into the warm, fragrant night.

He didn't know he'd been looking for her until he saw her in the chorus line of one of the saloons. Glory danced with the same joy-filled abandon she made love, her long legs kicking higher than the other girls, her violently scarlet-sequined costume clashing wildly with her riotous mane of red hair.

Adam took a place among the men at the long bar, ordering a brandy, sniffing it, savoring its scent and taste as he watched Glory. Her smile was broad, her sparkling eyes scanning her audience. He chuckled when Glory spotted him, leaning forward, throwing the girl next to her out of step. The others looked on, laughing as Glory waved happily at him. Adam raised his glass to her, his smile only slightly less broad than hers. For the moment the disturbing ghosts of Edmund Revanche and Wolf were banished.

Minutes after the show ended, Glory was draped over him, smudging his dark outfit where her powder made an outline of her body against him.

"Wasn't I wonderful, Adam!?" She touched her nose to his. "Did you miss me?"

Before an appreciative audience he kissed her soundly.

She touched the side of his face, her eyes already anticipating the night.

"Go get dressed, Glory," he advised, smiling, "and hurry."

She stared at him for a moment, then wriggled her hips against his. "What do I need clothes for?" She giggled and hurried off, returning quickly with a cape thrown over her shoulders, barely concealing the clashing scarlet costume. "I'm ready!"

"Christ! So am I," Adam muttered. She hurried along beside him chattering, telling him everything that had happened since she had seen him last. As they entered the hotel lobby, she said, "Oh! It's just like coming home! I missed you, Adam, I really did! Why, if I had any decency in me, just any at all, I'd forget all the others and love you always."

Ignoring the stares of the people in the lobby, some approving, others outraged, he scooped her into his arms and carried her to his room. "Just love me tonight, Glory. One night at a time."

"You're marvelous," Glory mumured, twining her fingers through his damp, curling hair. "Even when you're only half with me, you're marvelous."

He laughed softly. "Which half of me did you miss?"

She propped herself up on one elbow, staring down into his face. She said earnestly, "You've a mind full of butterfly ghosts."

"I'm half here, and I have butterfly ghosts." He pulled her down on his chest, nibbled at her ear, then whispered, "What are butterfly ghosts?"

She smiled. "Things on your mind or heart. Disturbing—"

"I've only got one thing on my mind," he said quickly. But she wasn't to be deterred. Without knowing how it happened or realizing he had wanted to talk, Adam found himself telling Glory about Edmund Revanche.

Glory curled herself into the curve of his body, then she sat up, her face animated. "Why you'll just have to do something to that man!"

Adam looked away. "I should have killed him the first time I met him."

"Kill him!" she squealed, her flame-red curls bobbing in disarray. "Oh, no! That wouldn't do any good. Once he was dead, he'd never even know he'd been killed."

Adam snorted, laughing as she shivered with indignation. "What the hell did you say anyway? That didn't make sense."

"Now, don't you tease me! Killing is just what a creature like that would expect you to do. Men are so obvious!"

Adam folded his arms behind his head, grinning. "What would you do to him, Glory?"

"I'd hit him right where it hurts—right in his insufferable, arrogant pride! And he'd be alive to know I'd done it, too!"

Adam, still smiling, was now listening carefully. "Go on. How?"

She hopped to her knees, then mounted him, sitting across his loins, her breasts bobbing as she gestured with waving arms, her eyes sparkling. "Well, doesn't he just think he's king of the anthill with all his little black ants to do his work for him? Take away his ants, and what's he king of then? Everyone in the whole South falls apart if one teeny little slave gets away. Just imagine if every black on his whole plantation vanished. Everyone would know! He could never hide that! You do haul slaves, don't you? Well, haul his."

"Clear out *all* his slaves?" Adam said slowly.

"Yes! Yes! Wouldn't it be fun? Think how completely just it'd be!"

Adam grinned. Soon he was chuckling, then laughing out loud. "Lord, but that would give me pleasure."

"You'll do it?" Glory squealed.

"Maybe. By God, maybe we will. I'll see what Ben and Beau think."

"Oh, I know they'll agree!"

Adam put his hands on either side of her head. "I wouldn't be surprised."

"Good! Now, let's make love!"

He moaned softly, shaking his head, but Glory's hands were already busy, and the rhythm of his breathing changed.

The following afternoon Glory and Adam met Ben and Beau at the dock. At first they listened quietly to the plan to rid Edmund of his slaves, but they were soon adding their own embellishments.

Ben said, "Damn! When do we go? We'll talk to that voodoo queen Ullah knew."

"Juneau Nuit," Adam said.

"There's not a darky in New Orleans that won't do exactly what she says. Jeez, Adam, it'll work!"

Beau had remained silent, his face sad. "Nothing I'd like better than to see that son of a bitch ruined. I'll go to my grave rememberin' those masks and . . ." His voice trailed off. "How do we work it, Adam?"

Adam spoke low. "Mostly everybody allows the darkies

to go to the voodoo ceremonies. I'll tell Juneau what we have in mind. During the ceremony she'll give the slaves instructions, and they'll slip away. We'll have to arrange to haul them to the ship, but—"

"Sounds easy as pie," Ben declared. "There's bound to be a hitch."

Adam shrugged. "We'll go armed and deal with surprises as they come."

"How soon?" Beau asked.

"As soon as the moon darkens again—next trip to New Orleans. Agreed?"

Ben and Beau put their hands atop each other's, and Adam covered them.

"Hey! Don't leave me out!" Glory covered their hands with her own.

They left for New Orleans aboard the *Liberty* the following month. "Damn, the only thing I don't like is that Revanche won't know it was us."

"Hell, Adam," Ben said. "Maybe you want that madman chasing around the world after you, but not me. Just take his slaves and let the bastard go crazy trying to figure out what happened."

"I want him to think of me every time he thinks of what he lost. Every time it hurts him, I want my name on his lips. He made Ullah know, he made Tom know. I want *him* to know."

Ben, looking at him, shook his head. "Send him a letter if it makes you happy. Just don't mention I was with you. I like living."

After an uneventful run they entered the noisy piers at Poydras Street. The military regalia of New Orleans increased with every trip, and interest grew steadily in the ordnance that Adam carried as cargo. Already the South was feeling the scarcity of manufactured goods. But the Southern way of gracious living continued as though there were no Yankees on Southern battlefields and no Yankee cruisers trying to close off the mouth of the Mississippi.

Ben, as captain of the *Liberty*, was immediately surrounded by agents and representatives. Adam and Beau were overseeing the removal of cargo when a small black boy raced up the gangplank, his smile wide, his eyes wider as they darted over the low, sleek blockade runner.

"Mastah Cap'n Adam Tremain!? Cap'n Tremain? Wheah Ah gwine fin' Cap'n Tremain, Mistah?"

Adam walked up to him. "What's your business with Captain Tremain, boy?"

The boy was craning to see more of the ship. "Lawdy, lawdy, ain't nothin' prettier dan dis ol' boat, is day?"

"Not many things," Adam tousled the boy's nappy hair. "I'm Captain Tremain. Think you can remember why you wanted to see me?"

"Oh, yassuh!" He handed a finger-smudged envelope to Adam. "Ah's s'posed to wait fo' yo' ansuh, suh."

Adam read the note, glanced up, looking over the dock area, then read it again. He carefully placed the letter in his breast pocket.

"Wheah's yo' ansuh, suh? Young miss, she say, 'Willie, you bring dat man's ansuh to me, or Ah's gwine tan yo' black behin' 'til it done tun white.' "

"She said that?" Adam's eyebrows raised. He grinned at the thought that she might very well have said that.

"She sho' did, an' she mean eve'y word."

"Well, I'm her answer. Deliver me, Willie."

The boy trotted ahead, looking back every two or three paces to see that Adam was still following.

Dulcie was nervously pacing the banquette outside Brennan's Restaurant. She was in as great fear of Aunt Caroline finding her as she was of Adam not replying to her letter. It had taken her all morning to become "lost" from her aunt and cousins and chaperones. She walked faster in frustrated annoyance at the relatives who protected her every move.

Adam stopped at the corner, watching her skirts swish as she marched back and forth, oblivious to the scene she created.

"Ain't you comin' wiff me no mo'?" Willie asked.

Adam eyes did not leave Dulcie. "I think I can manage on my own now."

Willie's face crumpled. "But Ah ain't gwine git mah penny. Missy say she won't give me nothin' lessen Ah brings her back a ansuh.".

Adam handed Willie three shiny pennies. The small boy's eyes sparkled to rival the sunstruck coppers in his hand. "Yassuh! Thanky, suh!"

Adam touched his cap as Dulcie whirled around for her return march. She halted, her mouth open, as he smiled and began to walk toward her. He placed her hand on his arm. "Shall we have coffee?"

She nodded dumbly. Confronted by him, she was bereft of words.

He ordered for them, then sat back. "Willie said you wanted him to bring me to you, or you were going to beat him until he turned white."

"Oh! I said no such thing!"

"Well, then, I owe both you and Willie an apology. My impression was that you wanted to see me. I'm sorry to have imposed myself on you." He made to get up from his seat.

She looked at him, horrified. Smiling sardonically, he settled back. He was tired of games, of bold advance and coy retreat. He never wanted to live through another time of her claiming to want something of him, only to regret her impetuosity as she had in the cabin at Mossrose. She had hated both herself and him that day, for wanting him and for being wanted by him.

Coolly he said, "When are you going to learn you can't be your daddy's sweet innocent and my woman at the same time? If you wanted me here, be honest enough to admit it when I come." He watched her trying to decide how she should answer him. Her eyes looked like liquid gold and her skin like cream. For a moment he thought she would burst into tears.

Visibly she rallied. "I wanted you to come here to meet me." She looked down into her coffee cup. "Will . . . will you tell me why you came?"

He reached across the table and took her hand, irritated by the glove that kept her soft silky skin from him. "I was surprised to see your letter. I didn't expect you to be here."

"I came to visit my cousins and Aunt Ca'line," she said too quickly, so he knew she was hiding from him again. Then she withdrew her hand from the protection of his. "No. I came because I knew you'd be in New Orleans."

"And I answered your letter because I knew you'd be here."

"You're not angry with me? You don't think I'm—that I'm one of those awful women who—"

"Don't say any more, Dulcie. Don't say it and don't think it."

"Adam—" she allowed her hand to steal back into his—
"take me somewhere. Let's walk. I just want to be near
you."

New Orleans was not Mossrose. It provided no solitary
path shrouded by crape myrtle. With each public building
they passed, Dulcie became more aware that Aunt Caroline
would learn of—and disapprove of—the coincidence by
which Dulcie became lost just as Adam came into port.

She was nearly in tears. Everything began to seem gloom-
ily impossible. Although she had mentally made her commitment to him, even to living a life of sin if need be, she
was finding the practicalities extremely difficult. Everything
from here out would have to originate with Adam. He
would have to provide a place where they could live together for the few days each month he would be in New
Orleans. He'd have to take her from her family. And no
matter how she tried, she couldn't visualize Adam as the
kind of man to keep a woman closeted away from decent
society.

She said wearily, "I've made a terrible mess of it again,
haven't I?"

He squeezed her hand. "Not a mess—but a dilemma."
He hailed a taxi. Seated beside her, he kissed her cheek.
"What am I to do with you now?"

"I don't know. How does one go about these things?"

"What things?" he asked warily.

"Well, you know . . . women, mistresses, and—"

He looked down at her, not sure whether to be angry or
amused. It was safer to be amused. "Well, most often
women come to my hotel room."

"Oh, no! I couldn't! I could never walk into a hotel in
broad daylight. Why, everyone would think . . . I mean,
they'd know—"

"Yes, they would. If it was the truth, you shouldn't mind.
But you do mind, Dulcie, so you'd better let me take you
home. Where does your Aunt Caroline live?"

Dulcie's mouth tightened. "I'm not goin' to Aunt Caroline's. Not after I've finally made up my mind and come all
the way to New Orleans."

Adam frowned. "Just what do you think you're going to
do?"

"If I must parade across a hotel lobby to please you,
that's exactly what I will do!"

"You don't know what you're talking about."

"Oh, yes, I do!"

"Just like that—" he snapped his fingers—"you're going to toss away everything you've been taught."

She glared at him, her eyes flashing defiance and resentment. "I didn't toss it away! You did it for me—at Mossrose, right under my father's nose. Or had you forgotten?"

Adam's eyes grew cold. He'd known girls reared like Dulcie. All such girls wanted—all Dulcie had wanted—was harmless flirtation. Now she saw herself as a tarnished woman, offering the lesser remains of herself to him, offering him the blame for her fall from purity as well as absolving herself of responsibility for her own passionate nature.

Suddenly the dark cabin at Mossrose, with her shrinking away from his touch, burst in his mind, a million painful fragmented pictures. "Hell, no, I haven't forgotten! I remember all too clearly that you said you never wanted me to touch you again."

"Since you ruined me for any decent man, I'm stuck with you, aren't I?"

The hurtful words found their target. He stared out the window, not trusting himself to speak. Watching her, his face tense and drawn, he forced himself to think of her as any other woman who wanted satisfaction, unwilling to admit it but willing to use any man to gain it. "All right, Miss Móran. I guess you're no worse than some I've known. You want your pound of flesh—you'll get it."

He knocked on the carriage roof. The driver's face appeared above him. Adam gave instructions, then sat back, his arms crossed over his chest protectively as he willed himself to think of anything but Dulcie.

Tom's cabin was in as bad shape now as it had been when he and Ullah first came. Swamp grass had reclaimed the yard. The tree from which Revanche had hanged Tom had split and blackened from a lightning bolt.

Adam told the driver to wait. He lifted Dulcie from the carriage. Without speaking or looking at her, he took her hand, forcing her to keep up with his long strides.

"Where are we? Where are you takin' me? Adam—what are you doin'?" She tugged at him, but he made no response. "Not like this. I didn't—"

He pushed her inside the cabin and closed the door. Slowly he began to unbutton his coat, making himself believe, childlike, that each brass button loosened meant that the words she had spoken in anger and guilt no longer hurt him. Each motion erased part of the insidious hold she had on his feelings. She stared at him in frozen facination.

"I forgot. You wanted me to tell you I love you—even if it's a lie, didn't you. Anything to please, Dulcie. It is your day. I love you."

He tossed the coat over a dust-laden chair, then removed his shirt. "Touch me, Dulcie. If you're going to be a kept woman, you're going to have to do better than this at pleasing a man."

She wanted to run, but she wouldn't. In spite of his coldness, his eyes blazed. He wanted her, and she knew it. She stood her ground. With the same deliberation with which he had removed his coat, she reached up, removing her hat. She took her time, defying him with her eyes, teasing him with the slight movements of her body. Her hair fell to her shoulders. She ran her hands through it, making it cascade down her back in waves of molten copper. Her fingers touched the buttons of her afternoon suit, loosening them slowly one by one, exposing the slightest path of creamy white skin in the dark of the velvet. She removed her fichu and stood waiting for him.

He managed to keep his voice level and cold. "Don't stop there, Dulcie."

"All right, Adam." She placed her hands flat against his chest. She caressed him, while he stood rigid as a cigar-store Indian. Her hands moved slowly over his torso, down to the lean, hard flat of his belly. Without a sound she shrugged out of her jacket. As the soft, warm skin of her breasts touched him, his fists clenched.

"Look at me, Adam. Kiss me."

He looked down at her, frowning. "How far do you expect to take this?"

"I want you to love me."

His look was sardonic. "Don't ask for something you don't really want. There'll be no interruptions this time."

"I know," she said softly.

He walked away from her. Briskly he went to the cupboard, dragging out a pile of quilts. He tossed them on the ruined bed, then with the same sardonic look on his face, removed his trousers and boots.

She couldn't look away from him. She gazed at his broad shoulders, the deep muscular chest, his narrow hips, his hard pulsing penis. "Are you ready to go home now, Dulcie?" he asked, his voice thick and husky.

She felt ridiculous and frightened standing in the ruined dusky room wearing only a skirt, while he stood before her naked and filled with desire, taunting her, cold and loveless in all his actions.

"Adam, please—don't make it so difficult for me."

"It shouldn't be difficult. Now that you've given up your dreams of marriage and love, you'll find one man much the same as another. If you want to begin your career as a mistress, you won't find anyone more patient than I."

Her hand flew to her mouth. She shook her head wildly. "I didn't mean that! I don't want to be anythin'. I just want you! I love you, Adam. Don't be angry with me, please!" She ran to him, throwing her arms around him, burying herself against him. "I love you," she whispered.

She felt the tremor run through him, then his arms closed around her, sheltering her. Her skirt and pantalettes fell to her feet. His hands gently caressed her body as he kissed her.

Dulcie reeled in a dizzying whirlpool of feelings she'd never known. He picked her up and placed her on the bed. He leaned over her, his face taut with passion, his eyes soft and loving. Slowly he lowered his weight down onto her, and instead of being heavy, his body seemed pliant to her, responding to her slightest movement. Her back arched small animal sounds escaped her as his warm, seeking lips touched her body, caressing with a deeper intimacy and heat than his hands had done.

She had never felt warmth like the warmth his body on hers created. He caressed her, slowly, gently parting her legs. She trembled, her eyes opening wide as he entered her, stretching her, hurting her, filling her until she was lost and everything including her own body was Adam.

Slowly, as he moved with infinite care and gentleness, the stretching and the pain eased. Other more delicate sensations pulsed through her, growing stronger, until once more she was there, and instead of Adam, it was she and Adam.

Where one began and the other stopped she didn't know. They were one.

He kissed each eye, her cheeks, and her mouth. Without knowing, she moved to the demands of these new feelings, moving with him, anticipating the leaping, living flame that rose and fell within her at every stroke.

"Adam . . . tell me, please tell me."

He embraced her tightly, trembling, his face buried in her hair. His voice was low and husky. "I love you, my darling. I love you."

Her blood surged, her heartbeat sounding in her ears.

She lay cradled in his arms, his body relaxed and moist. She snuggled closer, smiling, feeling more content and complete than she had known was possible. She said softly, "Tell me again, Adam. Tell me now."

He opened his eyes lazily, his mouth in a natural, easy smile. He touched her, his fingers tracing the curves of her body. Then he got up on one elbow looking down at her. "I love you, little one," he murmured. "But not as my mistress. You'll be my wife."

Her eyes teared, and laughter bubbled up inside her. She bit her lower lip to keep it all from tumbling out at once. He held her close, telling her he wanted her as he could never want any other.

Still smiling, she got into the carriage to return to Aunt Caroline's. But as he told her of his hastily formed plans, she became alarmed. "*No!* You'll never come for me. I know! Don't send me to Savannah, Adam. Something will happen. We'll never be together. Please. Keep me with you."

"Dulcie, I have business in New Orleans that can't be cast aside. I want you to return to Mossrose. I'll come there for you. It will only be a month, and we'll have the kind of wedding your parents want for you. I'll write to your father and ask for your hand, and let him know when I'll arrive. You——"

"Adam, no! I'm afraid. Don't make me wait. Now is our time. Please . . . don't let us lose it."

"Dulcie," he said sternly, "when I say something is important, you have to trust me. When I tell you I love you, you've got to believe me. Nothing will stop us from marrying—unless it is you."

"It's all I want. You're all I want, Adam."

"Then nothing will prevent our marriage. Be at Mossrose for me, darling."

Wiping her eyes, she nodded. "I'll see you until I leave, won't I?"

"Of course. As often as I'm able."

He took her to the Tilden's newly bought plantation, Marsh House. Caroline was swooning in a chair, and Jenny was waving smelling salts under her nose.

"Dulcie!" Gay cried. "Captain Tremain? Dulcie, where have you been?"

"She got lost on the Rue Royale," Adam said smoothly, looking at Dulcie as he might a naughty child. "Fortunately I found her before harm befell her."

"We—we were in the dress shop, Aunt Caroline, and all of a sudden I didn't see you. I hunted for you. Then I got lost."

Caroline blew her nose and dabbed at her reddened eyes. "Ah didn't know what Ah was goin' to tell youah poor mama," she whimpered. "Ah owe you mah heartfelt thanks, Captain Tremain." Her breath caught, and she sniffed again.

Robert watched as Adam's eyes sought and met Dulcie's. "You'll join us for supper, of course, Adam?"

"No, Robert, thank you, but I have an appointment. With your permission, Mrs. Tilden, Robert, I'd like to call on Dulcie occasionally."

Caroline Tilden, at Robert's slight nod, smiled her approval.

Robert walked out with Adam. "Our house is yours. You are always welcome. But, will you accept some advice from a friend? Marry her."

Adam nodded. "As soon as I'm able."

"I'm relieved. What I see between you cannot be held back for long—not with two people of your temperaments." Robert smiled, then became serious again. "Don't say anything I might not wish to hear. As her eldest cousin, my duty to Dulcie and Uncle Jem—"

"I understand that," said Adam heavily.

"I am responsible for her while she is here. I—I cannot permit you to be alone with her. I'm afraid I must be your chaperone. Dulcie is too clever at leavin' maids bewildered while she does as she pleases. Such a woman!"

During the following weeks Adam visited Marsh House as often as propriety allowed. Most of his time was spent with Robert, riding and hunting. It was no hardship; he liked Robert. But as the days passed, his longing for Dulcie grew. He couldn't look at her without reading in her eyes her love for him. Touching her hand while in a room crowded by watchful Tildens became an exercise in self-torture.

The days away from her were even less peaceful. Juneau Nuit had been Ullah's friend and was happy to aid

Adam in stealing Revanche's slaves. But, as with a project that depended on secrecy and the cooperation of many, Juneau and the three men spent many hours planning how to remove the slaves undetected, organizing the transport wagons, and finding anchorage in the Mississippi where they could board the *Liberty* unseen.

Juneau solved their most pressing problem. Edmund was not a generous man, nor one to give his slaves any unnecessary freedom of movement. Juneau and her voodoo doctor walked boldly onto Revanche's fields, carrying with them the most feared of all voodoo magic, gris-gris amulets and charms.

The field hands cowered before Juneau's powerful hypnotic voice as Dr. Beauregard walked along the rows of people in the cane fields. His hair, combed out, reached to his waist, but he wore it rolled into knots that formed little pockets all over his head in which he carried his magic paraphernalia, pebbles, shells, dried lizards, bird skulls, dried frogs, and hoot-owl heads. He pranced, weaving among the people, his wizened face grinning in satanic glee as he gave them glimpses of the gris-gris. Left on a doorstep in the dark of the moon, the gris-gris could work incalculable harm. Juneau instructed them to attend the voodoo ceremony the night Adam was to sail.

Juneau preached against the Yankee. She condemned Lincoln and his antislavery stand as evil, a strange, strange credo to be heard from Juneau Nuit's lips, but one that served its purpose that afternoon.

Sleath dared not touch or interfere with the powerful voodoo queen. Instead the overseer went after Edmund.

Dressed entirely in black, Edmund, slim and distinguished looking, approached Juneau with Sleath as she harangued to his slaves. She turned to greet him, her eyes wild and frenzied with the power of the spell she had cast on his people. "Ah gwine save dese peoples fo' you. We gwine celebrate Saint John's Eve dis summah—three times!" She thrust her fingers in front of Revanche, then she turned so that those in the fields could see the number. "Ain't no Yankee gwine live when yo' peoples sees him. De angels dey gwine p'tect us. Dey gwine join dey han's wiff ouahs, an' save de South. Dey gwine keep us true to ouah homes!"

Edmund listened, intrigued. He had always believed Juneau to be a dangerous nuisance, encouraging his slaves to run. Today she was saying exactly what he would have wished her to say had he ever dared dictate to her. *"Amen!"* rang out after each of Juneau's statements. Black faces shone with belief and the will to be led by this woman. That was to Edmund's advantage, and he agreed to allow her to hold Saint John's Eve service in the distant bayou where his plantation abutted Marsh House property.

Juneau raised her heavily braceleted arms in blessing and demanded the slaves' presence. Doctor Beauregard chanted and gyrated as he displayed the gris-gris that would end up on the doorstep of any man, woman, or child who did not obey the command of the voodoo queen.

Adam's single remaining worry was the slave grapevine. They couldn't prevent the slaves from speculating about Juneau's Saint John's Eve ceremony, the second one she'd have held that summer. Should they discuss the rarity of what Juneau was doing or in any way arouse suspicion, Revanche would end the plan before it got started.

The Sunday of the voodoo ceremony was the same day Adam had promised to take Dulcie to Circus Square with Robert and Gay. Ben was going too, escorting fourteen-year-old Jenny. They made a cheerful, fun-seeking group.

When they arrived at Circus Square, the slaves had already congregated. Black men strutted before their white spectators in castoff finery. The women in dotted calico skirts with bright-colored madras tignons competed with the brilliant colors of summer flowers. Children milled among the adults, their garments decorated with bright feathers and bits of colored string and ribbons.

Dulcie's hand stole into Adam's, her heartbeat quickening to the drumming of the bamboula. Her eyes fixed on the black man who wielded the bones, maintaining a steady, primitive rhythm. A slender black stepped into the center of the Square. Around his ankles were tied tinkling bits of tin and brass. His woman faced him, then other couples joined. The men moved back and forth, toward and away from one another, leaping into the air, then stamping their feet. Strongly accented Negro voices rang out, *"Dansez Bamboula! Badoum! Badoum!"*

The black women barely moved. Their eyes half-closed, their bodies swayed sensuously as they chanted an ancient song, monotonous, deeply moving.

Dulcie had never seen anything so primitive.

The dancers rested, allowing others to take their place, but the bamboula drummer never stopped. The calinda was a favored dance. Dulcie glanced about and saw that Robert and the others were entranced by the dancers. "Shall we get somethin' to drink, Adam?"

He led her through the crowd, weaving among the hawkers with their trays slung around their necks. He got her a ginger beer and a mulatto belly.

All afternoon he had dreaded telling Dulcie he was leaving New Orleans tonight. Now the moment had come, and he didn't know what to say.

She talked about the dancers, then spoke of the small, unimportant ways she filled her hours when he wasn't with her. "Aunt Ca'line and Uncle Webster are havin' friends in this evenin'. Will you come, Adam?"

He hesitated. "The *Liberty* sails tonight, Dulcie."

She looked accusingly at him. "Would you have told me if I hadn't asked you about tonight? Or would you simply have disappeared and left me to wonder?"

"I was going to tell you . . . today sometime."

"Then surely you'll see me tonight—alone. It will be so long."

"No, not long. Just one more month, Dulcie."

"Why won't you let me be with you? Surely I mean that much to you!"

"You mean everything to me. Dulcie, we can't talk here. People are already looking at you."

"I don't care. Let them look! I want to see you tonight."

"I have business to attend to, with Ben and Beau."

"Ben and Beau! You're with them all the time!"

"That's enough," he said harshly. "You've got to learn to trust me."

"Whatever you say," she said, subdued; but her eyes glinted with determination. They rejoined the others. Smiling gaily, Dulcie stood by Ben, leaving Adam trapped by the excited chatter of her cousins.

Dulcie was sweet flirtation itself as she pumped Ben for information about tonight's "business," hinting all the while that Adam had already told her about it. Piecemeal, Dulcie discovered that Adam would be attending Juneau Nuit's voodoo ceremony. To Dulcie a voodoo ceremony was just another version of the Circus Square dances, certainly nothing to take Adam from her on his last night in port. She directed Ben's attention back to the dancers so that she could consider what she had learned.

Chapter Sixteen

As soon as the Tilden carriage rolled out of sight, Adam and Ben hurried to the *Liberty*. They checked the cargo, which had been arranged on deck so that the ship appeared to carry a full load. The hold was clear for the human cargo to board later that night if all went well.

Dressed in gray, Adam and Ben blended into the night shadows as they approached the hut on the edge of Gray Oaks to join Juneau Nuit in her anxious wait.

The room filled slowly with about seventy people. Twenty-five Negro man and women separated themselves from the others and sat with their legs crossed beneath them on the floor. The women's heads were adorned with the tignon, the seven points directed heavenward, but all were aware that prayers said in darkness were said to the Devil.

In the center of the floor lay a small tablecloth at the corners of which were two tallow candles. Centered on the cloth was a shallow Indian basket filled with herbs. Outside the basket Juneau Nuit had arranged a number of small bones. Near the outer edge of the cloth were feathers.

The rest of the slaves sat along the wall. One man played a fiddle. Others beat with their thumbs on gourd drums.

Adam and Ben stood against the wall, watching Juneau Nuit go into her trance. The old fiddler stamped his feet three times. *"A present commencez!"*

From the shadows, near Juneau, a tall, heavy-set Negro of Herculean proportions stepped forward. His face strained with emotion, the Hercules began to sing in a soft, low voice. As the words flowed from him and the emotion built, he sang louder.

I will wander into the desert,
I will march through the prairie,
I will walk upon the golden thorn—
Who is to stop me?

The man seemed to grow in stature, rising larger and
more immense. His eyes rolled in wild frenzy. His words
came fierce, his gestures defiant.

I will wander into the desert,
I will march through the prairie,
I will walk upon the golden thorn—
Who is there to stop me?
Who is there who can resist me?

The fiddlers and drummers kept time, growing in violence and rhythm. He waved his arms, and all the room
cried, *"Malle air ca ya di moin!"*

They got to their feet, joining him in a march. In a
graceful, animal motion he picked up two candles and
began to undulate around the room, the others following.
Finally he stood before Juneau Nuit. With regal solemnity
she put a bottle to his mouth, and he drank from it. With
a blowing sound he spurted a mist from his lips, holding
the candles to catch the vapor. The candles flared up,
casting eerie fire reflections around the room.

Then he entered a trance, communicating with the
spirits of the dead, revealing the future. He spoke of their
voyage on a dark sea and the land of freedom that rested
at the end of that turbulent voyage.

Juneau Nuit signaled four men. She formed cabalistic
signs over them, sprinkling liquid from her calabash as
she murmured incantations. From behind a black doll an
old man brought forth a hidden receptacle. He withdrew
from it an enormous serpent, holding it aloft. He talked
to it, whispering, murmuring, mesmerizing. At every word
the snake undulated, darting its tongue, eyeing the old
man. Slowly the snake stood upright for about ten inches
of its body. In that position the old man passed the snake
over the heads of the four black men and around their
necks. *"Voudou Magnian!"*

Juneau snaked her way among the people, giving each
of them the feather of a black swan, a talisman to hold

them in the safety of her spell. Then she chanted, dancing around Adam, singling him out as an extension of her own power.

The old man handed her a ceramic pot. Juneau Nuit lifted it high above her head. Then she painted symbols of the Black Swan on all four walls, enclosing them within the safekeeping of Adam, the man she had designated as the Black Swan.

When it was over, the room reverberated with a howl of exaltation. The music began again, and they drank tafia, the rum of sugarcane.

The old man took the snake again, forcing it to writhe around the crowd of people. Everyone in the room cried, "*Voudou! Voudou Magnian!*"

Then the old man twirled the snake, tossing it into the fire.

Immediately a woman began to dance like the snake, writhing and twisting. She tore off her kerchief, a signal for the others to join.

The drum beat. Louder and louder. The fiddler thrummed faster. Adam felt as though the music were coming from inside of him. Burning herbs and weeds filled the air with a strange, heavy odor. His clothes felt tight, his body not his own. With the others he began to move, his body swaying.

As the noise increased and the passion of the ritual built, the women tore off their clothes, dancing nude like the serpent.

"*Houm! Danse Calinda!*
Voudou! Magnian!
Aie! Aie!
Danse Calinda!"

One by one the candles winked out, the only light coming from the pyre on which the serpent burned. The heat of the room was stifling, cutting off rational thought. Primitive passions unleashed controlled them now and drove the dancers on and into each others' naked arms.

Dulcie endured supper with the Tildens and their guests. Her eye was on the clock. It was nearly eleven when the Tildens stood on the front veranda bidding their guests goodnight.

Gay and Dulcie went upstairs, each retiring to her room. As soon as it was quiet, Gay slipped into Dulcie's room. Behind her trailed Jenny. "Go back, Jenny," Gay whispered. "I'll be there in a moment."

"Let me in, Gay. I want to see Dulcie too! Open the door, or I'll tell Mama!"

"Don't you dare!" Gay dragged her sister inside.

Dulcie looked helplessly at Gay. "We'll only be a minute. Why don't you wait in your room?"

Jenny's eyes were hurt and defiant. "Why can't I be here with you?"

"Oh, you are such a nuisance!" Gay said. Jenny flounced across the room with a flourish. "Jenny Tilden, you breathe one word to Mama, and I'll snatch the hair right off your head!"

Jenny gazed at Gay open-mouthed. "Hey! What are you up to? I want to be part of it too. Can I? Oh, please—I'm old enough now."

Dulcie, already in riding breeches, looked speculatively at Jenny. "You can come—" Jenny leaped up, smiling and clapping her hands—"but only if you're ready when we are. If you're not dressed quickly enough, then we leave without you. Agreed?"

"Agreed." Jenny beamed and ran for the door.

Dulcie nudged Gay. "Hurry up! Let's go. She'll never catch us."

The girls raced down the stairs, carrying their boots. They slipped along the darkened halls, then out the French doors. They stifled nervous laughter as they sat down to put on their boots. Once again they were running.

"Wait, Dulcie," Gay panted. "I can't run another step."

Dulcie paced back and forth impatiently. "Oh, now look what you've done!" Jenny was running toward them as hard as she could.

Gay jumped up. She and Dulcie zigzagged through the pines. Jenny's hoarse whispers followed them. "Gay, Dulcie, wait for me!"

"Dulcie, I can't leave her. She's scared."

"Gay, if you ruin this for me, I'll never forgive you!"

"What's so important? We watched the darkies all afternoon."

"That was different! I'm sure this is more excitin'."

"Ha! It's damp, and I'm cold, and it's scary out here."

"It's important to me!" Dulcie snapped. "Are you comin' or not?"

Gay glanced back at her sister, standing undecided and

frightened not twenty feet away. Hesitantly Jenny called, "Gay, Gay, where are you?" An owl hooted. Jenny squealed. She began to run for the house.

Dulcie and Gay plunged on into the dark woods. Night shadows and sounds stalked them, hurrying their steps over the mile of uneven terrain. With relief they heard the noise of the ritual long before they located the hut on the edge of the bayou.

"It looks creepy." Through the window they saw the eerie, licking flame-shadows of the serpent pyre. Dark forms of dancing, writhing bodies crossed and recrossed the shadow-flame. "Dulcie . . . I don't think—"

Dulcie moved closer. "Come on, Gay, it's nothin' but a dance."

Gay stopped at the door. She covered her eyes, peeking from between her parted fingers. "Dulcie—they're naked! Don't look!"

Dulcie looked. Near the front of the hut, his head back, eyes half shut, shirt open to his waist, Adam stood as Juneau Nuit danced before him with slow serpentine grace. Around them writhed naked blacks, crying out in ecstasy and the primitive *"Voudou! Voudou Magnian!"*

Dulcie threw off Gay's restrained hand and darted in and out of the twisting, dancing, copulating bodies, her eyes never leaving Adam.

Gay screamed for her cousin. Artless hands touched her. Drunken, half-understood words assaulted her ears, sinful, naked bodies assailed her eyes. She ran from the hut in panic, leaving Dulcie behind.

Without thought to direction, Gay lunged for the protection of the cypress trees, knobby and strange in the darkness. Around her the familiar seemed transformed and alien. Dark, without the moon, she could see none of the familiar patterns of the terrain. Sounds she should recognize and couldn't until they were almost upon her, frightened her witless. She huddled against a cypress trunk, hearing the rumble of wagons but unable to see them.

Gay spun and dashed in the other direction. She stifled a scream, her hand shaking uncontrollably. The black sky seemed to be breaking into a luminous arc. She watched as a column of horsemen, all carrying torches, came over the rise of a hill. They, too, headed for the hut. Gay ran deeper into the woods.

Behind her the night burst with angry voices and shouted orders.

Inside the hut everything happened at once. Adam opened his eyes to face Dulcie, trembling in excited anger. "Business!" she shouted over the rhythmic din.

"Dulcie . . . Holy Mother! What are you doing here?" The impassioned drowsiness left him. He straightened, alert, his thoughts marshaling on how he could get her safely away before Beau arrived with the wagons. He grabbed her arm. "You little idiot. You don't know what you've walked into!"

She struggled to free herself. "You lied to me! You said—"

He heard the first angry shouts outside. A gun went off. Horses neighed in fright. The door to the hut burst open.

Without looking, Adam knew what had happened. Pandemonium broke out inside the hot, incense-ridden hut. Someone kicked at the pyre, sending wild, weird shadows licking across the walls and ceiling.

"Start them out, Ben!" Adam screamed. The blacks were shouting, frantically trying to escape Revanche's men armed with whips and chains.

Under Beau's orders the *Liberty*'s crew charged the hut. Naked blacks rolled in fear, trying to avoid the indiscriminate lashing of the whips. Beau and the crewmen attacked and fought anyone clothed or having white skin.

"Hold tight to me!" Adam shouted at Dulcie. He pressed her against him, shoving his way to the door.

She screamed as a whip curled around Adam's back and bit the soft flesh of her arm.

Adam held her safe, acting as a shield, ignoring the bite of the whip.

She could feel his muscles involuntarily tighten at each lash. In the darkness she heard a man screaming, *"Tremain!"* as though it were the most cursed word in the language.

He shoved her out the door. "Run for those trees! I'll come there!"

She hesitated and saw him plunge back into the blackened hut. She ran for the trees, waiting, deathly afraid, until he emerged twenty minutes later. He grabbed the nearest horse, leaping onto the animal's back reining in only long enough to swoop down and grab her by the waist. Dulcie struggled, finally managing to get her leg across the animal's rump. She clung to Adam.

Adam leaned down, his head on the horse's neck, riding with reckless speed through the forest. At the Tilden's slave quarters he dismounted quickly, nearly knocking her off the horse. "For God's sake, do as I tell you, Dulcie. You could have been killed!"

"What was goin' on back there? Adam, you're hurt!" Her fingers were sticky from the bloodied ribbons that had been his shirt.

"Forget that! I'm not hurt." He kissed her hard and quickly and turned her toward the house. "Run, Dulcie! I've got to go back."

She took a step. "Let me go with you! I can help!"

Strained taut as a bow, he said, through clenched teeth, "Damn you, Dulcie!" He mounted the horse, looking down at her from that height. "Go where you belong, where I know you'll be safe."

"Adam!" she cried after him.

"Go home to Savannah, Dulcie!"

When he returned to the hut, the confusion had spread. Fighting, thrashing bodies rolled in the grassy turf. Beau's wagons filled and rolled into the darkness.

Adam pulled free a slave who cowered under the attack of Revanche's overseer. Sleath spun, his whip whistling through the air, curling around Adam's body to bite the flesh over his ribs. A gasp of pain was forced out. Again the whip lashed. Adam braced for the split second when the pain would bite and at the same instant the whip would be caught and held by its impact on his body. Then he grabbed, jerking Sleath, wrenching the whip from his hand. With the heavy handle Adam beat him senseless.

He tossed the whip away, racing for the area where Revanche's men had tethered their horses. Juneau Nuit and Dr. Beauregard followed. They freed and slapped each horse on the rump. The terrified horses snorted, scattering, then herded into the woods.

"Can you do one more thing for me, Juneau? Then Ullah will be avenged."

"You're de Black Swan, Cap'n. What's you wan' us to do?"

He handed her a small box of sulphur matches. "Fire his fields. Set Gray Oaks ablaze." Juneau chuckled, an eerie, satisfied sound in the darkness. "I wish I could do it myself, but I've got to get your people safely aboard the *Liberty*."

"Mebbe woan be yo' han' dat light de flame, but it be yo' matches an' yo' spirit dat done it. You jes' look back. De night gwine come alive. Juneau gwine bring on de fire o' de night sun."

As Adam raced for the wagons, Ben caught up with him. Running like madmen, they flung themselves onto the last wagon. They saw nothing until they were free of the woods. Then, like a halo in the heavens rose the hazy orange glow. The fire of the night sun. Gray Oaks was in flames.

The yellowish glow from the cane fields spread, flames licking up in the darkness. For once, Edmund Revanche found himself victimized. Totally helpless, he watched his beloved Gray Oaks turn into a conflagration. With a sickened heart he saw the walls give way to the intensity of the hellfire that consumed them. His frustration and fury were pale, insignificant, compared to the hatred he felt for the man responsible for his ruin.

The *Liberty* was anchored in the Mississippi. Adam's troubles began again. The slaves wouldn't leave the wagons. He implored them to get into the jolly boats. Faces turned from him. Men kept their hands folded, hiding their nakedness. Women clustered together, knees closed tightly, arms covering bared breasts. Adam looked dumbfounded. "What do we do now? They won't move!"

Ben winked at him, then a great laugh erupted.

"Damn you, Ben! It isn't funny!" he shouted, then burst out laughing. He leaned weakly against the wagon. A gargantuan hand clasped his shoulder.

" 'Scuse me, boss, suh."

Adam looked up into the dark, shining face of the Hercules who had communed with the dead spirits. He looked like a court jester with his head held rigid by a pronged iron collar Edmund had placed on him for being incorrigible. Bells on the ends of the prongs that clasped the sides and back of his giant head tinkled at every movement.

"What is it?" Adam asked.

"Iffen you got coverin' to hide dey nekkidness, Ah kin
gets 'em on de boat fo' you, boss."

"Ben, Beau . . . haul the bedding, linen, anything we've
got on the *Liberty*. Bring it ashore. Hurry!"

"Aye, aye, sir," Ben said, still chuckling.

"You think they'll come if we cover them," Adam said
skeptically.

"Dey sho' 'nuff will, boss. Ah be glad to he'p you. Dey
ain't a nigger heah who ain't afeered o' dis black man."

"Come on down. What's your name?"

"He be Rosebud," a woman giggled.

Adam looked at the enormous man leaping with his tinkling slave bells down onto the soft earth. "Rosebud!" he
repeated, suppressing laughter.

"Dat right, boss, Rosebud McAllister. Mah Mammy
done it 'cause she doan know Ah gwine grow an' grow an'
jes' nevah stop. Ah's right proud o' dat name. Ah be Rosebud McAllister, R.B. fo' sho't. Dey's only one like me."

"Welcome aboard, R.B." Adam grinned and shook the
man's hand. Ben and Beau returned with sheets, blankets,
tablecloths. Rosebud McAllister took the entire load, then
routed out the first group of slaves.

Rosebud began to move in the serpent's dance. "We
gwine fly on de wings o' de Black Swan."

The slaves echoed, "We gwine fly on de wings o' de Black
Swan."

Rosebud's voice grew louder, more confident. "We gwine
cross ober Jo'dan on de wings o' de Black Swan."

"We gwine cross ober Jo'dan on de wings o' de Black
Swan."

"We gwine soar to de Promise Lan' on de wings o' de
Black Swan." R.B. sang out until the words became a
chant, then a song, and the slaves began to follow the black
naked giant. They held the sheets up in front of them as
R.B. instructed and went singing to the *Liberty* completely
oblivious of their naked backsides.

As the last of the slaves boarded the ship, it rang with
song, low, melancholy prayers of hope and remorse and
fear. Men and women keened and moaned in self-conscious embarrassment. Some nursed painful if superficial
wounds, others sang because it made them feel better.

But for Adam it was chaos reigning. Leaderless again
once R.B. melted into the crowd, the slaves scurried madly
across the decks, several blundering onto the bridge, others

racing wildly seeking cover behind cotton bales. Jack-tars, mates, and firemen shouted futile instructions.

Adam bellowed for order. Ben tried to force several into a line. As soon as he released one to grab hold of another, the first man melted invisibly into the dark. Laughing and helpless, Ben retired to sit on a coil of rope, watching the frantic activities of crew and slaves. Everywhere was noise and confusion. Nowhere was there order.

The *Liberty* began to make its way to the Head of the Passes, only having to anchor again short of the forts. Adam paced the bridge, checking the navigation as he waited for the noise to quiet. "God, Ben, we can't run the blockade with them howling like this." Adam groaned, then turned and raced down the companionway to confront his noisy passengers. *"Quiet!"* he shouted, until he got their momentary attention. "Everyone must remain quiet, or the Federals will be able to find us."

They looked at him, agreeable and mildly attentive. It seemed they listened. He mounted the companionway. The keening and singing began anew. Adam spun around, ready to storm back, angry and outraged that they hadn't obeyed. Instead, he went to the shiprail, grasping the cold brass, leaning helplessly against it.

They understood nothing of blockades or Federal gunboats. Most of them were afraid of the ship. They were frightened and embarrassed and were consoling themselves.

But how was he to get them safely out of Louisiana? If they continued, the noise would carry for miles on the night air. He didn't dare take them past the Confederate forts. Just having them aboard was illegal. Easily identifiable, Negro voices would draw fire on the *Liberty* from Confederates as well as Federals. This night there was no safe harbor, no friendly ally. He was pirate, smuggler—enemy to both North and South.

As a crewman passed, Adam said, "Send Rosebud McAllister to me."

"Aye, aye, sir. Who is . . . Rosebud McAllister?"

"The big black with bells on his neck," Adam snapped, then chuckled helplessly.

Snickering, the young seaman went in search of Rosebud.

Adam explained to the giant why silence was absolutely essential. He looked beseechingly at Rosebud. "Can you quiet them?"

"Dat gwine take a pow'ful lot o' doin', but you done ast de right man. Seem like Ah better kick 'em all up de side o' dey haids, boss."

Adam groaned. "No-o—"

"Well, den, you got some spirits dat mighty potent?"

"Now you're talking!" Adam ordered everything alcoholic from the galley and the cabins. Swathed in blankets and tablecloths, the slaves were fed rum, brandy, wine, gin, and whiskey. Within an hour the ship was quieting. Some vomited over the side, some on the immaculately clean decks. Some snored gently. Others slept the sleep of the dead. No one spoke. No one sang.

Adam sighed. Rosebud tinkled at his side, the little bells unnaturally loud in the quiet. "We sho' nuff shet dem up, boss!"

Adam agreed, clapping him on the shoulder. "For God's sake, go below and have someone take that damned collar off you."

"Aye, aye, boss!" R.B. saluted as briskly as any seaman Adam ever had.

Just before dawn, much later than Adam wished, the Liberty slipped through the blockade at the Southwest Pass and steamed into the Gulf of Mexico, headed for New York.

Near dusk of the fifth day they were spotted by a Federal cruiser. Adam stood on the bridge, as Ben was at the helm. The Jack-tar in the crow's nest shouted, "Ship ahoy!"

Adam leaped down the ladder to the deck. R.B. gazed in consternation as the cruiser belched fire some eight to ten miles astern of them. The shot hit the water harmlessly, sending spouts into the air. "Dey shootin' at us, boss?"

"Nobody else," Adam said tersely as he rushed past.

Rosebud followed. "What we gwine do 'bout dat, boss?"

"We're going to build a mighty head of steam and run like hell."

R.B., wearing a shred of sheet tied precariously about his loins, marched to the coal bunkers with Adam. He grabbed the coal shovel from the smallest of the firemen and sent the man sprawling, shrieking as he crashed into the coal bunker. Adam spun around to face Rosebud's enormous grin. "Ain't nobody kin shovel faster'n a skeert nigger, boss!"

Adam watched the huge black man feeding the mouth of the furnace two shovel loads to the best fireman's one.

R.B.'s powerful chest and arms rippled, already coated with perspiration, as he established an easy but swift rhythm.

"Well, Chief, you got a new man." Adam glanced back at Rosebud. The furnace was glutted with coal. Sparks flew. Adam grinned, shaking his head. "Keep an eye on him."

"He looks like a willing worker," the chief said.

"All of that. Just make sure he doesn't feed it so full he blows us right out of the water."

Adam returned to the deck to check the rigging. Under full sail and full steam, on an evening like this with a favorable wind, nothing on the seas could outrun the *Liberty*, unless it was his own ship, the *Independence*. All he had to do was make certain no one made an error.

Astern, the cruiser steamed after them, the great gulps of fire and puffs of smoke spewing shot harmlessly into the air and water. Adam felt triumphant. Invincible. On this, his most disastrously chaotic trip, Adam felt like a king.

Chapter Seventeen

Dulcie was left standing in the driveway of Marsh House as Adam rode to the hut. Someday she wouldn't be left behind. But she recognized leadenly that Adam's life left little space for a lady used to drawing rooms and finery. Commitment to him was not so simple as it had first seemed.

Her whole life would have to change and expand to accommodate his dedication to what he believed right. She could live her life at home, waiting, wondering if he would return, or she could somehow become a part of what he did and believed in. Neither choice was easy, and both required courage. She would travel against the stream of her family's beliefs.

She turned resolutely toward the house. Her uncle walked toward her, a lamp held high. "What's the explanation of this, young lady?"

Webster Tilden was a humorless man she had never liked. Now she liked him less. "I went for a walk. I couldn't sleep."

"You went for a walk," he said with overbearing sarcasm. "Strange, considerin' I heard you comin' home by horse. How did you happen on a horseman at this time of night?"

Weak responses, easy replies flooded her throat. Uncle Webster expected her to beg his pardon, to be his sweet empty-minded niece seeking his guidance after an indiscretion. Then she thought of Adam; her back stiffened, her jaw set stubbornly. Her amber eyes glowed. "I have no explanation."

Webster was nonplussed. "Well, we'll see about this. Never—never has the Tilden name been so disgraced by the unladylike obstinacy of a female as it has tonight."

Dulcie shivered. She was too accustomed to her father and uncles having absolute command to be very brave in this, her first attempt at independence.

Webster muttered to himself. "It had to be someone you know. I knew you'd turn out no better than a trollop. I told Caroline we'd rue any society our girls had with Jem Moran's girl. Proved me right tonight, haven't you, girl."

She glanced at the house. Everybody was up. Aunt Caroline, looking pale and much abused, wafted her smelling salts in a little arc under her nose. Gay's face was blotched from crying. Only Jenny, flushed with triumph, enjoyed the scene.

Dulcie heard her uncle give sharp orders. A conch shell sounded twice, an eerie sound that sped over the damp night. "Robert and Phil are out huntin' for you, Miss," Webster said accusingly. "Since you put us to shame, and have placed Gay and Jenny in danger for your selfish motives, I believe you owe us all a complete explanation."

Dulcie remained silent.

Webster turned his eyes on his daughter. Gay burst into tears. "We went to the voodoo ceremony, Daddy. We didn't mean to do anythin' wrong!"

"I'm sure you didn't, but you can see the harm that has been caused."

"She did too know we were being bad!" Jenny cried. "She wanted to see Captain Tremain. She knew he'd be there. I heard them talkin'."

Dulcie sheltered in the babble of voices.

Webster silenced them with a harsh gesture. He stood combatively, legs apart, arms folded. "Dulcie, I'm waitin'. I am not a patient man."

Dulcie's eyes darted to Gay. Faced with Webster's anger,

her newfound courage drained away. "We—I thought it would be like Circus Square. I didn't know it was a—a religious ceremony."

"You expect me to believe that, of course!"

"It's the truth!" Dulcie blushed remembering blacks naked, giggling drunkenly, grappling on the floor.

"So you dragged your cousins along."

Gay was looking down. Jenny had found an interesting hangnail to smooth out. Dulcie took a deep breath. "Yes. I did."

"Daddy, it wasn't all her fault!" Gay cried. "We wanted to go—"

"*I* didn't! *I* came back!" said Jenny proudly.

"Now, let's hear about this Captain Tremain, who lures young women out at night. You met this—this man there?"

"I did not meet him! He knew nothin' about it. I may not be a lady, but he is a gentleman!" Dulcie blazed at him, her fear vanished. "I love him, and I'm goin' to marry him!"

Caroline's head lolled. The salts bottle rolled to Webster's foot. For once in a lifetime of ladylike pretense, Caroline had really fainted.

"*Marry him!* A brigand, who creeps about in the night? A man totally lackin' in honor or breedin'? I suppose your father knows about this! He has given his consent, naturally?"

Take what you want and pay the price, Adam had told her once. She had not counted price when she came to him, but she was beginning to guess what this evening's fiasco would cost her. What would Uncle Webster tell her father? And what would Jem do?

Dulcie stood straight and defiant. Once more she set her resolve. "My father knows and approves of Captain Tremain, Uncle Webster. We are to be married next month. And it—it was my fault that Gay and Jenny were disobedient. It was my idea to go to the ceremony. I wanted to say good-bye to him. That was all!"

"Shameless!" Webster hissed. "Brazen, bold-faced piece of baggage!"

Dulcie said rapidly, "I did a foolish thing. I know that now. I can only ask your forgiveness, Uncle Webster." Her aunt had revived and was looking at her coldly, her lip lifted as though something stank. "I am sorry, Aunt Ca'line."

Webster's chest expanded, seeing he had Caroline's agreement. "We extended our hospitality, Dulcie—generously. You've repaid our kindness by causin' us all to hang our heads in shame. You are no longer welcome under my roof. My letter to your father, with a detailed account of this escapade, will precede you home. Perhaps Jem will have some idea of what to do with you. That, fortunately, is not my cross to bear." He pointed dramatically upstairs. "Go to your room!"

Robert and Phil burst in. "Daddy! There's a fire!" Phil shouted. "It's Gray Oaks! Got to be—nothin' else around for miles."

Robert quickly crossed the room. "Dulcie, are you all right?"

"Robert! I do not wish her speakin' with any of our family!"

"Daddy! The fire—aren't we gonna—"

"Damn Gray Oaks!"

"Phil, get our darkies over there to help." Robert's eyes held Webster's. There was no compromise in either son or father. "I'll see Dulcie to her room."

Dulcie preceded him, suddenly tired; she kept her back straight, walking with a dignity Patricia would have been proud to see. But she had no feelings of pride or dignity. Uncle Webster had thrown her out of the house, something almost unheard of in a Southern family. She couldn't even whisper to Gay, her own cousin. And Robert—how long before he turned against her too? It had all been for Adam, yet he neither knew it nor could help her. Courage was a lonely virtue. But she would not let them see her cry.

Robert touched her arm. "What happened, Dulcie?" he asked quietly.

Dulcie met his look defiantly, and defiance melted. She was nearly undone by his eyes: loving, understanding, saddened. She said with great difficulty, "I-I wanted to see Adam once more. Oh, Robert, I've made such a mess of everythin'!"

"We must contact Adam at once. Perhaps he has not sailed. If he knew about this, Dulcie, he'd want to help you."

"No! No, I've caused him enough trouble tonight. Robert, please—"

"Dulcie, he'd want to be here."

Dulcie thought of the slaves. She didn't want Adam to leave them. And if he did, she knew, she'd have lost. "I don't want you to summon him, Robert. Just . . . don't hate me, please. I never meant to harm your family."

Robert kissed her cheek. "I can't pretend to understand you or Adam. But I am not my father, you know."

Dulcie could not speak. With his loving gesture, Robert had made her feel the shame that Webster never could. She had deliberately flaunted the tenets she had built her life around and thrown them at her aunt and uncle. Robert knew, and still he could forgive her.

She said finally, "Adam . . . asked me to marry him. Next month."

He looked relieved. "It would seem, after tonight, the sooner the better. My blessin's to you both—though you'll be tryin' to harness the wind."

When he had gone, Dulcie stood with her back to the closed door. Jem and Patricia would hear of her latest headlong venture, see it written down in every black, damning detail. Jem had forgiven her one unforgivable deed. But even if he were placable this time, it would not be enough to repair a ruined reputation.

Claudine's voice was querulous. "Miss Dulcie, wheah on earth you been?"

"You can start packin', Claudine. We're goin' home."

As the train moved toward Savannah, Dulcie remained quiet, her eyes fixed on the countryside. She knew she wasn't going to be absolved of this wrongdoing. Through the unholy network of cousins and uncles and aunts that linked Southern families, everyone would soon know Dulcie was of unsavory character. They would punish her and, by association, her parents. She could not put them through that.

She could not go home.

With an overwhelming sense of fright and loss, she thought of her promise to be in Savannah for Adam. And now . . . "Claudine, we're not stoppin' at Savannah. We're goin' to New York."

Claudine's eyes popped. "Miss Dulcie, you cain't do dat! Iffen we doan come home, Mastah Jem gwine be awful skeert. Ain't right you do dat."

"It isn't right that I bring this home to him either.

And it isn't right that I should arrive home simply to tell him I'm goin' to disappoint him again. And I am, Claudine. I'm goin' with Adam."

The trip, usually a matter of a few days, stretched out endlessly. Because of the war, schedules were abandoned. Every Confederate Army unit not already lining the southern banks of the Potomac River seemed to be traveling in that direction. Soldiers swarmed onto the train at every stop. Because of the urgency of moving the troops, civilians were shunted aside. They spent anxious hours in depots and sleepless nights in strange hotels in strange cities, waiting for a train not filled to capacity with supplies or troops.

At Wilmington Dulcie sent two telegrams. The first to Oliver. The second to Jem and Patricia: GOING TO VISIT AUNT MAD STOP LOVE YOU BOTH STOP FORGIVE ME STOP PLEASE UNDERSTAND STOP DULCIE.

She arrived at the Raymers' two hours before they were to attend a ball. Mad ignored Dulcie's confession entirely.

"As long as you're safe and no harm *actually* came of it, I don't see any reason to think about it for another minute. Do you, Ollie?"

"Of course not, dear Mad. In the instance of yourself or Dulcie, I am sure reflection upon past sins would produce no improvement for the future."

"Exactly what I thought," Mad said smugly. "Now, dear, you tell Claudine to unpack. We'll all attend the soiree."

"Oh, Aunt Mad, I couldn't possibly dance tonight! I'm covered with dirt. You can't imagine what the trains are like these days. Why, last night Claudine and I had to sleep in some man's barn."

Mad waved her toward the stairs. "That's all past, dear. A pretty gown and oodles of compliments from young men will set you to rights."

As Dulcie allowed Claudine to scrub away the grime of travel and massage her weary muscles, Adam sat in the comfortable study of Clyde Lewis, New York importer of fine wines. Lewis had concluded his business and left to join his guests. A gust of music blew in from the ballroom.

Rod Courtland carefully locked that door, and the one to the hall. Opening Lewis's safe, he withdrew a packet wrapped in oilskins. From it he unrolled a marine chart of the north shore of Long Island. "We'll have to change your anchorage, Adam. Sorry I had to ask you to meet me here. I'd already made my engagement for this evenin'."

Adam grinned. "Considering the lady's charms . . ."

Courtland's deep blue eyes sparkled impishly. "God bestows his gifts more lavishly on some than on others. Yes, well—enough of that." He pointed to Long Island Sound. "You'll sail in here, around Centre Island past Brickyard Point. Directly north is an abandoned manor house. Since it overlooks my dock area, I'll let you know about the tenants if it is taken."

To Adam an abandoned mansion seemed minor in an area of navigationally troublesome peninsulas and cul-de-sacs. Courtland's route made a landlocked hook, starting south in Oyster Bay, curling north again in the waters enclosed by Mill Neck, Oak Neck, and Centre Island. Along the south, a mile and a half from Courtland's home, lay the main body of Long Island. "I'm aware of the lengths to which you've gone to help, sir, but . . . once I'm in these waters, I can be cut off and helpless—"

Courtland jabbed at the sheet. "Here's Jones. Here's Pace. Van Meter. Maring. Crane. Van Loon. All good neighbors, all seamen, whalers, and smugglers. Others, like Baldwin here, are on my payroll."

"My pardon, sir. As usual, you've planned carefully."

"Protecting my investment, Adam. That includes you." His eyes met Adam's. Embarrassed by the emotion generated, he added gruffly, "I have a caretaker couple—Hans and Cateau. Hans is a former seaman, tough as they come. Both work with the Underground. I know you don't like sailing into these waters, but—"

Adam smiled easily. "I'd make a very scared blockade runner if I ran up the white feather every time I sensed danger."

Rod nodded once. "It's clear to you, then?"

"Perfectly. One or two more details and I'll be on my way. I've ordered another ship from Collie."

"Do you need a bank draft from me?"

"No, this time it is all mine. I just thought you should know. Watson, Collie's agent, has promised it to me in six to eight months."

Rod gave him a long, smiling, speculative look. "I envy

you young men. You take terrible risks with your lives, but a few runs through the blockade and you're wealthy. I am eager to see what you do after the war."

Adam shrugged, embarrassed at wanting to share with this man something he'd kept a private vision. "I have an idea of helping to build the South into what it could be. Start a shipping line, perhaps, or factories. A one-man revolution." He smiled wryly. "If I live."

"Just don't get careless, Adam. Oh, say! I have a message for you. You remember Oliver Raymer's niece? He had a telegram from her. She's to arrive any day. You're to be sure to look her up."

Adam looked away. If Dulcie was coming here, she would not be in Savannah waiting for him. He had said that only she could prevent their marriage. She apparently had decided. This time it was for good. He would not dangle on a string for any woman. He rose. "Thank you for the message, sir. I'll see you in a couple of months."

"She may be here tonight, Adam. I saw Raymer last week, and I know their names are on Lewis's guest list. Look for her."

Adam shook his head as he picked up his coat.

Rod put his hand on Adam's shoulder. "Adam, don't be a fool like I was. Don't let her get away if she means anything to you."

"I had no say in the matter. Dulcie decided to end it between us. It's just as well, though," Adam said briskly. "All's she's ever meant to me is trouble. I could use a lot less of that these days. Good-bye, Rod." He took the oilskin packet and strode into the ballroom, leaving the safe open.

Officiously attendant, the Lewises' butler entered the study, emptying the ashtrays and righting the precise angle of the chairs Adam and Rod had vacated. His eyes riveted on the open safe. Hurrying, he went back to the ballroom, watching Adam as he moved with grim haste and stayed suspiciously near the wall, excusing himself from all society with the guests.

Impatiently Adam wove his way through a group of chatting men. Everything had conspired to delay him. Having to meet Rod here in downtown Manhattan took him miles from the *Liiberty*'s anchorage. He'd arrived at the Lewises' late and would now be late getting back to the ship.

"Adam! Adam!" A lithe form in a white-embroidered

silk taffeta gown deserted her partner and flew across the ballroom.

Adam stopped short. "Miss Moran! Lately of Savannah, I believe. Fancy seeing you in New York."

"I can explain everythin'! Uncle Webster—" Interested eyes surrounded them. "Let's go somewhere. We can't talk here!"

"No, we can't. I am already several hours late." He tried to step around her, but she grabbed his arm, making him drop the oilskin packet.

"Adam—please—you must listen! You don't understand!"

With a muttered imprecation he stooped swiftly to retrieve the charts.

Dulcie screamed. Adam whirled at the sound of a shot.

"Stop that man!" A second shot rang out in the marble-floored ballroom, whistling over Adam's head and lodging in the heavy oak front door.

"Stop him, I say! He's a spy! He's robbed the safe!"

Dulcie jumped to Adam's side, ready to defend and stand by him. Around them women were screaming, running with zigzagging steps to their spouses. Potted palms tumbled in the flurry of skirts. Bold gallants, too old or infirm for real war, searched through coat pockets for weapons to bring to bay the vicious Southern spy.

"Stop him! He's a Rebel spy!" resounded in the chaotic room. Most were not certain which of the men in black dinner dress was the spy they were to capture. Others converged on Adam.

Instinctively, faced with pistols and men who had drunk too much to be sensible, Adam grasped Dulcie tightly. In his other hand he clutched the oilskin packet. Catlike, he backed through the door. Nearing a group of women grimacing in collective horror, he began to run.

"Stop, or I'll shoot!"

"No! The ladies!" The shot rang out. The room became a hell of piercing screams and scrambling figures. The huge, candle-lit chandelier crashed to the floor, throwing the small burning candles in frenzied sparking paths across the dance floor. Ladies hastily jerked up heavily hooped skirts before they caught fire. The men fought their way through the chaos trying to extinguish the flames before the house caught fire. Adam and Dulcie ran through the door.

"Stay by the driveway. Once they've calmed, go back

and act as though nothing happened," Adam shouted as
he ran for his carriage.

"I'm comin' with you!"

"No!" The carriage driver jolted to attention as Adam
vaulted to the seat.

"Adam!" she wailed, her heart in her voice, as she lifted
her enormous skirts, running after him. He told himself
she wouldn't run far. Then another shot sounded. He hung
onto the seat rail and reached out for her. She grabbed his
hand, and as the driver whipped up the horses, she managed to get into the carriage, falling to the floor, her hoops
blocking Adam's view. He pressed them down out of the
way and looked behind them.

"Ohh!"

"Stay down, or we'll both get shot! They're coming after
us and shooting at anything that moves."

"I'm not goin' to stay on this filthy floor!"

The carriage gathered speed. Dulcie, helpless in her
finery, bounced around as the wheels jolted over the bumpy
streets, careening and skittering around corners. Then she
felt Adam's boot in the small of her back.

"Stay down! They're shooting!"

Over the noise of rocks and mud that slammed against
the underside of the carriage, and the deafening rumble of
the wheels, Dulcie could barely hear. "There he goes!"
"Shoot the horse! Slow him down!"

The carriage lurched. A scream of pain sliced through
the clatter. Then they were streaking in a runaway carriage, crossing lamplit streets at a dead gallop, crashing
into garbage barrels, sometimes running over the piles of
refuse that lay along the sidewalks.

Behind them, all around them, wild shots thudded into
buildings and broke windows. Police whistles shrilled. Running feet pounded. Horses' hooves clattered recklessly on
the cobbles. Facedown on the floor, her ears drumming,
seeing dizzying glimpses of shadowy buildings and cross
streets, Dulcie hoped their careening ride was taking them
to safety.

Half a block away a fire engine was bearing down on
them, clanging its bell aggressively. Its six horses were
straining as they galloped full tilt, their eyes showing white
and their nostrils flaring as their driver plied the whip.
Around the horses' hooves ran three Dalmatians, accompanied by a score of baying, yapping curs. The long, heavy

steam pumper swayed dangerously. Men and boys ran
alongside, crying, "Make way! Make way!"

Adam's horses were galloping at top speed, out of control. If Adam's driver couldn't stop them, the two vehicles
would crash at the intersection. With six large horses
against the two smaller, the lethal tonnage of the pumper
wagon against a flimsy open carriage, he and Dulcie would
certainly die, mangled beyond recognition in a totally senseless accident.

The driver was out of his reach, past Dulcie's billowing
hoops. He lunged, his long body bridging Dulcie as he
grabbed the driver's waist, pulling back as the driver sawed
on the reins.

The horses veered unexpectedly, went one on each side
of a lamppost, and came to a lurching halt. The driver was
flung over the rump of a horse. Adam slammed against the
driver's seat, then was thrown back. In front of them the
fire engine rumbled unchecked across the intersection, pursued by its stream of dogs barking, men, and children all
yelling.

"Dulcie! Are you all right?" Adam shouted, trying to
find her beneath the tangled mass of hoops and silk. He
leaped from the carriage. "Give me your hand!" They had
to get across the intersection before the next pumper engine
passed.

"Adam, I can't! I'm stuck!"

He dragged her backward out of the carriage, avoiding
the wheels as the panicky horses reared and lunged. Her
skirt caught and ripped, but she was free, standing shakily
beside him, her hair wild, her arms scraped and bruised.

He grabbed her hand. "Run!" She pulled free, bending
down. He grabbed her again, and they ran, clumsily, her
hoops swaying against his legs. "Hurry up! Damn those
contraptions! They'll get us both killed!"

"Let go! I can run better without you!" She scooped her
hoops up and sped through the break in the traffic only
a step behind him.

The street was thick with carriages, running pedestrians,
mounted policemen, and running dogs and children. Their
pursuers would be stopped for several minutes by the
tangled carriages. But he still had to get them to the ship,
several miles away at anchor.

Dulcie ran beside him valiantly, taking three steps to his
long-legged two. He pulled her into a deep doorway. She

clung to him, her breath coming hard, her eyes sparkling with excitement. Trouble though she was, she had spirit and fire.

He grinned at her appreciatively. Then he frowned. "Oh, *Christ!*"

"What's the matter?"

"I left the damnable chart! I'll have to go back!"

"I picked it up!" she panted. "It fell out of the carriage."

"Good girl!" he said inadequately. "Now, if we can find a horse!"

He found several carriages tethered near the Happy Tymes Tavern. He was untying the animal when a rotund, slightly wobble-legged man came out of the tavern, heading directly for them. "Damn!" Adam muttered. Bewildered, the man looked at Adam, then at his horses. "Hunting your carriage, sir?"

"Ain't this it?"

"No, sir. They all look alike, you know." Adam smiled ingratiatingly as he led the man to another vehicle. Like the best of footmen, Adam secured the man in his seat, tucked a leg blanket around him, then hurried back to Dulcie. "Let's get out of here before the old coot realizes he never had a driver in his life."

He lashed the horse and took off at a run. The streets had quieted now. He looked over at Dulcie sitting tensely beside him. "Do you see anyone?"

"Not a soul." She giggled, slipping her hand under his arm, her cheek resting against him. "I always wondered what it would be like to be your wife, and now I know. It's bein' a horse thief."

He found himself laughing uproariously. "Miss Moran, whenever you're nearby, all hell breaks loose. Is it you, or what?"

"*I* didn't cause this! If you'd taken me along when I asked you in New Orleans, none of this would have happened!"

"Then I should have taken you . . . I did!" He laughed again.

Now that they were together, in spite of plans gone awry and dangers left behind, their hilarity bordered on the hysterical.

"Oh, Adam, what if I hadn't gone to the ball? I almost didn't!"

"And what if I'd met Courtland at his brownstone? I almost did!"

"What if you hadn't bent over to pick up the chart when that man shot at you!" She shuddered against him.

He squeezed her tight. "Dulcie *mea*, why were you in New York and not waiting in Savannah? Have you changed your mind about me?"

She burrowed against him like an insistent kitten wanting to be petted. "Never. Never! Adam, I love you. I want you, no matter what."

"The last time I heard you say that, I got trapped into a proposal."

She sat up, no longer pliant. "I did not trap you into anythin'! I merely"—she gulped, not having the right word.

Adam laughed. "Whatever it was, I liked it. So, Miss Moran, the moment we board the *Liberty*, we'll have Ben marry us."

"Why?"

"Why!? What do you mean, why?"

"I certainly won't become just another of your charities!"

"My charities! What in hell do you mean by that?"

"I mean I'm not goin' to be married out of obligation—just to keep your conscience clear."

He looked at her sidewise. In a formal tone he said, "Miss Moran, I do not wish to shock you with my precipitousness, but I should like to call your attention to the fact that for several reasons not at all clear to me, I love you very much. And because of that, and not some damn-foolish idea of obligation, I am asking you to become my wife."

Dulcie looked at him, her eyes holding his.

More softly, he said, "Dulcie, I need you. Marry me."

Chapter Eighteen

Beau was stalking around the dock when they arrived. "God Almighty, Adam, what happened to you?" He stopped short as he saw Dulcie, bruised and disheveled. "Dulcie?" Beau looked appealingly to Adam. "Adam? What—?"

Dulcie giggled. "Good evening, Beau," she said pleasantly. "Fine black night for an ocean voyage, isn't it?"

"Christ! You're both crazy as loons! Is *she* comin' with us?"

Adam grinned. "It's a long story."

"I'll bet. Jeez, Adam, I never know what's goin' to happen when you're around this girl."

"This time I'm going to marry her."

Beau stood open-mouthed, then grinned. "Yee-hoo! Welcome aboard, Dulcie!"

It was barely two hours before daylight. Once the congratulations had died down, Adam took Dulcie to a cabin. "Please, just stay in one place," he said urgently. "I promise I'll be back as soon as we're clear."

"It's so dark, I can't see a thing."

"Don't light a lamp or even a match. You could get us spotted by some Federal. We'll be lucky to get out unseen as it is."

Dulcie waited, not in the least convinced there was need for all the precautions Adam demanded. They were moving furtively past black shores, lined with blacker trees and occasional small shacks. She heard the engines turning, the paddlewheels slicing the water. She strained to hear commands, but heard none.

It was an uncomfortable, eerie feeling to slip through the night chancing obstacles, risking discovery, hoping, heart in mouth, that luck would ride with them one more time. And Adam went through this every trip!

Accustomed to the darkness now, she could make out shapes: the bed, a washstand. There was water, soap, and towels. When Adam returned, she would be fresh, smelling of soap, with her hair neat . . . and wearing what? Her torn and dirtied dress hung on her like a rag. Well, she'd wear her petticoat. It was attractive, the nearest garment to a nightgown she had.

If she hurried, she could have a basin bath all over. She wished Claudine was there to undo the forty small silk-covered buttons down the back of her dress. She reached around, found a loop and tried to undo it. After an irritating struggle she got one button free. If only she had a buttonhook. There, another one free. In a few minutes, with aggravating setbacks, she had undone those she could reach.

This left twenty buttons just below her shoulder blades.

Maybe if she took off her hoops and turned the tight-fitting dress around? The tape that held her hoops up was tied with one of Claudine's hard knots at the back. Nothing would move. She was stuck in her clothes.

Adam came in and locked the door. His arms found her, pulled her near. His fingers ran over the silk neckline. "You're not very eager, little one." He tugged gently at the bodice. "I had hoped . . ."

"Oh, Adam! I can't undress myself! I can't get out of my buttons or hoops or—"

He burst into laughter, then pulled the gown. Buttons popped and flew around the cabin, bouncing along the floor.

"Don't!" she cried frantically. "I don't have anythin' else to wear!"

His mouth was on hers, his hands pulling her dress to shreds.

"Oh, not my petticoat too!" She did not know this Adam, this laughing exultant rapist.

He skinned the straps off her shoulders, and her breasts were loosed into his hands. He caressed them greedily, then tugged at the tape that held her hoops fast. He unsheathed his knife. Her hoops collapsed to the floor. Petticoats and pantalettes followed. She stood naked as he shucked off his uniform. She looked at him with glowing eyes.

He smiled and reached for her. Bracing himself against the bulkhead, he put his hands under her rump, pulling her off her feet, entering her without preamble. Dulcie felt his heat within her, urgent, driving, demanding. She was helpless in his strong arms, her body opened to him, her own passion rising, soaring like a kite on the wind. He kissed her deeply, his tongue filling her mouth as his heat grew and throbbed. She ground against him, wanting him in her as far as he could go, wanting him to press her tighter and tighter to his body, wanting . . .

"Ohh . . ." she moaned. Her pulsations reached a delirious, unbearable peak and went on. Groans escaped Adam's lips as he drove into her convulsively, embracing her with trembling arms until his own storm had passed.

At length he released her. His breath was coming hard. Both their bodies were drenched in sweat. Against her mouth he said, "Oh, Dulcie, forgive me. I couldn't wait. I'll make it better."

She said dreamily, "I couldn't wait either. I had to have you."

He looked into her amber eyes, shiny in the gray dawn. "Thank God!" He laid her on the bed, then started to lie beside her. "Adam, lie on top of me, as if we're making love again. I want to feel you . . . grow hard inside me."

He rested on her, the end of his penis at the hot entrance between her thighs. He kissed her eyelids, the tip of her nose, her ears. With his tongue he teased her nipples to rosy erectness. Gradually he became harder. He went into her little by little, aware as he had not been before of the tightness and warmth with which she sheathed him.

He kissed her, tantalizing, touching her tongue, drawing away. His fingers caressed her, then went down to open her gently, fully.

She whimpered, and began to writhe under him, until he felt the sucking caress of her orgasm; but he made himself wait.

He eased down on her, his cheek beside hers, her long hair tangled around them. Her heart slammed against his as she caught her breath. Then tears flowed from her, onto his cheek. He kissed her tenderly. "Don't cry, love, don't cry."

"Adam, I'm so happy! And it's so wonderful. But aren't you—?"

"Never happier."

"But you're still . . . you haven't—"

"Not yet. Are you comfortable?"

"Mm-hmm. Oh, it feels so good. Don't pull away from me."

"Never." For a long time, then, he kissed her, caressed her smooth skin with his hands and his lips, murmuring love words, rejoicing in the feel of her. Her hands held him, played across the heavy muscles of his back and arms, teasing as she unsheathed him. He was throbbing with ardor, exquisitely torturing himself by holding back.

She made little noises, moving her head from side to side. Her fingers became claws, digging into his back. "Please," she whispered as if in agony.

His hands slipped under her, drawing her close to him. He moved in long, smooth strokes, and together they ascended to a golden plateau of rapture he had hardly dreamed could exist.

He stayed inside her afterward, pulling the sheet up over them to absorb the perspiration that wetted both their bodies. As they both sank into profound sleep, he murmured, "I love you, Dulcie."

He awoke in the sunny afternoon. Dulcie leaned on one elbow, trailing strands of her hair over his cheek until he grabbed her to him. He kissed her, and her hands began to work down his belly. He rolled over onto the floor, and she followed, landing on top of him with a surprised grunt. They laughed, lying in a tangle of arms and legs and the sheet and her hair.

He rolled away, scrambled up, and grabbed his trousers. "Up and out, wench."

She lay still, gazing at him with dreamy golden eyes, her delectable mouth curved in a soft smile. Pale freckles sprinkled her nose and her rounded breasts that rose and fell with her breathing. One leg lay straight, the other bent in an unconsciously seductive pose. She held out her hands, inviting him to join her on the floor.

Adam shook his head, still grinning. "Up, love," he commanded. "I'm so hungry I could eat an old sail."

She rubbed against him, feeling the harsh wool of his uniform against her bare flesh. "What am I goin' to wear?"

"I like you just the way you are."

"I notice *you* have clothin' on."

"Well, if you insist."

He was gone for half an hour. "Would you believe, you're the only woman aboard? This is all I could find." He held out much-washed blue duck trousers and a Garibaldi blouse, lavishly embroidered in red, white, and blue flowers. "These belong to the cabin boy. The blouse was for his girl friend."

She was aghast. "I can't appear in public . . . in men's clothing!"

"When you get them on, nobody will suspect the britches belonged to Carlos. Wear them as if they were riding britches. Put them on, Dulcie, they'll remind me of the beginning of my great downfall."

"Turn your back," she said primly.

He leaned against the bulkhead, his arms crossed, watching her. "Isn't it a little late for modesty?"

Her eyes flashed defiance. She blushed. But she dressed boldly under his gaze. She belted in the full blouse, arranging small tucks, and looked at herself in the mirror. "Do I look all right, Adam?"

The trousers fitted her snugly, nicely outlining her rounded rear. The blouse was spectacular, full across her firm breasts, and cinched in tightly at her tiny waist. Her hair bounced around her glowing face. "How can you possibly look more womanly in that outfit than you do in a gown? I'd better throw a blanket over you, or there won't be a man on board who'll get a lick of work done."

For the remainder of the voyage they spent much of their time on deck. The weather was warm, the sea breeze tender. He found it intensely trying not to be able to touch his woman when he wanted to. He also found it heightened his emotions when he was alone with her.

Nassau harbor was crowded with ships of every kind. Shouts, steam donkeys, the clank of chains and machinery blended into a not unpleasant din. To Dulcie, seeing it for the first time, it was enormously exciting. The trade winds carried the fragrances of spices and blossoms. The brilliant blues of sky and sea, the rosy gloss of sand, the rainbow hues of flowers and birds, expressed for her the happiness to come to herself and Adam.

Among the longshoremen were several women. Dulcie had glimpsed such creatures on the streets of New Orleans: gaudy, painted, overdressed in their expensive fashions. She was suddenly aware of her own casual attire, so at variance with Adam's severely correct uniform. Perhaps she could buy decent clothing before she had to meet Adam's friends.

"Yoo-hoo! Adam! Ben! Yoo-hoo!" One of the most flamboyantly gowned was jumping up and down on the dock in happy excitement, waving her frilly parasol. "Over here! Adam! Welcome home!"

To Dulcie's chagrin and distaste, Adam wasn't offended. Worse, he leaned far over the rail, waving, smiling. "Hey, Glory! Keeping it warm?"

"You bet! Piping hot and ready to serve!"

Dulcie shrank, shut out as Adam and Ben bantered with the woman whose hair was redder than her own.

Then Adam, grinning in a pleased way, said, "You'll like Glory."

Dulcie stiffened. She might not be gowned for the role, but she would show this—this frowsy woman a thing or two.

As soon as the gangplank lowered, the red-haired female picked up the skirts of her brilliant blue walking suit and rushed forward. She threw her arms around Ben, then flew to Adam. Adam hugged the creature happily.

"Dulcie, my dear, this is Miss Eleanor Brooker from Boston, now known as Glory Hallalooya of Nassau. Glory, Miss Dulcie Moran of Mossrose Plantation near Savannah, who is going to be my wife."

"Your *wife?* Oh, Adam, I'm so *glad* for you!" Her eyes turned quickly to Dulcie, taking in the blouse and trousers. "I'm so glad to meet you, Dulcie! Adam is a wonderful gentleman. I just know he'll make you a fine husband! I hope you'll consider yourself my friend. I'd like that!"

"Thank you, Miss Brooker," Dulcie said distantly.

Glory babbled on. "Is that the newest thing in the States now? So unusual—and on you so becoming. Would you mind terribly if I copied your outfit? In pink satin, it'd be a sensation!"

Dulcie hesitated. Adam laughed. "Enjoy it, Dulcie, Glory's always like this."

"They're still wearin' skirts and dresses in the States, Miss Brooker. However, you're welcome to copy it if you like."

Glory giggled and threw her arms around Dulcie, hugging her tight for an incredible moment. "You're so generous, Dulcie. We're going to have great times together! Now, come on, Adam, Ben, I've found a divine little café that serves turtle pie! I want you all to be my guests! I've got a new job." She wiggled her hips and winked. "So we're all going to celebrate!"

"Adam, I don't think we—" Dulcie's eyes pleaded with him. "I can't wear this on the streets."

He said, "Glory, lead us to the nearest dress shop. Dulcie came with me in such a hurry, she forgot her wardrobe."

"I know just the place. Madame Clare's prices are scandalous, but she has fashion right down to the dot."

"Hey, see you later, Adam," said Ben drifting off.

Glory clutched at his arm. "Oh, Ben, don't be such a crosspatch! While Dulcie gets herself fixed up, why don't I just—" She whispered something and giggled, and Ben's face lit up agreeably.

Adam bought Dulcie several outfits, for street, for evening, for afternoon calling. As Glory had said, the price was scandalous. Last he ordered Madame Clare to make Dulcie a silvery-white shirt in the Garibaldi style, and a pair of trousers of the finest gray gabardine. "If Glory thinks it's stylish, I want you to have it first!"

Dulcie smiled. He understood feminine rivalry better than she expected.

By week's end Dulcie was heartily tired of the eternal company of Glory Hallalooya. Every day Glory visited, expecting Dulcie to drop everything. "Can Dulcie come out and play?" Glory's version of playing was to visit the many shops that catered to blockade runners' ladies, and help Dulcie spend Adam's money.

"But, Glory," Dulcie protested, "he's not *made* of money!"

Glory said, in a rare quiet mood, "Do you know, Adam sometimes nets three hundred thousand dollars on a round trip—*profit?*"

"How would you know?" Dulcie was immediately sorry she asked, for Glory forthrightly told her.

"We were talking about it in bed one time." At Dulcie's stricken expression, Glory put her hand on her arm. "You mustn't mind about me. Nor the others either. We're all in the past. Your handsome Adam has been in bed with quite a number of women, and it's all been in fun 'til he met you. Don't you know? He's wildly in love with you— *much* more than he realizes. And, you know, he's the kind that will be true!"

"I hope so!" said Dulcie. Glory was a revelation to her. She wondered how many other "friends" like her Adam had. She did not know where he spent his hours away from her. He had business to attend to, he said. He came home when he had said he would, and each day they did something special together. During these times he was devoted to her, laughing, teasing, happy.

They were married on the *Independence*. Adam had given Dulcie leave to decorate as she thought appropriate.

He was pleased that she didn't turn his ship into a floating boudoir. Her feminine love of ornamentation confined itself to a semicircle of bright-hued tropical flowers, set on the deck where Beau would marry them.

Theirs was a motley guest list, mainly blockade runners dressed in a surprising variety of uniforms, and their female companions of the hour, gowned, gloved, and hatted according to *Godey's Lady's Book*. The crewmen from their three ships were all attired in blue cloth uniforms with proper straw hats. They stirred restlessly, waiting for the bride.

Dulcie arrived in a hired carriage open to the hot Bahama sun. Over her auburn hair was a Belgian lace veil that came to her shoulders, hiding her face entirely. Her dress was of Belgian lace over silk. Her wide hoops swayed as two of Adam's crewmen escorted her up the gangplank. She carried a bouquet of white and pink oleander and yellow hibiscus.

The ceremony, a reverent oasis in the bustle of Nassau harbor, was dignified, as they had wanted it. When Dulcie turned back her veil to raise her glowing face to Adam's hard, possessive kiss, the whistle blew on the *Independence*, to be echoed joyously by all the ships in port.

Glory hugged Dulcie, "If I ever get married, I hope it will be as beautiful as yours!"

Ben, looking stunned, said, "You did it, Adam. By God, you did it!"

Adam and Dulcie grinned constantly at each other, unable to let go of one another's hands, wanting to get away from the party, which had moved to the Royal Victoria's ballroom.

When finally, late that night, they were in their hotel room, Adam said, "Let's go to the ship."

"The ship? Are we leavin'?"

"No. I just want to have you, as my wife, there. A fit of sentiment, I guess."

"Oh, Adam. That's nice!"

In the morning they breakfasted in the captain's dining hall. "We have a busy day, Mrs. Tremain. We're going to see my solicitor. There'll be times when I'm not here to take care of our affairs, so you'll have to learn to manage on your own."

"You won't be here? What do you mean?"

"The business. I'll be making a run in about a week."

Her eyes widened. "Couldn't you . . . stay here—this one time?"

He touched her face lovingly. "There's a cargo of medicines and uniform cloth and necessities for the civilians. The South needs everything we can bring in, Dulcie. And there are the slaves. They're waiting for me to help them. I have to go. You know that."

"Could I go with you?"

"Not now. The situation is too uncertain. Maybe I can take you sometime, but for now I want to know you're safe in Nassau, waiting for me."

Dulcie discovered she had a very wealthy husband. Through Barrett the solicitor he arranged for her to draw ten thousand dollars a month. He also supported Zoe, whose funds from Paul Tremain's estate had dwindled. Mr. Barrett tried to unravel the mysteries of banking for her. "Any questions, Mrs. Tremain?"

"N-no."

"I'm always available should you encounter difficulties while your husband is on duty." He smiled warmly.

The days that Adam remained in port flew by, each one more precious than the one before. Nearly every evening they were invited to parties, balls, or musicales. The musicales were formal affairs at first, growing merrier, with everyone singing. A favorite of the blockade runners was

There are bonds of all sorts in this world of ours,
Fetters of friendship and ties of flowers,
But there's never a bond, old friend, like this—
We have drunk from the same canteen!
Think of your head, think of your head,
Think of your HEAD in the morning!

Their last night came. Adam was excited, as always, at the prospect of going to sea. Dulcie was depressed and trying not to show it. There was one last party, then life would be dull again for the blockade-running seamen would be gone. If she could get through this party without breaking down. All she wanted was to fling herself into his arms and weep wildly, and that would never do. The other captain's wives showed no such anxiety or feeling of desertion. She would be cheerful now if it killed her.

Having convinced herself, she was more depressed than ever. She was in the ornate bathtub, soaping herself. "Adam? Will you wash my back?"

It was a pleasant ritual, washing each other's back and sometimes washing each other all over, to their mutual excitement and gratification. She loved feeling Adam's muscles through a light coating of soapsuds.

Adam was stalking about naked. He dutifully washed her back, then dropped the cloth and began to rub her neck.

"Ummm, that's lovely," Dulcie murmured.

His voice was soft. "What do you really want to do this evening?"

"Be with you. Nothing else, only be with you." The treacherous tears were in her eyes and her voice.

"All right," he said, and climbed into the tub with her.

Dulcie burst out laughing and splashed him. He scooped up water, pouring it on her, making her gasp. She tried to fend him off, but in the end water was all over the floor and hardly any in the tub.

She eluded his grasp, hopped from the tub, and flung herself onto the bed. Adam landed beside her in a flying leap that broke both siderails. The tall headboard and footboard collapsed over them, forming a tent. Dulcie shrieked. Adam ducked and covered her head. When the noise had subsided, they cautiously looked up. He bounced experimentally. Nothing seemed about to fall any farther.

Dulcie giggled uneasily. "Let's get out of here."

He ran his forefinger from her shoulder blades down her back to the gentle curve at the bottom of her buttocks. "Why?" He smiled lazily.

"I don't want to get crushed."

"You'll be perfectly safe." He started kissing her. "You'll be protected by my body."

He made love to her for a long time, stroking, caressing her, being stroked and petted and teased to the height of ardor.

Afterward, lying still dovetailed, feeling one another's heartbeats gradually slow to normal, they talked in low tones, Dulcie able now to laugh, to enjoy being with Adam without thought of tomorrow.

"Let's go out on the town," he said. They wandered

from one watering hole to the next, drinking here, snacking there, taking a cab somewhere else. Dawn found them on the highest spot in Nassau, waiting for the sun to edge up out of the Atlantic and light Eleuthera Island.

The light seemed to spring up suddenly, red-gold and dazzling. Dulcie shut her eyes and leaned against Adam's shoulder. "D-d'you know, Adam . . . Adam, I think I'm jus' a li'l bit drunk?"

Adam laughed. "Dulcie, Dulcie, you're a whole *lot* drunk!"

"You're leavin' an' I'm happy. Why am I happy, Adam? I should be—"

"You're happy because you're drunk, and because you know I'll be back soon. And because I'll bring Claudine, and all your dresses—"

"And because I love you," she said, sighing contentedly.

She could barely remember going back to the hotel and Adam putting her to bed. She knew when he kissed her, for his moustache prickled a little. She did not hear the door close. When she woke, he had gone.

Chapter Nineteen

Adam set course on the Nassau Line, steaming almost north toward Wilmington. On the open sea the crew spotted no Federal ships. As the *Independence* approached the Carolina coastal blockade, Adam's tension mounted.

The blockade stretched in a forty-mile arc from New Inlet, twenty-five miles south of Wilmington, down around the Cape and Frying Pan Shoals to Old Inlet, just below Smithville at the mouth of the Cape Fear River. The ship was quiet, the crew alert. Adam made certain all hatches were covered tightly with canvas, letting no light from the fireroom show to give them away. The only light left aboard shone on the binnacle, and it too was shielded by heavy canvas. Satisfied that the ship was dark and blended in with sky and sea, he whispered orders down the tube. The *Independence,* her engines humming smoothly, steamed toward the line of blockading cruisers.

Adam moved cautiously through Onslow Bay. He heard nothing, smelled no telltale smoke, and yet he knew, somewhere out in the inky blackness, they were there. They were all waiting for him, having only to sit in their ocean anchorage and allow him to make a sound, show a light, make a single mistake that would present them with a target.

The Federals hung in as close to the shore as their drafts permitted, anchoring off the two main channel inlets of the Cape Fear. Old Inlet entered the Cape Fear at its mouth, guarded by Forts Caswell and Holmes. It was the closest, but navigationally the most dangerous. A boomerang-shaped bar called the Lump lurked just two to five feet below the surface. On either side of the Lump was deeper water, but the smallest miscalculation would run the *Independence* aground, leaving her helpless and exposed to the fire of the cruisers.

He decided to run for New Inlet, a channel opened by hurricanes a hundred years ago. Though it too had a bar of shifting silt and sand, it was the easier to navigate. And New Inlet had the added advantage of being protected by the small but scrappy fort of palmetto logs and railroad iron called Battery Bolles.

The *Independence* steamed toward Confederate Point, a few miles above New Inlet. Adam would work his way back south silently along the shallower waters where the blockading ships could not follow because of their deep draft. The shore was flat and featureless. At each quarter of the ship Adam stationed his leadsmen. Whispered measurements drifted to his ears. Twelve feet. Fifteen feet. Then as he himself felt the pull of the waters, twenty-two feet. They were almost at New Inlet. All eyes strained for sight of the Mound, a hillock no higher than a tree, and for the slight gradation of color that marked black ocean from black shore.

Adam's nerves were strung taut. Things didn't have the right feel. His eyes were everywhere. His ears strained for anything, voices, the sound of an engine . . . *there!* A change, just for a second, in the quiet purr of his own engines, reflected off some hostile surface.

Suddenly the night was brilliant. A Drummond light illuminated the sky. Two ships waited, anchored less than a mile apart off New Inlet. "Full speed ahead!" he ordered. The inlet, revealed by the flame, lay half a mile south.

Both Yankee cruisers fired, their shots landing heavily in the water near the *Independence*. Then the onshore battery opened fire on the Federal ships. Adam, seeming to crawl along at fifteen knots, felt a shot go past his head. It hit the edge of a large cargo box on the port foredeck. Loosed from its moorings, the cargo box slid toward the forward stack. Abruptly it stopped, pinning a seaman against the stack housing. Adam heard the man's harsh, agonized cry, then another shot fell astern.

"Three points starboard," Adam ordered. The battery continued to fire. There were no more shots from the Yankees. Within minutes he slid through the inlet into the Cape Fear.

Adam let out long-held breath. Now he could light his running lights. He steamed up the twenty-five-mile stretch of marsh-bordered water to the channel between Eagle's Island and Wilmington. Just inside the channel, a few yards from the east shore, stood a huge ancient cypress, a sure sign that his dangers were past. Sighting the Dram Tree, Adam perpetuated a tradition that had begun in early Colonial times, and broke out spirits for all onboard.

Shortly after anchoring in Wilmington, Adam showed his papers and got clearance from the port authority. Guarding against fugitives or deserters who might be concealed in the cargo, sentries walked their posts in the yellow lantern light, rifles at ready. A Confederate quartermaster materialized from the darkness and eagerly pounced on the arms and medical supplies. The luxuries were unloaded into one of the warehouses, consigned to Kidder and Martin, George Myers, Worth and Daniel. From Wilmington three railroads carried supplies inland.

Adam collected the money due him, paid his fees, and bargained for his return cargo of naval stores, turpentine, resin, tar, and pitch. The British were paying well for these now. He bought cotton at ten cents a pound, six hundred bales compressed to half-size by the new steam compressor. It would sell in Nassau for five times this cost.

In the gloomy afternoon of the following day he went to Smithville. It had the poignant unalterability of home.

Worries of cruisers and cargo fell away as he leaped the steps to the door. He hadn't seen Zoe for months. And he'd had word that Tom had a "cargo" for him.

Zoe greeted him with a glad cry. He hugged her tightly, surprised anew at her smallness and fragility.

Angela took wing from her seat on the piano stool and flew to hug and kiss him. She was still a child, in spite of the careful grooming of her blond hair, in spite of the sedate dress of pastel plaid that revealed a very womanly shape. But she would have to learn not to kiss men on the mouth. He returned her kiss, brotherly, on her cheek.

"Adam, I'm living here all the time now!" she crowed, hugging him, pressing against him.

"Well, Ma, you'd better set guards. You've got a belle in the making." He ruffled Angela's hair, amused when she quickly smoothed it.

Mammy lumbered in from the kitchen. "Mas' Adam, you bin eatin' reg'ler?"

Adam laughed. "Good old Mammy, still trying to pound me down to size. Don't you know I never missed a meal in my life? How's my favorite woman?"

Mammy's eyes tried to be severe, but they twinkled and betrayed her. "Mebbe iffen Ah knows who yo' woman is, Ah be able to tell you, Mas' Adam. But iffen you's jes astin' 'bout Mammy, she's fine, jes' fine."

"I brought you all something." He pried open a case and took out tea and coffee, condensed milk, quinine, soap, stays, and whiskey.

Zoe said, "Oh, Adam, we haven't had any tea for weeks. Mammy, ask Lucia to fix us some."

"Ah fix de tea," Mammy said belligerently. "Ah ain't gwine let some no-'count make it too thin fo' mah boy!" She bustled away happily.

"Now, let us hear all the news," Zoe began.

He took a deep breath. "I'm married now." Out of the corner of his eye he saw Angela's hand fly up to her mouth.

Zoe's astonishment made her voice squeak. *"Married!* When? Is she nice?"

Adam laughed. "She's of a good Savannah family, which should please you, and she's also intelligent, quick-tempered, and she likes me pretty well." Adam talked about Dulcie for some time. Even Mammy came in to listen. Angela, silent at first, ventured a question. She said, "I guess you aren't going to wait for me to grow up, are you, Adam?"

"With my luck, I'd be gone at the moment you grow up, and someone would steal you away from me. Don't tell me you haven't any callers yet!"

Angela blushed and lowered her head, a gesture reminiscent of Ullah. "Well, one or two—but they only come after Aunt Zoe's cookies!"

At bedtime Zoe asked, "Where do you go from here, Adam?"

"To New York. I'm to see Rod Courtland."

"What does he look like, Adam? What kind of man is he? You do like him, don't you?"

Adam looked curiously at her, speculating about her sudden interest in Courtland. "He's about my height. Stubborn jaw. Stubborn man, when he chooses. Eyes that can skewer you—but he's fair. He's always fair. I'd call him handsome, well proportioned, very fine features. A good-looking mane of silvery gray hair. He's also a good man to have on your side. Satisfied I'm not playing with the bad boys, Ma?" He smiled impishly.

She said primly, "Can't a mother pry a little bit?"

Adam chuckled. "It's good to be home again."

In the night Adam was awakened by two sounds. The first was a thunderstorm. The second was indefinable. Without changing the rhythm of his breathing, he listened. Though he heard nothing, instinct told him someone was in his room. Then, a white, formless blob burst from behind his door and hurled itself under the covers with him.

"Oh, Adam, I can't wake Aunt Zoe—and I'm scared!" Angela said, through chattering teeth. "Will you g-get me warm?"

Adam, acutely conscious of his own nakedness, hurriedly wrapped himself in the sheet. She was cold; her teeth chattered like castanets. He wrapped his long arms around her and snugged her up to him.

"Are you always afraid of thunderstorms?"

"Only sometimes. It sounds like the guns."

"Nothing will hurt you." He was aware of her warmth inside the curve of his body. "You're safe, Angela."

She soon drifted to sleep as he held her. He eased

away from her, rolled smoothly out of bed, and pulled on his trousers. He picked her up and carried her to her own room. As he tucked her in securely, she clung to him for a moment, then murmured, "Good night, Adam."

Next morning the skies were clear, washed clean and shining. Angela, though she smiled at him, made no mention of the storm.

Toward evening he found Tom at his cabin not far from Crusoe Island. When he heard about his marriage, Tom wrung his hand and congratulated him. They drank a glass of white lightning together and then got down to business.

"I got nearly twenty fugitives waitin'," Tom said in his hoarse voice. "I took a handful of 'em cross-country to Eben Cline's, but that's doin' it the hard way now. Most of 'em don't mind stayin' here, so I put 'em to work. Come on, I'll show you my new bunkhouse."

Adam inspected the long log house with ticks on the floor and a wide stone fireplace. "Looks like you're in the business to stay, Tom."

Tom shrugged. "Ahh, well, I got nothin' better to do. It's not too comfortable goin' to town anymore. Zoe and Mammy like seein' me, but not Angela. I don't know what's got into her. How'd she seem to you?"

"Grown up. I wouldnt' worry about her, Tom." He looked into his friend's white-scarred face. "She needs a father, no matter how she acts. Keep on seeing her."

Tom grunted, then changed the subject. "Where'll we take these people this time? Lockwood's Folly Inlet? You could anchor off Oak Island an' get 'em off shore in jolly boats."

"I don't want to stand so close to Old Inlet. The Yankees make their swing around there. If we'd miss connections or I have to run for it, you'd get caught with a couple dozen contraband and hang for it. And I'd be studying the cell walls up in Fort Lafayette, New York."

"We can quit anytime. You've more than paid any debt long ago."

Adam's eyes shone. "Speaking of debts, Tom, how would you like Edmund Revanche with no slaves, his crops and Gray Oaks destroyed?"

"Christ a'mighty, boy! You ain't gonna do that!"

"It's done. Ben, Beau, and I did it."

Tom's mouth gaped open.

"You remember Juneau Nuit, Ullah's friend? Well . . ." Adam told him everything. "There wasn't a stalk of cane standing."

Tom smiled slowly, his lips trembling as tears came to his eyes. "I wish Ullah could know. All the grief and sorrow that man caused."

"Now he's getting some of it back."

"Does he know you were in on it?"

"He sure does! He called my name. We painted the Black Swan on the hut."

Tom's face puckered in worry. "He won't ever forget."

Adam laughed easily. "Between him and the Yankees and a red-haired wife, I'm not safe anywhere."

Adam left early the next morning, taking the quickest way through the tangled Green Swamp to Smithville. He had plenty to do to get cleared out of Wilmington, figure out hiding places for twenty fugitives, secure an anchorage on the western bank of the river, and maintain it for however long he had to.

Tom, having to take a more circuitous route with his people, would arrive at the rendezvous sometime the following day. There were long stretches of soggy ground where they had to portage the boats. The women muttered prayers and cast suspicious eyes into every dark clump and every patch of piney woods that might hide 'gator or bear. They moved in constant dread of wildcats, rattlesnakes, and coral snakes, all plentiful in the pocosin.

"Whut you got dem big guns fo', Mastah Tom?" asked Verna, pointing to his heavy rifle and the pistols he wore. "Who you gwine shoot?"

"Nobody and nothin' if I can help it," Tom said.

But he held the rifle at the ready as they moved to the edge of the water. Gratefully the men put down the boats, and soon they were poling down a creek. Tom saw smoke ahead; he motioned for silence. Around the bend they came upon a small salt camp. Half a dozen people fed fires over which large kettles of brackish water were being boiled down for their salt content. One man hastily pointed a rifle at them, though Tom waved and smiled until they were out of sight.

They were sitting in the bushes along the shore of the Cape Fear when darkness fell. The *Independence* rocked sleepily at anchor, dark and soundless. At last Tom heard a boat being cautiously rowed in his direction.

Adam loomed before him. "Any trouble?"

"No, everythin's fine. These damn salt camps are gonna be the death of slave haulin'. I passed three of 'em on the way out."

"Let's start gettin' them on board. What salt camps?"

"Little one- and two-family half-assed operations. They go down to the shore and boil themselves some salt. I guess the swamp rats always did it, only now that it's gettin' scarce, everybody's doin' it. There's a bunch around Cove Creek and Dutchman's Creek, below Smithville. Hog killin' season now, you know, an' they need the salt to put up the meat."

The last of the fugitives went up the Jacob's ladder. Adam shook Tom's hand. "Take care of yourself."

Adam watched the ocean through New Inlet for some time. Nothing to be seen. He gave the order to weigh anchor, and they steamed out into the Inlet, running north close to the shore until they had passed New Topsail Inlet. He headed out to sea running smoothly, with no obstacles in sight.

A few nights later he slid into Long Island Sound to Oyster Bay and around the hook of Centre Island up into Courtland's Puddle, as he called it. Hans and Cateau welcomed him and took charge of the fugitives.

In the morning he saw Courtland, who inquired after his well-being and, upon being told of the marriage, congratulated Adam heartily. Later he took the carriage to Oliver's house. Oliver, blocking the doorway, glared at him with open hostility. "What have you done with my niece?"

"We were married, sir," Adam said, smiling.

"You picked a fine way to do it, I must say. Dragging her off in public, getting shot at. I don't suppose you bothered with a minister?"

Adam laughed. "No, sir. Ship's captain. First-class all the way."

Oliver smiled grudgingly. "Damn blackguard—you might as well come in. Mad! Oh, Mad! Come meet Dulcie's husband!"

Mad was not in the least taken in. "Oh, is Adam here?"

Only Claudine, standing with unusual diffidence in the

hall listening to their conversation, did not seem glad of his marriage or relieved that Dulcie was safe. She stared at Adam with eyes that held hurt—and challenge.

Whatever was bothering her, he'd like to get it settled before he was stuck with her in Nassau. He could manage Dulcie and Glory together, but he didn't need a sullen black girl to confound the problem.

Shortly he excused himself from Mad and Oliver. Claudine was in a bedroom packing two large trunks. She looked up at him, startled, then kept her eyes on her work.

"You heard me say Miss Dulcie wants you with her in Nassau?"

"Yassuh."

"You don't have to go unless you want to."

"Ah knows that." She was almost insolent.

"And I don't have to take you, no matter what Dulcie wants."

She stopped folding the cambric nightgown. "Nossuh," she whispered.

"How do you feel about it? Do you want to go with me, or stay here?"

"Ah does anythin' you tells me, Mastah Adam."

Damn women! Ladies were secretive and indirect enough, let alone their servants. He glared at Claudine's defenseless neck. "We leave in two hours."

Upon his return to Nassau he saw the two bright heads covered with frothy bonnets, one dressed in green, the other in blue. He expected Glory to come leaping to meet him, but it was Dulcie who sprang from the carriage, to run and collide with him breathlessly, her arms going around his neck, her bonnet knocked askew.

"Oh, Adam!" she cried between kisses. "It's been so *long!*"

"Did you miss me?" he teased.

"Oh, yes—*yes!* Did you miss me?"

"How could I not?" He kissed the end of her pert nose. "Missus Tremain, the captain's middlin' glad to see you."

Dulcie laughed. Then she saw Claudine, standing respectfully back, and reached out to hug her. "Claudine, you'll love Nassau! Did you have a good voyage?"

Claudine beamed, looking around. "Yes'm, Miss Dulcie, Mastah Adam jes' took that boat through them waves slick as a ironin' bo'd. Lemme fix yo' bonnet. You got it all caddywampus."

Dulcie set her own headgear straight. "Glory, this is Claudine, the best maid anybody ever had. Claudine, meet Miss Glory Hallalooya." She watched Claudine's face, waiting for the effect of Glory's name.

Claudine started to smile and quickly turned it into a cough with her hand over her mouth. But Glory laughed in delight, and the others joined her. In his absence, Adam noticed, Dulcie and Glory had become close friends. Not *too* close, he hoped, thinking of Glory's usual after-dark activities.

"What have you been doing?" he asked in the carriage.

"Glory and I went shoppin' twice, and she helped me serve tea to the blockade runners' wives one afternoon."

Adam raised his eyebrows. "Glory? Or Miss Eleanor Brooker?"

Glory's laughter pealed out happily. "I was Miss Brooker that day. *In a prim gray dress,* Adam! Can you imagine that?"

"I'd rather not. Sounds as if you've been under deteriorating influences."

Dulcie made a face at him.

In the hotel lobby Glory deserted them, explaining that Beau would be waiting. "He needs somebody experienced. He's so sweet and innocent!"

Adam, recalling some of Beau's more spectacular whorehouse feats, could hardly keep his face straight. He asked teasingly, "Like Johnny Packer?"

"Oh, but Johnny was just a little *boy!* Adam, you're *awful!*" Still giggling, she whisked around a corner.

In the suite Adam pointed to a small room. "You'll sleep there."

"Ah he'p Miss Dulcie with her dress," Claudine said, looking stubborn.

"Miss Dulcie will call you when she needs you."

Alone with him, Dulcie said, "Poor Claudine. Thrown out of her job by a big, muscular, gorgeous *man.*" She laid her head on Adam's shoulder. "Oh, my love, it's so empty without you. I've been so frightened for you."

He untied her bonnet and flung it onto a chair, then began plucking out the heavy horn hairpins until her hair tumbled onto her shoulders. He put both hands on her face, with his fingers up into her hair. With his thumbs he gently stroked the smooth freckles over her cheeks. "I'd come back to you, you know," he said earnestly. "No matter whatever might happen, I'd always come back to you."

Her eyes searched his. "Adam, do you love me as much as I love you?"

"Ask me in fifty years," he replied softly. "If you still need to ask."

Much later Dulcie said, "Are you ready for your surprise now?"

Adam lay on his back, his hands dangling over either side of the bed. "Didn't I just have it?"

She giggled. "I made somethin' for you. Every evenin' I'd think of you and work on it. It was somethin' to keep you close to me."

"A ball and chain."

She scrambled off the bed, and he watched the tilting motion of her rounded buttocks as she walked to the dressing room. She came back, one hand behind her, and as he watched her breasts bounce pleasantly, he said, "This must be captain's paradise."

She grinned, holding out a vest of finest white ribbed silk, hand embroidered with moss roses in shades of pink and cream.

He put it on. Over a shirt it would fit him perfectly. "Dulcie *mea,* you're a wonder." He laid the vest down carefully. "But modest as I am, I believe I deserve somebody as nice as you." He hugged her, his face buried in the sweet, perfumed place between her breasts. She held him there, stroking his hair, for a long time.

"Adam, did you mail my letter?"

"Yes, from Wilmington. Your parents may have it by now."

"Tell me about everythin'."

"The Yankees have replaced Major Anderson in Kentucky with General Sherman. Sherman's an Ohioan, a West Pointer, a Mexican War veteran. His last job was as president of a street railway in St. Louis. He's got some peculiarities, a nervous, twitchy man, I've heard. He probably won't last long in command, though it'll be a good thing for the South."

"Are there others like him?"

"I haven't heard. There's General George McClellan. He's the man who organized the Army of the Potomac.

Now he's general-in-chief of the army. If he continues as well as he started, the South's in trouble."

"And the battles since I left the States?" It came out so easily, she thought; none of the homesickness showed yet.

"The Confederates took Ball's Bluff. The Union officer, Stone, sent a regiment across the river without providing a way to return. We attacked from the bluff and slaughtered nearly half of them."

"Don't tell me more. Adam, did you get shot at?"

"Yes, love, and missed. Now let's plan for tonight. Any parties?"

"Beau mentioned a cockfight. Do ladies get to go here in Nassau?"

"They do everything else. I don't see why not. We'll go if you like." He stood up, pulling on trousers. "For now let's go for a horseback ride. I need the wind in my teeth today."

She dressed quickly in the silver and gray outfit he had had made.

As she entered the parlor, Dulcie was surprised to see Claudine rise from a straight chair. She had forgotten her maid's existence.

"Them trunks come, Miss Dulcie," she said sullenly.

"Well, unpack them, Claudine. We're goin' ridin'."

"Miss Dulcie, you ain't gwine on no street in no git-up like that."

Dulcie smiled. "All the ladies wear this kind of outfit now."

"Yo' hair's a mess too. Look like you ready fo' baid. Mastah Adam, Ah's s'prised you doan take a han' to Miss Dulcie. She doan look—"

"That will do, Claudine! We're in Nassau now, not at Mossrose. And I'm a married woman. If I displease my husband, he'll tell me so."

"Yes'm." Claudine turned away muttering to herself.

On their way downstairs Dulcie asked, "What do you suppose has gotten into Claudine?"

"Nobody, lately," he said.

"Adam, Glory was right. You're a low-minded man. How do you know that?"

"Guesswork. The dissatisfied look, the one you used to wear when you were still your Daddy's girl."

"What do I look like now?"

"The cat that licked the butter crock."

So they began a pattern for the months together in Nassau, Dulcie alone while Adam made his runs. Usually he went to Wilmington, sometimes to New York, though he liked that less and less. In spite of Rod's precautions he could too easily be observed entering Oyster Bay. From the empty house on Centre Island anyone could watch his activities.

He remained in Nassau to take Dulcie to the Junkanoo Parade on Boxing Day. The celebration began about four in the morning, after an all-night party. Festively garbed men and women gyrated to the music of goombay drums, cowbells, and horns. Dulcie and Adam danced and sang with the others until the merrymaking palled. Then with Glory, Ben, and Beau they dined royally on hot sherry-laced conch chowder, baked crabs from Andros Island, and guava duff.

"We'll have a happy year, Adam," Dulcie assured him. "If you take part in the *junkanoo*, you chase away the evil spirits and invoke the good ones."

"It's true," Glory said. "I went last year, and look how well I turned out."

"We can see that, Glory," said Beau, leering down her generous cleavage. "But I think you got your start a little before last year."

She giggled. "I think you did too, Beau."

Ben looked sharply at them. "I think it's superstitious nonsense."

"Well, well, there's always one sourpuss in every crowd. We certainly know who ours is!" Glory said.

Ben glared at her, then attacked his crab.

As the weeks passed, Dulcie became more irritated by Claudine. When Adam was gone and the exquisite tension that existed between them had gone with him, Claudine was easier to manage. She was not so outspokenly critical. But when Adam was around, Claudine was always helping, always underfoot. Adam couldn't do anything wrong. And Dulcie couldn't do anything right.

Yet, watching, she could see nothing in Adam's manner toward Claudine that would encourage her behavior. He didn't even go around naked anymore unless their bedroom door was locked.

She'd give Claudine every second night off. Knowing

Claudine, she'd find another 'Pollo and soon forget her attachment to Adam.

Before they knew it, April had come. Beau was going home to his sister's wedding. He would stay in New Orleans a month if the blockade permitted, visiting friends he might not see again until the end of the war.

Beau left an hour ahead of Adam, who had gotten a last-minute consignment of saltpeter. Though there were sources in the Confederate states, the quality the blockade runners brought in was thought purer for manufacturing gunpowder. As with everything in short supply, those who wanted it would pay handsomely.

Glory chirruped, "Don't you drag yourself back here all overworked and unable to enjoy yourself with me."

Beau laughed. "Just you keep the sheets good and hot for when I get back." He shook Adam's hand. "See you next month, Adam. So long, Dulcie."

Dulcie kissed Beau fondly, feeling his cheek smooth against her lips and smelling his lime tonic. He had grown dearer to her these past months, and there was a vulnerability about him.

Beau clapped his hand on Ben's shoulder. "Take care of yourself, Ben." His eyes twinkled. "And don't forget she's mine when I get back."

Glory threw her arms around him and crushed him to her. "Honey, you take good care of yourself. Will you, now?"

"You bet, Glory chil'." Beau strode up the gangplank. At the top he turned, smiling, and waved. He grinned, noticing Glory's hand already tucked under Ben's arm. Then slowly the *Ullah* steamed out to sea.

Adam said, "I'd better get on board. Behave yourself, Glory."

"I will—unless I get a better offer."

Adam kissed Dulcie briefly. They had said their good-byes the night before, making love with leisure and fervency.

Dulcie whispered, "Good-bye, love." In her eyes was the message *come back safe*.

In the carriage going to the hotel Glory wept.

"I always feel that way, Glory."

"Isn't it silly of me? I've fallen in love before—every night, sometimes—but he's the first man I ever still loved after he was gone."

Dulcie giggled. "That's what you said when Ben left last time."

"But Ben won't ever *need* me—and Beau might."

Chapter Twenty

The *Ullah*, loaded with Enfield rifles, Belgian muskets, percussion caps, bolts of serge, lead, tin plate, and steel, steamed uneventfully into the Gulf of Mexico. Beau chided himself for hunting trouble where none was. It was a beautiful dark April night, and for once he was having an easy run. He should be grateful, but it had been too easy.

He concentrated on the things he knew to be right and good. He'd never known Adam more contented or pleased with himself than he was standing on the Nassau pier with Dulcie. That was good, and Beau was happy for them.

Then there was Barbara. He knew she loved Morgan Longworth III with all her heart. Before the month ended, Barbara would wear the same glow that now bathed Adam and Dulcie.

But once more his thoughts took on an edge of doubt. He hadn't heard from Barbara since last October. It was unlike her. Both his mother and Barbara were regular correspondents, though the mails were anything but reliable.

Barbara's last letter told him that Morgan was stationed with the Beaufort Artillery under the command of Captain Stephen, manning the fort at Bay Point that guarded Port Royal and Hilton Head Island. As Beau well knew, Port Royal had fallen to the Yankees last November. Where Morgan was now, he had no idea.

The more he forced his mind over Barbara's letter, the more uneasy he became. Ceaselessly, he scanned the Gulf horizon. His keen ears, accustomed to listening for the slightest sound, could hear the telltale noises of other ships. But he saw nothing but the inky black night. No flare went up. No signal split the night sky. Nothing indicated the *Ullah* would be hampered in entering the Mississippi.

Again he brushed away the filaments of spider-web ghosts, superstitions, and expectations of trouble. He should take this run as a godsend. And still, he couldn't. The Federals were out there. Every nerve in his body sensed it. If they were, why didn't they stop him? The *Ullah* was not like the *Liberty* or the *Independence*. She could never out-run a cruiser. This trip she was heavily loaded, slower than ever. Though Beau would never tell Ben or Adam, he always took the *Ullah* out thinking it would be his last run. And tonight, by all reason, he should have been caught. Why hadn't he been? What had kept the blockading ships from guarding the Mississippi?

The *Ullah* slipped into the Pass à l'Outre without a shot fired or a flare to light the sky. It gave him the worst, most foreboding feeling he'd had since the war began.

After he discharged the cargo, Beau loaded a dray with special items for his family. Though the South was carrying on much as always, the shortages were being felt. Prices rose alarmingly as it became more difficult to bring supplies in. Beau had brought coffee, which his mother deemed too expensive at four dollars a pound. And he had several tins of tea, which sold in the South at eighteen to twenty dollars a pound. Muslin, even a bolt of silk, along with woolens and serge, he stacked in the dray. Last he put a box containing scarce items such as corset stays, toothbrushes, sulphur matches, needles, and an assortment of medicine, including a case of good French brandy for his father. Satisfied he had chosen well, Beau whipped up the horses and headed out of New Orleans for the LeClerc house.

Mavis, his mother's personal maid, opened the door. Her eyes immediately filled with tears. She drew him close against her bone-thin frame as he had when he was a small boy. "Mastah Beau! We gwine be all right now."

Beau disentangled himself. "What's the matter, Mavis? You spoil Ma's hair?"

"Ever'thin' gone sour, Mastah Beau. Ol' Mastah gone off to fight wiff Gen'ral Lovell's ahmy, an' Mastah Morgan got hisseff kilt. Ol' Miss, she workin' herseff to death, an li'l Miss, she doan think o' nothin' 'ceptin' Mastah Morgan an'-dem Yankees. She hates 'em fierce an'—"

Beau rubbed his cheek. "Morgan's dead, and Daddy's gone. I thought Lovell was in New Orelans. Where's my mother?"

"In de pahlah. She allers in de pahlah. Allers workin', makin' cloth fo' de uniforms. Ah cain't do nothin' wiff her no mo'."

His mother dropped the old hand card she had been

working with, her face a mixture of sorrow and joy at seeing her son.

Beau went to her, holding her, soothing her. She picked
up the hand card and began to work as she talked. As supplies of ready-made clothing ran out, women who remembered the old ways hand-carded. He stopped her hand. "I've
brought you plenty of cloth, even some wool. You don't
need to do this by hand, Ma."

She began to work again. "But I want to, Beau. There
are so many in need, and"—her face clouded—"it keeps
me busy."

"What happened, Ma?"

His mother shrugged. "There's so little to tell—and so
much."

"What about Daddy? Mavis says he's with General Lovell."

She nodded. "I don't know where. They were in the
city, then they left. He'll write when he's able."

"Why didn't you write to me, Ma? There was no need
for you and the girls to be alone. I would have come home."

"But I did, Beau! I write to you regularly."

Beau's feeling of foreboding grew. His mother recounted
the attack on Port Royal last November seventh; but she
used Morgan's words.

The island had been guarded by Morgan's Beaufort Artillery, a volunteer company on Bay Point, and by the
Charleston Company, manning Fort Walker. The Federals
sent a fleet of thirteen men of war and fifty troop trans-
ports. The *Wabash,* a double-decked steam frigate mounting sixty-two guns, was the flagship. The Confederates had
little chance. Port Royal fell.

Morgan had been shot in the first few minutes of the
bombardment. Seriously wounded and unable to move, he
had written all that he saw and heard to Barbara. He was
dead by the time the Confederates evacuated, but his letter
was sent on to New Orleans.

"How is Barbara, Ma? Is she . . ."

She rose from her chair, leading Beau into Barbara's sitting room. Barbara was with her younger sister, listening
and correcting as Sissy read *Ivanhoe* aloud. Sissy jumped
up, the book tumbling as she dashed to hug Beau. But Barbara remained in her chair. She was thin, and tired looking. It seemed impossible that she was the same radiant
sixteen-year-old he had seen last fall. When she spoke, her

voice was low, too mature, too expressionless, too contained to be his sister. Anguished eyes met and held Beau's. He released himself from Sissy and went to Barbara, cradling her as she cried and told him again how Morgan had died.

Next day brought word of the impending attack on New Orleans that Beau had sensed and feared. Federal ships gathered in the Gulf under the command of Captain David Farragut, whose objective was to gain control of the Mississippi, splitting the Confederacy in half.

Word spread like wildfire. The people were edgy and excited over the coming Federal defeat, for it was unthinkable that the great city of New Orleans would fall. With General Lovell ordered elsewhere, the citizens armed with whatever weapons they could muster. Beau was amazed by his mother and Barbara sitting in the parlor, two old muskets tucked neatly by their chairs. At Beau's inquiry Barbara's eyes blazed, haunting and fierce in her wasted face. "I'll do my part. We all will. Any Yankee sets foot on our soil will rue the day his mama gave birth."

"Barbara, you listen. If the Yankees come, you and Ma hide. Don't get fancy ideas about doin' your part with a weapon you can't handle."

"You talk like a defeatist, Beau. No Yankee's comin' here, 'cause New Orleans'll never fall. We're goin' to win, 'cause we got God on our side."

"You can't talk for God, Barbara, so you just do as I tell you."

"But I can talk for God. I know. God hates all Yankees."

Beau shook his head, annoyed and saddened at her adamant hatred of the Federals. His mother was equally stubborn if more rational. "No Yankee is goin' to drive a Le-Clerc from land we built up with our own hands. Whatever we lack, it will never be pride or self-respect. You keep that in mind. We're Southerners, and God didn't make a man any better than that."

Beau left his warlike family and went to the city. For the most part it was undefended, relying on Forts Philip and Jackson downriver to ward off Farragut's fleet.

Twice David Farragut had had to postpone his attack, waiting for conditions to be right. Then, on April 23, 1862, at a signal of two red lights from the flagship *Hartford*, Farragut's fleet of twenty-five wooden ships and nineteen mortar schooners moved into the Mississippi. The first division, under Captain Bailey headed for Fort Philip. Ten minutes later Bailey's guns were replying to the concentrated fire pouring from the fort.

Captain Boggs, on the *Varuna*, accompanied by the *Oneida*, hugged the shore, avoiding the heavy fire of elevated guns set to protect the midchannel of the river. The Confederates sent the Louisiana State gunboat *Governor Moore* and the River Defense ram *Stonewall Jackson* against the *Varuna*. The two Confederate craft forced the *Varuna* into shoal water, where she sank to her topgallant fo'c'sle. But the two Confederate vessels were ablaze and ran to shore. The crew of the *Governor Moore* under the command of Commander Kennon surrendered to the Federal cruiser *Oneida*.

The Confederates sent pyres on rafts into the river. The Mississippi was clogged with ships and rivercraft. The *Brooklyn* nearly ran afoul of the smaller *Kineo*. The ugly turtle-back ram *Manassas* appeared under the *Brooklyn*'s bows, glancing off the large ship, her chain armor taking most of the impact. The ram steamed on, and the Federal *Kineo* met her. The bulky, awkward *Manassas* continued her erratic journey up and down the river, eluding most damage, until the *Mississippi* struck her a broadside that knocked her into deep water. On fire, the ram moved past the mortar boats and blew up.

Farragut's flagship the *Hartford*, trying to avoid collision with a fire raft pulled by the Confederate tug *Mosher*, grounded. Captain Horace Sherman, master of the tug, managed to lodge a huge torch along the side of the *Hartford*. Flames sprang up the ship's sides and along her rigging. But Farragut, screaming orders, would not give up his ship, and his mate fought to put the fire out and refloat her. The little tug *Mosher* was broadsided and sunk with all aboard.

The mortar schooners were situated about two miles below the forts. From that strategic position they bombarded them ceaselessly. The air vibrated with noise. A thick cloud of suffocating smoke covered the area, its sulphurous sting blinding men and choking them as they struggled to identify friend from foe. The flashes of the guns were their only guide.

In New Orleans, north of the battle, the people were in the street shouting their betrayal. General Lovell's troops should have been defending their city. In the stead of three thousand well-led troops, Wilson's Rangers were sent to help defend the forts.

Wilson's Rangers were riverboat gamblers organized into a unit better known as the Blackleg Cavalry. Ordinarily they were dandy-dressed players of games. As they rode down the streets, ladies handed them bouquets. The citizenry shouted approval and encouragement.

Beau was not cheering. Inwardly he seethed. It was criminal negligence to allow New Orleans to fall to the Federals. Jefferson Davis had no concept of the importance of the sea and the Mississippi. Like Adam and Ben, Beau believed that the army that controlled the Mississippi and the ocean was the army that would win the war. To allow the Mississippi and New Orleans to fall to Farragut was something Beau hated deep inside. Along with the others he felt betrayed.

Just short of the forts the Blackleg Cavalry was greeted by a salvo of shot. With admirable speed the regiment of riverboat gamblers snipped the distinctive buttons from their uniforms along with their dreams of heroism. They headed ignominiously back to the city, to melt unseen into the population.

The fire bells began to peal in New Orleans. Twelve strokes four times repeated. Farragut had passed the forts. The city's defenses had crumbled.

Beau felt desperate. For once he wished he had joined the army. He wished he were in one of those forts, any fort just to be able to stop Farragut or any other damned Yankee who dared threaten his city. As it was, he felt helpless and useless when New Orleans needed him most.

The closer Farragut came, the more chaotic the city grew. Bestirred men and women shouted patriotism, reaffirming they would never surrender, cursing the cowardly imbeciles who had allowed the city to fall, and declaring the Yankees would burn, loot, and pillage. It would be Carthage again. With typical Southern flamboyance, shopkeepers flung wide their doors, inviting the citizenry to cart away whatever they could.

"Not one damned lick of molasses to the Yankees!"

With frantic greed, people fought over the spoils that lined sidewalks and streets. Some hired drays to haul loot home. Beau cringed as Barbara, her shoes covered with molasses that ran in the gutter, fought to destroy the goods in New Orleans rather than let a Yankee belly be filled.

Beau left the destruction, dodging the flying firkins of butter, spilled coffee, tea, potatoes rolling crazily down the cobbled streets. He went to the piers, where steamers under the direction of Governor Thomas Moore were being loaded with ordnance and military stores to be taken up-river to safety.

Beau rounded up half a dozen of his scattered crew. When he arrived at the pier, several steamers were already on their way north. He approached the government official overseeing the loading. "Load your ship with cotton," the man ordered in distracted haste.

"My ship is the large steamer, sir! She can haul stores upriver."

"Don't need her," the man said curtly. "Load her with cotton and set her adrift with the others. It'll slow them down a little."

Beau felt he might choke on his own spittle. Managing only to bark out clipped orders, he joined his crew in loading the cotton that stood on the wharf onto the *Ullah*'s decks. Quixotically, he loaded the *Ullah* as compactly and neatly as she had ever been.

Beau's face was grim as they worked through the morning of the twenty-fourth. Bonfires burned on the piers and streets. The hideous scent of burning ham and sugar mingled with the more acrid odor of scorching cotton. People heaped piles of provisions ready for the torch. Fifteen thousand bales of cotton would burn on the streets or be loaded in ships like the *Ullah*.

After Farragut passed the fortifications at Chalmette, there was little to stop him from coming directly to the city. Beau gritted his teeth. For one horrible moment he thought he would cry. His hand trembling, he tossed the first sputtering torch onto the damp cotton on the *Ullah*. His men handed him others. One by one he lobbed the torches onto the old ship's decks until she was ablaze and drifting out into the current of the Mississippi.

Beau watched her become a giant ball of flame, great bursts of cotton exploding from her decks into the suffocating haze of smoke. As much as he wanted to, he couldn't look away from her until he saw her hit by shot from an unseen vessel. The planking of her spar deck and one of her stacks flew high into the air. The *Ullah* shuddered as she was broadsided again. Then she listed gently, still burning, a fiery beacon in the haze.

Feeling empty and sick at heart, Beau didn't wait to see Farragut's fleet. He returned home. Sissy, eleven and full of the wonders of a world that hadn't touched her yet, looked frightened, her eyes darting from the smoke-smudged face of her brother to that of her pale, strained mother.

"I saw Barbara at the docks," Beau said wearily.

"She told me when she came in. She said you had to fire your ship. I'm sorry, Beau. I know what the ship meant to you—all of you boys."

"It couldn't be helped. Adam or Ben would have done the same. What hurts is that the *Ullah* went for nothing. New Orleans was already lost. It was such a waste—the cotton and food, and the ships."

"What is lost to us is gone. There's nothing you can do now."

"I think I'll go wash up . . . and talk to Barb. She'll have to curb these feelings of hers. There'll be Yankees everywhere. They won't tolerate her saying whatever she pleases."

Beau's mother sniffed. "Defenders of the Constitution they call themselves. Barbarians! Uncouth barbarians!"

"Not all Yankees, Ma. One of the men who got Adam and Ben and me started with the *Ullah* is a Yankee. I'd never be ashamed to bring him home or have it known that I'm his friend."

She said nothing, but her eyes damned all Yankees. Beau went slowly from the room. Sissy tagged along. "Will they come, Beau? Will they rob and—"

"I don't know, Sissy. A lot depends on who commands the troops. If he is an honest man, I doubt we'll have trouble." He pulled her pigtail, then disappeared into his bedroom. He lay down and was sound asleep in minutes.

As Beau slept, David Farragut was having his own problems. Soon after one o'clock he entered a virtually defenseless city. The battle was won, but the New Orleanians set about to show this Yankee conqueror how empty victory could be. They refused to surrender.

They flaunted Confederate colors, they sang Rebel songs, they shouted invective against the bluebellies, they spewed hatred and defiance, daring Farragut to do something about it.

What Farragut had gained was responsibility for a city

aflame with spirit of the Southern cause. Farragut finally threatened to bombard the defenseless city, hoping to extract from New Orleanians an admission of defeat. But, a wise man, he did nothing. He, like they, awaited the ground forces.

General Benjamin Butler arrived on May 1, 1862, and took the beautiful St. Charles Hotel for his headquarters. As greedy and dishonest as he was incompetent and disagreeable, Butler had the misfortune of looking his part. He was a short, overweight man with heavy jowls and a red-veined face. One eyelid drooped noticeably, and if "Cock-eyed Ben" chose to alter his sullen, irritable expression with a smile, even that was crooked.

Immediately upon arrival he set about making himself the most hated man in the South. The St. Charles's gold table service shortly disappeared. For that coincidence he was dubbed "Spoons" Butler. For more serious offenses, he was called "Butler the Beast."

A man less impressed with himself might have won the cooperation if not the hearts of New Orleanians. They were a people who lived by a code of honor, their lives governed by graciousness. Butler offended them at every turn as he set about to humble them. As military commander he took what he wished and did as he wished. He was supreme. All he lacked was recognition of that supremacy by the people.

General Butler had handbills made with his picture on them. His unlovely face could be seen everywhere in New Orleans. Then he issued orders that would humble the people and bring order to "his" city.

All persons over eighteen were required to take an oath of allegiance to the Federal government or surrender their property and leave the city.

No citizen was permitted arms. Butler's soldiers were to search the homes of the citizens for weaponry. Any slave offering information against his master regarding the possession of firearms was freed.

"The wretched beast!" Barbara spat as she tacked rosettes of Confederate colors to her dress. "He can strut and posture, but he'll never stop a Southerner from being a Southerner!"

"Antagonizing him won't help," Beau said quietly. Barbara was changed and hardened since losing Morgan. The word *Yankee* or *Union* or *Federal* set her eyes to blazing. He just hoped she wouldn't insult the wrong Yankee.

"Beau, why are you so willing to accept Yankee rule? If you weren't my brother, I'd call you a coward for what you said."

"I'm no coward, but I'm no fool either. A lot of women parading the streets wearing Confederate colors and bonnets won't harm General Butler. It won't help the South either."

"How little you know!" she said bitterly. "It's an expression of our spirit." She touched her heart. "Men may ride off to war. They may shoot the guns and load the cannons, but women are the ones left with burned-out houses and the graves to be dug and filled and the fatherless children to raise. Whether you accept it or not, Beau, it is our belief in our men, our spirit, our willingness to sacrifice that will defeat men like Butler. He can shoot us, imprison us, starve us, but he can't stop us believing and hating all the Yankee stands for!"

"The outcome of the war will be determined by guns and battles."

She snorted. "How easy for a man to say. Look to the streets, Beau. Battle hasn't defeated our women! And those who obey Butler are not real Southerners. *Our* men are fighting for the cause."

Beau didn't argue. She was partly right. The women were Butler's worst headache. They defied him. They insulted his men. Should a soldier come near, the women pulled in their skirts, making a show of their fear of contamination. From open windows Confederate songs rang out. Never had the spirit of Dixie been so vibrantly displayed as it was in New Orleans that spring and summer.

Butler was livid. He issued Order Number 28, aimed at the women. No one was permitted by action, word or gesture to insult a Federal soldier on pain of imprisonment. Women were forbidden to flaunt Confederate colors or sing Confederate songs.

Soon his order was tested. A woman was sentenced to Ship's Island for laughing during the funeral of a Federal officer.

The women were furious. Butler's pictures disappeared. He lived in constant irritability. His men were busy day and night trying to discover what had become of his pictures.

In one of the few times during the month of May that Beau, his mother, and sisters could laugh, he told them about Butler's difficulties. Though Butler's order was aimed primarily at the ladies of New Orleans, it most annoyed the prostitutes, and they put up a resistance of their own design.

Beau sat comfortably in the parlor savoring the story. "Butler has been going mad trying to discover what dastard stole his likenesses. Then, I heard, one of his less intelligent officers, relayed a vile rumor to the general." Beau paused, took a long sip of brandy, and leisurely lit a cigar, his eyes dancing as they met Sissy's.

"Beau, stop teasing and tell us!" Sissy shrilled.

"Well, it is rumored that . . . the ladies of the evening did some confiscating of their own."

"His pictures!" Sissy concluded excitedly.

"Yes, and it is further rumored that, being imaginative young women, they pasted the pictures . . ."

"Where, Beau? Where?" Sissy prompted, edging nearer.

"In the bottom of their tinkle pots."

Barbara began to laugh, softly at first, then as hard as Beau had ever heard her laugh. "Oh, Beau, is it true? Have they really?"

"We'll know by morning," he said mysteriously.

As Barbara laughed at the general's expense, his foot soldiers were suffering in acute embarrassment, marching through the streets of the red-light district, knocking on every door and demanding to inspect every chamber pot in the house. Those bearing General Butler's illustrious image were confiscated and taken back of the St. Charles Hotel, where General Butler personally smashed each one with a heavy hammer.

News of the night's work reached every house by the following morning. New Orleans had something to laugh about. But no one was fooled, least of all Beau. The women had made a fool of "Cock-eyed Ben," but he had the power to crush them. Searches of private homes would increase.

So would confiscations of private property. One man had already lost his entire stable of prize racehorses, ostensibly for military purposes, but actually to be sent north to Butler's own stables. Butler had brought his brother, A. J., into the city. Between them, nothing was too small to tempt their greed.

Beau knew it was a matter of time before the LeClerc home was searched. Mavis and the house servants would say nothing, but what of the field hands? Who could be sure a slave wouldn't believe a hollow Yankee promise of wealth and "freedom" when all his master could offer was another year of cutting cane.

Beyond that uncertainty was the stubbornness of his mother and sister. They insisted on keeping their loaded muskets within easy reach.

"Americans have the right to defend themselves," his mother said. "And we *are* Americans, Beau. We fought for this land a hundred years ago. No white-trash Northerner can make me give it up."

"I'd rather die than allow that beast to know he'd made me afraid for one moment," Barbara added.

Strategically they were wrong. Still, he admired them. He admired many of the women of New Orleans. In them was a fierceness of spirit that couldn't be ignored. Their weapons were their tongues, the look in their eyes, the unmistakable censure in their attitudes. Small weapons when compared to Enfield rifles, Parrot guns, and cannons, but for all that, he thought theirs might be more enduring. Generations of Southerners had suckled at their breasts, been guided by their soft Southern voices whispering fierce words of honor and lessons of Southern pride. It would be these same softly fierce voices who taught generations of the future. It was a force no Parrott gun could boast.

By the beginning of June they were lulled into a sense of security. The soldiers had never come. No LeClerc had been forced to pledge allegiance to the Federal government. No one had attempted to harrass them or search the house. Beau began planning to return to Nassau.

He sent a telegram to Zoe informing her he would be in Wilmington at the end of June. She would give the message to Adam.

His sea chest was packed. He'd already ordered Joachim to hitch the dray he'd drive to Wilmington. At noon Barbara and his mother prepared ham.

"A toast to the most beautiful women in New Orleans." He raised his glass lovingly to his mother, then Barbara, and last Sissy, who grinned into the crystal goblet, the first wine she'd ever been allowed.

They smiled, accepting his compliments, when Mavis rushed to Mrs. LeClerc's side. "Dey's here! Oh, Miss what we gwine do? Dey's come!"

"Who's here?"

Beau was on his feet, his face taut. "The Federals. Stay where you are. Don't make a sound."

Six blue-uniformed men milled in the hallway. At a glance Beau knew this was not the normal call. There was no ranking officer. They had all been drinking. He was certain the search was something the six of them had thought up themselves, but there was nothing he could do to stop it.

"Who're you?" One man asked, singling Beau out. "I wuz tol' three ladies live here." His accent was harsh, Northern, clipped.

"I'm Beau LeClerc. This is my home."

"Ah'm Beau La Clair. This is mah home," the man mimicked, then burst into a loud guffaw. "Well, now, Beau La Clair, I s'pose you know this here city is part of the U-nited States of America agin, don't you?"

"No sir, I do not. The state of Louisiana by will and consent of her people is part of the Confederate States of America."

"By Jeez-zuz, the way this guy talks. Hey, fellas! Lookie here. We found us a real live Reb traitor." The man moved nearer to Beau. The smell of whiskey was strong and sour. "I want to hear you pledge allegiance to the U-nited States of America right now, Reb."

Beau hesitated, quickly licking his lips. "I can't do that, sir. I'm a loyal citizen of—"

The rifle butt smashed into his mouth so quickly, Beau hadn't seen it coming. Blood and teeth gushed from his mouth.

"The pledge of allegiance, Reb!" He swung the rifle into Beau's stomach. Beau went to his knees. "Well, boys, this fella ain't gonna co'perate. Gen'ral Ben'll be sure 'nuf happy to know we got us s'more Reb propitty." He kicked Beau. "Tell him, Jake."

As Beau tried to rise, Jake clubbed him back to his knees with the rifle. Two men began to fill potato sacks with family silver and heirlooms.

Beau lunged for another man as he made for the dining room. Jake kicked him viciously in the head. Beau groaned and fell to the floor.

Jake, unconcerned, recited Butler's order that anyone over the age of eighteen not taking the pledge of allegiance to the Federal government would forfeit all property and leave the city. "That means now—tonight, Reb. I see you here tomorrow, and you're a dead Reb, you unnerstan'?" Beau lay motionless. The man prodded him with his foot. "He unnerstan's."

"Hey, look what we got here," a man yelled from the dining room. "Don't mind if we help ourselves, do you ladies?" He settled into Beau's chair.

"Be my guest. It's hemlock," Mrs. LeClerc said.

The man heaved his legs up. His filthy boots came down on the white lace tablecloth. The wine decanter wobbled. He grabbed it, grinning. "Can't let that spill!" He took a long swallow. Three men stood in the door. "Ain't we gonna git any o' that, Luke?"

Barbara's face was as white as the tablecloth. With unnatural calm, she took a long drink of wine, then spat it into Luke's face.

"Jeez-zuz! We got a spitfire and an ol' witch!" He sputtered, just drunk enough to have both his anger and sense of humor roused.

The last two men entered, leaving Beau semiconscious in the hall.

Luke's tongue lapped at the drips of wine. He came round to Barbara. He grabbed her by the chin, forcing her to face him. "Little Southern belle. Too good for Yankee scum, ain't you?"

"Leave her alone!" Mrs. LeClerc said.

"Keep out of this, ol' witch." He thrust out a beefy arm, backhanding her across the throat. Mrs. LeClerc gasped, strangling. Barbara lurched back in her chair, kicking at Luke.

He grabbed Barbara's wrist, pressing until she cried out. He continued the pressure until she screamed. "Lock the old witch up," he growled. "Them too. I got some talkin' to do with the spitfire."

Two of the men dragged Sissy and Mrs. LeClerc screaming up the stairs. At a roared order Mavis scurried after them.

"I hate you!" Barbara hissed, barely audible for the pain in her arm.

Luke ripped the front of her dress. "I don't see nothin' special. Wha's so special about a Southern gal that's too good for a Yankee? *You show me!* What you got that's too good for the likes of Luke Baker?"

She spat at him again. He slapped her so hard, her head

rocked. She was dizzy, her balance precarious. She groped for the table, her fingers closing over the handle of the carving knife.

Beau, left for unconscious, struggled to the sitting room and the muskets. He grabbed both, then dug his Colt out of his mother's sewing basket. He staggered to the dining room. Leaning heavily against the doorjamb, his mouth still pouring blood, he fired into Jake's surprised face.

Barbara leaped, driving her knife deep into Luke Baker's belly.

The other two men grabbed for their pistols as Barbara, screaming, shoved the dying man from her. Everything in sight she hurled across the room. Three guns went off.

Beau discharged the second musket. The Federal's head splattered on the wall.

The other Federal moved toward the window, wary of Barbara and Beau. As Beau fired, the man leaped, crashing through the glass.

Beau ran to the darkened parlor. He could hear scuffling and shouting upstairs. He moved into the hall. Legs braced, feet spread, hands together steadying the Colt, Beau aimed for the heart of one of the men at the top.

Mrs. LeClerc, her arms outstretched, butted the other Federal, pushing him down the circular staircase.

The two soldiers lay in a tangle at Beau's feet. One man was dead, the other dazed. Without hesitation Beau cracked his skull.

Barely able to speak through his ruined mouth, Beau motioned to his mother and Sissy. "One got away," he muttered, all but unintelligible. "He'll bring help. Got to get you away. Can't come back."

Mrs. LeClerc nodded. She couldn't nurse Beau now or help him in any way but to obey without question. She gathered food, matches, and necessities, thinking of the Federals who would hunt Beau down. Shortly the women were headed for the stables as Beau instructed.

Joachim had the horses hitched and waiting. Beau handed his mother a paper bearing directions to Tom and Ullah's bayou house. "Don't tarry, Ma. You have to be there before dark, or you'll get lost."

"Beau . . ." his mother cried.

"I'll come there, soon's it's safe."

"Beau . . ."

He tried to smile. It became a grimace of pain. "I'll be careful."

She cried openly as he helped her on to the wagon. "Beau, we love you, dear. Don't . . . just remember we love you."

"I know, Ma. Me too," he said, then nodded to Joachim. The wagon lurched, then rumbled at a slow pace down the driveway. Beau glanced back at his home once, then returned to the stables and saddled a horse.

With a boldness that defied his own reason he rode to the St. Charles Hotel. Not bothering to conceal himself, he walked to the flagpole, looking up where the Stars and Stripes fluttered in the late afternoon sun. Then, with the catlike agility that had once won him the task of placing the shingles on Tom and Ullah's roof, he shinnied up the flagpole.

Two guards gaped at him in astonishment. "Halt!"

Beau looked down. From his pocket he withdrew three sulphur matches. He struck one and held it to the end of the flag.

"He's burnin' the flag!"

"Desist, or I'll shoot!"

Beau lit the second match and held it to the cloth of the flag.

Two shots rang out.

Beau plunged to the ground, the flaming flag tight in his hands.

"Look at the damned bastard," said one guard as they rushed over, grabbing the flag and stamping out the remaining flames.

The second man kicked savagely at the body. "Killin's too good!"

"Jeez-zuz, I tell ya, ya never know what one o' them crazy Rebs is liable to do."

Chapter Twenty-One

Ben knocked on the door of Adam and Dulcie's suite at the Royal Victoria. "Good morning, Mrs.—" Dulcie's face was white and strained, her eyes watery, her lower lip trembling. "What's wrong? Where's Adam?"

"Oh, Ben, it's so awful."

Ben stepped inside. Adam, hard-faced and grim stared down at his hands. He held two letters. A short one from Zoe said that Beau would be in Wilmington at the end of June. The other was from Beau's mother.

"Tell me what's got you both lookin' like you're at a funeral." Ben said.

Dulcie put her hand over her mouth, her breath catching on a stifled sob. "I'll . . . I'll go send Claudine for some coffee."

As Ben uneasily sat down, Adam silently handed him the letters. He read Zoe's first, as had Adam. "He lost the *Ullah*." Ben looked up. "Is that what's got you all worked up? Jeez, Adam, we knew it would come sometime. We ought to be whoopin' it up! Beau's all right. What's a ship?"

"Keep reading." Adam's voice was deep and thick.

"Oh, God. Oh, my God." Ben looked stricken.

"This God-damned fuckin' war!" Adam exploded, his face tight with hurt and shocked anger.

Ben walked aimlessly. "Look . . . uh, Adam, I've got to get out of here for a while. Uh, tell Dulcie . . ." He dashed for the door.

As it closed, Dulcie came back into the front room. "He knows?"

Adam walked to the window. Standing behind him, Dulcie slipped her arms around his waist and laid her cheek against his back. "Thank God it wasn't you. Come sit with me, talk to me, Adam."

"Not now. Let me alone, Dulcie."

"You'll feel better. We can write to Beau's mother. We must let her know she's not alone. Come, tell me what you'd like to say. Oh, Adam, you can't brood. You have to go on a run soon."

He turned from the window, pushing her away. "Dulcie, not now," he repeated tensely. "Leave me alone!"

"I can't. I'm your wife."

"My wife, not my keeper, Dulcie!"

"Adam . . ."

"I don't want to talk to you." His voice was cold, his eyes hard.

Dulcie stared at him, helpless and hurt. There was a

great part of himself he still kept closely guarded. The
years of his growing up, the events that had made him
the man she loved, he refused to share with her.

She fled to the bedroom before he could see her crying. She waited expectantly for the front door to close.

Adam was torn between the need to leave, walk, run,
heal himself until the kinks of pain and memory eased
and the need to go to Dulcie. He walked hesitantly to the
bedroom. She was standing by their bed, waiting, he knew,
for him to leave. He went to her, closing her inside his
arms. "I'm sorry."

"Oh, so am I, Adam," she cried, holding herself against
him. "I'll never ask you to tell me things you don't want
to tell me."

"Beau . . . Beau was like my brother. I can't believe he
won't be coming into port any day now, that I'll never
see or hear his voice again. Oh, God, Dulcie, why? He
had such plans, so much to do, and now . . ." he straightened and moved away from her again. "It's all a waste.
The destruction and misery . . . it's a bitter, rotten war.
So much death."

"It's not all death, Adam. There's life too."

"Life? Poverty. Illness. Hunger. Painful, useless life."

"No, you're wrong. I didn't think this was the time to
tell you, but perhaps it is the best time of all."

He didn't look at her. She went on alone. "We're goin'
to have a child, Adam," she said softly. "He'll never see
any of this war or misery. We'll make a fine home for
him. Perhaps if we gave him Beau's name . . ."

Adam stared as though she were a marvelous stranger.
She laughed nervously. "I—it won't happen until next
spring. You are pleased? Adam, say *something!*"

He nodded like a small boy, then smiled uncertainly.
Dulcie laughed and threw herself into his arms. "Oh,
Adam, I love you!"

He held her close, kissing her, then stopping to look at
her, his fingers moving across the exposed areas of her
flesh, perhaps to see if she had altered in that moment
she told him she carried their first child. He took her to
the bed, undressed her and then himself.

Dulcie giggled as he lay down beside her. His desire
to see her all over, to find and marvel at the slightest
change her pregnancy might have brought was obvious.
She had done the same thing before her mirror, looking

at her breasts to see if they had yet begun to swell, sticking her small, still-flat tummy out to see what she would look like months from now.

Adam's hands moved across her breasts. "I think they are already a little larger," she said. "Can you tell?"

He put his face between them, then moved down to her belly, his hands caressing her. He kissed the smooth skin above the triangle of hair. "Will it be a boy?" he asked softly, wanting to hear that it would.

"It must be, Adam. And we will name him Beau. Beau Tremain."

He kissed the soft skin over the child again, then lay with his hand covering her belly. "I love you."

Late that afternoon they walked down Bay Street toward Rawson Square. Adam talked easily now, telling her of years in school when he and Beau and Ben heckled teachers and ran free in the bayous playing at Indians or hunting alligators.

They spent a leisurely afternoon, walking in and out of stores, buying things they neither wanted nor needed. Their talk flowed, and while it was tinged with a sense of Beau's death, it drew them closer together.

Dulcie looked up at her husband, her eyes filled with admiration and love. She wanted Jem and Patricia to see him through her eyes, to know him as she did now, to know how happy she was with him. Letters were not enough, particularly with the way she had left home, running first from New Orleans and then the harrowing escape with Adam from New York, and now Beau's death. Life was too uncertain, family too impermanent not to touch them whenever she could. Perhaps when the war was over, they wouldn't be there.

"Adam, could you take me home when you make the next trip? I wouldn't get in the way. I know the rules of your ship now."

"You want to go to Mossrose," he said softly, a fact not a question.

"I'd like to see Mama, and of course Daddy will have instructions as to what our child must look like. You realize, Daddy will insist on a full head of red hair like his own, freckles, and—a Moran temper."

"Poor man's in for a disappointment. Beau will have a Tremain temper and no freckles *anywhere*. Those are cute only on girls."

"Then you'll take me?"

"I'm due in Savannah in August. It won't be an easy trip, Dulcie. Think it over before you decide. The river is closed off by the blockade. I'll have to come into Charleston and go to Savannah by land."

"Oh, good!"

"Good? No, you don't understand. We—"

Dulcie giggled and pressed his arm against her. "I'll have you all to myself across an ocean and then all the way from Charleston to Savannah and then at Mossrose and all the way back. Now, who doesn't understand?" she asked impishly. "Maybe we'll have twins."

Ben left for Wilmington the night before Adam and Dulcie were due to sail for Charleston. They went to the pier to see him off.

"Godspeed," Adam clasped Ben's hand with greater fervor and meaning than ever before.

Ben's eyes met his. "You too, Adam." He smiled at Dulcie. "You take care of yourself and your family, Dulcie. Watch out for the captain here."

When the *Liberty* steamed into the channel, Adam said, "You're certain you want to make this trip? I can carry letters to your family for you."

"I'm sure, Adam."

"I thought you would be, so I had your trunks put aboard. Dulcie, what about the baby? And why must you travel without Claudine?"

She shook her head stubbornly. "I won't need Claudine." Then she smiled. "Don't you remember, I want you *all* to myself? No one but us."

Pleased and loving every minute of her adoration, he looked no farther than her words for her reasons for leaving Claudine behind.

Dulcie boarded the *Independence* while Adam saw to last-minute arrangements. As she organized her own belongings in the cabin and struggled with unaccustomed practicalities, she knew that when she and Adam returned from Mossrose, something would have to be done about Claudine. Claudine was in love with Adam. She had not done anything Dulcie could criticize, but the knowledge was always there. So was the possibility that one night Adam would come in late when Claudine was not by Dulcie's side. She knew she couldn't stand that. Even if

Claudine weren't with Adam, the suspicion would be. And if Claudine were with Adam, she'd rather die than know.

The only reasonable solution was to bring a new maid back with her from Mossrose. She would give Claudine her freedom. Adam would approve. And Claudine would have to agree that her freedom didn't include Nassau or anyplace near Adam. Perhaps she would like to return to France.

The following evening Dulcie stood on the quarterdeck beside her husband, waving happily at Claudine. The twinkling lights and gay noises were behind her. Claudine looked tiny standing beside the gargantuan Rosebud. Dulcie knew she felt abandoned and confused. For a moment all Dulcie's resolve melted. No one could replace Claudine. She would not send her away. Claudine was the best friend she ever had.

Then Adam waved to the small black girl, and Claudine's face changed. The lost-child look vanished as her attention riveted on Adam. She smiled, her whole being coming alive. Dulcie watched and felt a little sad. No matter how much she cared for Claudine, she cared for herself and Adam more. Claudine would leave on their return.

The *Independence* steamed out of the harbor, leaving Nassau a dim, misty mirage behind them. Adam set course for the North West Providence Channel. Dulcie was alert, tense, momentarily expecting to see a Federal cruiser. As the crew lounged without concern on the watch and Adam was relaxed and gazing contentedly out to sea, she tugged at his sleeve, her eyes full of questions. He laughed, and the sound was loud, carrying on the evening air.

"You said I wasn't allowed to talk!" she accused. "And here you are—"

"We're still in British waters—no Federals allowed," he said, still chuckling. "As soon as we clear the islands, then it's all quiet."

"How long until we're clear? Will it be completely dark by then?"

"I certainly hope so. We want to slip past the cruisers that lie in wait just beyond the Bahamas. They like nothing better than to catch some unsuspecting runner steaming right into their path."

"You mean they cruise clear out here?"

"Sweetheart, they cruise anywhere they think they might catch a prize."

"Oh, Adam, I think—I think I'm frightened. I never knew how much danger you were in. You never told me. They won't catch us, will they? You said no one could catch the *Independence*."

He hugged her against him. "That's what I said."

Together they walked the decks, Adam checking the rigging and security of the cargo lashed to the deck, Dulcie asking questions at every stop. Patiently he explained the equipment's function. She began to feel his love for the old square-rigged wind-driven ships he had learned his craft aboard. She heard in the undertones of his voice and the words he chose the forward look of his whole philosophy. He had become a steam man because steam was the way of the future. Adam had a fondness for things of the past, but his vision was set firmly on what was to come. He was ready for change, welcomed it, gloried in its challenge.

At dawn they passed the Berry Islands and altered course to west northwest, the final leg of the channel to the Atlantic. Adam checked his charts and made navigational corrections. The contrary waters and currents of the Bahama area slowed their progress more than he had reckoned. As often as he had made this trip, he knew he could never count on the sea here. It was a strange region, plagued by sudden storms, peculiar mists that allowed no visibility, peculiar water spouts that rose without warning, capable of destroying a ship. And this time it had slowed the *Independence* so that he would be coming into the Atlantic exactly when he didn't want to be. He lost his casual ease and ordered the sails of the brigantine-rigged steamer to be set.

He would be sailing out of the protection of British waters in daylight, and he didn't like the look of the morning sky. There were no storm clouds, no heavy seas, but the feel was wrong. He had sailed too many times in these waters not to respect his intuition of trouble just as he did the readings of barometers or indications of the compass. He had seen the sea whip to a froth so quickly a man could lose sight of the horizon, becoming lost in a world in which there was no visible difference between sky and water. It was a sea in which ships vanished without a trace.

The *Independence* leaped ahead, her sails filled with the wind. Adam eased off the engines, then posted lookouts at each quarter of the ship. The hours passed, and the sea became cloaked in mist as the warm waters of the Gulf stream mingled with cool air. The crew stood by, alert and tense, awaiting the inevitable cry, "Ship ahoy!"

It came just after noon. Adam swung to look in the direction of the call. The cruiser heaved into sight. The heart of every man aboard the *Independence* thudded. The cruiser had the weather gage of them. She was on the windward side of the *Independence* which allowed her to pick her time and angle of attack.

In a fleeting instant Adam considered his options. With British waters so near and Dulcie aboard, he decided to run, counting on the superior speed of the *Independence* to carry them back to the islands before the cruiser could do much damage. He shouted the new course to the helmsman and demanded full steam.

The *Independence* shot forward, set for the waters off the Great Bahama Bank. The cruiser angled in toward them, signals flashing. "Heave to, or I'll sink you!"

The sea changed, the blue-green water churned white, the wind current became contrary and inconsistent. Adam shouted orders to the crew, moving the great sheets, taking advantage of the additional speed the sails gave before the sea became too heavy to keep them set. The *Independence* was doing sixteen knots, pulling steadily, if slowly, away from the cruiser.

The cruiser signaled again.

The shouts and the sudden increase in the movement brought Dulcie from the cabin. Adam's voice cracked across the air like thunder.

"Keep her clean full." The ship slammed across the wind. Then Dulcie heard the shots from the cruiser. Above the howl of the wind one of the crewmen shouted. "Get below, ma'am. We're runnin', an' there's bad weather ahead!"

Dulcie stood frozen to the spot. The wind whipped over the deck. Before them the sky was turning ominously dark. The waves crashed against the *Independence*, sloshing and sending spray over her decks. Dulcie clung to the cargo lashings, gasping and struggling for balance.

The sea heaved and tore at the lightly built hull of the *Independence.*

"Ready about!" Adam shouted, knowing that the time he could use the sails was in fact done, and still the cruiser was within gun range. Tacks and sheets of the courses were cleared for the yards to swing.

Dulcie pulled hand over hand along the cargo lashings, then struggled to the companionway. She glanced up in the direction she knew Adam to be, though she couldn't see him. Until this trip she had never accurately imagined what his being master of the *Independence* meant. Each member of the crew sprang into action at the sound of his voice. There was no hesitation, no look of doubt. They trusted him entirely. Only then did she realize the scope of Adam's power aboard the ship. There was no one above him. No one to whom he turned for direction or decision. He was alone. He was absolute ruler of the *Independence* and responsible for all the lives aboard it. And he had said he needed her. Now she knew why.

Tears of pride came to her eyes. At another urgent cry from the crewman to get below, Dulcie carefully picked her way back to the cabin. Dutifully she sat down to remain safe. But she wanted to be with Adam.

On the quarterdeck Adam shouted, "Lee oh! Down helm!" The helmsman spun the wheel in the direction of the wind. The foresheet and jib sheets eased. The weight of the wind lessened as the ship flew quickly into the wind's eye. The canvas shuddered, then slackened as the *Independence* crossed the wind.

"Mainsail haul!" The yards came round. The hands wound the brace winches frantically.

"Let go and haul!" The foreyards ground around on the winch. Adam glanced at the full sails. The rain was steady but not heavy. He looked at the cruiser, still coming and much too close. With a wary eye he checked the darkening mass ahead. For a moment he considered surrendering his ship, and then reconsidered. The squall was moving rapidly. He couldn't avoid it by surrendering to the cruiser. He pulled at the edge of his moustache and tried to think of something they could do to avoid the storm and the cruiser. It was futile, and he knew it. If Dulcie were not aboard, he would never have thought about it at all.

The cruiser was as harshly buffeted by the heavy seas as the *Independence*. Her shots fell wide, and Adam prayed silently for the squall to hold off long enough for the *Independence* to make use of the sails to outrun the cruiser. Slowly they were gaining distance. If it could only last a bit longer.

The cruiser captain began to fire hot shot at the *Independence*, knowing her speed would eventually leave the cruiser behind. The first shot was short, but Adam heard the ominous hiss as it sunk into the sea. The next shot sliced through the topsail. The canvas flashed into flame. Adam swore under his breath. The shot, a cannonball heated red hot before firing, was capable of sending the ship up in flames.

Within moments the next cannonball struck, shearing the foremast. Grape and canister spewed across the decks. The fire caused by the hot shot blazed like a beacon, presenting the cruiser a clear target in the darkening murk.

Thunder began to rumble. Lightning flashed, great bolts of fire slammed into the heaving, white-capped breast of the ocean. Adam chewed tensely on the end of his moustache. The *Independence* was built for speed but not endurance. She began to yaw in the heavy seas.

The crew worked frantically hauling in the remaining canvas. The cruiser, astern of them, suddenly disappeared into the pelting rain and rolling ocean, only to appear again several points starboard of her last position. In spite of the storm and though they were in British waters, she showed no sign of giving up the chase.

Adam adjusted his course once more, running for Andros Island, hoping to round it and return to the safety of Nassau harbor.

The fury of the storm mounted. Adam began to suspect that it was not merely a storm but one of the enormous, dangerous squall lines that plagued the ocean here and could extend for as much as one hundred miles.

With the cruiser hard on her heels, firing shot, the *Independence* was running before the sea, the most dangerous position she could have. Both steerage and power were lost to her as she was lifted by the stern, carried forward on the breast of a sixteen-foot wave. Adam abruptly checked the speed, to stop the wild yawing of the low blockade runner, never designed to take such punishment. Green water swept over her decks. The ship nosed under, then struggled back to rights. Carried forward again, she broached and broadsided into the seas, helpless as the next wave rolled over her. They seemed to shoot straight to the bottom of the ocean as the waves parted and then snapped closed over them. The hull trembled and shook as though she would tear apart.

The helmsman met the swelling sea by quartering into it, receiving the force of the crest on the windward bow, then as Adam shouted, he straightened course, taking advantage of the momentary calm that follows a heavy sea.

"Man overboard!" They heard, heeded, then forgot as the ship pitched and yawed slithering into the next trough.

As the sea crested and washed over the *Independence,* he heard screams and then silence. The green water enveloped them and washed away as the ship righted. The forward deck was empty. No cargo, no man.

With a panicky fear he had never known since Ullah's death, he realized he couldn't get to Dulcie. There was only one chance of keeping the ship together and afloat; he must remain as he was, directing from the helm. And if he lost the ship, he also lost Dulcie—and their unborn child.

The hull of the *Independence* strained, the ship shuddered as one of the engines quit. Adam grimly ordered the first mate to signal an SOS to the cruiser. They hadn't seen the cruiser for the past half hour, but Adam was certain the heavier-built ship was weathering the storm far better than the *Independence.* Prison was far preferable to dying in a white sea. Repeatedly between crests the SOS was sent, but he saw no answering flash.

Adam checked the compass, no longer certain of direction. The compass jerked erratically, not showing north. He ordered the SOS sent from every quarter of the ship without stop, and again his mind raced to Dulcie and the child. He sent two crewmen below to see to her. He ordered the second mate to take out their supply of flares and to shoot them up regularly so the cruiser could find them if it were anywhere near.

Poring over charts, checking and rechecking the few indications of position he had, Adam judged they were near the Tongue of the Ocean. The ship lurched, then rose, yawing and broadsiding once more into the trough.

The green seas washed over them. The charts swept from the table. Adam was flung to the deck. The helmsman lay sprawled unconscious, the helm spinning wildly as the ship was buffeted by the sea.

Adam pulled himself painfully up, grabbing the helm.

The first ominous sounds of the hull grinding against reef or rock came but seconds before the water crashed in on them. The *Independence* listed, teetering on the reef. Then she was lifted high, free of the barrier, only to be sent crashing down into the sea to break apart.

BOOK III

The Black Swan

1862-1865

Chapter One

Pale points of starlight set deep in the black heavens lit the sandy shore of Andros Island. The Tongue of the Ocean roared ceaselessly. The dark forest crept toward the angry waters. A large square native hut stood near a smaller round one, both with thatched roof and walls. At a distance, several other huts were clustered raggedly together. Near the ocean's edge shadowy figures moved stealthily out of the protection of the dense growth, away from the security of the huts.

Cautiously, following the woman who led them, they approached the two bodies lying on the wet, littered sand. The voodoo queen, a woman short and wide, said, "Tek de 'oman to Mam'bo Luz hut."

The natives looked at her, fear and doubt on their faces.

Mam'bo Luz raised her huge arms. With her head thrown back, she praised Erzulie, goddess of the Moon. Then she turned her intense gaze to the natives. "Erzulie speak ter Mam'bo Luz. 'Oman be good speerit Erzulie sen' from lan' ob Ife. We call 'oman Guédé Vi, chil' ob de gods."

Satisfied Luz had the blessing of the gods, the natives lifted the limp woman, carrying her with care to the voodoo queen's hut.

Mam'bo Luz's attention focused on the other body. Moving sinuously, she circled the man, then stopped, holding her body rigidly still, listening for the words of the gods as she had before. Again she nodded her head quickly and turned to the natives. "De man evil speerit. He de Guédé l'Orage, god ob de stawm. Bring bad time."

Luz watched their faces, her expression shrewd and crafty. It had been a long time since she had been able to perform one of her black miracles to impress them. For months she had fretfully watched her powers being usurped by her archrival, Lucifer. Now, with the gift of the woman of the red sun and the man of the black storm, Luz could once more demonstrate her power—and crush

Lucifer's hold on her people. Luz would perform her black miracles with Erzulie's gift.

She spread her arms wide, encompassing the crowd of brown people who stood tentative and waiting. "Luz 'tect you. Tell you what ter do. Tek de man 'roun' de ben' where he doan see de village. Buil' ring ob fire 'roun' 'im. Buil' it high, high, high! Fire, fire, fire!"

The men hung back, circling the powerful guédé who had been washed ashore, afraid to touch the evil spirit.

The woman was contemptuous. "No lissen ter Mam'bo Luz? No lissen ter Erzulie? Git dat man 'roun' de ben' 'fo' he wake up. I gib you a charm, keep you safe lak de bat in de cave." She mumbled an incantation, and the men moved away, carrying the man far down the beach, around the bend to the empty desolation of an empty shore.

Luz smiled in satisfaction, then shouted after them. "You git back, I talk *ol'* storee. I tell you what you doan know. Ol' storee calm de water."

Later, near a small fire in the clearing, Mam'bo Luz began her "old story" in the traditional way:

> Dis was a time, a very good time,
> Not in my time but in ol' people time,
> Monkey chew tobacco an' spit white lime.

"Dere was a king, big king 'cross de sea. King say to Gilmartin, I gib you some lan'."

In the strange singsong cadence of her language Luz wove the story of the white man's invasion of the isolated native world of Andros Island. The first of the luckless Gilmartins had been given a land grant by an English king. Gilmartin had brought with him men from the Congo to clear the wild jungle. Before he could enjoy the riches gleaned from his new mahogany plantation, he died. His son inherited the wealth as well as the curse that seemed to hover over the Gilmartin family. The son, too, died young, leaving behind the riches of the plantation and two children, William and Kenneth, to lust after it. William, the oldest son, inherited. At his untimely death his property went to his young son, Justin.

"Kennef t'ief de lan' from boy Justin. Den Kennef tek a wife. De wife Helen. Helen gib Kennef li'l girl baby. Helen look on Mam'bo Luz while she got baby in belly." Mam'bo Luz smiled now, remembering how her power had soared when Helen had given birth to Dorothy and the child had had a birthmark that remained bright red all her life. Helen had looked on Luz, and the natives had believed Luz had marked the baby. They still talked of it today.

Luz chuckled maliciously as she told of Helen's second child. "Helen belly git fill up one odder time. Sen' Mam'bo Luz away 'cause Luz be pinto woman. Helen doan wan' pinto spots on baby. Mam'bo Luz call on de gods. Call Erzulie. Call *guédés*. Mek de ritu'l when baby git born. Mam'bo Luz mek de baby speerit evil!"

Mam'bo Luz's laughter rang out in the dark night. The natives shivered, sensing her maniacal aura. "Luz pow'ful! Luz han'maid ob Erzulie! Kennef know dat. Dor'fy know."

Luz, insane with the notoriety the Gilmartin's misfortunes gave to her, took credit for everything that befell them. Her people witnessed her incantations, calling down the spirits to plague the Gilmartins further.

Luz performed her rituals day and night. The Drum of the Thunderbolt split the heated night air. The wild singing and dancing went on and on until Luz triumphed.

Helen Gilmartin had died giving birth to the deformed child, whom Kenneth had hated on sight. Drinking and raging over his land like a madman, Kenneth had shouted blasphemous vilification at God. Deep in the woods he had cursed the land, pounding on the earth until his hands were bloody. He renamed his plantation Satan's Keep and his only son Lucifer.

Seventeen-year-old Dorothy, horrified by her baby brother and the drunken raging insanity of her father, had run in panicky fear to the dense junglelike forest and become lost.

"Dor'fy disappear—poof!" Luz smiled slyly. "Nobody know 'bout Dor'fy. Mam'bo Luz know. Mam'bo Luz wise, eh, eh."

The old story went on. Luz described how, bloated with success, she turned her attention to the infant on whom she had placed an evil spirit. "Lucifer so ugly nobody touch. Fadder no touch 'im. Boy Justin no touch. Nobody touch ugly evil speerit. *Mam'bo Luz touch 'im.* Feed 'im. Ten' 'im. Mam'bo Luz got de power ober Lucifer.

"Frum time Lucifer li'l boy, Luz tek de life juice from he root. Sometime she suck it out. Drink de life juice. Mek Lucifer weak. Mek Mam'bo Luz strong, strong, strong'r. Sometime Mam'bo Luz tek he root inter she Sacred En-

trance down below. Hol' he root tight. Tight. Mam'bo
mount Lucifer an' ride 'im till he root gush he life fluid
inter Mam'bo Luz. Mam'bo t'ief he power. Mek Lucifer
weak, weak. Put 'im in de Mam'bo power."

The others murmured, then quieted, waiting for her to
tell them of the future, in what new way she would weaken
the fearsome Lucifer.

"Ternight de speerits come in on de stawm. De man
come fo' Lucifer. De 'oman come fo' Mam'bo Luz. De
gods funnin'. See which serbant be bes'."

Luz's narrowed eyes were hard. The gods had sent two
bodies from the sacred land of lfe. One for Lucifer, one
for Luz. She saw a contest of strength. Luz or Lucifer
would win to reign supreme on the island.

"De man speerit, Guédé l'Orage. No good!" she said
violently. "Man he ready to gib he body so Lucifer hab
body like a god. Big. Strong." She looked at them slyly.
"But nobody tell de man how Mam'bo Luz t'ief de power
from Lucifer." She snickered. Her people giggled and
poked each other.

Luz stood, her fist stabbing the sky. "Gods punish de
man! Put 'im in de pit. Mam'bo Luz pow'ful, eh, eh." Then
she swung her attention to her people. "But Luz kin'. We
tek keer ob dat man speerit. Treat 'im good, lak he a real
people. Mek de medsin on 'im. Mek de food offerin'. Put
man in de sacred ring ob fire. Three days. Den we put 'im
in sacred boat an' sen's 'im back to de sea. Say, 'Man
speerit, git on back ter lfe.' Dis way Lucifer no git de
strong body ob de stawm speerit. We do dat, doan we, Pa
Bowleg?"

Pa Bowleg smiled toothlessly, nodding. "We do dat, eh,
eh."

Mam'bo Luz then told her mesmerized people how she
would take the body of the woman as her own. Luz planned
her greatest triumph of all. She would enter her own spirit
into the beautiful body of the red-haired woman Erzulie
had sent on the storm-tossed sea.

Then Luz's eyes became slits as she warned her people to
keep her plans secret. "Mam'bo Luz doan wan' ter lay de
oberlook on her brown peoples 'cause dey tell de storee to
Lucifer!"

Heads shook in negation. "No, no, Mam'bo Luz. Doan
gib de oberlook!"

The short, wide woman smiled. "Mam'bo Luz gib her peoples big trick dis night. We mek Lucifer de ritu'l."

Faces lighted with sensual appreciation. This was a special ritual, one they highly enjoyed, performed on the ground outside the *oum'phor*.

"I talk de ritu'l. Den biddy biddy ban, dis storee en'. Fus' de *ogantier* clap he bell, mek de big noise dat wake up Lucifer. Den de drums begin. Summon Lucifer. Brown peoples dance. Sing. Happy.

"Be brown mens git de strong hard root like de Sacred Tree. Brown 'omans want fo' root. Brown mens mount brown 'omans. De drum go boom boom boom boom boom. Mam'bo mount Lucifer. Mek Lucifer less, less. Mek Mam'bo Luz strong, strong, strong'r. Mambo use de speerit power to gib her peoples good times."

Smiles wreathed the faces, even as some cast apprehensive looks into the dark beyond the low fire.

Mam'bo Luz shook her *asson,* a gourd rattle. The *organtier* struck his bell with an iron rod. Then the Drum of the Thunderbolt began its demonic beat.

The brown people waited tensely, chanting, wanting to move, to dance, but not daring. The drumbeats stirred their blood with passions of fear and lust.

Mam'bo Luz began to dance, her plump body writhing like the serpent. Her people danced, their faces growing dreamily sensual.

The drum assumed a new note, wild, *loa*-ridden, uncontrollable. The dancers froze, heads turning to the dark forest path.

Lucifer had come.

Chapter Two

The sun beat down mercilessly, a ball of fire in a shimmering sky. The air hummed, a low, soft buzzing burr that made Adam's head pound. Around him everything undulated, shimmering, unstable.

The ball of fiery sun seemed to be both inside and outside him. Burning with a cold fury from within, scorching him from without. His leg, swollen from the knee to his toes, shot pain all through him. He shivered, in spite of the hot sand burning his flesh. He moved, and fell back groaning. His stomach heaved with waves of nausea. The sea water burbled up into his throat. He rolled over, pressing his swollen leg, cut by the coral, into the gritty hot sand. He vomited until his body curled, clutching with the effort. Slowly the compulsive spasms subsided. He fell back exhausted, moaning with pain. Against his closed eyelids everything was flaming red, red and pulsing, red and hot, red and deathly cold.

He stirred restlessly in semiconsciousness, his hands weakly searching the sand for water. He drifted into and out of sleep. Nightmare followed nightmare. Dulcie tossed on a green sea. Himself dashed beneath the surface to be dragged along the dark, sharp coral. Shapes dancing and glittering in the eerie light of a ring of fire. Himself left there thirsty to burn from its heat. The blazing sun, burning and peeling Dulcie's flesh. His own skin burning. Hellish faces gyrating, leering, putting hands all over him, lifting him. Itching. Cold. Sun fire. Ring of fire. Blackness. Redness.

Days later he awakened to a gentle rocking and thought he was in a bayou. He lay still, confused, searching the sky for the cool green protection of overhanging trees. Above him was an endless sheet of blue broken only by wisps of shredded cloud. Hunger gnawed at him. The thirst was unbearable.

He drew his breath in sharply as he scraped his injured leg. He reached down to protect it, then he sat up examining himself carefully. The blue duck trousers were tattered, the right trouser leg in ribbons. A long ugly gash ran from his right knee to his ankle. The remains of a poultice clung to the wound. He touched it gingerly. It was not a new wound.

Adam hardly breathed. He felt as though a thousand pairs of eyes watched him, though he could see no one. Shaking himself free of superstitions and fear, he touched his face, his fingers working back and forth over his heavy beard. Five days' growth, perhaps more. Again he felt chilled. Where had he been? Where was he now?

His attention shattered as he saw fruits and nuts, food in clay pots, coconuts and roasted meat in the bow of the craft. Greedily he wolfed down chunks of bread, wetting it with coconut milk. Glancing about, he craftily shoved the remaining food back into the protection of the bow.

He felt clear-headed and unfevered; still, he didn't trust himself or what he saw. It might be yet another of the hellish nightmares. The ring of fire seemed more real than the food or the gently swelling blue sea. He looked around quickly and fearfully to see if the fire ring were anywhere near him.

Behind him was the ocean. In front of him was the ocean. To his left was the endless ocean. To his right lay a long shoreline. For nearly an hour he let the boat bob along, staring apprehensively at the low, desolate shore. There were no signs of habitation or human activity. Behind sand beach lay a dense wall of deep forest as forbid-

It was as if he had been plucked from some past time and placed here, ignorant and alone in an unpeopled world. The sun was riding low, the sky turning a dusky blue-violet overhead, scarlet and gold nearer the horizon. He lay back tired and fevered again. Without knowing to what he was resigning himself, he shut his eyes, knowing it was easier to let gods or demons control him than it was to try to reach that desolate, unfamiliar shore.

Adam fell into a restless sleep. With darkness came the nightmares. Sound pounding, pressuring, crushing, drumming against his body. He was slammed against the curling wall of green water. The *Independence* came apart, great pieces of her planking thrown into the ocean. He was thrust down, pinioned and torn on the coral reef so close beneath the raging surface. His oilskins swirled around him, trapping his arms. Screaming in soundless, water-stifled screams, he fought to the surface. His chest burned with liquid fire as the water closed. Again he was thrust onto the lashing coral, the moving water sawing him across the sharp points.

Things touched him in the watery darkness. Then in the clarity of a blazing sunlit day he saw Dulcie swept away from him, her red hair wet and darkened like aged rust, fanned out on the green water. He reached for her, pushing with all his strength for the surface and Dulcie. He was spun head over heels until one darkness became all darkness. He no longer cared if he breathed in the rain-pelted air or the salt-laden sea.

He awakened, his stomach heaving. He leaned over the side of the boat and vomited up all he had eaten from his cache. Shaken, he lay back, trying to separate reality from nightmare. Then with a shrieking moan that stabbed the night air, he remembered clearly everything that had happened. All that was missing were the fevered days of the fire ring in the night and blazing sky fire in the day. He must find Dulcie.

He ran the boat up on the shore. It was a native longboat a crude, primitive craft designed to skim the shoals and coral-strewn shallows. He took his cache of food and hobbled up the sandy beach, stopping to rest every hundred feet or so. His still-swollen leg began to ache, blood oozing through the poultice. He began to gether driftwood but gave up, falling down exhausted to sleep in the damp sand.

During the days that followed, Adam grew stronger. He wandered the beach, searching for wreckage of the *Independence*. He found flotsam, but nothing bearing the name of the ship, no sign that anyone had survived and passed this way, no old campfire or refuse. Nothing.

By the third day his apprehension for Dulcie's survival grew stronger. She would not know how to find food or fend for herself. Every moment he spent tramping the miles of beach he counted as one less moment she had to live. Finally, he realized that while he had lain unconscious and fevered in the longboat, he had probably been traveling northward, with the current of the Tongue of the Ocean. Likely he had been wrecked somewhere south of the area he now searched.

He went to what he supposed to be Andros's North Bight and speared several bonefish, then smoked them, stowing them in the bow of the native longboat. Then he set out south, staying close to the shore, beaching the boat often to walk the shoreline, hunting for signs of life or evidence that he had finally found the spot where the *Independence* had gone down.

He came to Middle Bight and knew then that he had indeed been on the northern section of the island. Andros was a collection of islands, an archipelago within an archipelago. Stopping just long enough to fish again, he crossed the bight to the largest of the many small islands that made up this section of Andros. Some of the tiny cays were only three to five acres, just small protruberances sticking up above the level of sea and reef.

A stop at the native settlement at Mangrove Cay lent

no encouragement. The natives had not heard of a ship-wreck. Adam again headed south, searching the beaches on the north tip of the southernmost island of Andros. At last he found the grim evidence: the remains of a jolly boat, skeletal and partially sand covered. *Independence* was clearly marked on its good side. The other side and the bottom were stove in. Tucked under the prow was an oilskin.

He picked it up, his hands trembling with the impact of this first sign that someone besides himself might have survived the wreck. He laughed aloud, then he broke into a run, heading for the dense forest that crowded in against the salt grass, certain he would find Dulcie or a crewman from his ship.

Adam tore through the rich growth, ignoring wild briars that ripped at him. Colonies of flamingoes scattered. Pelicans, ducks, black parrots raised an alarm. Screaming "Dulcie," he slashed through the mangroves, sisal, and pawpaw, and trampled over wild cotton, bay lavender, and poppy.

From the dense foliage iguanas scurried to safer domains, and frightened eyes in brown faces watched him. He was the Guédé l'Orage—the evil spirit who had appeared in the storm. Thin and haggard, his black curling hair matted and encrusted with dried sand, he looked imploringly at the trees, raising his hands in supplication. Mam'bo Luz had underestimated the powers of this spirit when she set him adrift in the longboat. Mam'bo Luz said she had the power to keep him from giving to Lucifer the body he needed to make him the earth-bound servant to Legba, the voodoo god. But she had been wrong. He had returned.

Adam slumped to the ground, lying back against the trunk of a cabbage palm. He buried his face in his hands, desolate and half-crazed. He no longer knew what he was doing. His mind would take him no further than two simple thoughts—keeping alive and finding Dulcie.

Wanting to appease the tormented *guédé*, an elderly native crept silently and fearfully from the heavy underbrush. He placed coconuts and grapefruit about ten feet from where Adam lay and vanished back into the wilderness.

Birds screamed overhead, small animals slithered through the ground cover, as Adam remained hour after hour, his head tucked protectively in the shelter of his arms. He was tired, filled with the despondency that offers no hope but

refuses to allow a man to stop trying. It was dusk before
he had the courage to come out of his refuge.

He nearly stumbled over the coconuts and grapefruit.
He stared, puzzled at the small pile of bounty; then hunger
overcame thought. He ripped open the grapefruit. He took
the three coconuts to the ruined jolly boat. He wrapped
them in the oilskin, using it as a knapsack.

He continued his search for Dulcie. He rowed south
about two miles before he realized that someone had had
to bring the food. Just as night fell, he beached the craft
and ran back across the open expanse to the woods. Before he had gone a hundred yards, he was hopelessly lost
and confused.

His nerves drawn beyond endurance, Adam stood in the
dark virgin forest and screamed his frustration. There was
nothing. No sound. No human. No hope. No peace. He
pounded the trunk of a papaw until he brought down the
fruit and bruised and bloodied his hands. For the rest of
the night he wandered, trying to make his way back to
the beach.

The watching eyes were fearful. The small offering had
not been enough to drive the spirit back to the sea. The
offerings must be greater. The ceremonies seeking the aid of
the moon goddess, Erzulie, though her handmaiden,
Mam'bo Luz, must be more holy, or the Guédé l'Orage
would offer his powers to Lucifer. Mam'bo Luz would make
them pay dearly if that happened.

As Adam slept, a small band of them crept, laying out
in ritual fashion the foods most likely to please this spirit
from the sea. Just before dawn, they placed dried twigs
around the Guédé l'Orage, a protective circle to keep his
powers inside and away from themselves. Then they set
fire to the twigs. Immediately there blazed around Adam a
ring of fire that brought him screaming from sleep.

Wild with memories of the nightmares, he thrashed
through the blazing circle before the natives could gather
their wits to run. One by one they eluded him, vanishing
into the dark foliage, leaving no sound nor track to follow. Adam ran after one, then another. He managed to collar one small, wiry boy. The youth's eyes rolled deep up
into his head, showing only the whites as he sank to the
ground, muttering and praying in a strange tongue.

Adam shook the boy. "Did you take me from the sea?"

The boy muttered uncomprehendingly.

"Was there a woman?!"

Trembling, nearly senseless, the boy bobbed his head indicating first yes then no.

Adam shook him until the boy cried out, gasping for breath. "Answer me! Answer me! The woman! Did you see her? Did you send her out to sea too? Oh, God! What did you do with her? Answer me!"

The boy began to jabber and gesture, pointing west.

"She's farther in the woods? You lead me to her." He held onto the boy as he pulled at some vine to tie the youth.

Securely bound to Adam's waist, the boy sat meekly down. Adam pointed to the sky. "At first light you take me to her."

The boy smiled slightly, then curled up to sleep. Adam sat next to him, his back rigid against a tree, trying to remain alert.

At full dawn Adam awakened, the vine still around his waist. The other loop lay empty beside him. The boy was gone. As before, in a ceremonial configuration lay a supply of fruits, prepared meats, and vegetables. Adam ate slowly, scanning the brush. There was no sign that anyone was there.

Perhaps it was the forest that gave him the feeling of being followed and observed, and the legendary chick-charnies who left food for him. Perhaps it was a nightmare, and he was not really on this primitive, largely unexplored island at all. Perhaps the *Independence* had never gone down in a storm off the Andros coast. Perhaps he was completely mad. But perhaps the boy *had* seen Dulcie.

He tossed the remainder of the chicken away and walked deeper into the woods, heading westerly. Before long, he found distinct paths, and the going became easier. He walked for hours, wishing that the little Androsian chick-charnies would feed him again. Hopefully, he lay down and feigned sleep. After an uneventful hour he searched for food on his own. Each sloping, twisting trail took him deeper into the heart of Andros.

He went on, determined not to give up until he had found Dulcie. He continued through the woods, going down one path to its end, retracing his steps until he dropped to the ground exhausted. In the morning food lay beside him. Drawn in the earth was a picture legend

that he read with ease. He was to return to the sea. The
figure of a man lay on the beach. Himself. In front of the
man's outstretched hands was a native boat. Behind the
figure of the man, representing the past, was the stick
figure of a woman with flowing hair. Dulcie. The head of
the woman was a skull. Angrily he swiped at the drawing,
obliterating it with his hands. Then he stood and stamped
the earth until no sign remained.

He ran down the path, desperate to reach its end. Perhaps it was only madness, but every instinct told him
Dulcie was near. He tore down the long twisting, tangled
path, his mind wildly racing with hope enlivened by the
natives' efforts to discourage him.

The sun was almost directly overhead when he burst out
of the woods. Before him lay a wide expanse cleared of forest growth, a large emerald island surrounded by a sea of
dark pine and mahogany trees. In its midst blazed a
pinking white mansion, unreal and dazzling in the bright
light. Intimidated by the sight of a house such as this in an
unexplored wilderness, Adam retreated to the forest, peeking out from the broad sisal leaves. Twice he ventured
out, determined to go boldly to the house. Twice he retreated. He was no better than the natives, as apprehensive of the unfamiliar as they.

He tugged at his beard. His clothing, what there was of
it, was torn and stained from the nights spent in the forest
and the water. It was no wonder the natives were afraid
of him—but how was he to regain his veneer of civilization
and approach this house? It was amazing how quickly he
had become a wary, stealthy animal.

Yet Dulcie might be inside that house. He started across
the great lawn. Without the cover of the trees he felt exposed, watched at every step. Furtive and wary, he kept
looking over his shoulder as he approached.

A slender, plainly dressed Indian woman answered his
knock, her dark eyes widening for a moment before her
face became a mask again. Her hair was black and straight,
knotted at the back of her head. "You come ter see Mistah
Gilmartin?"

Adam didn't know whom he had come to see. Tiredly
he rubbed his forehead. "I was in a shipwreck. My wife . . .
my wife went down with it. I've been told . . . a native indicated this house—"

"We find no woman. No woman here."

"Have you heard anything? Has anyone seen—"

"Maybe she be buried. Always give the dead to the Lord of the Cemetery, Baron Samedi."

"Amparo! Who's that?" a strangely resonant tenor called.

Amparo looked at Adam, her dark eyes filled with warning. "You go now. You go back ter sea. You go."

Adam's hand shot out, holding the door. "No, wait, please. Help me. I must find my wife. Please. You know something. Tell me—tell me!"

A dog nosed past Amparo's legs. The petulant tenor voice demanded, "Move aside! I can't see! Who is it?"

Her eyes scolding Adam for not having left, Amparo stepped aside.

Staring up at Adam from his seat on a dogcart sat a malformed youth. His black beadlike eyes were moist and staring. On his head bristling black hair sprouted. The boy's ears stood out, small winglike protuberances. His mouth was a gaping slit. His torso was large. He had no arms or legs. From his shoulders grew finlike hands, flapping gleefully as he laughed his odd, mirthless cackling. At his groin were two other growths, feet, useless, fleshy.

Amparo said, "This be Lucifer Gilmartin."

Adam mouthed the boy's first name.

Lucifer smacked the lips of his gaping mouth twice. "Didn't you know you've come to Satan's Keep? The home of the damned? I am lord of Satan's Keep. Lucifer. Do you know Lucifer?"

"Yes, I know of Lucifer," Adam said quietly.

The boy cackled. "You may think you know, but you don't. Lucifer outsmarted God. How, then, could you, a mere man, know anything? Or are you smarter than God too?"

"No, I'm not." Adam turned to Amparo. "Could I see Mr. Gilmartin?"

"No!" Lucifer cried. "No! Talk to me! Talk to me!"

"I need help. Your father can help me."

"My father can do nothing! I have the power, not he!"

"Lucho!" Amparo said chidingly. "We'll take 'im ter your father an' let 'im see for himself."

Lucifer commanded his dog to back the cart up. His eyes never left Adam's. An expression of venomous hatred was on his face. "He's like all the others," he said to Amparo. Then he spoke to Adam. "What you want to know, I know. I could have been your friend."

"What could you have told me?"

"That you were in a shipwreck."

"You heard me say that to Amparo."

"You're looking for a woman," Lucifer said.

"My wife."

Lucifer laughed. "She's not your wife now. She's with the spirits."

The blood rushed to Adam's head. He wanted to smash his fist into Lucifer's leering face. "Amparo, take me to Mr. Gilmartin." He hadn't come this far to be turned back by a boy and a housekeeper.

Amparo motioned Adam to enter. Adam stalked past, not daring to look at the monster boy. Lucifer called after him. "I know everything. You've killed all hope of ever knowing your fate or hers." His laughter rang through the crude adobe inner walls.

Amparo led him to a doorway, then disappeared into a corridor. Adam fought down the impulse to shudder. The deformed youth watched him.

"Costa!" the boy shouted. A wizened old servant crabbed his way to the boy, walking in a crouch that made his thin, sinuous muscles stand out like cords. Lucifer stared at Adam. "You see, I am all-powerful. Costa! Lie on the floor!" The man fell to the floor. "Roll over!" Lucifer looked up from his obedient servant, grinning broadly at Adam. "Have you such power over any dog or man? Have all your straight limbs ever given you command? Go see my father, mister fool. Talk to another of your kind." The dog sprang forward. The servant Costa followed, crabbing along behind Lucifer.

Adam entered Gilmartin's study. A fire burned in the overwarm, airless room. In a large threadbare chair sat a drunken wisp of a man, Kenneth Gilmartin, thinning white hair barely covering his pinkish scalp, his clothing soiled and neglected.

He looked up as Adam crossed the room. Gilmartin waggled his hand vaguely. His speech was slurred. "Justin'll have that order ready t'morra, or I'll have the boy's hide. Tha's a promish." He offered Adam a drink out of his own bottle. "Tell me about London now."

"Sir, my ship was wrecked some time ago, maybe weeks.

Can you tell me anything about that wreck? Did your men find wreckage? Or survivors?"

"Your ship wrecked? Tha's strange. I jush got a letter yesterday. You been with Mam'bo Luz? You ain't one o' them livin' dead o' hers?"

"I know no one named Luz. Who is she? Would she know of a woman being washed up on shore?"

"Dorothy?"

Adam sat up alertly, once more hoping. "No—not Dorothy. Dulcie."

Gilmartin's eyes leaked pathetic tears. "She'sh losht. Losht."

"Think, sir, please. Could her name have been Dulcie, sir?"

"Saw her long time ago, day that son o' Satan was born. God-damned demon, he is. Now I can't fin' her."

Adam was on the edge of his seat. "Have you seen her!"

Gilmartin kept drinking from the nearly empty bottle. "Long time ago . . ."

"Damn it, stop drinking, man!" Adam shouted. "I have to find her! She's my wife. She's carrying my child!"

Gilmartin was crying pathetically, cradling the whiskey bottle against his chest. "So long ago . . . Search. Always search. Never give up until she'sh found."

Adam rushed from the study. He went to every door, peered into every room, opening closets, examining the contents of drawers, hunting for anything that might reveal Dulcie's presence. The mansion was a rabbit's warren of passages, one wing of the house connecting to another. Nothing hinted at Dulcie's presence, yet his feeling remained strong that she was there.

At every turn he was stymied by Lucifer, smiling his evil knowing smile, waiting for the opportunity to tell Adam he was a fool. "I am the one to whom you must supplicate. I am the one to answer your wishes. It is to me you must pay homage to gain your desires."

After Adam had wandered through the house several times, Amparo came up to him. "You must leave now, man. Nobody here to help you. Go back to the sea. Go back where you came."

At the edge of the woods he stopped to look back at the strange isolated mansion called Satan's Keep. Thank God Dulcie hadn't been there.

* * *

The next day he walked south down the beach. He found several pieces of wreckage. One of his charts, ruined by sun and water, lay buried in the sand. In a small inlet a jolly boat rocked, caught on a snag. Inside was the gruesome cargo of two crewmen, blistered by the sun, torn by scavenger birds, covered with insects. Adam hauled the rotting corpses from the boat and buried them in the forest.

Beaten, no longer knowing where to look, and afraid of what he would find, Adam returned to the native boat. Inside it was a fresh supply of food. He had come to take it for granted. He laid his oilskin on the sand and went to sleep.

The sun was high when he awakened. He lay still, a shadow long and dark falling across his face. He blinked, squinting against the sun, and looked around. All manner of things had been carried to the beach and now encircled him. At his feet was a scarecrow figure, black and eerie against the sun, almost unidentifiable against that blinding brilliance. Behind him a small banana tree had been planted in the sand. Around him lay a circle of banana leaves. From the circle the leaves formed a path to the native boat at the water's edge. To his right was a pole, a *joukoujou* painted black, a sign of death. As he stood up, Adam saw the pile of black clothing laid near the pole, apparently for him to don.

His attention went to the scarecrow hanging against the light of the sun. He moved out of its shadow. On a crudely made cross hung Dulcie's gown. Perched at the top was a skeleton head.

Adam stared in horror at the grotesquery, then lunged forward, ripping the figure down.

From the forest the natives came forward. Slowly and rhythmically their drums beat, and their low, fearful voices chanted to the Guédé l'Orage, the god of storms, the spirit of death and cemeteries. Slowly they advanced on Adam, the Drum of the Thunderbolt never faltering or stopping, the low thrum of their voices growing in intensity.

Adam screamed at them and hurled the cross garbed in Dulcie's clothing. Their line parted, the scarecrow figure falling to the sand, and they came on. The line of natives began to curve, enclosing Adam in a circle formed by themselves and the sea behind him.

Slowly he backed up, unsure of their intent. The dark

faces appeared to be entranced by him and called him
Guédé l'Orage. In unison they murmured as one of their
members saluted to the four directions of the earth. Whenever Adam misstepped, taking his feet from the ceremonial
path, the human barrier moved in, forcing him back to the
leaves. His calves touched against the hull of the native
boat. It, too, had been lined with banana leaves. Around
the bed of leaves lay the food he had come to expect from
his mysterious benefactors, who until this moment he had
imagined cared for him.

Somehow they had gotten Dulcie's gown. They could
take him to her—if only to show him where she died and
where she now lay. He put his hands out to them. "Where
is the woman?" he asked softly.

Cries of alarm, a break in the rhythm of the prayers.
But they pressed on, walking steadily toward the water as
though they would walk right through him.

Adam backed into the small craft and stood waiting for
them to approach. A native handed him the black grab.
Without question he put the robe around his shoulders.
Flag bearers came forward, oriented themselves to the
cardinal points, and saluted the boat and Adam as its precious cargo. Amid a cacophony of drums, seashell trumpets,
and chanted rituals, they pushed the native boat into the
water, sending the Guédé l'Orage, the god of the storm,
back to Ife, fatherland of the gods.

Three natives walked out into the water over the coral
shoals, pushing the native craft from shore. Adam felt the
current of the Tongue of the Ocean begin to propel the
boat north. By nightfall he would be bobbing along the
shore of northern Andros as he had been that first morning of consciousness after the sinking of the *Independence*.
If the craft continued unhindered, he would eventually
reach Nassau and help from Ben.

Adam beached the boat near the Nassau pier. He ran to
the docks chuckling madly under his breath as he saw the
Liberty at anchor. He raced for the gangplank, shouting
orders. "Prepare to weigh anchor!"

Several seamen working on deck glanced up to see a tall
gaunt man in flowing black robes, his long unkempt hair
streaming around his face, his beard scraggly, his eyes burning with the same intensity that was in his commanding
voice. The four crewmen moved forward barring his way.

The largest one solicitously took Adam's arm. "Easy does it, mate," he said jovially. "You're in the wrong berth."

"Take your hands off me and do as you're ordered, Carson!" Adam swung around to face the others. "Prepare to weigh anchor!"

Carson, bewildered, backed off. The other three stared, open-mouthed. "Captain Tremain? Bejasus—can it be you, sir?"

The second crewman crossed himself. Carson ran for the quarterdeck.

"Since when can't you recognize your captain, Billings?" Adam snapped.

The man's eyes shifted uneasily from Adam. "Beggin' your pardon, sir!"

Adam sneered and stalked off toward the companionway. He had mounted the first steps when Ben appeared at the top of the ladder.

"Adam! Holy Mother, it is you!" Ben rushed down the ladder, forcing Adam to back away. Ben grabbed his hand, then clasped Adam by the shoulders. His smile was filled with relief. "Christ, we thought you were lost. Some of the crewmen made it—and then, when you never returned —Christ! You're really here!" Ben beamed; then he looked carefully at Adam. "Jeez, you look like hell. What happened?"

Adam's eyes grew wild and fevered. "Weigh anchor, Ben. We've got to go back. I know she's there. Those damned natives are hiding her from me." He faced the gaping crew, who had stopped work and come to stare. "Weigh anchor, damn it! I command you to get this ship underway!"

Ben motioned the men away, saying, "You're got your orders." Worriedly, he touched Adam's arm. "We'd better plot the course, Adam," he said gently. "I need a little more information than you've given me."

Adam shook him off. "The southern tip of Andros. That's where they are. We can take the men ashore and get Dulcie. No one can stop us."

Ben sighed, "We're not going anywhere, Adam."

"Ben! I've got to go back. They have her, I know they do."

"Come into the cabin. We'll talk as you bathe and eat."

"For God's sake, man, don't you understand? They have Dulcie."

"Come with me, Adam. We'll do it my way or not at all. I don't know what you're talking about."

"Will you help me after I've told you?"

Ben nodded. "I'll do anything I can, but you're two steps from collapse. You're not making sense."

Adam followed him and did as Ben asked. He bathed and dressed. Ben handed him a razor. "I don't have time! You said—"

"I said I'd listen and then decide what could be done, if anything. Where did the ship go down? What happened?"

Without realizing it, Adam picked greedily and steadily at the food the mate put before him as he told Ben all he remembered about Andros. Even he was aware that it sounded garbled and fantastic. So many days had never come clear in his mind. He was no longer certain that Kenneth Gilmartin and Lucifer were real. Perhaps they were creatures of his tortured imagination.

Ben rubbed his temples. "Do you know how long you've been gone?"

"What difference does it make?" Adam asked shrilly.

"You left Nassau six weeks ago. You say you went down that first night. God! I don't know how you survived. But Adam, a woman couldn't. Dulcie, if she made it through the wreck, is—she's dead."

"No! No, she's not! Others survived. She did too. The natives—"

"Over a hundred crewmen and all the officers were lost. Every crewmember who survived has made it back here. They returned days after the wreck. That's how I knew the *Independence* had gone down. The first eight men returned, and each thought he was the only one. Dulcie couldn't have helped herself. And . . . she couldn't have foraged—Christ, look at yourself! You're half-dead!"

Ben had seen Adam meet defeat with cold fury, with hot-blooded anger, with calm, but never had he seen Adam with helpless tears in his eyes, humbly begging him to make Dulcie be alive.

His voice breaking, Ben again refused to take him back to Andros. His story about the ring of fire and the Guédé l'Orage and the spirit queen and the monster boy were all the stuff of nightmares.

Above all, Ben suspected Adam had buried Dulcie himself and was unable to face it. He had told Ben of finding bodies and of finding Dulcie's gown. Ben was certain it had been Dulcie Adam had buried in the forest. There was no question that Adam was on the edge, his eyes burning blue coals sunken deep in his head. He was exhausted and overwrought.

He prepared himself and Adam a drink, slipping a potion into Adam's without the slightest twinge of bad conscience. It was only minutes, but it seemed like hours to Ben before Adam slumped in the chair, the glass rolling from his slack fingers.

Ben ordered the mate to bring Rosebud McAllister to the cabin. As he waited, Ben sat quietly in his chair. A deep ache coursed through him.

Rosebud lumbered into the cabin, his eyes fixed on Adam. "Praise de Lawd, he done led de Boss back home to us!" Rosebud lifted Adam from the chair, holding him tenderly as a baby, and placed him in Ben's bunk. "Ah specks Ah be resignin' fum de *Libutty*, Cap'n. Look like Ah got me a job lookin' aftuh de Boss."

Ben watched the giant man place a coverlet over Adam with infinite care. "He'll need a lot of caring. Mrs. Tremain died when the ship went down. The captain hasn't been able to accept that yet."

Rosebud let out a low, sorrowful moan. Shaking his head mournfully back and forth, he rocked back on his haunches, his hands clasped in front of him. "Oh, Lawd, lay yo' peaceful han's down on de boss. He done been yo' servant, de Black Swan. Now, what dat ol' black swan gwine do when he ain't got his li'l ol' firebird to come home to? Ain't right you leave him all 'lone here, Lawd. You done better bring dis boss man peace fo' his soul."

Chapter Three

"You feelin' better, Boss?"

Adam opened his eyes, staring uncomprehendingly at Rosebud. He moved too quickly. His head throbbed. "My God, what did Ben give me?"

"Ain't nothin' gwine hurt you much." Rosebud grinned.

"Ol' Cap'n Ben got hisseff all worked up wiff you. He put you to sleep."

"Where'd you come from, R.B.? I don't remember seeing you."

"Ah come aftuh you asleep, Boss. Ah go gits you somethin' good to eat, now you 'wake an' feelin' better."

"Rosebud, will you go with me? Help me find Mrs. Tremain."

Rosebud watched him sadly. "Ah goes anywhere you wants me to, Boss. But Ah gwine tell you what you oughter know fust. Dem natives is voodoo. Now, Ol' Rosebud here, he done a lot o' witchin' an' spellin' folks. Dey done give you a warnin'. Dey doan want you on dat islan', thinkin' you be one o' dem guédés an' all."

"I don't care what they think. They have Dulcie."

"No, Boss. Effen dey sen's you back to de sea, dey mo'n likely sen's her back, too. Cap'n Ben say you fin' her dress, an' mebbe her body—"

"Not her body! The natives—they put her dress on a cross and planted it in the sand beside me. You see, Rosebud? That proves she's there. How else would they have her gown?"

"Gowns is mighty temptin' gahmints even fo' de Mam'bos. Ain't no woman Ah know kin turn her back on a purty dress."

Adam shook his head mutely. Rosebud went on, "Miss Dulcie, she jes' a li'l bitty woman. Ain't no big strong man like you be."

Adam remained silent, unable to argue with Rosebud, unable to face having to agree with him.

"Effen you still wants to go, Boss, Ah go wiff you. We hunt dat ol' islan' fum one side to de odder, effen dat's what you want."

Adam left the ship without speaking to Ben. Rosebud didn't believe Dulcie was alive any more than Ben did, but Rosebud was willing to help him. Though Ben might come, too, if he insisted, Adam felt betrayed.

Adam turned into one of the grogshops along Bay Street, pouring two quick rums into himself. He was thinking nonsense, and he knew it. Still, the feelings of betrayal and depression wouldn't be chased away.

Rosebud stuck to him like a mustard plaster. Where Adam went, Rosebud followed, clearing the way, shoving grumbling seamen from barstools, placing silver on the counter when Adam forgot to pay.

Erratically Adam wandered down Bay Street, drunk enough now not even to remember that Dulcie wouldn't be waiting at home. The more he drank, the more it seemed that nothing had changed. He laughed and joked with the other men, shouting cheers at the woman who danced bare-breasted at the Halyard Light Inn.

Rosebud yawned and settled back, waiting. Adam could hardly stand and was incapable of walking unassisted when he was ready to leave. He clung to Rosebud's arm, slurring, "You gonna folla me all—alla time?"

Rosebud placed his arm around Adam's waist and near-ly carried him from the Halyard Light. "No, Boss, Ah's jes' gwine take you to yo' do'. Miss Claudine'll know what to do wiff you den."

"Miss Claudine?" Adam gurgled, laughing. *"Miss* Claudine . . . you been steppin' out with Claudine? Dulcie'll laugh about that."

Rosebud grunted, steering Adam up Parliament Street. With relief he reached Adam's suite. Claudine was silent as Rosebud dumped Adam onto the sofa. Her eyes were tear-filled. She had thought him dead. Now here he was, drunk as a lord and grinning like a happy cat.

Adam blinked sleepily, his legs sprawled. "Claudine, tell Miss Dulcie the captain's home an' middlin' anxious to see her."

"Miss Dulcie ain't here, Mastah Adam. She went with you. She . . ."

Rosebud frowned, shaking his head. Adam's head nodded. Rosebud said, "She daid, but de boss doan wan' to think so. He jes' keep on a-sayin' he gwine fin' her an' woan give up fo' nothin'. Look like we jes' have to wait 'til he sees hisseff she ain't comin' back to him no—"

"She's not dead!" Adam heaved himself unsteadily from the sofa, his fists clenched, swinging at Rosebud. The huge man did an agile dance, sidestepping Adam's thrashing arms. Claudine squealed, her hands covering her ears as Adam hit the floor like a felled tree.

Rosebud chuckled. "Dat be de onliest man ain't skeered t' come at me wiff boff his fisses a-goin'."

"Oh, you killed him!" Claudine wailed.

"Ah din' touch him. He knocked his ownseff out." Rose-bud carried Adam to the bedroom, dropping him onto the coverlet. Grinning, he shook his head. "He gwine think de cavalry been a-rompin'- an' a-stompin' on de inside o' his haid when he wake up."

Claudine's eyes were huge with questions. "Miss Dulcie ain't daid? He ast—"

"Now, doan you start thinkin' things, Claudine. Ain't no way Miss Dulcie gwine be livin' now. Cap'n Ben tell me de boss bury her hisseff" Rosebud tapped his head. "It done made him funny, but he know, an' we gotta he'p him when de time come fo' him to tell us he know. Miss Dulcie she daid, an' we's all he got now."

Claudine placed a coverlet over Adam, sat down quietly on Dulcie's chaise, and watched as he slept.

The Lawd had strange ways, Claudine thought. She loved Miss Dulcie as well an' true as one person could love another. She done give Miss Dulcie her most faithful devotion through all the years. 'Til Mastah Adam come to Mossrose. She never did know 'zackly what went on 'tween Mastah Adam an' Miss Dulcie that time, but Mastah Adam done need her after he come from Wolf's cabin. And she was there for him. Miss Dulcie wasn't there, but Claudine was. She guessed that was the beginnin' of the time when she knew she'd do anythin' fo' Mastah Adam.

Claudine thought some of Dulcie and cried for the lost years at Mossrose, the days when as children they had gone to Fellie's shop and been given candy, the days when she and Dulcie visited the Saunderses and Dulcie always got Glenn into trouble. She thought of the night they had helped Fellie and Ester and Darcy escape. That was the first time she'd seen Adam. Claudine had known then that Dulcie never belonged with a man like Adam. A woman had to be willing to sacrifice everything, and Dulcie hadn't even known then what that meant. But Claudine had known. She knew now. She was willing to give all of herself to him and ask nothing in return.

Adam lay still. Familiar kitchen sounds—a woman softly humming, a cup clinking pleasantly against a saucer—dragged him back, forcing him to think, to want something he now knew was not to be. His head was throbbing from the liquor, and he was no longer able to deceive himself. Dulcie was dead. In infinite detail he went over their last moments together. He saw her in the captain's cabin fussing over her things, showing him the layette she had

sewn for the baby. He remembered half-heartedly trying
to convince her to remain in Nassau and then how
pleased he had been when she had repeated that she
wanted him all to herself. He had killed her wanting her
with him. He shut his eyes and again listened to the sounds
of a woman preparing a meal for a man.

It seemed like Dulcie. Claudine's low, soft voice became
the high, clear soprano he wished he was hearing. With his
eyes closed and his mind tightly locked, he *knew* it was
Dulcie.

Claudine smiled as she pulled back the draperies, letting
in the bright morning sun, a favorite motion of Dulcie's before she leaped back into the warm bed beside Adam.

Against his will, he opened his eyes, squinting against
the blaze of light. Claudine's slender frame was silhouetted
against the window.

"Mawnin', Mastah Adam. Ah brung you a good, good
meal. Aftuh las' night you gwine need yo' stren'th." She
placed the bed tray over his lap, then stood back and
surveyed her work, complete with a small red flower. "You
hungry?"

Adam hesitated. "It's fine, Claudine."

Bolder, perched on the bed, she pushed the tumble of
hair from his forehead. "Ah gwine take keer o' you. Ah
nevah gwine leave yo' side. Ah watches out fo' you jes'
like Miss Dulcie'd want."

Adam closed his eyes against the soft flow of words.

"You ain't et yet," Claudine protested. "Ain't you hungry?"

He shook his head, and she took the tray, looking at him
with loving patience. "Mebbe you be wantin' it aftuh a
bit. Ah fix it fo' you then."

Adam waited until she left the room. Then he got out
of bed, still dressed from the night before. He slipped out
of the apartment.

The streets were bustling and busy. Everyone had someone to see, business to attend to, someplace to go. Adam
wandered the side streets, avoiding the places he and
Dulcie had visited together. He entered the Halyard Light.
It was quiet in the daytime, only a few men sitting in
varying stages of dissipation at the back. The stage where
the Halyard Light's main attraction, Ramona Rose, danced
every night looked ludicrous in its empty crudity. By day
it was simply a dingy little grogshop, bleak and forgotten.

By night it throbbed with the passions Ramona Rose was hired to excite. The Halyard Light then reeked with sweat, stank with the sour breath of lusting, drinking men, while Ramona Rose stripped and danced and sang, egging them on with her low, husky voice, teasing them with her voluptuous body.

Adam sat on the end stool. The barman brought his rum. Adam sipped, his mind blank, staring at the empty stage where the woman would be that night. He loathed the sight of her. She was the lowest sort of female, and he wished she were there. He wanted her to dance. He wanted to hear her low, throaty voice. He wanted to watch her, and hate her.

His head buzzed mildly when he walked into the afternoon sun. He ambled toward the shore. The native boat still sat at the water's edge. The banana leaves, wilted and turning brown, were still in the bottom. He kicked the side of the boat and wondered what would happen if he got in and headed back toward Andros. Perhaps he would reach his destination and find Dulcie. Perhaps he would never reach his destination. Perhaps he would sink beneath the sea. Perhaps he would never find Dulcie. Maybe that was all there was to be the rest of his life: always wanting to search for her and being afraid to for fear he would learn the one thing he didn't want to know.

Rosebud found him there, staring into the cloudless blue sky, lying back across the seat, his feet hanging over the side.

"Where you been, Boss? Ah been lookin' all ovah de whole islan'," Rosebud grumbled good-naturedly.

"I've been right here," Adam said shortly.

"How long?"

"How should I know how long? What do you want, Rosebud?"

"Ah wants you to gets us back to work. We got a big ol' boat jes' settin' and waitin' fo' usuns to fill 'er up an' go to Wilm'ton."

Adam moved, shading his eyes to look at Rosebud. "What ship?"

"Doan know, Boss. She ain't got no name 'til you gives 'er one."

Adam was on his feet, striding toward the docks. Rosebud smiled, following him. Anchored down from the *Liberty* was the third sidewheel paddler Collie and Com-

pany had built for Adam. It sat low in the water, gray
and sleek like a night hunter built for speed.

"See, Boss, do whole worl' ain't stopped. Dey's a lotsa
things jes' a-waitin fo' you to go an' do 'em. An' a lotsa people. My people, dey's a-waitin', too. You ain't forgot you
de Black Swan, has you?"

Adam bounded up the gangplank with Rosebud at his
heels. He ran his hands over the brass rails, grasped the
companionway ladder, released it, and stood back to
examine masts and rigging. "I haven't forgotten."

"Dat mean we's gwine sail soon?"

"I don't know, Rosebud. I don't know anything right
now."

Rosebud said ponderously, "Dat jes' be a tempe-airy
sitchy-ation. What we gwine name dis ol' boat?"

"*Ship,* for Christ's sake—when will you learn to call it a
ship!"

"What we gwine name dis ol' ship, Boss?"

Adam, laughing, gave up. "R.B., I think you've already
named it. As you said, I'm the Black Swan, and your people are waiting. We might as well make him big enough to
see from a long way off."

"Yassuh Yassuh! Dat what we gwine do. We gwine sail
on de *Black Swan,*" he chanted, dancing around the deck.
"We gwine soar on de wings o' de *Black Swan.* We gwine
sail to de promise' lan' on de wings o' de *Black Swan.*"

"What's going on up there?" Ben shouted. "Someone to
see you, Adam."

Rosebud preceded Adam down the companionway, sing-
ing and chanting. "Dis ol' boat she be name de *Black Swan.*
Hey, Boss! How kin dat be? De boat she's a girl, an' de
Black Swan he be a man! What we gwine do 'bout dat?"

Ben looked at Adam. "You really going to name it the
Black Swan? I know how you felt about Ullah, Adam,
but after what we did to Revanche, it's just like wearin' an
advertisement for him. You don't need—"

Adam's face set. "I hadn't thought of it. But it's the
best damned reason I know for naming her the *Black
Swan.* Who wants to see me?"

"Glory. She's on the wharf. Damn you, Adam, I swear
I don't understand you one bit. Why make things harder
for yourself? If I didn't know better, I'd think you wanted
Revanche to skin your hide off you."

Adam grinned, then slapped Ben on his back. "What makes you think you know me so well?"

Ben eyed him suspiciously. "Shit, I don't know. You sound all right, at least you did 'til now. You do know about—I mean, you're not still wanting to go back to Andros . . . for anything?"

Adam's face grew hard. "No, I'm not going back to Andros."

Ben clasped Adam's hand. "You know how I feel . . . about Dulcie."

"How do you feel, Ben? Why wouldn't you go with me to find her?"

Ben spoke in a whisper. "She can't be alive, Adam. Not after all that time, and you—Jeez, Adam—look at yourself. You're a scarecrow! The men didn't even recognize you. How could I agree to go to that God-awful island and let you go through that again when I know in the end you'd come back without Dulcie?"

Adam watched him for a moment. "Let's go see Glory."

Ben held back. "Adam? You do understand? There's nothing I wouldn't do to help you if I could."

"I understand, Ben. You believe she's dead, and you're doing what you think is best."

"Adam, you believe she's . . . don't you?"

"I don't know what I believe."

Glory, her gown a tame shade of gray, stood on the dock. She put her arms out to him. "Adam, I'm sorry, so sorry."

He allowed her to kiss his cheek, then pulled away. "We're all sorry," he said flatly. "Let's think about other things, like christening my new ship properly. Come on, Ben, you can tell me why I shouldn't name it the *Black Swan.*"

Ben looked at Glory, his face grim, but he followed along with the others. Adam headed directly for the Halyard Light.

Ben stopped outside the door. "Not here, Adam. This is—"

"It's as good a place as any. Don't you like associating with the common man, Ben? Being a ship's master gone to your head?"

"I was thinking of Glory. It's not a place I'd take a lady."

"Well, Glory, we'll leave it up to you." Adam's smile was hard.

Glory matched him stare for stare. "You can't fool me, Adam Tremain. I know what you're doing. I'm not that easy to shake off, and I'll tell you something else. I'd like to know why you're trying so hard to get rid of every friend you've got. Let's go. I've been in tougher places, for worse reasons."

A gust of smoky air burst out of the Halyard Light as Glory pulled the door open and was engulfed in the murk of the interior. She minced her way to the back of the smoke-clogged room and sat down at the farmost table. Her eyes met Adam's. "Aren't you going to sit down, Adam? Don't tell me your enthusiasm has waned."

"My enthusiasm hasn't waned, Glory." He waved at the bartender.

Glory laughed. "Am I supposed to think about that reply, figure out I've been insulted, and flounce out of here in a huff?"

Adam shrugged. He poured himself a drink, offering none to Glory or Ben. "Do as you like." He drank quickly and refilled the glass with equal speed.

"Look, Adam," Ben began. Glory shook her head. Ben leaned toward her, saying low, "Enough is enough. I don't know what the hell's come over him, but I'm damned if I'll sit in this stink hole and listen to him all night."

"I don't recall forcing you to join me, Ben. Matter of fact, seems like you came to my ship and interrupted what I was doing."

"You son of a bitch! I was trying to help you. I've known you all my life—'til now, Adam. And we've been through a lot together, but no one, not even you, is gonna talk to me like that!"

"No? Then you'd better leave now." With a bottle before him he was feeling playfully mean. It was better than feeling haunted.

Glory coughed. "I do hope you gentlemen are enjoyin' yourselves. I'm certain you're making my stomach turn. I've never seen the like of you, Adam Tremain. Your wife dead, and here you are—"

Adam slammed his fist down on the table. "She's not dead. She is *not dead!* Don't say that again. Not ever!"

"Come on, Glory. I've had a bellyful of this."

"Adam—what do you mean she's not dead? Ben told me—"

"Oh, yes," Adam said sarcastically. "Ben said. Ben should learn to keep his mouth shut about things he knows nothing of."

"Dulcie's dead, and I'm done with listenin' to you blather crazy nonsense about chickcharnies and natives and devil children!"

Adam swallowed the contents of his glass, "Get away from me, Ben."

"Stop it!" Glory cried. "Adam, what makes you think she's alive? Oh, Ben, listen to him! If there's the slightest hope—"

"There's not," said Ben.

His speech thickening, Adam concentrated on Glory and repeated the story of his weeks on Andros.

Glory listened avidly. "Adam, she must be in that terrible house. Who in their right mind would name a house Satan's Keep? Are you certain you looked everywhere? Cellars! Were there cellars?"

Adam shook his head. "No cellars."

"What about the native huts?"

"Couldn't. Ben wouldn't go back with me, an' Rosebud would—"

"Well, we *will* go! We'll search every hut in every village on Andros, and we'll find her!" Glory reached out to take Adam's hands.

His eyes on Glory were bloodshot, poorly focused. "We'll all go," he whispered. "We'll . . . bring her back."

"Oh, yes! There is hope! We'll keep looking until—we find her."

Adam held fast to her hands. "You go, Glory. You go and . . . find her for me." In a strangled whisper he added, "I can't."

Ben turned away, not able to watch or listen any longer. Adam went on in the same slurred, hoarse whisper. "I wanted her to make that trip. She went because I wanted her with me. I should have surrendered to the Federal ship. My God, if I'd just surrendered. Why didn't I, Glory? Why did I go on?"

"You did what you thought was best, Adam."

He shook his head violently. "Captain's responsible . . . responsible. I killed her. I killed the baby—my baby. Christ

Almighty, why did I do it?" He put his head down on the table. His shoulders heaved. "Find her, Glory. Please go find her. Make her come back."

Glory said pleadingly, "Adam, it wasn't your fault. Please, honey, you couldn't help what happened. It was the storm. You can't stop a storm. Adam—please."

Ben put his hand on Adam's shoulder. He said gently, "Come on, Adam. It's time to go home."

"No! No, don't want to go back there," he muttered.

"Then come to my place."

Adam groped for the rum bottle, sloshing liquid into his glass. "Gonna celebrate th' new ship."

As he spoke, a drum rolled, giving his announcement inadvertent fanfare that pleased him. Ben slumped back, determined to wait until Adam's mood improved or he passed out. He was certain he wouldn't have to wait long. The rum bottle was already more than half empty.

Ramona Rose, the Halyard Light's claim to fame, stepped up on her rickety stage, clad in many layers of colorful robes. With each drumroll she shed one garment. Tonight, unlike other nights, she stepped from the stage and moved through the room, teasing the patrons at the tables.

Her coarse hair hung down her back like writhing cottonmouths. At the center table she sat on the lap of a prosperous-looking seaman. She thrust his head back. The man's mouth hung open. Her deep, sensuous laughter floated across the room as she poured his malt down his throat. Laughter burst out. Ramona, quick and elusive, was on her way to another table before the seaman could grab her.

Glory watched her, wide-eyed. "Oh, Lord, Ben, to think I wanted to be a stripper. My God, she's horrible."

Ramona slithered out of a pale green robe and left it twined around the head of the next man she approached. Two tables away from Adam, Ben, and Glory, Ramona was assisted in removing her golden robe by a leering drunk, whose hands and eyes were so busy, he never felt her remove his money pouch, carelessly tucked in his belt. Over his head, Ramona dangled the bulging pouch, encouraging derisive laughter. As the robe floated to the floor and the man's hands reached for the last garment, Ramona dangled the pouch in front of his nose, moving away in quick dancing steps as his expression changed from lust to anger. She dropped the pouch and watched as he scrambled to retrieve his scattered gold coins.

She sauntered to Adam, only a virginal white robe covering the scanty costume she wore beneath. Her dark eyes snapped with disgust. "Well, gentlemen and *lady*, is he alive or dead? Shall we find out?"

Deep in his morbidity, head slumped on his chest, Adam was only vaguely aware. Ramona, bumping her hips at Ben, whirled and swiftly straddled Adam, pulling his head against her chest.

Drunkenly, he shook his head, smiling vapidly.

"Pussycat, pussycat, where have you been?" Ramona purred. She pulled his head up by his hair, looking deeply into his eyes. "Wanna go see the queen, pussycat?" She laughed, and the others joined her, hooting and stomping.

Adam watched blearily as Ramona wriggled on his lap, pleasing her audience, driving them to frenzy. He grasped her robe at the neckline and ripped it from her as he stood up, thrusting her away. "Slut!"

Ramona lay stunned, then she began to laugh, running her hands through her hair, rolling and moving on the floor as suggestively as she had while dancing on the stage. "Now there's a man!" she shouted. Quickly she went back to the stage, murmured instructions to the musicians, then looked to the back of the room where Adam sat. "This one's for you, pussycat! All for you!"

The drummer rolled a fanfaronade while Ramona Rose gyrated her hips in voluptuous suggestion. Her long, sharp fingernails moved sinuously along her body, caressing her breasts. Then as the drummer hit three hard echoing licks, Ramona swung her pelvis forward, in a movement obscene and explicit. Her eyes never left Adam. "I can do that all night with you, pussycat!" Her audience cheered lustily.

The band played a rocking, bawdy tune. Ramona paced the small stage, her steps calculated to inflame her audience's lust. At intervals the drummer hit a hard note echoed by a soft one, and Ramona flung out one thigh and held the pose, running her hand up to caress the scanty sequined green triangle between her thighs. The gaze from her black-fringed eyes compelled Adam's on her.

A husky seaman cried, "Come on, Ramona! Whirl them tits!"

Ramona moved one shoulder, and her breast lifted and fell, lifted and fell, while she watched herself in apparent surprise. Then the other breast moved in a partial circle. To the cries of "Take it off!" she flung away the last transparent veiling.

She stood nearly naked, her long black hair in stringy ringlets down her back. A muscular woman past youth, she still had a good body. On each nipple was a long green tassel that glimmered in the smoky light. Her teeth flashed white at Adam. The music began again, and Ramona moved her breasts, rotating first one, then the other, while lowering herself to a half-squatting position.

As she rose effortlessly, the tassels twirled, in wild abandon to the sensuous beat of a single drum. The rotations slowed down and stopped. Ramona stood still, smiling.

"Christ, Ramona, ain't you a-gonna set 'em on fire?"

"I don't see any coins falling all around me," Ramona spat. Gold pieces pelted her, and she smiled again. "That's more like it, you tight-assed bastards!" She looked at the drummer, who wearily accompanied her through a brief series of bumps and grinds and swaying tassels.

Ramona went to the far side of the stage and bent over, giving the gawking men a clear view of her naked buttocks. Ceremoniously she lifted a stemmed glass and dipped her tassels in it, stripping out the extra fluid. The husky seamen sprang to help, quickly lighting each tassel with a match, and grabbing a quick feel for his trouble.

Ramona whirled her tassels, first in one direction, then the other, until the blue flames dimmed and went out. Then, to screaming applause, she danced off the stage, picking up the coins as she went, each motion provocative. The drummer stayed with her to the very last coin, the last sensuous bend, the last glimpse of bare breasts and rounded buttocks. With a final obscene gesture, Ramona Rose vanished behind a door.

Ben stood up. "We're leaving, Adam. I'm done with coaxing, and I'm done with groveling in this hellhole. You coming or not?"

Adam looked up blearily. Ramona was in view again, smiling, teasing him with her eyes, taunting him with her body. He shuddered, and stood unsteadily, knocking the rum bottle over. "I'm coming."

On the way home Adam was quiet, thinking of Ramona and himself. God! she turned his stomach. And yet, how many times had he gone to the Halyard Light these past few nights just to see her?

Claudine, her face anxious, opened the door to the suite. "Ah take keer o' him, Mastah Ben. Doan you worry none, he be jes' fine now."

"My newly appointed keeper," Adam snarled as he sprawled on the sofa.

She bathed his face, her nose twitching at the scent of Ramona. "Who you been with, Mastah Adam?" she asked lightly. She handed him a towel and a steaming cup of coffee, then settled on the floor at his knees. "Why you go to some no-'count woman, when you knows Ah's heah fo' you?"

Adam saw the look of hurt in her eyes. His own were cold. "I was with no one, Claudine, I don't want to be with anyone. *Anyone*."

"Dat ain't true. Ah knows you, an'—"

"You know me. Then why don't you know I don't want you mooning over me like a sick cow?"

Claudine stood up, her back straight, her face etched in pain and hurt. "You ain't got no call to say dem things to me. Mebbe Ah ain't no Miss Dulcie, an' mebbe Ah ain't white, but Ah keered fo' you, an' Ah been lovin' you fo' a long time. Ah ain't done nothin' to make you say dem things to me." Tears streamed down her face. "Ain't no woman gwine love you like Ah done. Ah neveh ast you fo' nothin', jest wantin' you to keer fo' me now 'n' den. Ah knows you doan love me. Dat was fo' Miss Dulcie, but Ah lovin' you jes' de same. All Ah'm wantin' is to do fo' you when you needs me. Ain't right you go to some white-trash slut when you's hurtin' an' needin' fo' a woman."

Adam did not speak. Claudine began to cry softly. He stared up at the ceiling, finding cracks and discolorations in the smooth plaster. Hearing her sobs, his chest hurt, and his mind racked him. Once, he would have soothed her, comforted her. Once, he would have done so many things. Now, he realized, he was incapable of even the simplest act of kindness. Each breach of his hard façade by kindness made his thoughts of Dulcie and his responsibility in her loss more intolerable. Sometime it had to end. He had to become a man again.

He went to Claudine where she had curled up sobbing out her love for him. "I'm sorry, Claudine," he said, less kindly than he meant. "It isn't you. I just don't want a woman. Dulcie . . . was all I needed."

Claudine looked up at him. "Dat's jes' why she be wantin'

you to turn to me, Mastah Adam. I love Miss Dulcie 'most as you. We both love her, an' now all we got lef' is us. You an' me."

Adam touched her cheek. He shook his head. "I'm taking you back to Mossrose, Claudine. That's where you belong, with Jem and Patricia. They have to be told, and . . . they'll need you, much more than I will."

"Doan do dat to me, Mastah Adam. Doan sen' me away from you. Ah promise Ah nevah say dese things to you again. Let me stay by you, jes' take care o' yo' house. Ah woan nevah say nothin' agin."

Adam sat down heavily. "I wouldn't want you to be here and be afraid to talk to me or worry about angering me. But every time I see you, I think of Dulcie. When I come in this room or sleep in my bed, Dulcie is all around me. I don't want to stay here or see these rooms ever again. Next week when the moon is dark, you and I are going to Savannah. I'll tell her parents that I—that she . . . I'll tell them. And then, Claudine, I'm going to try to forget."

The next morning Adam dressed carefully, wearing the uniform of a ship's master. The clothing felt strange and out of place on him. The well-tailored jacket fit him, but it felt larger than he did. It was as if Adam Tremain had somehow shrunk and the frame of the man had become larger than the man himself. But he walked past the Halyard Light, resisting the temptation for one quick drink.

He bargained for a load of civilian goods guaranteed to bring high profits, something he had never done before. He took on as cargo only the one-third load that Confederate law required of a blockade runner. He would carry the heaviest guns the agent had available: three Whitworth rifles, one long-range cannon, and five Parrott guns.

Adam took the *Black Swan* on her maiden voyage without benefit of a trial run in November of 1862. Adam knew the odds were turning against the runner. The Federals had closed many more ports. They guarded the sea with more ships and a growing familiarity with the peculiarities of Southern waters. The few slim advantages the blockade runner had were vanishing.

Adam was mildly surprised to find that he didn't care. When the *Independence* went down and the sea had spewed him up on Andros, he was a different man, a man with different fears, different desires.

He entered Charleston harbor using Maffitt's Channel. Fort Moultrie squatted on his right as the *Black Swan* steamed past Castle Pinckney for the Cooper River piers. He wasted no time clearing his papers with the Confederate agents, who speedily relieved Adam of his cargo of ammunition and heavy guns. The civilian goods were consigned to an honest warehouseman Adam had met the year before through Melody Cox.

Adam and Claudine left for Savannah in a rented wagon. The hundred-and-thirty-mile trip stretched to a one-hundred-and-fifty-mile ordeal as Adam took old trails, avoiding wandering bands of Confederate and Yankee troops who had been separated from their companies or deserted.

Adam saw neglected cotton fields dry and barren, fields that bore the signs of having been burned, fields that had been stripped and left with naked broken cornstalks. The prosperous farming South was taking on the air of a patched, war-ravaged old vagrant. In other places he saw plantations that looked criminally prosperous in contrast to those the war had touched. But no matter where he looked, the evidence of the devastation of the South was irrefutable. Slowly, a battle at a time, a raid at a time, a day at a time, the bounty and resiliency of the South were being destroyed.

By the time they reached the River Road, Adam's mood was contemplative and sad. He was more than just a man born in the South. He loved it. Its spirit was as much a part of him as his bones and muscles. This inexorable wasting of its vitality ate at him, twisting inside of him, paining him with an unassuageable hunger.

Claudine shivered, her eyes darting from one side of the road to the other. Then she drew in her breath. "Oh, Lawd, Mastah Adam—de Chilcotes' house—"

Adam looked over the top of Claudine's head. Ghostly and blackened beyond the row of charred, naked trees, stood the shell of the Chilcotes' plantation house. The west wing was caved in, the east wing standing tall with its broken, darkened windows looking blankly toward River Road. Five of its seven Corinthian pillars stood alone, separated from the fallen roof.

Adam tightened his hands on the reins. He hurried the horses toward Mossrose at a brisk trot. The crape myrtles stood as always, suggesting nothing amiss. Involuntarily, he released held breath and slowed the horses to a more leisurely pace.

Claudine whispered. "Turn back. Ah doan wanta go on. Mebbe . . ."

Adam stared, waiting for the road to curve and give him sight of the softly hued pink-brick façade of Moss-rose.

"Ah doan like this, Mastah Adam—doan feel right. Ah doan wanta go on. Please, we doan gotta go heah, does we? Ah doan wanta see it."

Adam said hoarsely, "Stop it, Claudine!"

"Ah cain't! They's daid people heah. Ah feel it in mah bones."

Adam grabbed her roughly, the reins held in one white-knuckled fist. "Damn you, womàn, don't say another word!" He shook her violently.

Claudine's eyes were frightened. "Ain't gwine change nothin', you shoutin' at me."

He thrust her away. His mind was playing tricks. With each slight curve he was looking at Mossrose. He could hear the sounds of children playing. He heard the slave bell ringing. There were songs in the air. "Can you hear anything? The slaves . . . children?"

Claudine's mouth set tight. "Dere ain't nothin'. Jes' de hants."

Adam scowled. "If you'd shut up long enough to listen, you'd hear."

They took the last turn, and Mossrose loomed against the sky. Claudine looked away, but Adam stared bleakly, not even surprised by what he saw. An upturned wagon lay in a deeply grooved rut in the front lawn. The windows were broken out. Along the frames were the telltale black, licking scars of an interior fire. He glanced at the folly, his memory of it gleaming white in moonlight strong. But for a flickering of his eye he showed no feeling as he looked at the charred remains of the five columns that had sup-ported its roof.

In the sturdy brick walls of Mossrose were gaping holes where field pieces had bombarded it. One such field piece stood abandoned, mired deep in the path to the slave quar-ters. Adam shrank from it. Waste. Everything was waste. Broken wagons. Barren fields. Burned-out shell of a house. Everything was gone. There was no noise, no singing in Mossrose, no running feet, no bright red-haired girl to ride up the path on Strawberry with the wind in her hair and the roseblush on her cheeks.

Adam got down from the wagon, his mouth set, his eyes dead. Expecting only more death, more destruction, he walked into the front hall. Mossrose was gone. Even its scent had vanished. This place smelled like a stable, and evidences of its use as such remained on the once brightly polished floor. His boots sounded loud, echoing in the strangely empty house. In the main parlor, where he and Dulcie had danced, were ashen remnants of a huge fire that had been set in the middle of the floor. Across the papered walls and ceiling crept dark smoke streaks.

Claudine stood in the entrance hall, her eyes watering from the acrid, damp smell. She hadn't wanted to come back. There was nothing here. She was terrified to find out whose spirit it was that she sensed wandering restless and unhappy along these grounds. Perhaps it was 'Pollo. Perhaps it was her own mother, Rosaleen. Her eyes followed Adam, but she stood where she was.

Adam circled the parlor, touching the charred ruins of the furniture. The piano had been hacked to pieces, some of it burnt for firewood, other splintered remnants left to lie on the floor. He kicked at the twisted keyboard, then squatted down, his fingers caressing the ivory rectangles, remembering, trying to bring back the sounds of Dulcie playing and singing.

The house was filled with strange, empty noises. Leaves skittering across the floors, blown there by wind and storms. Mice busily claiming what man had discarded. Stray, scraggly chickens pecking at threads of once luxurious carpets. Soft padding noises of unknown origin mingled as Adam strained to hear the past sound again in his mind.

From the back hall the woman moved slowly, blending the telltale sounds of her cloth-wrapped feet with the rustling of the wind. She pressed against the wall, her face shining with nervous sweat, her eyes white-walled with fear. She had done this before. Abandoned plantations lay unguarded and tempting to every passing deserter, every band of marauding refugees, gangs of runaway slaves, impoverished whites.

She slithered around the corner, her eye on the intruder. She raised the ax, renewing her grip on its broken handle.

The man didn't move. He hadn't heard her. She moved quickly, taking small running steps toward her victim, the ax held above her head.

"Ludy!" Claudine's shrill voice pierced the air. "Ludy, no!"

Adam spun, still on his haunches, throwing himself off balance. He half-lay on the floor, his arm up protecting his head.

Ludy, the midwife, stood poised, wild-eyed, the ax held aloft directly over Adam. Her body was still tensed, ready to strike, as she turned toward Claudine.

Claudine moved forward, stopping as Ludy moved the ax. "Ludy . . . no! It's me, Claudine."

Ludy glanced down at Adam. He made no move to defend himself.

"That's Mastah Adam. Ludy, put that ax down." Claudine's voice trembled.

Slowly Ludy lowered the ax, still staring suspiciously at Claudine. "What you doin' heah? Wheah you comes from?"

"Nassau. We been livin' in Nassau. Mastah Jem tell you 'bout that, ain't he? You kin see who Ah am, Ludy. Look."

"Mastah Jem gone," Ludy said warily.

Claudine, frowning, approached her. "What you mean, he gone? Wheah Mastah Jem go? Wheah Miss Trishy?"

"She gone too. Ain't nobody lef'."

"Dey daid?!"

Ludy shrugged her shoulders. She placed the ax in the corner. Adam sat on the floor, silent, staring at the broken keyboard. "Dey lef' an' doan come back. Mastah Jem say he comin' back, but he doan."

"What happened at Mossrose, Ludy?" Adam asked softly.

"Cain't say 'zackly. Lot's o' feet come trampin' thoo heah. Lots o' death an' sorrow stay behin'."

"Where's 'Pollo? He ain't—"

Ludy smiled. " 'Pollo make he daddy happy. Dem black sojers know 'Pollo somethin' special fust dey sets dey eyes on him. He a lootenan' in de Affican Ahmy," Ludy said proudly. "He march off wid dem sojers headin' fo' South Ca'lina to meet up wiff de ahmy o' Gen'l Rufus Saxton. 'Pollo gwine be de instrum'nt dat end dis ol' war."

"And the others?" Adam asked.

"Some done run off. De raiders hack some to deff fo' de sport of it," Ludy said bitterly. "Dey burn Mossrose an' tells us we's free." She picked up the ax. "So Ah free, an' Ah defen's mah home. Dis ol' ax know de way thoo plen'y white-trash skulls dat tells me Ah's free an' den take de food from mah fiel's an' de clo's offen mah back. Ludy ain't no fool. How Ah s'pose to live effen dey burn an' kill eve'y thing dey sees?"

Adam slowly got to his feet. "Who is left, Ludy?"

"Violet. Barney an' Dick out in de woods diggin' up de supplies we done hide away. Grace hidin' in de spring-house. Hosea. Hersel an' 'Simmon, dey in de qua'ters. Ain't much o' de qua'ters lef'. Dem white trash dat run from Gen'l Rosecrans' ahmy done burn ever'thin' dey cain't eat or take wiff 'em. Den dey piss on what's lef'. Dey's de chilluns ob de debbil, dose mens."

"The men who came through here are deserters from Rosecrans's command? He's supposed to be in Tennessee."

Ludy looked blankly at him. "Doan know wheah Tenny-see is. Dem mens say dey come a long way ovah de moun-tins to bring us freedom. Dey say we ain't wu'th all de mis'ry an' de hell dey livin' thoo. Dey say dey ain't nevah gwine back. But dey doan bring us no freedom."

Claudine looked disgustedly around the room. "Dey make dis mess?"

Ludy nodded. She looked at Adam, her eyes fierce, her mouth set. "We took keer o' Mossrose like Mastah Jem say, but we ain't stayin' no mo'. Barney an' de mens fixin' de wagons. We gwine leave heah tonight. Fellie an' Ester an' Darcy up Nawth. We gwine fin' 'em."

Claudine looked at Adam. "You knows wheah Fellie an' Ester is?"

Ludy's mouth grew firmer, small lines forming. "We fin's 'em."

"Mastah Adam, ain't you gwine do nothin' 'bout this?"

"What do you want me to do, Claudine?"

"You jes' gwine let 'em go?"

"How many of you are there, Ludy?"

"Barney an' Dick an' Hosea an' Violet an' Grace an' me. Hersel woan leave 'Simmon. Ol' 'Simmon he done got burnt when dem sojers fire de qua'ters. Hersel say he an' 'Simmon gwine die wiff Mossrose. Dey too ol' to be gwine Nawth."

Adam thought of Hersel, the little groom whom Dulcie used to plague by riding Strawberry out into all kinds of weather. He remembered 'Simmon, the purple-black old man who worked in the fields beside his old stick-woman wife. He hadn't the heart to walk to the quarters to see these old men who had lived long enough to watch their world die and now waited only to die with it.

He stared blankly outside, then roused. "Ludy, tell them to come in. I'll be sailing for New York. I can get you that far safely."

Ludy looked suspiciously at Adam, then to Claudine. Claudine broke into a wide grin. "Doan you worrit none, Ludy. Folks eve'ywheah calls him de Black Swan. Ain't you nevah heard o' de Black Swan?"

Ludy's eyes filled with tears. "We heahs, but ain't nevah thinkin' he gwine come to Mossrose. Thanky, suh. We does what you say."

Adam went outside. He walked to the ruin of the folly, his feet moving over the grass where he and Dulcie had danced. Without thinking, he headed for the burned-out stables, half-expecting the blue roan to be saddled and waiting. He stood in their ruins and looked down the row of slave quarters. The cabin that had been Wolf's stood out from the burned shells of the others.

Adam remained staring at the cabin for some time. How different would his life with Dulcie have been if Wolf hadn't interrupted them with his obscene display that day in the little hut in the woods? For a moment it seemed to Adam that Dulcie would still be alive, happy, and waiting for him at Mossrose if it hadn't been for Wolf.

All the guilt he had been carrying he mentally transferred to Wolf. It was Wolf's fault that Dulcie had followed him to New Orleans and come to be in Nassau. It was his fault that Dulcie had had to sail across the ocean to see her parents. It was Wolf's fault that she was on that particular voyage.

It seemed real to Adam, until Grace's shrill voice pierced his thoughts. He started, blinking, seeing Mossrose as it really was—abandoned by Jem, its fields trampled and scorched, its stables charred rubble. He shivered thinking of Dulcie here, or rather lost from here, wandering he didn't know where. Lost like Jem and Patricia.

Grace streaked across the lawn shrieking, " 'Simmon daid! Ludy! 'Simmon daid! Hersel say he gwine die, too! Make him stop! Oh, Ludy, come quick!"

Chapter Four

The cortege of slaves buried 'Simmon and Hersel in the slave burying ground behind the peach orchard. Adam walked slowly after them with Claudine. With the last spade of dirt thrown into the grave and the last prayer murmured, all faces turned to Adam. They were ready to leave, and they looked to him to lead them to safety and bounty in the North. They had finished with Mossrose.

Adam told each one what was needed. Quickly they went to gather the provisions for a long journey. Hosea brought to the front entrance of Mossrose two rickety, hastily repaired wagons. Adam walked briskly from one small pile of provisions to another, mentally tallying the additional risks their makeshift vehicles would create in an already dangerous trip. The wagons were held together with wood patches and wire. Hosea had done the best he could.

But Adam doubted that the wagons would make the hard trip. Roads that had once been cared for by the plantation owners were now left to the whim of weather, use, and time. They were badly rutted, in some places nearly impassable because of fallen trees, debris, and heavy rains. On those same roads, they would be the target of hungry marauding bands of runaways or deserters. They had shoes on their feet, clothes on their backs, supplies in their wagons, and horses. Any single item was enough to tempt those who had nothing.

Adam decided to leave behind the weaker of the two wagons. They would use one of the big Mossrose wagons and the wagon he had rented in Charleston. It was too small, but it was sturdy. Hosea led two horses, sorry creatures that Jem had put to pasture two years before— all that was left of the Mossrose stable, once second to none.

They set out at sundown, keeping to the main roads to spare the rickety wheels of Hosea's wagons. Their route was merely a choice of evils. On the main roads they were liable to be stopped by patrollers seeking runaways. Along back roads they could be accosted or attacked by nearly anyone. There was no place of safety in these times. Law, what little there was of it, was arbitrary, dependent on the mood and condition of the lawmaker. Of lawlessness there were endless varieties brought about by necessity, hunger, meanness, and war.

The first dawn they stopped near Beaufort, just miles from the Federal refueling station at Port Royal. No one slept. Adam prowled the surrounding area, his hand on the Colt at all times. Barney and Hosea worked feverishly repairing the left rear wheel of the wagon.

Her tread so light it made no sound on the pine-laden turf, Claudine came up to Adam. He whirled, grabbing for her. "For God's sake, Claudine, don't come up on me like that."

She rubbed her hand along her bruised upper arm where he had grabbed her. "We gwine be all right, Mastah Adam?" she asked quietly.

"We'll be all right." He watched her hesitate, frightened but not wanting to show him, uncertain but already cowed by his determination to be rid of her. He reached out and took her chin in his hand. "We'll be all right, Claudine."

"What you gwine do wiff me?"

"Would you like to go North with the others?"

"Ah jes' wants to stay wiff you. Ah woan be in yo' way. Ah woan do nothin' what you doan wan' me to."

Adam's eyes roved over the dark area, searching for movement in the shadowy woods. "You can't stay with me, Claudine. We've already talked that over, and my mind is made up."

"Ah ain't gwine Nawth!"

"You'll do as I tell you."

"Nossuh! Dey's suhtain things you cain't tell me. Ah cain't he'p what Ah feels fo' you, an' Ah cain't he'p you doan wan' what Ah gots to give you, but Ah ain't gwine Nawth! Ah's stayin' jes' as nigh to you as Ah kin!"

"Lower your voice!"

"Ah ain't gwine Nawth," she repeated softly.

"All right! I've already told you, you can stay in Wilmington with my mother. Now, for God's sake, go with the other women and sleep."

But none of them could sleep. Adam, as restless as his passengers, decided to chance being stopped and questioned. He could always say the wagon load of slaves belonged to him and pray no one asked him for papers. Nearly anything seemed better than the waiting and the constant fear of surprise.

From then on they traveled day and night, stopping only for meals and short rests for the drivers. The miles seemed to bring Charleston no closer, until finally Adam recognized plantations they passed. "We'll be there by nightfall."

Adam drove the wagon to Melody Cox's millinery shop, as close as he dared to the well-guarded dock area. He went to the ship alone. "Rosebud!"

The big black man loomed out of the darkness. "When you git back, Boss?"

"I've got six fugitives waiting behind Melody's shop. Not a one has papers. Have we any cargo that hasn't been loaded yet?"

"Ain't much, Boss, jes' some turpentine, an' some mo' naval stores."

"Rouse six of the men. As the slaves load the stuff on board, one of our men will go back down the gangplank and take the last of the supplies. Oh, and Rosebud, gather three sets of men's clothing for the women. A very large set—yours—for Violet."

Rosebud whistled. "Yas, Boss! I meet you at Miss Melody's. You gwine stop an' say hello to her fo' a minute?"

Adam scowled at him, then hurried back down the gangplank into the darkness. Rosebud heard him call out a cheerful greeting to one of the Confederate guards patrolling the area.

Shortly after, Rosebud ran along the Charleston streets, the bundle of seamen's clothing tucked under his arm. All the women, dressed in the trousers and shirts of the crew, followed Adam and Rosebud back to the dock area.

"Grace, you open your mouth just once and I'll smash you!" Adam rasped, his raised fist clenched. Grace's head bobbed mutely.

Rosebud handed her a small cask and lifted one of the large kegs. "Y'all jes' folla aftuh me," he said. He waved a large arm at the crates, kegs, and boxes. "Eve'ybody take one an' walk along like you knows what you's doin'."

Silently the train of six blacks followed Rosebud, Violet huffing and straining under the additional weight of a cask of turpentine, Rosebud's trousers pinching painfully into her monumental girth.

As each black reached the companionway to the hold, a

crewman took his cargo. The slave slipped off, edging along
the deck to Adam's cabin. The crewmen finished loading,
cheerfully waving or shouting farewell to the marching
guards as they normally did.

Above, hung the sliver of a new moon. Adam looked
skyward warily, then gave orders to sail.

"Ain't we gwine wait 'til de moon is right, Boss?"

"Not unless you want to do your waiting in a Confederate
prison. We stay and someone is going to find these people. We go and we just might make it. No Federal will expect us tonight."

Rosebud's eyes walled. "Ahh, Boss, we all gwine git kilt
fo' sho'!"

Adam punched him playfully. "I've never gotten you
kilt yet, Rosebud. Trust me."

"Ah trusses you, Boss, but Ah doan trusses dem Yankees."

The engine of the *Black Swan* started. Adam pored over
his charts until every light aboard was covered or put out.
He set the course for Maffitt's Channel. He reversed engines, staring at the moving cloud bank, waiting for the
mass of black clouds to cover the silver moon.

He ordered full steam, and the *Black Swan* leaped forward and ran for the Atlantic. They had passed the first
tier of blockading ships before they were spotted. Suddenly the sky lit with the eerie golden and red and white-
blue blasts of cannon fire, flares, and grape and canister.

Rosebud grabbed the fire shovel and began digging into
the coal bunkers. The boilers of the *Black Swan* steamed
and blew hot, wet air, forcing the ship through the water
faster and faster. She sat low on a gently rolling sea, cutting her way farther from land.

In Adam's dark cabin Violet's pudgy hands clasped in
what she was certain was the last prayer in her life. Tucked
under her arm and wriggling furiously was Grace, silenced
but struggling for air. Around them were the earsplitting
sounds of the Yankee guns.

On the quarterdeck Adam felt an exhilaration he had
never experienced before. He watched the gun bursts exploding, hot shot pounding into the sea, and grape and
canister tearing at the main deck, while he stood boldly
unsheltered at the rail, daring one of the shots to find
him. Without Dulcie, without the substance of his life intact, it was easy to believe the legends about himself that

the slaves had begun to create. Adam Tremain was merely mortal, with all a man's weaknesses, sorrows, and failings. The Black Swan was of the gods, an invincible force that could carry the blacks through fire and out unscathed. To-night, aboard this ship, there was no Adam Tremain who hurt and sorrowed; there was only the force, only the Black Swan.

He had no difficulty entering the Cape Fear. He knew the currents and the shoals as well as any river pilot. He chose his time and ran for the surf line and the protective guns of Fort Fisher. He and Rosebud toasted the success-ful voyage as they passed the Dram Tree.

The fugitive slaves were taken from the ship under the cover of night the same way they boarded. Each man and woman carried a piece of cargo. Once on the darkened pier, they slipped away into the darkness.

By the time Adam reached Zoe's house with the blacks hidden in a dray loaded with civilian luxuries, he was tired. The wild, invincible sensation of being the Black Swan had left. He leapt from the dray at the front door as Rosebud took the slaves and Claudine to the barn.

Adam knocked tentatively, suddenly unsure that Zoe would be there. Unreasonable doubts crowded his mind as he thought of Beau leaving on an ordinary run and never returning; of Dulcie, warm and loving beside him one night and the next swallowed for all eternity into a rag-ing white-water sea; of Mossrose, burned and empty of life.

Zoe's eyes opened wide, then she burst into happy laughter. Adam paused, then swept his small mother into his arms, holding her close as he buried his face in her shoulder.

"Oh, Adam! Each time you come home, I feel as though it's been years." She expected him to release her and set her gently on her feet. But he didn't. He held her fast, em-bracing her in a hurtful, almost desperate grasp. His breath caught as a great tremor ran through him.

"Adam," she said, in a soft, worried voice. "What's hap-pened?"

Racking sobs tore out of him. His voice was broken and muffled. He pressed his face deeper into the curve of her neck. "Dulcie's . . . dead."

Zoe's eyes prickled and stung. She wrapped her arms around him.

"Oh, darling. I'm so sorry." Nothing she could say would change or ease it for him. She pushed herself away. "Come to the study, Adam. Hurry, dear, before the others learn you're here."

His eyes averted from his mother's gaze, Adam sank into a chair, his head in his hands. Like a dam bursting, words flowed from him, thick and anguished as he painstakingly told of his and Dulcie's life together. He calmed when he talked of the shipwreck and Andros. Zoe listened to him blame himself. Red-eyed and tortured, he looked up at her. "Why couldn't it have been me, Ma? Why Dulcie?"

Zoe said nothing. Her face contorted as she fought not to cry.

Adam looked down at his hands. "She carried our child with her." He said it so softly Zoe wasn't sure she had heard. He seemed to forget she was with him, his voice low and choked with emotions he had never allowed anyone to see before, speaking of things he had always kept tightly locked inside himself. As he spoke of the loss of the daughter-in-law she had never met, Zoe learned the depth of her son's love for Dulcie.

When he had finally talked himself out, Zoe rose, coming to kiss him tenderly on the forehead. "Stay here, Adam. I'll keep the others away from you as long as I can."

Adam felt better for having talked. But he knew it was not merely the telling that had made him feel better. It was being home. It was not being alone. It was being loved no matter what he had done, no matter how weak he was, how responsible for Dulcie's death. Zoe would have forgiven him anything. And though he knew he could not tolerate her unquestioning absolution for long, just now it was what he longed for, what he needed.

He emerged from the study nearly an hour later. From the kitchen he heard angry voices and remembered belatedly that he had said nothing to his mother about the six fugitives or Rosebud or Claudine.

"Ah ain't stayin' in no barn!" Claudine's voice was shrill.

Angela's low voice replied, "Well, well, where do you think we keep fugitives? For someone who's begging shelter, you certainly put on airs."

"Ah ain't beggin' nothin'!"

Adam looked on amused as the dark, tiny-statured Claudine, her jaw thrust out, her brow furrowed, argued with the delicately blond Angela. Ignoring their agitated shouts, Adam came up behind Angela, slipping his hands over her eyes.

She straightened, her mouth open, then twirled and wrapped her arms around his neck. "Adam!" She covered his face and neck with rapid, chaste kisses. "I'm so glad you're home! Why did you go hide in that ol' study? Aunt Zoe wouldn't let me near you!"

Chuckling, warmed by her ingenuous greeting, Adam gently began to remove her arms from around his neck. She stood on tiptoe, laughing and teasing, kissing him on one cheek, then the other. "I'm glad, glad, glad to see you!"

Adam began to laugh, his hands gently resting on the curve of her waist. "Enough! Enough!"

Claudine said sourly, "Mo'n enuf, iffen anybody was to ast me."

Adam removed himself from Angela's grasp, his eyes still smiling. "Angela is . . ." He was about to say, "like my little sister." Confused, he realized Angela was no longer the Angela of his memory. At fifteen she was tall, at least five feet seven inches, and there was nothing small about her. The curves of her breasts and hips were pronounced and womanly, the gleam in her eyes that of a temptress, her mouth sensuous.

"Angela is what?" Angela looked at him from lowered lashes, a playful smile on her full lips, her hips thrust toward him. "What's the matter, Adam? Cat got your tongue?"

"Angela Pierson!" Zoe bustled into the kitchen trailed by Mammy and Rosebud. She reached up and tweaked Angela's ear. "How dare you behave like a tart in front of Adam! Shame!"

Angela pulled away, her feet spread apart, hands on her hips. "Who are you to tell me what I can and can't do? You let me alone!"

"Angela!" Zoe gasped.

"That's enough, Angela," Adam said. "You'll obey my mother without question and without insolence."

Angela's dark eyes flashed angrily. "Yes, Master. Whatever you say. Should I see 'bout the washin' now, Miss?"

Red to the roots of her hair with anger, Zoe stepped forward and slapped Angela resoundingly. Angela's head jerked, but the hateful defiance remained blazing in her eyes. She turned her other cheek. "You've never hit me on this side; wouldn't you like to?"

Wilted by the girl's blatant, unyielding hostility, Zoe said sadly, "Go to your room, Angela."

Angela smiled slowly, her last glance provocative and warm on Adam. "Anything you say, *Aunt* Zoe."

"I'm sorry you witnessed that, but sooner or later it had to happen. I don't know what to do. Angela is head-strong, and so bitter."

Before Adam could reply, she turned to Claudine, speaking softly to her, explaining how the household ran, what would be expected of her and what she could expect from Zoe. Claudine would be happy here with Zoe. To Adam it seemed impossible that anyone given the oppor-tunity would not want to stay with his mother, taken care of in this quiet, orderly house. It now seemed strange that he hadn't spent more time here. This time he would. When Ben came into port, he'd tell him not to expect him in Nassau before the new year, perhaps not even then.

To Zoe's surprise Mammy took to Claudine right away, sitting back in her rocking chair before the open kitchen fire peeling potatoes while Claudine scurried back and forth from sideboard to oven.

Claudine looked pensive. "Mammy, who's dat Angela girl?"

"Miss Angela be Mastah Tom's daughter. Mastah Adam save dem from a bad, bad man long time ago."

Claudine weighed the wisdom of speaking or keeping her mouth shut; but instinctively she trusted Mammy. Within minutes she had known Mammy loved Adam every bit as much as she did. "She's no good."

Mammy concentrated on her potato.

"She's hankerin' aftuh him," Claudine persisted.

Mammy sighed. "He ain't heah much. She be a li'l sis-ter to 'im."

"All she need is one night. Mastah Adam's a-hurtin', an' she—"

"Ain't nobuddy gwine do nothin' to mah boy! Not while dey's breaf in dis ol' body."

Claudine smiled and turned back to the preparation of the meal.

* * *

As Claudine brought in the large platters of food and deftly removed the first course from the table, Zoe smiled up at her. "Claudine, you're a blessing. Mammy works herself to death. You're the first person she has ever permitted to help her."

Claudine glared at Angela, sitting unnecessarily close to Adam. "Mammy an' Ah unnerstan's each odder."

Puzzled, Zoe smiled tentatively. "I'm glad you do."

After eating, Adam sat back comfortably, sipping a brandy. He was relaxing for the first time in weeks. There were no unwanted thoughts to hound him, no twisting feeling of hopelessness or loneliness writhing inside him, because the adoration of these two women made it easy to live only in this moment.

By the end of the first week Adam was certain that staying in Smithville until after Christmas was the wisest and most healing thing he could do. He manufactured small responsibilities that he magnified into large duties only he could perform. All his reasons seemed important and pressing when he talked to Ben. Clapping his friend on the back, Adam insisted Ben come home for supper. But Ben was not fooled by Adam's hearty cheerfulness. He spoke about it alone with Zoe.

"He's not himself," Ben said urgently. "He wants me to haul the slaves north for him while he stays here and—and takes care of what he calls his responsibilities to you. I'm sorry, I didn't mean he shouldn't help you, it's just that—"

"There's no need to apologize, Ben. I agree with you. But you said he was drinking heavily in Nassau and associating with the lowest sort of people. He isn't doing that here. Aside from his brandy after supper, he rarely drinks. What harm can come to him when he is with his mother? There are times in all our lives when the only safe haven we know is the haven of our parents' love. Don't press him to leave. Let him think he is necessary to me for this short time. Adam is not a man who can delude himself for long."

Ben nodded, but he felt uneasy. Adam was not one to seek the aid or comfort of any person. All his life Adam had sought solitude when he was confused or hurt. But anything was better than the drinking and nightly carousing in the Halyard Light.

Ben stayed for two days, then with Adam's help got the

fugitives aboard the *Liberty* and sailed to New York.

Adam put off what he considered his duties. Lethargically he moved through each day, showing hearty good humor to his mother and Angela. The rest of the time he felt inert.

During the last week in Advent, as Zoe made frantic preparations for Christmas, Adam talked to Angela. Without thought, he took her to the beach. The cool misty wind blew Angela's hair free from her scarf. She looked lovely. Her skin had a golden, creamy softness. She might have been Ullah, except that even in Adam's exaggeratedly mellow memory, he knew Angela was prettier.

He was jolted when her first words were accusatory. "Zoe made you bring me, didn't she!"

"She knows you're unhappy. I thought perhaps you'd want to talk to me. You used to tell me everything."

"What makes you think you know so much about me?" she asked sullenly.

Adam looked out across the teal mist-shrouded water. "We always know about the people we care about, Angela."

"You care about me? You admit that?"

He looked quickly to her upturned face, the questioning eyes that demanded an answer. "Of course I do. Ever since you were just a little tiny thing who laughed when I gave you a ride on my shoulders."

She turned away sharply, a sardonic smile on her lips. Nearby the water made soft slapping sounds against the shore. "Adam, will you marry me?"

Adam went white. "I'm married."

"You *were* married. Were! She drowned!"

Through stiff lips he said, "Stop talking about her. She—"

Angela went on, heedless, "All my life I expected to marry you! You promised you'd wait for me, and you broke that promise! That's why she died!"

"I was teasing," Adam whispered. "Teasing is not a promise."

"Next you'll deny you love me!" She took a step back. "Adam, look at me. You have said I am too young for you. What do you think now?"

She turned before him, like Glory or Dulcie, pleased with a new dress. Adam's head buzzed, looking against his will at this woman he had considered a child. She was tall, willowy, her pose seductive. In her pretty face, so reminis-

cent of Ullah, there was none of her mother's unquenchable innocence. In her body there was no babyish softness.

She saw it in his eyes. She said triumphantly, "I'm ripe,
Adam, like a peach ready for picking. I'm ready for a
man. Ready for you."

"God." He swallowed. "Angela, you can't do this . . .
go around putting yourself on the market like a—a slab
of bacon."

"The market has only one prospect, Adam. I won't have
you marry some other woman like last time. I'm grown
now. There's no reason to wait. You're free, and I'm
ready."

"Don't talk like that!"

"Why not? Who's to say I can't, and who would care if I
did?"

"I care." He tore his eyes away from her. "Your Aunt
Zoe cares. Your father cares. Oh, God, Angela, I care!"

"How do you care, Adam? Do you want me? Or are you
just helping another little pickaninny?"

Mouth open, he pivoted to face her. "What are you
saying?"

She laughed contemptuously. "Oh, I know! I'm a nigger, Adam. Tom told me. Even showed me Zoe's letter to
my mother."

"Did he tell you . . . everything?"

"She was a slave, and they murdered her. Tom would
be dead, too, if it hadn't been for you." She shrugged,
her hard, angry eyes on the ocean. "If he'd died, no one
would ever know I'm not white. Not even me. You owe
me something for that. You made me suffer for what I
am."

"Damn you! What you would have been is a slave, if
your father hadn't loved her enough to make her his wife."

"And killed her because of it. Some love."

He grabbed her shoulders. Her insolent smile remained.
"There was no woman finer than your mother! You remember that and try to live up to her. Tom loved your
mother as few men ever love any woman."

"Will you love me like that, Adam?"

He released her. "I love you as an uncle . . . a brother."

"You're a liar!" She ran, stopping halfway up the beach.
"You want me! Liar, liar!"

* * *

During the holidays an uneasy reserve lay between Adam and Angela, dampening Zoe's festive celebration. Angela was more cooperative than she had been in months, but Adam was restive and ill at ease. Zoe suspected what was bothering him. Gently she brought their conversations around to his ship, Nassau, the war, the blockade, anything that might stir him to leave. Though it tore at her, she wanted her son to leave. She couldn't send Angela away, therefore it had to be Adam.

By the end of January Zoe was nearly out of her mind with worry. Adam showed no signs of wanting to go back to sea, and the tension generated by himself and Angela was all but unbearable. It was only a matter of time before something happened.

By the first week in February Zoe decided to tell Adam bluntly that she wanted him to leave.

She found him in the study. He hadn't shaved, and for the first time since he had been home, he was drunk. His eyes were red, his face haggard as though he hadn't slept in days. Zoe's nose crinkled at the heavy alcohol smell. She sat rigid-backed on her chair.

"Adam, this has got to stop. Dulcie's death was an accident. I love you, dear, but I will not be a part in your blaming yourself."

He wiped his hand across his forehead and then reached quickly for his glass, downing the bourbon with a grimace.

Zoe snatched the bottle. "Stop it! I won't tolerate this! I won't have another drunk under my roof, never again!"

It was as if she had slapped him. He had not thought of his mother's feelings. To her he must seem like Paul Tremain, that ghostly figure whom Adam remembered as a drunken, vindictive man. As a child Adam had run from his father's hot temper and unjust punishments, But Zoe had lived with that man, suffered through days and nights as his wife. Adam's red-rimmed eyes filled with tears. "What's the matter with me, Ma?"

"There's nothing wrong with you, Adam. This time will pass, dear."

Morosely he shook his head. "Am I like *him?*"

"Who?"

"My father."

Zoe's hand fluttered to her breast. "Paul? Oh, no, Adam!

Never. There is no similarity between you and Paul Tremain. None!"

Adam shut his eyes tightly. "Something *is* wrong with me. Oh, God! Ma, I wanted her; I wanted her. She's like my sister, but I wanted her."

Zoe's knees gave way. Last night she had heard a woman's soft tread in the hall and had pulled her quilt tight around herself. Perhaps she had even known it was Angela going to Adam. Stammering, she asked, "Adam . . . n-nothing happened? You didn't—?"

Wildly he shook his head. "No. No. She's a child."

Zoe sighed in relief. "Angela's no child. She never really was."

Adam shuddered. He could still feel the smooth, silky softness of her bare skin against him, smell the clean, unsophisticated fragrance of a young girl. He stared down at his hands with disgust and felt again the sensual stirring of his blood as he remembered how he had touched her and how, with his hand once on her breast, he had given way to the fierce surge of passion, the fire that coursed through his loins, his mouth hungrily seeking the solace of hers.

He stirred uneasily, glad the desk blocked his mother's view of his body. "I can't stay here, Ma. I have to leave."

"I know," Zoe whispered.

Chapter Five

Dulcie opened her heavy eyelids. In the red wavering light the Face stared, heavy brows shadowing all-seeing eyes, a long nose, and down-turned open mouth. The forehead was grooved deep with judgment and disapproval. It moved sometimes, changing expressions, but it had not yet come near.

She closed her eyes so she wouldn't see the Face anymore. Her groping fingers explored the hammock upon which she lay. Around her body were wound strips of crisscrossed cloth. Her hair was plaited into a coronet. She was chilly in spite of the choking, steamy warmth that

rose from the pit beneath her, some cauldron of hell that
issued bubblings and hissings, that blew steam to coat
her with a malodorous sheen of moisture.

Tears slipped down. She didn't want to be dead. The
dead suffer pain; they hurt, punished for earthly sins. Pain
and burning. She burned. Her chest was freshly seared by
every indrawn breath. Low in her belly a squeezing cramp-
ing drew her tighter and tighter into a spiral of pain that
issued from her in a hot flood, and still the pain remained.
Her skin burned, aching in a thousand places that throbbed
at a touch. And inside was the terrible empty longing for
something, someone.

Her eyes ached as she strained toward a soft footstep, a
singing voice. It was the woman. The woman's fingers were
skilled as she cleansed Dulcie's wounds, feeling her forehead with calloused hands, pressing on Dulcie's belly. Her
monotonous rhythmic chant cajoled and soothed. It eased
the awful loneliness.

'Oman ob de red sun, Mam'bo Luz ten' you, eh, eh.
Gib you medsin, mek you speerit float free
Out ob you body.
Luz let you do de dance fo' Erzulie, eh, eh.

Dulcie let her eyes close. It was the woman who placed
the heated stones in the pit. The woman was her imp of
hell, pretending to help, but instead keeping her prisoner
unable to touch the earth, unable to go to those warm,
loving memories that were too vague to grasp. She could
only feel, and let the salty tears stream uselessly down
her face.

The woman was wide and plump, with pale hair hacked
short. Her skin was that of a serpent's, mottled, brown and
pink. Pinto . . . a pinto woman.

Dulcie stiffened against the bindings, some deep-buried
instinct awakened. Cold. Wet. Wind. Water. Pinto woman
. . . coming, bringing indignity, hurting, the abysmal sense
of loss, taking away all good, taking her. She would escape,
run from this red-black place of light.

A gray streak opened in the dark walls. The woman
came in, singing her strange song about floating and dancing. She was there, her rough palm on Dulcie's chest above
the swaddling. How long a time had passed? When had
she come?

She began to clean Dulcie's infected coral wounds. As she poured on her powerful herb concoctions, the pain struck deep. Dulcie gasped, her weakened body retreating from this new torture. She watched as if from a distance, feeling but shutting out the feelings.

Dulcie looked up at the woman, unable to make herself known. The woman did undignified things to her body, chanting her monotonous song. Dulcie squeezed her eyes shut against the hideous sins she suffered, unable to stop what took place. It was hell. A place of powerlessness, indignity, evil.

Dulcie's head was raised. Broth wetted her lips. In her trancelike state she wanted to drink of it as of a river flowing sweetly through herself, but the vessel was taken away. A fruitlike substance rolled endlessly over her tongue and down her thoat, quenching the ungovernable thirst. Dulcie shut her eyes tight, waiting for the medicinal herbs to work further sorcery, waiting for them to carry her to that Other World.

Perhaps she was becoming like the imp-woman. Suddenly her other-self floated free of the bindings. From some high place she looked down on that bound figure of herself and saw a sprig of oleander on her breast. The pit yawned empty now. The room lost its stifling warmth. The Face stared. As she watched, the Face leaned over and looked at the self in the hammock.

The thatched walls sparkled and glowed, in geometric patterns, merging and emerging, forming new patterns, dripping, cooling, disappearing into thatch again. She slid down a beam of pale light into herself, content for body and spirit to remain prisoner awhile longer.

Her hazy mind groped for her past, for someone taken from her. Like the geometric pattern, the memories emerged, then merged once more into the gray nothingness that filled her. She stiffened. Green water swirled at her, tumbling, tearing, filling her mouth and nose and ears, spitting her out upon the sharp cutting coral shore.

Time seemed endless, yet nothing. The woman came and went in the same instant. When Dulcie could think at all, her thought was only of hell. She lived there now, endlessly, timelessly. There had been water, then the fire and brimstone, the scourging of the body, and now the chanting and the scourging of the mind. She was being created again. When she was but a husk, the Devil would take her. Lucifer waited.

Sometimes Dulcie's personal imp spoke understandably. Dulcie didn't know if she understood the language of Hades or if the imp spoke her language or if it was merely another satanic refinement of her torture.

Sometimes in the blood-colored night grotesque dreams leaped before her eyes, dreams of a smiling black-haired man near enough to touch. When she reached for him, he became dust. She dreamed of a child, crying because it was lost. Awakening, she sorrowed all the deeper because she knew not for whom she sorrowed.

The days passed. The infections tightened their sharp-clawed grip. Down, down she sank into unawareness, except of the consuming fire.

She no longer knew of the pinto woman's ministrations. She lay breathing shallow, her skin hot, her eyes glassy and unseeing.

The pinto woman worked over Dulcie, affirming what she already knew. It was time to consult higher powers. In the *oum'phor*, the temple room, the pinto woman sprinkled cockleshells and studied them intently. The red-haired one had been given to Baron Samedi, Lord of the Cemetery, and two dead-spirits sent to collect her. If she, Mam'bo Luz, did not act quickly, not only would Lucifer be cheated of a beautiful body to house his soul but Mam'bo Luz as well. The woman from the sea would die.

Luz assessed her considerable powers. Baron Samedi would not give the woman up easily. What if Luz made an *exchange?* Baron Samedi wanted a body and a soul. Luz would offer him her own ugly-like-a-frog body and the sick woman's useless soul. Then, through ritual, the powerful spirit of Luz would enter the body of the red-haired woman and continue its earthly journey housed in shining beauty.

Such a transformation, properly proclaimed, would make her powers unmistakable, for she would have successfully bargained with the Lord of the Cemetery. She could become handmaiden to Mama Moon, Erzulie, as in her heart she had always been. Her spirit, cleansed and revitalized, would be more powerful than Lucifer.

Luz spat contemptuously. Desperate to change his hideous appearance, Lucifer lacked the audacity of Luz,

Daughter of the Sun and the Dark Night. Lucifer's powers were of earth, not of the spirits.

She shook the cockleshells again. The voodoo gods— the *mystères*—would be with her.

At dark Dulcie was carried, barely breathing, into the ritual hut, the *oum'phor*. She was laid, properly oriented to the cardinal points, on a mat near the center post of the thatched hut.

In the *caille-guédé*, an inner chamber, ritual drums beat softly. A *veve* representing a coffin was traced on the floor with ashes and coffee grounds. Two small mats covered the cabalistic design. With ashes, the sign of the Cross was made over the mats.

"I call fo' de red hair 'oman," Luz said. "Mam'bo Luz command de red hair 'oman ter walk inter de *caille-guédé*."

The *ogantier* made an insistent clangor on his flattened bell. Dulcie's attendants shed their garments and put them on inside out. Dulcie's lips, crackling with fever, parted. The brown people listened for the dead-spirits that inhabited her body to speak through her. "We abide. We abide. We not depa't."

"We be strong'r!" chanted the natives. "Mam'bo Luz be strong'r!"

Luz shook her *asson*, a calabash rattle. The spirits mumbled. Two attendants, supporting Dulcie, forced her in a shuffling travesty of a walk into the inner chamber. Her head was placed at the foot of a large black cross. She lay naked on the mats covering the coffin design. Her eyes were unseeing, her skin waxen.

Mam'bo Luz crossed Dulcie's entire body with ashes, placing small *couis* with burning candles in a triangle, one at her feet, one at each shoulder, Nearby burned sesame seeds, incense, and asafetida. On the altar burned a candle, its light flickering on *couis*—bowls—decorated with skull and crossbones, shovels, picks and axes, all dedicated to the barons and guédés who served Baron Samedi.

Mam'bo Luz invoked various gods, the saints, the dead, and the *mystères* and *loas* to grant success. Next she addressed herself to certain *mystères* whose business it was to aid the ritual.

Corn and peanuts were placed on Dulcie's belly, chest, and forehead, and in each upturned palm. Luz oriented a black duck to the cardinal points, then held it over the

grain, moving right to left, from abdomen to forehead,
encouraging the fowl to peck at each pile.

Muttering incantations, Luz did the same with a white
drake. "All dat be evil, depa't. All dat be good, enter.
Enté, té, té." A magnificently spurred red rooster was in-
duced to peck, then was placed between Dulcie's legs. The
ducks were set on her breasts. Luz, still muttering, passed
the fowls over Dulcie. After each passage the birds were
shaken to remove the evil they had absorbed.

Dulcie shuddered, raising herself violently. She was
pushed back down. Mam'bo Luz instructed the spirits to
take Dulcie's soul, to permit her own stronger, wiser soul
to enter the body.

The white drake was released, free to roam until the
evil spirits made it vanish. The three *couis* were passed
over Dulcie, moving from head to foot, then over her forehead in a circle.

The stone of Brisé was passed over her, Luz chanting,
"By the power of Brisé of the Mountain, Break-bones,
Break-limbs, Mam'bo Luz command evil speerit depa't,
strong wise speerit enter. *Enté, té, té.*"

The drums increased in tempo and loudness. The *ogantier*'s bell clanked fiercely, deafeningly. The *trianglier*'s instrument dinged. Luz shook her calabash *asson,* with its
shells and reptile vertebrae swishing inside, its strings of
beads tapping outside.

She swooped down to a basin, splashing handfuls of bath
liquid at Dulcie's face. Others joined, splashing her with the
odd-smelling liquid, while Dulcie moaned and squirmed.
When the liquid was all used, Dulcie fell back unconscious.
Luz's calloused hands clapped tightly at her breasts. The
dead-spirits had departed.

Mam'bo Luz worked more quickly now. She filled her
mouth with liquid from a *coui* on whose side was a
graven image of Erzulie. With a spraying sound she quickly blew the liquid into the Nine Sacred Entrances of Dulcie's body, chanting, "Evil speerit, go live with Baron
Samedi, strong wise speerit, enter the body of 'oman
Child of the *Guédés.*"

In a frenzy now, Luz tore her clothes, screaming incantations. Dancing like Danbhala, the serpent god, she
writhed, flicking out her tongue. She danced faster, faster.
The drummers, the *ogantier,* and the *trianglier* played
ecstatic accompaniment. Lithe and agile, Luz touched each

of her own Sacred Entrances to Dulcie's, eye to eye, navel to navel, genitals against genitals. Rising, she whirled in a brown and pink blur, circling Dulcie, faster, faster until, with a hair-raising scream of *loa*-ridden exaltation, the mottled woman fell to make a cross with Dulcie's body.

Mam'bo Caille guardian of the inner chamber, stepped forward. With ashes she outlined the bodies, chanting above the frenzied excitement, "Evil speerit of red hair 'omen, stay with Baron Samedi, Lord of the Cemetery. Strong wise speerit of Mam'bo Luz, live in peace in 'oman fum de sea." She sprinkled ashes over the bodies. She sprayed liqueur over Luz and Dulcie. Mam'bo Caille screamed, "Mam'bo Luz! Is it Mam'bo Luz? Is Mam'bo Luz dar?" Mam'bo Caille lighted the liqueur and passed the burning liquid over the crossed bodies. Then she scooped up the blue flames and washed Dulcie and Luz.

Luz lay deathly still, foam dribbling from her slack mouth. Ceremoniously she was laid facedown onto a large mat and covered with ritual ashes, shells, and meal. Two candles were set in the earth to burn out, symbolizing the return of her body to the earth.

Mam'bo Caille perfumed Dulcie, massaging her, chanting, "Mam'bo Luz, rise! You speerit lives in 'oman fum de sea! Mam'bo Luz, dance!"

Dulcie struggled to her feet, water in all her limbs. Her head reeled. Dizzy, she staggered forward, her face and arms heavenward. Around her the celebrants danced and swayed, their expressions dreamlike and exalted.

The men approached her, offering themselves as her partner. Her vision blurry, she groped toward them. Then she stumbled and fell to earth.

The black duck lay dead. It was laid beside Mam'bo Luz's body, sprinkled with ashes. The red rooster had flown to the top of the cross where it perched in beady-eyed alertness. A blanket was held in flames until it was scorched, then her attendants placed it over Dulcie. She was carried from the inner chamber. She would remain in the outer chamber until she was well, or until she died.

On the third day the white drake vanished. Closely watched by the natives, he dived into a shallow pool and failed to come up.

Days later, free of fever, Dulcie began to feel hungry and restless. She chafed at her little-understood confinement. She was not allowed outside the room, nor could

she enter the inner chamber where Luz's body lay guarded
but untended. Day after day she was forced to wait—wait
for something.

Then Mam'bo Caille and several attendants appeared.
She was led into the sunshine. It was warm and golden,
edging every leaf and blossom, every shell, every grain
of sand, with blessed light.

She was placed on a thronelike eminence at the head of
a circle. Dulcie nibbled at ceremonial dishes. The gleaming
brown faces split in approving smiles. Hesitantly they began to talk in their incomprehensible tongue that murdered
English yet did little credit to either the Africans or Indians from whom they were said to be descended.

Weak and light headed, she watched these strange brown
people. She was different from them, yet she seemed to be
a part of their lives. Confused, she speculated on her
presence here. She had no recollection of coming here. She
had only a vague, fear-filled sense of having escaped
something dreadful.

She was facing the *oum'phor* when a strange-looking
woman came out. Her brown face was covered with cloud-
shaped pale patches. She staggered, as one drunk, to the
festive circle. Those by Dulcie gasped, their eyes bulging,
too terrified to move.

The pinto woman greedily stuffed her mouth with the
ceremonial food. Fearfully the others looked everywhere
but at her. She said, "Mam'bo Caille gettin' shif'less Mek
m'stakes. Ritu'l doan tek."

The words meant nothing to Dulcie. She moved away
from the strange woman.

The woman looked hard at all her people. "I be de body
ob Mam'bo Luz. I be de walkin' daid. No peoples kin kill
me 'cause I daid."

The natives moaned in fear and shrank from Luz.

"I talk *ol'* storee. I tell you whut you doan know. I got
de power now, de power ob de walkin' daid. Baron Samedi
come get peoples whut doan come to de fire dis night." Luz
resumed her ravenous eating.

That night Luz built a fire in the barren space in front
of her hut. For some time she sat, looking into the flames.
Then she went in to Dulcie. "I mek you ready fo' *ol'*
storee."

She approached Dulcie, holding a bowl of the herbal
medicine.

Dulcie backed away, her eyes wide in fear. "No! No! I won't drink that!"

"Mam'bo Luz say you drink."

"It makes me feel strange. I—don't know who I am!"

A ferocious scowl appeared on Luz's face. "*You drink!*" She struck a gong by the doorway. Pa Bowleg and another man hurried into the hut. At Luz's command the two men seized Dulcie, one holding her head back as Mam'bo Luz poured the mirage-inducing tonic down her throat.

Dulcie became docile, willing for Mam'bo Luz to slip off her gown and rub on ointment that made her body tingle. Then, clothed once more, she sat by the fire where Luz told her to.

Luz stood chanting.

> Fire, burn! Light de da'k night
> Brighter dan de Moon, warm lak de Sun.
> Fire lak de 'oman hair, burn high an' never die.

Dulcie watched the flames. Something was happening to her vision. The flames became bits of brighter paper, drifting upward. As Luz flicked out her fingers, the fire leaped tall. Luz's flesh became transparent, providing a ghostly housing for the bones and the grinning skull.

The people glided forward, their eyes huge and white and rolling. They sat at a distance. Luz motioned them closer. The fire died down to a steady shower of sparkling metalic shapes. Dulcie seemed to rise, to be in two places, sitting by the fire and suspended above it.

Luz settled herself comfortably, prepared to amaze the natives as she pieced together the story Dulcie had revealed in her delirium. "I talk *ol'* storee.

> Once on a time, a very good time,
> Monkey chew tobacco an' spit white lime.

"Dis was a man got red hair. Now dis man he got black peoples do his wo'k. He got red-hair 'oman daughter. Seem to 'im her shif'less. Man say, 'Daughter, why ain' you do no wo'k?' She say, 'Poppa, I setten out ter be a speerit queen.' Man doan lak dat. So man put her on a big long-boat. She sail up an' down, up an' down in de sea.

"She knows 'omans got to have man. She doan see no man what light her eye. Fin'lly she see de longboat cap'm.

She say, 'Cap'm, I goin' ter be de speerit queen. You come erlong me an' I mek you de speerit king.'

"De cap'm say, ''oman, you too fool. I got me a boat ter sail.'

"Red-hair 'oman eye light up. Say, 'Cap'm, I goin' ter run off fum you 'til I cotches you.' Red-hair 'oman go home ter Poppa, an' she set an' she wait. Quick quick come de cap'm to git her. She run off, an' de cap'm follers. She run one place, an' she set an' wait. Run off, set an' wait. De cap'm he git weary, he say, ''oman. I goin' ter mek you inter a wife. Dat be wo'k you kin do.'

"So 'oman mek inter a wife. All dis time she mekkin' plan to be de speerit queen. She say, 'Husban' Cap'm, tek me on de boat!' So Cap'm teks red-hair 'oman on de boat. She wo'k witch, an' de sea monster he eat dat boat. One man lef'. He be Guédé l'Orage, master o' de stawm. But Mam'bo Luz strong'r dan Lucifer. Drive Guédé l'Orage inter de sea, back to de lan' ob Ife.

"Red hair 'oman crawl up outen de sea. She sing.

Farewell, Poppa! Farewell, Cap'm!
I got to be de speerit queen.
Mam'bo Luz tek me from de sea an' mek me queen.
Farewell, Poppa! Farewell, Cap'm!

"Mam'bo Luz hear de sing. 'omen's speerit be outen she body, hangin' up in de air. Speerit say, 'Mam'bo Luz, how come you doan ten' ter me? I goin' be in limbo effen you doan safe me.'

"Luz say, 'Speerit, I come fas' I kin, so you doan be in limbo. You git back in de body, so de red-hair 'oman be de speerit queen.'

"Speerit he foxy. Say, 'Mebbe not. Mebbe I pesticate Aunt Inuna.' "

An old woman at the edge of the fire pulled back, her eyes frightened. Her arms made an X on her breast. Those near her made the same motion.

Luz went on, "But Aunt Inuna foxy too. She keep speerit out. Speerit say, 'Mam'bo Luz, you pooty good Mam'bo. How come you doan mek de ritu'l so you speerit be in red-hair 'oman body?"

"Mam'bo Luz t'ink on dat. She say, 'Where my body goin' ter be?'

"Speerit say, 'Mam'bo Luz, doan you know nuthin'?

Body be daid, but it still walk, talk, mek medsin, mek de ritu'l. Be strong, strong, strong'r, 'cuz you speerit got a new shell.'

"Luz say, 'Speerit, whut my new name goin' ter be?' Speerit say,

> Mam'bo Luz ol' body walk aroun' daid,
> Luz done lef' de earth.
> Red-hair 'oman tek Luz speerit,
> Red-hair 'oman born again,
> Call her name Guédé Vi.

Luz stood, arms upraised, face to the brilliant stars. Those around the dying fire watched her, motionless. Luz looked dreamily at the black forest. Though no one moved, eyes rolled in fear and expectation, following the pinto woman's gaze. She crooned, "Speerit ob de speerit queen, de 'oman o' de sun an' de moon call you! Guédé Vi, come fo'th." Luz's hands pointed upward. Every head followed her outspread fingers.

Dulcie, in her extraordinary duality, felt the eyes upon her spirit-self as she hung above the dying fire, felt the waves of their shock and terror as they saw her for what she was, a reddish mist spiraling up from nowhere, an element raw from the fire of rebirth.

She saw the triumph on Luz's mottled face. She knew the warmth of her spirit-self, the frozen chill of her body seated motionless upon earth. She *was*. She existed. She was not dead.

The pinto woman turned her hands with outspread fingers down. Dulcie's spirit-self drifted toward the fire until she was pulled into it. The fire blazed high, and Dulcie knew blackness, elation, and exhaustion so deep it carried her beyond death.

Afternoon light came weakly into the hut. Her head hurt. The light was hostile, a sword in her eyes. Her skin felt prickly, her tongue thick.

Dulcie eased out of the hammock. She would walk up to the Face, talk to it, tell it to stop staring at her. She reeled across the sandy floor. The Face was carved of wood. But it *had* moved. She touched its deeply grooved contours.

"Doan tetch dat!"

Dulcie jumped away.

"Dat de guardeen speerit mask. Ol'! So ol' he come down to Mam'bo Luz fum she gran'fadder. Gran'fadder be a Bowleg Indian."

"I'm sorry." Dulcie was afraid of Mam'bo Luz. She was evil.

"Git back in de hammick, Guédé Vi."

"That's not my name. My name is . . ." To her horror, she could not speak her name.

Mam'bo Luz smiled. "You name Guédé Vi, chil' ob de guédés. You do t'ing Mam'bo Luz tell you."

"Who are you? Why do you keep telling me what I must do?"

Luz, pouting, pointed toward the hammock. Dulcie obeyed. She looked at Luz from the hammock, tears starting. If only she knew who she was or what this place was, perhaps then . . .

Dulcie slept again, waking after dark. Someone was in the hut. Not Luz. Luz always sang. Dulcie held her breath; hands touched her. A soft voice spoke low. "Mam'bo Caille ast de Guédé Vi ter wek up."

"Wh-what do you want?"

"Mam'bo Caille tek you ter de oum'phor. We goin' ter mek de ritu'l."

"I don't know anything about rituals!"

"Den you goin' ter fin' out. Mam'bo Luz speerit enter your body, so we mek you body strong, strong fum Lucifer."

"No! No! I don't want to see the Devil! I didn't do anything!"

Mam'bo Caille's voice was contemptuous. "Fine speerit queen you goin' ter be. Feered ob you own magic. We goin' ter tek you to Lucifer, so you goin' ter lak dat."

Inside the oum'phor, heavy with incense, candles flickered. On the wall hung an elaborate ritual design of two serpents standing on their looped tails, facing east. Between them were three eight-pointed figures, on the right a cross.

Dulcie shuddered. In this place those serpents might come alive.

"We mek you ready fo' de ritu'l. You goin' ter please Lucifer."

"But I don't *want*—" These people were in hell as she was. If they said she had to please Lucifer, she had to do it. They feared Lucifer, they schemed to steal his power, but still Lucifer ruled.

Mam'bo Caille had Dulcie lie naked on the stone altar. Lucifer's altar. She began to smooth an ointment onto Dulcie's arm.

Chanting interspersed with the *huh* sound of people dancing and singing. The drums rose. The chanting stopped abruptly and began again.

There was commotion outside the *oum'phor*. Mam'bo Caille blocked the entrance. "De Guédé Vi ain't ready."

A tenor voice with a strange timbre said, "Move out of my way, old woman! I am Lucifer, lord of Satan's Keep!"

Dulcie sat up, fear mounting into her dry mouth. She saw Mam'bo Caille thrust down. A tall being glided in, a personage of immense presence. Sharp red horns grew in his bristly black hair. His ears were pointed like bat wings. A black satin robe covered him from his red collar to the ground.

The gaping slit that was his mouth opened in an evil smile. "I am Lucifer. You are mine." The head went back, issuing a mocking laugh.

Dulcie whispered, "No—no! I can't—!"

"You *will* serve me!" The robe jerked. "You will! Costa, the robe!"

The old man swept Lucifer's robe off. He was revealed. A barrel-chested thing with no arms and no legs except the pale growths that dripped over the edge of the wheeled throne. On his belly was drawn an enormous phallus, half his own width, with its purplish bulbous end forming a point level with his reddened nipples.

Dulcie drew in her breath and began to scream. Half on the altar, half off, she was petrified, her arms crossed protectively over her breasts. Then from between Lucifer's feetlike protuberances rose another phallus, pointing at her with terrible purpose. She could not stop screaming. Lucifer glided toward her, laughing exultantly.

"You are mine!" His mouth gaped; his tongue hung out through the gross aperture. With Costa close behind, he moved toward Dulcie.

Dulcie scrambled down off the altar. Costa and Lucifer blocked her escape. She stood pinned between the satanic thing and the altar. The finlike hands trembled at his shoulders, wanting to touch her.

"Oh, God! Oh, God!"

"Don't say that name!" he screamed. "I am greater! I am *Lucifer!*"

Dulcie, mindless with terror and revulsion, shoved at his barrel chest. Shrieking, Lucifer toppled onto Costa and Mam'bo Caille.

Dulcie ran for the tunnel that led out the back of the temple. The tunnel was pitch black and reeked of mold.

If Lucifer pursues me, catches me in this stinking place, I'll die. But I am in Lucifer's own dwelling place. He will catch me!

She ran faster, crashing heavily into the rough walls, losing her sense of direction.

She came out of the tunnel into Luz's hut. The Face stared at her.

The drummers, the *ogantier,* the *trianglier* pulsated in frenzied din. The natives shrieked in ecstasy as the animal spirits possessed them. Dulcie heard Lucifer's and Mam'bo Caille's shrill cries.

She darted out of the hut, running toward the blackness of the forest. She would hide there. Hide from Lucifer. Hide from hell.

Her feet sank into clinging sand. Then she plunged into the forest. Her side hurt. Air sucked coarsely into her bursting lungs. Pain struck her right side, struck harder, sharper. She doubled up with it.

She had to hide. Lucifer would come. Luz would come. They would find her. Bent over, she moved along the path like a hunted animal, her progress tiny pain-racked steps. Dulcie's eyes darted at shadows, her ears strained for rustling of the foliage.

The drums stopped.

She began to run again. Vines tore at her long hair. Long grasses like satanic claws reached up, cutting and tangling around her feet and ankles. She stepped barefoot on terrible, unknown, squishy things. Webs of unseen spiders clothed her in their filaments. Creatures leaped from the darkness, searching the warmth of her bare flesh. She shook them off, clamping her mouth shut against the revulsion.

He was coming. Luz was coming. The brown people were coming. She could hear them. Hear their voices still excited from the drums and the dancing. They knew this strange land. It was theirs.

Then their voices hushed. The unknown reaches of this vast Hades cowed even its own inhabitants.

She must run—run faster, deeper into the forest, away from the light. Go where even demons feared to follow.

She ran from the sound of their feet, from the frightened sound of their muted voices. She was breathless, her heart and head pounding. The path was gone. She might be running back. Back to Luz. Back to Lucifer.

She stumbled to a halt, her breath harsh indrawn sobs. "Oh, God, please. Please. Hide me. Don't let *him* find me. *Please,* God!"

The sobs burst forth. What was the use? How could God be in hell? "I am greater than God!" Lucifer had cried. "Greater than God! You are mine!"

She splashed through clinging muck up to her ankles. Then she was in water, still trying to run, her arms flailing. The water became deeper. She struggled toward the bank she had lost in the blackness.

Her feet slipped on the slimy bottom. Her breath sounded like demented laughter as she clawed and plunged in the murky swamp water. Her fingers closed around the snakelike tendrils of the mangrove roots. She fell, supported by the roots, her hair fanning out dark on the dark water. She was so tired. She couldn't run. Couldn't hide.

The thudding feet, voices, torches came near. A strange feeling of peaceful resignation came over her. Her breathing eased. Her body was at rest, suspended by the water. The brown people pounded past.

She lay there for eternity, waiting for them to return her to Lucifer.

The forest became quiet. The winking lights of manmade fire were gone. Dulcie clung to the roots, afraid to move, too cold to stay in the water. She groped among the snaking mangrove roots until she found the bank. On hands and knees she crawled to the path.

When pale green morning light came, Dulcie was stumbling along the hard earth. She could barely think. Danger no longer had meaning—but she shied away from a cave, shuddering at the thought of what might lurk there.

Trees were as ominous. Chickcharnies lived there. At length Dulcie climbed a large-leafed tree, looking up warily to be certain she hadn't invaded the sanctuary of one of the three-toed, red-eyed birdlike goblins. Satisfied, she slept fitfully.

That afternoon she ate fruits she recognized. Braver because she had survived this long, she moved on. Then she saw the tracks of cart wheels.

She must get as far away as she could from Lucifer and his tribe of demons. She ran, stopping only at nightfall to sleep for minutes at a time, waking in terrified starts at forest noises. At daybreak she moved on.

At noon she heard sounds that forced old memories, disembodied, but some comfortable, lost part of herself. Axes rang. A saw chattered. Men talking, work talk. Black men, speaking. Her language. Another voice—one of authority.

Tantalized by familiarity, Dulcie peeked through the broad-leaved sisal. She was tempted but wary that all things in Lucifer's forest were another trick. He was Satan. He might have wanted sport with her feeble efforts to elude him. He might be playing with her now.

Behind her the forest came alive. Odd little creatures hung from limbs by three toes. They were all around her, laughing, crying. Wizened little faces leered. Some had feathers, some had beards and tails. Their small evil red eyes glaring, they chortled, "Chick-charny, chick-charny."

One came nearer. It chattered at her. Her eyes shifted from the vile little creature of Satan to the men. Was the white man a disguise of Lucifer? She didn't know. But she feared the man more than the thing that hung upside down staring at her.

She developed a pattern for her days; waiting for the men, watching them work, waiting for a sign that it was Lucifer wearing the body of an attractive man. She made a game of staying hidden and then coming into the freshly made clearing at night.

Once the man hung his shirt on a limb, and Dulcie stole it. She smiled to herself while the man complained. That night she felt warm and close to the stockily built, well-muscled chestnut-haired man, smelling his particular odor wrapping around herself like another skin.

One day the men did not come until noon. She heard them approaching. The white man was singing.

The heart bowed down by weight of woe
To weakest hopes will cling,
To thought and impulse while they flow

That can no comfort bring; That can, that can no comfort
bring

Dulcie peered from behind her tree. He sang old English
and Irish airs she remembered from childhood. The men
began to invade her forest. They searched, while the brown-
haired man sang.

She was very frightened. The chickcharnies flew in agitation from limb to limb, chattering loudly. The men were
thorough, looking everywhere on the ground, up into the
trees. She stayed motionless, invisible.

His singing made her more and more afraid, stirring up
memories of herself as a child, when her red-haired father
had sung to her. Why did she think her father was red-
haired?

He stopped singing. And that was worse. He looked
for a long time into the forest. He saw her, she knew. She
must run, but her legs would not obey. Softly he began;

> *Shule, shule, shule agra!*
> Only death can easy my woe.

She felt trapped, as unable to move or think as when
Mam'bo Luz rubbed the strange ointment on her body.
She could run no more. She had been alone for so long,
living with fear, with nobody, nothing that she knew,
watched by a hundred red beady eyes, waiting.

He knew she waited. His longing was a palpable thing.
And he knew her. He sang the song Jem had sung as he
rocked her on a summer's evening.

The men had passed her. The chickcharnies quieted, huddling together, their unblinking red gaze inimical. Soon
they would descend on her, biting, scratching, destroying
her.

She left the tree, feeling them ready to spring, and ran
on shaking legs toward the chestnut-haired man. She
stopped, cornered, confused.

"My . . . God!" he whispered. "Dorothy? Is it . . .
Dorothy?"

Her voice, unused for so long, came out in a croak.
"I'm Dulcie."

Looking into his face, poised for flight, she repeated,
"My name is Dulcie."

"Come nearer. Let me touch you. Let me see if you are real."

Dulcie drew back. "No."

"But you are wearing my shirt, and you came to me." Tears flowed down his cheeks. "I have loved you all these years, Dorothy, even when I knew you had to be dead. Oh, my beloved, for God's sake, let me—"

"Are you Adam?" she asked, bewildered.

His gaze grew bitter. He wiped his tears. "No, I'm not Adam. I am Justin Gilmartin." He sighed. "And Dorothy is still dead."

"Am I dead? Am I"—her voice broke—"in hell?"

"I've wondered that myself." At her look he said hastily, "No, you aren't dead. You're on Andros. So you can't be in hell, can you?"

"But I saw the Devil."

"Who knows what's in that forest? Where have you come from, Dulcie?"

"Why did you call me that?"

"Twice you said it's your name. Why are you hiding in the forest?"

She thought of telling him everything; but then he might deliver her to Lucifer after all. She said craftily, "I live there."

There was a little smile on his face. He was not handsome, but he had a strength that Dulcie trusted. "Would you like to sit down?"

Dulcie refused, her eyes wary. "Do you live in a house?"

"Yes. Would you like to come to my house? You could live there."

"Would you protect me?"

"Yes, I'll protect you. I promise. Will you come with me now?"

"No. No. I can't."

He stood in front of her, holding out both hands to her.

She did not know why she took his hands, but she did. She walked through the cut forest with him unafraid.

The large white house loomed in front of them. She pulled back, apprehensive. Justin said easily, "Nothing will harm you."

Wtih the greatest of effort she continued. Something evil was here. It wasn't the man. He would keep her safe. He had promised.

Amparo met them at the door. Her eyes flicked over Dulcie. Her lips curled at Dulcie's muddy hair with twigs stuck in it, her fair skin stained with fruits and berries. "What you goin' ter do wid 'er?"

"Amparo, this is Dulcie—my guest. Prepare Dorothy's room."

"Hmph!" Amparo grunted, and turned away. "No good comin'."

Dulcie hung back, holding tightly to Justin's calloused hand. He got her into the house. They walked past a room where there was a lot of noise—random thumpings on a drum, bells ringing, a dog howling. "Lucho's started his birthday party already," said Justin.

Kenneth Gilmartin looked up eagerly at Justin, not seeming to see Dulcie. "Did you find her? Any trace of her? Anything?"

"No, nothing. But I found this girl in the forest. She calls herself Dulcie. Doesn't know, or won't say, how she came to be there."

Kenneth Gilmartin's voice filled with awe. "Dorothy— my dear child." He stumbled forward and enfolded Dulcie in an embrace that smelled of bodily neglect, liquor, and bad teeth. "So long . . . so long." He looked at her blearily. "My dear, you are improperly gowned. You must have Am— Amparo . . . your mother would not like . . . So good to have you home again, Dorothy, so good."

He fumbled away and sank back into his chair, lost in his dream.

"I wondered where you had gotten to," came a voice from the doorway.

Dulcie jerked around to look behind her. He was sitting on a dogcart, the nightmare creature who said she was his. The gross body cheated of proper appendages, the mouth that yawed in a sneering smile.

Dulcie edged to the perimeter of the room, like a hunted animal. Justin ran to her. She screamed, her hands drawn up like claws.

Lucifer howled with laughter, his oversized torso reeling drunkenly.

"Shut up!" Justin yelled. He lunged, grabbing Dulcie. Her eyes rolled back, she tore at him, biting his hands, clawing him with ragged, torn fingernails.

"No! I'll die! I won't be his! No! No! No-o-o!"

Chapter Six

Lucifer laughed insanely. Justin pulled Dulcie tight against him, smothering her cries. "Stop it, Dulcie! Stop it!"

"He's Lucifer—the Devil—chasin' me. The woods . . . everywhere!"

Justin's hand covered her mouth. "Shut up and listen!"

Dulcie fought, her small body straining in Justin's unbreakable grip. She bit the hand pressed tightly against her mouth. She went limp.

Justin held her upright. "Will you listen?" he said hoarsely. "He's not the Devil. His name is Lucifer Gilmartin."

Dulcie struggled weakly, her mouth working beneath his hand.

"Don't struggle. I can hold you silent far longer than you have strength to resist. It's Lucifer's fifteenth birthday today. He's known enough tragedy. I won't let you make it worse. He won't harm you, do you understand?"

"I will! I will!" Lucifer screamed. "I'll work a spell on her. She'll get sick, and she'll die—very slowly!"

Dulcie wriggled like a small trapped animal against Justin. Her breath grew shorter. The room began to spin. Sounds stopped.

She regained consciousness in a bed with clean white sheets. Someone was washing her. Luz?! There was no staring mask. Another memory stirred. "Claudine? Claudine?" An Indian woman was scrubbing the berry stains and forest muck from her skin. Her eyes smarted with incomprehensible sorrow. "What happened to Claudine?"

A voice spoke from near the window. "Is Claudine your nurse, Dulcie?"

She couldn't think who Claudine was, but she longed for her.

Justin moved closer. Dulcie tensed. "Where is he? Don't let him take me!"

"No one is here but Amparo and me," Justin said gently.

Amparo laughed. "She mean Lucifer."

Dulcie looked suspiciously at the door.

"Costa ain't bringin' 'im. Costa too ol' for carryin' Lucifer."

She stared up at Justin; there was no choice but to trust him. "Am I safe?"

Justin's hand brushed along her naked shoulder. "You're upstairs, Dulcie. Lucifer will not come. You're safe."

Amparo's lips worked soundlessly as she slapped a towel over most of Dulcie's naked body. Bitterly Amparo glanced at Justin, then dropped her eyes to hide the burning jealousy flaming there.

"Are you hungry? Would you like something hot to drink?"

Each kindness he offered dragged her further into his power. She shouldn't trust him, not with Lucifer so near. But her stomach cramped with hunger. "Please I'm so hungry."

Amparo moved with quick, angry motions. Roughly she pulled a yellow nightgown over Dulcie's head.

Justin ordered her to bring Dulcie food. Amparo left the room. Justin sat on the edge of the bed. The gesture was a familiar one of some warm time, some dear person who lived just beyond the limits of memory.

He smiled at her. "You've come to a strange house, Dulcie."

Dulcie pulled the sheet up a little more.

"I can imagine how we look to you. Let me tell you about the Gilmartins. You may not judge us more gently, but you can rid yourself of the idea that you're in hell. Our failings are human ones, Dulcie. Greed has been the family downfall. Uncle Kenneth stole this land from me when I was four years old, when my father died. Now he says the land is Lucho's. You've seen Lucho—Lucifer. He's a bright boy imprisoned in a hideous body. Everyone is half-afraid of him because of his appearance—and because he . . . imitates that damned voodoo witch, Mam'bo Luz. Poor Lucho. He hates us all because we're not like him."

"He said he would make me—"

"Die? He's threatened us all, but we're still here. He pretends he has powers, but the only people he frightens are those so ignorant that they listen to him. He won't be able to harm you unless you're afraid."

"But I *am!* You weren't there. You don't know. The first time I saw him he had red horns, and he was tall.

He had a thing like this on his chest." Dulcie gestured, her hands shaking. "And a black robe."

"Damn that old woman! Did Mam'bo Luz involve you in a ritual?"

The memories were sharp. "Yes," she whispered. "Lucifer was going to—he came toward me—he—I kept running, and running and . . ."

Justin took her hands away from her face. "Dulcie, listen to me. That couldn't have happened. You've seen Lucho. He could never be tall. He can't even get around without help."

"But it was Lucifer! He was there! I didn't imagine him!"

"I believe you, Dulcie. At least I believe what you think you saw." He shrugged. "Perhaps it *was* Lucho."

Dulcie looked at him, doubting, then asked, "Who is Dorothy?"

"Dorothy was Lucho's sister. She's dead. You'll have to believe that, because everybody in this house—including me at times—wants her to be alive so badly we believe she is. The eternal fount of hope," Justin mused. "Somewhere she's out there, still alive, still whole."

"Perhaps she is."

Justin glared at her. His voice was bitter. "She disappeared fifteen years ago. She ran into the forest and became lost on the day that Lucho was born. Fifteen years ago her mother died bearing Lucho."

"He *can* make people die!"

"No, he can't. His mother was always frail. She nearly died bearing Dorothy." Justin paced back and forth. "An ignorant savage tended Aunt Helen. If anyone is from hell, it is Luz. She let Aunt Helen bleed to death."

"Perhaps she didn't know," Dulcie said shakily.

Justin whirled, his fists clenched tight. "She knew! Dorothy saw the baby. Luz told her it was a curse. Dorothy ran. She didn't know the woods; she'd been in school in England. We never found her."

"But you did try? You hunted?"

"We searched the area for miles, calling her, lighting the forest with torches. Weeks later we gave up. Uncle Kenneth kept hunting. He despised the baby, blamed him for what had happened. He named him Lucifer. Now we have an annual search, on the day Dorothy disappeared. I couldn't believe my eyes when you walked out of the forest."

"Why were you singin? Why weren't you lookin'?"

"Dulcie, *she is dead*. Uncle Kenneth's mind may have broken under the tragedy, but I don't want to end up as he is. It would be so easy here in Satan's Keep. For years at a time we have no society with the outside world. I dream constantly of Dorothy. I can't believe . . . but I can't stop hoping."

"But you were singin' for her."

"She taught me music. Everything good and beautiful I know, Dorothy taught me. It's my way of letting her know I remember her."

"And you still love her."

"It isn't difficult to love a ghost when there is no one else to love. We were going to be married. Since she left, there has been no one else to . . . love." His eyes were questioning. "You remind me of her, a little."

"Here's de food you ast fo'. Took a lot o' trouble." Amparo banged the tray down on a table. "Kin you feed youseff?"

Dulcie eyed the food greedily. "Give it to me, Amparo."

"Mistah Kennef wan' you, Justin."

"Tell him I'll be down soon." His look dismissed Amparo.

"He ain't goin' ter lak it, you bein' all twit-eyed on de girl."

"I said I'd be there later!"

Meaningfully she gazed at him. "You fo'gittin' what you got, Justin."

Dulcie ate everything. At last she pushed the tray away. "Justin, do you know . . . who I am?"

His expression flickered. "I know you came to me. You're mine now. That's all I want to know. That's all you need to know."

"Will I ever remember?"

He smiled down on her. "Try to sleep. I must go see my uncle. Shall I send one of the servants to sit with you?"

For the next days Dulcie rested, not leaving the room. Zara, the old Indian servant Justin had sent to her, kept her company, always with sewing or mending in her gnarled hands.

Justin took his morning and evening meals with Dulcie.

They spent the lamplit evenings in her bedroom or his. After Justin would bid Dulcie goodnight, he would bolt her bedroom door to the hall, leaving the door that joined their rooms open. Her dependence on Justin grew.

Sunday was the one day of rest at Satan's Keep. Justin had insisted she be always at his side. Hesitantly, she donned one of Dorothy's gowns. Then, trembling, she sat next to Justin at the dinner table.

Kenneth, after an initial embrace, lapsed into his vague world. Today Lucifer was on good behavior. He watched Dulcie constantly but seemed only to want to be talked to.

Kenneth spoke unexpectedly. "You are looking much better. You will take your meals with us now."

Justin said quickly, "Only dinner, until she gains more strength."

"Strength." Kenneth sighed heavily. "Your mother has no strength. You must see that she has better care."

"My mother is dead!" cried Lucho shrilly.

Kenneth eyed him. "Here is Dorothy. You said she was dead, too."

"Lucho, shut your mouth," said Justin coldly.

Lucho spewed a mouthful of food at Justin.

Justin brushed his clothing. "Take him, Costa. He can eat alone."

"I won't go!" Lucho flapped his fin hands, rocking, trying to avoid Costa. He tumbled heavily, yelling in rage and frustration.

"Let him lie, Costa!" Justin took a bite of fruit. Lucho continued to scream, to roll around, until Kenneth rose unsteadily and delivered a sharp kick to the boy's rear.

The strange tenor voice said, "I will make you die, old man."

"I'm dead already, dwelling here on the dump heap of civilization," said Kenneth. "Dorothy, I'll have a small serving of that trifle."

Dulcie shakily spooned out the dessert. Costa watched Lucho, watched Justin. When the boy had been quiet for several minutes, Justin lifted him onto his seat.

That night Dulcie heard the drums. The *ogan*'s penetrating clank traveled over the damp night. Then, as the drums called, a door closed, and she heard the light rumbling sound of Lucifer's cart.

Dulcie hid in the bed, her fear of Lucifer overwhelming. She couldn't think of him as a human being imprisoned in a creature's body. He was the Devil. She pulled up the cover, shivering with unconquered fear.

Justin stood in the adjoining doorway, "Is anything wrong?"

She strove not to let her teeth chatter. "I'm all right, Justin."

"It's only the drums, you know."

Dulcie fell asleep knowing that he was protecting her.

Sometime before dawn she became aware that someone, something, was in the room with her. Strong flowery incense hung over her. Something rustled, like a taffeta gown. Dulcie lay rigid, listening. Frightened of what she might see but still more frightened not to know what menaced her, she opened her eyes.

A figure, shimmering, gossamer, with a pale mottled face moved slightly, leaning toward her, reaching.

"Adam! Adam, help me!" She began to scream.

There was a great thudding as a heavy body hit the door. Justin broke the bolt that unaccountably had been fastened on Dulcie's side. The figure darted for the window and vanished.

He was there, holding her with harsh strength against his bare chest. "Dulcie, wake up, wake up. It's only a nightmare."

"Oh, Adam, I'm so—" *He* wasn't Adam . . . no. He felt different, he smelled different. She tried to pull away from him.

He held her closer, crooning, "There, there, my darling, you're safe." His rough hands turned her covers back, and he took her into his arms to hold her like a child, murmuring softly, kissing her face, rocking her as he stood. Dulcie moaned softly as long-forgotten feelings stirred in her. She longed for the comfort that she remembered of some man's arms, some man's voice, some man's love. "It was a bad dream, my love, nothing but a bad dream," Justin murmured.

Dulcie gripped his neck harder, as if by the pressure she could make him something he was not. "Justin, don't leave me alone."

"I won't—I've been waiting, hoping. Anything you say —anything." He carried her into his bedroom. He pulled her against him, his mouth forceful, insistent. Dulcie tried in vain to push him away, tried to turn her head.

"Don't turn from me. I've waited. Dorothy . . . I've needed you so. Why—why did you leave me? I would have protected you."

"I'm not Dorothy!"

His mouth closed over hers, his tongue compelling, his hands under her nightgown. Then he tore the nightgown from her. His embrace became harsher, more demanding. His hands pressed her body to his, the hardness of his penis hot against her belly. The room reeled around her. Inside her head repeated the silent cry, *Adam, help me!* Aloud she screamed, "Justin! Stop! *Stop!*"

But there was no stopping him. He threw her down on his bed, forcing his knee between hers. He entered her, stroke by stroke until Dulcie sobbed, her mind a blurring whirl as her body reacted to his urgent motions. Pulling, flexing, thrusting . . . then his cataclysm of heat.

His hand fumbled on her breast. "Good God. What an animal I've become! Doro—Dulcie, Dulcie, forgive me! I've needed you so."

Tears rolled from Dulcie's eyes. Long ago she had been a part of such a thing as this. It had been an act of love, not of violation.

He lay beside her, putting her head on his shoulder, his arm possessively around her. He brushed the hair from her temple. "I love you. I'll always love you. Don't try to remember. Be mine."

Dulcie cried, harsh tears for the life she could not remember, for the man, whoever he had been, who had loved her. She cried for Justin's taking her roughly and calling it love. He stroked her, petted her, he spoke with tenderness he could not manage before. After a long time Dulcie released herself from the yearning for that other loving man. She made herself feel once more safe with Justin.

Dulcie's memory brought back fragments of other nights, vignettes of feelings, sensations, loving and being loved, sharing passion, rising to heights of earthly glory, nights that were gone because she was lost, *he* was lost—the man she had once loved was lost.

Her hand slowly slid down his body, feeling the heavy muscles, the strong, prominent bones, stopping as her fingers closed around his thick, hot penis. She wanted that now, wanted to feel it throbbing within her, wanted to find the lost glories.

He did not hurt her, did not hurry this time. Dulcie felt

the rising sensation of pleasure as he went into her, holding her tenderly, rocking easily against her. She felt his spasms of fulfillment, but for her there was not the sense of completion she sought.

Justin rained kisses on her face, murmuring ecstatic words of endearment. Dulcie pretended to share his feelings, as though her own burning passion had been quenched. This man who desired her was her only protection in this strange and fearsome house. She clung to that.

She woke in the morning with Justin beside her. He reached out, to make love to her another empty time.

When he had gone, Dulcie felt more sure of herself. She didn't know what diabolical fate had brought her to Satan's Keep. For Kenneth she was his long-lost daughter, and for Justin she was to lie in his arms fulfilling long-held dreams. She would perform both tasks. In doing so, she'd learn about this house and its inhabitants—and herself. Perhaps the key to her past was here, needing only to be recognized.

Dulcie's ambitions reckoned without Amparo.

"You ain't s'pose ter be trackin' 'roun' the house when Justin ain't here! You stay in that room!"

Dulcie gave Amparo a level look. "I want to visit with Mr. Kenneth."

"He drunk as a hoot owl. Justin lock 'im up."

Since Amparo never called him "Mr. Justin," Dulcie surmised her services to him were all-inclusive. She took a new approach. "Amparo, I'm feelin' better, and I don't like bein' idle. If you'll bring me clean cloths. I'll begin on the parlor."

"What fo'? Nobody care 'bout how it look."

"I care! It's filthy," Dulcie replied coldly. "You can help me."

"Justin didn't say I take orders from you."

"Shall I tell him you refused to help me clean the parlor?"

Amparo worked in slovenly fashion, eyeing Dulcie suspiciously. Dulcie worked hard, in an attempt to set an example. That evening she would speak to Justin, suggesting a thorough housecleaning.

But that night she was so sleepy that she went to bed without dinner.

Justin, trying unsuccessfully to rouse her with kisses,

went raging to Amparo. "What did you do to her? I told you she was to rest!"

Amparo shrugged. "She tell me ter clean. I clean."

"You gave her something, you bitch!" His hand clutched Amparo's shoulder hurtfully, and she winced away.

"Miss is sick, won't lissen. Amparo can't help she won't lissen. She get tired too quick." Amparo touched his shirt where it exposed the curling brown hair of his chest. "I take care o' Miss bes' I kin, Justin, but I ain't got the power to do what can't be done. Miss's body don't rightly b'long to her. De *guédés* sent it ter Mam'bo. You let her go back where she b'long. Amparo make you fo'git."

"I don't want to hear the name Mam'bo Luz in this house. Dulcie's none of your bloody business, and you keep out."

"Justin, I bin your mate fo'teen year. You an' me's got two boys. We good as married. I don't 'tend to fo'git that."

Justin thrust her hand away from him. He walked in cold silence up the stairs to lie beside Dulcie.

Dulcie had wild dreams that night, of water rushing into her room and bearing her out on its tide, dreams of a faceless man who stalked the beaches and the forest paths seeking her. Things that came and got her, herself running after an unknown something. By daylight the memory faded, and only desolation stayed.

She got through the weeks and months, some days feeling strong and energetic. Other days she was depressed and vague, tormented by weird mind pictures. Everyone was her enemy.

On her clear days she cleaned the house. She tried to take Dorothy's place. She even tried to see Kenneth as her father. Then recollection would taunt her with Jem's smile, his turn of phrase, his unexpected irascibilities . . . and slither away. The harder she tried, the less she could remember.

She became fond of Justin in a superficial way. He was not a happy man, having little to be happy for. But he was kind to her—except when he came to her at night, taking her with rough desperation. Then she endured Justin's approaches as the price of her protection.

On her depressed days she stayed in her room, unable to face Lucifer. He had a way of silently appearing on his wagon, without warning sound. Dulcie might relax, then look up to find him behind her, loosing his maniacal laughter.

But when she paid him consistent small attentions, he was less apt to indulge in his peculiar misbehavior. She set out to know him better. She read to him, asking him questions about the story. She played dominoes with him, making his moves as he directed. As Justin had said, the boy was bright, quick-witted, and shrewd. But occasionally she caught a look of intense lust that took her back to that night in the *oum'phor*. He wanted her. He would come at her again.

She didn't know how long she had been in the Gilmartin household. Probably several months, for it was now springtime of 1863. She had regained her strength but was afraid to go outside without Justin. And she had failed to reach back in her memory beyond the dance of rebirth. Justin knew something, but his usual answer was another question: What did she remember?

Nothing. Nothing.

One evening at dinner, for no apparent reason, Lucifer was excited, talking a great deal, interrupting rudely, slopping his food. Justin reprimanded him but did nothing. Kenneth sat in the parlor, drinking and talking to himself. Dulcie, feeling depressed and helpless, could not eat.

"Miss, you ain't goin' ter git strong without you eat," said Amparo.

"I am not hungry, Amparo."

Justin pushed his plate away and rose. "Goin' to bed," he said thickly. His foot kicked a table leg, upsetting a water glass. He grabbed at the table for balance and fell heavily to the floor.

Dulcie ran to him. His eyes were glassy; he was hardly breathing. "What's wrong with him? Help me get him up!"

Amparo stood still and smiled. "Justin sleepy."

"Help me! He's ill, terribly ill!" Dulcie tugged frantically at Justin. "Amparo! Costa! Can't you understand? Justin is sick!"

Neither moved.

Lucifer began to laugh, a mean chuckle that grew, one breath after another, into a loud, hysterical clamor of fiendish glee. His face grew red. His truncated form heaved. His weblike hands flapped as he rocked on his seat. The demented sound filled the room.

Dulcie, on her knees, stared at him. He was looking beyond her. She turned, and her blood froze in her veins. Mam'bo Luz barred the door. Justin had been drugged. They had come for her.

She would not let them have her.

She had barely moved before she was tripped by Costa's outthrust foot. Then Amparo was on her, holding her face down on the floor. Dulcie struggled, managing to roll from under Amparo. She tried to crawl under the heavy oak dining table, but Lucifer, still laughing insanely, launched himself and fell onto her.

They grabbed her. Costa's grip was surprisingly strong. Amparo, her eyes fierce with hatred, straddled her stomach so that Dulcie could hardly breathe. "Goin' ter git you outer here. Back to Mam'bo Luz, where you b'longs."

Dulcie fought madly, pinching, scratching. She screamed as Lucifer bit her arm. He laughed exultantly and tried to do it again.

"Gib her de juice ob de herbs," said Mam'bo Luz. "Keep 'er still."

Dulcie tried to keep her lips closed, jerking her head about. Grasping her jaw, Mam'bo Luz poured the potion. Spitting and gagging, Dulcie swallowed some of the drug.

"Doan let 'er choke ter deff," said Mam'bo Luz briskly. "She goin' ter come erlong nice now. Git up off her belly, Amparo."

Dulcie lay still, gasping, dizzy and disoriented. Mam'bo Luz squatted beside her. "Lay quiet, Guédé Vi. We goin' ter tek you back to de *oum'phor*. Hear dem drums? Dey's drummin' de welcome fo' de speerit ob Mam'bo Luz, wearin' a new body. You goin' ter lak dat, Guédé Vi."

"Why do you call me that? My name is Dulcie Moran!"

"Mebbe so one time, but now you Guédé Vi."

Dulcie sat up, her head reeling nastily. "I'm goin' to my husband, Captain Adam Tremain! He's a blockade runner. He'll come and find me."

Their eyes were all on her; even Lucifer, lying on the floor nearby, was watching. In Dulcie's fuzzy vision Justin seemed to rise. She said urgently "He'll kill you—like he did Wolf!"

Mam'bo Luz's blotched lips spread in a superior smile. "Luz put de oberlook—" Justin's balled fist struck her. Luz lurched and sprawled on the floor.

Justin was all over the room, reeling, staggering, swinging with his fists. With an open-handed blow that made her head rock, he knocked Amparo down. Lucifer rolled into a corner and watched, bright-eyed. Costa crouched under the table, his arms protecting his head.

Dulcie, sick, her nose bleeding, grabbed the bread knife. Lucifer's eyes bulged as she staggered toward him, the thick blade upraised.

"Dulcie! No! Get—study!" Justin grabbed desperately for support, knocking over a chair. He crashed into the doorframe, his legs sagging.

Kenneth looked up from his stupor. "Kill him, 'swhat I say. Meant to, day he'sh bo-born. Sh-spawn a Sha-satan."

Dulcie and Justin staggered into the windowless study. Justin fell onto a chair. Dulcie, blood gushing from her nose, could hardly see to lock the door. She pushed the divan in front of it, then collapsed onto the floor.

The house was unnaturally quiet when they both regained consciousness.

Justin said, "Ohhh. My head."

Dulcie lifted her eyelids with effort. Ben? Had he stayed overnight? What kind of party—? It came back to her. "Justin?"

"Are you all right, Dulcie?"

She said, "Yes," wondering if it was a lie. She ached. Her ribs felt smashed. Blood was caked on her face. Her nose was swollen. "Are you?"

"God knows. *Christ,* what a head! I hope I killed those ghouls."

"They were goin' to give me to Lucifer!"

"We're not out yet. If Luz is dead, Lucho will have us killed. I've got to get you away from Satan's Keep." Into Justin's mind flashed pictures of Lucifer raping her, his sadism unleashed and vengeful; of Dulcie, torn asunder, her parts used in savage rituals glorifying Lucifer's demonic powers. "I love you very much."

"You mustn't! Don't love me, Justin. I'm not free!"

He said harshly, "You must let me protect you! Marry me."

"I remember everything—who I am, where I lived, how I came to Andros. Adam will come for me."

"You don't know! No one will come!"

"He-he promised. Adam said no matter whatever might

happen, he'd always come back to me. He wouldn't break his word."

"Your husband is dead."

"He can't be dead. He's very strong—and he knows the ocean, and . . ."

Justin waited. "A man came here last summer. Amparo told me after—well, afterward. He'd been in a shipwreck, and he looked through this house, hunting for his wife."

"Adam!? Was it Adam? A big man? Tall, black-haired?"

"He looked for a red-haired woman. Luz found you both on the shore. Luz saved your life because she . . . wanted her soul to enter your body."

"Dear God," Dulcie whispered.

"She calls you Guédé Vi. It means you're a child of the gods. She wanted a beautiful body like yours, so when you were washed ashore, like a spirit from the sea, she seized her chance."

"How could I have her soul and still be alive? Still remember Adam?"

"Dulcie, I don't know. I've lived with voodoo all my life, and I know some strange things are made to happen. But this? Luz looks and acts the same as before, even if she does call herself the living dead."

"But Adam? Tell me! Did she . . . she didn't have him—"

"Mam'bo Luz used him to gain power. There is something between Luz and Lucifer. She was his nurse, you know. She taught him the black arts from infancy, and Lucifer believes. He'd do anything for a handsome body such as they say Adam had. Luz cheated him of his chance. She told her people that Adam was an evil spirit of the storm, the Guédé l'Orage. She had them . . . get rid of him."

Dulcie's breath came in whimpers. "No—no—no—"

"They murdered him, Dulcie. I tried to keep it from you."

"He can't be dead! He can't! Adam was too—". She choked. She had said *was*. Adam *was*. "He *is* alive! I'm goin' to have his child!"

"When?"

"In the spring." She began to weep bitterly. It was already springtime, and she would have no child. "Luz killed my baby too."

Justin held her while she wept. "I hoped you'd never

remember. I hoped you'd love me as I love you, that we could have a life together."

Dulcie shuddered. "Never. Not—not with . . . anybody else."

"I can be the man I once was, Dulcie! With you, I can live again!"

"No! I belong to Adam. It couldn't have been Adam who was here. He'd never have given up 'til he found me."

"It was Adam! Think, Dulcie! He's dead! It's been months. If he were alive, he'd have come back. He hasn't come. He never will! It's like Dorothy. They're both gone. The dead have given the living to each other."

Dulcie shook her head, frightened by the possibility it was true.

"Look at me. Listen. I've got plans for us. This land belongs to me. I inherited from my father. Uncle Kenneth controls it, but I'll appeal to the courts in England. They have the original records. I'll win, then I'll be a wealthy man. This will be ours alone!" His eyes searched hers in the murky light. "Ours. Think of it!"

Endless years stretched out before her. Years of living with Justin alone on this island, never an escape, never human companionship. She saw herself old, saw herself dying, alone with Justin. She wanted to scream, to tear from the room, even to throw herself on the satanic mercies of Mam'bo Luz. Forcibly she made herself calm as a small hope formed. "When will you leave for England?"

"I'll go with the mahogany shipment, late in the summer."

"You won't leave me here, will you?"

Laughing, he crushed her against his chest. "Of course not. We'll be married in England, in a church, and there'll be an organ. Do you like music? Dorothy wanted music at our wedding."

"I like music," Dulcie said weakly. "Why must we wait until summer?"

"I need the money from the mahogany. You don't think Uncle Kenneth allows me to have money of my own!"

"But summer is so far away. Justin, I can't stand it."

"You want to marry me! You'll say yes?"

She squeezed his hand and tried to put life into her voice. "I will. But please give me time to mourn."

"It's been months."

"But I didn't know! Please!" Dulcie's voice rose to shrill hysteria.

He considered a moment, then said, "Keep in mind that I am waiting."

They unlocked the study and crept out, Justin holding the bread knife. He locked Dulcie in her room. He found Amparo in the kitchen. She looked at him fearfully. "Where's Mam'bo Luz?"

"She went clean outer her haid, doan know nothin'. Pa Bowleg took her back to her hut."

"Lucifer? Costa?"

"Costa got Lucho lock up. Costa in de bed with sharp pain in his heart. He goin' ter die, can't draw breff."

Justin put his hands on Amparo's neck. "You can die, too." His thumbs caressed her throat, harder, harder, until she was gasping and struggling to breathe. When she was half-fainting, he let her drop to the floor. "That's how you'll die, if you give me your stinking herbs again." His boot prodded her ribs. "Did you hear me?"

Justin went to Costa's room. The old man was in bed. He began to gabble apologies.

"Shut up, Costa." He stood staring at him. "From now on you'll work in the forest with my men. At night you'll be locked up. You're not to go near Lucifer again."

Costa turned his head away so that Justin would not see his tears. Only he, Costa, loved Lucifer just as he was.

When Justin's men had finished, his and Dulcie's rooms were fortified with gratings over the windows, heavy bars and locks on the door. Dulcie lived in the rooms. At first she slept long hours, feeling safe at last. Awake, she dreamed of Adam and combed every memory for some clue that would assure her he still lived. At night the drums sounded, distant reminders that she lived with danger, and she believed Adam was dead.

By day Justin made a show of elaborate patience. But at night he came to her bed, his mouth hot and searching as he tried to force desire awake in her. But she belonged to Adam Tremain.

Hot summer came, and Justin lost his patience. "You've had time a-plenty to wallow in your grief, if that's what it was."

"You, of all people, ought to understand about mournin'

for someone you've loved and lost," Dulcie replied shortly.

"Very well said, my sweet. But I don't mourn now. I need you, and you need me. You owe your safety to me." He put his hand on her neck. "I burn, Dulcie. I burn, and you've made me wait long enough."

He jerked her out of her chair and kissed her roughly. He forced her backward onto the floor. Then he raped her.

For Dulcie, it was worse than that other time. Then she had not known she belonged to Adam. Now she knew, and the knowledge made it more brutal and punishing. She was Justin's vessel of gratification. He showed not the faintest essence of love, or of loving desire. He knew she wasn't Dorothy. She was Dulcie, still grieving. He lusted. He used her.

Panting, he got to his hands and knees, still between her spread thighs. "There'll be more like this. You might consider before you refuse me again."

Dulcie said coldly, "Did you find it satisfyin'? I didn't!"

He slapped her on one cheek, then the other. She flinched but did not cry out. "You'll beg me to take you next time."

"Never! If you rape me a thousand times, I'll still never beg!"

His lips curved upward. "You'll change your mind, I promise you."

He adjusted his clothing and left, coming back shortly with Costa. With a few taps of a hammer upon a thin-bladed chisel, Costa removed the hinge pins from both doors. He carried the doors away.

Dulcie said, "J-Justin—you can't. Luz can come in. P-please—put them back on! I'm sorry! I'll do w-whatever you say."

He looked at her without concern. "I'm sure you will. Sleep well."

"Where are you goin'? Justin—please! Justin! I beg you."

He went down the stairs. She heard a key turn.

Far away, but sounding ponderously on the night air, the *ogan* and the drums beat. Dulcie scuttled back to her room, sitting tightly curled in the wardrobe. When morning came, Justin did not appear. By noon, hungry and thirsty enough to dare, she crept downstairs.

There was no one about, not even Lucifer. Constantly watching for the eyes she felt upon herself, she snatched bread and fruit and a jug of water, retreating hastily to the wardrobe. She ate a little, hid the rest from the mice, and sat down facing the door.

After a few sleepless days and nights, her nerves were taut beyond endurance. She had to escape from Satan's Keep, but she couldn't do it alone. She didn't know where to find a ship or how to stay away from Mam'bo Luz. Amparo had hidden the food. She would starve to death.

On the fifth evening she went to dinner. Justin put a large piece of meat in his mouth. Lucifer watched, excitement making his black eyes glitter.

"Justin, I've come to ask you to put the doors back—please."

"Doors?" asked Kenneth. "Something's happened to the doors?"

"I haven't heard any apology." Justin crammed in a large spoonful of vegetables.

Dulcie's stomach growled. "I'm sorry for the things I have done to displease you. In the future, I will do what you want me to."

"You'll do that anyway."

"Justin—I beg you . . ." She could not say it.

His eyes were on her, desiring her, hating her. He waited.

Her glance darted to Kenneth, holding his fork suspended; to Lucifer; to Amparo, whose looks were daggers. She met Justin's gaze again. "I beg you to take me . . . make love to me. I . . . want you, Justin."

"You're interrupting my dinner."

"Justin, please—I can't go upstairs. I can't stand it anymore."

"I'm very sorry, Dulcie. Amparo, please bring me a clean spoon."

Amparo said sourly, "Since when you sayin' please to me?"

"What do I have to do? Please don't make me beg anymore! I'm crawlin' now!"

"You haven't even begun."

"Justin, I don't know what to do!" Defeated, she walked to the stairs. She looked up, into the yawning blackness. She turned and ran to him, throwing herself at his feet. She clung to his leg. "I'll be anythin' you want! I'll love you—do anythin', be anythin' for you!"

"Get up off the floor."

"Justin—don't send me away! Love me—here—anywhere you want."

He dragged her to her feet, shoving her up the stairs. The doors were propped up against the wall.

The thought of making love in an open room, where Lucifer would watch, repulsed her. "Could we—wait until dark?"

" 'Love me here, anywhere you want. Isn't that what you said?"

Dulcie had never hated herself more. She put her arms up around Justin's neck. "Make love to me. I want you to." She closed her eyes and put her mouth on his, expecting him to respond. "Please," she whispered.

His voice was cool. "Make love to me as though I were Adam. Give me what you gave Adam."

"I can't. It's you I love and want, Justin." She kissed him again. "Now and always."

Dulcie was unable to bear thinking of him as she undressed herself and Justin. When he stood naked she whispered, "Lie down, please."

He lay on his back, and she knelt over him. When she had stroked, caressed, and kissed him to the peak of tension, she joined his body to hers, moving against him, feeling his fingers dig into her buttocks. She shuddered as he moaned in ecstasy.

Afterward, in his embrace, she was filled with shame. If she wanted to survive, she had to be Justin's whore.

Once convinced that Dulcie had forgotten Adam and loved him instead, Justin became the considerate husband-to-be. Though Dulcie lived locked in the two rooms, it became less onerous, for each day she was nearer to leaving Satan's Keep.

They kept their departure plans secret. If Amparo found out, she and Mam'bo Luz would stop them from leaving.

She began pressing him to take her to New York. She could not convince him to go to Savannah. But one evening, unable to hold back her longing, she began to speak of Patricia and Jem, Mad and Oliver, evoking aching memories of Mossrose. Then she talked of New York. Overcome with homesickness, she burst into tears.

"What's wrong with you?"

Dulcie cried harder, gulping out her words. "Oh, Justin,

I know you won't understand. But I love my father and m-mother. I miss them terribly! I'm so homesick, I could die!"

"After we're married, I might take you to see them—if you please me."

"It's been so long! Couldn't we be married in New York? You'd like my family, Justin. I want them to meet you."

"Impossible. I'll be busy. I must get top price for the cargo."

That night Dulcie was her most loving, doing everything that she knew would heighten Justin's pleasure in her. It no longer mattered how deeply she had to degrade herself. She was determined to get to New York—and away from Justin Gilmartin.

Chapter Seven

Adam entered Nassau harbor feeling like an exile from all the people and places of his past. From the bridge he watched the off-loading of the cotton. Once, the bustling excitement of the docks and the bawdy rowdyisms of the shore crews had set his blood racing, his mouth watering with the taste of adventure.

What had happened to the man he had been, Adam didn't know, but he was gone. In his place stood a man whose eyes viewed the people, the times, and the war with a stark reality devoid of humor. He was missing the spirit of adventure that had made "the business" important to the Southern cause and essential to assuage a youthful hunger for danger and bold fun.

Now, in March 1863, the bold fun was over. The festive lights and colors of Nassau had a tarnish, a glitter of falsity, as he made his way to the offices of Fraser, Trenholm and Company to draw his salary—five thousand dollars—for a single run. The bulk of the money was deposited in an account in Liverpool.

Not even Fraser, Trenholm knew Adam's identity. They were not aware that Adam Tremain was not an alias. False names were the rule in "the business." In the beginning Adam, Ben, and Beau had tried to identify the mysterious

owners of blockade-running fleets. Many men on leave from
the British Royal Navy were particularly anxious not to
be identified. Others were Northerners for whom the
politics of war translated into the politics of profit. And
there were Southerners, some dedicated to the cause, some
to lining their pockets. All wanted their names kept secret.
One alias led to another. While Adam had always dealt
straightforwardly, using his own name, that was less believable than if he had chosen an alias. He had thought it a
fine joke that his own name as ship's master was accepted
as false.

It no longer seemed a joke; the thrill of making so much
money had gone. The agents deposited nearly four hundred
thousand dollars per trip—the profits over and above his
salary—into the account in Liverpool. He had felt like a
child counting multihued sugarplums when he reached the
first million. Profits had not been so great at the start of
the war, but they had seemed more fairly earned.

Now, with Confederate paper money all but worthless,
he could buy one ounce of quinine in Nassau for two dollars and eighty cents in gold and sell it for twelve hundred
Confederate dollars in the Carolinas. With deflated Confederate currency he then bought Southern cotton for eight
to ten cents a pound. Twelve thousand pounds of cotton
would sell in Nassau for nearly ten thousand dollars. The
profits grew of their own volition. Making only one run a
month, Adam would make five million dollars each year
the war lasted.

He also knew that with each increase in the fabulous
profits the South was weakening. He was tempted not to
make the runs, yet if he didn't, needed supplies wouldn't
get through. Nor could he undercut the other runners'
prices. Not only would he make them his enemies but the
auctioneers would raise the prices as soon as Adam discharged his cargo. And yet, such profit had clouded his
patriotism. When men had to pay one hundred thirty-five
dollars for a dozen brown cotton shirts, and soldiers walked
barefoot across snow-covered mountains in Tennessee for
lack of supplies, where was the nobility in his work?

He turned on Bay Street, pausing at the Halyard Light,
then went on down the line of boisterous grogshops, entering the raucous, murky interior of the Red Beacon. It
was packed with an ill-smelling, ill-tempered crowd of
packet-rats formerly on the Liverpool–New York run. Un-

shaven, surly-mouth men with ears pierced for gold loops, necks bedecked with bright silk kerchiefs.

Adam shouldered his way to the bar. He ordered lager ale, downing it thirstily, his eyes lighting with a perverse excitement, as he surveyed the men around him. Theirs were wary faces. Belligerent faces. Brutal faces. Faces of men who had lived so long by need and instinct, they knew nothing else. Perhaps the only honest men. For didn't all men hide beneath their civilized outer shell a primitive beast capable of hate, murder, destruction? Didn't Adam himself?

He had believed himself better than some men, certainly better than Edmund Revanche. He had thought himself honest, decent, honorable until grief, drink, and war had turned him into a man capable of lusting after Tom's fifteen-year-old virginal daughter. Even now he had difficulty admitting his base animal lust without providing himself with heady excuses.

Ale sloshed from the mug onto Adam's tunic as a thick-set man backed into him. "You God-damned bastard! Look what you did!" Adam bawled, and shoved his hand in the face of a squat ship's fireman.

"Watch who ya calls a bastard, ya motherfucker!" The man rolled forward, ramming his fist into Adam's stomach with the full force of his two hundred fifty pounds. Adam doubled over, coughing, spewing beer, and gasping for air. Then he heaved upward, the heavy mug tight in his right hand. Like a glass hammer he slammed it under the fireman's bulldog chin. The man reeled, arms outspread as he cushioned himself against the crowd.

"Kill the tar! Kill him!"

The fireman was slow to regain his feet. Belligerently Adam eyed the other men, daring them to come near him. One blond brute sneered in disdain and lifted his mug to his lips. Adam's fist shot out, smashing the man's cheekbone.

Pain shot through Adam's arm as his knuckles connected with firm, yielding flesh and hard, unyielding bone. He fought like a madman, not even knowing whom he hit. It was a catharsis, a cleansing by pain and fire. His instinct was to hurt and be hurt.

The Red Beacon became an arena as its patrons joined the flailing, brawling melee. Men skittered across the floor on their bellies like fallen ten pins. Jaws were dislocated, eyes blackened, skulls cracked. Knives, ice picks, awls, flashed sharp deadly spears in traces of lamplight. Blood dripped on the already dark-stained floor.

Dodging the enraged blond brute whose cheekbone he had smashed, Adam kicked viciously at the man's hand, missing and throwing himself off balance. The blond roared, and lunged forward to take the advantage, his sailor's sheath knife broad and sharp. Adam twisted, rolling to his left. The knife nicked the bony crest of his shoulder, lodging hilt deep in the paneling, pinning him tight to the wall by his tunic. The blond's left fist streaked before Adam's eyes as his head snapped back, slamming dizzily into the wall. The man's right fist pounded into his abdomen. Hand stiff, Adam thrust with all his strength to the man's diaphragm, bringing his knee up hard into his attacker's face as he doubled over. The big blond crumpled. Adam ripped away the fabric that held him captive, kicked aside the unconscious man, and left the brawling to the others.

His step was brisk as he swaggered into the Halyard Light. He felt good. He was a man who knew what he could do and had done it. Tonight he knew who he was: Adam Tremain, who could and would beat the devil out of any man who dared challenge or interfere with him. He had recognized the blond, a back-alley fighter who boasted of carrying no marks and having no losses. He'd carry marks now. And he'd know who put them there.

Ramona Rose was onstage, her hips swaying. Her black eyes found him in the smoky dimness. "Turn down the lamps an' light up my tassels, boys. Here comes Ramona Rose's pussycat!"

Ramona sauntered toward him. Adam kept right on walking, his eyes linked with hers until their two bodies met. Ramona stood flat against him, her bosom thrust forward, her legs planted firmly. Only a fragment of what had once been a diamond-hard beauty remained in her sensuously cruel face. "Whatta ya gonna do now, big fella?" She tilted her head back, looking at him through deep-set shadowed eyes.

"Ay! Ramona baby!" a drunk howled. "Sweetie! Come back 'ere!"

Adam's arm shot out, catching the drunk in the throat as he staggered up to reclaim Ramona Rose.

Adam moved forward again. Ramona moved her body

in perfect timing with his, moving back as he moved forward a step at a time, until her back was to the last table. "I've danced as much as I will. Is there anything more to you, or are you all tease and no deliver?" Adam said.

She cocked her head, hands on hips. Then she thrust her head back, her pendulous breasts quivering as she roared with laughter. "What makes you think you're man enough for Ramona, Pussycat? All I've heard from you are a couple o' lousy drunken boasts. I don't see you got anythin' no other man ain't got."

"Then call my bluff, bitch, or I'll call yours right here. I'll lay you out like a piece of meat on the table."

They had the attention of every man in the Halyard Light. At Adam's threat they began to chant, "Yeah, yeah, yeahyeahyeah," pounding their tables, urging Adam on.

Ramona Rose hesitated, her tongue making a slow, obvious circuit of her wide mouth. "Why not? I'll take you on."

Adam grasped her arm, heading for the door.

"Naw! Nawww! Do it here!" the men howled, banging the mugs harder.

Ramona linked her arm in Adam's. "Ya all jes' be sure you're here tamorra night. I'll tell you all about it. Won't be any secrets then. Ramona Rose'll know all this boy's got an' all he wished he had."

Adam shoved her out onto the street. He followed her through a narrow maze of back streets until she entered a one-room house. She pushed the door inward. Adam closed the door, slipping the cross bar into place. He wasn't going to be caught unawares by one of her Halyard Light cronies who thought to rob him while Ramona kept him occupied.

Ramona groped across the room to light the single lamp on the table.

Adam stared, then came for her. He grasped her by the jaw, his fingers and thumb pressing cruelly against the joint until Ramona whimpered in pain. "Breathe a word about me in that dump and I'll unhinge this for you and you'll never talk again."

Ramona could barely move her head, but she nodded, eyes watering.

Adam released her. He began to look around the small room.

Ramona rubbed at her jaw, moving it gingerly. "Who in hell d'ya think y'are?"

"This is a pigsty." He kicked at a pile of discarded clothing.

"So what?"

"Clean it up! I don't like dirt."

"You don't like dirt," she said slowly and emphatically. "What a laugh. Who do you think you're kiddin', Pussycat. I *know* you. You're just like the rest o' us at the Halyard Light. Dirt! We're all dirt! Scum! An' you're no better!"

He grabbed her arm, forcing her to bend toward the pile of filthy clothes. "Clean it up!"

She twisted away, throwing the clothes in his face. Quick as a cat, she leaped forward, pounding against his chest. "Get outta here! Go on! Go back to the rock you crawled out from under. Beat it!" She sidestepped his enraged swing, putting the table between them. She hurled a crock of dried, rotting chili. Adam ducked the bowl, swiping its moldy contents from his clothes and face.

Her eyes were wildly bright, her cheeks flushed, her nostrils flared. She hurled every object she could lift at him. He dodged and deflected spoons, candles, a flat iron, hats, dresses, shoes, and all her firewood.

Her rage surfeited, she slumped onto her cot laughing. "All right," she panted. "So you won't get out. What in the hell do you want?"

"Not a damned thing!" He glanced at the door. "Fresh air."

Ramona was there before Adam. "Don't be too hasty, Pussycat. Maybe you're more man that I figgered." Her long beringed fingers fanned out across his chest, pressing against him, digging through the fabric of his tunic to the flesh beneath; then her touch gentled, racing across his chest soft as the touch of goose down.

Adam felt a chill of revulsion. He removed her hands, pressing them hard against her sides. Ramona came up on the balls of her feet, arching toward him, her head back as she bit his lower lip, holding it painfully between her teeth. Adam let go of her hands, grasping both sides of her head. Deep in her throat Ramona laughed.

Adam squeezed the sides of her head, his arms trembling with the force he was using, Ramona's long fingers worked into his tunic. Her sharp-filed fingernails chilled him, making his muscles jump and twitch as she clawed along his ribs, then moved closer, encircling him, clawing down his spinal column. Without meaning to, he released his grip.

In spite of himself, in spite of his revulsion for the woman, his breathing quickened. Hot, growing response came unbidden into his loins. She worked at the placket of his trousers, teasing, probing. As he grew hard and tumid against her hand, she demanded in her husky voice, "Kiss me, Pussycat, Don't say you don't want nuthin'. This'll say you're a liar." She pressed her hand against his hot, exposed penis. "One thing a man can't lie about, ain't it?"

"I don't want *you*," he said through clenched teeth, trying to force control on his own body.

Ramona laughed, her wicked fingers moving everywhere at once. Adam hadn't the will power to move away. He writhed, squirmed, and groaned, his breath panting gasps as she had her way with him. She shrugged out of her robe. She wore only the tassels that covered her taut nipples and the G-string. She moved her hips slowly, her belly rolling forward to touch his penis, then away, touching again, caressing, her eyes sparkling in malicious knowledge. "You're a man an' I'm a woman, Pussycat. That's all it takes. That's all that matters. You don't have to like me, an' I don't have to like you. Anything else is a Goddamned lie. There's fuckin' an' hurtin' an' that's all."

Adam, his eyes shut against the sight of her, licked at the blood trickling from his raw, torn lip. Ramona's voice beat at him as though she were inside his skull, pounding on him, hammering as though he were a white-hot horseshoe being beaten on an anvil. She writhed sensuously, her words bitter as gall, twisted from her own cruel despair.

"Come to Ramona, Pussycat. There's jes' you 'n' me. Your pisser an' my cunt. That's all you need. That's all I want."

Sun-darkened hands stroked him, moving along the length of his penis. Her dark hair fell over him as she bent, touching him with her lips then her tongue. Adam drew in his breath as her tongue circled and teased him. Then something inside snapped. He felt nothing.

He saw her as she was, an aging woman, whose curves were sagging rolls of flesh. Her hair was coarse and dry, her hands unclean and ill-kempt, the fingernails filed to points, weapons. She was pathetic and loathsome.

And this—this was evil and dirty. As was he. All night he had been building up to this, to coupling with her just as she said. To do it out of brutish anger and self-hatred. To use her to punish himself and to use himself to punish her.

But to hear her low, sultry voice speaking of coupling, of tearing at one another, claiming that was all there was of goodness between a man and a woman . . .

"I haven't fallen that low, Ramona. Not yet," he said almost in awe. Awkward as a schoolboy, he fumbled with his tunic and trousers.

"What's the matter with the pussycat? Can't you keep it up? I know a little trick." She went to a container of white powder. "Lick a little of this on an' you'll have the damndest, longest hard-on ever."

"No. It's not that—"

"Now, look, are we gonna fuck or ain't we?"

His anger had vanished, wiped away by her words. Without the armor of the deep self-loathing or the anger, he couldn't talk to her. He had no means to reach into her base, primitive world. She trusted only the animal. Ramona neither knew nor understood anything but the brutish treatment he and the other men had given her at the Halyard Light.

Helpless and mute, he moved to the door. He fished in his pocket, grasping a handful of coins. He dropped them onto the table. Ramona's eyes widened in surprise, then narrowed. "What's that for? What kinda queer dick are you? What do you want me to do for all this money?"

Adam shook his head. "Nothing. Not a thing. Oh, God! I'm sorry!" He ran from the house, Ramona Rose following into the lane.

"Hey! What is this? What the hell you doin'? You! Bastard! What do you think you're buyin'?"

Her voice followed him down the narrow street of crowded little houses, echoing with his running footfalls, hounding him. He could still hear her when he turned the corner and zigzagged through the narrow streets. He ran until he reached the water's edge. Out of breath, his chest heaving, Adam dropped to his knees in the cool, wet sand, digging his fingers deep until the water bubbled up and covered his hands.

He shuddered, squeezing his eyes closed. What had he nearly made of himself tonight? He stripped off his clothing.

scrubbing himself with wet sand, until his skin stung and burned. He waded into the deeper water and washed again.

Adam slept aboard the *Black Swan*. With the first light of dawn he rose, bathed, and shaved his face clean of the unkempt beard. He studied his reflection. His face was hard and lean, the bronzed skin paler where the beard had hidden it from the sun. The flesh was drawn tight on his cheekbones. He was thinner and more angular, and to the sensitive curve of his mouth was added the unrelieved look of hurt in his eyes. Even he could see it. But now he knew he hadn't killed Dulcie, not by carelessness, not by poor judgment. He would have died to save her. And that was what had hurt so much. He never had been given the chance.

Studying his image with the same intensity he would a stranger's, he knew that by turning his life into a battle-ground of self-hate and guilt, he was destroying the good-ness of the rest of his life, denying the few precious months he and Dulcie had had. Ramona had flung that at him with such ferocity he couldn't hide from it. He had become afraid to trust anything good or loving. But no more.

Dulcie was gone. He accepted it. But he wouldn't forget her. He would never again make of himself or his life something unworthy.

Adam dressed quickly. "Morning, R.B."

"Well! *Good* mawin'. Boss! Lawd, kin dat really be de man?"

"No one but." Adam tossed Rosebud one of his favorite small cigars, then squeezed the black man's shoulders. "Thanks."

"You's welcome, Boss. You sho' is welcome."

He spent the day mending fences with Ben and Glory and with the people who had been his friends before the shipwreck. That night he walked down to the Halyard Light. He stood in the street, looking in through the open door. The yellowish light of the lanterns gave the smoky haze a muted look. The men's dark-colored shirts, the bright neckerchiefs, brilliant fire colors of harlots' skirts, all grayed out. The raucous sounds and the odors of sweat and liquor wafted into the street. Ramona Rose's husky, sensual voice blared out as she sang and danced on her rickety stage. The loud jeering voices of drunken men blended in with her deep alto.

Adam stared, forcing himself to take note of every sign of decay. That ramshackle building, the floors crusted with tramped dirt and stains of years, the men whose faces showed the constant abuse of their habits, Ramona's voice that told so much more than the words she spoke. He had sought solace in that hellhole. It was important that he know it for the falsity it was. As Ben had said, he had to have been half out of his mind to seek comfort in Bedlam.

Adam made his next run into Wilmington without making his usual stop at Zoe's. Though he didn't expect Tom to be there, he decided to anchor below Price Creek. The *Black Swan* was positioned so Adam could see the Union ships surrounding both New Inlet and Old Inlet.

Shortly after ten o'clock Tom clambered up the Jacob's ladder Adam had left swinging over the side of the ship.

"Adam, boy!" he cried, clasping Adam's hand, then drawing him close in an awkward, affectionate embrace. "Zoe told me you were here the better part of six weeks, an' I was off huntin' in that damned swamp with Seth an' his boys. She tol' me what happened to Dulcie, son." His hoarse voice choked with emotion. "To some it might seem you 'n' me don't have much luck with our women, but don't you fool yourself, Adam. The only gift God gives any man is love. Mebbe you 'n' me didn't have it long, but we did have it. We had the real thing. An' what's more, we knew it."

Adam turned away.

"Aw, Christ, don't be ashamed of tears." Tom sniffed and laughed, slapping him on the back. "Come on, you ol' horse turd, gimme a drink. I know you got the best."

Tom settled himself on Adam's bunk. "This is somethin'," he said admiringly. "Come up a step or two since the ol' *Ullah*, ain't you?"

Adam shrugged. "A little more carving, a little more brass."

Tom stared into his brandy, sniffing the nutty aroma. 'Shor' don't smell like that firewater Seth brews up. If Ol' Jeff Davis had any smarts, he'd pass out a ration of Seth's brew to every Yankee soldier. Afore they got to their feet again, we'd wipe 'em off the earth."

Adam laughed and changed the subject.

"What effect do you think Lincoln's Emancipation Proclamation will have on us?"

"We'll still get some darkies wantin' to pack for the North."

"What will you do, keep them in the swamp 'til we get six or so?"

"I don't think you ought to make the run into New York for any fewer. It's not as safe as it was before, is it?"

Adam shook his head. "There are Yankee ships everywhere. They cruise from here to the Bahamas. Damned bastards lurk beyond the Out Islands just waiting for some runner to move out of British waters. Mostly though, it's that place of Rod's that spooks me. His harbor is really boxed in. I don't seriously think anyone is going to follow me in there, but all it would take is for someone to spot me, alert the Yankees, and let them wait for me to come out. I'd have one hell of a time outrunning them, even in this ship."

"Mebbe it's time you 'n' me got out of the slave-haulin' business."

"I'm not ready to put up the white feather yet," Adam said. "But a little caution won't hurt. I keep feeling things are closing in around me."

"Boy, you are givin' me a bad case o' the cowardlies. If you're gettin' anxious, I want you to stop. Forget the whole thing."

"Not yet. The only kin of Dulcie's I know live somewhere on Manhattan. Every trip I've made, I stopped at the Raymers', but they're out of the country. God, Tom, everywhere I looked for her people, there was nothing left. It's as though all trace of her, her family, everything—it's all gone."

"I'd like to tell you not to think like that, Adam, but I remember when Ullah died, I left like someone had emptied the whole world of everything good and left me behind with nothing. Ullah was all there was, and she was gone like she had never been."

"But at least you have Angela. Ullah is in her, too. You have something left."

Tom shifted restlessly. "There's two sides to that," he said. Then quickly: "It's near eleven o'clock, the tide's right, an' you gotta sail."

Adam handed Tom a thick envelope. "Give this to Ma for me, will you?"

"I was wonderin' if you was jes' goin' off without a word to your ma. She an' Mammy have damn near wore out their knees prayin' for you. Zoe'll be mighty pleased to hear you're all right."

"See you next trip, Tom. Say hello to Seth for me, and Johnnie Mae."

"She always asks about you. That woman's the damndest toughest individual I ever did see. She can outhunt, outshoot, an' outrun any man in those swamps. Make her happy to hear you think of her."

When Glory Hallalooya cared about someone, she left no doubt. The moment Adam stepped onto the pier, she threw her arms around him. "Oh, Adam, I have a surprise for you!"

"I'm afraid to ask."

"Ha! Well, I'm not going to tell you either. Not until Ben comes back."

"You're a wretched little tease. Why isn't Ben back? I thought he was due in from Charleston."

Glory batted her eyelashes exaggeratedly. "He was detained from leaving."

Adam roared. "Poor Ben. He has no idea what a minx you truly are."

"Adam, if you ever tell him, I'll never forgive you." She was smiling, but she was half-serious.

"Why, Miss Glory Hallalooya, I think you care more about Ben then you've let on. Which of you is it who cares? Glory Hallalooya or Eleanor Brooker?" He helped her into the waiting carriage.

She fussed with her parasol. "Oh, Adam, I don't know. Ben could never . . . I mean . . . oh, shoot! Glory Hallalooya has always been fun—for everyone. But I'm Eleanor Brooker, too, and Adam, I think I love him. I mean, really love him. What am I gonna do?"

"Keep right on being yourself, Glory. Ben doesn't keep coming back to you just because you're *fun*. He's not like that. Anyway, how long's it been since Glory Hallalooya has been *fun* for anyone but Ben West?"

"Since Beau died. But Ben doesn't know that."

"Would you like to bet a new bonnet against a box of Havana cigars?"

The horse swerved as Adam's hands jerked on the reins.

Glory bounded up to hug and kiss him. "Oh, Adam, I love you!"

"I know," he muttered.

Glory's surprise for Adam was a young woman.

"Glory, I appreciate what you're trying to do, but I want you to listen to me. I don't want a woman, and certainly not just any woman."

"But Adam, you just don't reailze how much better off you'd be with some nice girl who'd be waiting here for you, so happy to see you whenever you got back."

"You're more than enough."

"But I'm not. It's not the same as it used to be when you'd lean over the rail and tell me to keep the bed warm. You know I'd do that for you even now, Adam, but I don't think you'd want that, and it'd make Ben unhappy, and—"

"I want you just as my friend," he finished for her.

"Yes, so you do need someone else. She's so sweet, Adam, and I've invited her to dinner tonight, and if you say you won't go, I'll just die!"

Adam looked at her through lazy, narrowed eyes. "Besides Dulcie, you're the most persistent, conniving female I ever knew. What's her name?"

Glory's face clouded. "Well . . . she doesn't know. We call her Apples 'cause of her pretty red cheeks, but no one knows who she really is."

"What do you mean? Doesn't she know who she is?"

"She came to Nassau while you were gone. Captain Drover found her floating around in the waters off Bimini in one of those little boats you use to haul the cargo ashore—a lightboat or—"

"Lighters. Where had she come from?"

"He doesn't know. She was nearly dead when he got her. Captain Drover and Ben figured she must have been a passenger on one of the runners' ships that went down. The way you men come and go, not always returning to the same ports, no one can keep track of you. How many blockade runners do you know that we haven't seen for the last year? We don't know if they're alive or not."

"Were there any other survivors?"

"Captain Drover ddin't see anything else, no survivors, no wreckage, just one lighter and the girl."

"You've already told her I'd be there tonight?"

"Oh, Adam, I do so want to see her with a good man.

She makes me think of myself when the Packers left me stranded here. I wasn't so brave as I led you to believe. I was frightened, but I had more in my favor than Apples has. I always liked men—and you know I just love making love. But Apples isn't like that."

"Then, what do you want me to do, be her old uncle?"

Glory giggled. "No, silly! I just don't want her to think all men are like some she's met. The longer this war goes on, the more water rats it seems to bring to Nassau. It's not like in the beginning when you could count on the captains being gentlemen."

"You don't say."

"Don't you go making fun of me! You will come?"

When Adam was introduced to the girl, his first thought was that the name Apples did not suit her. She was a delicate beauty. Her hair was a soft brown, which she wore atop her head. Light waves arched gracefully, framing her high forehead and the gentle oval of her face. Her eyes were a serene blue, her coloring fair. Everything about her bespoke quietness, muted emotions. Her smile was a slow one that lit her eyes and remained there long after her mouth had relaxed. Adam hadn't expected to like her, but he was drawn to her from the outset.

Throughout dinner they talked of the war. From time to time Glory, Ben, or Adam would mention something about their past or their homes. The girl, though she showed interest, said nothing personal about herself.

As the evening wore on and they had played cards and guessing games, Glory and Ben became more interested in each other than in their guests. Adam took the girl to a small sofa. Outside the open window a street band played. The music was pleasant and soft. Adam leaned back, looking up at the night sky. He turned, found her eyes on him, and smiled. "Isn't there some name that belongs to you? Something for me to call you?"

Her eyes were the softest shade of blue, altering with her expression, shading from gray to a muted lavender. Her expression was far away. She was quiet for so long he wasn't certain she had heard. When she spoke, her voice came as though from a great distance. "I . . . I'm Le-Le-Leah. Leah."

She made him feel calm. He didn't even think about it being her real name. He repeated it softly. "Leah. Leah, my lost girl."

"I'm Leah Haynes," she said slowly. "I'm Leah Haynes
. . . from Mobile, Alabama. Adam—that's who I am!
I'm Leah Haynes, and I live in Mobile, Alabama!" She
put her hands up covering her rosy cheeks, her eyes wet
with tears and shining. "Glory! Ben! Adam made me remember! I know who I am!"

Glory wrapped her arms around the girl, crying, "Apples, Apples, I'm so happy for you. App—what is your
name?"

Ben looked in awe at Adam. "How'd you do that?"

"I just asked her if there wasn't something I could call
her other than that awful nickname."

"Asked her? You just asked her, and she told you? Why,
we've inquired in ports in the States about any female
passenger bound for Nassau, Bermuda, or Havana in the
past year. There's never been a hint from anyone. And
you *just ask her,* and she *tells you!* Christ, Adam!"

"What else do you remember, Leah?" Glory asked.

"Well, I'm from Mobile. And I'm nineteen—I think. I
. . . oh!" Her eyes were frightened. Quickly she reached
for Adam's hand. "I can't remember any more. I can't
think. Nothing is clear now."

He forgot Ben and Glory. All he saw were Leah's eyes
changing from the dark gray-blue they were when she was
troubled. He scooped her into his arms. Her hair was silky
and fragrant, the color of buckwheat honey. "You'll remember, but not now. Just talk to me. Tell me about the
things you like best. Tell me about the flowers and the sun-
sets and your favorite hat and what makes you laugh."

"Why would you want to know all that?"

"For no reason, except that I do."

She began, her voice as melodious and gentle as a warm
misting rain. The three of them listened as though Leah
told the most fascinating story in the world, and all she
spoke of were the most commonplace things of the life of
any girl who had grown up in the deep South before the
war.

Throughout the month, Adam continued to see Leah.
Each time she remembered a little more. She knew she
had a brother. Her father had died early in the war. Her
mother had been dead since Leah was ten. She still didn't
recall why she had been on a boat. She guessed, offering
many possibilities, but she didn't know.

Adam was almost sorry when it was time to make the

trip to Wilmington. He didn't want to leave Leah. She always seemed so lost when he wasn't near. But she surprised him. As did all the women of the blockade runners, Leah, too, seemed perfectly resigned to the peculiarity of their schedules. They followed that pattern, and Adam found Glory had been right. He had missed having a woman waiting for him upon his return, a woman whose eyes scanned the myriad masts and could unerringly pick out the one belonging to her own man's ship.

By July he had put off going to see Zoe long enough. Confronting Angela now didn't seem difficult. Leah had restored his perspective. Angela was a child. He had looked on her as a child except for that one moment, and even in that he could now be fairer to himself. He had been sound asleep when Angela had entered his room. He hadn't been fully awake when he responded to her caresses. It was time to go back.

Zoe's worries about Adam vanished the moment she saw him. One day home and he was as normally restless and fidgety as ever. He repaired the carriage house and mended the back step that threatened to collapse every time Mammy approached it. But once those tasks were finished, he was eager for a dark night when the clouds would cover the moon.

For days the skies were vivid blue by day, bright indigo by night. Then slowly the clouds and wind and rain began to move in, and Adam judged he'd have three days at the most to wait for a truly dark, foggy night. His talk with Angela would wait no longer.

In the past four months Angela had gained an amazing amount of poise. Too often he had the feeling he was being skillfully handled, and by a woman of some experience. Yet she was only Angela, just fifteen years old. He was imagining things.

Claudine came to the carriage house as he mended the broken stall.

"Mastah Adam, kin Ah talk to you?"

"Sure, Claudine. It's been a long time since you and I have talked."

"Dis ain't 'zackly jes' talkin'. Dey's somethin' you ain't gwine like."

"Uh-oh," he said solemnly. "What've you gotten into?"

"Ain't me, it's Miss Angela. Miss Dulcie was allers head-

strong but never was bad. She got herself into a plen'y o'
fixes but no matter what she done, she stayed a lady. Mastah Adam, Miss Angela ain't nothin' but white trash! She
kin be mean an' nasty. Ooo-eee kin she! An' she got a
hankerin' fo' de mens. An' dey's not all white mens. She
doan care 'bout nothin' 'ceptin' she git what she want."

"Claudine, I don't think you need to say any more."

"Yes, Ah do! 'Cause I ain't so sure Ah wants to stay
here. Well, that ain't 'zackly true. Ah likes yo' mama
and Ah likes Mammy, but Ah'm sick to mah stummick
ovah tryin' to hide from yo' mama all de times dat gal
sneak out an' doan come back in 'til mawin'."

Adam rubbed his forehead. "You're sure about all this?"

Claudine switched her bottom in annoyance. " 'Course
Ah'm sure. When you ever know me to carry tales that
ain't true? Now, what you gwine do 'bout her?"

"I don't know what I'm going to do."

He sent Claudine after her and stalked into the study,
still uncertain. How did one tell a headstrong, bitter girl
that it was her own life she was destroying?

Adam paced the study, rehearsing the way the conversation should go. He could not be gentle, could not be
subtle, or Angela wouldn't listen. If he skirted the issue,
she would make it a flirtatious game.

Nearly half an hour later she breezed into the room.
"Well, well, Adam! Imagine you looking for me. Aunt Zoe
must be out. Isn't that cozy?"

Already it was going badly, and he hadn't opened his
mouth. "Sit down, Angela," he said gruffly. He wondered
how Rod Courtland would handle something like this and
wished he had the older man's presence.

Angela wore one of the new-style hoopless dresses many
Southern women had adopted. On Angela it was discon-
certingly revealing, made of a soft material that clung to
her, outlining every curve of her body. The low neckline
—too low for the early afternoon—displayed Angela's well-
formed bosom.

When he didn't speak immediately, Angela fidgeted, then
crossed her legs, making the dress perform even greater
feats of revelation. "Well, Adam, you seem to have lost
your train of thought. Or did you simply want someone
to keep you company?"

"I have not lost my train of thought, and if I wanted
someone to keep me company, it would not be a child. I

have something to say, and I don't intend to let you make a game of it. A lady cannot do as she pleases just because she pleases, Angela. If you are to marry well, as your mother wished for you, certain proprieties must be observed."

"My, my, but you do sound pompous! I'm not interested."

"Sit down, damn it!" He shoved her back into the chair. "Wipe that look off your face, and the rouge and lip coloring as well!" He tossed his handkerchief into her lap.

"Who do—"

"Do it, Angela, or I'll wipe it off for you with the back of my hand. You may want to ignore it, young lady, but I can't. You're Tom's and Ullah's daughter—two of the best people to walk this earth, and no one, not you or anyone else, is going to dirty them! I don't know what's gotten into you, but you'd better get it out of your system. Because, Angela, I'm stopping here next month, and if I hear you've been near any man my mother has not invited into the house as a suitor, I'll thrash you within an inch of your life."

"That little bitch!" Angela snarled. "That dirty little bitch. Lies! All lies! Did she also tell you she hates me because you prefer me to her? Did she tell you she loves you and dreams about you? Can't you see she's trying to make you—"

"Shut up! The last time I was here you told me you were like a peach ready to be picked. That's no longer the case, is it? How many men have there been?"

"So what? You didn't want me. I told you I wouldn't wait."

"What I do has nothing to do with this. I'm talking about you, and the man you'll someday want to marry. The right man, who has a right to expect to be the only man his wife lays with."

"And what man will that be?" she asked bitterly. "If you don't marry me, there'll be no man who cares if he's the only man I've ever been with. Darkies can't be as particular as the whites."

Adam frowned. "What in hell do you mean by that?"

"You know what I mean. I'm as much a nigger as Claudine. A Gray Oaks nigger. What white man can I marry and risk his finding out what I am? With what white man could I risk bearing a child with dark skin? Who is this marvelous white man who will want me? There was only you. I believed in you all my life. I thought maybe to you it wouldn't matter. But it does matter, doesn't it, Adam? You don't want a nigger wife, either. No one does!"

"My God, Angela, what are you doing to yourself?"

"It's been done *to* me! I didn't ask Tom to love my mother. Why couldn't he just have used her like other men do with plantation women? Why couldn't I have grown up always being nigger? Then I wouldn't want the things I want now. Do you know what it's like having Aunt Zoe talk about how it will be when I marry?"

"Angela, there is no reason you can't marry well. You're not nigger."

"I am!"

"You're one-eighth Negro. Seven-eighths of your blood is white."

"One-sixteenth blood is nigger! Or don't you know the law?"

"Don't degrade yourself. There's no need—"

"Don't degrade myself? How? By saying I'm Negro? I thought that didn't matter to you. Which is it, Adam? Degradation or pride? It's hard to feel both at once."

Adam was speechless. Her face was bitter and hard, her eyes glassy with tears she'd probably never shed.

"You don't understand. I don't know why I expected you to. I guess I thought you cared. I wasn't just being bold when I offered myself to you, Adam. I love you. I've loved you so long I can't remember when I didn't. I think I still do, except now it hurts."

He put out his hands to her. "Angela . . ."

She shook her head wildly. "Oh, no! I don't want pity from you. I want you as a man or not at all!"

Adam stepped toward her. Angela stepped back. "Just stay away from me. What's between us is between a white man and a black woman. I know I stir you. I found that out. So it must be my blood that makes you hesitate. If it is that, Adam Tremain, I'll get even with you. If you spurn me because of my mother, I'll make you pay, because it was you more than anyone else for whom I wanted to learn how to be a 'white lady'."

"Angela," he said in a low, calm voice, "Can't you conceive of reasons other than your blood that would stop me from marrying you? I'm twenty-six years old. Nearly

double your age. I've been married to the only woman I
ever wanted for a wife. Most of my life I've thought
of you as a sister. Don't those reasons mean anything to
you? Or are you so wrapped up in self-pity and the desire
to hurt that all you can see is one thing and that alone?"

"Yes!" she hissed. She left the study, slamming the door
behind her.

Adam continued to linger in Smithville. Somehow the
girl had to be controlled. He told Zoe only enough to make
her understand that Angela must never be allowed to go
out unescorted.

Zoe stared down at her needlepoint, uncomfortable, biting her lower lip. "Oh, Adam, I don't know how to tell you
this, dear."

"Just say it straight out, Ma."

"It's too late to keep Angela . . . I mean an escort with
her won't—Oh, Adam, she sneaks out at night. She thinks
I don't know. Tom will be so hurt when he finds out.
Adam, I feel so wicked. In a way I've helped her become
a—a tart. I've been too weak to stop her, and I sit upstairs
like a wicked old woman and say prayers that that little
harlot won't bear a child by one of those men she—"
Zoe sobbed, her needlepoint falling to the floor. "It's only
a matter of time before word gets around, and whatever
chance she has left will be gone."

"If people don't find out on their own, Angela will make
certain they do. She's like a cauldron inside. She hates what
she is, what Ullah was."

"Ullah was so good—and she loved Angela."

"I'm not sure even Ullah could have done anything
with Angela. But she's not staying here to ruin herself.
You and Mammy and Claudine keep her in this house at
night if Mammy has to sit on her. When I come home in
October, I'm taking Angela to Tom. Let her cool her heels
in the swamp for a while. I don't think Seth's boys will
appeal to her. She may be easier to handle after she lives
with her father for a while."

"But what will you tell Tom? Adam, it'll kill him."

Adam paused, remembering: *"You have Angela. Ullah
is in her too."* And the hurt look on Tom's face: *"There's
two sides to that."* "Ma," Adam said softly, "I think he
already knows."

* * *

Adam returned to Nassau in mid-August. Seeing Leah waiting in the suite was more welcome than he had realized. He wanted and needed the balm of a gentle woman's understanding, and Leah gave that in abundance. He lay in her arms, listening sleepily as she sang. Her voice was childlike in its sweetness. Everything about her was light and sweet. There were times she hardly seemed real to him, and her strange arrival on Nassau seemed perfectly logical. How else would a creature like Leah come to be anywhere? She'd simply appear, like a naiad in the middle of a lake.

She made him lazy in his contentedness. One day slipped into another, and he barely thought of the cargo he'd have to gather to run into Charleston in September or of the problems in Smithville he'd have to solve in October. For now there were only the warm, hazy days of August, and the breeze-cooled nights with Leah.

In September, on the night of his return from Charleston, Leah clung to him. She had had nightmares while he was gone, and this night, even in his arms, she trembled and wept in her sleep. Just before dawn she slept peacefully, and Adam lay watching her, wondering what had caused her fear. Though he recognized he was not in love with her, not as he had been with Dulcie, he hadn't realized how much he cared about this small, gentle girl, whose eyes spoke far more eloquently than the tongue of a philosopher.

He took her on a picnic the next day. They sat atop a hill overlooking the ocean. "Do you remember what you were dreaming last night?"

Leah stared past him at the thick wall of flowers behind him.

"Tell me what it was, Leah. We'll talk about it and then throw it away, throw it far out into the sea so it'll never frighten you again."

She looked directly into his eyes then. Hers were sad, her deep-lavender sad. "If I tell you, everything will change. My lives are not two halves of a whole, Adam. I will have to choose. And no matter which I choose, I shall only have half."

"You've remembered?"

"Yes," she said, in little more than a whisper. "I remember it all now."

He swiveled around, resting his head in her lap. "Don't

wait for some other time, some *right* time that may never come. Tell me now, Leah. Let me be a part of whatever it is."

"Perhaps you're right. I shall have to decide sometime. My brother, Carter, and I had sailed on the *Mercy*. He thought we'd be safest on a British ship. We were sailing for Bermuda. It was night, and there was a storm. I was below in my cabin. It seemed as though everything exploded. I don't know if we were attacked or if the boilers blew up. Carter came to the cabin, screaming at me to hurry; we had to abandon the ship. He released one of the small boats, and we climbed down a rope ladder. The *Mercy* was already sinking, and men were screaming. There was fire . . . bodies in the water and—"

"God! I'm a stupid fool! Of course it had to be something like that."

"I want to tell you. I want to tell you just this one time and then . . . then we'll never talk about it again. Adam, please."

He sat up, taking her in his arms, holding her as she talked. "We were in the small boat for days. I don't know how many. Carter took food from the galley, but it wasn't enough. We had almost nothing to drink. Carter had grabbed two bottles of wine. We sipped at them, hardly daring to do more than wet our tongues. During the day we saw ships so far distant they were like specks on the horizon. At night we could hear vessels, but they ran without lights, and we couldn't see them. We tried to call out, but our tongues were swollen and our throats so dry it was like whispering. No one heard. Carter even tried beating on the side of the boat with his empty wine bottle.

"I don't know how long it was before Carter began to drink seawater. I still had some wine, but he wouldn't touch it. The seawater made him sick at first, then it . . . I think it drove him mad. He—I was dozing. The sun was so hot . . . and Carter stood up. He was staring at the wine bottle. I lifted the bottle to give it to him, but he lunged for it. He fell over the side. I saw him come up. He wasn't far from the boat, and Carter was a good swimmer. I knew he could get back. But he didn't swim toward the boat. I tried to call to him. He didn't seem to know where he was. He'd swim one way, then he'd turn around, searching for the boat, and he'd be looking right at me and then swim farther away. He seemed to do that forever, and then

—then he disappeared. He went beneath the water and . . .
I don't remember how long it was before Captain Drover
found me. I don't remember days, just the sun and the
darkness and the sun."

Adam became more aware of the fragility of the girl he
held. She was like a delicate Dresden figure, dainty and
perfectly formed. He doubted she weighed a hundred
pounds fully clothed. There was so little of her, and yet
somewhere there had to be a strength, a purpose for living
that had brought her through that ordeal. "We won't talk
about it ever again. It's over, and you're safe now."

"I haven't told you why my brother was taking me to
Bermuda, Adam. After that it is over. Before the war my
father arranged for my marriage. I've loved Hugh Larkin
since I was a child. I wanted to be married in Mobile.
But then my father was killed, and Carter knew he would
be leaving for Tennessee soon, and I would be left alone.
Hugh works in the Confederate Agents Offices in Bermuda, so it was decided we would be married there."

"Then Hugh has been expecting you since March?"

"We didn't know exactly when we were coming. Carter
was to get leave whenever he could. Now you see the two
parts of my life can never become one happy entity. I must
remain the Leah who lives here in my garden paradise with
the sea captain who led her back to memory and forward
into the most lovely days I have ever known, or I must become again the Leah who journeys on and marries Hugh
Larkin."

Chapter Eight

Dulcie had left New York with Adam in October 1861.
After two years in the heat and riotous bloom of the Bahama Islands it was strange to come into the port of New
York in September 1863. The sun had not the strength
it boasted farther south. Dulcie, noting that the maples
had turned red and yellow, shivered in Dorothy's cotton
dress.

Over the whole city hung a black cloud, product of

thousands of chimneys and industrial smokestacks, and an overpowering stench of garbage, slaughterhouses, and the dung from horses and the pigs that roamed the streets. The noise was appalling: the rumble of drays and carriages, the shouts of the drivers, the shrill whistles of policemen, the heavier, more alarming sounds of emergency vehicles with their ear-shattering bells, the din of factory machines, and the clamor of the dock activity itself.

Grasping her arm as though she might flee and leave him alone in this strange and frightening world, Justin pulled Dulcie toward a row of waiting carriages. The first driver stared at their clothing and demanded payment in advance. Angrily Justin clutched the driver's coat. Hastily Dulcie intervened, and they took another carriage. The first driver, staring after them, puffed out his lips and wiped his brow with a dark bandanna.

"Justin, you can't settle things with your fists," Dulcie said severely. "You could be locked up in jail for assault."

"He was insolent."

"Well, we don't resemble a lady and a gentleman much right now. We'll have to buy you a proper outfit today."

"And a warm coat too." He did not think of clothing for her.

"We'll have to borrow from Uncle Oliver." *What if Mad and Oliver should be out of the city?*

She refused to consider that. She concentrated on the sights. The vehicles they passed shone, the horses looked well groomed. Soldiers on the street wore crisp blue uniforms. There was an air of bustle and prosperity. Northerners moved more quickly and purposefully than Southerners.

She leaned forward and spoke to the driver. "What can you tell me about the war? I've been out of the country for two years."

"We trounced the Rebels at Gettysburg, last summer. Heard they lost twenty-eight thousand men," the driver began. "Right away we had four days of draft riots. Man wasn't safe in his own home. They did terrible things to the coloreds. Strung 'em up, cut 'em, burned 'em in the streets. I could tell you stories that'd curl your hair. They beat up the nigger-lovers, wrecked their houses too. Even blew up the armory. They had to call our soldiers, fresh from Gettysburg."

Justin pulled on her arm. "Stop talking to him. This has nothing to do with you. We'll be in England. There's no war there."

"Justin, don't you understand? We're not isolated on Andros now. The war does affect us. It's affecting trade between nations—you'll probably get more money for your mahogany. If our ship hadn't been properly registered, we couldn't have come into port, or we might have been captured. This war is involving the whole civilized world."

"Civilized," Justin grunted.

Dulcie knocked at Oliver's door, feeling queer and breathless.

Her father opened the door. "The trade entrance is—" he began, seeing her clothing, then finished in a whisper, "Dulcie. Dulcie Jeannette." He held out his arms, his face very white.

"Oh, *Daddy!*" She hurled herself at him. His embrace nearly broke her ribs. She was home.

Her father was crying, and so was she. "We thought you were dead. We heard the ship went down, Dulcie Jeannette. Patsy—"He cleared his throat and bellowed, "Patsy!"

Patricia's voice floated in from another room. "Comin', Jem! Ah'm not deaf." She whispered, "Mah baby?" and passed out on the Oriental rug.

"Mad! Oliver!" Jem cried.

Dulcie knelt by her mother, rubbing her wrists.

Mad and Oliver came in together. "There, Ollie, what did I tell you? Dulcie is perfectly all right." Mad hugged and kissed Dulcie for so long that Oliver simply put his arms around both of them.

Patricia's gentle tones penetrated the uproar. "Dulcie, come to youah mama."

"Oh, Mama, it's so good to be home!"

"Honey, wheah have you been? Why didn't you write? We were afraid—"

"Mama, I've been very ill—"

Jem held out his hand to Justin. "I'm James Moran, Dulcie's father."

"Justin Gilmartin, of Satan's Keep." Justin ignored Jem's hand.

Mad's eyes grew round. "Dulcie, where's Adam?"

Dulcie tensed. Justin watched her sharply. She turned away, looking blindly at Aunt Mad's huge Boston fern. "Adam is—"

Justin said clearly, "Captain Tremain is dead."

There were tears in Mad's voice. "H-how? When?"

"A year ago—" Justin began.

Jem interrupted him. "Mr. Gilmartin, allow my daughter to reply."

Every word tore a piece out of Dulcie's heart. "We—were on our way to Savannah—last August. We were shipwrecked—on Andros Island. Adam died. I was rescued by some natives. For the past year I've lived in Justin's home.

"As my woman," Justin said defiantly.

"You don't leave much to the imagination, do you?" Oliver said.

Mad, her eyes streaming tears, said, "Dulcie—tell us about Adam."

"We don't have much time, Dulcie," said Justin.

Oliver said smoothly, "Mr. Gilmartin, among gentlefolk you may have to curb your impatience. Dulcie, we are listening to you, my dear."

"We were washed ashore. The natives thought he was an evil spirit, so they k-killed him." Her whispered words fell into stunned silence.

"Tell them you've forgotten him, Dulcie. Tell them about *now!*"

"Justin and I are goin' to England to regain his property from his uncle." Then she added, whispering, "We'll be married."

"We'll be leaving tomorrow," Justin said.

"*You* may be, Mr. Gilmartin," said Jem. "But if Dulcie wishes to go with you, I expect her to say so. We are hopin' she will visit awhile."

"I'm not good enough for Dulcie? Is that what you're saying?"

"Nothing of the kind," said Oliver. "We got off on the wrong foot, Mr. Gilmartin. Everybody is emotional, hard not to be. You're taking Dulcie away when she's barely gotten here. Perhaps you'll tell us what is your hurry?"

Justin, slightly mollified, explained about the mahogany shipment.

Oliver eyed him. "Suppose you could sell your lumber in New York? You'd avoid shipping costs and make a tidy profit."

"I'll make one, you can bank on it."

"And with the profit, you buy grain. There's a crucial

shortage in Europe. You stand to get an enormous price for it."

Justin looked intently at Oliver. "How much?" he began, then, suddenly distrustful, turned on Dulcie. "He's trying to trick me out of taking you with me—"

"Dulcie hasn't said whether she wants to go," Jem cut in, his anger rising, "And we are not goin' to discuss that now."

Dulcie turned gratefully to her father. "Daddy, have you been visitin' here long?"

"We left Mossrose over a year ago."

"Left Mossrose? Daddy—Mama—it's our *home!"*

"We'll go back to it after the war if we can. We might have stuck it out another year, but your aunt and uncle persuaded us to leave."

"But the servants—the horses—Strawberry?"

"We sold everything we could. I'm sorry." Jem smiled sorrowfully. "But you should be glad to know I freed the slaves."

"Not that we don't miss Mossrose," Patricia murmured. "Mad an' Ah go visitin' an' shoppin', an' we work with Mrs. Algernon Sullivan, who has established a soup kitchen foah Confederate prisonahs out on David's Island. Theah isn't enough time in the day to get homesick." She smiled weakly at Jem.

Dulcie asked, "Do you have any news of the county people? Glenn? Leroy? The Whitakers? And Robert—what do you hear of him?"

Patricia said, "Leroy proved to be a fine soldjuh, very darin'. Befoah we left Mossrose, we heard of his exploits. Glenn is a prisonah on David's Island. I talked to him jes' the othah day. Addie Jo has two little boys."

Tears came to Dulcie's eyes for her own lost child. "Robert—?"

"Robert is a courier," Jem said. "You must remember, Dulcie, that our only chance for news is seein' someone from home. The mail service and the telegraph can't be depended on between North and South."

"Andrew Whitaker. He's dead, isn't he." Dulcie, remembering that chaste kiss in the garden, wished she had not been so prissy.

"How did you know, honey? He died in his fuhst skuh-mish. The man behind him fell and accidentally shot Andrew in the back. Youah cousin Phil . . . ran away to join up. He . . . lost a leg. Only a boy, an' he—"

"Mama, don't think about it." Dulcie clenched her jaws. "If anybody can cope with that, Phil can."

"We haven't even given you a chance to refresh yourselves," Mad said. "Are your trunks comin?"

"We don't have trunks, Aunt Mad. I'm wearin' a borrowed dress that's nearly as old as I am, and Justin is wearin' his father's frock coat and breeches. We had to conceal our departure."

"My goodness." Mad's eyes sparkled with curiosity. "You must tell us about it. Come along, Dulcie, you can have your old room."

As Mad steered her toward the stairs, she heard Justin say, "I will accept your proposition, Mr. Raymer. When can we see these men you spoke of?"

That night Dulcie slept alone and fitfully, accustomed to much different night sounds. Toward dawn she was startled awake by the din of the *ogan* and drums. She sat up in bed, her heart pounding. Mam'bo Luz! She lay back; it was merely the rumble and clanging bell of the fire wagon.

In the morning Justin, resplendent in a borrowed checked suit and a brown worsted Chesterfield, left with Oliver. Jem went to his office.

"We've got to take you shoppin', Dulcie honey," said her mother. "You look like an orphan in youah Aunt Mad's dress."

Dulcie hugged her mother fiercely. "It's so *good* to hear you fussin' over trifles! Mama, if you'd seen me on Andros —I look like a queen now!"

"Just the same, weah goin' to buy you a whole new wahdrobe!"

Mad said the thing Patricia was studiously avoiding. "Dulcie, you aren't goin' to England with that man, are you?"

"No." Dulcie looked at her mother, and words died in her throat. "Mama, Aunt Mad, will you excuse me? I forgot somethin'." Dulcie hurried toward the stairway.

"That's a relief," Mad said, her eyes still on the staircase where Dulcie disappeared. "I'll get my wrap. Then we'll be on our way."

Mad swept into Dulcie's room and scooped her niece into an embrace. "Now, what is all this, Dulcie? Tell me, dear. You know there's nothin' your old Aunt Mad can't hear."

"I can't marry him, Aunt Mad. I just can't!"

"Then you won't."

"But if it weren't for Justin, I wouldn't be alive!"

"But my darlin' girl, that doesn't mean you must marry him."

Dulcie sobbed into her aunt's ample bosom. "Help me, Aunt Mad. Help me. I want Adam so. If he were dead, wouldn't I know it? Wouldn't I feel it? Aunt Mad, let's go see Mr. Courtland. Now. This afternoon. He'd know about Adam."

"This afternoon? Well, I don't know, Dulcie."

"Please go with me!"

"I'm barmy as an ol' bedbug, but I'll go."

Dulcie, the height of fashion in a green poplin walking-dress and matching cloak, walked with outward confidence into Roderick Courtland's office. "I should like to see Mr. Courtland, please."

"I'm sorry, Madame. Mr. Courtland is out of the city. He did not say when he will return."

"You *must* know when he'll be back!"

"Mr. Courtland is frequently called out of the city. You must understand, Madame, that his holdings are extensive."

"Would you know about my husband, Captain Adam Tremain?" Dulcie, trembling, put her gloved hand on the counter for support.

"I'm sorry, Madame, I am not at liberty to say."

Dulcie wished that she could grab this pompous ass and wring the truth from him as Justin would. "What is your name, please?"

"Daniels. Homer Daniels."

"Mr. Daniels, a year ago my husband and I were shipwrecked. I've been back in the States only one day. I am tryin' to find out if my husband is alive or dead." Her voice cracked. She fought to regain her control.

"C-come into Mr. Courtland's office, Mrs. Tremain, ladies. I didn't understand." He took down several ledgers. After some time Daniels said, "The last record of Captain Tremain was written in June, 1861. In October 1862, there is a notation that the ship *Independence* sank. You can read it if you like."

In the carriage, Dulcie said, "I still don't believe it." In her heart, she was beginning to.

In three days Justin had sold his mahogany at an excellent price. He bought grain and watched it being loaded for London. Then he came for Dulcie.

It was the moment she had dreaded. In his harsh way Justin thought he loved her. She owed him her life, for if the natives had not eventually killed her, they would have maimed her mind beyond healing.

Thinking of all these things, weighing them against her certain misery, Dulcie said, "Justin, I'm not goin'."

Justin stared at her, uncomprehending.

"I could lie to you as I have these past months. I could make you believe me, because you want to. Now it's no longer fair for me to pretend."

"You used me! You never loved me!" His face was tense, his nostrils distended. "I saved your bloody life, and this is the thanks I get."

Dulcie bit her tongue on a caustic retort. "I know you did. But I can't repay you in the coin you demand."

"You used me, you bitch."

Dulcie grasped the back of a chair. "I'm sorry—please understand."

In the late-afternoon sunlight their eyes held. Justin's were hot and bitter. "It did work! You did love me! I know you did!" He clutched her arms, shaking her with a force that made her teeth rattle. "It's this stinkin' city that's changed you! I'll make you come around."

Dulcie's voice quavered on a high note. "Dad-deee!"

"You're coming with me!" He let go of one arm. She slapped him as hard as she could, squirming to get away.

"Let my daughter go!" Jem's pistol pointed unwaveringly at Justin. His face was suffused with rage.

Dulcie recognized the steely look. "Justin, he'll do it!"

"Bloody lot you care!" He sent her hurtling into the marble-topped stand.

"You misbegotten whoreson!" Jem yelped.

"Daddy, don't! I'm all right!"

Justin looked at Jem, then at Dulcie. "Is that supposed to make us even? I save your skin and you save mine?"

"Justin, take my gratitude—it's all I've got to give you!"

Justin snorted. "Gratitude makes a cold screw. You can put your gun away. Keep your ass-licking daughter."

Jem was advancing on Justin. "Get out of here before I kill you!"

"Justin, I didn't mean to hurt you. I had to do what I did."

He raised his eyebrows sardonically. "I suppose you did. It was the only *civilized* thing to do."

When he had gone, Dulcie went to her room. She lay across her bed staring at the wallpaper, trying to justify what she had had to do.

September went by, with cool, bright days. Dulcie got government approval for good character and a permit to visit the Confederate prison on David's Island. Glenn was gaunt, one arm in a sling, and pathetically happy to see her. When she told him Adam was thought dead, he was as sorrowful as though Adam had been his boyhood friend.

To lighten his maudlin thoughts, Dulcie said, "Mama tells me you have two little boys."

Glenn's face brightened. "I haven't seen the baby yet. Addie's living with her parents. They'll take good care of her and the children, but I worry. The war's gettin' closer to Savannah. Dulcie—and there's nothin' I can do. I could go home—if I live—and not find a trace of my family."

"Miss, you've overstayed your time," the guard broke in.

"Please—just another minute."

"Rules, Miss."

Glenn took her hand. "I hope you come again, Dulcie."

With the gentle guidance of Patricia and Mad, Dulcie spent more time visiting the prisoners and working in Mrs. Sullivan's soup kitchen. Though it didn't stop the gnawing hunger for Adam, it gave her purpose, and in a way made her feel closer to him.

Mrs. Burris, one of Mrs. Sullivan's workers, drew Dulcie aside one day. "I'm delighted to see another staunch Southerner aiding her fellow man. Your mother and aunt are such marvelous ladies. Isn't Molly Sullivan wonderful? To have the gumption to think up such a brilliant idea as this soup kitchen and then to persuade the Federal authorities to permit it!"

"Yes, indeed. She seems a fine, kind lady."

"Oh, but I completely forgot what I wanted to ask you. We have formed a literary society, the Jeffersonians. Mad suggested you might like it. I am so sorry, Mrs. Tremain, your aunt did mention that your husband is missing. It is all so sad. There are so many. But for that reason you might wish to join us. We gather news from the South. Occasionally we obtain outstanding speakers."

Dulcie could hardly speak. "You gather information?"

"Yes, as much as we are able."

"I'd like very much to come."

"Splendid! This month our speaker is a man who travels throughout the South. He has just come back from a harrowing adventure and will tell us about it Tuesday evening. Mr. Revanche is our best source of information. He understands how we yearn for our loved ones and takes the time to bring back whatever news he can. It will be a real treat for you to meet a man of his caliber and know he is fighting for *our* side."

Dulcie thought Tuesday night would never come. Her thoughts in the intervening days were all of the stranger named Edmund Revanche, a new source of hope. She rehearsed what she would say as she asked him to help locate Adam. More than ever it seemed he had to be alive.

Several carriages lined the street in front of Mrs. Burris's handsome townhouse. Inside the brightly lit parlor ladies and gentlemen clustered around a tall foreign-looking man in black. He was dignified and reserved, speaking with courtesy but little animation. His hair, black tinged with gray, formed a deep V at his forehead. Unlike most men of the day, he wore no moustache. He had charm in plenty, as Mrs. Burris had said, but a rather automatic smile, which he seemed to switch on as he deemed appropriate. The man was experienced in handling numbers of admirers at once. His dark, magnetic eyes found Dulcie. After a deliberate stare he returned to his conversation.

Mrs. Burris hovered anxiously, waiting to introduce the latest arrivals. "Mr. Revanche, may I present Mr. and Mrs. Oliver Raymer, Mr. and Mrs. James Moran, and their daughter, Mrs. Tremain?"

The hooded lids over the dark eyes flickered. He pressed his cool lips overlong on Dulcie's hand. "The name is very familiar. Is your husband a Southerner, Mrs. Tremain?"

Faced with the man who might help her, Dulcie's throat tightened painfully. "He . . . was." To his questioning, sympathetic gaze, she managed to go on. "He is—missin'. Perhaps. They say he died at sea."

"My condolences Madame. So many brave men have died. But you have hope. You did say he is missing? Perhaps we can—" With an apologetic half-smile Edmund turned to be introduced to a noisily insistent woman.

Dulcie had all she could do to keep from grasping his coat sleeve. Perhaps he could—what?

"Come sit down, dear. You're so pale. Dulcie, truly you must not go on like this." Mad held her hand tightly.

"Aunt Mad, I must talk to him! He was about to say he would help me! I knew he was, and then that old cow interrupted." Dulcie squeezed Mad's fingers until she cried out.

She sat back at Mad's insistence, waiting until Mr. Revanche had spoken. Then she would talk to him. She'd talk to him if she had to follow him home!

Mrs. Burris was saying, "Mrs. Meadows, would you be kind enough to take Dulcie around and introduce her? We want her to feel right at home with the Jeffersonians. Oh, and she must meet Mr. Revanche's companions."

Mrs. Meadows skillfully moved Dulcie among the guests. She met Chad Kaufman, a powerfully built, stocky man who hadn't the grace or the elegance of his mentor. His eyes, ice blue, assessed Dulcie as he spoke. A hard, cold man, Dulcie thought, relieved that it was not Chad Kaufman whose help she would request in finding Adam. Edmund Revanche's other companion was Josiah Whinburn, a pale, lusterless man who seemed ill at ease. Neither could claim Edmund Revanche's charm or his concentrated interest in the people to whom he spoke. Both had had considerable to drink.

As Mrs. Meadows led her to another group, a Mrs. Downing said indignantly, "The Abolitionists are worse than ever, now that wet rag Mr. Lincoln has issued his Emancipation Proclamation. I notice he didn't free any slaves except those of Confederate citizens!"

"It's hard to believe that man was a Southerner by birth."

"A Kentucky mule, I've heard him called," said a mutton-chopped man.

"Let me tell you the latest," said Mrs. Downing." A blockade runner—calls himself the Black Swan—has been stealing people's servants by the *boatload* and bringing them into New York. In broad daylight!"

"He must have a secret harbor."

"I have *heard* he comes into Long Island."

"He wouldn't dare. The Yankees would have him in a second."

"Oh, but he has to be in league with them," said Mrs. Downing. "No sane man could be so bold and daring! They say he goes into Wilmington as regular as clockwork, and soon after, he's here in New York with the fugitives. I've heard this man cares *nothing* for his own life, that he risks *everything* to free those darkies! And friends, the worst is still to come. I have *heard* that the Black Swan is *himself a Southerner!*"

"A traitor!" gasped one woman.

"Ought to be lynched," the whiskered man agreed. "Who is he?"

Dulcie stood very still. They might have been describing Adam. Or Ben. Still, such recklessness did not fit either man.

Mrs. Downing whispered, and every head bent toward her. "No one knows his real name. His ship is called the *Black Swan* too."

Dulcie released held breath with a sob she covered with a cough.

"Cowardly traitor!" the muttonchopped man declared.

Another man said, "I hear that without the drugs, arms, and ammunition the Black Swan daringly brings to the South, General Lee's army would long ago have had to surrender."

Mrs. Downing said frigidly, "I don't believe we are talking of the same person, Mr. Bates."

"Did I hear someone mention the Black Swan?" asked Edmund. "Hardly any decent Southerner but would like to see him hanged."

"Oh, Mr. Revanche, do you know him?" Mrs. Downing fluted.

"Yes, dear lady, I know him. He is a low troublemaker. Even as a boy he was disrespectful. As a young man he ruined a business arrangement, and when he was challenged because of his interference, he refused that challenge! I was personal witness to that. The dastardly fellow hid behind the skirts of two women! As for stealing slaves, he ruined a very fine gentleman of my acquaintance. Yes, I know the Black Swan."

"Has he done you harm, Mr. Revanche?" Dulcie asked boldly.

"He has done *me* no harm, Madame. But such men are pernicious influences on Southern society, which is suffering cruel enough blows. But I will say no more, lest I have nothing left for my lecture." He bowed, smiled, and turned to his associates.

As a lecturer Revanche was superb. Using maps, Revanche showed the area still in Confederate hands. He demonstrated the curve of land that swung from Virginia to New Orleans, land Union forces had gained.

"They are trying to squeeze us out of our homes," he said. "They will force this line to the sea—unless we stop them. And, ladies and gentlemen, we can stop them." He shook his fist menacingly at the air, and his listeners cheered. "We can brighten the spirits of our loved ones still in the South. A small way, taking but moments of your time, a little paper, and ink. Letters, my friends! I am in a position to ensure that your letters will reach your families and friends.

"Those of you who would like to communicate with your loved ones will be interested to know that I am going to Wilmington shortly. If you will speak with me or my associates, we will arrange personal delivery of letters."

"What does Mr. Revanche do?" Dulcie whispered to Mrs. Downing.

"My dear, I thought everyone knew. He's a spy for the Confederacy."

"But appearin' in public like this—"

"He deals only with loyal Southerners! He is here to raise money for supplies. He has brought us beautiful letters from Confederate officers who have personally thanked him for his esteemed services. He is quite an important man, invited to the best homes. We trust him implicitly."

Several people flocked around Mr. Revanche. Dulcie waited until she could speak to him alone. She didn't want the other sympathetic, curious faces watching her, listening as she talked to him. As the group surrounding him dwindled, Dulcie stood close by.

Edmund, relaxed and at ease, smiled at her. "I am sorry you were the one to have been kept waiting, Mrs. Tremain."

Dulcie lowered her eyes. "Mr. Revanche, you say you'll be goin' to Wilmington. Would you carry a letter to my . . . late husband's mother? She lives in Smithville. That is thirty miles south."

Revanche's eyes were warm on her. "I know it well. The entire area is a smuggler's paradise, and as you know, the North is not the only side to be harassed by traitors."

"Then it wouldn't inconvenience you too much?"

"It would be my pleasure, even if you were not so lovely a woman."

Under his admiring glance, Dulcie blushed, which annoyed her, for it only showed that she was unaccustomed to civilized company. "I did not expect this—this service, so my letters are yet to be written. May I send them to you?"

"I could come by for them tomorrow afternoon. Or, if you prefer, send them by messenger to Mrs. Burris."

"I'll have the letters in Mrs. Burris's hands tomorrow morning."

His laughter was soft, private. "So, you'll deny me the pleasure of a visit with you."

"Oh, no, it isn't that. I am in your debt, Mr. Revanche. This means so much to me. I wouldn't dream of puttin' you out of your way!"

"Then by all means, Mrs. Tremain, we will arrange it as you wish. Now, dear lady, if I am not mistaken, there is more troubling your mind. Is there something else I could do for you?"

Dulcie hesitated only for a moment, then said, "Yes." She looked around. Many others stood nearby, watching, listening.

Edmund motioned with his eyes. "I believe the bay window would afford us some privacy, Mrs. Tremain."

Heads turned curiously as Edmund led her to the shelter of the heavily draped bay window, but Dulcie was determined not to let this one chance of finding Adam slip away because of a bunch of nosy-bodies. In a low voice she said, "I believe . . . I hope, Mr. Revanche, that my husband did not die at sea. He might have been cast ashore."

"My dear, I do not wish to discourage you, but the chances of a man—"

"I know. I've been told before, but please listen to me."

Edmund touched her arm, his smile sympathetic and encouraging.

"I—I was on the ship with my husband . . . and I survived. I was washed ashore. You see, I have reason for my hope. I am not merely indulging myself in wishful thinkin', am I?" Dulcie's golden eyes were full of appeal as she looked into Edmund's onyx bright ones.

"I can't answer Mrs. Tremain, but let me say I envy your husband. Your love and faith in him is something any man, even a hardened traveler like myself, would give his life to know. Rest assured, dear lady, that if there is any information to be gleaned, I shall ferret it out."

Dulcie couldn't hold back the tears. Embarrassed, she blinked, pretending there was something in her eye. Edmund placed his handkerchief into her hand. "Don't hide your tears from me. They do you credit. You have shown strength and courage in your undying search. After the sights of our war-ravaged South, it is a comfort to see a beautiful woman longing only for her man. For the most part I see hunger, despair, hatred. Love is far more refreshing."

Dulcie murmured her thanks, trying to regain control. Her eyes shone with gratitude. "How can I thank you, Mr. Revanche? Not only are you the only person who has offered to help, but you understand. I think . . . there must be someone you love very much."

Edmund looked out the window, his fine profile to her, "There was. My wife. But she died a long time ago. Since then "—he turned to look fully at Dulcie—"there has been no one to compare with her."

Dulcie's hand rested lightly on his arm. "I—I understand that."

"I am sure you do, Mrs. Tremain." Edmund frowned slightly, his face contorting into worry. "But there is one thing."

"Yes?"

"Of course, I hope only for the best news. But there is no telling what I'll find. He may be dead. Or it may be something else."

"I want to know. I must know. Please promise me that whatever you find out you will tell me."

"It may not be pleasant."

"But it may be! It may be the very thing I've hoped for."

"I would never withhold that from you, Mrs. Tremain. It is the other sort of news that I fear. I would rather tear the tongue from my head than have it bear ill tidings to you."

"You are a kind man, Mr. Revanche, but I am much stronger than I look. I have lived through many experiences I didn't think I could. The hardest thing I have ever borne is not knowin' if Adam is alive. Whatever your news, I want to be told."

Chapter Nine

Edmund Revanche traveled south in comparative luxury because he had Northern trains and passes available to him. Chad Kaufman, blond and Nordic, expanded under preferential treatment, his expression haughty as he sat across from Edmund. Both men were impeccably dressed. Edmund, as usual, was clothed in black, the severe tailoring accentuating the hard, long lines of his body, his aristocratic paleness, his proud inbred delicacy. Chad, though he emulated Edmund in other ways, dressed as a dandy. His compact, pampered body was swathed in a silk shirt and pastel brocaded waistcoat, topped by a fur-trimmed mauve frock coat.

Watching them with an inner revulsion was Josiah Whinburn. Ever since he had become indebted to Edmund Revanche in a brag game eleven years ago, Josiah had become increasingly, inexorably dependent on Edmund's hard, cruel strength. Tom Pierson had tried to save him once by lending him twenty-five thousand dollars to keep Marsh House from being sold. He might have succeeded in turning his back on gambling and drink if only Tom had remained in New Orleans.

But Tom had left New Orleans. And Josiah had never been strong enough to run Marsh House on his own. It had only been a matter of time before Josiah had become a slave to Edmund's bidding.

Only once had Josiah gotten the better of Edmund, and he had paid dearly for that piece of rebellious independence. Edmund had coveted Marsh House. But Josiah, after holding it for years at a great loss, had sold it to Webster Tilden in 1860. Through the years Edmund had reminded Josiah repeatedly of his ungrateful, spiteful act.

Edmund had made Josiah pay by hours of humiliation, by performance of tasks odious and menial. Edmund controlled Josiah's life.

Though Edmund had not indicated that this trip was different from others, Josiah looked at his smug expression and knew it was. Edmund's dark eyes burned with an inner glow. The harsh linear mouth twitched in private amusement.

"Why'd you tell Mrs. Tremain we'd deliver her letters?" Josiah's tongue was thick with too much liquor, his words running together. "We're not goin' to Charleston, and Smithville is out of the way. We head inland from Wilmington."

Edmund looked at Josiah down the length of his nose. "Would you have me disappoint the lady, Josiah?"

"You've disappointed others."

"Oh. Have I? But perhaps I view this particular young woman differently. Perhaps she has touched my heart."

Chad smiled. "Ah, love. It seems capable of humbling the mightiest."

Edmund sneered at him. "You can be such an abominable fool, Chad. Here, dispose of this." He handed him Dulcie's letter to Zoe. The letter to Ben he tucked into his breast pocket. "The young lady can be told we went to great lengths. This letter was undeliverable."

"Why tell her anything?" Chad imitated Edmund's pedantic inflection.

"Because I choose to. Keep your mind on things you understand. Which reminds me, devise a more clever code. We need details of Lee's plans this next month and a map of the supply routes between Wilmington and Lee's army. Should we be stopped by a Confederate with even minimal intelligence, he could decipher your code."

Chad smoothed his waistcoat and performed a small ritual with the ends of his moustache. "I—I beg your pardon. I'll change the code, of course, but we've had no difficulty. No one has questioned us."

"Of course not, you idiot. We're known as Confederate agents. But in case your powers of observation have failed entirely, I shall remind you the complexion of the war is changing. The great Southern cause is badly bruised. Our compatriots may not be so trusting and naïve as in the past. You might also keep in mind, Chad, that since the value of Confederate currency is near nothing, the information we have been bringing them is also worth nothing. Confusion has been our ally, but I would expect one of these days someone will note that agents Revanche, Kaufman, and Whinburn are somewhat less than adept."

"So why're we makin' the trip at all?" Joseph slurred. "We turned complete traitor? Bad enough we been sellin' secrets on both sides. Now we jes' gonna help the Yankees destroy our lan's an' people?"

"Perhaps it would ease your conscience to join one of our fine Confederate fighting units, Josiah."

"Would. Would, by God. Least I could die like an honorable Southerner. Least I wouldn't be bitin' the hand o' my own people. Least I wouldn't be foolin' some pore l'il widow, makin' her think I was goin' to fin' her los' husban' fo' her."

"Ah, Josiah, you wound me. How could you think me so heartless? I intend to bring definitive information of the missing Captain Tremain to his widow. I shall ascertain when and how her stalwart husband died. I shall also make certain his widow happily recovers from her sorrows."

"E'mun', what you gonna do? Why don't you let tha' pore li'l lady alone?" Josiah whined. "You don' know nothin' 'bout her husband. Let her be."

"You're mistaken, Josiah. I know her husband quite well. If my information is correct, Captain Tremain should be in Smithville any day now."

Adam docked at Wilmington and left the discharge of cargo in Rosebud's capable hands. By early morning he was in bed in Zoe's house. It had been a sleepless, harrowing run. The blockade around the Cape Fear was formidable, with the Yankees increasingly eager to capture the invaluable supplies being carried by the blockade runners. Without Colonel Lamb's tireless vigilance at Fort Fisher, the odds against the unarmed blockade runners would have been insurmountable.

There was no longer any such thing as an easy run. The main mast and bunkers of the Black Swan had received heavy damage, yet Adam considered himself lucky. The carpenter had cut away the spar and made temporary repairs, but before he could leave port, major repairs would have to be made.

Adam yawned, his body aching. Disquiet remained with him. The edginess was becoming a constant part of his life. Except in Nassau, he never felt safe. The nagging feeling of something amiss dogged him—something overlooked, some danger ignored, something lurking just around the next turn, the next mile of open ocean, the next run. Something was there, just waiting for him to make a mistake.

He tossed in bed, punching at his pillow. "You're beginning to jump at shadows," he muttered into the gloomy dawn light. He sank back to stare at the ceiling, relentlessly retracing each mile of the last voyage, until, exhausted, he fell into a fitful sleep.

He was groggy when he awakened. He went searching for food and Zoe.

"I have to take advantage of every moment Mammy and Claudine aren't around, or I'd not be allowed in my own kitchen." She laughed. "Sit down like you used to at the kitchen table, and I'll fix something."

"Where is everyone? Ma, did you tell Angela?"

"I gave you my word, dear. But don't take her to the swamp today. We'll have this evening at home. I've baked pies, and there'll be an extra for Tom."

"Ma, I told you I was taking her first thing. There's no use in putting it off."

"Adam, I'm not weakening. Honestly. Angela needed some things, and I sent her shopping with Mammy and Claudine. Anyway, Tom won't be at his cabin until tomorrow. Someone has been attacking the saltworks of the swamp people, and Tom has gone to help."

"Who'd attack the swamp salt camps? Yankees wouldn't bother. The swamp folks don't have works big enough to be worth their while."

"Tom says whoever it is has a grudge against you. The work has been attributed to the Black Swan."

Adam shook his head. "Probably some local who sees a good little salt camp and wants it for himself."

"Well, it's a good thing it was Seth's and Johnnie Mae's people, or they might have believed those rumors. They're saying the Black Swan has turned traitor and is being paid to disrupt salt production. Oh, Adam, I wish you'd be more cautious. Why can't you—why does everybody have to know about you, dear? Couldn't you be more secretive about your—your work?"

"Nobody'll believe those stories, Ma. I wasn't even here

when the attacks happened. My comings and goings are easily noted."

"All of them?" Zoe asked, eyebrows raised.

"Enough of them," Adam said sheepishly.

"That is exactly what I meant! Why can't you be more cautious? O, fie! I don't know why I waste my breath. You'll do as you please anyway, but we are having supper together tonight. In that I'll have *my* way."

"So Angela gets a reprieve. But a short one."

Angela was sullen as she sat on the wagon waiting for Adam and Zoe to stop arguing over how many supplies would go with Angela into the swamp. Three times Claudine had patiently taken off and put on packages as the argument shifted first one way then another.

"I'm taking her to Tom's cabin, Ma! She won't need all this stuff."

"Humor me, dear. A woman doesn't stop being a woman just because she's not in a town. I wouldn't feel right sending Angela off without—"

Adam threw his hands into the air. Claudine giggled and drew his frustration on her. "Shut up!"

"Adam!" Zoe gasped.

"Not you, Ma. Christ! Deliver me from women," he muttered. "I'm sorry, Ma. Put your packages on." He kissed her, helped Claudine onto the back of the wagon, then took his own seat next to Angela.

"I won't stay with Tom," Angela said savagely. "I'll run away."

"You can do anything you damned well please, but sit still and shut up!"

"You don't care about anyone! You're mean and rotten, Adam Tremain!"

They traveled by wagon as long as the log roads through the swamp were passable. The scent of open fires was heavy as they passed several small saltworks. Rough-looking men, armed and wary, guarded the perimeters of the salt camps, eyeing Adam and the two women suspiciously.

A few miles from Tom's cabin the roads were mere rutted, spongy paths. Adam reined in the horses and leaped down to search in the thick brush near one of the swamp water channels. The last miles would be traveled by flatboat.

Settled in the boat, Angela gazed up at him with eyes that implored him not to shut her away from everything she knew and liked, and Claudine's dark eyes accused him of forcing her to go somewhere she didn't want to go, to serve someone she didn't want to serve. He hadn't a moment's peace of mind.

When they arrived at the cabin, they found it empty. Tom and Seth's men had not returned from searching for the men who had disrupted the saltworks. Gruffly Adam ordered Claudine to fix them something to eat and Angela to help unload her things from the boat.

"It's awful here," Angela pouted.

"It's your home."

"It's not my home! It's Tom's."

"Look, I'm tired of arguing with you."

Angela dropped the small bag she carried and ran to him. "Adam, I'll be good. I'll do whatever Aunt Zoe wants. Please! I promise."

He patted her awkwardly. "You're better off here. Give yourself a chance, Angela. You'll like the swamp."

"Never!" she moaned.

"You've just forgotten. Remember the house on the bayou? the flowers? Your mama was always worried you'd pick up a snake because you loved the pretty colors."

"You're not angry with me anymore, are you?" Teary eyes gazed hopefully into his.

"I can never stay angry with you. You're still my first girl."

"I wish you meant that."

"I do, but—"

She sighed gustily. "I know. Your sister."

Claudine produced a good fish muddle for supper. "When Mastah Tom gwine get heah?" Her eyes darted to the window where close-growing vines and branches rubbed, made eerie rustlings. "How long we got to stay heah?"

"I have to stay here forever," Angela said dramatically.

"Well, Ah doan."

"Go on to bed, Claudine. If Tom were coming tonight, he'd have been here already. He's probably holed up at Seth's or Winnabow's place."

"Wheah Ah'm gwine sleep? Ah ain't gwine out to dat big ol' cabin by mahseff." Claudine shivered, glancing at the fugitives barracks.

"You and Angela sleep here in the house. I'll sleep out there."

"You gwine leave us alone in here!"

"Nothing's going to get you, Claudine."

"But dey's *things* out dere. Ah kin heah 'em tippy-toein' 'roun' an' scratchin' at de winders."

"Just branches."

Adam waited until there was quiet in Angela's room, silence from the loft where Claudine slept. Then he went across the yard to the slave building, weary from his sleepless nights and the long journey. He stripped off his shirt and boots and fell into the first bunk. Within minutes he was sound asleep.

He dreamed. Disturbing dreams, making him shift on the bed, restless and trapped. His arms, thrust over his head, began to prickle. He grew still, his eyes opening slowly to bright sunlight and complete awareness.

"Don't struggle, Captain Tremain. You will find Chad has done an excellent job of securing your hands and feet to the bed. For a man accustomed to attack you have a remarkable faculty for deep sleep."

Adam tested the rope on his wrists. It was secure. He strained, raising his head. A disheveled, sorrowful man slouched in the door. Another, muscular well-dressed blond man stood at the window, his back to Adam. And Edmund Revanche sat, relaxed and urbane, chatting with him.

"What do you want, Revanche?"

"Oh, now, Captain! Surely, you can surmise what I want. Once you challenged me. Remember? Yes, I thought you might. Perhaps, then, you will also recall another meeting. At Gray Oaks. I see you do. That is commendable. There was also an earlier occasion. Three times you interfered in my life, Captain Tremain, and three times you disrupted it badly. You deprived me of my livelihood as well. I cared a great deal for Gray Oaks. I spent years making it a showplace any man would envy. Don't you agree I owe you something? It is only fair that I should have my way with you. Once. Just once."

Adam remained silent. He wouldn't give Edmund the satisfaction of hearing him ask what he intended. Let the man enjoy his moment. Let him talk in his quiet, cold, sophisticated manner. Tom and Seth and the others would return. Time was on his side, and Edmund did enjoy talking. He liked seeing the effect of his power.

Edmund smiled as he watched Adam's face. "No one will come." He played with a piece of rope, methodically twisting the splayed end. "Men will do nearly anything for money—gold, Captain. I have hired five ruffians to go from one salt camp to another creating havoc in your name. It is an odd thing—people love a hero, but they love better to find he has feet of clay. Given sufficient evidence, they are eager to believe the vilest of rumors. At the moment your friends think they're chasing the Black Swan. Quite a hero until he turned bad for the sake of filthy lucre. I hear the Yankees got to him. They say he's being paid fabulous sums for each saltworks he closes. Some even claim he's been promised a political post in Lincoln's government."

"No one will believe that. Certainly not the swamp people."

"No? You think my men are not adept enough to make it believable? Perhaps not. But it won't matter to you, Captain." Edmund smiled again. His fingers formed a steeple against his lips. He looked up at Chad. "The Captain and I have chatted long enough. Take him outside, Chad, and be careful. Captain Tremain has a reputation as a brawler. Do whatever you must, short of killing him."

Chad, his eyes cold blue and expressionless in his florid, broad-planed face, examined Adam impersonally. He flexed his heavy shoulders, straining beneath his frock coat, as he carefully fitted his kid gloves to his hands. From his pocket he drew a knife, snapping the blade open. He sliced through the rope at the top of the bed.

Adam clenched and relaxed his numb fingers to get the blood circulating. Chad cut the rope at his feet. Adam's feet were still hobbled, and his hands bound together, but he was free of the bed.

"Get up, Captain. Move slowly, please. I should not like to mess my beautiful coat by having to punish you for foolhardy disobedience."

Adam eyed him warily, then glanced at the pale, sweating man by the door. Adam drew his legs up, kicking at Chad's stomach. The man reeled back against the other bunks. He crashed to the floor.

Adam was on his feet, hopping and staggering against the hobble on his ankles. As he had guessed, the other man made no move to stop him. He pressed against the wall, giving Adam room to get out the door.

Edmund watched, amused as Adam awkwardly leaped and hopped toward the swamp. "The man has the instincts of a moth near flame." Edmund put out his hand to prevent Chad from racing after him. "Barefoot, he couldn't survive an hour. Perhaps we should let the snakes perform our task for us. But no. We'd not have the pleasure of watching. Give him a few moments to enjoy his freedom, Chad."

"W-why we gonna do this, E'mun'? C-can't we jes' let 'im go?" Josiah stammered.

"Bring him back now, Chad."

Chad, his anger turned cold and hard, sauntered to the horses and took from his mount the bullwhip Edmund insisted they carry wherever they went. He glanced at the soft earth, noting the direction Adam had taken. He felt no need to hurry.

Adam didn't dare stop to untie himself. He thought only of putting distance between himself and Revanche. He didn't see or hear Chad step quietly onto the path behind him. With the first curl of the bullwhip, Chad wrapped the eighteen-foot black coil around Adam's waist, jerking back, bringing Adam down hard and flat on his back.

"You disappoint me, Captain. You were hardly any sport at all. Edmund led me to expect far more pleasure from you."

Adam groaned, shaking his head groggily as he struggled to regain his breath. Above him loomed Chad's broad, unfeeling face. Deftly he released the whip from Adam's midriff and began delicately flicking the tip down his naked torso, each painful bite drawing blood. "Get up, Captain. This time perhaps you'll be wise enough to obey me."

Adam didn't move. "Carry me if you want me."

"Stubbornness is foolish. It can gain you nothing." Chad took several paces backward, uncoiling the whip to its full length. The black coil sliced through the air, whistling before it bit into Adam's neck and chest. Before he could catch his breath, the whip clawed down again, slicing the trousers from his leg. Adam cried out as the whip bit again. He rolled to his stomach. The whip flayed across his back and buttocks. Chad kept the rhythm mercilessly regular and quick.

Adam's bound hands clawed the earth. "Stop! For the love of God—"

"Crawl, Captain! Crawl!"

Adam writhed on the ground as Chad worked up a sweat and rage that lent greater power to his arm. Agonized cries ripped from Adam's throat as he obeyed. Inch by painful writhing inch, he dragged himself along the spongy earth, away from the whip, back into the clearing and Edmund Revanche.

"Enough, Chad! Leave something for our beauties." Edmund looked around the area. "Tie him to that sapling. Josiah, bring the beehive."

Claudine and Angela knelt on the bed, peering out the window. Claudine wild with fright, stared at Adam's bloodied body.

"Who are they? What do they want?" Angela clung to Claudine.

Claudine began to tremble, her eyes showing white, her teeth clamped together. She pulled away.

"Claudine! What are you doing?" Angela wrapped her arms around the small black girl. "No! No, you can't go out there! I won't let you. They'll see us! They'll know we're here!"

"Leggo o' me! Ah's gwine he'p him!"

"Let him take care of himself! You know what they'll do to us! Listen to me, Claudine. Listen! Adam was going to leave us alone. He ran away, into the swamp. He didn't care about us—"

"Lemme go! Ah doan care what he done. Dey's hurtin' him!"

Josiah placed a large box hive and a package of clothing near Edmund, Sweat poured down his face and body, staining his olive green frock coat black under the arms. "We don' have—have to do this. We done enough, E'mun'. please, please, for God's sake, please!"

Edmund donned the beekeeper's suit over his black clothing. On his head he placed a hood with a black tulle veil.

Adam watched in horror as the three men rapidly became unrecognizable. He struggled uselessly against his bonds, but fear was now coursing through him, and common sense gone. Nearly paralyzed, he watched Edmund Revanche calmly don a mask as he had done years before in preparation for committing murder.

Adam choked, gagging as he strained against the leather strap Chad had affixed around his neck and the sapling.

Around his waist was another strap. His legs were bound with rope. His arms were free, but his hands were tied together in front of him.

Of the three, only Josiah had not yet donned the long, heavy drill canvas bee gloves. Reluctantly, his eyes darting nervously from Adam to Revanche, Josiah picked up a small pail and paintbrush and began to daub sugarcane liquor on Adam's body. The sticky sweet substance mingled and coagulated with the blood that oozed from the lacerations of the whip.

"I'm sorry . . . sorry. Don't want . . ." Tears streamed down Josiah's face under the black tulle, the back of his hand frequently sliding under the mask to smear across his nose. He blubbered excuses as he continued to coat Adam with the liquor that would attract the bees. "God forgive. I didn't want to. So sorry . . . sorry."

Josiah dropped the empty pail and scurried back to Edmund, still sobbing. He pulled on the heavy gloves and stood by Chad waiting for Edmund to loose the bees.

Edmund's face was all but obscured by the heavy veiling. "Put your hands out in front of you, Captain Tremain."

Adam looked at him, his jaw clenched tight in a futile attempt to still his fear.

"Come now, Captain. I'm only going to free your hands." Edmund pulled Adam's hands forward, then sliced through the rope. Immediately Adam grasped the leather thongs tied around his neck, trying to free himself.

Edmund shrugged. "I dislike taking undue advantage of you, so I shall give you some valuable advice. Bees do not like motion. Don't swat at them or try to fend them off. Test your mettle, Captain Tremain. Stay calm and motionless. Allow them to crawl over you. They will sting only in defense of their hive or themselves. One sting and they die, so they sting only when necessary." Edmund bowed mockingly.

Sweating, his fingers numb and trembling, Adam picked at his thongs.

The beehive had been sealed for the two days that Edmund had been traveling. That alone was enough to excite the bees. Leisurely, Edmund poked about the clearing until he spotted Tom's ax. He moved the hive to within fifteen feet of Adam. He picked up the ax, delicately testing its balance. Lightly he struck the hive. A humming arose, fearsome, belligerent, menacing.

Edmund waited, veiled head turned to the other masked figures, one standing in expectant stillness, the other fidgeting uneasily. "I shouldn't try to run, Josiah," he warned. "After all you might be our next victim."

Josiah's voice was a whimper. "No . . . oh, please. Jes' git it over—"

Edmund smiled into Adam's terrified face. "Josiah is such a coward," he said regretfully. With the butt of the ax he knocked sharply on the hive. The humming increased. "But I'm sure you can set him an unparalleled example of courage. Can't you, Captain?"

Adam, his jaws clenching, glared at Edmund. But his gaze fell to the box with its angry voice as Edmund took a workmanlike hold on the ax and began slowly to chip at the hive.

Tap. Tap, Bits of wood flew. The axe took on a life of its own, raging and vengeful, the strokes more forceful until the hive splintered.

A dark ribbon of angry buzzing bees streamed endlessly from the damaged hive, spiraling up to blacken the bright blue of the sky and then curling into a descent. Edmund was motionless as the bees streamed toward him, toward Chad and Josiah. Josiah, panicking as the bees covered his protective clothing, ran screaming in ragged circles.

Adam stood bound against the sapling, his hands pressed tightly against his face. In seconds he felt the first bees light. Their bodies swarmed over his skin, the touch of their feet ghostly. Their buzzing, vibrating, trembling sounds were everywhere. Sweat poured from him and ran down his body to mix with the sticky cane juice.

A bee stung his lip. Then another stung his neck, his ear, his shoulder. The scent of the stings left behind excited the other bees. The signal went through them.

He was stung in several places at once, each sting a separate pain, each pain demanding attention. Adam lost count, lost knowledge. The stings and the pain were everywhere. They were in his ears, inside his trousers. The milling, crawling, stinging insects covered his belly. The brown-striped bodies moved and buzzed over his face, his head, his back.

Unable to remain still, he screamed as the pain became agony. Involuntarily he began to flail. In spite of himself, he clawed at the bees. Yet they came on, thicker than before. One would sting and fall away, to be replaced by two others until he knew nothing but pain. The maddened insects crept into his nostrils. Already his eyes were sealed shut. He screamed hoarsely, and in closing his mouth his teeth squashed the buzzing demons. He dug at himself, no longer aware of the bees, only wanting to destroy his own agonized flesh. His hands crushed the bees, driving them against him.

Claudine burst from the cabin, a long butcher knife in her hand. The bees came, swarming around her, darting in angrily to sting her. Claudine ran for Adam, shrieking and slapping bees clinging to her. Adam, still screaming in horror, was concealed by the insanely buzzing, moving mass.

She swept at the front of him, wiping clear long patches that were covered again immediately. She sawed at the thong that held his head fast to the sapling. She screamed, shivering and crying as the pain of the stings crescendoed, wrapping her in mindless agony. But she kept on, her fingers cut and bleeding where she slashed herself with the knife as she hacked through the leather straps.

As the strap around his neck gave way, Adam curled forward, his and Claudine's voices agonized whines. She finally severed the strap holding his waist, and he slumped to the ground, his ankles still bound to the tree. Claudine wiped frantically, trying to get the bees off him. Her sight and strength failing, she flung herself on him, protecting him with her own body.

In another part of the swamp Tom Pierson swore. "Seth, where in hell did those bastards get to? I thought sure we had 'em treed."

"Mebbe so, but we ain't got 'em treed now."

"What's the fun in tearin' up little piddly-assed salt-works? We got a bunch o' amateurs that don't have the guts to smash up somethin' big?"

"Ah, ye be squanderin' yere substance," a husky female voice declared. "Oi'll be a-leavin' ye."

"Would it be too big a favor to go by the cabin, Johnnie Mae? Adam ought to be there by now. Tell him I won't make it 'til dark."

Johnnie Mae smiled. It had been a long time since she'd pleasured her eyes on Adam. "Aye. Oi'll that." She shoved off, poling her flatboat with casual expertise.

As she neared Tom's property, the birds were excited,

flying up, cawing, calling. Johnnie Mae reached for her
shotgun. She checked its load, her eyes squinting and keen,
searching the wild swamp growth. She heard hoarse screaming. A man's voice. A woman's. Drawing nearer, she heard
the angry mumbling of the bees. Single bees darted toward
her, lit, and stung.

She moored the boat and grabbed a limb of dry brush
pine. She struck one of the precious sulphur matches Adam
always brought back for her on his runs, and made a torch.
Shotgun in one hand, in the other the smoke torch, she
came from behind Tom's cabin. Three men were riding
down the path toward town. Johnnie Mae balanced the
shotgun against her bony hip and fired. She didn't bother
to look to see if she had hit anyone at that distance. Her
attention jerked to the two figures, who looked more like
bee-swarmed logs than humans.

She gathered dry pine and moist leaves, building a ring
around the sapling and the two people. She set it afire,
watching it blaze up, then begin to smoulder as the moist
leaves dampened the flare of dry pine. Thick clouds of
smoke went up. She lit another torch and ran the fire
across the bodies, burning bees the smoke was not pacify-
ing. The air was thick with heavy, acrid smoke. The bees
began to calm, retreating to their damaged hive. Those that
remained Johnnie Mae killed.

Choking, her eyes streaming, Johnnie Mae freed the
man's legs, then dragged the woman from him. Adam was
barely recognizable, a bloodied, swollen mass of angry
red flesh, covered with brown stingers.

Johnnie Mae's thin, workworn hands touched him tentatively. "Dereling," she gasped. "It canna be. Dereling,
dereling, ye canna be dead. Ye canna be."

She leaned over him. Finding a pulse, she fled along the
swamp path. In minutes she reappeared, poling her flat
swampcraft. She struggled with Adam's weight, dragging
him unconscious to the boat. "Oi'll git ye there," she muttered, straining with him. "Oi'll git ye home. Oi toted ye
once to t'loft when ye was nowt but a boy, dereling, when
we was young. Oi'll tote ye now. Oi'll not let ye die. Not
yere Eve. Yere Eve'll keep ye safe. Oi'll not let ye die."

As Johnnie Mae panted and muttered to herself, struggling to get Adam onto the rocking boat, Angela snuck
from the cabin. "Help me. Please, help me. Take me away
before they come back."

Johnnie Mae straightened up, startled. "Who be ye?"

"I'm Angela Pierson—Tom's daughter. You must help me! You can't do anything for him now!"

Johnnie Mae, her pale eyes blazing, spat at Angela. Her attention swerved back to Adam. She'd seen venomous bites before, and she'd seen shock. She knew a man could die from a single sting of a bee, or he could survive over a hundred. The Lord decided. Adam was still alive. She counted on his size and strength, if only she could keep him unconscious so he wouldn't attempt to kill himself because of the pain. She'd seen that happen too, aye.

She packed Adam in mud, then raised his feet higher than his head. "Oi be takin' him home. Effen ye be a-comin', fetch the woman."

"I can't . . . the bees—"

Johnnie Mae shrugged. "Fetch her, or ye kin swim home, girl. Oi got no need fer ye."

Angela ran to Claudine. Gingerly, loathing to touch her, she dragged Claudine to the boat. Johnnie Mae's hard eyes drilled into Angela. "Ye be nowt but a bitch."

Johnnie Mae got Claudine aboard. Angela watched the thin, spent hag place Claudine at the far end away from Adam. Then Angela reached out for Johnnie Mae to help her aboard.

Mirthlessly Johnnie Mae laughed, her mouth gaping in a toothless grimace. Her long sinewy body leaned on the pole. Slowly the boat began to move.

"Wait! You can't leave me! I did as you asked! Oh, don't leave mè—please!" Angela hesitated, still expecting Johnnie Mae to soften.

The swamp woman leaned harder, moving the heavily loaded flatboat. "Ye feckless maumet! Ye didna he'p him, an' ye coulda!"

Angela leaped, barking her shins as one leg went into the water. She clung to the boat. The flatboat dipped into the black water, then righted. Angela, soaked, huddled on the bottom, panting and whimpering.

Johnnie Mae's mouth worked grimly as she shoved the pole into the mud and withdrew it. "Stop yere caterwaulin'! Put water an' mud on them two. Keep 'em cooled down."

"I can't! The snakes . . . my hands—"

Johnnie Mae thrust the pole at Angela, stopping just short of sweeping her overboard. "Ye will! Else Oi'll make 'gator bait o' ye, an' smile fer the chanst! Ye'll do what must be done! Moi dereling willna die!"

Johnnie Mae's lean, hard body moved in relentless rhythm, guiding them tirelessly through the swamp toward Smithville. She had never been farther than the edge of the swamp. Towns terrified her. And still she poled on.

Adam awakened screaming, his hands digging and gouging at his head and eyes. His face was an indescribable mass of swollen pulp. He ripped at himself, crying out in agony. Johnnie Mae squinted against what she must do. She struck him on the head with the short oar once, then again. "Ye'll not die, Adam Tremain, ye'll not die by yere own hands or by theirn. Yere Eve'll git ye home."

"What was that, a love tap?" Angela asked sarcastically.

"Oi'll give ye the same, only better, ye useless slut! An' dinna be temptin' me, fer it'd be the one pleasure o' this day!"

Johnnie Mae ignored Angela then, seeing only that she kept renewing the cool water and mud on the two swollen forms. As she poled without rest or pause down the swamp channels, she talked as if to herself. "P'loike ye be a big ol' bear, Adam. Play like Oi be a foine lovely loidy. Play wie me, Adam, Oi be yere Eve. There be a stane to mark our passing. There be a tryst stane fer the man an' his Eve. There be a bond no man kin break. Oi'll take ye home, dereling, Oi'll take ye home."

Twice more on the way to Smithville she knocked him out to keep him from killing himself with the pain. It was dark when Johnnie Mae's little flatboat rocked in the stronger current of the Cape Fear River.

"Ye'll go to his cabin, an' bring his ma wie a horse an' wagon."

Angela nodded and began to get from the boat. Johnnie Mae's hand clenched her wrist in a painful grip. Her eyes burned into Angela's. "Oi be but the sow to the rutting boar, but fer this man. Ye'll bring me the wagon, girl. Ye'll bring it swift an' true, or on the blood o' moi love, Oi'll kill ye."

"I will—I will—I'll bring Aunt Zoe! I promise! And the wagon—I'll bring them!" Angela's voice rose to a high, hysterical whine.

"See ye do it, girl. Oi make no idle threats."

Angela ran up the sandy path, her skirts flying. Hysterical, Angela pounded on the door. Zoe, wrapped in her nightrobe, opened it but a crack.

"Let me in! Johnnie Mae—! She's going to kill me!"

"Where is Adam?" Zoe shouted. She grabbed Angela's arms and shook her until her teeth chattered. "Tell—me—where is he!"

Johnnie Mae dipped her hand into the cool water, constantly bathing Adam's fevered flesh. "Oncet ye tol' me, dereling, there was more to a man's love than Oi knew, an Oi tol' ye there be'n't. Oi tol ye we be like the rain seed, our freshet let an' gone wie the mawnin' gloam. It be'n't true, Adam Tremain. It be'n't true. The rain seed be wie us always. The lovin' comes agin an' agin. Ye canna die now, dereling. Oi be wie ye, a-watchin' fer ye, a-keepin' ye, an' lovin' ye."

Chapter Ten

Zoe shook the information from Angela, then left her sobbing on the stoop. Zoe raced to the stables still in her nightclothes.

"Rosebud! Rosebud! Wake up!"

Rosebud sleepily rubbed his eyes with ham-sized fists. Zoe dashed from the stalls to the tack room. "Rosebud, Adam needs you. There's been trouble."

Rosebud clambered from the loft and began to hitch the carriage.

"No, no, the wagon. Johnnie Mae said a wagon."

"What you needs a wagon fo'? What de boss got into?"

Zoe repeated the disjointed story Angela had told her.

"Ah git de boss, Miz Zoe. You gits ready fo' him. Wheah Miss Angela? She gotta show me wheah de boss is."

Angela was loaded into the wagon, screaming that she couldn't go back.

"You gwine take me to de boss," Rosebud said, his jaw jutting out. "Which way Ah goes?"

Johnnie Mae's suspicion quickly turned to approval as Rosebud carefully lifted Adam and Claudine into the wagon bed. Johnnie Mae told him what had happened.

Zoe and Mammy crowded in the doorway watching their slow progress, Johnnie Mae burdened with Claudine, and Rosebud carrying Adam. Zoe clapped her hands over her mouth and swallowed, pressing back sick bile as Rosebud brought the hideous distortion of her son past her.

"Lawd, Lawd," said Mammy, shaking her head. Then she gave brisk orders. Adam was laid on his bed. A cot was brought for Claudine.

Johnnie Mae remained silent and watchful. Then, shoving Mammy aside, she moved her hands over Adam quickly. She placed her ear to his chest, her body taut and listening. His chest seemed to curve inward, his face was ashen and slick with sweat, his breathing making a loud sucking noise.

Mammy lumbered forward. Together they pried his mouth open. His tongue was swollen, almost blocking the air passage.

"Bring col' watuh, soder, an' all de rags we gots." Mammy's eyes never left Adam as Johnnie Mae's strong, bony fingers mercilessly depressed his tongue until the bluish cast left his lips.

"Rub his wrists," Zoe cried. "Here, let me help."

Johnnie Mae's hand shot out. "Don't ye rub nothin'. Ye be forcin' t' pizen through him the faster. Fetch me yere skinnin' knife."

Zoe stared in disbelief. "Poison? What poison? What are you going to do?"

"Do whut she says, Miz Zoe. We gots to git de stingers outer him."

Johnnie Mae quickly scraped the brown lancets from Adam's flesh. Mammy directed Rosebud to shift Adam's body so that Johnnie Mae could work without stop.

Zoe stood back helplessly watching this strange trio work on her son. Rosebud McAllister, Mammy, and Johnnie Mae were all that stood between Adam and death. Zoe's hands automatically folded in prayer.

Johnnie Mae looked at Zoe as she worked on Adam's leg. "He willna die."

"No, ma'am!" Rosebud asserted stoutly. "De boss gwine make it!"

"He sho' will," Mammy declared. "Ain't nobuddy dyin' roun' heah."

Johnnie Mae made a sour face at Mammy, her head

cocked toward Claudine. "T" wee 'un's a-gonna. The pizen be too strong fer 'er."

Rosebud shifted uneasily, his eyes filling as he looked at the cot.

Mammy scowled. "Miz Zoe, you pack 'im in dese col' rags. Git dat swellin' down, you heah? We gots to ten' to Claudine." She grabbed Johnnie Mae's arm and steered her to the cot.

Zoe nodded, feeling strangely calmed by these people whose love for Adam permeated the room. She packed the cold cloths against Adam's skin, having to replace them nearly as fast as she could get them on him.

With Rosebud helping, Johnnie Mae worked on Claudine's small body, scraping off stingers. "She ain't never wakened," Johnnie Mae said quietly. Claudine's face was gray, her lips purple. Mammy tried forcing life into the girl, willing her to keep breathing.

All of them stared as Zoe screamed. "He's strangling!"

Johnnie, Mammy, and Rosebud all rushed to the bed. Zoe leaped aside as they forced his head back, his mouth open, pressing against his tongue, letting the vomit out. Still, he didn't breathe; his pulse was ragged, and his heartbeat wildly irregular. Johnnie Mae forced her breath into his lungs, and Mammy forced it out. Then the hoarse whistling noise filled the room again as Adam gasped for breath on his own. For hours they rushed from the crisis on the bed to the crisis on the cot.

The moon was high before all the stingers were removed and Adam and Claudine were packed from head to foot in cold packs soaked in laudanum.

Mammy and Johnnie Mae talked in hushed tones, their eyes shifting from one bed to the other. Claudine lay still as death, her small frame bloated in an ugly, shapeless mass. To Johnnie Mae's mind there was no help for her, but Claudine had earned her loyalty. She had helped Adam, and for that Johnnie Mae worked tirelessly.

Adam moaned, just below the threshold of wakefulness. With regularity his body tensed as pain gripped his abdomen, then the dangerous vomit would come, threatening to choke him or back up into his lungs. As the night passed, their hope held only because Adam continued to struggle.

As first light came to the sky, Adam's periods of agonized

consciousness became more frequent. He would wake up
with shuddering yells, turning his grossly swollen head on
the pillow, frantically clawing his puffed eyelids, jerking
and whirling from one side to the other. Cold cloths flew
in every direction as Johnnie Mae and Mammy tried to
hold him down.

Unable to see or hear, imprisoned in his private hell of
unendurable, unending pain, Adam's whole remaining
strength was concentrated on escape. Drunkenly he rolled
from his bed, eluding the grasping hands. His arms whirled
like windmills, fighting off the swarming bees. Even with
his eyes swelled shut he knew where escape was. He
plunged for the window.

Rosebud shoved between Zoe and Johnnie Mae to fling
his considerable weight at Adam, bringing them both to
the floor with a bone-shaking thud. Cunning and determined as a madman, Adam fought, screaming and choking, trying to free himself from Rosebud's strong grip.
His words were unintelligible; the pleadings of a soul to
be delivered from its agony.

Suddenly Adam gasped for breath. Rosebud, lying awkwardly atop him, moved away for Johnnie Mae to clear
Adam's throat. When his breathing was restored, Rosebud
lifted him as though he were a child and tenderly returned
him to bed. The women were there immediately, replacing
cold cloths, lending him what comfort they could with
tender murmurings and the muttered "Lawd, Lawd," that
was a prayer in itself.

Rosebud stood by the bed, his teeth bared in a grimace
of tears, saying, "Boss, Boss, Ah ain' nevah mean to hurt
you, nossuh, nossuh!"

Adam lapsed into unconsciousness again. The women,
panting, straightened up, their eyes meeting and sliding
away.

"De pain gots to stop," said Mammy wearily. "One dese
times Rosebud ain't gwine be heah to he'p." She lumbered
out, returning with her medicinal herbs. "Some say dis de
bes' dey is fo' de poisonin'." She showed Johnnie Mae a
jar of blistering flies steeped in spirits.

Johnnie Mae nodded curtly. One at a time she removed
the cold packs. On each swollen sting they applied drops
until each one showed angry red. "De poison be ha'mless
once de blister rises. Lawd, Lawd, he'p us git thoo dis
day."

Claudine died the second night. Adam lingered on, hovering between consciousness and coma. To Mammy's delight the blisters on his skin were rising. Rosebud, not so certain of the cure, sat slumped in a corner like a huge black mountain. Slow tears ran down his face for Claudine and for Adam, who had no rest no matter what they did for him.

Zoe prepared Claudine for burial. The fear that had been growing threatened to engulf her. Claudine is dead. How long will it be before Adam dies? *The Lord giveth. The Lord taketh away. Please Lord, I beg you most humbly, don't take away my son.*

Mammy and Johnnie Mae reassured each other countless times a day by saying positively he would live. And countless times each of them had rushed to Adam to keep him from strangling as his swollen throat closed.

Reassurances did not soothe Zoe. She had only questions. How long before they were unable to keep the air passage open? How long before they got to him too late? How long could he stand the ceaseless pain that racked him? How long before she had no son?

After they buried Claudine, Zoe stood in the cold moonlight remembering the night years ago when they had buried Ullah. How similar this night was. Angela had described the men who attacked Adam. Two of them meant nothing to Zoe, but the third did. The cruelty of the deed, the man's sadistic pleasure, was too familiar, too hatefully unforgettable. No one had to say Edmund Revanche's name. She knew he had been there. Years ago she had sensed they hadn't seen the last of him. She felt the same fright now.

"Mammy," she said shakily. "I . . . I want Adam's fa-father to know him before—before it's too late."

Mammy put her arm around her favorite child. "You jes' got de mizzer'bles now! Tomorra things seem diffunt."

"I want him here, Mammy. I want him to know Adam."

"You cain't do dat, Miz Zoe. Dat man ain't knowed all dese yeahs he gots a chil'. An' Mastah Adam, he doan know nobuddy 'cep' Mastah Paul. How you gwine tell him now?" She shook her woolly head mournfully. "Uhh-uhhh. You done kep' yo' secret. Ain't no time fo' tellin' now. What's people gwine say?"

"I don't care now, Mammy. I'm not ashamed of Adam, or of giving birth to him. Why should I be ashamed of how

it happened? I shouldn't have listened to Papa. He said I
sinned then. I think it was the rest of my life that I sinned.
I kept Adam from a father who might have loved him.
Maybe this wouldn't have happened if—"

"No, ma'am, Miz Zoe. You daddy woulda kilt you. Ah
'members ol' Mastah Horace. You done right, yes, ma'am!"

"Mammy," Zoe pleaded. "I couldn't live with myself if
Adam died and—"

"He ain't gwine die! Ah woan have you sayin' dat, callin'
down de evil eye on 'im. Mastah Adam be jes' fine."

Mammy stomped off, leaving Zoe to her thoughts. For
once, Zoe's resolve didn't weaken in the face of disapproval.

Mammy muttered to herself, her old head shaking as
she remembered the night and young Miss Zoe. *Lawd, dat
was a turrible time, turrible. Upstandin', pious, self-right-
ous, y'all could call Mastah Horace all dem things, an'
he jes' flang 'em all on Miss Zoe.* Mammy clucked, shaking her head. *An' now Miz Zoe wantin' to staht it all up
agin. 'Tain't fittin'. 'Tain't a good notion no-ways, an' it
jes' ain't fittin'. No, ma'am!*

As Mammy came to the bed, preoccupied with the past,
Johnnie Mae said, "Oi be a-goin' back to the swamp now."

Mammy's jowls shuddered. "He ain't fit yit!"

"Oi be a-goin' to fetch Tom an' Seth. Mayhap we fin'
them who did this. Mayhap Oi kilt one wie moi gun. Oi be
a-leavin' now, an' a-comin' back."

Mammy considered for a moment. "Ah ain't one to hol'
wiff killin'," she said gravely. "But effen you fin's 'em,
you come git Mammy. Ah gwine do 'em in whiff mah
choppin' knife. You come git Mammy, you heah?"

"Oi'll git ye," Johnnie Mae promised.

Late the next afternoon Tom was pounding at Zoe's
front door. His pale face was covered with perspiration.
"Where is he? I saw that get-up an' I knew. It was Edmund, wasn't it, Zoe?" He watched Zoe's face, feeling a
deep, hot emotion he'd believed long dead, boil up inside.

She nodded.

"Oh, yes, it's Edmund's way all right. The whole place
stinks of him. Johnnie Mae finished one of 'em. Blond
bastard I never seen before. Bled to death. Christ! I hope
he took a long time doin' it." Tom laboriously climbed

the stairs. Once during the yellow fever epidemic in 1853, he'd started after Revanche. Weakness and grief had overcome him then. Not this time. Whether or not Adam lived, Tom vowed Edmund Revanche would not. He would find him—and fittingly destroy him.

"Tom." Zoe's voice halted him halfway up. "You . . . you know the Confederate agents, don't you?"

"Sho', I know 'em. Why? Adam hasn't got trouble there? Nobody believed those fool rumors."

"It's nothing like that. I—I want to get a telegraph message through to . . . to the North. Can you do it for me?"

Zoe's cheeks were blush red in her pale face. Her hands were clasped tight. Tom patted her awkwardly. "You look like you better sit down, Zoe, before you fall. What's on your mind?"

She turned from him, biting her lip. If she couldn't tell Tom, she'd never be able to carry it through. But it was so hard to say, to make her wicked secret public. And what if she were wrong? "I need to get in touch with someone. Tom, will you help me?"

"You know I will. Anythin' I can do. But you gotta tell me more'n this. Who is it?"

Zoe was silent for a long time, then she whispered. "Roderick Courtland."

"Courtland? Why Courtland? Did Adam—?"

"Adam has said nothing. He dreams of Dulcie. He calls only for her."

Tom shook his head, clearing the cobwebs. "Well, what's the message?"

Zoe stared at her hands, her words coming out singly like extracted teeth. "Tell him . . . tell Mr. Courtland to come. I need him desperately. And Tom, you must be certain to sign my name Zoe McCloud Tremain. That will tell him all he needs to know. He'll understand then."

"Maybe it'll tell him, but it sho' don't tell me anythin'."

"He . . . he's Adam's father."

During the next days Zoe prayed and took her turn nursing, anxiously awaiting Rod's arrival. Mammy, gray and sagging with fatigue, remained at Adam's side. Her bed was the cot left in his room after Claudine's death. Mammy hardly slept an hour at a time, barely closing her eyes before Adam's fevered nightmare cries would awaken her and bring her to him.

Mammy's potions had worked, but she took little comfort in the receding of the swelling and the healing of the bee stings. Fever lived in Adam, high and constant and debilitating. The lacerations from the whip, embedded with swamp mud, were largely ignored those first crucial nights. Now each laceration was a stripe of infection, with teeth of pain in its yellow-gray center bordered by angry red flesh.

Mammy's old eyes, grayed over with cataracts, strained as she cleaned the festering wounds. Several times each day she asked of Rosebud, "Do Ah git it clean out?"

"Ain't no way fo' keepin' it clean, Mammy. It jes' full wiff pus."

"Den we gwine warsh him again. De bees doan kill 'im, we ain't gwine let no festerin' do it. Johnnie Mae say she gwine bring de herbs fo' de poultice. Den he be fine. Do Ah got it clean?"

Roderick Courtland's hands trembled as he read the telegraph and the name of the sender. His mind was a jumble, trying to connect two images. One out of a far-distant past and the other from the present. Zoe McCloud . . . Tremain. She had run away from him twenty-seven years ago. He had never seen nor heard from her again, until this day. Adam Tremain. Her son. *His son!* It was possible —more than possible. Why else would Zoe write to him now? What else could explain the coincidences of their last names? Why else would he have felt such a strong liking—no, love—for the young man who should have been merely a business partner?

It took Rod two days to find a supply ship going through the Cape Fear blockade, and a great deal of influence peddling to wangle permission aboard. He refused to perform services for the North while he was in the South. He would not spy for his own country or against his son's.

That he was a civilian, and one who refused to serve the Union as well, was almost fatal to his desires. Rod was nearly to the point of agreeing to anything, when he gained permission as a personal favor from a friend.

"I don't think you have any idea of what you're walking into, Rod. You've taken a lot for granted. There are no friends between North and South now. There aren't even fathers and sons."

"I'm going, with your help or without it. My son *is* there, and nothing is going to keep me away. You could make it a lot easier."

"I've said I'll help you. But a man doesn't like to send his friend on a suicide venture."

Three days later Rod stood on the deck of the supply ship, looking out across a dark ocean toward a dark, undistinguished shore. His clothing was dark. Everything was dark. This nightwork in an unpredictable sea, in a hostile environment, was in stark contrast to his own world of Manhattan banks, lunches in crowded oyster bars, the Stock Exchange, theater, and balls. This blackened, eerie expanse of nothingness was his son's world, and Rod found himself intimidated by its quiet, lurking violence.

The second mate lowered a longboat and helped Rod aboard. "Good luck, sir." Then he disappeared. Rod was alone, heading toward a shore he couldn't see. Unfamiliar with the tides and ways of the ocean, Rod ran aground. To his unaccustomed eyes he seemed to be miles from shore. He sat perplexed and undecided until the rhythm of the incoming tide began to impress itself upon him, and his eyes began to take note of the waves, watching them roll in lighter than the unseen sand.

As though he'd been doing it for years, Rod swung his legs over the side of the boat and pushed it off the sandbar, continuing to the shore. He was disproportionately proud of himself as he beached the boat and ran quickly across the sand to the pines. He didn't know if this was Molasses Creek, but he could hide here until Tom found him. Already he was clammy and cold in his wet, clinging clothes. Silently he cursed himself for having gotten on the sandbar, then Tom for not arriving with the promptness of his New York driver.

Tom waited with the wagon sheltered in the woods, expecting Rod to march boldly toward the main road. Both men waited, cold and uncomfortable until first light, when Tom could easily see Rod's tracks heading for the copse of pine not thirty yards away.

Annoyed enough not to care who saw or heard him, Tom yelled at the horses and ran straight for the pines. "I've been waitin' for you by the road half the night!" he growled.

"I was told the road wasn't safe."

"How in the hell was I to know you'd have the sense not to walk right down the damned road. Get in. Zoe's like to think we both got our heads blowed off."

On the way to Smithville Tom told Rod what had happened. Having had several hours to think while he waited, Tom was in no mood to minimize any of Edmund's deeds. Rod received a full and bluntly honest summary of his son's life during the time Tom had known him.

He listened in near silence, his shoulders slumped, and he stared bleakly ahead. "She never told me about him, not even when she knew we had met."

"I don't expect it'd be too easy for a woman to come right out an' tell the world her son's father ain't his father a-tall. Seems like she's talkin' now because she thinks he's dyin'."

"Is he, Tom?"

"Don't know. He's strong as ten ornery mules, but it's been a long siege. Fever's taken a lot outa him, but my money's on him. Hell, Rod, everythin's ridin' on that boy makin' it."

They entered the main street of Smithville in pensive silence. Tom reined the horses in front of the house. "This is it. You go on in. I'm gonna rub down the horses."

Zoe knew he was there before he touched the door. It had been twenty-six years since she had given birth to this man's son, nearly twenty-seven years since she had last seen him. Her hands fumbled with the lock. "Rod . . ."

He stood on the top step, changed, older, and yet the same youthful, brilliant blue eyes stared into hers. The same sensitive mouth turned upward in the shy, yet bold smile she remembered.

She moved back as he entered the house, dwarfing the entry hall with his size and presence. He was dressed in dark clothing similar to Adam's. He removed his watch cap, exposing a mane of waving silver hair.

"Tom told me." His voice—how could she have forgotten? Perhaps she never had. Perhaps that was why she so liked to hear Adam talk or read to her. She grasped at a small table. "Zoe—are you ill?"

"No, no, I'm fine. I . . . Rod, Adam is—"

"I already know, Zoe. I knew as soon as I saw your name on the telegram. May I see him now?"

"Oh, please." She led him to Adam's room.

Mammy sat snoring in a chair by Adam's bed. "She won't leave his side. She . . . she's always looked after him, from the time he was a baby. She—" Zoe sniffed, and regained control. "Do you remember her, Rod?"

"I remember her." Rod's eyes were on Adam. He murmured in a restless, fevered sleep, talking of drums and fires and Dulcie. The swelling from the bee stings and the blisters from the cantharides had nearly disappeared, but the odor of infection had not. Adam was thin, hollow-cheeked, flushed with fever. "How long has he been like this?"

"Days. Ever since Johnnie Mae brought him home. But Mammy says he is better. She says—oh, Rod, I'm so afraid. He's going to die, isn't he? He—he doesn't even know me."

Rod stood by the bed several minutes, then sank into the chair near Adam, his hands limp between his legs.

Zoe fought back tears looking from one man to the other, so alike and yet so different. In Adam there was enough of herself to soften the craggy sharpness of Rod's features.

"Why did you keep him from me, Zoe? Whatever you thought of me, you couldn't have thought I wouldn't want my own son."

"I—Papa—I didn't know what . . ." she stammered, then took a deep breath, and said in a low, nearly steady voice. "There didn't seem to be anything I could do at the time. I wasn't sure of so many things."

"I wanted to marry you. Didn't that mean anything to you? Or was that what you ran away to avoid?"

Zoe was speechless, her throat and eyes thick with tears.

"There's so much of you in him, Zoe. You reared him well," Rod said quietly. "I loved you. Didn't you know—or didn't you care?"

"I . . ." Zoe shrank from him. She didn't know this man. She'd hardly known him that summer so long ago. She'd been so filled with love for him then, she'd allowed herself to be swept along. Now here he was again, throwing it all at her, urging her to talk, to explain, to reveal her innermost secrets when she no longer could. The hideous, hateful years with Paul Tremain had robbed her of words and feelings of love. Through those years the memory of Rod had become only an idealized dream of a summer's love long past. But Paul had been real. His criticism of her, his drunken demands on her, his loathing of her. That had

been real. But the lovely summer with Rod . . . she didn't
know what that was, fantasy or reality. "It was all a long
time ago, Rod."

Rod shook his head. "I don't understand you. I don't
suppose I ever did, but I didn't think I could be that
wrong."

"No."

"Well, thank you for this, Zoe." He touched Adam's
hot forehead.

Rod slept in the front room on the sofa, insisting he
would be quite comfortable. Zoe went to her room, her
mind a wild montage of days past. She wandered about,
unable to settle down enough to prepare for bed.

Before her danced another self, a seventeen-year-old Zoe
sent to visit her older sister, Faith, in Boston for the summer. Mammy, younger, and as excited as she to be taking
a train north, sat by her side. Faith had been pregnant and
homesick. Walter, her husband of two years, was stationed
in Boston as adjutant to General Denker. Zoe, the youngest
and the most willing daughter, was sent to her sister.

Zoe had been wildly excited. Paul Tremain, her fiancé,
was still on his Grand Tour, and Zoe missed the excitement of parties and young men paying attention to her. She
was often invited, but her father had said she must go to
social functions only with Paul, lest she fall prey to tempta-
tions too strong for a weak-minded female to resist.

Horace McCloud was strict with his daughters, but especially so with Zoe, the child who had entered woman-
hood without her mother's guidance. Horace prided himself
on having arranged her marriage to Paul. It would unite
two fine families. Though she had not been consulted,
Zoe looked forward to the wedding. Obedience to her
father was second nature. She took on faith that Paul
would be an ideal husband. He was courteous, pleasant
looking, and attentive, with prospects of a fine future.
There was little else a woman could ask. Her life was well
settled when she left for Boston. In October she'd return
home and marry Paul. Meantime she had an entire summer
to be free of her father's all-seeing eye, and a city to explore.

Her first week there had been ordinary, unmarked until
Walter and Faith had taken her to a dinner party. She
didn't remember the people there that night. She remembered nothing except the young man who had arrived late.

He had come in the middle of dinner, laughing his apologies as he seated himself in the empty chair to her left.

No one introduced them, so he turned boldly to her, his vivid blue eyes sparkling with deviltry. "I'm Roderick Courtland. You don't know me yet, but I know you. You're the loveliest woman in Boston. Have you a name?"

Zoe blushed, causing her to giggle so that she couldn't speak.

"You're Ann—Beth—Carrie—Diana—Ellen—"

"Oh, you've a long way to go if you're going to guess by that method, Mr. Courtland."

"S—Sylvia—Teresa—"

"Still farther—"

"Yvonne."

Zoe shook her head.

"Zita?"

"No."

"But I've fallen off the end. There are no more letters. You must not have a name."

"Zoe. Zoe McCloud."

He took her hand, the blue eyes engulfing her, his mouth turned up in a slight smile. "Zoe. Soft, soft Zoe."

"Mr. Courtland—"

He looked sincerely ashamed. "I know, I'm as bold as brass and as objectionable as—the devil. But I know when I've met the woman for me."

"Mr. Courtland, really, I don't like this conversation."

"But your eyes are shining, Zoe, and your cheeks are flushed, and—"

Zoe pulled her hand from his warm one and scooted to the far edge of her chair to look up and see amused faces watching the play between herself and Rod.

After that evening it seemed there was a party every night, or perhaps it was just those nights she remembered, because Rod was always there. Zoe lived for those nights. He always spotted her the moment she walked through the door. When his eyes sought hers, she knew she was the loveliest woman in Boston. Rod's eyes told her so.

Then on a hot night in July he told her he loved her. Zoe had never known what it was like to be in love. She had thought of, and been taught, only what to expect of marriage. She knew how to be a hostess, to sew fancywork, to play the piano and the harpsichord, to sing passably well, to organize servants and run a house. Of her

blood racing and her heart performing magical feats of
rhythm, of her eyes seeing only one man's face in a
crowded room, of longing for the sound of one voice, of
being satisfied by the touch of one hand, she knew nothing until now. Rod began to fill her whole life, awake and
asleep. Paul Tremain no longer existed for her. There was
only one man, and she was in his arms, and he loved her.

All Zoe remembered of the ball that July night was that
it was given in General Denker's honor, and the lovely
flower-filled ballroom opened onto a great veranda. Below
the veranda were the gardens. Endless pathways of sculptured privet hedge wound around the grounds. She and Rod
had walked through those dark arched tunnels of green
and had finally come to a Greek temple built at the edge
of a pond.

They had sat in the temple for a long time, hearing the
music softly in the background, and the closer sounds of
nightbirds and crickets. One minute became another, one
kiss became so many they never ended, one caress and Rod
telling her he loved her and needed her.

Zoe felt no shame as he undressed her and touched the
moonlit contours of her body. She felt nothing but happiness. Even the sharp initiating pain of his joining with
her had been lost in the strange, pulsing feelings of delight. She was aware of nothing and no one but him. And
later, after he had helped her to dress and fix her hair, she
reentered the flower-filled ballroom and the presence of her
scowling older sister, aware of nothing but Rod at her
side, his hand gently caressing her waist at every step.

Now she knew that that evening Faith had seen and
understood things Zoe had not yet come to grips with. Already her days with Rod had been numbered, but at seventeen and in love Zoe had known none of that. Faith had
been cool toward her, making acid comments about both
Zoe's exit and her reentry to the ball. And Mammy had
taken but one look and known what had happened.

"Lawd, Miss Zoe, Mastah Horace gwine th'ow hisself
into a fit! He gwine lock you up fo'evah effen he fin' out
what you done. An' what Mastah Paul gwine think when he
fin' out his bride be used goods?"

Zoe had only smiled. Paul and her father were far away.
From then on she had tempted fate beyond recall. Faith
knew Zoe was religious. Three, sometimes four times a

week, she told Faith she was going to a church meeting. Escorted by Mammy, Zoe went to meet Rod.

Halfheartedly Mammy scolded, prayed, harangued, and nagged. She approved of Rod. And Zoe had never been happier. To Mammy that was justification for nearly anything—so long as they didn't get caught.

"Oh, you is bad!" she chided each time before she disappeared into the kitchen of Rod's apartment, leaving Zoe and Rod alone. Mammy believed as did Zoe, that Rod would marry her, and soon. Soon enough to forestall the trouble that was bound to come when they returned to Wilmington in the fall.

Rod often spoke of marriage. He had only one more year of school, and he was certain he could study and work at the same time, thus being able to support a young wife who promised to eat very little.

On the fifth of August Zoe returned from her "church meeting" to find Faith and Walter waiting for her.

"I've already notified Papa of your behavior, Zoe. You'll be sent home as soon as Walter can arrange it. Mammy, I want her packed tonight."

"Faith . . . I don't want to go home. Papa said I was to stay until—"

"Stay!? And have you completely ruin our reputation? Walter is a very important man, Zoe. How do you think it has been these last weeks with you acting like—like a— with that Mr. Courtland? I can hardly look my friends in the eye. They think perhaps I am like you!"

Zoe had tried to plead with Faith to let her see Rod before they left or to write him a note. But pleading was fruitless. Faith was as single-minded and adamant as their father. When Zoe arrived home, her father was at the depot. She was never free to write to Rod. Even Mammy's attempts to sneak out with Zoe's letters had ended in failure and greater bouts of rage from Horace McCloud.

In desperation she told her father she couldn't marry Paul. She was in love with another man. Horace took a strap to his daughter, threatening her. Forbidden to see him, even to speak his name, Zoe retreated into old habits of obedience and meekness, no longer daring to think of Rod somewhere in Boston.

By the end of September Zoe knew she was pregnant.

She married Paul Tremain in October. She tried to be a

good wife and thought she had succeeded until she told him she was pregnant. He showed no sign of pleasure in the coming child. Soon after, when he was drunk with courage enough and animosity enough, he told her he had known she was no virgin and had suspected she was pregnant. He wanted to know who the man was.

Zoe endured his verbal and physical abuse, but she never mentioned Rod's name again. From then on, Paul drank more and more. He first resented the thought of the baby, then the baby himself. The older Adam grew, the more Paul hated him. For all the years of their marriage he made their lives a hell.

Zoe had clung to the memory of that summer until she could no longer separate facts from imagination. Her love she poured onto Adam as much as she dared without calling down Paul's wrath on the boy. Except for that one summer, Zoe knew nothing but fear and abuse from a man. She wasn't sure there was anything more. Paul had claimed to love her. Rod had claimed to love her. She knew about Paul. But she knew nothing of Rod.

And now he was back. She had called him back into her life.

She didn't sleep all that night and was in the kitchen at first light. She had dressed with care, and now, nervously, she prepared his breakfast, her mind whirling, testing the sound of phrases she might say to him. When Rod came sleepily into the kitchen, drawn by the odors of bacon and coffee, Zoe was almost beside herself with tension.

He grinned and slouched into a chair. "Smells awfully good."

Zoe's eyes were wide, her face pale. "Rod—Rod, I didn't run away," she said breathlessly. "Faith—Faith sent me, and Papa. I didn't want to marry Paul! I tried. I—"

Rod got up, hurrying to take her by the shoulders. "I had no right to talk to you as I did last night. It was unfair and foolish of me. As you said, it was a long time ago and better forgotten."

"No, please. I should have told you. And Adam too. After I was married, I didn't know how. I thought Paul would—I never believed Paul would hate him so, and by then Adam thought he was Paul's son and I didn't know where you were after you left school. Oh, Rod, I didn't want to leave you!"

"Why didn't you come to me while you were still in Boston?"

"I couldn't! Faith kept me locked in my room, and the next morning Walter put me on a train. Then Papa was at the depot when I got off. Faith—no one would even let me write to you."

"In all that time you couldn't write just once?"

"No! Papa . . . I just gave in. I was so weak and stupid!"

"Not half so stupid as I was."

"But it wasn't your fault. It was mine. I—"

He put his hand to her lips, shushing her. "We were both very young and not very astute, Zoe. I went to your sister's house when you didn't come to the apartment the next night. She told me you'd gone home because you didn't want to see me again. I wasn't hard to convince, not with my hurt pride, too much youth, and too little sense. She told me you'd been engaged the whole time we'd been seeing one another. That was all it took to make me swallow the whole story. Like a fool, I believed her."

"How could you? You knew—"

He shook his head. "No more than you."

She looked into his eyes. "Rod, would you really have come for me?"

"Yes."

"Even after what Faith told you?"

"Even then."

Slow tears rolled down her face. Rod smiled slightly and wiped them away. "Twenty-seven years, Zoe, and I swear you're no older than when I met you."

"I just wish I had done everything differently."

He shrugged. "I don't believe in trying to recapture the past. Neither of us is free of blame or guilty of all of it. But what remains is the present. So, shall we do with it what we can?"

"Rod . . ."

"We can begin with breakfast. It smells good, and I'm hungry. After that I want to see Adam. I don't suppose you've told him about me?"

"No. He hasn't been sensible enough to understand anything since—since it happened. And I haven't known how to tell him. What do I say?"

Rod ate slowly, nibbling on a piece of toasted bread. "You needn't tell him at all. I know. That's enough. Adam and I have become good friends. He has my respect, and I believe I have his."

"Rod, it isn't enough. Tom knows, and of course Mammy. How could I decently keep it from Adam? I want him to know you, Rod, as his father. Every time he'd return from New York and talk about you, I wanted to tell him. I used to ask questions. Sometimes when I hadn't the courage to ask, I'd sit and pray, hoping he'd talk about you so I could hear what he thought of you. And then I'd feel so guilty for what I had done. Adam might have been spared so much if I had been less of a coward."

Impatiently Rod shoved his plate away. "It's done, Zoe. I don't want—"

"Good morning, Aunt Zoe."

Zoe started, and Rod turned to see an attractive young woman leaning against the door.

"Angela—you startled me," Zoe said uncomfortably, her eyes sliding away from Angela's. "I've told you not to come up so silently on people."

"I wasn't so silent. You were just so busy talking you didn't hear."

"Were you listening to a private conversation? Angela—"

"The food smelled so good, I just followed my nose. I wasn't trying to listen to anything. I'm not interrupting, am I?"

"Certainly not," Rod said. "We were talking of kingdoms lost for want of a nail."

Angela wrinkled her nose prettily. "What?"

Rod laughed. "All that means is that it's nothing of interest to someone as young and pretty as you. You're Tom's daughter, aren't you?"

Angela listened to him with her head cocked to one side, her face alight with amusement. "Why, you're a Yankee! Aunt Zoe, I never thought you'd let a Yankee in your house."

"Your breakfast is ready, Angela."

Angela pouted. "Why are you so angry?"

"I'm not angry, and there is no need to start that up again."

Angela sat down, her eyes narrowing. "Are you still holding it against me because I didn't die out there too?"

"Angela! Don't be ridiculous!"

"I'm not being ridiculous. That's what you're really saying. I should have done what Claudine did, and then I'd be dead too."

Zoe removed her apron, tossing it on a chair. "If I felt that way, you wouldn't be in my house, and you are. That's enough."

"I did nothing wrong. What makes you think you'd have done differently?"

"He took care of you—watched after you." Zoe's voice rose. "You wouldn't be alive if not for him. And the one time he needed you—"

"Well, I needed him plenty of other times, and he didn't care then!"

"Whoa! Ladies—quiet. What is all this?" Rod raised his arms, pretending to separate two pugilists.

Zoe walked hastily to the washstand. "Nothing. Just a family argument."

"She hates me because I didn't die trying to save Adam like Claudine. That's what they all think. That's what they all want!"

"You've said enough, young lady! As long as you're Mrs. Tremain's guest, you'll keep a civil tongue."

"I'm not a guest! I live here—or I did. Do I live here, Aunt Zoe?"

Zoe walked angrily from the kitchen. Rod followed her. "Zoe, what is this about?"

"It's too long a story, and I want to see Adam."

"Your whole life seems wrapped up in long stories and secrets. Pardon me. I thought I could help you. Wasn't that why you asked me to come?"

Zoe looked at him tearfully, then ran up the stairs.

Adam moved restlessly on the bed, his voice hoarse and all but unintelligible, an undercurrent that mumbled of limbless monsters and chickcharnies and Satan. When Zoe came in, he opened his puffy-lidded eyes and seemed to see her. "There was a . . . shipwreck."

"Yes, dear, I know," Zoe said shakily.

"Red hair—she had red hair. See her? Wife . . . red hair . . ." He drifted off, then his gaze found Rod's. "May-maybe you saw Dus-Dussie? Dussly? Wrecked. *In'pend-pendas.* But not Dussie . . . find her."

"We'll do that," Rod said heartily.

"Red—like fire. All 'roun' . . ." Adam's eyelids swung shut.

Biting her lip, Zoe forced herself not to go to Adam to try to make him recognize her. Mammy sat listlessly in her chair, her face gray with fatigue, her clouded eyes sunken deep in her head. "Mammy, I want you to go to your room. You're not getting any rest."

Mammy didn't move for so long, Zoe thought she hadn't heard. Then the old woman took a deep breath. "Ah resses when he resses. You jes' leave me set wheah Ah is, Miz Zoe. Dis wheah Ah b'long."

"Mammy, I want you to do as I ask!" Zoe said shrilly.

Rod come up behind her, moving her toward the door. "Let her do as she wants, Zoe. She wouldn't sleep if you made her go to her room."

Zoe pulled away from him, nerves raw. "Don't meddle, Rod. I know what's best."

"Damn it, Zoe, if anyone should go to her room and rest, it's you!"

"Don't raise your voice to me in here!"

"Then get out in the hall because I am going to raise my voice to you!"

Mammy's tired eyes lit briefly. "Y'all bettah do what he say, Miz Zoe."

"Zoe!"

She whirled to face him.

"You and I are going to get a few things cleared up. If you want my help, I'll give it willingly, but I sure as hell will not be shoved into the background to watch a woman scream at every member in the household. I'm accustomed to running things—and running them smoothly."

"Well, I'm not accustomed to being run!"

Rod's eyes bored into her. "Maybe it's time you learned to be."

"I should never have sent for you! Never! You're just as pushy and crude as any Yankee. If Paul Tremain taught me nothing else, he taught me never to trust any man, and certainly no dirty Yankee!"

Rod grabbed her arm. "Don't you ever confuse me with Paul Tremain—or any other man, Zoe!"

"Let me go!"

"Not this time." Rod walked quickly to her sitting room.

Chapter Eleven

It was an anxious six weeks for Dulcie before Mr. Revanche returned. While he was gone, General Lee had attacked the Army of the Potomac near Bristoe Station, Virginia. Union Major General Thomas, called "The Rock of Chickamauga" for his bravery there, replaced General Rosecrans as commander of the Army of the Cumberland. General Grant became supreme commander of the western forces and within ten days had opened a supply line to Chattanooga still under siege by Bragg.

"Look at this, Patsy," said Jem, shaking his newspaper. "Lee has been fightin' without a decisive battle for the past month, so now he's withdrawn his troops to winter quarters on the Rapidan River. Can't our generals do anythin' but skirmish and retreat?"

"And die of disease." Oliver shifted his gold toothpick. "Twice as many men die of disease as of wounds. The Union has its Sanitary Commission to minister to the sick and wounded and its Christian Commission to look after their spiritual welfare. But the South hasn't got money for that."

"I heard a good one about a chaplain at Chickamauga," said Jem. "This so-named man of the cloth says, 'Remember, boys, he who is killed will sup tonight in Paradise.' One soldier yelled back, 'Well, Parson, you come along and take supper with us.' Then the shelling began, and the chaplain spurred his horse to the rear. The soldier says, 'Parson ain't hungry, an' he never eats supper.'"

The others laughed, but Patricia said, "That chaplain had to be a dirty Yankee. No Southuhnuh would—" She stopped, reddening. "Oh, Oliver, Ah beg you to forgive me. Ah don't mean *all* Yankees—an' heah you an' Mad are bein' so kind."

Jem patted her as she sat stiff in her chair, tears flowing in mortification. "There, there, Patsy love, Oliver knows you don't mean him."

"Of course not," Oliver declared heartily.

The front door knocker sounded.

Dulcie's heart jumped and began to beat with slow, heavy thuds.

Edmund entered the room, as impeccably dressed and at ease as always. He exchanged pleasantries with each one. Jem was too willing to talk about the war, and Oliver expounded on economic matters. Edmund accommodated them, graciously accepting a drink.

Dulcie could not stand it any longer. "Mr. Revanche, is there . . . did you learn anything of my husband?"

Edmund set his glass down. His voice was soft and regretful. "You are all hoping for good tidings, but none of you wish more than I that I could bring them. Unfortunately, I am not able to do so." His eyes remained on Dulcie.

She became pale, holding her breath.

Mad bristled. She was one of the few upon whom Edmund Revanche's charm had no positive effect. "As you have nothin' encouragin' to tell us, Mr. Revanche, perhaps it would be as well if you refrained from tellin' us anythin'."

"No, Aunt Mad," said Dulcie tensely. "I want to know. I . . . must know."

The sympathy in the room almost overwhelmed her, but she would not cry. Not here. She wouldn't break down, not until she knew.

"I gave my word that I would tell you anything I might find out, but Mrs. Tremain, I beg you, don't call me upon my honor to keep that promise. Let it be enough that I have verified that Captain Tremain is dead."

"He didn't die in the shipwreck—did he?"

Edmund looked at the others, appealing to them. Mad snorted. "Really, sir, you are drawin' this out into a three-act tragedy."

"I am loath to speak, Mrs. Raymer. I was hoping to spare your niece, for whom I have the greatest esteem, the sordid details of the death of a man who was patently not good enough for her."

"You are mistaken, Mr. Revanche. Either you have been misinformed or we speak of different men. No one was finer, kinder, or more honorable than Adam. I should like to hear your story. I think you have located information about the wrong man."

"I am seldom in error, Mrs. Rayner. Information is my

business. Were I not most precise and capable, the South would not wish my services."

Jem said impatiently, "Get to the point, Mr. Revanche."

Edmund breathed deeply, letting out a great sigh of resignation. "I bow to your wishes, sir. Mrs. Tremain, as you surmised, your husband did not die at sea. In fact, he died only last month."

Dulcie's head swam. Through dry lips she said, "Yes?"

"It was the talk of Wilmington. The respected, shall we even say idolized, blockade runner Captain Tremain met his end in a sordid brawl."

"If you please, sir," said Oliver angrily. "Where was this event said to have taken place?" He had greatly admired Captain Tremain, and his heart ached for Dulcie sitting so white and proud.

Edmund said sorrowfully, "In the Green Swamp, Mr. Raymer. A salt patrol was searching for him. It was reported that his men, led by him, had destroyed and disrupted several camps. There were rumors that Captain Tremain sold the stolen salt back to the Confederacy at tremendous profit to himself."

"I don't believe that!" Dulcie cried.

"Nor do I!" Mad agreed emphatically. "Adam Tremain would have nothin' to do with traitorous white trash. Stealing salt! The very idea!"

Edmund shrugged. "I am not making this up, Madame. Nor am I in a position to discern what is true or not true about Captain Tremain, not having known him myself. But, perhaps you did not know him as well as you thought."

Dulcie sat in stunned silence. *Tom lived in the Green Swamp.*

"Go on, Mr. Revanche," Jem said. "Painful as it may be, I think my daughter should hear it all. Perhaps then she will see what I saw from the beginnin'. This man was never right for her."

"The patrol found Captain Tremain with two women. They tried to arrest him, and he fought them. I was told he died of his wounds. The white woman, evidently a swamp creature, escaped."

Dulcie shook uncontrollably. "The other woman—?"

"She was killed, trying to save the captain. She was known to be his . . . companion." Edmund paused for the full effect of his words to hit Dulcie. "She was a nigger wench. Claudine, I believe they said."

Dulcie's vision dimmed. The room grew black, disappearing while she watched. Sounds dimmed. The shelf clock that ticked so loudly softened to nothing.

Dulcie put up one hand pushing away the acrid smell stinging her nostrils. She moved her head from side to side. "Stop. Don't."

Mad chafed her wrists. "Dulcie honey, can you hear me? It's your Aunt Mad. Sit still, dear. You'll be all right in a few minutes."

"A terrible, terrible blow," Edmund said mournfully. "I feel responsible. Mrs. Tremain insisted. I did not want to tell her."

"We understand, Mr. Revanche," Jem's face was red with anger. "Dulcie had to know. I told her he'd break her heart. An adventurer, that's all he was—"

Mad said, "Jem, you hush. This is gossip!"

"He was a good man, a fine man," Oliver declared. "Pity he had to come to such an unfortunate end."

"At least it won't be known here in New York for a while," Jem said. "Dulcie won't have to face our friends and defend the rascal."

Dulcie stood up, though her arms and legs were jelly. "I don't want you talkin' about Adam. If . . . if Mr. Revanche is correct, then Daddy is right, and I made a mistake in marryin' him. But—" She looked at them all, seeing none of them. "Can't you understand? I love him."

Oliver, without comment, handed her a glass of straight whiskey.

"Ollie Raymer! Dulcie, don't you take—"

Dulcie sipped the whiskey defiantly, wanting it to take hold as it had that one night—with him—when they had watched the sun come up over Eleuthera.

Had he gone to other women on each trip away from Nassau? Was it carousing and wenching that gave his face such a haggard look when he came back to her? And Claudine—with him at the last.

Beneath the doubts was a deeper hurt. Adam had never really tried to find her. He knew Oliver was in New York, and he had not sought him. He knew her father lived at Mossrose, and he had not sought Jem.

She held out her glass for more. Yet, she still loved him.

The longing didn't ease. Knowing he was dead didn't change it. Knowing he was not the shining knight she had believed didn't lessen it.

It seemed to her that she spoke very clearly. "Mr. Revanche, I realize this will be hard to keep secret, but I'd be grateful if you said nothin' to anyone else. I will need time to—"

Edmund was at her side, bringing her hand to his lips. "I'd protect your reputation with my life. Not all men are—"

"I don't want to talk about it anymore."

"No, no, we won't talk about it. Forget. Begin anew, Mrs. Tremain."

"Oh, yes," Dulcie sighed. "Tomorrows are made for beginnin', aren't they? My tomorrows used to be so . . ." She shook her head. Her tongue felt thick. "No, no, I mustn't think that. Did you deliver my letters?"

"Mrs. Tremain's letter I delivered myself. The lady was not at home, so I gave it to a servant girl. The other I wasn't able to deliver." He reached into his pocket. "Captain West is not known in Charleston." He handed Dulcie the worn-looking letter.

She stared at it, dizzily speculating on the source of the travel stains on it. She tore it slowly across and put the pieces in the fire. She laughed, a low mirthless chuckle. "Tomorrows are for beginnin', and yesterdays are for burnin'. Burn, yesterday, burn!"

She noted with surprise that her legs were misbehaving. "I—don't think I feel quite well. Excuse me, Mr. Revanche, I must . . ." She looked around stupidly, wondering what it was she must do.

"Mrs. Tremain—forgive my boldness—may I tell you that never in my life have I met a woman braver or more poised than yourself? Will you permit me to call on you tomorrow? I should like to offer you whatever small crumbs of comfort my presence will provide."

"Certainly." Holding Jem's arm, Dulcie mounted the stairs. The maid undressed her, and she lay in bed feeling unpleasantly close to the rawness of life. Her mother came in. "I don't feel like talkin' Mama."

Patricia bent down and kissed her daughter fondly. "Earth has no sorrow that Heaven cannot heal. Remembah that, dahlin'."

"I'll remember. Good night, Mama."

"Theah's nothin' we can do fo' you now, but dahlin', woman have always found strength in theah Makuh. It's moah than a platitude, Dulcie."

After Patricia tiptoed out, Dulcie shut her eyes. Vignettes of Adam . . . Adam . . . Adam drifted before her like a magic lantern show. Adam cruel yet desiring her in Tom's bayou house. Adam comforting her on board the *Tunbridge*, talking with her in the storm, entering the tournament because she wanted him to, catching Andrew Whitaker kissing her. The night of the terrible fire at the plantation. Adam and herself laughing like two fools running from their pursuers in New York. Adam making love to her under the canopy of the broken bed. Making love, making a child together, dying together—all of them. And only herself left—dead. Tomorrows with no beginnings.

Edmund Revanche came calling the next afternoon. He provided her a deliberately pleasant respite, speaking charmingly but not vivaciously of his travels. Some things, he said piously, he could not reveal for his own safety. "There is a large group of Southern citizens usually called the Peace Society. This seditious organization wants to overthrow the Confederacy and restore all states to the Union."

"Surely someone in authority would heah of theah meetin's an' arrest them all." said Patricia.

"They have no meetin's. Men known as 'eminents' travel the South, conferring the degree on others. Each member is an independent. They have passwords, secret codes, every shady means of operation."

"It doesn't sound like much of an organization to me," said Mad.

"It is highly organized," Edmund smiled. "They work alone, encouragin' desertion, askin' famiiles to refuse to serve on the home front. Some of our soldiers are bone fide members of these Peace Societies."

"What is ouah world comin' to, when loyal Southunuhs can't be trusted anymoah?" Patricia asked.

"There are always misguided souls who cannot see the common good, Madame. But there are many women like yourself who nurse the sick, who never sit down without their knittin' so that our gallant men in gray may have socks and scarves. One woman like you is a credit to the entire Confederacy." Edmund's eyes rested on Dulcie, who had said little. "You are looking much improved to-day, Mrs. Tremain."

"Do go on talkin'. I am content just to listen."

"It is such a bright and pleasant afternoon, may I take you ladies for a carriage ride through Central Park?"

"Thank you, Mr. Revanche, but Patricia and I have obligated ourselves to finish several pairs of those socks you spoke of."

"I will go with you, Mr. Revanche," Dulcie said.

Though the mid-November day was chilly, it was warm under the plaid lap robe Dulcie shared with Edmund. The cool wind was invigorating.

"Will you be in New York long this time, Mr. Revanche?"

"Until the New Year, Mrs. Tremain. May I call you Miss Dulcie?"

"Why?"

"I know how you must feel about the man whose name you use."

"I'm sure you don't, Mr. Revanche. Do you have business in the city, or will you be takin' a holiday?"

"If you must be so prickly, why did you come?"

"Because it's better than knittin' socks."

Edmund laughed. "How refreshingly honest you are, my dear."

"Mr. Revanche." She chose her words carefully, allowing them to reflect her bitter emptiness. "When I first met you, I thought I might learn to like you very much. Now that I know you better, I discover I am totally indifferent."

"You are hardly being fair, my dear. It was you who extracted my promise to tell you whatever I discovered. If you recall, I tried to dissuade you from listening. I might remind you that no matter how despicable the captain's behavior toward you, I had no part in it. Shall you punish me for what he did? And shall you end what might have been a pleasant friendship between us?"

"How could you possibly want a friendship with me when you know . . . I really don't care to continue this conversation, Mr. Revanche."

"Come now, Dulcie, even widows have friends. You have had a grave shock, but I tell you, the best way to recover is to go on with your life. Fill it with new things, new people, new ideas."

"Mr. Revanche, truly, I don't care."

"That must change. Immediately . . . Dulcie. My name is Edmund. I'll expect you to use it. As a matter of fact, I shan't answer to anything but Edmund coming from your lips."

Dulcie smiled in spite of herself. "Does nothin' put you off?"

"Very little. I am a man of select tastes and of great determination. I seldom forget a woman of beauty, or an enemy, and I pay proper homage to each." He laughed, pleased with himself, confident of her.

"No wonder you're such a success. They say you are a spy. Are you?"

"Where did you get that romantic notion?"

"One of your lady admirers whispered it to an avid audience. If you're not, you'll disappoint at least two dozen loyal Southerners."

"Ahhh. Then by all means we'll foster the idea. I always find it best to be whatever is wished by one's admirers. It makes them so much more ready to support my causes."

Dulcie looked at him from the corner of her eye. "Mr. Revanche—Edmund, sometimes you seem far more the cynic than the idealist."

He laughed, flicking the buggy whip. "You're a perceptive woman."

"I didn't pay you a compliment."

"As I said before, your honesty is refreshing."

"And yours is disconcertin'."

"Why? My life is such that cynicism comes readily. Except when I am in New York lecturing and raising money, I see little that bolsters one's idealism. But I seldom have the opportunity to speak with an intelligent and beautiful woman capable of understanding my temporary disillusionments."

"Are they temporary?"

"Of course. Once this cursed war is over. I have dreams . . . and home."

Dulcie smiled, glad she had come, glad to hear a man speaking in such a fashion about his future.

Unobtrusively, Edmund moved closer. "Have you ever roller-skated?"

"Ever what?"

"It's like ice-skating, except it's done on wheels. It's the latest craze. The social leaders of New York are trying to confine it to the educated and refined classes and so are making it fashionable."

"I'd like to try that."

On Friday evening Dulcie went skating with Edmund, falling down several times before she learned to glide on wheels. He was fairly expert, skating either forward or backward. Relaxed and enjoying himself, he was at his most charming. Though he seemed always aware of his effect on people, superficially he was an uncomplicated, pleasant, attractive man who drew women's eyes. Dulcie found herself smiling, having fun almost against her will.

"You are lovely tonight, little one," said Edmund.

I love you, little one, Adam had said. Dulcie forced a smile. "I am enjoyin' myself, Edmund."

"Tell me, have we been fashionable long enough? Surely everyone has noticed us by now. Shall we have a late supper at the Astor House?"

In the following weeks Dulcie went out often with Edmund. At Wallack's a stage presentation creaked with old castles, titled lords and ladies, and missing heirs. During one scene, when Lady Upsnoot still lay on the floor from her suicide, someone threw her a corsage. The dead lady arose and bowed, clutching the flowers, as was the custom. Then she lay back down and continued to be dead. Dulcie laughed and laughed.

At Thanksgiving (officially proclaimed by Mr. Lincoln as the fourth Thursday of November) the family, with Edmund as guest, dined at the New York Hotel.

"Ah don't s'pose, if we wuh in Georgia, we'd be eatin' this well, Jem."

Jem laid a small bone in the bone dish and licked his fingers. "Possibly not, Patsy love. But Mossrose quail are sweeter than these."

"One thing I miss in the North," said Edmund, "is genuine Southern salt-cured ham. What we get here is but a pallid substitute."

"If what you said about salt is true, Edmund, they aren't havin' too much of your favorite ham in the South, either," said Dulcie.

He smiled at her. "Your memory is very accurate, my dear, especially when one recalls how the subject came up."

"Do you visit your home when you go South, Mr. Revanche?" asked Mad.

His eyes kindled briefly. "I lost my home by fire."

"How dreadful!" said Patricia.

"What will you do after the war, sir?" asked Oliver.

Edmund preferred cigars from a gold case, selected one, clipped the end, and lit it. "Politics. In essence I want to build up the country again. Win or lose, the Confederate States will be in need of repair."

Dulcie was thoughtful. Adam had such an idea. It was incredible that two such different men would seize upon the same idealistic notion.

From Thanksgiving until New Year's Day Revanche came almost daily to see Dulcie or to take her out. When he was lecturing, he liked to have Dulcie with him. He always had Josiah Whinburn along at lectures as well. Dulcie wondered sourly if Edmund wanted to assure himself of a sympathetic audience. She found no redeeming qualities in Josiah, who seemed driven and unsure of himself.

Edmund was famous in expatriate Southern circles, for his oratory was compelling, his fund of heart-wrenching stories bottomless. His ability to wring yet another dollar for the collection was ingenious.

On the way home late one night Dulie said, "Edmund who really gets the money you collect?"

"Why, the South, of course."

"Humbug. Those letters you show are false. I'd bet my teeth on it."

He was amused. "How did such a dishonest notion enter your head?"

"What you say and what you do don't add up. Somehow you are cheatin' people."

"And as a loyal Southerner you are protesting?"

"I want to know what you are up to."

"I am concealing nothing. Every penny goes into Confederate funds."

"After your expenses, of course?"

"My dear Dulcie, your late husband's perfidy has made you hard and cynical. With such an unwomanly character developing, how can you hope to attract suitors?"

"Edmund, you always make remarks as if a widow is in a position of beggary or not allowed to think unkind thoughts about men. My . . . late husband had his short-comin's, but he treated me as an equal. I *don't* like bein' patronized by creatures in britches."

Edmund laughed. "I'll add stubborn and sharp-spoken to your charms."

"You're evadin' the issue. Josiah pockets part of the collection money. Is that helpin' starvin' Confederates?"

His face darkened. "What will you do about these suspicions? Whisper them about? Or are you asking for your share?"

"If I wanted a share, I'd say so in plain words."

"If my assistant is stealing, I must put a stop to it. The piddling contributions are too small to interest me. I turn them over to Confederate agents. I don't know how the money is spent."

Dulcie stared at him. "If you don't care, why do you lecture? Why go to all this trouble? For you do work hard at it, Edmund."

"I wish to make friends, a great many friends, among Southerners and Yankees alike. There is one error many of our people make, Dulcie, that I shall not. The South will need not only the best of its Southern people after the war, it will require the good will and financing of the North. I shall be in a position to call upon that good will when it is needed."

"And that does not make you feel disloyal?"

He frowned at her. "Of course not! It is for the South I will make use of their influence and their money."

Dulcie fell silent. He seemed to make good sense, but still there was something terribly calculating in Edmund.

She looked up to see him smiling at her, his eyes warm and admiring. "You are a beautiful decoration to any man whose arm you hold, Dulcie. Especially now that you have left off wearing that ludicrous black armband."

"Why do you bring that up again and again? I believe you mention it more than I do. You tell me to forget, and then you remind me."

Edmund's voice was cold. "Forget and forgive. I no longer believe you can or should do either. How can you, when he deceived you so cruelly, deserted you for a skinny little nigger wench—"

"Skinny? How do you know if she was skinny, Edmund? Is there more you haven't told me? Were you—there—when he was—killed?"

"Rumor has a long tongue. For all I know, she was quite plump. What is the difference? She remains a nigger, fat or thin."

"Possibly, but what is the purpose in mentionin' Adam?"

"Must I have a purpose for everything? Very well, I have one. I am merely pointing out that love, so called, is a useless commodity. Having similar goals is a far more valid reason for marrying."

"I don't believe I need such instruction."

"I think you do. You will marry again. Women like you need that relationship."

"Oh, you are infuriatin'! Puttin' me in a box labeled 'wife.' Why not label me 'broom'? I sweep. Or . . . or washboard? I scrub."

"I am happy you find me infuriating. Not long ago you claimed indifference. I am making admirable progress."

"Take me home. I have had enough of your egotism."

"As you wish, my dear." They drove on in silence, Dulcie annoyed, Edmund smugly satisfied.

At Oliver's home Edmund helped Dulcie down from the carriage. Before she knew it, he had embraced her, his lips pressed against hers, softly, then compelling. After an instant's startlement, Dulcie found herself responding. It was so long since she had been kissed.

Yet, why should she be unsettled because a man had kissed her? Compared to the greater liberties she had endured, a kiss was—should be—nothing. She was a free woman, out in society to have a good time, and if a man's idea of a good time included a kiss, why not?

She knew why not. Never again would she be subservient in love, yielding to the man's need while denying her own. Justin had taken her—no, made her beg him, for what she didn't want. What Edmund felt she didn't know, but what she felt for him was not love. In Edmund's kiss there was no fire, just a vague reminder of what once was. One man had fed her fires with his own, counting her desires and their fulfillment as important as his—but that man had never belonged totally to her and had died unfaithful after abandoning her.

Edmund said she needed marriage. He was wrong. She would never marry again, never lie with another man. She was done with all that.

She did not see or hear of Edmund for several days. Her family never mentioned him. Aunt Mad had a gala party on the Saturday before Christmas, inviting several young people. As Dulcie's table partner she chose Oliver's assistant, Parley Tobin. Oliver, beaming, introduced him as a very bright young gentleman, rising fast.

Parley was soft-spoken, a loyal admirer of Oliver. "That man is my ideal, Mrs. Tremain," Parley confessed. "He has taught me so much. He can attend to several things at once, yet remain perfectly calm and efficient."

Dulcie giggled. "You should have seen him dealin' with a bandit while we were in France. He was so calm, he even *snored!*"

Parley's pleasant face fell. "Surely you are joking. A gentleman would not . . . you must be teasing!"

"Yes, I'm teasin'. Uncle Oliver is a bulwark, a man without fear."

Suddenly Dulcie realized why she was attracted to Parley. His gentle manner reminded her of Beau, sure of himself yet having that endearing vulnerability that tore at the heartstrings. "Call me Dulcie? I'd like that."

He blushed, glancing at Oliver, far down the table from him. "I—I'd like to—Dulcie—it's a beautiful name."

They smiled at each other. After a moment Parley said, "I don't want to seem forward, D-Dulcie, but your uncle tells me you're out of mourning now—"

Dulcie smiled. "Yes. I am."

"And I wonder if you'd enjoy seeing a minstrel show? Next Wednesday night? The Bijou Theater is specially presenting *Christmas on the Old Plantation*. Since you're from Savannah—"

"Oh, yes! They're such fun!"

Later, when they grouped around Mad's grand piano to sing, Dulcie kept seeking Parley's smiling eyes. She never caught him looking elsewhere but at herself. And Oliver, watching, beamed.

Parley was the last one to say good night. When they were alone in the parlor, with the gaslights low and the coals burning rose-gray in the grate, he said, "I won't embarrass you by lingering, Dulcie. But—I just want you to know—you're the most beautiful woman I ever met, and the sweetest, and I—"

Dulcie looked at him raptly, her eyes wide, her lips parted. She guessed his next words and was disappointed when he did not say them. Once, a lifetime ago, she would have asked him coquettishly. Now the hunger for endearments drove her beyond coquetry. She whispered, "Go on . . ."

"Dulcie—forgive me. I've been forward."

Dulcie said lightly, "You may kiss me if you'd like."

His blushes left, and his face became pale. "I wouldn't dream—" But Dulcie continued to look at him with a half-smile, her eyes soft. Parley gingerly touched her arms, gently found her lips with his. His mouth was warm; his breath smelled not unpleasantly of the spirituous punch that had been the good-night toast. He was moustached, clean, and attractive, with Beau's apparent unworldliness.

Dulcie put her arms around Parley's neck. She wanted this gentle man to kiss her out of her mind, make her forget the man she could never forget, wanted him to be tender and harsh with her at the same time, take her, touch her, use her, make her fall in love with him.

But Parley Tobin, assistant to Uncle Oliver, had better sense than she. He wanted what she did—it had been in his eyes all evening—but he was aware of his position. Parley's kiss was tender, yearning—and brief.

"Dulcie—I'm sorry," he gasped, holding her away from him. "I forgot myself. I won't do it again. Will I see you Wednesday night? I wouldn't blame you if you—"

She said softly, "I'll be ready at seven."

After he had gone, she tried not to think of herself as the fool she must be for throwing herself at the first appealing man she met. What must he think of her? Bold? Brassy?

He liked me, she argued with herself. *And I liked him. I want to see him again. I want to have a good time with him.*

Mondays and Tuesdays she worked at the soup kitchen. Wednesdays she joined Patricia and Mad at their sewing circle. Loyal Southern women did these things, but Dulcie's heart wasn't in them. After the war, whoever won, what would there be in the South for her? She loved her nation, but how could a widow work to restore its crumpled grandeur? A woman alone was suspect. A lady was expected to live in the shadow of a husband, or of a father. A lady was not supposed to earn her living or be independent. Only men had that option.

Well, she'd manage it somehow. She'd start learning about business as soon as she could. When her opportunity came to be of real help to the South, she'd recognize it. She would be ready.

The minstrel show was enjoyable; the evening with

Parley was not. Dulcie had not forgotten how to coquette, but now it seemed silly and pointless to pretend lack of interest or to wait months before he dared kiss the back of her hand. She kept wanting to move their relationship along faster.

After the show they talked of the war over hot mince pie and coffee at Delmonico's. "What are your chances of being drafted now, Parley?"

"Oh, none at all. I never wanted to serve in the first place. When my call came, I simply went down and paid for a substitute. Let someone else fight this war. I don't believe in it."

Dulcie said carefully, "What don't you believe in?"

"Any of it. I don't believe the Rebels had to secede. The North would have compromised. And it's silly for a slave owner to say he has to have a hundred niggers to pick his cotton. If they weren't so lazy, they could get along with fewer."

"Have you ever seen cotton fields, Parley?"

"No, but—"

"Cotton raising is hard, backbreaking work. It's not a matter of droppin' a seed on the ground and pickin' a box-ful of handkerchiefs off the bush a few months later. The plants must be cared for. The little cotton bolls, about this big, must be picked, one or two at a time, by hand from mid-summer until after New Year's. The best pickers can pick three hundred pounds a day. That's a bale if it's not compressed. That's thousands of times bendin' and stoopin'. It's at least as hard as factory work."

"I take your point." He smiled. "But if the Rebs would use modern methods, this idiotic war would never have started."

"And if the North had been fair with the South, instead of tryin' to impose Northern methods on a country that's entirely different, we wouldn't have had to secede."

"It's all the same country, Dulcie."

"But it isn't. We don't have snow and ice, we have a constant growin' season, and we're a hundred years later in developin' our section than you are yours. When Northern lawmakers try to legislate the way we shall live in our section, we don't like it very well."

"I—you're taking this personally, Dulcie, and you needn't. It's the whole South, not yourself, that I'm angry about."

"Well, it's my nation that's bein' torn up because yours butted in. If I take it personally, it's because I love my nation."

His fingertips touched the back of her hand lightly. "Don't let's argue, please? We're each entitled to our own opinions."

"I took that for granted."

He smiled at her, his blue eyes sparkling. "For a lady, Dulcie, you're a mighty independent person."

"My—my late husband taught me I was the equal of any man. And someday I'll prove it."

"For what purpose? As a wife you won't be needing any—any such manly ambitions."

Dulcie looked at him stonily. She had thought him more broad-minded, but he was ordinary, respectable, unimaginative. "You think just like every other man I've met but one. The little woman's place is in the home—and she's to keep her mouth closed even there." She grinned. "So much for educatin' the female."

"There are so many things we agree on, I feel sure."

Dulcie continued to smile. "Yes, many."

"I-I thought Mr. Bones was very amusing, didn't you?"

"Shuffles was my favorite. He reminded me of 'Simmon, a little old man I knew."

"Is it true that Southerners consider their darkies family?"

"Some of them. Wouldn't you if your servants lived in the house with you and served you all their lives?"

"I-I never could. I was reared to feel that servants were servants. All ours were white. Father wouldn't let a darkie on the place. The freed ones are totally worthless. They don't know how to work, and they don't want to learn."

Dulcie smiled faintly but said nothing. The gulf between herself and Parley was uncrossable.

On Christmas Eve Edmund came calling. Behind him, staggering under a load of gaily wrapped packages, was Josiah, his gaze sliding away from Dulcie's as she greeted him. *It's almost as if he's ashamed,* she thought. She smiled warmly, wanting him to feel happy.

"Dulcie, my dear, you are more beautiful than I had remembered," said Edmund, taking her hand and admiring her gown of green silk. "I hoped, in my absence, you'd grow pale and poetically wan."

Dulcie laughed. "Did you expect me to pine away for you, Edmund?" She eyed the gaily wrapped packages. "Are these for me? Shall I beware of Greeks bearing gifts?"

"Perhaps not Greeks, but of gentlemen of French extraction."

The evening passed gaily, with friends dropping in to bring gifts of fruitcake and homemade dainties, staying to visit and accept a highball, or, if they were ladies, a glass of blackberry cordial. At times the discussion got lively, as when Jem, the rabid Southerner, met an equally rabid Northerner head on.

It was long after midnight when Dulcie and Edmund were left alone. Dulcie sat daintily on a chair, weary to the bone, wishing she could sprawl with her knees apart and her hands hanging down. Edmund stalked around, still excited from the evening, smoking his cigar. His eyes sparkled. "I've brought you a small gift, a token of my esteem. I'd like you to open it now."

"I have nothin' for you, I'm sorry to say. I really didn't expect to see you again. You haven't been here for some time."

"Did you miss me?"

She grinned, playfully slapping at his hand. "Don't be so in love with yourself, Edmund. I hardly knew you were away."

"Sometimes, my dear Dulcie, you are so insouciant I could shake you."

"Violence will get you nowhere," she said lightly. "I grew up fist-fightin' with all my best friends. The knack stays with—"

"Open the package, and tell me if I must return it."

Dulcie slid the bow off the gold-foil-wrapped box. Inside a satin case, nestled on a white velvet cloth, was a bib necklace of teardrop emeralds, each surrounded by small diamonds. There were earbobs to match. Dulcie stared at the lavish display, her heart thudding.

"Put them on, so we can see if they become you."

"I-I can't. They're too expensive. I don't want them."

"Poppycock. Most women would leap at the chance."

She had been holding the box in her hands; now it seemed heavy, and she rested it on her lap. "You're . . . trying to buy me."

"Is the price insufficient? You haven't heard my terms yet."

Dulcie closed the box and held it out to him. When he did not offer to take it, she put it on the floor. "I don't want your jewelry or your terms. Just—just take them back."

He sat across from her, watching her keenly, enjoying her distress and bewilderment. He smiled lazily. "It's an honorable offer. I'd advise you to take it."

Dulcie glanced at the box. "It can't be."

He withdrew a smaller case from his pocket, snapped it open, and held it out to her. An emerald and diamond ring glittered there, beside a wide gold wedding band. "Are you convinced of my intentions now?"

Dulcie felt hypnotized, as though the glittering rings were swaying in front of her. She blinked and looked elsewhere, her head light.

He smiled. "After this war is finished, there will be opportunities to make staggering amounts of money in the South. Perfectly honest money."

"What has that to do with . . . those?" She gestured.

"Patience, my dear, I shall explain. Railroads are going to have to be rebuilt. New lines will be established. Now, someone will have to furnish materials. There will be plantations upon which taxes are overdue. I propose to pay those taxes and make the owner a decent offer. The South is going to change, become more industrialized like the North. Many Yankees will go South to make their permanent homes. I will have lumberyards and sawmills, and laborers who will be grateful to get work at my wages. I'll be rebuilding the South. No, Dulcie, I'll be leading it. Perhaps as governor."

"Buyin' low, sellin' high, and takin' advantage of people's ignorance."

Edmund shrugged. "Ignorant people have always been taken advantage of. But I am kinder than most and will offer a better bargain."

"You don't need a wife for that."

"But I do. A Southern woman, one who is so strikingly beautiful that men won't suspect her intelligence. One who is clever enough to listen, to feign ignorance while obtaining information to further our aims. Once established, I will go into politics, where your talents as hostess and private informer will benefit us handsomely."

"You do mean a legal marriage?"

"Of course."

"But still a . . . business arrangement."

Edmund lit a fresh cigar. "I think you have made it abundantly clear you want no more than that. So I shall abide by your restrictions. If you choose to cling to your romantic ghost, I'll accept that."

"But why? Why should you want a wife under those circumstances? You know I don't love you—I never could."

"I don't need a bedmate if that's what concerns you. I . . . am not that way inclined toward women." His eyes seemed veiled by the hooded lids.

Dulcie's mind whirled. "Edmund, I could never consider such a . . . a thing."

"Don't be hasty, Dulcie. I am offering you exactly what you want. A home, jewelry, an opulent life, no husbandly demands. All I ask in return is that you use your excellent mind of which you are so proud. I want you to look beautiful for me. I want you to help me in rebuilding the South, creating an empire of our own. And I do not ask that you give up your memories of Adam Tremain, although I think them foolish."

"I couldn't. It's so . . . calculatin'."

"It is honest. Our desires are well matched, our goals similar. We needn't pretend to love to have a fulfilling life."

"I can't believe that you would want such an arrangement or be long satisfied with it."

Edmund sighed, his patience deliberate and forced. "I have told you I have . . . select tastes in women. I don't believe you wish me to be more explicit. I have also an abhorrence of children. I would never permit my wife to have a child. If that does not assure you, my dear, I don't know of anything that would. For yourself, you would have complete freedom, so long as you did not interfere with my plans or my need of your services as hostess and helpmeet. And so long as you are discreet, a lover would pass my eyes unnoticed."

Dulcie swallowed. *Never permit a child.* Edmund's first wife, dead, leaving no children. How had she died? Trying to rid herself of Edmund's child? Or of another man's child? Dulcie blinked. "I would be your employee. In public I would be your devoted wife—but with separate bedrooms? I would be helpin' you make yourself wealthy—"

"I am already. Take these baubles to Tiffany's and have them appraised if you doubt that. However, I intend to acquire more wealth, and with it a great deal of power—that is true coinage, my dear. Does my proposal interest you? If so, we will be married in April."

"You've even planned that?"

He smiled at her, cupping her chin with his fingers. "Don't look so appalled. Can you deny that you and I have enjoyed one another's company? Come, now, answer."

"You-you've always been kind, and you understood when no one else did."

"That won't change. I've merely taken away the impediments to your feeling free to remarry."

"But Edmund—" Dulcie made a helpless gesture. "I've never heard of such a proposal."

Edmund laughed. "Where is your forward-thinking independence? Perhaps you are more conventional than you thought. I will let you think about it until New Year's Day. We will announce our plans then, or . . . Now, put those gems on. I want to see you attired as you should be."

Dulcie fastened the jewels on. "The rings too," Edmund insisted. "Now look at yourself. That is the way I would have you, Dulcie, the way a woman like you should be treated always."

She stepped back from the long mirror. The green silk gown in the daring new hoopless style fitted her perfectly. The necklace was tiered, resting just at the cleft of her pale breasts. The earbobs swung and shimmered. The cluster of stones on her left hand glittered.

The man behind her smiled, "Ah," he said softly. "The perfect picture of the wife of a wealthy man. Think of that, Dulcie." He picked up his greatcoat and top hat, gloves and stick. "A powerful man."

The front door opened and closed behind him, letting in a rush of icy air. As one in a dream, Dulcie moved from the mirror to turn the key in the lock, then returned to the mirror, posing prettily, admiring the rich sheen of her hair in its festive ringlets, pretending to herself that she was not going to look at the expanse of priceless gems that would be hers if she agreed to marry Edmund Revanche.

He had not told her everything, she knew. His business dealings would not be so lily white, his wages not so generous as he portrayed. Undoubtedly he intended to seize a plantation here and there for the tax moneys. In politics he would be very successful, with or without her help.

And how well would he live up to his share of the bargain? He had promised her a certain freedom, treatment as an equal, and cash for her private use. She would be expected to serve on committees, to head causes, to work for the sick and the homeless. Her freedom would be a hard-won privilege. But she would not have to be his whore. Edmund was not a warm man, but he had always been kind, even indulgent toward her. And he appreciated her intelligence—even was willing to buy her for it.

Dulcie turned her head yet another time, watching the pretty fall of the earbobs, seeing the gaslight reflected endlessly in the facets of the diamonds that lay cool among the green emeralds on her breasts.

She tried the words on: "I will marry you, A . . ." She saw her face turn pale and sad, and she stretched her mouth into a deliberate smile. The man whose name she had so nearly said was gone, and her love for him was dead. But they had shared a dream together, to rebuild the South. It was the one untarnished memory of their short marriage. In her own way, no matter how small, she would keep that dream alive. And Edmund was offering her the opportunity.

Christmas dinner was a gay affair with twenty at the table, including Parley. Dulcie, strangely depressed, put forth hardly any effort to be witty or entertaining.

Parley said solicitously. "Are you unwell?"

She managed a smile. "A silly little headache. I . . . had a sleepless night."

"Waiting for Saint Nicholas?" he asked mischievously, and she giggled.

After their guests were gone, Mad found Dulcie in her bedroom. "You don't treat poor Parley very well, Dulcie," she said mildly.

"Aunt Mad, you're up to somethin'. I know it's against your principles, but could you tell me without beatin' around the bush? My head is splittin' and I'd like to go to bed."

"I'm not at all pleased to see you goin' out socially so much and havin' such a gay time."

"Aunt Mad! You've always been first to say what's past

is past! What do you want me to do, huddle in my black shawl and nurse my grief?"

"I'd a sight rather you did that than cover it all up as if Adam never meant the snap of your fingers to you."

"Cover it *up!* I—"

"All this frantic rush, your giggles and gaiety. It's as if you're trying very hard to hide from yourself. I'll bet you have never just given in and bawled over Adam. Now, have you?"

"No," said Dulcie angrily. "Nor will I. He could have found me—not left me to save my own life on that God-forsaken—horrible—" Her voice trembled, and she had to stop.

"What makes you think he didn't try? Why do you believe he is dead?"

"He *is!* Edmund told me how he died."

"I'll admit I believed him at first, and I cried a lot over it, but now I'm not so sure. Dear, that Mr. Revanche is—"

"I know you don't like him, so don't start criticizin' him! You're bein' unreasonable, Aunt Mad, and I don't want to hear it!"

"Goodness me, you needn't get *shrill*. What exactly did Mr. Revanche say that made you believe him?"

"He mentioned the Green Swamp, and Adam has a friend there, Tom Pierson. He spoke of the saltworks, and I know about them from Adam. He said two women— Aunt Mad, you know how women cluster around Adam like flies around a honeypot. Then he—he m-mentioned—" Dulcie bit her lips. She was very near to crying, and she could not, for it would destroy her.

"Claudine," Mad filled in smoothly. "I'm sure there are several in the South with that name."

"He said she was little and skinny and that she died for him! Oh, Aunt Mad, it *was* Claudine. She was in love with Adam, and I was a-afraid—Claudine—you don't know how she used to sneak out—"

"Of course I know, dear," said Mad placidly. "I'd have sent her home from Europe if I could have. So you were afraid. Afraid of what?"

"To leave her alone with him! Afraid I'd never be enough woman for him. I couldn't trust—I didn't know how to!" Dulcie's tears were flowing now, her words only partly intelligible. "We left her in Nassau. I was goin' to free her, send her away when we got back—and then . . ."

Mad stroked Dulcie's hair. "There, dear, let it all out."

"And I was on Andros—with savages—and—Lu-Lucifer. I was so frightened, and I needed Adam so. Oh, Aunt Mad, why? Why did he leave me there?"

"That wretched Mr. Revanche has made you think all this!"

"Edmund is so . . . he . . . it's almost as if he had seen Adam. Everything—it was so like Adam. I even asked if he had been there."

"I still don't think one man's story is proof," said Mad stubbornly.

Dulcie sobbed. "If he is alive, why doesn't he come for me? I loved him so much, Aunt Mad. All I ever wanted was him! He could have found me. He knows you and Uncle. Even if he couldn't find me on Andros, he could have come here."

Mad awkwardly patted Dulcie. She didn't quite know herself why she was so insistently on Adam's side. She thought of the times she had seen them together: on the *Tunbridge,* talking intimately together, and in each other's arms outside Dulcie's cabin; playfully sparring at the theater; at the ball, when he had tried to protect her and then taken her with him. Perhaps it was no more than the fact that Mad believed wholeheartedly in the power of love and couldn't conceive that what she had seen between Adam and Dulcie could die. "Perhaps he did come here. Perhaps Ollie and I were away—we were! We went to Canada last year, Dulcie. I'm sure Adam must have come and—"

"Aunt Mad! Adam is dead. I *know* he is dead. He's gone! Oh, Aunt Mad, I'll never love anybody else the same way. But I can't go on lovin' a ghost. I can't always go on hopin' for somethin' that isn't there. Edmund has shown me that. I don't want to be a widow for the rest of my life." She took a deep breath. "I've decided to marry Edmund Revanche. In April."

Mad, horrified, whispered, "Dulcie—you *can't!*"

Chapter Twelve

Throughout November Adam slowly regained health. Once the worry of a constant life-and-death crisis was over, Zoe and Rod were drawn more to one another. Nearly every day they quarreled and made up. Zoe felt by turns either bullied or entirely feminine. In the space of a moment she could shed years of responsibility and care, appearing before Rod as a young girl naïvely eager for his affections.

Rod behaved little more sensibly. He prided himself on his sophistication, his knowledge and savoir-faire. Yet he found himself waiting nervously for her to appear at suppertime, gazing at her diffidently, seeking a response in her eyes.

The days ran through their fingers like raindrops, peculiarly combining the renewal of their love with the vigilant worry over their son's inadequate and slow recovery. The bee stings were healed, the blisters small fading marks on Adam's skin. The infected whip lacerations were healing, but Adam was not well.

He grew stronger, able to sit in bed or in a chair part of each day. He was conscious, aware of people, and certain of their identity, but none of his reactions were normal.

Rod had visited him daily. Neither he nor Zoe, however, knew if Adam realized that Rod's presence in Smithville was peculiar. They were not even certain Adam knew he was in Smithville. After the fever had broken and he was lucid and carrying on a weak but steady conversation with Mammy for several minutes, Rod and Zoe came in to see him.

"Someone is here to see you, Adam," Zoe said softly.

He frowned. "Have you found Dulcie?"

Zoe glanced quickly at Rod, standing beside her in plain view. "No, dear, it's Mr. Courtland. He's come all the way from New York."

"The natives have her. They wanted her for some reason. That's why they drove me off. I shouldn't have let them do it. I should have gone back."

"Adam," Rod ignored the rambling. "It's good to see you awake for a change. How do you feel?"

Adam stared, his eyes fearful and troubled. "The bees . . . I couldn't—"

"That's over."

"Over . . ." His voice trailed off uncertainly.

"Adam, do you know me?"

Adam looked at him blankly, then laughed. "I ought to! You owned half my ship." Then he looked away, his face troubled again. "She went down in a storm. We were being chased and—Rod—I left Dulcie on Andros."

"No, you didn't. It's just a nightmare. You've been very ill. The ship went down a long time ago, Adam. Dulcie is not on Andros."

"Yes, she is!" He struggled to rise, then fell back weak and exhausted.

"Don't fret now. We'll have plenty of time to talk later."

"I've got to find her. I shouldn't have let them drive me away."

"You can't sail now. The moon—it's a full moon. You can't sail."

"First dark night," Adam murmured, his eyelids already falling shut.

Rod and Zoe went back downstairs. "He simply accepts me as part of his surroundings, Zoe."

"Maybe if we tell him why you are here, it'll make him—"

"No. This is no time to shock him with any more news."

"But, Rod, suppose he stays like this forever. There must be something we can do. He's always been so bright. He'll realize Dulcie isn't on Andros. Or if she is, it would only be her remains."

"Stop going over it, Zoe! I don't want you to tell him —not yet. I forbid it!"

"Then what are we going to do?"

"Give him time. He's still living those nightmares. God, I'd hate to be him."

Adam clung to the idea of going back to Andros. He had the fixed notion that Dulcie was merely waiting for him to find her. About that he talked incessantly, but about other things he remained mute. After his single mention of the bees he showed no further sign of remembering. Slowly he regained strength. He became cheerful and coopera-

tive, wanting to spend time with Zoe and Rod, teasing and
talking.

Adam said casually, "I didn't know you knew my
mother."

Rod laughed. "Would it surprise you to know I knew
her before you did? What would you think of that?"

"I think Ma's been holding out on me. How many other
men have you got tucked away in your life?"

"None! What a terrible thing to say to your mother,
Adam Tremain!" Zoe smiled. "Oh! You are getting well. I'm
leaving before you both gang up on me. Tom is here, so
don't tire yourself too much. He'd like to visit with you."

"Tell him to come up. I'm anxious to talk with him."

After visiting with Adam, Tom joined Zoe, Angela, and
Rod. "He wants me to go to Andros. Can you imagine
running that damn ship of his? But he's got it all planned.
Knows just where he wants to land, how long it will take
to find Dulcie, and the day he plans to be home again."

"He's asked me the same thing," Rod said. "What'd you
tell him?"

Tom rubbed his jaw. "Mebbe I did wrong. I told him I
wouldn't go, an' he was a darned fool for thinkin' o' goin'
himself. Guess I gave it to him straight. Told him Dulcie
was dead—there weren't anythin' for him on Andros."

"How did he take it?"

"I dunno. I expected him to try to knock my head off.
That's what he'd usually do. But he wasn't angry or nothin'.
Seemed like he expected me to say no. Said it didn't matter, he knew what he was doin' an' he'd find someone to
go with him. Ya know, the funny thing is, Adam don't
usually want anyone with him. Seems like he's makin'
damned sure he never sees that island alone again."

Rod put his arm around Zoe. "He talked to Rosebud,
and he said no too."

Zoe lost herself in another world, gazing up at Rod.

Tom grinned, "You tell him about you two yet?"

"Tell him what?" Angela asked.

Tom ruffled her hair. "None o' your business. Didn't anyone ever tell you children are to be seen and not heard?"

"Since I'm no longer a child, that doesn't apply to me.
What haven't you told Adam? Are you going to get married? Is that it?"

Rod smiled down at their joined hands. "I don't know.
Is that it, Zoe?"

Tom chuckled. "Well, Zoe, what about it? It wasn't very purty, but I believe the cussed Yankee is proposin'."

"He did no such thing!"

Rod slid onto his knee, his hand holding hers. "Yes, he did."

"Oh, Rod, get up off the floor!"

"Come on, Zoe, you got Angela an' me sittin' on the edge o' our seats. Ya gonna make him an honest man?" Tom's face split wide in an expectant grin.

Rod's eyes held the question without teasing. He seemed so far away.

"Do you really want to marry me?"

"Are you going to say yes this time and mean it?"

"Oh yes, yes." At once she was in his arms.

Tom filled two glasses with brandy for himself and Rod and two with blackberry cordial for the women. "Ever seen anything like that, Angela?"

Angela watched Zoe and Rod embrace. Zoe, who had chastised her and come near to calling her a scarlet woman, was now, right before her eyes, making a spectacle of herself with the Yankee whose illegitimate son she had bore. "Never," the girl said acidly. "I thought only white trash behaved like that."

"No, sweetheart, white trash act the way you are right now. I guess you're too young for this anyhow." Tom dumped the cordial back into the decanter. "Run along to your room. No sense in havin' a happy occasion ruined by a spoiled youngun. Go on, now, we got some serious celebratin' to do."

Angela raised her head, glaring at her father, then walked unhurriedly from the room.

At the top of the stairs she hesitated. Light showed under Adam's door. She turned toward it, her mind made up. "I saw the light."

Adam put down the chart he had been studying. "I'm glad you did. You don't often come to see me. Sit down. Talk to me."

"I can't. I've been sent to my room."

"What have you done this time?"

"I haven't done anything."

"So, your wicked stepmother sent you to your room for nothing."

"I haven't got a stepmother, and it wasn't Aunt Zoe. It was Tom."

"Ohhh. You really are in trouble, then."

"Aren't you smug! You always have all the answers."

"Not all, but some. You might do better if you listened once in a while."

Angela laughed. "That's right. Just listen to you and Aunt Zoe, and all the bad things will disappear. My mother won't be a nigger anymore. I'll be like any other white girl. Then I can marry the handsome white prince and live happily ever after." Angela shook her head, a disdainful smile on her face. "You think you know everything. Well, I could tell you a few things if I wanted to."

"Like what?" Adam smiled.

"Like all that stuff, those maps you read, are just a waste of time. No one is going with you to that island. They're all going to say no. They think there's something wrong with your head. Even Aunt Zoe thinks you're daffy, and she's always on your side."

"They'll change their minds when I explain the facts."

"*She's* dead. Why do you keep thinking about her?"

"She's not dead."

"Oh, yes she is, and you might as well be! Even if she were alive, she wouldn't want you now. I don't know why I ever thought I loved you either. I don't! I don't anymore!"

"Whoever sent you to your room had the right idea," Adam said wearily. "Get out of here, Angela."

"Oh, listen to the captain giving orders. He really thinks he's somebody! Captain Adam Tremain, fine ol' Southern family with all the trimmin's—even the skeleton in the closet. Isn't that grand!"

"Shut up, Angela."

"Shut up Angela," she mocked. "Don't tell any secrets, Angela. Don't mention dear, sweet, pure Aunt Zoe is a harlot and the good, gallant captain is a bastard. Don't talk to your betters, Angela. Shut up, Angela. Shut up, Angela. Well, I don't have to shut up. Not now or ever. You're no better than me. And neither is Aunt Zoe!"

Adam stared at her, stunned into silence by her vehemence.

"Do you know what's going on downstairs? They're celebrating—they're laughing, making a joke of *your father* proposing to your mother. That's what they're doing. Just like it was all right, and my father is right there with them. And you were going to send me away because I wanted to

marry you. I loved you! I didn't do any of the things Aunt
Zoe did. So, why was I so bad? What did I do that was
so wrong?"

"What are you—? Go to your room, Angela. I have
charts to mark."

"You don't like to hear that do you? Or maybe it's too
complicated for you. I forgot, your brains are scrambled.
I'll make it simple. Mr. Courtland is your father. Aunt Zoe
is your mother. Finally they've decided to get married.
Does that mean you'll be legitimate from here on out?"

Adam stared at her in bewilderment. "Where do you get
notions like this?"

Angela smiled slyly. "Oh, I don't know. I guess I must
have made it all up. Y'all are always sayin' I'm a liar.
'Night, Adam."

Angela walked lightly down the corridor to her room.
She rummaged in the back of her cupboard, bringing out a
low-cut gown she had stolen from Zoe's wardrobe. Pleased
with the effect, Angela concentrated hard as she looked in
the mirror, changing her childish hairdo into a sophisticated
style she had seen the fancy women of the waterfront
saloons wear. Then she tugged at the neckline until it was
far off her shoulders, showing an expanse of creamy skin.
Quietly she slipped down the servants' stairs.

Adam's pen lightly traced the course from Wilmington
to Andros, but his mind wasn't on his charts. Background
noises intruded. Laughter. The sounds of clinking glasses.
Voices raised happily.

He got out of bed unsteadily. Angela's words lodged
in his mind. Rod was his father. Shakily he walked down
the stairs toward the light and laughter. His mother's voice
was high-pitched and gay.

From the parlor door he watched Rod's arms close
around Zoe. She held a cordial glass first to her own lips,
then turned it for Rod to drink.

"Can't kiss through a glass. Give your bride-to-be a
proper bussin'," Tom said, taking the glass from Zoe.

"Don't you dare, Rod Courtland! It's not proper in public," Zoe giggled.

"Since when am I the damned public?" Tom howled.

Adam stood trembling in the doorway as Rod's lips
possessed Zoe's.

"Well, look what showed up for the celebration," Tom

said coming to Adam. "It's about time you got your ass down here. There's congratulations in order. Your Ma and Rod are gonna be married. You always told me you'd make a Rebel out of the old sod. Took your Ma to do it."

Dizzily Adam met Rod's eyes. The room wavered. "You're my father?"

The smile on Rod's face became fixed. He wasn't sure if it was a straigthforward question or simply another of Adam's lapses into a nightmare world that combined past and present indiscriminately. Cautiously he said, "I guess marrying your mother would make me your father." Rod led him to a chair. "Here, sit down. You shouldn't have come down those stairs. You look ready to pass out."

Adam leaned back, his face ashen and covered with a moist sheen. Tom shoved his brandy to Adam's lips.

"You're my father," Adam repeated. "Angela . . ."

Rod considered, then took Zoe's cold hand in his. "Yes, I am. Your mother and I have always loved one another, and both of us have loved you. I don't know what else to tell you. You've always thought of Paul Tremain as your father, but he wasn't. It's that simple."

"Adam, I want you to be happy about this," Zoe said earnestly. "I am, dear. I've never been so happy."

"We'd like your blessings, Adam, if you're able to give them."

Adam nodded, unable to do more. The brandy had hit his stomach like a hammer blow. Voices all blended together. The room swam, colors bleeding into one another, then fading to a misty gray.

Rod and Tom carried him back to his room. "Hell of a way for him to find out." Tom scowled. "Where the hell is Angela? Damn! I sent her to her room. I've got some talkin' to do to that young lady."

He ran down the hall in his crab-legged way. "She's not in her room! I knew it, damn it, I know that little heifer has gone out on the town."

"Slow down, Tom."

"I'm gonna find her. Then I'm gonna beat her."

Zoe said, "She'll be back soon. I don't really think she does anything bad. She just runs when something upsets her."

"How long's this gone on, Zoe? You never told me why Adam was bringin' her to the swamp. It was this, wasn't it? There's men."

"I don't know for sure. Adam—"

Tom's face screwed up. "Of course, Adam! She's always been hankerin' after him. What'd she do?"

"Nothing! Tom, please, you're excited and angry. We were just worried that she was going to get into trouble. She is very open with . . . everyone. I don't think she realizes what some of these soldiers are capable of. She's familiar with honorable men. She is just young—"

"Zoe, you're a good woman, but you're dead wrong. I been keepin' my eyes closed tight against everythin' that li'l girl has been doin' an' thinkin' for the past two-three years. But not after tonight."

Angela came in the rear entrance of the house shortly before two o'clock in the morning. Zoe, half-asleep against Rod's shoulder, awakened, alert to the change in the house noises.

Tom was heading through the kitchen before a word was spoken. Zoe moved to follow. Rod pulled her back. "She's his daughter. Let him handle it. I haven't been alone with you all evening."

"I don't understand Angela, Rod. Why does she do the things she does?" Her eyes turned toward the angry voices emanating from the kitchen. Rod pressed her against him, pressing his hand over her ear.

"Mind your own business, Zoe."

She wriggled against him, then smiled up at him. "What is my business?"

He kissed her, his hands warm and searching over her bodice. "I'm your business. Can't you concentrate on that?"

"I have been—for years."

"You don't suppose, in your ponderings, you could find a more comfortable place for me to sleep, do you?"

She giggled, "I thought you liked the sofa. You said it was the most comfortable sofa you'd ever slept on."

"It's the only sofa I've ever slept on. You see I never lie."

"So where do you propose to sleep? There's the cot—"

"There's Zoe's bed."

"Rod, that's sinful."

"What I'm feeling is just as sinful. Shall we share one sin, or shall we both commit our separate ones?"

She was laughing when Tom stormed back into the room. "Have you seen what your sweet little protégée looks like when she gets herself all done up, Zoe? Get in here, Angela! Get in here, damn it, or I'll bring you in myself."

Reluctantly, her face smeared with tears, her heavy makeup smudged across her face by Tom's ungentle hands, Angela stood in front of Rod and Zoe, her eyes blazing.

Zoe drew in her breath. "Angela . . . oh, Angela—your pretty face. How could you do that to yourself?"

Angry tears gushed from Angela's eyes. "You didn't care. None of you cared about me. I found someone who does."

"You go near him again and I'll break every bone in your head. We'll see how pretty you are then," Tom said savagely. "She's been galavantin' with some black buck."

Zoe swallowed hard, not knowing what to say. Tom himself had married a black woman, but Ullah had never seemed any color to Tom. Angela's young man did. "Go to bed now, Angela. In the morning . . . it'll seem better."

Angela's fists were clenched. A tremor of rage ran through her. "Ohh, I hate you! I hate you!" She ran past her father.

Tom glared after her. "I'm sorry. We sure put a damper on your night. Best thing I can do for you is get myself out of here."

"You're welcome to stay, Tom."

"I know that, Zoe, but I want to get outside. I got to do somethin' about her, an' right now all I can think of is beatin' her to death."

Angela awakened with puffy eyes, humiliation and resentment hot in her breast. She opened her door and listened. Mammy padded toward Adam's room with a breakfast tray. From below she heard Zoe's voice and Rod's, animated and happy. Outside Rosebud shouted to another man. He, too, sounded happy. She shut the door, crying bitter tears of self-pity. She cried softly at first, then louder. No one came. No one asked how she was or comforted her noisy tears.

By noon she was certain no one was going to bother about her. They would never let Adam go without two meals. Everyone in the house would have been beating a path to his room trying to tempt him with delicacies.

Zoe had never really cared. Angela could see that now. Right from the beginning Zoe had befriended Ullah only for Adam's sake, and later she had gotten stuck with Angela. Even Tom didn't want her. He seldom came to see her, and then he never really wanted to talk to her or take her places. And Adam had made it clear that he wanted no part of her.

Miserable and building a convincingly sad case, Angela took on the air of an abandoned heroine. Sentimentally she stroked Ullah's tattered box of treasures Tom had given her on her fifteenth birthday. She ran her finger over the box, imagining it to be something of great value.

Angela had no clear picture of Ullah. It was easy to make her mother beautiful by Angela's standards, make her white, whiter than Zoe, make her rich and powerful. Angela imagined her so seductive that all men, even Adam, had loved her.

Angela opened the box and took from it Ullah's colored pebbles and shells. Each one was a gem. A ruby sparkled in the palm of Angela's hand next to a sapphire and an emerald. Jade jostled carnelian and moonstone. Diamonds sparkled and winked next to onyx. For a long time she played, making the stones and shells what she wished they were.

Then she took out the letter from Zoe. It was dog-eared and yellowed. Angela read it as she had so many other times. This time she imagined Zoe was a poor old woman thanking Ullah for permitting her, a woman fallen from grace, to attend her barbecue on Saturday.

But Angela had drawn her game out too long. The image wouldn't hold. She kept seeing Zoe's shocked face last night when Tom dragged her into the parlor to be humiliated and judged. She saw the clay doll Ullah had saved from her own childhood. Viciously Angela tried to stab her hatpins into the doll, wanting it to be Zoe, and Tom and Rod and Adam.

Around Angela were all the tawdry, simple things that had meant so much to her mother. To Angela the gems no longer glittered or promised dreams of an impossible future. They were dirty little stones anyone could pick up on the street or beach. The letter was an ordinary acceptance note. Angela ripped it in half, then shredded the paper into jagged pieces. She ground it into the floor, hating the sight of it.

Still glorying in her own anger, Angela postured before her mirror, her face haughty and superior. Then the expression crumpled into that of a lonely child. "Nigger. Nigger, nigger, nigger, nigger." She backed from the mirror. She reached for the clay doll. "Nigger! Nigger! Nigger! Nigger! NIGGER!" She hurled the doll at the mirror. Glass and clay slewed over the floor, tiny shards cutting her feet. Crying, Angela picked up the shells and stones and threw them, the small sharp objects making hard popping noises as they hit the walls.

Still no one came.

Late that afternoon Angela dressed and went out. No one stopped her.

She went to find Jubal Lerner, a man who wanted her, a man who cared enough to be there when Angela needed him. And he was black. She needn't fear discovery with him. If their babies turned out black, no one would care. She needn't fear that either.

When Tom arrived at Zoe's, Angela was gone. "Where in the hell did she get to? I didn't know they walked the streets in the daytime."

"I don't even know how long she's been gone. Oh, Tom, I'm so sorry."

"She can't do nothin' she hasn't done a dozen times before, Zoe. Don't waste yourself on her."

Angela reappeared after supper. Rod answered the door. Calmly he stepped aside for a gaudily dressed Angela in a newly bought gown to enter, followed by her equally gaudy escort. "Jubal, make yourself comfortable. I'll pack what little I've got and be down in a minute."

Tom barged into the parlor, his face a mask of disgust. "Get your black butt offa that sofa. Servants in the back, boy!"

Angela came halfway down the stairs. "Be careful what you say, Mastah Tom. That black boy's gonna be the father of your grandchildren."

Tom started for her. Rod grabbed him, talking in hushed earnest tones. Roughly Tom pulled free. "If she wants him, she's welcome to him. Damn bitch. Let her go!"

Zoe joined them, leaving Jubal dressed to his teeth in a stiff collar, suit jacket, and spats and uncomfortable about being in the parlor alone. "Tom, you don't mean that. You can't let her go. She's throwing her life away. She's too young to know better."

"No whore is born young, Zoe. Sorry to put it that way to you, but there isn't any other word for my—for Angela. Forget her. She's no good."

Angela, with second thoughts, came slowly down the stairs, her air of superiority less certain. "Well, I guess I'm ready now. Haven't you anything to say to me, Daddy? No blessings? No celebration for me like there was for them?" She walked to Tom, standing near, her eyes seeking comfort in his.

"I'm glad she's dead. You dirty little bitch, I'm glad your mother isn't here to see you."

Angela was taken aback. Tears sprang to her eyes.

"Go on! Take your nigger buck and get out of here!"

Angela was too shaken to feel her burning humiliation. That would come later. Now she looked pleadingly at Tom. "I just wanted someone to love me."

"You found him." Tom stalked from the room.

Zoe placed her hand on Angela's arm. "We *do* love you, Angela. Stay with us, dear. It will be all right."

Angela shook free of Zoe, her eyes blazing now as they hadn't before. "Don't touch me! You—you made fun of me, made me want—oh! I hate you! I hate you! Jubal! I want to leave!"

Zoe followed. "Angela—if you ever want to come home—"

Rod pulled her back and slammed the door. "No, Zoe, we won't be here for her if she wants to come home."

"But Rod, she's a child. She doesn't know—"

"We'll be in New York." He tilted her face up. "There won't be any more little girls to raise, unless they are ours."

The wedding was held on Christmas day. Tom gave the bride away. Adam was best man, handing a plain gold band to his father as Rod married his mother.

Whether the wedding made a sensible impression upon Adam, no one knew or dared question. He seemed happy and joined in the festivities. He embraced Zoe and Rod, expressing happiness for his mother.

Then, tired, still unable to remain on his feet for long, Adam returned to his room. He slid under the quilts, pulling them close against him. Slowly plans began to form again. The charts he had going over played themselves before his eyes like a series of pictures. Quick little visions of the beach at Andros, the sound of the drums, the forest, flashed and were lost to him. Faces came and went: Ben, Rosebud, Rod, Tom, all the people who had refused to help him renew the search for Dulcie.

At last once face remained. One man, one last hope. Oliver Raymer, an almost forgotten face, now came clear. Oliver had taken Dulcie to Europe. When she was in trouble, Dulcie had run to the Raymers. When she was worried about Jem and Patricia's reception of some bit of news, it was to the Raymers she turned. Oliver loved Dulcie as a daughter. Almost as much as Adam loved her. He would seek Oliver's help.

He fell asleep with the idea planted firmly in his mind, a slight smile on his lips. For the first time since he had lost her, he felt some hope. Oliver would not refuse him. All he had to do was get to New York. Find Oliver.

Chapter Thirteen

As he boarded the *Black Swan*, Adam's legs trembled, and before his eyes danced little bright spots in the darkness where there was nothing to be seen. Above him a sliver of the quarter moon slipped behind boiling dark clouds. He would have preferred a blacker night. At least a third of his men were not on board. He'd miss R.B., though he knew the smiling black giant would have kept him from sailing.

Adam stalked the deck as usual, his eyes missing nothing, checking every detail as though the first mate were lacking in competence. Occasionally he leaned on the rail more heavily than he wanted to admit, drawing strength from the salt air, his voice repeating with the wash of the water that he'd be all right. He'd be all right. The important thing was to find Oliver.

Oliver would see that the only course left was to go back to Andros and search until they found her. She was there. He should never have believed . . .

The first mate stood in front of him, saluting. "Steam's well up, sir."

"We'll wait 'til midnight, Mr. Compton."

"It's just past, sir."

Surely he hadn't stood in one spot so long. "What does the lookout report?"

"Three Federals out about two miles, sir."

"Very well. We'll hug the shore. Give the orders, Mr. Compton."

They crept in the shallows mile after mile, then just before dawn struck boldly into the shipping lanes.

Luck rode with them through the sleepless days and nights until they reached the Long Island coast. Adam hung well offshore until dark, then steamed into Oyster Bay and up into Courtland's cul-de-sac. Someone now occupied the large house, whose bulk loomed against the night sky, staring and ominous like a night bird watching. Adam stared tiredly at the house for some time, then pushed his imaginings aside. There was no enemy in that house, no one watching, no one wishing him ill. Rod would have warned him. After all, Adam thought, managing a weak smile, Rod Courtland was his father. Fathers were known to protect their sons.

He walked to the foredeck. Rod hadn't known he was leaving Wilmington. . . . Adam shrugged. He had made voyages before without knowing what awaited him. This was no different. He climbed into the jolly boat and kept his eyes fastened on the approaching shore.

Hans was waiting for him. "Well, Cap'n Tremain! Nice seein' you again, sir. I was afraid we were out of the business."

Adam stared at him, stupefied with fatigue.

"With the slaves, sir," Hans explained.

"Oh, I . . . I don't have any this time, Hans."

"Say, Cap'n, not gettin' the grippe, are you? Been a lot of it about."

"No. Hans, I'll be needing a horse right away. I must ride to the city."

"Can it wait 'til mornin', Cap'n?" He stared hard at Adam. "You ain't never found that Mr. Raymer home yet."

Adam rubbed his face. His head was buzzing, the little lights danced before his eyes like fireflies, his skin prickled with old sweat and the memories of bees—hundreds of them angry stinging—swarming. "I need the horse tonight. It's been too long already. I can't wait any longer."

"Then, it'll have to be my carriage, Cap'n. With me in the driver's seat."

Adam swayed. "Hitch up, Hans. I've got to get there as soon as possible. Dulcie—she—she's lost. I've got—"

"I know, Cap'n. I know."

Adam woke up to a gray, rainy dawn. Hans had stopped the buggy, and they were partly sheltered in a grove of bare-branched trees. "What's wrong?" he said, alarmed. "Why did we stop here?"

Hans opened his eyes. "I got sleepy, Cap'n. We'll hurry along now." He flapped the reins; the captain looked little better for his six hours' sleep.

"Why keep tryin' to see that man, if you don't mind my askin'?"

"My wife and I were shipwrecked—on Andros. I've got to find her."

"You went down a year and a half ago, Cap'n," Hans said mildly.

"I . . . know what I'm doing."

"Beggin' your pardon, sir, I just thought—God almighty, Cap'n Tremain, you ain't acted like yourself since then. You look like you been through a cider press. If there's gonna be trouble, you ain't up to it."

"No . . . no trouble. Her uncle'll go with me. Everything will be fine."

Hans grunted. "Git along, hoss!"

The winter rain gusted over them as the horses moved along the rutted, muddy roads. "Had a spell o' nasty weather. Reckon it's goin' hard on the boys in the trenches. Heard the lung fever's pretty bad."

"How much longer 'til we get there?" Adam asked irritably.

"I reckon two, three o'clock. You know it's purt near a daylong trip in winter, Cap'n. Don't you want to rest?"

"No—just get there."

It was raining hard when Hans stopped in front of Oliver's house. Adam got down slowly, surprised at his stiffness. He was tired beyond reason. Oliver's house seemed miles away, distorted by distance as he walked the few yards to the front stoop. He clacked the lion's-head knocker.

Fred opened the door. "Yes, sir?"

"Is Mr. Raymer at home?"

"Certainly, sir. Come in and warm yourself while I give him your name."

"I don't need to be announced. He knows me well."
Adam walked unsteadily toward the sound of voices. His
eyes fevered, he thrust open the parlor door, looking
blindly around the room until he spotted Oliver. "Mr.
Raymer—I must talk to you. You're the only one left I
can talk to."

Before him was a tableau with all the performers frozen
in place, their eyes fixed in amazement on the tall, gaunt
man, dressed in a damp, rumpled captain's uniform. Under
his cap his black curls hung in strings. His piratical black
moustache accentuated the pale hollowness of his cheeks
and his wild, fevered eyes. His movements were jerky, like
a puppet manipulated by an amateur.

Adam's gaze fixed on one of the people. *Revanche.* Oh,
God, he had to get away—run. But his legs . . .

"A-Adam!" came a hushed voice. His frightened eyes
met the golden eyes—eyes that haunted him in dreams.

With swift clarity every person in the room came into
sharp focus. All the people he had searched for were there.
All of them. It was another nightmare, fever-ridden, taunting, wounding, laying new scars across old ones.

His breath came out in a horse whimper of awful fear.
This was Death. It stared at him out of Dulcie's dead eyes,
smiled at him with Revanche's mouth. Adam grasped the
doorframe, his legs trembling and threatening to give way.

"Adam—good God, it is really you!" Oliver smiled, his
hand out.

Adam backed away. "Don't come near me." His gaze
darted to Patricia, who had fainted, and to Jem, who was
patting her hands absently. Mad stared at him, her face
alight.

"Edmund, let me go!" Dulcie said angrily.

With liquid grace Edmund rose from his seat beside
Dulcie. On his face was a courteous, pleased smile. "Captain Tremain," he drawled. "I must say you are quite a
surprise—and not wholly a welcome one." Edmund offered him a small, thin cigar. Adam, his back against the
door, shook his head. "Too bad. I thought if anyone would
appreciate a good cigar, it would be you. I seem to mis-
judge you on all counts."

Dulcie came up to the men. With authority and the easy
proprietary air of a man sure of his woman, Edmund took
her hand, speaking low and firmly in her ear, telling her to
leave him to talk to the captain.

"Adam . . ." Dulcie hardly heard Edmund, her eyes filled with moisture, her words choked and held back by shock and leaping joy.

Edmund moved uneasily, his laughter harsh. Adam slowly raised his hand, his fingertips barely touching the unruly curl at Dulcie's cheek. The room pulsated with hushed, pent-up emotions that threatened to burst into flame.

Edmund broke the silence. "Captain Tremain should be told our news, Dulcie. Arrangements must be made now that he has made his untimely return from the dead. Shall you tell him, or shall I?"

"Dulcie . . . I thought I'd never find you again. I thought—"

"Oh, Adam." She tried to go to him. Edmund's hand clasped her wrist hurtfully, making her wince and draw back.

He said, "I see that I shall have to be the bearer of the glad tidings. Dulcie and I are going to be married. Your resurrection is unfortunate. However, you have abandoned your wife for over a year, so I presume we can take that as a statement of your feelings. I feel certain you will give us your cooperation in annulling your marriage."

Adam listened to Edmund as though hypnotized. Sweat beaded his face. He mouthed, "Married . . . married . . ." He looked at Dulcie's white, strained face. "Bitch! You God-damned bitch!"

"It's not true! Adam! He's lyin'! Don't listen to him!"

Edmund thrust her left hand toward Adam. The emerald and diamond sparkle pained his eyes. "This is the ring *I* gave her, Tremain. And she *will* be my wife. There will be no legal problems. You deserted her. I can arrange—"

"Whore," he whispered. "Whore—"

"Here, now, Captain—" Oliver began.

Dulcie pulled away from Edmund. "Please—let me explain. Let me—"

Adam paid no attention to Oliver, who was trying to put his hand on Adam's shoulder, or to Jem, who had sprung to protect his daughter. He did not see Jem's gun or Mad screaming, "Don't! Not Adam!" His eyes were only for Dulcie. And his eyes were hot with hate. "You God-damned whore. You put me through hell."

She held out her arms to him; he backed away for every step she took forward. Finally she stood still, tears streaming, not able to understand the names he called her, only seeing him retreat. "I love you!"

Adam stared at her, her words more hypocritically searing and hated than Edmund's ring on her finger.

"I've never stopped lovin' you." Her golden eyes spilled tears.

Adam turned and ran blindly. "Bitch! Bitch! Bitch!"

Dulcie ran after him. "Come back! Come back! Adam! Please *listen* to me" She splashed through the filthy street heedless of the cold drenching rain.

Adam shouted for Hans.

Dulcie, staggering, ran recklessly after him.

Hans, watching them, moved with purposeful slowness. As Adam entered the carriage, Dulcie grabbed his muddy boot. He jerked his foot away. She slipped in the freezing mud, her face smeared with tears and rain, going to her knees. She held her muddied hands out in supplication. "I do love you. I always will. Why are you doin' this to me? I thought you were dead. Adam—why won't you come back to me? What have I done?" Her voice broke. "Oh, Adam, please, please don't do this to me. Please. Oh, God, Adam, I can't live without you—"

"Go back to *him*," Adam snarled, his mind filled with pictures of Dulcie and Revanche, the ring gleaming on Dulcie's finger. He glanced at her hand seeing the mud-dulled gleam of the emerald against her white skin.

"No—no! Edmund lied!"

"Lied? Lied, bitch? Who lied? You'll get a divorce as soon as it can be arranged. My wedding gift to you!"

Dulcie burst into fresh hysteria. "I don't want a divorce! I love you! Adam, all I ever want is you!"

Adam grabbed the whip and laid it across the horse's rump. Dulcie sprang back awkwardly, her slipper sucking deep into the mud as she fell to the street. The buggy wheels sprayed gobbets of mud and dung over her.

Dulcie picked herself up, brushing clots of filth off her gown and transferring them to her hands. "Adam . . . Adam . . ."

Jem helped her up the steps. Her rain- and mud-soaked gown weighed her down, wrapped around her legs, and made her stumble. "I saw it all," Jem said. "He's lower than scum, Dulcie Jeannette. Praise God, you're rid of him at last. He's shown you once and for all what he's truly like."

She jerked away from him. "Let me alone!" she screamed.

Dulcie entered the parlor like an avenging fury, her hair and clothing dripping water and mud and reeking of the barnyard. Her red eyes streamed tears. Oliver stepped back in alarm as she headed straight for an angry, white-faced Edmund.

"How dare you make a spectacle of yourself in a public street—?"

Quick as a cat, she put out both dung-smeared hands and raked her sharp fingernails heavily into Edmund's cheeks.

Edmund cried out in pain and surprise, automatically lashing out, sending Dulcie sprawling into a small table.

Her hand closed over Mad's Jersey Turtle paperweight. Screaming in inarticulate rage, she ran at him, the paperweight tight in her hand as she brought it down on his cheekbone.

Edmund, stunned, grunted in pain, then his face twisted in anger. Blood spurted onto his shirt and pale gray frock coat. He lunged and grasped her hands, squeezing until she let the paperweight drop, then thrust her away, making her fall onto the sofa. His hard, dark eyes never left her, his expression one of deep contempt. He appeared calm as he smoothed his clothing, his hand touching the cut, bruised place on his cheek.

"Mr. Revanche—" Oliver began.

"Take your hands away, sir. I've suffered enough of your hospitality."

"I'll kill you!" Dulcie bounded up from the sofa. She reached out to claw him again. Edmund grabbed her, pinioning her arms across her breast. "You thankless little trollop!" he breathed, his face hating and mean close to hers. "Let me leave you with something to contemplate."

She spat in his face. She screamed, struggling and kicking him. "You drove Adam away from me! I'll kill you! I—"

"You'll do nothing! . . . but listen," he hissed. "I found you thinking yourself a widow, parading around with your little mourning band, enjoying your charade. I gave you life, you bitch, and you've thrown it back."

"I hate you!"

Edmund laughed. "Cherish it, Dulcie. It's all you'll have,

because this time, this time, when I leave you, you will in truth be a widow. You have my word."

"Liar! Liar! Liar!"

His laughter rang in her ears.

"Let me go! Get out of here! I hate you!"

"Hate me, Dulcie, hate me until you're shriveled and worthless to any man."

She let out a strangled scream of rage, writhing in his grasp. Suddenly Edmund released her, watching with cold amusement as she stumbled and fell. Slowly he drew on his immaculate white gloves. "I know the spot where Tremain moors his ship—an incredibly stupid location. From my house atop the ridge I can see every move he makes. A simple, anonymous message to the Federals, and your Captain will be captive the moment he emerges from that cul-de-sac." Edmund walked quickly from the room.

Dulcie threw off her father's restraining hands, shoved aside Oliver, and ran down the hall screaming vilifications at Edmund's back. Suddenly, overwhelmed and helpless, she covered her face with her filthy hands.

Aunt Mad was at her side. "Come on, honey. Let's go back into the house and get these wet clothes off you."

"He'll get Adam killed. He'll do it, Aunt Mad."

"He's nothin' but a liar. Now that we know Adam's alive, we'll find him."

Dulcie looked where Edmund's carriage had been. "We've got to stop him—stop him right away." She ran, stumbling toward the stables. She would stop Edmund—kill him herself with her bare hands.

Mad shouted at her to stop. Jem and Oliver ran through the rain toward her. The stable doors were shut tight against the winter wind. The old groom peered out the window with frightened eyes. Dulcie pounded on the stable door and then the window, her fist hammering the glass as the man drew his head back. Then she leaned against the wall, the bricks digging into her forehead, crying and wringing her hands. Edmund was gone.

They took her into the house. Patricia, very pale, stood at the foot of the stairs. "Oh, baby, youah just all ovah mud!"

"Trish, shut your mouth," Mad said grimly.

"Well, Ah nevah!" gasped Patricia, threatening to swoon again.

"Mad, that's no way to talk to your sister," Jem said severely.

"*God's blood!*" shouted Mad. "Your daughter has had a shock that would be the death of most women, and you're both mealymouthin' over trifles! Ollie, Ollie! Help me get Dulcie undressed!"

"Ah'll help you," said Patricia. She gingerly took Dulcie's arm.

Dulcie jerked away. "I don't want you. I don't want anybody! Just let me alone!" She started up the stairs, but her wet skirts wrapped around her legs and made her fall.

While the maid ran the bath water, Mad cut her stinking dress off her. "Into the tub, Dulcie. That's it, Marie, pour the water over her hair."

When Dulcie was bathed and shampooed and her hair wrapped in a towel, Mad held her nightgown for her. "Here it is, dear, nice and warm and dry."

Dulcie brushed it away unseeing. "My habit. Got to have my habit. Most girls would have the sense to stay indoors, but I like the storm." She rummaged in her wardrobe, grabbing a shirt and a divided skirt. "Oilskins," she murmured, rummaging again.

Mad whispered to Marie, who slipped out the door and downstairs.

"Dulcie, what are you goin' to do, dear?" Mad asked calmly.

"Find Adam. He'll understand. Adam understands me. He'll see I couldn't help it. Aunt Mad, where did you put my oilskins?"

"I haven't seen them, dear. I expect they're in Nassau."

"Nassau. That's it. Nassau. He's got to go there sometime. Aunt Mad, I'll go to Nassau. Tell Marie—where did she go?"

"Downstairs. I thought we'd enjoy a cup of coffee."

"Tell her to pack. I'll go right away."

"We can talk about it in the mornin'."

"No. No! I'm goin'! I want Adam! Don't you understand?"

"You're not goin' this evening, Dulcie. Tomorrow will be soon enough."

"Edmund's goin' to kill him! I've got to stop Edmund! What'll I do—I can't even think!" She paced frantically, babbling. "He lied every step of the way—to the Jeffersonians—those letters. Oh, God, God, why couldn't I see it? Edmund lied to me. I believed him, Aunt Mad! I stopped believin' in Adam!" Dulcie sank to the floor, sobbing. "I doubted him. All the time he was gone I thought the worst—worst things about him. I didn't want him to be dead. I don't want to live without him!"

"Dulcie—Dulcie! We'll find him, do you understand? We'll find him!"

"No—he'll never forgive me! Never, never, never!"

Mad bent over her. "Sit up, Dulcie, and let's dry your hair." Briskly she began rubbing Dulcie's damp hair. "Of course Adam will forgive you. He loves you! If he didn't, he wouldn't have come here."

"Never . . . never . . ."

Marie came in with the coffee. Mad drank hers. Dulcie set her cup down after one sip. "Amparo," she said accusingly. "You've got Amparo here."

"What's that?" asked Mad.

"Did she tell you to drug me? *Did she?*"

"You're in New York now, remember? That's all past."

"I'm goin'! I'm not goin' to wait any longer! I've got to get to Adam before Edmund." Dulcie ran to the door, only to find it locked. She pounded on it with her fists, crying Adam's name over and over.

No one in the Raymer household slept that night. Patricia trying to comfort Dulcie said all the wrong things. Dulcie wouldn't let Jem in, screaming at him, "You hate Adam, and I hate you! I hate you!"

When Dulcie tried to leave via the window, Mad sent Marie after Oliver. Dulcie, in the presence of two unruffled people who loved her very much, achieved a measure of calm. But she couldn't sleep. She sat in a chair endlessly rocking and hugging herself.

Sunlight was coming weakly through the windows when Marie knocked.

"I don't want any breakfast," said Dulcie, her eyes fearful.

Oliver, smiling, held out his arm. "You shall serve yourself, Dulcie. Pick out whatever you like."

Dulcie walked down ahead of them. Her mother and father were already seated. Patricia, puffy-eyed, toying with French toast, said, "Good mornin', baby." Jem pulled out her chair, patting her shoulder awkwardly. Dulcie flinched away.

She took portions of everything, but food gagged her.

She sat tensely, her eyes darting, seeking a way of escape.

"I'm going to see if Roderick Courtland is back," Oliver said. "Perhaps you'd like to come along, Dulcie?"

"Yes. Let's go now! Uncle Oliver, hurry!"

"You'll have to dress a little differently," he pointed out.

Dulcie jumped up, jarring the coffee cups. "I'll hurry, I'll be ready, I won't make you ashamed, you'll see—"

"Oh, Mad," Patricia moaned, "What ah we evah goin' to do with mah baby?"

Mad patted her hand. "Don't worry about her, Patricia. She'll manage somehow. Dulcie is a survivor."

"That damnable man—" Jem began.

Oliver said, "Now see here—"

Patricia's soft voice overrode Oliver. "Jem honey, ahn't you the one who taught Dulcie to think fo' herself? She was doin' just that when she married him, so he must have some redeemin' qualities."

"But he's out of his head!"

"Neither Adam nor Dulcie is in very good condition," Oliver reminded him. "We'll have to keep watch on her in case she gets the notion of going after him. Perhaps Courtland can tell us if Adam is as wild as he seems."

Homer Daniels was all attention when Oliver came in, bowing and bidding him good morning.

"Daniels, is Mr. Courtland in today?" Oliver asked.

"Mr. Courtland is out of the city. I'm sure he won't mind my telling you the happy news. He was married at Christmastime."

"Married! Rod?" Oliver chuckled. "Tell me, Daniels, who is the lucky lady?"

"We don't know, sir. His telegram didn't mention the lady's name."

"When will he return? My niece and I must see him as soon as possible."

"He didn't say."

"Mr. Daniels, do you know where Mr. Courtland is?" Dulcie asked.

"Yes—Mrs. Tremain, isn't it? I believe he's in—that's it, Smithville, North Carolina. The telegram came from there."

Dulcie, already pale, clutched at Oliver's arm. "You've been very helpful, Mr. Daniels. Thank you." She walked out and got into the carriage.

"I must send a telegram message, Uncle Oliver. Adam's mother lives in Smithville. That must mean Mr. Courtland *must* know somethin' about Adam. He's there because something terrible happened to Adam—I know it. I don't mean yesterday. Before that. If Adam were in trouble and Ben or Tom couldn't help, he'd send for Mr. Courtland. They're more than business partners. There's a great affection between them."

"It would have to be strong if a staunch Unionist like Rod decided to go South and stay."

"Oh, Uncle Oliver, I haven't been thinkin' clearly since I saw Adam. But things are comin' clear now. Adam was weak, even sick. Why else would he warn you away? Why back away from me? Why did he look so terrified to see Edmund? I'd expect him to be jealous—but not frightened."

"Sure you're not imagining, Dulcie?"

"He was frightened of everyone in the room. But Adam isn't a fearful man. Somethin' has happened to make him that way. What?"

"I wish I knew. Possibly he's been captive. Maybe he escaped from prison. Or perhaps . . . Dulcie, has it occurred to you that Adam might not be the man you once knew?"

"I'm not the giddy girl he married either. If he comes back to me—"

"Worse than that, my dear, he may be insane. The way he acted yesterday—if I'd never known him before that—that's what I'd call him."

"If it's true, then he needs me. No matter what he says. I can't desert him now. He has to have somethin' to depend on. Oh, Uncle Oliver, I'll never doubt him again."

Dulcie sent several copies of two telegraph messages. The first, to Roderick Courtland, read: SEEKING INFORMATION ON ADAM TREMAIN STOP URGENT STOP MUST FIND HIM STOP REPLY C/O OLIVER RAYMER SIGNED DULCIE TREMAIN.

The second went to Adam in care of Zoe: PLEASE COME BACK STOP I LOVE AND NEED YOU STOP FORGIVE THE PAST STOP I WILL WAIT AT OLIVER RAYMERS HOME STOP I AM YOURS AS ALWAYS SIGNED DULCIE TREMAIN.

Hans halted the weary horse in the barnyard. "Don't know about you, but I'm sure ready for a mess of Cateau's sausages an' hot biscuits with honey. C'mon in. Gettin' too near daylight to make a run for it."

Adam had slept part of the way, the turmoil in his mind seething over into his dreams. Dulcie and Revanche. His hand on her wrist, his ring on her finger. Her hands covered with street slime. The falsity of her tears and declarations of love for him. Bitterness filled his heart. It was too stunning an emotion for him to overcome.

"I'm leaving, Hans," he said. "I don't give a damn what happens."

"That's your decision, Cap'n, but if you're as good as your reputation, you might consider your men. Maybe they ain't all ready to get blowed out of Long Island Sound."

"If I've got any cowards aboard, I'll leave them with you," Adam said coldly.

"Then farewell, Cap'n Tremain, and a safe journey to you."

Despite his worries about the dangers of Courtland's chosen anchorage, Adam's mind was not on Federal cruisers this night. He steamed into the Sound, staying near to the shore as he rounded Lloyd Neck.

Calling for speed, Adam touched the wheel, steaming toward deeper water. As soon as the *Black Swan* was in a ship channel, the sky lit up with flares and the deep-throated roar of Parrott guns.

On deck, the crew of the Black Swan raced like madmen to answer Adam's sharp, fear-edged commands. "Full sail! Full steam!"

Fire spewed into the sky as the forward stack exploded under the impact of a hot shot. A line of men showered buckets of water on the flaming deck as the firemen continued to feed the *Black Swan*'s boilers. Sparks and cinders blazed to the deck, showering the crewmen.

There would be no hiding from the cruisers tonight. The *Black Swan* steamed over the dark ocean, her stack a golden wavering torch lighting the way. Shouting orders, Adam scanned the sea astern of them, locating the two cruisers by the flare of their guns. The *Black Swan* yawed, sliding into a trough, shuddered, listed then righted as shot crashed into the upper hull.

Unarmed, and with the dawn approaching, Adam could only rely on the *Black Swan*'s speed. He shouted again to the crew, making adjustments in the topgallants, then set course for Bermuda, the nearest safe British harbor.

Throughout that dawn and the following day and into the darkness of the next evening, the *Black Swan* raced across the heaving Atlantic just barely ahead of the lethal range of the two Federal cruisers hounding her.

An hour before they entered British waters, a heavy rain began to fall, with blessed fog rolling over the sullen, heaving ocean.

Adam remained in Bermuda long enough to make repairs on the *Black Swan* and allow the ardor of his Federal pursuers to cool. At the end of the week he cautiously set out for the Carolina coast.

He slipped into New Inlet under fire from a Federal cruiser that had spotted him late. The guns of Fort Fisher boomed out reassuringly, scoring minor damage on the cruiser.

Adam anchored in Smithville. Before dawn broke he was on a flatboat on Price Creek. At his feet lay a bundle of clothing, blankets, and oilskins. In a box were provisions. In his pain, as he had done so many times before, Adam returned to the swamp for solace and healing.

Chapter Fourteen

Zoe jumped as the doorbell rang. Then she raced to the door, hoping it was Rod and Tom returning from the general store. She didn't like being alone these days. All she could think of was Adam. Was he safe? Was he well? Was he mentally fit?

As she flung the door wide, she was greeted by the black, grinning face of a messenger. He thrust into her hands a sheaf of crumpled telegraph messages, all addressed to Adam in Zoe's care.

Hastily she closed the door, clutching the yellow papers, her heart pounding, her hands trembling. She stared down at the multiple messages Dulcie had sent in hopes of getting one through.

She was still standing in the entry hall when Rod returned. Her face ashen, she handed him the telegraph messages.

Debating, Rod read them, then handed them to Tom. "What do you make of it, Tom? I was under the impression Dulcie was dead. Adam certainly thought so."

Tom raised his eyebrows. You don't think that no-'count snake belly Edmund would use a thing like this to—"

"That's just what I'm thinkin'."

"But suppose it *is* from Dulcie? Suppose Adam saw her. Suppose something happened that we know nothing about. Rod, please, we should answer this."

Rod pulled Zoe near to him. "You're getting worked up over nothing, Zoe. If Adam did find Dulcie, she wouldn't be sending him messages. He loves that girl so much he'd never leave her."

"Are you going to answer it?" Zoe persisted.

"No. It's not addressed to me, and I had no business opening it. And we don't know who sent it. If it is from Edmund Revanche, he won't have the satisfaction of knowing that it was received. If Dulcie sent it, she'd want a reply from Adam, not from me."

As they stood talking, the bell sounded. Zoe received another telegram.

Rod opened it. His mouth set hard, a look of satisfaction in his eyes, "I'll answer this one. If I send a reply to Oliver Raymer and it is not a hoax, he'll give the message to Dulcie. If it is a hoax, I'll certainly mystify Oliver, but I can't help that now. How does this sound? 'Adam Tremain has left the area stop have no information stop signed R. Courtland.' I'll also telegraph Daniels and see if he knows anything."

Next morning the *Black Swan* stood at anchor in the Cape Fear. Zoe, on her way to the church to roll bandages for the Wilmington hospital, stared in joy, then in disbelief. The crew moved languidly about their tasks.

She turned the buggy around, hurrying home to find Rod. "Please go to the ship and find out about Adam. Something's not right, I'm terribly worried."

"Calm yourself, sweetheart. He's safe, then."

"No! Rod, I know he's not on that ship. I can tell!"

Rod returned to the house to confirm what Zoe suspected. "The first mate says he disappeared after they docked last night. No one knows where he went or when he's coming back. Zoe—"

"He's gone to the swamp. When he was a boy and things went wrong, he always went to the swamp. I used to worry so. I was always afraid for him. But he knows the swamp. He'll be all right—I guess."

Rod stirred uneasily. "He wasn't well when he left here. If he's made the trip to New York and back, he's in worse shape now. I don't think he's all right. He's in no condition to be in the swamp alone."

"Oh, Rod," Zoe burst out. "You can't know—you don't know Adam this way. All my life I've had to let my son go—when I wanted to be the one to comfort him, when I wanted to tie him to me because he was all I had of you. I'm frightened when he takes such chances. But it's his way. Nothing has changed now. I must let him go—and so must you."

Rod held her, petting her, comforting her. "I'm new to this, Zoe. You have learned to let him go, but I haven't. Adam may be perfectly safe and happy back there in the weeds, but I won't be satisfied 'til I've talked to him. What kind of a father would I be if I cared so little for my son that I would not even make the effort to see that he is all right?"

Zoe dropped her head onto his shoulder and nuzzled him. "I'm so grateful for you, Roderick Courtland," she whispered.

After a heated discussion Tom said bluntly, "What I don't need is some damned fool city Yankee gettin' hisself chewed by a 'gator while I'm tryin' to fin' Adam. I'll go alone, or you can go alone."

"Then I'll go alone," Rod shouted.

"You do that! You jes' go ahead an' you're gonna be givin' that boy a daddy all snake-bit an' good for nuthin'."

Zoe looked at them in alarm. "Oh, Rod, listen to him. You don't know the swamp—and something might happen to you. I couldn't stand that."

"I'll give him your love an' any other message you want to send him, Rod," Tom said earnestly. "This is my country. I know its ways better'n you."

Tom returned in two weeks. He'd found Adam, living in a lean-to. He was far from well, very thin and wasted, but he was managing. He refused to read Dulcie's telegram or talk about her, save to say that he had seen her and never wanted to see or hear of her again. "He don't want to see anybody, he don't want to come back, he jes' wants to be left alone. So I'm lettin' him alone."

"But you do know where he is?" Zoe asked.

"I know where he *was*."

"We've had another telegraph from Dulcie. Oh, I wish we knew what happened. Perhaps we could do something if only—"

Tom looked grim. "Zoe, if it was me, I'd let that girl stew. She's done somethin' to our boy that's cut him up worse'n I ever saw him. He'd be a sight better off if he'd found her dead."

"Tom! We don't know what happened. People who love each other—"

"You're a forgiving woman, Zoe," Rod said. "It's your nature, but I agree with Tom. Adam's been through all manner of scrapes and troubles, but nothing has ever felled him like this."

"But that doesn't mean it's Dulcie's fault!"

"What else could it be? Who else means that much to him?"

As the days went by in New York, Dulcie's hopes grew irrationally. Everything would be all right. Somehow everything was always all right. Even when she was on Andros, helpless, ill and at the mercy of Mam'bo Luz and Lucifer, help came.

And when she had had to submit to Justin, her father and Uncle Oliver had come to her aid, and that had come out right. When she had had no hope of finding information about Adam, Edmund Revanche aided her. And when Adam returned, even though Edmund had caused a terrible scene and driven Adam away in anger, she had rid herself of Edmund. Now she knew Adam was alive. She was no longer helpless. She was free to seek him, to love him, to make him love her again. It would be all right.

After a nerve-wracking ten days Rod's telegraph answering hers arrived. With blind fear she clutched desperately to dreams, never testing or facing reality. Her certainty that everything would be all right grew stronger and less rational daily.

"Mama, Aunt Mad, we're all goin' on a shoppin' spree. Adam is not goin' to see me in anythin' less than the finest, prettiest, most fashionable dress ever! None of those ol' drab war colors for me. I want to look gorgeous for him. Everythin' new! And pretty!" She twirled around the room, pausing momentarily to appreciate herself in the mirror. "He likes me to look pretty."

"Dahlin', when have you ever looked anythin' but pretty?" Patricia cooed.

"Dulcie, do sit down. You're givin' me a headache," Mad said irritably.

"Oh, don't be a fusspot, Aunt Mad. Can't you see I'm happy? I'm really happy again! Everythin' is going to be all right, and Adam is safe and—"

"And he told you he never wanted to set eyes on you again."

Dulcie closed her eyes against the memory of Adam's face as he drove away. She frowned. "He didn't mean that. He—he wasn't well, and Edmund acted like a horrible cad, and—and Adam was simply jealous."

"And a pretty dress and a few smiles will put it all right?"

"Mad, Ah sweah, youah bein' about as sour as curduled milk. Ah simply cannot undahstan' you. All the time you were tellin' mah baby to cheer up, an' now youah actin' like she should be back in mournin'. Ah think a shoppin' spree is just what she needs. Adam will come 'roun' when he's feelin' a mite bettah, an' after all, it isn't Dulcie who should be a apologizin'. Ah've nevah seen a man worse behaved than Cap'n Tremain. Imagine usin' language like that in front o' ladies, an' to his own wife!"

"Batterin' her eyes at him like a toad in a hailstorm is not goin' to cure what ails Adam and Dulcie, Patricia! That's the trouble with you Southerners! You're always lookin' to appearance and ignorin' the meat of the matter!"

"Why, Mad Raymer, you're as much a Southerner as ah am!" Patricia scolded.

"I'm not! I'm a level-headed Yan—woman! And I won't be sidetracked nor will I go on this shoppin' trip. Dulcie Jeanette, as much as I love you, I am tellin' you, you are makin' a terrible mistake. If you truly love Adam, then go to him and set things straight, and for that you need a humble and truthful heart, not a lacy fichu!" Mad stormed from the room with the parting exclamation, "You know I'm right! Ollie agrees, and Ollie's never wrong!"

"Well! What's gotten into her?" Patricia breathed.

Dulcie looked pensively after her aunt, then smiled. She couldn't allow Mad to shake her new confidence. Adam would come back. Adam loved her. His feelings couldn't have changed over one unfortunate incident.

Dulcie and Patricia planned a wardrobe designed especially to please the eye of Adam Tremain.

By the end of the month packages were arriving from the dressmaker daily. Dulcie reveled in the pleased expressions of her father and Uncle Oliver as she modeled each new creation. By night she thought of Adam, and only then did doubts come to her brought on by long days of waiting for Roderick Courtland to return to the city. Through Courtland she could contact Adam in New York, or failing that, he could tell her what Adam's sailing schedule was. She assumed he still used Nassau as a base, but many of the blockading captains had changed to Bermuda, and others had gone to Cuba. If everything failed, she could go to Nassau if she could find a Northern ship willing to take a female passenger into a port notable for its Southern sympathies. She tossed in her bed fighting the worries that overtook her only in the dark, when she was alone and unable to keep herself brittlely gay and fussily busy.

The next morning Dulcie leaped to her feet, dropping her collection of fashion drawings when Fred announced a visitor. Her face fell. It was Josiah Whinburn. Then, as she composed herself and waited for Edmund's protégé, her thoughts turned entirely to Edmund and his cavalier treatment of her.

Josiah's hat was clutched in his nervously sweating hand. He had tried to wash his tension away with liquor. He stood before her, uncertain and appalled both at himself and at Edmund. "Emmun' sen' me to ge' his jool-joolery back, Mrs. Tremain." Jem stared in amazement at Josiah's words. Josiah's coloring alternated from beet red to turnip white. "Emmun'—Emmun' says it was part of a—of a bargain—an' you di'n't hol' youah end up."

"Edmund Revanche has sent this rapscallion to take back gifts he gave to my daughter?" Jem said hotly.

"Daddy, please," Dulcie's eyes glittered in cold amusement. "Josiah doesn't really want to be here, do you, Josiah?"

"No, ma'am. This ain't mah ah-dee of a decent visit."

"Of course not. You tell Mr. Revanche that I will return his jewels—gladly. He may pick them up at Tiffany's on Thursday."

Josiah turned scarlet with relief. "Th-thank you, Mrs. Tremain."

Jem stood by the door, signifying the visit had ended.

Josiah murmuring excuses and good-byes, stumbled his way out.

"Dulcie Jeannette, I wouldn't give that blackguard the satisfaction of tellin' this to that no-'count boss of his, but you are actin' very unwisely. Those gems are worth a fortune. You have every right to keep them."

"Maybe I do, Daddy, but I made a bargain, and I intend to honor my word to Edmund, just as he honored his to me."

"What kind of agreement could you have with a man like that?"

"Oh, Edmund had great plans—to help the South, he said. I was to work with him. I mean to keep that agreement, or at least some parts of it. In his own way Edmund will appreciate what I am goin' to do, even if it will hurt his pocketbook a bit. I'm goin' to get the money back for those jewels in the form of a bank draft made out to your friend, Mr. Young."

"The Confederate agent?" Jem looked at her amazed. "I can't say it's not a fittin' use for the money. And I've got to admit that Edmund Revanche has it comin', but Dulcie Jeannette—what's become of you?"

"Not a thing, Daddy. I am still the same Dulcie I've always been. I'm just usin' my wit. It's about time women did more of that."

"I'll be the first to tell you, you have a mind the equal of any man. I might say a bit more devious, but daughter, I wonder if it's what you want."

Dulcie raised her chin. "Women have to be devious, or they'd never get along. You saw how far honesty got me with Adam."

The slow days became weeks. Every Monday Dulcie visited Courtland's office, to be told there was no news. Each time she wore one of her new, carefully designed outfits.

After each visit, she sent another telegraph to Adam. Occasionally she sent messages in care of Fraser Trenholm: PLEASE COME TO ME AT OLIVER'S STOP I NEED YOU AND WILL WAIT STOP.

Each telegram became more difficult to send, each trip to Courtland's office required more mental preparation to endure. At the beginning she made her trips uptown expecting to see Mr. Courtland, expecting him to aid her, then hurried home expecting that Adam would be waiting for her at Oliver's house. Now the face of hope required she put on more makeup and strain her cheeks in greater and longer-lasting false smiles. Hope became more slender and more difficult to trust, but she clung to what little she had, making the greater effort, never allowing a minute of the day to find her downcast or pessimistic. She became the perpetually gay optimist, spending her laughter and her flirtations with the abandon of a larcenous keeper of the mint.

Finally there came a Monday when she could hardly force herself to leave the house, so overwhelmingly tired of being cheerful was she. It was a March day when the snow sagged under the onslaught of a cold, driving rain, a day when fireplaces and hot tea and heavy shawls were not warm enough, when even gaslights could not dispel the gloom that sulked in every corner.

But she could endure giving up no better. An hour later, dressed carefully in a camel-colored silk suit, Dulcie was pushing open the door with Roderick Courtland's name painted on it in bold black letters. Mr. Daniels gave her the wary look she had come to recognize. On other days she had shrunk from the officious, long-suffering smirk, but today she smiled brightly, as she had learned to do and raised her voice to its bright, sociable level, her golden eyes fixing Mr. Daniels in his place like a butterfly for inspection. "Good day, Mr. Daniels. Have you heard from—"

His face showed relief. "Mr. Courtland has returned, Mrs. Tremain."

Dulcie's legs threatened to buckle under her. At last— after all the trying and the waiting, he was here. "Then announce me. I must see him."

"Oh, I'm terribly sorry, Mrs. Tremain. That would be impossible. If you had an appointment—"

"An appointment! I've been comin' here regularly, and I won't be turned away today. If you were any secretary at all—"

"I am not a secretary, ma'am, I'm a—"

"What does it matter what you are! You should have made an appointment for me. I must see him, and I *will!*"

Mr. Daniels cleared his throat. "Be seated, Mrs. Tremain, I'll ask him if he can spare you a few moments."

Dulcie, too nervous to sit, tears threatening and thoughts in a panicky jumble, paced in front of the high counter.

Half an hour went by, and Mr. Daniels had not returned. Seething with anger and humiliation, she paced faster until a sheen of perspiration covered her upper lip. She made herself sit down, forced herself to remember Mr. Courtland had been away for a long time and would naturally be busy. Her attempt at reasoning lasted only minutes, then she was on her feet again. She'd tell Mr. Roderick, Courtland—supposed friend of her uncle, supposed gentleman—a thing or two about his office and his Mr. Daniels and his own behavior toward a lady!

Her breath catching, she sat down again. She couldn't do that. He was her only link with information about Adam. She'd be charming—the loving, worried wife. At least until she got the information she needed.

At last Mr. Daniels returned. "Mr. Courtland will see you now."

The handsome man behind the desk rose and bowed, but his manner had no warmth. "Good morning, Madame. Daniels says you have been inquiring as to my whereabouts."

Dulcie smiled brightly. "I certainly have! Why, I was beginnin' to think you had left the country."

Rod noted her high color, her nervous brilliance, her beauty, and was moved by none of it. "I don't wish to be rude, Madame, but this is a busy day. Daniels said your business was important."

"Yes," Dulcie smiled winningly, her eyelashes dropping to shadow her eyes. "I'm sure it sounds silly to you, but I assure you it means a great deal to me—even though I am embarrassed havin' to come to you and—"

"The matter, Madame, what is it?"

Dulcie stared at him. Why should he be angry? If anyone had a right to be angry, it was she! She tried to quell her own anger and disguise her acute embarrassment. "I wish to know where I can reach Captain Tremain. When do you expect him in port? Or perhaps you can tell me if he still uses Nassau as a base?"

There was a look of sardonic amusement on Rod's face. "Captain Tremain? Madame, you have come to the wrong man, and certainly for the wrong purposes. He *is* your husband, is he not?"

Dulcie felt the heat mount in her cheeks. "All I'm askin' from you is information, which, as his partner, you must have."

"My partnership with your husband does not extend to his personal life, Madame. If Captain Tremain thought it best to absent himself from your comfort, that is his business, and I will not interfere. If this is what you wished to see me about, you have wasted both our time."

Dulcie's hand shielded her eyes as she bit back tears. "Please, Mr. Courtland—you don't understand. I must find Adam. We—we had a terrible misunderstanding and—"

"I don't want to hear your private business! I suggest you see your priest or minister. This is a place of busi—"

"Will you at least tell me if he received my telegrams? I've been sendin' them—oh, but you wouldn't know." Dulcie fiddled with her gloves, drawing them on her hands, then removing them again. "Mr. Courtland, my uncle, Oliver Raymer has spoken so highly of you—and so has Adam. Won't you please hear me out? I know you're an important man, and busy, but it is vital to me." She looked at him appealingly. "Perhaps even to you. I know Adam is upset, and if I could just see him to explain, then everythin' would be all right again. I am sure he would do a much better job for you once we have settled our differences."

Rod's eyes glittered, "Do go on, Madame. I find this fascinating. Please, do tell me how you expect to make a better man of Captain Tremain."

Dulcie laughed. "Oh, I didn't mean quite all that. It would be a bit presumptuous of me, wouldn't it?"

"It would, but don't let that deter you. What is it you want of me?"

"Only that you tell me how I can see Adam."

"I've already told you I won't do that."

Blushing prettily now, as she had been taught to do as a young girl, Dulcie glanced at Rod from beneath a fringe of dark lashes. "I can see a lady must tell all with you, Mr. Courtland. It was all so silly. I hate even to talk about it. There was a misunderstanding between my husband and me. We were shipwrecked. I—I thought he was dead. And then I met a man—Edmund Revanche. Of course, I didn't love him, but he asked me to marry him anyhow. Well, he was at my uncle's house one afternoon and—and Adam just showed up. Well, you can imagine my joy! Here he was—and after all that time I had nearly died of grief and loneliness thinkin' him dead. There—was a terrible scene. Edmund, of course, was stunned, and I'm afraid he didn't handle it well." Dulcie talked on, not noticing the warning flash in Rod's eyes or the hard line of his mouth. Brightly in her best party voice she chattered on.

Rod's head nearly burst as he heard her description of that afternoon Adam had walked into the Raymer house. If he heard her speak Edmund's name once more in that soft, slow drawl of hers, he'd wring her neck. "Shut your mouth!"

Dulcie stared at him open-mouthed.

"Get out of here and don't utter another word."

"Wha—Mr. Courtland!"

"Leave, Madame."

Suddenly Dulcie's temper flared. "Whom do you think you are? My uncle will certainly hear of this! Perhaps you have returned to your office earlier than you should have, Mr. Courtland. You are not fit to deal with decent people. I came here in good faith—to talk to a gentleman."

Rod was shaking as he glared across the desk at this young woman, who matched him stare for stare, unintimidated and defiant. "Do you have any idea of what decency is, Madame? I doubt it, or you wouldn't have come here with your gamin ways and your flirtations to tell me of a *slight* misunderstanding between yourself and—and my *son!*"

Dulcie took a step back, her hand on her frantically beating heart. "Your son?" she breathed. "But you can't be! Adam's father was Paul Tremain. They hated one another. He—he—"

"Paul Tremain was not Adam's father. I am."

"Ohh. But I didn't know. I thought—"

"I question that you have *ever* thought, Madame. Perhaps it is time you did."

"But I—I don't know what to say."

"Then try listening. Sit down, Madame. It is time someone enlightened you to what you are and what you have done." Rod paced, talking with great animation and anger, telling Dulcie everything he knew of the time Adam spent on Andros, his trip to Mossrose, his search for Jem and Patricia, his search for Dulcie.

"Do you think that I didn't search for him, Mr. Courtland?"

"Where, Madame? Tell me to what lengths you went to find your husband."

"I wrote—everywhere I could think of. I wrote to Mrs. Tremain, and to Ben. I tried to see you. I did all I could!"

"And made certain that all the while your own precious hide was well clothed, well fed, and warm!"

"You have no right—"

"And found yourself another man to take his place as fast as a snake sheds an old skin!"

"I won't listen to this! I didn't know what Adam went through! I didn't know he searched for me! And how do I know now that you are tellin' me the truth? I was told he was with—was with my maid and they were—they were closely associated. There are many things you simply do not know, Mr. Courtland. I am not so black as you paint me. It wasn't easy livin' as I had to live to survive. I could tell you—"

"Sit down! *I'm* going to tell *you!*" Without mercy Rod launched into the long history of the animosity between Adam and Edmund Revanche, sparing Dulcie no detail of the beating of Tom or the death of Ullah or the attack with the bees on Adam. "And now, you little hussy, you have the audacity to come to my office to tell me you had a slight misunderstanding with my son! It was because of you Edmund Revanche set those bees on him. But for an old swamp hag and two darkies, Adam would be dead, and Revanche would be bedding the grieving widow. Now, Madame, leave this office before I assist you out the door!"

Dulcie, bewildered and frightened, looked at him in stunned silence. "No . . ." she whispered. "You're lyin' to me . . . You're lyin'. It's not true."

"I don't lie, Madame."

Dulcie's face was gray. "He loved me—"

"Yes, he loved you. I hope it *is* in past tense. You've done enough."

Her eyes would barely focus. "Is—is he all right now?" she asked inanely, remembering the gaunt, wasted man who had greeted her in Oliver's house, then turned on her with fear and hatred.

"What difference can it make to you now?"

Pathetically she looked up at him. "I love him, Mr. Courtland. Oh, don't say anymore! I know! I know! Everything you said about me is true! I—I won't ever try to see him again. I promise." She dabbed at her eyes. "Mr. Courtland, please—if you ever see him again, tell him— please tell him—I didn't know—I didn't know. I never wanted to hurt Adam. He's . . . I love him. But I'll never go near him again. You're right. I've done nothin' but hurt him. I didn't mean to. I . . ." The tears came down in streams. Everything that had happened to Adam had happened because of her, because he loved her, because he risked anything and everything to find her. And she had distrusted him and had sought solace in a sham marriage with Edmund Revanche, a man she should have recognized as despicable and hateful. But she had wanted to survive, to fill a life devoid of Adam with some substitute, and she had fooled herself into believing that Edmund's bargain was an extension of Adam's dream. Her stomach churned in self-hatred as she thought of the mockery that was.

Dulcie swayed, sweat running down her face, the room going gray.

Rod hesitated, baffled because he could not ignore the sincerity of her self-loathing and her love for Adam. Confused and moved to compassion, he put his arm around her shoulders. "Dulcie . . ." He led her back to her chair, then brought her water. "Drink this. I'm sorry. I shouldn't have told you."

Dulcie shuddered and removed his hand from her shoulder. "Don't touch me! How can you stand to touch me! You know what I am, what I've done!"

"No! No, I was wrong. I don't know if I can help you and Adam. But—let me think about it. Let me see if there is anything I can do."

"No! I don't want you to tell Adam! Nothin'! I must be goin'. I—"

Rod forced her to remain seated until some color returned to her face.

"I'll drive you home, please. You can't go this way," he said. "Forgive me, Dulcie. I'm a bumbling old man who has become a father to the man before he knew he had a child. I had no right to talk as I did."

"You are not a bumblin' old man, Mr. Courtland, and lyin' now to save my feelin's won't help. What happened was for the best. Who knows what greater harm I might have done Adam if someone had not stopped me?"

Rod ran his hands through his hair. "Why can one never undo what has been done?"

Dulcie murmured sadly, "I wish it were possible. Goodbye, Mr. Courtland."

"I'll see you home."

"I'd rather be alone. You—you've given me a great deal to think about. Please—understand. I need to be alone."

"But you'll come back? I—I would like to know you better, Dulcie. I misjudged you badly. I'm sure there is something we can do. After all, what chance has a man against his wife and his father?" Rod asked with false cheer.

Dulcie managed a smile. "What chance indeed."

Dulcie asked the carriage driver to take her through Central Park. She was pale and abstracted, muttering to herself, "I didn't know. God forgive me. God forgive me. God—God—God—"

By the time she reached home, she had no recollection of having ridden through the park or anything else that occurred after she left Rod's office. Nothing was important now. Nothing. No one. Her mind was blank. She entered the house, spoke to Fred, and went directly to her bedroom. After staring out at the slushy street for a long while, she sat down at her desk and took up a steel-tipped pen. Dipping it occasionally into the ink bottle, she wrote a few short letters, one to her aunt and uncle, one each to her parents.

Last of all she began a page

My dearest Adam,

Perhaps you will never see this, but it will ease my heart to write it. I have just seen your father and from him learned of the abysmal wrong I have done you all unknowing. Although it is far too late to beg your forgiveness, I will need it if my soul is to rest anywhere except in purgatory. Be assured I have loved you dearly, beyond all circumstances of parting and misunderstandings, and that my love for you will surround you even beyond death.

I cannot tell anyone save yourself the things I am about to reveal. Read them carefully, my dear one, and try not to judge me too harshly. I have wanted to live, to find you again, and so I have done many things which were repulsive to me and contrary to my nature. I make no apology for myself. These acts had to be done, and by me, and I did them.

I first became conscious, after the *Independence* went down, in the hut of Mam'bo Luz, a voodoo priestess.

Dulcie went on for page after page, telling Adam of her year on Andros, not leaving out Justin or the drums that echoed in the two locked rooms. She told him of meeting Edmund and of giving up hope after hearing Claudine's name mentioned with his death. She conveyed as well as she could the shock of seeing him again only to be parted, and the worse blow from Roderick Courtland.

She concluded

> My love, I wish you a happiness in the future that you and I were never destined to know. Try to understand me, and judge my circumstances along with my actions. Do not be bitter, my dearest one, for I am not. Think of me kindly if you can.
>
> Yours throughout eternity,
Dulcie Tremain

She sealed the letter and propped it up with the others on her desk. She cleaned the pen and laid it straight. She had left her kid gloves out; she straightened the fingers and put them away. Everything else was neat.

Dulcie went into the bathroom and ran the deep lavatory nearly full of hot water. Rolling back her sleeves, she plunged her hands in up over her wrists, and kept them there until they were quite hot. She reached into the medicine chest and took out Jem's razor and let it warm in the water. Perhaps when she used it, it would not hurt so much.

It did not. She scarcely felt the cuts across her wrists. She stood there dreamily, feeling the water grow colder, watching it turn quickly from pinkish to brilliant red.

It was late in the afternoon. Mad and Patricia were laughing when they came in the door. "Ah decleah, Mad, Ah'm chilled to the bone: Ah'm goin' to change mah clothes befo' Ah make mahself sick. Wheah's Miss Dulcie, Fred?"

"Upstairs, ma'am. She's been in her room since before lunch."

"Oh, that po' chil', Ah wish Ah could think o' somethin' to amuse her. Evah since she saw Adam, she's just gone fathah an' fathah into a de-cline."

The bathroom door was closed, but there was no answer

to Patricia's knock. She pushed the door, but it was stuck. She shoved hard until it gave slightly, and peered around the edge. She saw the deep marble lavatory filled with blood and the straight razor. Dulcie lay on the blue and white tiled floor, blood all around her. Patricia began to scream.

Mad, with Fred following, dashed up the stairs. Patricia clung to the doorframe. "In theah—on the floah."

Fred managed to push open the door, and Mad slid in behind him. "Mother of God," she knelt by Dulcie, her knee in a pool of blood. "Where is it all comin' from?" She took Dulcie's hand, and more blood flowed. Mad saw the cuts. "Oh, *no!*" Frantically she tried to stem the bleeding with her hands. Dulcie's blood flowed over Mad's fingers.

"Mah baby—" Patricia began.

"The other wrist too, ma'am," Fred said applying pressure on the cut.

"Trish, don't you *dare* faint!" Mad commanded. "Dulcie'll die if you do! Get into the linen chest and give us towels—quick! Move!"

"Make a pad, Fred," Mad told him. "Fold it and press it right on the spot." He moved as quickly and calmly as she did. The towels soon became soaked with blood. "More towels!" Mad said.

"We should look at her throat, ma'am."

Patricia gagged. They turned Dulcie over and were relieved to find no other wounds. They continued to apply pressure. There was little else they could do. "Patricia, send Marie for the doctor and then for Jem and Oliver."

Dulcie's chest rose and fell shallowly; sometimes it seemed not to move at all.

By the end of another hour the doctor had arrived. They moved Dulcie to the bed where the doctor could work better. He showed Mad and Fred the pressure point inside her upper arm, so that he could stitch the cuts unimpeded. He dressed the wounds. The bleeding had almost stopped. He examined her, listening to her heart, noting the sweaty pallor of her skin and the inside of her lips and the bluish tinge of the whites of her eyes.

"It will be a near thing," he said. "A very near thing. She is extremely weak and debilitated. You'll need to keep her warm. If she regains consciousness, begin giving her liquids. If there is any change during the night, send for me. I'll come past early tomorrow morning."

"Is there anythin' else we can do for her, doctor?" Mad asked.

"Say your prayers, Mrs. Raymer."

Patricia sat beside her daughter. Dulcie's breathing was very light. Occasionally she would take a single long breath and let it out with a semblance of a moan. Her eyelids stayed shut, not even fluttering. Around her mouth were faintly blue lines. Patricia prayed, *Please, Lord . . . she has so much to live fo'.*

Mad went downstairs with the doctor and met Jem coming in.

"Doctor! Is she—?" His face puckered.

"Your daughter is alive, Mr. Moran. There is always hope."

Jem wrung the doctor's hand effusively while tears coursed down his cheeks. Then he went up to see Dulcie.

Patricia reached out to him. Holding hands, they watched the weak motions of their daughter's breathing. "Ah want to stay by her, touchin' her all night. If Ah've got any strength in me, Ah want to give it all to mah baby."

Jem, choked, gripped her hand and swallowed tears. "We'll . . . both . . ."

Oliver came in to find Mad, her skirt stiff with blood, lying on the horsehair chaise-longue. Fred was bathing her forehead with cold cloths. "She just fainted, sir."

"Dulcie?"

"Alive, Mr. Raymer. The doctor's been and done all he could."

"I'll go up. Stay with Mrs. Raymer, just as you're doing. I won't be gone long."

Oliver saw the envelopes first. Quietly he gripped Jem's shoulder and kissed Patricia's cheek. He kissed Dulcie, whispering, "You're going to make it, Dulcie, do you hear me? You're going to be fine." He straightened up, not looking at anyone and stood with his back to them for some time.

Dulcie took in another long fluttering breath and let it go.

Oliver picked up the envelope addressed to himself and Mad. He lifted Adam's, weighed it in his palm. He turned to Jem. "Whatever happens, I think Adam should get this letter—intact. It's between them, don't you agree?"

Jem nodded. Oliver placed the letter in the desk drawer.

Then he left the house. He sent multiple telegraph messages to Adam Tremain, Smithville, and others in care of Confederate agents in Wilmington. All read: DULCIE TREMAIN HAS ATTEMPTED SUICIDE STOP DO NOT KNOW IF SHE WILL LIVE STOP FOR GODS SAKE COME IMMEDIATELY SIGNED OLIVER RAYMER.

Chapter Fifteen

The trip from Long Island seemed endless. Adam was silent and pensive. He hadn't felt as he did now since he'd first seen Satan's Keep. Then he had believed every moment he was unable to find Dulcie was one moment less she had to survive. But she had survived—somehow, by some means, and without him. She had returned to New York showing no ill effects. If anything she had been better off than he. She hadn't needed him then, nor did it appear she had wanted him. Quickly he shut his eyes against the memory of the flashing emerald-green and diamond-white stones on her hand.

But this was now. Both his father and Oliver had asked him to return to her as quickly as he could. Neither man would bring him back to New York if Dulcie were with Edmund Revanche. Surely not his own father. Rod had written only of her love for Adam. Nothing more. Yet it was still too late.

Oliver's message had brought different news. Dulcie had attempted to take her own life. Why? He cried inside himself and then shrank from the memory of Dulcie on her knees in the mud, her hands raised in supplication as she begged him to listen. He hadn't. He had run from her.

And now what would he find? A woman? A funeral? An end to everything? All the loving gone? All the longing, the bitterness, the disappointment locked in time with her death?

Tense and straight-backed, Adam continued his silent

brooding. Each strip of road brought back vanished days with Dulcie. Precious few days by which he valued his life, a slender line of time that told him who he was. His life was wrapped tightly, bound like swaddling in that young girl, that small red-haired creature who had looked at him from eyes of liquid gold, who had taunted him and every man with her smile and so seldom understood the invitations she offered. So easily she had become a part of him, yet he'd had her for so short a time, and she had never truly been his. He knew that now. Dulcie belonged to the moment, never to him.

It was dark when he finally pulled up in front of the Raymer house.

Oliver answered Adam's knock. "Adam, thank God you have come."

Adam grasped his arm. "Sir, Dulcie—is she—?"

"She's alive," Oliver said quickly.

"Will she see me?"

"Oh, I'm sure she will—but first Mad wished to speak to you."

"May I see Dulcie first? Please. I know you must be wary of granting me anything, but since you telegraphed I hoped you'd accept my apology for my behavior the last time I was here."

"Oh, it's not that at all. Mad wants to talk to you before you see Dulcie. Tell you— Oh, damn and blast, this is not . . . I—I am quite at a loss.'"

"There is something—you said Dulcie is alive!?"

"She's written a letter—left it to you, I mean. Mad and I think you should read it before you see her."

Adam looked at the long staircase, listened for a moment to the sound of footsteps in the upper hall, the soft murmur of voices around a sick room. Reluctantly he followed Oliver into Mad's sitting room.

Mad hurried across the room. "You came! I knew you would! I just knew it!" She hugged him close and planted a perfumed kiss on his cheek. "I told Ollie I couldn't be wrong about you! And I wasn't—was I, Adam?"

He looked at her for a long moment, unwilling to have this woman know him so readily. "You weren't wrong. How is she? Does she know you sent for me?"

"We thought it best not to tell her."

"In case I didn't come."

"We never doubted you, dear. The telegram might have

gotten lost. They do so often these days. You might not
have been in Smithville to receive it. So many things
might have gone wrong."

"May I see her now?"

With a hrrumphing sound deep in his throat Oliver
handed Mad the thick envelope, then excused himself and
left the room.

"Sit down, Adam." Mad poured each of them a demi-
tasse, trying to sort out what she should say. "You must
know that I care a great deal for Dulcie. Often I've envied
my sister her child. You must promise me, dear, when you
do go upstairs, that you'll be kind. Don't see her unless
you can go lovingly, Adam." Mad looked at him expectantly. "Dulcie has told me a little about her experiences
after the shipwreck, and they were horrifyin'. But I know
nothin' of what happened to you, Adam. What I have
counted on is that the love I saw between you before that
awful time is still strong enough to overcome all that has
happened to you. You are here, and that must be a good
sign."

"I don't want her to die, Mrs. Raymer," he replied softly.

"Is that all—the only reason you came?"

"No, that is not all, but it is all I can be sure of. Dulcie
is going to be married shortly, and . . . and I—"

"Bosh! You know as well as I that as soon as she set
eyes on you, there was never any question of another marriage."

"It isn't that simple."

"It is! And I might point out that you've made no
arrangements for a divorce. Or did you expect she might
commit bigamy?"

"I'll give her a divorce if she wants it," Adam said,
scowling.

Mad set her cup down with a decisive click. "Young
people are as unyielding as granite, I swear. Neither you
nor Dulcie has given the other a minute to explain. That
much you would grant to the most unruly of your crewmen. Can't you accord the same kindness to your wife?"

Adam stood up. "May I see her now, Mrs. Raymer?"

"No, you may not!" Mad picked up the letter. "Dulcie
wrote this to you the day she—that day. She would demand it be destroyed if she knew I had it, but she doesn't
know." Mad walked slowly away from him. "Dulcie is
every bit as stubborn and proud as you are. Perhaps I am

doin' her a grievous wrong by givin' this to you. Perhaps I'm disfavorin' both of you. I don't know what she wrote, but it must be the truth. She never thought she'd be alive to see you again after you had read it. I think you should, but I won't force you to do so. You may see Dulcie."

Adam took the letter. He was tense, awed by the weight and feel of the thing she had written just before she had decided she preferred death to living. He could barely bring himself to read it.

For a moment he stared at her handwriting, the ink making designs of curving lines, row upon row. The scent of her perfume lingered faintly on the paper. Then he forced his eyes to read. *"My dearest Adam, Perhaps you will never see this, but it will ease my heart to write it. I have just seen your father . . ."*

Before his eyes was a picture of Dulcie sitting at a desk in a room he had never seen, writing this letter to him, keeping nothing back, saving no shred of pride, offering him no blame, absolving him, a man who had turned his back on her pleas, on her love the moment he had first found her again.

He forced himself to read on, to learn of the life she had led since the shipwreck. Every word carried her message of longing for him, her undying will to survive anything that they might one day be together again, and finally her desperate misplaced trust that Edmund would help her find Adam.

Adam's mind flitted back to memories of himself trying to drown sorrow and despair in the arms of the slut Ramona; how he had sought peace in the arms of Leah— Leah, who offered him the same promise of being able to live without Dulcie as Edmund Revanche must have offered Dulcie.

Both of them had gone through the fires of torment and loneliness and longing. But how had they come to such cross-purposes? How could either of them forget what the other had done? Even now, he could not remember Dulcie sitting beside Edmund Revanche, her life pledged to him, without feeling the hot searing grip of anger around his heart. Nor could he believe that Dulcie could ever erase from her mind the names he had called her in anger, his rejection of her, the humiliation he had dealt her when he left her with Revanche, promising to divorce her and never see her again.

He stared at his hands. "She won't want to see me, Mrs. Raymer. You asked me to be kind. I would be kindest by leaving now."

"That's for you to decide, Adam. That's why I thought you should read the letter first."

He folded the letter and tucked it into his breast pocket, then he took his seaman's cap from the stand, and looked back to Mad. "It isn't that I don't want to see her . . ." His eyes were moist, his face set as his words trailed off.

"Go up to her, just for a moment."

He shook his head.

"You love her, don't you? Adam—no harm ever came from love. Go to her."

He looked toward the staircase, the letter hard and thick against his breast. Slowly Adam climbed the stairs.

As if by instinct he turned toward the slightly ajar door at the north end of the hall. He entered the room, quietly shutting the door behind him.

Dulcie lay pale and thin, lost in the large bed. Her skin had the translucent pallor of the very ill, her cheeks unnaturally flushed, her auburn curls pulled back into long pigtails not unlike those she had worn as a child. The freckles across her nose gave her the look of an innocent.

Adam remained motionless, unable to bring himself to move or disturb her. The ticking of the clock was loud, the sound of her breathing soft. Then she stirred, her hand weakly smoothing the pillow by her cheek. As she turned her head to find comfort again, her eyes opened, and she saw him standing by the door.

She stared at him, showing no surprise or sign of greeting. It was as if she always saw him wherever she looked, and that he should be in her room now was nothing strange, neither was it real.

He couldn't make his throat work to bring out the words, so he took her hand, holding it in his own two, gently, marveling at the feel of it against him. He kept his eyes down, aware that she watched him, but unable to meet her gaze. When he did, it was to see tears ready to fall.

"You shouldn't have come, Adam. I bring you nothin' but pain."

It was a long time before he could control his voice. Even then it came out a whispering rasp. "I don't want to be without you." His face worked, and he looked away from her. "Don't . . . don't ever do that to yourself again, Dulcie."

She took her hand from his, turning her face into the pillow. "Adam, don't say any more. Please. Leave me. Let me think I was dreamin'. I can't stand to hear you speak to me this way. Adam . . . please go."

He touched her hair and cheek. "I don't want to lose you ever again, Dulcie. I'll be here in the city. I'll wait for as long as it takes. Don't—don't leave me alone now, Dulcie. I need you."

She did not see him leave, but her senses followed him until the front door closed.

Adam went to Rod Courtland's brownstone.

"Adam!" Rod's hand shot out to take his son's in a bone-crushing grip of welcome. "Come in, come in! Did you get my letter? I mean did Zoe get it to you? Obviously you got it, or you wouldn't be here. Have you been to see Dulcie?" The look on Adam's face finally stopped him. "Oh, hell, I'm sorry, Adam. Come into the study. We can have a drink and talk in private."

Seated, a drink untasted in his hand, Adam told Rod about the message from Oliver and his hasty trip to New York. "She frightens me, Rod. So pale, so—transparent. As if she has already left me."

Rod cleared his throat. "I heard, from Oliver."

Finally Adam sipped his drink. "I'm staying in the city. After she's recovered, if she still doesn't want to see me, I suppose I'll accept it."

"What about Edmund Revanche?"

Adam walked restlessly to the window, drawing back the heavy drapery to stare out into the bleak March drizzle. "I don't know. Mad says Dulcie never wanted to marry him. Dulcie said—oh, hell! She probably fell for every lying word he fed her. She would. If she really believed he was trying to help her find me, Dulcie would have trusted anything the bastard said."

They fell silent, each of them thinking. "You'll stay here with me, of course. Your mother will be arriving soon."

"Thanks. I'll be grateful for your companionship."

Rod scratched his neck, self-conscious, trying to think of a way to phrase what he wished to say so that Adam would not know how much it meant to him. "You won't like being idle. Not for long, anyway."

"I've had more practice at it of late," Adam said lightly. "I'll manage."

"Be better if you had something to keep you occupied."

"I can't leave here. Not until she's well."

Rod harrumphed. "Ever think about working on land?"

Adam swung around to look at his father.

Rod's cheeks pinkened, and his hand tugged at his collar in agitation. "Well, hell! You are my partner, and you aren't bringin' in a damned penny sitting here on your tail! And—damn it—you are my son. Courtland and Son." He looked diffidently at Adam.

Adam stared at him as the fact of Rod's parentage slowly sank in and became something real and immediate. The words had been so easy to accept. They hardly had meaning other than his mother was happy. Now the father was speaking to the son. Slowly the smile that started inside crept to his face, his own cheeks flushing in self-conscious pleasure. Then he thrust his hand into Rod's. "Courtland and Son."

Rod pulled Adam toward him in a hard masculine embrace, which hid the tears that both hastily blinked away.

Adam went to the office with Rod each morning. Before the second week had passed, both knew that Adam was not suited to working with paper transactions; he was, and would remain, a man who required action.

Daily he waited for Dulcie to call him to her, but no missive came. Often that month he visited Mad, making her promise that she would not tell Dulcie he had been there. "I don't want to force her back to me, Mad. I want her to come only because she wants to be with me. How is she?"

Mad's reports varied little. Dulcie had been out of bed. Dulcie had felt strong enough to eat her supper sitting up in a chair. Dulcie needed Adam, Mad insisted. At the end of each conversation she urged him, "Go see her just once more. It will be different this time. Don't let pride stop you."

"It isn't pride. She'll ask for me if she wants me. If she doesn't, I'll give her her freedom."

"Divorce her! Just let her go, without even seein' her again!"

"If that's what she wants."

"It isn't! I know it isn't. She needs you. She loves you, Adam."

"She hasn't asked for me. I told her I'd wait, that I didn't want to lose her."

Mad, her eyes filled with questions, looked sadly at him. How many times had she tried to talk with Dulcie about Adam and been confronted with Dulcie's stubborn silence. Yet Mad knew Dulcie listened with eager attention to every sentence that contained Adam's name. Mad's face twisted as she burst out, "I don't know why she doesn't ask for you! Neither of you makes sense! Why do you fight so?"

Fight so? Adam walked away from the Raymer house. Was he fighting? He didn't think he was. All he wanted was to give her a free choice for once: Come to him or remain away. Neither of them had ever had that choice, it seemed. Always they had been thrown together, acting out of the heat of a moment, first loving in forbidden, out-of-the-way places, then marrying as they fled his pursuers, living in the midst of a war that made everything urgent and impermanent.

His feet took him unknowingly toward the Hudson River. As he had come to do so often the last weeks, he stood on the bank of the Hudson, staring sightlessly across its expanse. The bustling sounds of the dock intruded not at all on him. They were the pleasant background noises of "home," sounds that were less intrusive than the soft scratch of Daniels's pen across his papers.

April came and fled with no word from Dulcie. It was long past the time Adam had promised himself he would set her free if she did not wish to see him again. Still, he waited, wading methodically through the days in Rod's office, gaining skill and expertise but no feel for the work. He seemed to have come to a complete stop, unable to be at peace where he was and unwilling to take the final step that would take him away from Dulcie for good. He temporized, promising that if tomorrow didn't bring what today denied, he would give up and return to his ship and the dying cause of the South. With everything that was in him, he knew that was where he belonged. Yet he continued in New York, waiting and hoping, for what he didn't know. Mad told him Dulcie was stronger, even able to be out of the house when she chose. But never had she mentioned Adam's name, never asked for him.

One evening, the end of a warm, singular April day when the blossoms on the trees showed tender green against the weak sun-filled sky, Adam walked home. He had given

up using a carriage, needing both the exercise and the feel
of wind in his face. Hannah opened the door, her face in a
perpetually hopeful pout as she hung up his coat. "There's
a visitor for ya."

"Where is he?"

She brushed the coat with the greatest care. "It's not a
he, it's a she—some brazen she-goat that hasn't—"

For a moment Adam's heart rose, then he pushed the
feeling down. "Who is it?"

"How should I know? She'd not give *me* her name. I
told her neither you nor Mr. Courtland tended business in
the home. But did she listen? No, she did not! Sashayed
into the study and sits herself down like the queen. Shall
I be tellin' her you'll not have the time to see her?"

Adam was tempted. He was tired from a long day of
clients whose voices droned on monotonously about their
endless investments. But he said, "I'll see her. Tell cook
Mr. and Mrs. Courtland won't be in for supper but to prepare a collation for six after the theater."

"Miz Zoe di'n't say nothin' to me. This is my night off."

"That is why she sent the message home with me. Now
you will be needed tonight," he said with irritable deliberation.

Hannah flounced toward the kitchen, defiance in each
jolting switch of her hips.

Adam stepped inside the shadowy study, lit only by the
light of a single lamp that stood on Rod's desk. Deep in
the shadow of the leather armchair he could see the shape
of the woman. He walked purposefully toward another
lamp. "Hannah could have spared you enough light to see.
My apologies, Madame." He turned, the match still burning, to see Dulcie's pinched, uncertain face.

Drawing in his breath sharply as the flame touched his
fingers, Adam shook it out, his eyes never leaving her. Taking some command of himself, he walked toward her. It
had been almost two months since he had seen her. Weeks
since she had been well enough to see him had she wanted
to. Now he would not allow himself to hope. "You're the
last person I expected to be sitting here. Hannah prepared
me to do business with a lady dragon."

Dulcie smiled. "Hannah took an instant dislike to me."

He had nothing to reply. The silence in the room became awkward. Restlessly he got up. "Rod must have some
cordial."

"I don't care for anythin', thank you; Adam. It was you I came to see.

Unreasonably he didn't want to hear the reason for her visit. He didn't want to hear her speak the final words that would end it between them. He had promised her he'd give her her freedom when the time came. He didn't want to hear her ask for a divorce, which he would be bound to grant. "You're looking well, Dulcie. Nothing seems to alter you. You look beautiful no matter what."

"I can't stay much longer. Mama and Aunt Mad will worry if I'm not home soon. It is already dark. I told Aunt Mad where I was goin', but Mama and Daddy don't know. They still look after me as though I might break."

He poured her the unwanted cordial. He handed her the glass, his hand drawing back hastily as his fingers touched hers, as though he had done something wrong.

Again the awkward, heavy silence fell, blanketing them, smothering their ability to say the common words because their feelings rose and choked them. Finally Dulcie shook her head, her eyes misty. "Oh, Adam, this is so awful! I shouldn't have come. I knew I shouldn't." She struggled trying to rid herself of the glass and draw on her gloves.

He was out of his chair and at her side in a moment. "Why did you come?"

She rose, her gloves on her hands again, her suit smoothed. "Aunt Mad said you had stayed in the city. She said you are workin' with—with your father. I'm so glad you found him, Adam. I—I'm happy for you."

He stood close to her, so close the smell of his tobacco and shaving lotion filled her nostrils, his arm so near she could feel the heat of his body. She suddenly looked up at him. "Oh, Adam, why did you do it? Why did you stay? You don't belong here. Your ship—I'm sorry, I shouldn't have said that. I keep gettin' tangled in the past. The doctor said I might for a while. I keep thinkin' of things and people as they were, not what they have become. I couldn't imagine you in that office with Mr. Daniels bustlin' in and out, and you with all that smell of ink and paper and no—no sea."

His voice shook. "Dulcie, why did you come here to-night?"

Dulcie's head buzzed with the weakness and pounding of her blood. She shivered, trembling as she had with the fever. "I love you, Adam. I tried not to—I did! I tried and tried to forget. Oh, Adam, hold me, just for a little while. I won't ask for anythin' else. Just hold me."

His arms enveloped her, and he held her close against him, rocking gently with her. After a few minutes Dulcie drew back. He pressed her to him, his voice soft and blurred with emotion. "Don't move away from me, my love. Stay near, stay near." His words were lost as his lips touched her hair, her neck.

Dulcie's hands ran the length of his back, feeling again the long, lean hardness of him, her fingers seeking the well-remembered curves of the muscles of his sides and chest. There was no part of him that she didn't want to touch, to remember, to see as she once had.

She began to cry and laugh with joy. "You want me with you? Do you truly want me, Adam?"

"Yes, I want you, want you always." He kissed her again for all the nights and days they had been apart. His hunger grew as he held her in his arms. "Don't ever leave me, Dulcie. I love you. I love you. I need you. Stay with me. Don't go back to your parents. Stay here with me."

His breath caught, and his mouth was on hers again, his tongue tasting, seeking.

Dulcie stirred in his arms, feeling the male hardness of him, allowing the words of his love to wash over her, healing, forgiving, possessing. "Love me, Adam. Hold me closer . . . closer."

They moved to the sofa. Dulcie, her lips parted, looked up into his eyes dark with wanting. Her fingers worked at the buttons of his waistcoat. "I won't break, Adam. I'm well. You won't hurt me."

He undressed her with care, his hands touching her with a leisurely, attentive loving he had never expressed, perhaps never even felt, before. His lips moved delicately over her, caressing her forehead, kissing the soft, tender flesh at the corner of her eyes and mouth, learning again the delicious hollows of her neck, feeling her warm, erect nipples rise to his mouth.

Though one part of him was eager to join his flesh to hers, in all the rest of him he wanted to prolong the love-making, to express his desire for her with every passionately tender gesture. He drank in the scent of her hair and skin. He saw and felt the fineness of its texture. His eyes strayed over her with new awareness. As never before, he was alive to the most subtle nuances of her yielding. His love for her welled up almost like tears within him.

Dulcie's hands roved over Adam's body in a glad dream, her fingers remembering the curling hair on his neck better than she could recall her own face. She heard his heartbeat and knew herself sheltered there. Her senses roused to an almost mystical awareness, she felt the strength of love flow from her fingers, from her breath, from every pore of her skin, into Adam, and Adam's love flow thus into herself.

Her fingertips brushed lightly down his arm to the back of his hand, pressing his hand more tightly to her, and running on to caress his lean belly. She began to stroke the inside of his thighs, with gentle fluttering motions that grew more insistent until Adam placed her hand on his thick, throbbing penis. Dulcie felt it surge between her fingers and palm, felt to the very core of her being the depth and urgency of his desire for her.

She shifted her body, raising one knee to make herself vulnerable to him. His palm moved across her groin in slow strokes, his fingers flattened and outspread, moving downward, seeking the hot moistness of her, caressing, teasing her to burning hunger for him. She yielded under his hand, her breath coming in little moans of pleasure.

Then when neither could wait any longer, he entered her, sheathing his length in the warmth of her. As one, they broke the bonds of earth, winging to the heights of rapture, sustained, exalted.

The sensation was so profound that they slept, still joined, breath mingling with breath, hearts beating together. When they awoke, Dulcie murmured, "I have never loved you so much . . . or felt so loved."

Adam looked at her, the sleepy contentment still in his eyes. "Will you marry me, Dulcie?"

She laughed. "We're already married."

"I know, but would you marry me—tonight? Will you stay with me? Live with me, Dulcie. Never go back, never leave again."

She turned in his arms on the narrow space of the sofa so that she faced him. "I've wanted to hear that for so long, to know that we'd be together, like this always. I love you, only you."

Later, under Hannah's disapproving pout, they mounted

the stairs to Adam's bedroom. "We'll take supper upstairs,"
Adam said. "And Hannah, when Mr. and Mrs. Courtland
return from the theater, tell them that Mrs. Tremain will
be staying here."

In his room were all the trappings Dulcie had missed
about him. He had brought his logbook, charts, and small
instruments and placed them where they would be convenient to use. His uniform hung, neatly pressed, at the
end of the wardrobe. Everything was familiar, everything
spoke to her of Adam.

"Now I'm home! This is *you*, this is really you!"

His smile was graver than hers. "Yes."

"Even a picture of the sea."

"Rod had it hung up here for me."

"Why did you leave the ship? You've always needed it
so. And the sea. Being on the sea was so important to you,
not having a dry paintin' of it on a wall. Why are you
workin' in the city?"

"Because you are in the city. Because of all the things
I need, I need you the most."

Her eyes sparkled with happy tears. "Oh, my dear, my
dear. And I need you." Her arms went around him; her
face, shining with gladness, looked up at his. Their mouths
met, open, seeking. The flame swept them again, making
them blush and shiver with wanting each other.

Adam's fingers were at her blouse, Dulcie's hands at his
waistcoat. They caught each other's eyes and laughed, kissed,
and stopped laughing. Fingers flew with remembered expertise, her clothing lay in a careless heap with his. Then
naked, Adam picked up his wife and carried her to bed.
He stood over her, his eyes knowing every inch of her, his
heart yearning for her as though this were to be their
first time together.

He said softly, "Have I told you that I love you?"

Softly she replied, "Come lie with me, and let us tell
each other."

She held up her arms, and he went into them easily, murmuring secret things into her ear and against her breast,
hearing her voice, neither of them needing the words, only
needing each other.

Chapter Sixteen

Zoe was awake before the birds. Just down the hall, one door away, slept her son and his wife. Dulcie was *here!* Dulcie, whom Zoe had never met. She shivered happily, snuggling closer to Rod's warmth. What would she say when she met Dulcie? Would she like her? Would Dulcie seem as lovable to her as she did to Adam? And how would Adam look? Would the lines of strain be eased in his face? Most important of all, would Dulcie like her?

By six o'clock Zoe was on her way to the kitchen to oversee the preparation of breakfast. She would never get used to these Irish girls, who in no way had the understanding of running a household as Mammy did. Zoe had been gamely trying to get along without Mammy, but it hadn't been easy. Everyday of her life she had had Mammy to turn to and depend on. She missed the old woman's stolid good sense and her reassuring bulk. She wished Mammy could be here to see Adam and Dulcie.

But Mammy had refused to come North with them. "Ah's too ol', Miz Zoe, chil'. W'en dese bones is laid to res', dey gwine be laid in Ca'lina earf."

Zoe had thrust aside a sudden clutching of her heart. Mammy couldn't die! She said brightly, "Oh, that'll be a long time yet, Mammy. Besides, I need you to help me get Master Rod's household organized."

"Yes, it's been a bachelor establishment for so long, it needs a good firm hand," Rod admitted. "Better come along with us, Mammy. There's a big job for you North, and nobody can do it better."

"Ah thanks you, Mas' Rod." Mammy's eyes twinkled. "You tries to git 'roun' Mammy jes' like Mas' Adam, an' Ah like dat. But Ah ain't gwine be got 'roun' dis time."

"Mammy, please!" Zoe cried, putting her hand on the old woman's shoulder. For the first time she noticed that Mammy was no longer heavy. Extreme old age was stealing her substantialness away.

Mammy's arms encircled Zoe as they had so many times. "You doan need yo' Mammy no mo', chil. Mas' Rod, he gwine look affer you. Mammy need to be heah. Mah boy might come back an' need Mammy. Whut he gwine do effen Ah ain't heah to do fo' him? Now, you go on to Noo Yawk, an' leaves Mammy to do what mus' be did. An' Miz Zoe, you prays he doan evah gots to come back heah. He needin' his woman jes' like you needin' Mas' Rod. Time you boff movin' on. But yo' Mammy be heah, waitin' 'effen you needs to come home."

Zoe, on this happiest of mornings, blinked away tears, and sighed once more as she thought of what love and devotion had been lost when the South was torn apart. There had been great evils, true, but there had been good as well. Zoe's own mother had died so young she scarcely remembered any mother but Mammy. And this day, given a choice of parentage, Zoe would have chosen the woman who had mothered her throughout her life.

She awakened a reluctant Hannah, crisply gave her orders, and waited until the lazy girl had gotten up.

Zoe was straightening the table settings, lining up napkins and cups in precise order, when she heard a happy giggle and Adam's low voice reply. Zoe sucked in her breath, holding back tears, laughter, anticipation, until Adam and Dulcie came into the kitchen.

She was reminded of the day Adam had come home after receiving his master's papers. She hadn't seen him for four years; he had been a stranger to her. She had nearly gone out of her mind with pride that day. And he had been so pleased and full of his accomplishment.

He looked much like that today. The vivid sparkle was in his eyes. He walked with the broad-shouldered, straight-backed pride that personified him. Quick, lithe animal grace was in all his movements.

At his side was a jewel of a girl. Zoe couldn't think of her as a woman, for Dulcie's face shone with the dewy luminousness of a flower opening to the sun. Her riotous auburn curls were vivid against the dark masculinity of Adam, her delicacy complementing his ruggedness. Together they were complete. Zoe was left misty-eyed and speechless when Adam said, "Mother, may I present my wife? This is Dulcie."

Laughing, she hugged Dulcie. "Oh, my dear, dear child!" she whispered. Holding fast to Dulcie's hand, she hugged Adam. "And you too!" As Rod came sleepily into the room, she flew to him, throwing her arms around his neck, laughing-crying as she buried her face against him.

Rod blinked, then grinned at Adam. "Getting to know your mother again is quite an experience." He hugged her, raising her feet off the floor. "I take it she just met Dulcie?"

Adam's face glowed as he gazed on his wife. "She has a way of affecting people like that, Rod."

They all laughed, teased, and chattered as Zoe struggled to recover from her emotion and embarrassment. Breakfast was all but forgotten. Hannah stood at the serving board as instructed, her face pained and sullen. Then in spite of herself Hannah, too, was smiling, chattering, and scolding them as she served. "Sure none of ye'll eat a bite, if I don't bring it to you myself."

By the time she and Adam were ready to go to Oliver's to see her parents, Dulcie was nearly in a trance. "She likes me, Adam! She honestly likes me!"

Bemused, he said, "Of course she likes you. Did you expect otherwise?"

Old feelings of guilt assailed her. "I think I would have acted differently had I been she. She loves you so, and I . . . I have not been a good wife to you. How can she forgive me so easily?"

Adam's big hands swallowed up her shoulders. "There's nothing to forgive, Dulcie. There's nothing to talk about. My mother loves you, and"—he pulled her against him— "I love you. No more questions and no more doubts."

There was more jubilation and merry making at the Raymers'. Mad looked like a demented Cupid with her perpetual grin as she offered them too much to eat and drink. Patricia was her usual light-hearted, accepting self, once she was convinced Adam was sane and therefore worthy of Dulcie. Jem alone wore a downcast face. He took Dulcie alone into Oliver's study.

Without words he held his daughter. His voice was thick and choked. "I'm an old fool, Dulcie Jeannette. He's your man. Can you forgive me?"

Jem had changed. Time and worry and the war had robbed him of vitality. Even his hair was tempered with gray. Missing from his eyes was the warm, abiding pride for his dream, Mossrose. She saw the deep sorrow and fear that he'd lost the love of his daughter. And Dulcie knew that he loved her more than his own life. Whatever he had said or done in the past, he'd done thinking to protect her from the heartbreak that was to come anyway.

"Daddy, there's nothin' to forgive. That's what Adam said to me, and I'm goin' to believe it. We're goin' to start all over—all of us. Oh, Daddy, a whole new world is beginnin' for me! I don't ever want to look back. I love you now. I'll love you always!"

During the following days Dulcie felt herself surrounded by the love of Adam's family and her own. Though she basked in it like a sun-starved flower, it made her sad as well. Adam had said they would begin again and never look back. With him she did that. He made it easy for her. There wasn't a moment when she couldn't feel or be aware of his love. He left notes on her pillow. She found flowers beside her plate at the breakfast table. He brought her small gifts explicit in their sentiment. His eyes followed her into and out of a room. His hands spoke to her whenever he touched her. In his every move he made her know he loved her. He made the future promise a lifetime of starlit nights and soft hours of making love and long days of being loved.

But he couldn't stop her from questioning. Adam had found a way to close the door of the past, but she hadn't. In the beginning she thought it was because Adam was stronger than she. He always had been. When she had struggled and compromised herself merely to survive, he had been able to keep looking ahead, to see farther than the boundaries of himself. Adam always had a capacity to see and feel beyond himself, that she never had. Humbly she followed his lead and obeyed him, never looking back, never referring to what had happened to them, and never thinking the name of Edmund Revanche.

They had been together only two weeks when Dulcie became convinced that there would be no future unless she and Adam lived to themselves and found their way back through the past.

She broached the question coyly, waiting until she was snugly curled in the curve of his body in front of the fire. "Wouldn't it be marvelous if we had a house of our own? A yard that was ours—furniture, walls, floors all ours?"

"We will someday."

Dulcie feigned a carefree attitude she didn't feel. "Why

wait for someday? Everybody in New York moves in the spring. Mrs. Burris says it's a near ritual, the rite of a New York spring. People begin now to hunt for new places, then on May first the whole city packs up and everybody trades houses. Let's be a part of it, Adam!"

Frowning, he said, "You mean it." He got up, busying himself with the first papers he could lay hands on. "We have a perfectly satisfactory arrangement here."

"Really, Adam! I'm not one of your stuffy clients, that you should talk to me that way. Won't you even consider it?"

"I see no reason to uproot ourselves because you want to be out on the streets with the rest of the city on May first."

Dulcie bit her lip, trying to keep the anger out of her voice. "You're bein' unreasonable. I would not move simply to be a part of the crowd. We need to have a home. Some place that says Adam and Dulcie live here. I love your mother, and Rod likes havin' us here, but it is their home, not ours."

"This isn't something I want to discuss, Dulcie."

"Do you have some good reason for not wantin' to move?"

"We'll only remain in New York as long as it takes you to get well."

"I'm not sick!"

"I've said all I'm going to say." He picked up his coat. "I'll be back later."

"Where are you going?"

"For a walk. I'd ask you to come, but you tire too easily," he said nastily and left the room.

Dulcie made ready to throw the pillow after him, then let it fall. They were going to find a house. She would see that they did. Adam simply would not risk trying to understand the painful past year and a half. He was hiding as surely as if he had disappeared into his beloved swamp. Yet, neither she nor Adam could long endure the pretend world of no disharmony he was trying to create. She might lose him again if she pressed him. She would lose him for certain if she did not.

Dulcie feigned sleep when he returned. She ignored the caress along the line of her hip as he slid under the blankets. She made no response to the tickling of his breath as he kissed her neck and ear.

All the next week, in every way he could devise, he apologized. Dulcie accepted them all and did not mention the house. She counted on his sensitivity. And she was proved correct. Adam sensed that no matter what he did or how yielding Dulcie became, there remained between them the barrier of the house.

He gave in with better grace than she expected, but it also became another thing they weren't to mention again. He was totally unwilling to give importance to anything that showed tension between them. He ignored that side of their life as though it didn't exist.

Jauntily he brought her flowers, bowing low before her. "Madame, would you take a carriage ride with a gentleman who adores you?"

He took her to see several houses that were for sale and others that were for rent. They saw nothing that satisfied them. Dulcie was ready to believe they never would.

New York's traditional moving day came and went. She and Adam saw it only as amused spectators. It had been a day Dulcie would remember, for they had walked the streets, gawking at the immense stretches of storefront and cobblestone. People hurried in New York. They hardly had time to take a deep breath, so busy were they keeping up with the tempo of the city. The flurrying bustle to get ahead, to move from one place to another without time to stop along the way to enjoy the day, grated on Adam. She had never known him to judge people or criticize, but of late he frequently complained of this client or that. He, too, hurried more and enjoyed less what he was doing. The small things collected, and each day Dulcie felt greater urgency to thrash out the problems that stood untended between them.

Not until the end of May did any house satisfy them both. Through Mrs. Burris's special fondness for Dulcie, they found a furnished ten-room brownstone. Mrs. Burris helped them arrange a lease, smoothing the way so that Dulcie felt as though she were living in a hotel again. Even the servants went with the house. The arrangement was less than she'd hoped, but it pleased Adam, particularly because it was not permanent.

Once they had moved into the house and properly christened it with a party, to which they invited Dulcie's family and Adam's, they settled into a routine. Adam made a great show of the Yankee clothing he had had made for himself. He was the prosperous young businessman. Disturbed, Dulcie watched him set up a grinding, unnatural regularity to his movements. He went to the office at a particular time each day and returned home at a precise time each night. His rigidity lent an air of importance otherwise lacking in his way of life.

In her own way Dulcie fell into the same trap, filling her days with charity work, needlessly doing her own shopping and making certain their evenings were crowded with social events. Both of them were standing still at a very great rate of speed.

Dulcie had heard Mad and Patricia speak of the deplorable conditions at the Colored Orphan Asylum. Perhaps as a kind of penance she chose that as her particular charity. Though it was odious and exhausting work, it became the one thoroughly satisfying part of her life.

Small dark faces looked appealingly to her for aid and comfort. It was the closest she could get to "home" in the North. And it was there, away from him, surrounded by a sea of black-skinned children that she felt closest to Adam. It hardly made sense to her. Why should a bunch of pickaninnies be able to give her a sense of complete loving that sleeping beside him could not?

She didn't have many answers, but she clung to the few instinctive truths she had, trying to sort out where her hopeful imagination ended and truth began. Adam sometimes chose to leave the office early on the days she worked at the orphanage. His visits to meet her were not regular, and she couldn't count on his coming, but he did it often enough for her to know there was something particular that drew him. And when he did come, he was a different man.

He strode through the grounds with a pack of prancing, chattering children at his heels, every inch the sea captain as he delighted them with tales of frightful voyages and stories of their people making free.

Yet, he wouldn't talk to her about what drew him. He refused to admit that it was more than a visit to the orphanage for her sake. He talked to her of nothing of importance. With growing severity, he was closing Dulcie out of his inner life. He had thrown up a glass wall, and though she could see through it, she couldn't penetrate it.

Often they joined the parade of Sunday strollers along Fifth Avenue. The avenue was a stage upon which New York's changing character was displayed. Bold new edi-

faces occupied the spaces where beautiful old homes had
been torn down to make way for the march of commerce.
Many of the elite had moved farther uptown, developing
the city as they ran from its commercial heart. New de-
partment stores crowded against old mansions where die-
hards lived in crumbling majesty, hanging on to the simple, elegant life of a Dutch city that had long since
vanished.

New York was the North. It pulsated and shimmered,
its heart a ticker tape, its limbs long roads of cement and
stone, its tongue that of the marketplace.

In small green patches of yard boxed-in May flowers
struggled to bloom among iron-front buildings and miles
of paved land, Bridlewreath spirea drooped in thick, foamy
lace, dragged down by the weight of its own bloom into
the uncleaned streets. The tulips had come and gone, their
leaves already braided by hired gardeners. A few tenacious
crocuses smiled skyward. Robins hopped across cobblestone
to the small grassy patches, cocking an ear for worms in
the soil left wet by last night's rain.

But Adam scarcely noticed. He was restless, unable to fit
himself into the Sunday ritual of a city that had already
lost touch with the earth on which it sat. Thoughts of other
places and times tormented him. Tears threatened as Dulcie
remembered the endless expanse of green trees and white
cotton fields on the red earth of Mossrose.

Quickly Adam hailed a carriage. "Rod's having a get-
together to introduce Ma to some friends she hasn't met.
We might as well take part in the festivities. Ma doesn't
know it, but this could go on for years. Rod knows everyone who ever lived in New York."

Dulcie smiled. "I think it's nice. He's proud of her, always wantin' to show her off."

Adam squeezed her arm. "Today Rod and I will show
our women off together."

The day was spent in being exhaustingly friendly to innumerable strangers and acquaintances. She and Adam
had not spent a moment alone since the aborted walk on
Fifth Avenue. There seldom was a time when they were
alone, and when those moments did come, Dulcie found
herself too tired to take advantage of them.

She was exhausted when they returned home, and
fiercely determined to hide her weariness from him. Yet,

when he sent her upstairs with a peck on the cheek and a murmured excuse about business that waited, she did not resist.

Dulcie propped herself up in bed and opened the book she'd been trying to read for the last week. She wanted to be awake when Adam came upstairs. He wouldn't bother her if he thought she was asleep. He was so considerate of her need to recover that she wanted to scream at him, "Did you think how much you hold me back by tellin' me I'm too tired or that I'll make myself sick again? I can't fight both of us! Let me decide when I'm too tired and when I'm not! I'm fine! I'm fine!"

She wasn't fine, but she reasoned she would never be well if she didn't keep trying. So, she pushed a little harder each day, and each day concerns for her health were shoved into those dark recesses that hid things the Tremains no longer talked about—Andros and Justin Gilmartin and Mam'bo Luz and Edmund Revanche, a cache of unforgiven sins.

Dulcie pulled herself away from the edge of those forbidden thoughts to look up and smile as Adam entered. "Did you finish your work?"

"Mr. Bailey won't be happy, but all his bills and information are in order. Shippers are charging whatever they damned well please these days. If that damn fool thinks his wife can't live without a marble floor for her ballroom in the middle of a war, then he should expect to pay many times its value."

"I do believe, Captain Tremain, that you do not favor the estimable Mr. Bailey."

"As far as he's concerned, there is no war! All he thinks of is that damned monstrosity of a house he's building in the country. Marble floors! Why the hell does he need a marble floor? Why take a whole ship to bring a dance floor to the North? That ship—"

"If you feel that way, why don't you do somethin' about it? Tell the man what you believe."

"What good will it do? Will it stop the South from being crushed? Will it bring back the burned fields and the ruined cities? The dead are dead, Dulcie. Talk won't revive them." He sighed and flopped back on the bed, turning so that she would rub his back. "I don't suppose Mr. Bailey's marble floor will do any harm either."

"Perhaps it will, and that's what's botherin' you," she said hesitantly. "Perhaps any idle ship makes a difference to the South."

"One ship makes no difference. A flotilla wouldn't help. The South can't hold out much longer. You read Ben's last letter. The blockade is tighter than ever. We lost six runners in the first nine days of February this year. It used to be a good pilot could run through those Yankee cruisers with no more than a fast rowboat."

Dulcie's hand massaging his back faltered. Why was she trying to make him return to blockade running, when everything he said told her his chances of being captured or killed were greater than his chances of success? "I'm glad you're here, safe and beside me."

His voice rumbled on. "Last month the Confederate Government passed an act prohibiting the importation of civilian luxuries. The runners can't carry anything that isn't necessary or of common use. Runners aren't men who like being told what they can do. Davis also said that a full half the cargo space must be Confederate freight at a fixed price, all to be paid off in cotton. Between the blockade and the restrictions, a lot of men won't run it anymore. The greatest profit has always been in civilian goods."

"But you've always said the runners are a dedicated lot. They won't quit now that the South needs them more than ever."

"It was easy to be an idealist at the beginning of the war, Dulcie. There was money to be made, and the South was bursting with life, a man with financing could be anything he wished. Many thought they'd return after the war and live like kings. But it's all changed. There is no South, not as we knew it. The war can't be won now. And once a man's made his fortune, more money is hardly incentive to take the risks he must now take. A dead man can't spend much. I wouldn't do it for the money. Ben doesn't."

"But you would do it for the South."

"The South is dying. Blockade running doesn't help as much as it used to. A good portion of what's brought in never reaches the Confederate soldier. Sheridan and Grant and Sherman destroy in a week what it would take Ben and me a year to haul in."

"Well, somethin' must be done!" she said shrilly.

"What? It becomes impossible to take them everything they need. Arms, equipment, clothing, food, drugs, the list is without end."

"But, Adam, they are *our* people! Your family—Mammy, Leona and Garrett, and Angela are there—and my cousins. What will happen to them?"

He said nothing.

Dulcie curled her body to fit his. "Maybe we're just feelin' dire tonight. It can't be that bad. Ben hasn't stopped tryin'. As long as there are men like you and Ben, the South will get along. We have spirit. We have a cause worth fightin' for. We have faith and the land and—"

"All gone—or going. The land is burned and fallow, and the spirit is in the same tatters as our uniforms. The North marches proudly against a land of ashes and rags." His bitterness was overwhelming.

June saw New York sweltering in hot, humid weather. The city was sweating, dusty, and oppressive. The weather reminded Dulcie of the South or Nassau, but there wasn't beauty in New York. There wasn't the easy grace of those lost southern days, nor the boistrous cameraderie of the last days of Nassau. She longed for Nassau so often, she felt she had divined Ben's letter.

Dulcie sat on the arm of Adam's chair peering over his shoulder as he read. Ben chronicled a slapstick run into Wilmington. It was amusing, but there was nothing of substance, for Ben and Adam had lost their common ground. Unwritten but easy to read was Ben's hope that Adam would return to the sea and Nassau. Each letter brought home with galling clarity the emptiness of Adam's life in New York. He criticized the Southern sympathizers living in New York, men who bemoaned the heartrending breakup of the Great Cause, while secretly fondling money belts bulging with their war profits.

Yet, deep within, he knew he was the greatest hypocrite of them all. He had the power to do something, and he did nothing. He went from one mindless social function to another, watched endless plays, savored French brandies, dressed his wife in the finest fashion, while Ben carried medicine, munitions and food to those who fought for his homeland. They were being crushed. The South was already in its death throes, writhing in the agonies of inevitable defeat, being laid open to the onslaught of vengeance and hatred that was sure to follow a bitter war. But Adam Tremain sat warm and useless in the North, a missing pall-bearer at the funeral of the land he had always loved and had pledged himself to serve.

The more fiercely he felt his abandonment, the more precarious became Adam's and Dulcie's hold on their marriage. They slept touching each other, they made love with an undertone of desperation, trying by sheer physical contact to repair a marriage endangered because neither of them could open his heart for the other to see.

Dulcie prayed. Adam was slipping away from her just as surely as she felt herself slipping from him. With no purpose or direction in their lives they had no life. Denying the idealism and dedication that was an essential part of him, Adam didn't exist. He wasn't Adam.

Dulcie was rushing as she wrote the last of the weekly menu and handed it to Bridget. She was due to meet her mother and Aunt Mad fifteen minutes ago. They wouldn't expect her to be prompt, but neither of them would be in a pleasant humor if she left them standing in front of Stewart's in the sweltering June heat. She was running down the stairs when the door knocker sounded.

"Bridget! Answer the door. If it is someone for me, tell them I've already left!" She slipped inside the study just off the hall, listening.

"The Missus isn't here, sir, and Mr. Tremain is at his office."

A hoarse voice rasped, "*Mr.* Tremain? When'd he get demoted? Isn't this the home of Captain Adam Tremain?"

"He gave the sea up, sir. Will that be all, sir? The Missus isn't here."

Tom shifted his weight irritably. This bright-faced girl seemed in an unholy hurry to get rid of him. "Write down the office address. I want to see the captain before I leave the city."

Bridget hurried to the table in the hall, glanced at Dulcie hiding impatiently in the study. "I can't get the bloke off the stoop, Miss."

"Who is he? What's he look like?"

Bridget rolled her eyes heavenward. "Aaah! Blessed saints but he's a brutish-lookin' fella. Not the sort we'd be wantin' 'round here."

Dulcie paused, thinking for a moment. "He didn't give his name, did he? Bridget, ask him his name. No! I *know* who that is!"

Dulcie pulled the door wide.

She saw a burly man in his forties with thick sandy hair shot with gray, hair that waved with an intense vitality all its own, for it did not seem to belong on this battered wreck of a man. His complexion, ruddy, wind-burned, was disfigured by crisscrossed white scar lines, like a mud puddle that had dried and cracked.

His big scarred, misshapen hands held a wide-brimmed new hat against the vest of his elegant brown suit. Not the most expensive New York tailor could hide the drooping left shoulder and the arm whose muscles had never regained normalcy.

Dulcie realized she had been staring, her eyes wide, her mouth ajar.

There was warmth in Tom's mild blue eyes, and his smile was friendly and genuine. "Take a deep breath, close your eyes tight, then open them again, and I won't be so bad to look at."

Dulcie blushed down to the roots of her hair. "Oh, I am so sorry! Adam told me, but—please come in, Tom. Please. I've wanted to meet you for so long, and I've already made a mess of it."

Tom stepped inside, looking around as he followed her to the parlor.

"Sit down, I'll just be a moment while I tell Bridget to have a message sent to my mother and Aunt Mad."

Tom stood up again immediately. "Here, now, don't let me keep you from anythin'."

"Don't you dare try to leave! After all this time of hearin' about you and knowin' how much you mean to Adam, I'm not goin' to miss an afternoon with you. Of course you'll have to stay for supper. Adam would be disappointed if you weren't here when he gets home." She hurried from the room.

Tom stared at her long and hard when she returned. "So you're Dulcie."

"Yes, I'm Dulcie."

"I coulda picked you outa a hundred fillies an' known you were the one."

Pleased, Dulcie blushed prettily. "Why, I'm flattered, Tom."

"You're bright as a penny an' hard as nails. Just the sort to keep him jumpin' after you."

Dulcie sat stunned under his unblinking gaze. Finally she looked away, her voice shaking as she said, "You're not goin' to let me off as easily as Zoe and Rod have, are you? You've already set your mind against me."

"Zoe's always been a forgivin' woman. There's not much she won't take just the way it's given to her. Rod? Well, he don't hardly know anythin'. He's bein' a new husban' an' daddy all together an' that's 'about all any man can handle. But me—all I am is an ol' swamp rat who learned the hard way. Don't trust nothin' right off. Log might be a sleepin' 'gator. Face of a friend might be hidin' the heart of an enemy."

"A lost wife might be a faithless woman?"

"I didn't get round to sayin' that, not even thinkin' it yet. Ullah—that was my wife's name—Ullah she'd say, 'Tom, you white folks never could tell your own kind even when you's eyeball to eyeball.' Ullah had a sense for people, so I learned to wait before makin' up my mind."

Dulcie sighed, a sad, faraway look on her face. "At least you say what you feel. It's almost a relief to hear contempt. I know what to fight."

Tom cocked his head to one side, waiting. "Feels like I'm gettin' a twitch o' familiarity in my eyeball, Dulcie. What you got all bottled up?"

Dulcie started out of her thoughts, her face pinkening. "I shouldn't be talkin' to you like this. I'm sorry, Tom. I don't seem to be doin' anythin' right today. You're travel stained, and you must be tired. Let me have Bridget prepare a room for you. You can rest and freshen up before Adam comes home. Then we can all have a nice evenin' together. My goodness, I haven't even asked you why you are visitin' New York, or how long you're stayin'. What you must think of me! All I've done is talk about myself."

Tom rubbed his eye. "Guess it was jes' a fleck o' dust, after all. For a minute there I thought you might have somethin' to say worth hearin'." He stood up, his hand gropin' for his carpetbag. "Well, le's see that nice room so's I can get all them nasty travel stains washed off me."

Dulcie looked into Tom's severe, disapproving face. "I can't just talk to you about Adam and myself. I don't even know you. How can I tell you about Adam and me?"

"Hell, lady, if you can't talk to Adam and you can't talk to me, maybe you better start askin' yourself what you're doin' here! Playin' house is for kids."

"Now you're just bein' cruel!"

"Wouldn't be the first time."

"Well, for me it is. Adam told me so much about you, I always thought we'd like each other immediately."

"An' if you don't get what you want right off, then what?" Tom snapped.

Dulcie stared at him open-mouthed, then said angrily, "I don't have to listen to this, Mr. Pierson. You're a vulgar man. Bridget will show you to your room."

"You're damned right I'm a vulgar man! An' if you *ever* talked to Adam at all, you'd know he's the same. He belongs to the people an' the soil. Locked up heah in one o' your sweet an' pretty drawin' rooms, he's—hell! you might as well put him in a cage for the loonies to laugh at. He's nothin' heah. He don't belong. If you wanted a stuffed shirt, whyn't you marry one o' those cotton-assed dandies I seen hoppin' around on Wall Street today?"

"You've said enough, Mr. Pierson!"

"I'm jes' gettin' good an' warmed up! There was a time I thought you were jes' about the best thing ever happened to him. Then you went and cozied up with Edmund Revanche an' came as near to killin' Adam as I ever want to see."

"Edmund lied to me! I had no way of knowin' what he was like. His deceit nearly killed me as well!"

"An' ain't you jes' proud of it! Put a cottonmouth to your bosom an' then yell for sympathy when the critter takes a bite." Tom moved aggressively toward her, poking his index finger against her breastbone.

The incessant thumping of his blunt finger was unbearable. She fought tears, shaking with frightened anger.

"What's the matter, Missus Tremain?" Tom snarled. "You don't much like bein' on the receivin' end, do you?"

"Don't touch me again! Adam won't stand for you treatin' me like this! He won't have you in this house!"

Tom's eyes glinted as he bared his teeth in a mirthless grimace. "Mebbe not, lady, but you succeed in drivin' a wedge between Adam and them who loves him, an' what you got left for yourself won't be worth twice-chawed tabacca."

Dulcie stared at him, inarticulate. Tears sprang from her eyes. She ran to her bedroom to fling herself on the bed, weeping in rage and self-pity.

It was afternoon before she regained control of herself. Adam would be home, and Dulcie looked like a grief-ravaged hag, her eyes so swollen they were barely open.

Worst of all, though she could never forgive Tom, she recognized the truth of his words. She couldn't drive a wedge between Adam and those who loved him, particularly not Tom. Adam would defend her, but he'd never forgive her or forget the rift she caused. There would be nothing left between them.

She hurried to the bathroom, filling the basin with cold water. She pressed cold compresses on her face until she was numb.

She stared at herself in the mirror, assessing with a cold eye how normal she could make herself with powder and rouge. Her eyes still glinted with anger. She'd never forgive Tom. "I hate him!" she hissed at the mirror. "He's a low, mean man—not fit for Adam. Not fit—"

Her eyes filled with tears again, Tom's words echoing in her ears. She'd never have Adam to herself. He'd never be completely hers. She'd always have to share him. Share him with people like Tom, people she'd never met, people she didn't understand as Adam did, black people, ruthless men, politicians, visionaries of a time to come that Dulcie couldn't truly comprehend. Was there any man worth that?

She patted at her face, making herself smile into the mirror. Think about dancing, flowers, and fun. She tried to force herself to imagine she was preparing for a gala dinner. She tried to think of anything except herself and Adam and the people and ideas Tom symbolized to her, and she couldn't do it. It came back to her, pressed urgently, demanding that she know what she wanted and what she wanted to give to her life with Adam. Or that she decide that life with him was not what she wanted at all.

With greater calm than Dulcie could ever remember feeling, she sat down to deliberately consider what she wanted to do with her life. Always she had rushed headlong after things of the moment, racing in a blinding whirl of desires and gratifications. Now it was as if Tom had put his hands out and stopped the earth from spinning on its axis. Everything had stopped, waiting for her to decide.

She thought of herself growing up at Mossrose. The lazy sunlit days of teasing Jothan and braving the wrath of Mammy and Ester. Days of playing in fertile meadows with Birdie and Blythe, teasing Glenn past human endurance. She thought about the love she'd always known

from so many people and for the first time questioned
what she had ever given them in return. The big things
were easy to recall. She had never been ungenerous. It
was no hardship to give Birdie or Blythe a shawl she particularly admired. Jem would buy her a dozen more. She
had always shared possessions with never a moment's hesitation, but now she wondered if she had ever shared herself with any kind of depth or honesty. The moments of
her giving unselfish love to her friends, her parents, even
Adam, were infrequent ones. There were some, and they
stood out among her most treasured memories, but most
often her gifts of love had been tainted. The coin of exchange to buy the lady her heart's desire.

Suddenly she turned on herself, her criticisms more
cutting than Tom's had been. She was merciless until she
reached the point where even she recognized she had
passed reason, and was able to think clearly again. She
began to rebuild.

Adam loved the South, but had she loved it less? His
dreams and visions were of a future in which he worked
and devoted himself to rebuilding his land. Were hers different? She hadn't the muscle and the skills he had. Perhaps her contribution would not be so far-reaching. But
did that make it less valuable? It was what she had to
give. And she had one other thing that Tom could not
deny nor anyone else take from her. Adam loved her. He
had chosen her above all else in his life. So, in effect,
Dulcie had Adam to give.

Adam and Tom were already in the drawing room when
Dulcie came downstairs. Resentfully she listened to the
sounds of their voices talking in easy friendship, rising and
falling in animation and excitement. It was another part
of Adam's life she had never shared in. It was Tom's part,
the part that had started in New Orleans when Adam was
just a boy. With jealousy nipping at her, she entered the
room, her brightest smile on her face.

Adam and Tom both stood, appreciating her with their
eyes. She nodded toward Tom, her eyes sliding away
hastily, then she stood on tiptoe to accept Adam's chaste
kiss. Irritably she wished he had swept her into his arms
so that Tom could see she had not caged him within the
confines of some drawing-room life. All he had done was
make it seem that Tom was correct.

"Tom tells me you two had a nice chat, Dulcie," Adam said.

Dulcie's eyes flashed as she glared at Tom's amused face. "It was by merest chance I was here when Tom arrived. As a matter of fact, Tom can thank my inability to be prompt for our afternoon visit."

Tom chuckled. "There's always someone up there makin' sure good things happen when they're needed."

Throughout dinner Tom and Adam talked rapidly, sometimes using only half sentences, laughing at private jokes. She concentrated on holding her temper. She was sure Tom was doing this on purpose, showing her she didn't belong with Adam, that his world lay somewhere beyond her realm. She began to listen carefully, fixing names and places and events in her mind. Tom would stay with them for a few days, and the three of them would talk again. He would not find her so silent the next time.

"Ben writes that there was considerable cotton damaged in Wilmington last May," Adam said.

"Yep, about six thousand bales of cotton burned. Damned shame. How is ol' Ben?"

Dulcie started to attention. "We got a letter from Ben? You didn't tell me. Was there a note from Glory enclosed?"

"There was no message from Glory."

"Still, you might have told me. We always read those letters together."

"You wouldn't have been interested in this one—all business."

"I'd appreciate it if you'd permit me to decide what I find interestin', Adam."

"Well said, Dulcie. He always was too smart for his own good." Tom chuckled. "An' seein' as how we're jes' three civilians jawin' about a war none o' us has a part in, seems like you could have a say now and then. Ain't like it used to be when Adam knew firsthand of what he spoke."

"I won't rise to the bait that easily, Tom," Adam said.

"'Let men not ask what the law requires, but give what freedom demands.' Know who said that, Dulcie, an' why?"

Adam angrily tossed his napkin aside. "Yes, I know who said that. But there's a limit to everything. I've done all I could. Now I want a home and a wife. It's time to settle down."

"I was askin' Dulcie."

"It was Jefferson Davis, I think," Dulcie said hesitantly, her eyes shifting uneasily from Adam to Tom. Tom's face was as hard-set as Adam's. "He . . . he knew this war would be a long, thankless struggle and we'd all have to give well beyond what we were prepared to give in the early days."

"That about says it," Tom said grimly. "But it don't look like there's many who heed it. News is our lines get thinner everyday. Men losin' faith in our leaders. Men wantin' to go back home to see their loved ones. It's been a long, bloody siege. Hardly a family hasn't lost someone to the cause. Not too many can boast havin' all their limbs in good health. Now that the goin's gotten rough, our men are lookin' away, thinkin' they done enough, gave enough. You agree with that, Dulcie?"

Dulcie's food lodged in her throat. Adam's dark, angry eyes were riveted on hers. Tom had thrown her the opportunity to confront Adam with leaving New York. And she sat paralyzed, unable to say a word.

Adam shoved his chair from the table. "I'm going for a walk. But before I go, Tom, I'll mention I haven't been fooled into thinking you just moseyed up North to greet old friends. If you came to talk me into returning to the business, I might as well take you to Hans tonight. He'll have you on the first ship South."

Tom leaned back, relaxed, sucking on his toothpick. "Nope. What you do is your business. I'm here 'cause your daddy's got a whole wad o' my money tied up in Yankee greenbacks. I jes' don't trust all that paper. I'll take my money in gold."

"Most of your money is in gold," Adam said.

"Most ain't all," Tom said. "You still goin' for a walk?"

Adam looked at him sharply, knowing Tom was not telling the truth but unable to tell where the flaw was. Tom's face was unreadable. "Yes, I'm going. Would you like to join me?"

"I think I'll just sit here an' enjoy prettier company."

The next morning Tom went with Adam to the office. He was out of sorts when he returned to the house after lunch.

"Did you and Adam argue again?" Dulcie asked.

"Hell, no!—beggin' your pardon, Dulcie. What's the use o' arguin' with a fool who's got his eyes an' ears stopped up? If he's got the stummick to live in a place like this, I ain't got anythin' to say to him."

"You dislike New York that much, Tom?"

"Damned right I do! Not a one o' the pukin' bastards—beg pardon—can say a straight sentence. Went to lunch with some mealy-mouthed do-gooder talkin' about the sin o' the South an' the retribution o' God. Yep, I'll be glad to get home—if there's a home to get back to. Sherman's already stompin' 'round, gonna teach all us Rebels a lesson. Got those damned "Bummers" o' his goin' out ahead o' his army burnin' an' lootin' an foragin'. Once they come through a place, there ain't nothin' left. They're thinkin' to make us sorry. Only thing we'll ever be sorry about is that we lost."

Dulcie watched pensively as he talked. "Why did you come here?"

His eyes twinkled. "Mebbe I came jes' to see if I could dislodge Adam from you. Get him up off his ass an' back on his ship where he belongs."

"Yesterday I would have believed you and gotten my feelings hurt, but not today. Why did you come?" Tom sat down heavily. "You still haven't answered me," Dulcie said.

"If you was to nag Adam like you're naggin' me, he'd be on his way South afore the end o' the week. Or don't you want him back in the business?"

"I want him back in the business. And I want to go to Nassau with him, but not until he wants to go."

"Now we're gettin' somewhere. Sorry I was so rough on you yesterday."

"You didn't ask my forgiveness; and I'm not givin' it. You were vile and cruel. But I accept your apology."

"Kind o' you."

Dulcie smiled. "Not very. And you still haven't answered me. Why are you in New York?"

"You might say I'm here on Adam's account, an' you might say I'm here on mine. I got a little unfinished business to tend. Been long overdue, an' now I mean to handle it."

At supper Adam and Tom talked as they had the night before. War news intermingled with sharp, probing questions. Adam always trying to get Tom to give his true reason for being in the city. Tom trying to force Adam into admitting he wanted to be back running supplies into Wilmington.

Later in their bedroom Adam was wakeful and irritable. Dulcie turned the gas lamp on again. "We might as well talk. You're not goin' to allow either of us to sleep until your mind is settled."

Staring expressionlessly at the ceiling, he said, "I may have to be gone a couple of weeks."

"Where are you goin'?"

"I'm going to take Tom back to Wilmington. He won't go any other way."

"He asked you to take him home?" she asked, baffled.

"No, he didn't ask! I'm taking him!"

"And if he doesn't want to go?"

"I'm taking him!"

"Adam, what's wrong with you? You've never been like this before. What business is it of yours what Tom chooses to do?"

"Mind your own business, Dulcie."

"This is my business! You can't make people do what you want against their will."

"I know what he's up to, and I won't let him do it."

"Do what? What's he doin', Adam—I don't understand."

Adam's eyes were dark and coldly accusing. "He's trying to help me—protect me."

"Don't look at me like that—Adam—"

"He's come to hunt down Edmund Revanche." Adam turned on his side, his back to Dulcie.

She turned the gas lamp off and slid, shivering, beneath the blankets to lie awake long into the night.

She was hollow-eyed and drawn the next morning. Adam left early for the office. Tom was teasing Bridget unmercifully.

"Mawin', Dulcie, you look like you wrestled with the Devil last night and lost."

"I think I did, Tom. Adam believes you've come to have it out with Edmund. Have you?"

Tom rubbed his brow, a smile playing on his mouth. "Adam thinks that, does he? Well, Dulcie, looks like my visit has jes' ended. It'd be a sight better if I weren't here when your captain comes home tonight."

"Then it's true."

"It's true."

"He won't let you do it. He thinks you're tryin' to protect him at your own risk. He's goin' to take you to Wilmington."

"He can't take me anywhere if he can't find me."

"Tom, please don't look for Edmund. Adam would find you. He'd go with you if he had to. Tom, please, I don't want any more trouble with Edmund. I couldn't stand it if anythin' happened to Adam now."

Tom sat quietly looking at her for a long time. "That's why I'm goin' after him, Dulcie. Edmund's caused all the heartache he's ever gonna cause. I been hidin' from him for near twelve years. Man like Edmund can put fear in you that ain't natcheral. He killed my Ullah jes' as mean an' cold. Stood there an' watched her be torn apart. An' he was likin' it. I seen him. I know. I could feel the laughin' inside o' him while she was dyin'." Tom's eyes stared into the past, fixed and large and blue. "Stood there with that ice-man smile on his face an' watched her screamin' for mercy."

Dulcie felt sick listening to Tom paint a vivid picture for her of what Edmund was. She kept looking against her will at the thick, ugly scars on Tom's face and neck. She kept thinking of his crippled, painful walk. She kept remembering the suave, dark-haired, charming man who'd been the cause of this pain.

Tom's voice rumbled on. He gestured broadly, indicating himself. "Mebbe I coulda forgiven him this. When I married Ullah, I knew Edmund was gonna take it outa my hide somehow. He's got a powerful lot o' hate in him, an' I'd made him look a fool. Edmund was bound to come for me. But I can't forgive what he done to Ullah. She was helpless. An' he killed her." Tom looked up suddenly, gazing earnestly at Dulcie. "There's only two people in the world I love bettern' me, Dulcie. He killed one an' he damned near killed the other. Weren't for Johnnie Mae, Adam woulda died too. There ain't no way for you to know Edmund less'n you saw Ullah or Adam when he was done with 'em. He don't jes' kill, Dulcie. He likes the pain an' the sufferin'."

Dulcie was shaking. Tears streamed down her face and Tom's.

"Did you know it was Ullah that named him the Black Swan?"

"No," Dulcie choked.

"First time she ever saw him. He come up on us when we was swimmin'. Naked as two jays—an' him an' those whippersnap friends o' his were peekin' at us through the bushes. I damned near ruptured everythin' I got chasin'

him, but I caught him. I was mad enough to kill. An'
Ullah she jes' looked at him an' got all mooney-mouthed,
tellin' me stories about a pack o' white swans swimmin' on
a lake an' in their midst is one black one. 'You jes' knows
God made that one black swan somethin' special,' she says.
An' then she says that's Adam. He's one o' God's special
ones. Ullah always did call him her black swan. Seemed
fittin', kind o' like it was meant to be when Juneau Nuit
an' Rosebud picked up on it. Now he's the Black Swan
to all her people."

"Tom, he has to go back to sea. He's not happy. He
thinks he's stayin' here for me."

"Don't you worry none. He'll go back."

"What if he doesn't? He says he's finished—that he'll
never go back."

Tom smiled. "You let him say what he likes. It won't
change nothin'. There won't be no new South lessen there's
Adam Tremain to build it. He's goin' back 'cause that's
where he's needed."

Dulcie watched him as he climbed the stairs to his room.

Less than an hour later Tom stood in the entry hall, his
portmanteau in his hand. "I'm happy I got to know you,
Dulcie. You take good care o' our boy, you hear? Tell
him good-bye for me."

Chapter Seventeen

Adam carried a bottle of Tom's favorite brandy under his
arm when he came home from work. He was in high
spirits. A bottle of brandy, an evening of ribald humor
and reminiscing, and by midnight Tom would be properly
drunk and tucked securely aboard the *Black Swan* sailing
for Wilmington.

"Dulcie! Tom! Where is everybody?"

Dulcie emerged from the parlor. "Tom isn't here, Adam."

"When will he be back?"

"I don't think he intends comin' back—here. He'll go
home, I suppose."

He set the brandy down. "You didn't let him leave!"

"Did you want me to lock him in his room?"

Adam's face contorted in anger. "You meddling little bitch! You told him! You talked to him behind my back!"

"Yes, I told him you intended to stop him. You had no right to make decisions for—"

Adam shook her. "Where did he go? Where is he? Tell me! You know!"

"I don't know! He said nothing! Adam! You're hurtin' me. I don't know!"

He thrust her away and ran into the street. He went to every major hotel, then cursed his stupidity. Tom would never go to one of those. He'd seek some small, out-of-the-way place. A rooming house, a place along the docks, a place inhabited by Tom's kind of people. He'd go to any one of a thousand hidden holes in the wall where Adam might stand two feet away and never know because anyone Tom trusted could be counted on not to betray him.

Adam felt defeat long before he was willing to admit it. He didn't return home, feeling bitter toward Dulcie, blaming her for allowing Tom to slip away. He slept at the office sitting in his desk chair. At first light he began again asking questions, haunting restaurants, quizzing anyone he saw about a mutilated man with a strange crablike walk.

By the third day Adam knew without doubt that Tom had come to New York in search of Edmund Revanche. It was no longer a guess. Several of the Jeffersonians confirmed that they had seen Tom and he had been interested in meeting Mr. Revanche. Mrs. Burris had given Tom an itinerary of Edmund's speaking engagements for the next six weeks.

"I didn't know there was such a list. As you know, Mrs. Burris, my wife is an admirer of Mr. Revanche's."

"Oh, my, yes, Captain. We all know he was instrumental in reuniting you and Mrs. Tremain. He's helped so many—"

"I've never gotten to thank him properly. I'd appreciate it if you'd give me his itinerary, Mrs. Burris. I'll be doing some traveling."

"Since it is you, I'm sure he wouldn't mind. He doesn't like me giving information too freely. Mr. Revanche is so deeply involved in our war effort, he must be very careful."

Edmund was on a tour covering several major stops. He would be in three upstate towns, then would travel by canal to Buffalo, then into Ohio. He had stops in Cleveland, Columbus, and Cincinnati before entering Kentucky and gradually heading South.

Adam felt strangely enervated by the black print staring up at him from the list. Quite suddenly he realized he had no fear of Edmund. Perhaps in deciding to follow Tom, it had vanished. Whatever the cause, he was free.

Tom had a three-day start and might be waiting in any one of the cities on the list. If Tom met up with Edmund in one of the upstate communities, there was nothing Adam could do. But that was unlikely. Tom would pick a larger city, where the odds favored him more. From Buffalo on, Adam intended to stick as close as an extra skin to Edmund Revanche's schedule. If Tom found Edmund, he'd also find Adam. From there they'd go on together and do what had to be done.

He returned home after seeing Mrs. Burris. Dulcie ran to the door. He strode past her heading for the staircase. In their bedroom he tossed clothing into a portmanteau while Dulcie watched, her eyes huge with fright, and the knowledge that she had already lost him.

She stood in the doorway, her hands clasped tightly in front of her. "It's not fair that you should go after him, Adam. What Tom is doin' is important to him."

Adam didn't even look at her. He gathered up his shaving equipment and rammed that in on top of his clothes.

"He's never tried to stop you from following your beliefs. Can't you give him the same trust he's given you?"

The bag was packed. Adam stared at her coldly, then picked up the portmanteau and left the house.

Dulcie waited day after day. There was no word from him. She kept hoping without real expectation. It was almost a habit she couldn't break. She supposed it was inevitable that it should end this way, as tempestuous and filled with passions and angers and unfulfilled dreams as it had begun.

He had tried to settle into an ordinary life, to be an ordinary husband with an ordinary occupation, and had failed miserably just as she had failed at being the wife of a dedicated visionary man. And now it was over.

Adam was free again. He wasn't at sea, and he wasn't working for the South, but Dulcie knew that it was only a matter of time. He was once more active and fighting for the people he loved and causes he believed in. The rest would follow.

She put off telling her parents and Mad and Oliver that Adam had left her. But after he had been gone for three weeks with no word, she began to pack the things that had belonged to them. By the end of July she'd leave the rented brownstone and return to her parents. She was deliberately slow going about her work, knowing that once the house was closed, her life with Adam was also finished.

On the table in the hall sat a lonely letter from Ben that had come the week after Adam had left. It was addressed to both of them, but Dulcie hadn't opened it. A letter from Ben might have the power to draw Adam back if for no other reason than to read it. She no longer placed hope in such childish fantasies. It was just a letter, and she didn't want to read it; it would only make her long for things that would never be again.

It was almost a month to the day when Adam returned to the brownstone. It was late at night, and he let himself in. Dulcie had long since gone to bed.

The rooms looked ghostly in the moonlight that filtered through the curtains. The sofas and chairs had been carefully covered with sheets. The ornaments and decorative bric-a-brac that Dulcie loved were gone. The house had a cold impersonal air of abandonment. Those who once lived here were gone.

He stood for a long time in the dark, dreading the thought of finding the upstairs shrouded and empty too. Suddenly he ran, taking the steps two at a time.

"Dulcie!" His voice rang through the draped house, bouncing off the walls to mock him. "Dulcie!" He grasped the doorframe to their bedroom, holding on to it, but not daring to step foot over the threshold. "Oh, God, Dulcie be here."

"I'm here, Adam." As she reached out for him, his cheek and clothing still had the damp chill of a rainy night on them. "I didn't think you'd ever come back," she said.

"And I didn't think you'd be here."

She took a deep breath that caught in her throat, knowing it was too late to turn back even if he was in her arms again, making her ache inside with happiness. "I won't be here after this week. I'm leavin', Adam."

He sat up, holding her at arm's distance. "Where will you go?"

"Back to Mama and Daddy—or with you if you're goin' to Nassau."

"But I'm not going to Nassau. I'm home. We can wait out the war here and then decide."

Dulcie shook her head. "We're not happy here, Adam. You're not happy. Don't you understand, I'd rather be without you than to live as we are now."

"You really want to go back? After all that happened to you? Nothing would be different now, Dulcie. If anything, it would be worse. I'd be gone more often. You'd be alone and less certain than ever."

"What happened doesn't matter. Everyone has suffered in some way because of the war. That's what I was tryin' to tell you the night you left. Tom made me understand. A man can suffer, and he can survive that. But he can't survive seein' those he loves destroyed, Adam. He must die inside too or come to the point he must do somethin' about it.

"I know your chances of runnin' the blockade are no better than two out of ten. I may lose you. But if you don't go, Adam, if we stay here and you continue to try to be somethin' you're not, then your chances of runnin' that blockade are nothin' out of ten. You're not the same man here, Adam. I'd much rather worry about Yankee boats gettin' you than Yankee ways. Whoever heard of a Yankee duck outsailin' a Black Swan?"

Adam's eyes grew deep and dark as he stared at her in wonder. "After everything—you'd still go with me?"

"I love you, Adam."

"And I love—"

She put her hand against his mouth, stopping him. "Don't say it so easily. You see, I've only just found out how much I love you. I'm still a little in awe of what I am sayin' with those words."

They stayed up the rest of the night talking. Adam told Dulcie he had found Tom in Buffalo and had gone as far as Cleveland with him. Edmund was not expected in either of the cities.

Adam had argued, "You might as well come back with me, Tom. It's obvious he's changed the whole schedule—if he ever intended to use it. He probably gave this to Mrs. Burris to keep her happy—and flattered."

"He'll be comin' sometime. These people are waitin' for
him, an' hopin', an' they got money in their pockets. One
thing Edmund can smell from any distance is money. He'll
come sooner or later, an' I'll be here."

"And suppose he doesn't."

"Then I'll find him wherever he's hidin'."

Doggedly Adam stayed with Tom until one night over
a cool schooner of beer, Tom said, "How long you gonna
hang around muddyin' up my waters an' makin' a dry hole
of your own pond? You got a wife waitin' for you."

Adam lifted his mug, taking a long, deep swallow. "No, I
haven't."

Tom sucked air in through his front teeth. "Too damn
bad you didn't marry Johnnie Mae. Leastways she coulda
beat the shit outa ya when you're bound to make an ass o'
yourself."

They kept drinking until they got silly, then maudlin,
then at last the morning came with pounding heads and
sick stomachs, and the unvarnished truth.

Adam's thoughts had all turned to Dulcie. His anger
turned to fear that what he had said earlier would be true.
She would have left him. She'd be gone, this time for
good.

Tom saw only the past and what that heralded for the
future. "Adam, don't take this away from me. Edmund's
mine, an' if I die tryin' to kill him, it's all right. I'll take
my chances with the Lord. I'm doin' what ought to be done.
He took Ullah from me, an' he damned near took you.
Don't make me have to start soundin' like a fool tryin' to
explain how I feel 'bout you. Only thing I got left to give
you or me is freein' us all o' Edmund. Don't take that from
me. Go home an' love your wife. She's where you belong.
Love her like I loved Ullah, Adam. Don't matter what happens then. They can take your money, stomp on your
boat, blow up the whole damned worl' an' you'll still have
the only thing worth havin' right in your arms."

Adam wrapped his arms more securely around Dulcie.
"I left for home that evening."

"Tom would say somethin' like that." Dulcie smiled,
thinking back to the first day she had met him and thought
she hated him. "I could envy Ullah. What was she like,
Adam? Tell me about her."

She snuggled down in his arms, contented as she had

never been before. She put her head against his chest, as
he told her of leisurely times in the bayou, of days of
hunting and nights of singing and dancing by Ullah's
campfire.

"Was it because of Ullah you started takin' runaway
slaves North?"

"I hardly thought of slaves in those days. Except for
Ullah and Mammy and a few others, they didn't seem like
people to me. They were just the darkies who worked the
fields. And the ones I did know didn't seem to be slaves."

"Then how did you ever come to be so involved with
them?"

"I first got to know the runaways at Aunt Leona's.
She and Garrett worked for the Underground, and I was
the only one around one night when a group came through.
But I think it started before that. I just didn't know it. In
a way I can thank Edmund Revanche. To Tom Ullah wasn't
a slave. She was the woman he loved, so he married her.
But to Revanche she was always a slave. Even after Tom's
marriage to her she remained a piece of property to
Revanche. I don't think he ever considered what he did as
the murder of a woman. Ullah was no more human to him
than a horse gone bad."

Dulcie shuddered. "How can he be so charmin' even
sincere, and then commit such heinous acts?"

"Because he doesn't see them as heinous acts, Dulcie.
Edmund Revanche is one of the demons of life who speak
nonsense and make others believe it. He teaches the doc-
trine of hate and sells the souls of others to it. His is an
easy voice to listen to. That's the great tragedy of slavery.
Neither master nor slave can find the truth. When one man
claims ownership of another, there is no truth left. There
is only mistrust and finally hate."

"Surely you're not in sympathy with the abolitionists?"

"No. They've claimed ownership over the morality of
other men. There's no freedom in that either."

"Then, what do you believe, Adam?"

He sighed, letting out the breath with a soft laugh. "I
don't know what I believe, only what I don't believe. I don't
believe in slavery. The black man was brought here against
his will, and yet we have kept him so long, through so
many generations, he can no longer return to his own
land. Now we must find a place for him where there is no
place."

"But there is—you bring so many North. You find places for them."

"I help them make free because God never meant a man to wear another man's yoke. But to what do I send them? Freedom? All the North offers is hunger for freedom intensified, but no reality of it. It doesn't exist, Dulcie. Not here. Not yet." She looked up into the strong planes of his face, at the bright blue eyes that blazed with the visions in his mind. "You can feel their hunger, can see it. It isn't just the darkies, Dulcie. It's us as well. When one man pains, even if I don't recognize the ache in my own belly, his pain is mine."

"Adam, I don't know you," she said in wonderment. "I've lain by your side, slept in your arms, carried your child within me, but I don't know you."

His eyes burned deep into her.

"Then learn to know me, Dulcie. Where I am is a lonely place. I don't know where I'm going, and I have nothing to offer you but long years of uncertainty and searching for answers when I barely understand the questions. Love me, Dulcie, because I need you, because I can't stop trying. We're a nation massacring ourselves trying to find the truth. Somewhere, sometime, there must be a healing. God, Dulcie, I long for that. I long for you."

Dulcie looked at him through a mist of tears. "You'll find what you seek, Adam, and you won't be alone. Never, not as long as I live."

He leaned over her, his fingers touching the tears that stood in the corners of her eyes. He kissed each eye, his hand seeking the softness of her flesh beneath her nightgown. "I want you," he whispered.

"Yes, yes. Now. Love me, Adam, love me."

He removed her gown. It slithered off the bed in a whisper of silk. Her breath quickened as he looked upon her with such new tenderness it seemed a living thing. She parted her lips to receive his kiss and placed her hand on his as he moved over her breast and down to her belly. His hand looked dark resting warm against her skin. She pressed it harder against her softness, feeling the faint memory of a child stirring within her.

She caressed the inside of his thigh, until her hand closed around him. She trembled at his sharply indrawn breath, her body arching to meet him, her hand still pressing his into her abdomen. She opened her legs as he

moved over her. He leaned down to kiss her, his lips barely touching hers, lingering moist with the intermingling of
their breath. He entered her slowly, filling her, pressing
deeper, heating her body until she cried out. He kissed her
deeply, filling her mouth with his tongue, seeking, driving,
consuming her.

Adam thrust against her arching body again and again,
his mouth seeking hers, as he touched the depths of her. She
clung to him, pressing herself against him, gasping and
whimpering in the joy of release.

They lay exhausted in each other's arms. He kissed her
eyes and cheeks, tasting the light, salty tang of her perspiration, then he fell back, his breath still coming heavy and
deep. He laughed softly. "I love you." Then he said it
loudly so it echoed in the room. "I love you!"

At noon Bridget knocked at the door and poked her head
inside before Dulcie could answer. She grabbed the sheet,
pulling it over Adam and herself.

"Oh, I'm sorry, Ma'am. Saints preserve us! I didn't
know. Welcome home, sir! I'm ever so sorry." She hastily
backed out of the room.

"Bridget!" yelled Adam.

"Yes, sir!"

"I'm starving."

"Bridget, please bring Captain Tremain and me somethin' to eat—oh, and the letter from Captain West."

"Yes, Ma'am."

Dulcie got out of bed, humming as she searched through
her wardrobe.

"What do you think you are doing?" Adam asked.

"Pickin' out my prettiest dress to please you, Captain."

"The prettiest dress you own is the one you were born
in."

She switched her hips at him, smiling wickedly. "But
dah-lin', it's hardly suitable foah daytime weah."

"Then pull the drapes and make it night again."

Dulcie dropped her teasing pose. She stood still, watching him, feeling suddenly self-conscious and unfulfilled.
She ran across the room, throwing herself into his open
arms. "Oh, Adam, I want a baby. Our baby."

He buried his face in her neck, his hand moving down
to her thigh, his voice a low caress in her ear.

Bridget knocked tentatively at the door, her ear pressed
to the panel. She waited, then knocked again. She shifted

the heavy tray tó her other hand, inching down the hall. Undecided, she stepped back in front of the door. She glanced at it, then down at the huge dish of scrambled eggs she had prepared for Adam.

A sly grin crossed her face, then she looked furtively down the empty hall and scooped a fingerful of eggs into her mouth. A small giggle escaped. She knocked softly again, then walked downstairs humming dreamily between bites of Adam's breakfast.

The letter from Ben lay forgotten on the table in the entry hall until the next day. For the first time in months Adam wore his captain's uniform. He opened the letter as he waited for Dulcie, who was having a difficult time finding where she had packed her long-unused riding outfit.

He burst out laughing as she came downstairs. "Listen to this!" He flipped her a note in Glory's scraggly handwriting, then he held up Ben's short letter: "Come home, you son of a bitch! I turned out to be the better man, but I need you to be my best man."

Dulcie read Glory's note, "Dear Dulcie, Miss Eleanor Brooker requests your presence at her respectable transformation into Mrs. Ben West. Don't fail me, Dulcie. You just drag that handsome oaf here if you have to. You're the only woman in the world who wouldn't laugh at the idea of Glory Hallalooya wanting to be a real wife to her man. This is going to be my only wedding, so it's got to be done with the people I love."

"I've never had a more gently spoken invitation from Ben," Adam grinned. "I don't think I can refuse."

Dulcie squealed, her arms coiling around his neck. "We're goin'! When? How soon can we leave?"

Adam sent one of Hans's smuggling friends after Rosebud, then began rounding up enough men to crew the *Black Swan*. Dulcie finished closing down the house and settling the lease. Finally, they made last-minute visits to the Raymers. Dulcie said good-bye to Jem and Patricia, this time receiving their blessings and leaving them knowing she was happy. Their last stop was at Rod and Zoe's house. As always, Zoe fussed over Adam, begging him to be careful and then wishing him well. She was used to him going. And he was used to her ritual of worry. All that was left was for Hans to pick up Dulcie's trunks of clothing and household goods.

Adam took Dulcie to the harbor the day before they

were to set sail. He showed her the *Black Swan* for the first time, finding he had competition from Rosebud, who wanted to be certain Dulcie heard of every adventure the ship had been through.

Dulcie found herself laughing and smiling throughout the day. She'd almost forgotten the exhilaration of feeling really and thoroughly alive. Rosebud, Hans, Cateau, the crewmen—it was as though all of them were just returning from a long limbo of sleep. The air crackled with purpose and excitement. And at the very core of their renewed faith stood her husband, commanding, leading them all into something new and unknown.

Dulcie smiled as Adam drew in deep gulps of sharp, salty air. He glanced up as a brisk breeze sent the furled sails shuddering against the spars.

"Prepare to sail, Mr. McAllister. Lift anchor."

"Weigh anchor!" Rosebud barked at the crew.

He was returned to her. He was Adam as he had been when she had first seen him aboard the *Ullah*. She had entrusted Fellie and Ester and Darcy to him that day because she had instinctively known he was a man in whom authority lived beside personal integrity.

She slipped away unnoticed into their cabin. From her own sea chest she took a pair of blue duck trousers and a Mexican peasant blouse she had bought in New York. Dressed, and pleased with the effect, she walked boldly up to the captain standing on the bridge.

"Captain, sir! Your cabin boy reportin' for duty, sir. First mate Rosebud McAllister signed me on this mornin', sir."

Adam leaned back against the rail, his arms folded across his chest. The wind whipped his hair forward, brushing the black curls against his cheek. The dark gray tunic fit tight across his shoulders, the dark trousers stretched taut across his narrow hips. Her mouth dry, Dulcie said, "How may I serve you, Captain?"

A smile played at the corners of his mouth; his eyes, a deep sea-blue, darkened. Lazily he walked toward her.

She galloped on, knowing nothing would make her return. The wind rushing past was cold with approaching night and the grayness ahead was studded with stars. Alone out here with the great striding creature beneath her, why should she not leap from the summit of the hill right up to one of those beckoning lights? She urged the horse on with a fevered cry. Her eyes on the stars, she was aware only of her desire to escape. She did not hear the sharp challenge.

"Who goes there? Halt!"

Victoria gathered herself for the leap into the sky as the horse took off. There was a deafening shot and the animal stumbled as it landed on the other side of a small water-course, then slowed, flanks heaving, whinnying with pain. For a few moments she sat motionless, then slid from the saddle to bury her face in the warm glossy neck in despair. She would never get away now.

Hooves thundered up, then someone was beside her.

"Victoria, you are not hurt? *Tell me you are not hurt!*" He seized her shoulders and forced her around to face him. He was white and the hands that held her shook.

Her heart cried out against this cruellest of blows. With a moan, she pulled free and began stumbling away. But he was after her in a second.

"What do you mean riding out beyond the lines? Dear God, do you realize my troops could have killed you?"

"It would not have mattered. I am nothing. I have always been nothing."

"How dare you say that when, to me, you are *everything?*"

She spun to face him. Her great need was to hurt—to break him on the wheel of her own love, to scourge him with the lash of her jealousy. He stood before her, tall and strong with the scar of courage upon his cheek, but she wanted to witness his suffering. The thickness of tears in her throat forced the words out in jerky contempt.

"And what of her? Is she *everything* to you, also?"

He covered the distance between them in two strides. Even in the gathering darkness it was clear he was ablaze with passion.

"What do you want from me? What would you have me do? You will never be free and I am only human."

"Then take her," she cried. "Take her into your life and your very soul. Let her diminish you until your life is colorless and your soul is no longer your own. Take her."

"I cannot, Victoria," he said. "You are there between us all the time."

The very night held its breath as they exchanged their pain, their joy, their helplessness in a long glance.

"I . . . I am so sorry," she whispered.

He took her against him in a swift movement and held her there. "No . . . no," he murmured in anguish against her mouth. "Never apologize to me."

Sweet rioting pain beset her as she was drawn against him in crashing surrender. His mouth touched her hair, cheeks, throat, and closed her eyelids, took her lips with gentle savagery. She moaned softly. Her breasts burned beneath the pressure of his body. Her hand went up to twist his hair. Victoria found herself swung up in his arms while he began to walk into the darkness. Her fingers stroked the scar on his cheek and went on to trace the outline of his lips, until they parted and teeth gently bit against her flesh. Her hand dropped to tear open the gold-encrusted collar of his uniform to expose his throat. It was fever-warm beneath her kisses, and the pulsating thud of his heartbeat sent a wild message through her, to set her whole body throbbing.

With a groan he brought her face up to meet his once more, letting her feet slide to the ground, crushing her against him in an embrace that washed away her subjugation to her husband and put her very life into this man's keeping forever. There was so much of her that should belong to him.

Drugged with desire, he gathered her up in his arms once more and began walking into the cloaking darkness.

Victoria knew there would never be another night like this when a skyful of stars witnessed their love. She was reluctant to pull herself from the soft mood of submission as she leaned back against his solid strength, his left arm encircling her as he held the reins. She was still wrapped in a joy of surrender, she could feel Hugo's tenseness in the way he held himself in the saddle. She longed to turn her face up to his and caress his mouth with hers; she dared not. Did he blame her for forcing a surrender that had made a mockery of his honor? After tonight, how could they go back? He would find it either impossible to forgive her, or resist her.

Suddenly he pulled the horse to a standstill.

"How can I take you back to him?" he demanded in despair. She said nothing, only pressing closer against him.

In the starlit darkness his face was a rigid shadow. "How can I take you back to him?" he repeated in a soft groan. "It is too much to ask of any man."

She knew he was asking the question more of himself than of her. "How can you *not* take me back to him?"

Charles stood up when they entered, a flush dyeing his face darker in the pale lamp glow. For a moment there was silence, then he said, "So, you ran to him. Have you no pride?"

"By God, Charles, if I had not been commanding the watch and recognized your charger, she could have been fired upon by every guard along the river. Do you care nothing for her safety?"

"Get out."

Victoria began to tremble. She could only guess what had passed between the brothers in the past, it frightened her to see such naked aggression now. It occurred to her that love and hatred were conceived in the same womb; that a caress could destroy as surely as the sword. Putting a hand on Hugo's sleeve she said, "Please go," but he was past listening.

"Victoria is a woman, entitled to your care and protection. She is not part of your *legal property.*"

Charles gripped the table to steady himself. *"She is my wife!"* He was shouting now. "You still refuse to accept that. I shall drive the lesson home in such a way that you will . . . and I shall break you in the process. I swear it."

There was a paralyzing moment while Hugo took the full force of the words in his face. Charles was fighting unsuccessfully for command of himself. "You shall pay for it this time, believe me."

Victoria ran between the two men. "No, Charles. No!"

He pushed her aside so roughly that her foot twisted and she fell across the table with a sharp cry. It grew unnaturally quiet, and she just had time to see the brothers staring in horror at her as she lay there, before Charles said, *"Now* will you get out?"

"Please, for all our sakes, go," Victoria begged through a torrent of tears.

He gave her a long look from a face grown haggard, then turned to Charles: "I swear, if you ever harm her again, I shall take her from you. I shall forfeit my future, my profession, my honor . . . but I shall take her as surely as if she had never borne your name." He spun on his heel and strode out, his sword swinging against his leg.